G000080074

GOLDENMARK

By Jean Lowe Carlson

The Kingsmen Chronicles, Book Three

COPYRIGHT

First Print Edition, 2018
ISBN 978-1-943199-26-6

Edited By: Jean Lowe Carlson and Matt Carlson.
Proofread By: Matt Carlson and Stephany Brandt.
Cover Design: Copyright 2018 by Yocla Designs. All Rights Reserved.
Maps: Copyright 2018 Jean Lowe Carlson, edited Matt Carlson. All Rights Reserved.

Chapter Graphics: "Typo Backgrounds" by Manfred Klein: http://www.dafont.com/ Free Commercial Use.

ACKNOWLEDGEMENTS

To everyone who made this labor of passion come true, you are awesome! Special thanks to Stephany Brandt for her fantastic and dedicated proofreading. Love to my parents Wendy and Dave for their ongoing encouragement. Thanks to my friends Marc and Claire, Josh and Lela, Sam and Ben, and Amber for their constant support. Thanks to the amazing marketing guru Ryan Zee for his mentoring and a special shout-out to J.R. Frontera and all the ladies of the Epic Fantasy Romantic Authors group – you are all the best!

Special thanks to my amazing Launch Team – Sankalp, Mary Birchenall, Linda Ilin Wilson, Gene, Mari, Umer, Norman C Stone, Tom, Dawn, Kelly, Pat, Louise Flowers, Deb, Rebecca Hamilton, Helena Legakis, Richard, Matthew, Fern, Karina, Steve, Brittania, Jessica Salafia, Barbara, Deny, Lorraine Wells, Cindy, Kenneth, Emilia, Evelyn, Penelope, Stella, Geoff, Nadia, Brenda, Vaishnavi, Tiffany, Edwin, Frank, Doug, Susan, Amy Manny, Cheryl Johansson, Amy, Tina, Tyson, Marshall, Abbie, Kimmy, Turbo, Dawn, Vanessa, Eylene, Barbara, Alan, Brian Chris, Ronda, Jessica, Sandra, Ronald, MarIanne, Robert, Theresa, Phillip, Sunny, Marta, Sarah, Sasha, Roxann, Kat, Wayne, Eileen, Debbie, Gayreth, Carleigh, Seraphia, Gavin, Julie-Anne, Martin, Celianne, Valerie, Susan, Joy, Tom, Dennis, Wendy, Barb, Alice, Simon, Rachel Jean Smith, Joe Roach, Kim, Andrew, Mary, Alina, Linda, Fiona, Amber, Nikhil, Juan, Vue, James, Valjandra, Queen Nuba, Georganne, Tony, Ari, Jim, Judith, Sarah Hughes, Derek, Jules, Matthew, Marcos, Brad, Kimberly, Corinne, Ross, Jan, Teresa, Phil Smith, Bill, Roger, Suki, Sean, Mohammad, Debbie, McKenzie, Tanya, Stephen, Sue, Paula, Paulo, Stephanie, Jackie, Gina, Shannon, Lynn, Lana Turner, Cath, Malcolm, Bertha Alicia, Thomas, and Jen – you guys rock!!

And as always, the most incredible thanks to my husband Matt Carlson. You are a wonder in everything that you do, and I love you through the cosmos and back!

Join Jean's New Releases newsletter and get free books!
Visit https://www.jeanlowecarlson.com/

OTHER WORKS BY JEAN LOWE CARLSON

The Kingsmen Chronicles
Blackmark
Bloodmark
Goldenmark
Prequel: Crimson Spring

Short Fiction
The Man in White
The Grasses of Hazma-Din
Darkling's Cove

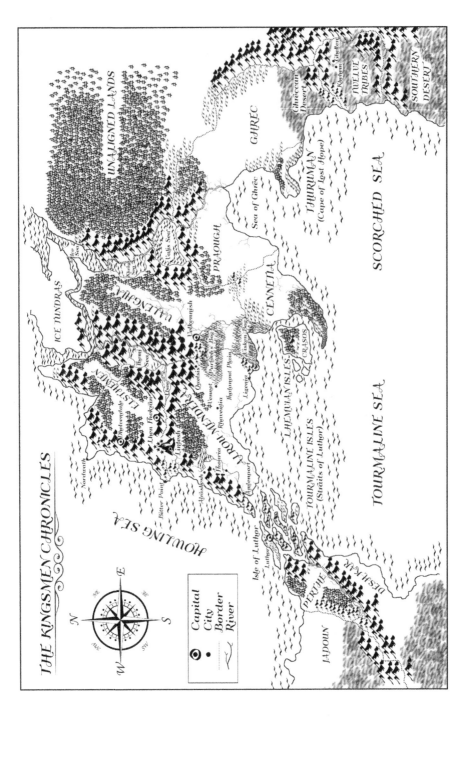

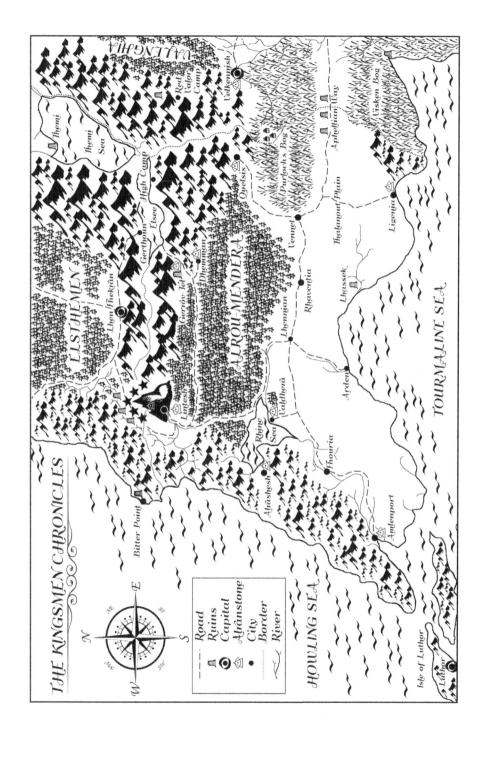

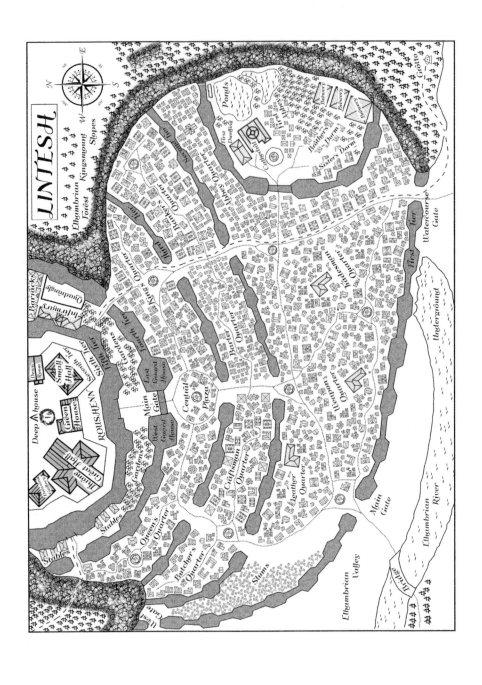

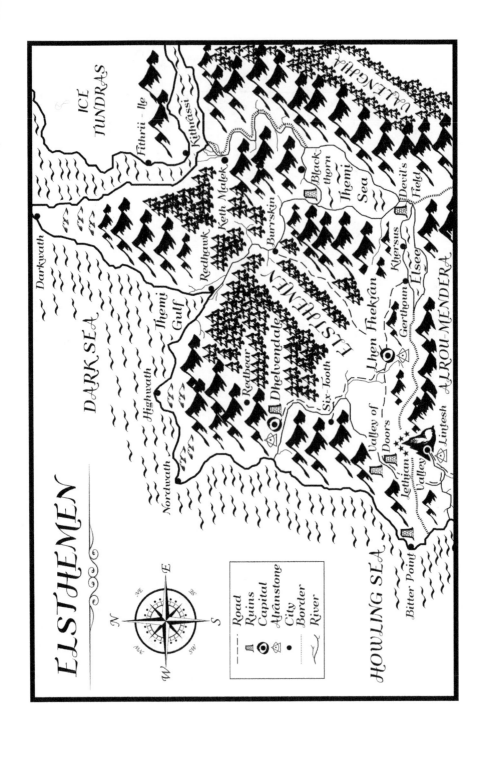

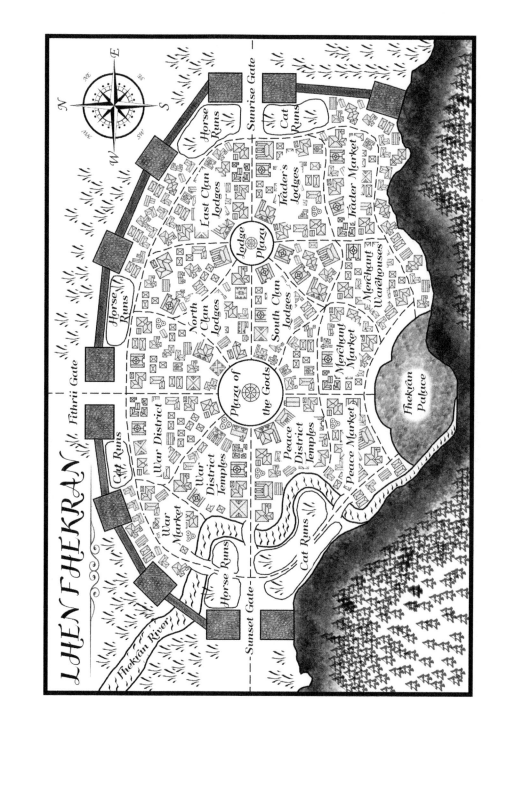

PROLOGUE – THEROUN

All around, General Theroun den'Vekir watched men fall.

The battle for Lhen Fhekran was not combat; it was annihilation. Annihilation of a country, of a city, of everything and anything that made a person human. Theroun could only watch from atop his mean black ronin cat as the sun set over the Kingsmountains – roaring out commands to shore up this barrier, to put more men on that avenue, to follow him to the next breach or the next. But despite Theroun's desperate strategy, the army of Alrou-Mendera walked right into Lhen Fhekran.

And tore the Elsthemi Highlanders apart.

With a wave of their hands, Kreth-Hakir mind-benders at the head of the Menderian army marched into the capitol, causing Elsthemi to take their own lives in droves. Blood washed the cobbled avenues as Highlanders slit their own throats. Lime-whitened red braids scattered crimson blood as Elsthemi fell. Battle-cats yowled for their falling riders, going rogue with no one to command them, racing into the chaos. Ferocious Highlanders turned against each other to the unspoken commands of the Kreth-Hakir, gutting their comrades with horror in their eyes – that their body was no longer theirs to command.

Theroun wheeled his black ronin cat, watching the city fall. Burning engulfed the rear of the invasion. Flames took the night as the sun died over the western mountains. Homes caught fast, straw and thatch flaring high in the gloaming. Stout ironpine and yitherwood went up like matchsticks, popping from resins. A sea of brown and cobalt-clad Menderians advanced with Kreth-Hakir in their herringbone-black leather armor – toward Theroun's failing knot of Elsthemi with their bloodstained furs and snarling cats.

"To me!" Theroun roared, coughing into his sleeve, his throat bedeviled from the black smoke that towered into the crimson sky. A wretched light consumed the underbelly of the evening, a ferocious knot of keshari fighters surrounding Theroun, death in their pale blue eyes. General Merra Alramir in her ruined white battle-armor flanked Theroun, her elite keshari riders holding their fall-back position at the palisade of Fhekran Palace.

The Menderian column advanced before billowing towers of red smoke. Like an army of ants they advanced upon the gates of Fhekran Palace, not a man faltering. Their eyes were dulled, reflecting the bitter sky, too uniform to be men in charge of their own minds. They were a hive tonight, not a trace of fear or bloodlust or any human emotion in their faces. Ten thousand Menderian soldiers, mind-ruined just like the Elsthemi who succumbed to their own blades.

Controlled by the black arts of the Kreth-Hakir Scorpions.

A familiar face walked at the head of the column, a dark twist of dominance upon his smooth lips. A lack of emotion poured through High Priest Khorel Jornath, leader of the Kreth-Hakir Brethren, as he stalked Theroun down in the roaring night. Hulking of stature, the man stepped over the fallen as casually as a lion in a field. Rather than riding his glittering black scorpion into the red night, he came afoot at the head of Lhaurent den'Karthus' cursed army. His scorpion was dead from its encounter with Theroun just a day ago at the Elsthemi-Menderian border, but the man who'd ridden it was very much alive. He had a bloody bandage around his upper chest, stained nearly as black as his silver-studded armor in the burning dark.

But where his Kreth-Hakir comrades assessed the three hundred vengeful Elsthemi and their battle-cats amassed before the palisades, this man held a cold stare only for Theroun. Khorel Jornath halted his comrades with one upraised hand, then spoke out in his rumbling baritone. "General Theroun den'Vekir of Alrou-Mendera! General Merra Alramir of Elsthemen! I have terms for you!"

"Terms!" General Merra sat tall astride her blood-washed white battle-cat to Theroun's right, her two remaining Captains, the brothers Rhone and Rhennon Uhlki, mangled from battle and riding snarling cats just behind her. Merra turned her head and spat. Blood and soot ruined her white armor, her wild red-blonde braids and high cheekbones feral. A proud woman of battle, Highland defiance sat in every vicious gesture as she gave a laugh from atop her mount.

"Fuck ye an' yer terms! Fight and face yer death!"

A dominant sneer twisted Khorel Jornath's lips. Towering over his taller-than-average comrades, his dark grey gaze regarded General Merra with disdain. His haughty features and cutting cheekbones were cast in fire and shadows, the silver studs on his armor glittering in the late evening as much as the flat black weave devoured the night.

"You will die as I tell you to die, whelp."

He raised two fingers. Merra's hands suddenly spasmed to her belt-knife, pulling it from its sheath. She cried out as her hand flashed to her throat. Jornath held her, her blade pressed so close to her sooty skin it drew a line of blood. He stared into her eyes, his dark gaze empty. Showing her that her life was utterly his, and Theroun knew enough of the bastard to understand he wanted to see fear in the eyes of Elsthemen's finest commander.

Submission.

"I'll hear your terms!"

Theroun barked it as casually as he could, interrupting the demonstration. Jornath's gaze flicked to him. Every gaze in the Kreth-Hakir battalion flicked to him. Every gaze in the Menderian army. Theroun felt the weight of that mass mind, like the crush of an ocean a hundred fathoms into the black. His breath came hard under that great weight. It hammered his chest and spiked pain through his body, but Theroun did not break his gaze from the Kreth-Hakir High Priest.

A subtle urge washed into him like a smooth rip tide. To raise his blade. To rip it across his own throat. So nice. So smooth. So good, to die by the blade as a commander should.

Holding onto his will, focusing it into a black spear so vicious Theroun could almost see it, Theroun forced his hand to pause at the hilt of his blade – not raising it. Shivering from the crush of minds, Theroun's body blazed with a pain so bright he saw stars. Chin down and eyes focused, he held onto that black lance in his mind, barbed like a scorpion's tail. Forming the essence of his defiance against the Kreth-Hakir – even though it was just imagination. He had nothing but his will against these men. But if that could keep Merra hale, keep even the tiniest fraction of the Elsthemi forces intact, he would use it.

He would do what he had to, to keep Queen Elyasin and King Therel's people alive.

"I'll have your submission, General." Jornath's cold gaze pummeled Theroun. "The rest can go their way if you agree to my terms. Personally."

Fear slid through Theroun's gut, tight and cold. He'd never really felt fear when faced with an enemy before. Even long ago, staring into the jaws of madness upon the Aphellian Way. But this was an enemy he couldn't fight. Not bound as they were into a mass consciousness; all of it focused upon Theroun's demise. Certainty shone in the High Priest's gaze. This was not about warfare, but about lessons. Jornath was here to see to Theroun's education – that the Kreth-Hakir Brethren were impossible to oppose.

Days ago, Theroun had gotten his blade into Jornath when they'd faced off in single combat. He'd left Jornath bleeding out in the grasslands. But to think a man dead and to know he was dead, were two very separate things. A fatal mistake that might mean death for the Elsthemi people, not to mention what was left of Theroun's defected Menderian forces.

Somehow, Jornath had survived the Black Viper's strike. And though one Scorpion alone upon the grasslands had not been able to take down the Viper, there were now nine. Nine herringbone bastards to reflect Jornath's commands through an entire army, bolstering the aggressors while breaking the defenders.

Until Lhen Fhekran was nothing but black ash and cold blood upon broken stone.

Theroun saw that reality in the High Priest's level gaze. Theroun hadn't been many things in his bitter life, but he was a good General. And a good General always knew when the day was lost.

"I will give you my submission, personally," Theroun barked, beginning the negotiations, his hand yet upon his blade. "And you will release the remainder of the Elsthemi forces. Immediately, and without damage of any kind."

General Merra's gaze flicked to him from atop her battle-cat, but she kept silent. The keshar-cats behind Theroun were still as ghosts in the roaring red evening.

"We've taken five hundred Elsthemi captives," Khorel Jornath's baritone was flat, his gaze level. "Five hundred of your best warriors, the ones that impressed us with their mind-resistance. They are to be tribute to my Order. We would take the last three hundred here," his thick lips turned up in a smirk, "but my people enjoy a challenge. If you can fight me in single combat, Theroun den'Vekir, and best me a second time mind-to-mind... I will allow these three hundred and their cat-rider General to go free. Immediately and without molestation."

"And the defenders behind the palace gates?" Theroun pressed, digging into the negotiation.

The Kreth-Hakir smirked, his dark eyes amused. "Yes. We feel your five hundred fighters inside the palisades, trembling as they watch our slaughter." His gaze roved the fortress-wall. Some of that oceanic press lifted from Theroun. A thoughtful smirk lifted one corner of Jornath's lips, and his gaze returned to Theroun, along with all its weight.

"You drive a clever bargain, General Theroun. How much do I want the glory of capturing eight hundred of Elsthemen's best fighters versus how much I want the satisfaction of breaking you? But I am a reasonable man. The fighters behind the palace walls may go with your Elsthemi battle-General and her retinue. I give my word." He nodded to General Merra. "However, Lhaurent den'Alrahel was specific as to my appointment upon this campaign. To uphold my end of our alignment, I must remit the King of Elsthemen and the Queen of Alrou-Mendera into his custody. Alive, preferably."

"Naturally," Theroun growled.

His mind raced. He was out of options. Khorel Jornath would storm the palisades of Fhekran Palace with or without Theroun's bargain. It was just a matter of how many lives would be lost. Theroun set his jaw, hoping he'd stalled long enough to give King Therel Alramir and Queen Elyasin den'Ildrian Alramir enough time to escape through the tunnels beneath the palace, into the mountains.

To enact their plan for the survival of their nations in this time of madness.

Theroun took a deep breath, feeling the crushing weight of the minds Jornath wielded. Setting his jaw, Theroun swung a leg back over the rump of his keshar-cat, dismounting with grace and keeping his exhausted body from twitching. Theroun's Black Bastard cat yowled in a forlorn rage, lashing its tail. Stepping up to its blocky skull, Theroun let the mean beast butt heads with him. It opened its mouth, putting Theroun's entire head in its jaws – though it didn't bite, only marking him with an inundation of saliva. Pulling back, the black keshar raked the stones with dark claws, swinging its jaundiced yellow eyes to Khorel Jornath.

Strangely, the Kreth-Hakir leader nodded to the great beast. The cat gave a nasty growl, raking the paving-stones to chips with its claws. "Your beast claims you, Theroun," the herringbone-clad man chuckled, "but you must surrender to me if you wish your warriors to live."

At his words, the eight Kreth-Hakir raised their hands. A shearing sound rasped the air, swords and axes and knives drawn from leather scabbards. The keshari defenders behind Theroun cried out. Theroun saw from the corner of his eye that all those weapons had been put to throats. But Theroun heard no gurgles, no screams. The man before him was playing a game of dominance and submission, not of life and death.

It was Theroun's debasement Jornath wanted.

Stepping from his ronin-cat, Theroun walked forward with steady strides. Khorel Jornath's haughty eyes watched him, a pleased smile twisting his thick lips. He lowered his hand and the rest of the Hakir did also, in a smooth unison like a hive of bees.

An eerie silence held the ranks as Theroun approached.

"I agree to your terms." Theroun stopped fifteen paces from Khorel Jornath. "Single combat. And all the men and women behind me go free, including those behind the palace gates. But single combat means you take no other minds into yours while we do this, just as I would let no other fighter into the ring with us for a duel of swords. Break your word, and lose your honor."

Theroun had made an astute guess. Jornath's eager eyes darkened. Not in rage, but in a quiet thoughtfulness, his head tilting as if regarding Theroun anew. Slowly, his lips curled up in a smile of pure pleasure. The press of a thousand minds lifted from Theroun's body, the ocean rolling back. Standing tall, Theroun twisted his neck to crack it, then took in a deep breath.

"Then let us begin," Jornath spoke.

"Let us begin."

A roaring silence filled Theroun's ears. The fighters around him were spectrally quiet, though burning filled the city. Red flames scorched the night, casting a diabolical glow over the black company of the Kreth-Hakir and the Menderian army. Through drifting char Theroun watched his opponent. Khorel Jornath did nothing at first, only eyed Theroun with a watchfulness in his gaze. He made no move to draw the two-handed broadsword that rode his back, nor to claim the knives at his belt; only crossed his arms over his herringbone jerkin and stood there, waiting to see what his opponent would try.

Had it been a battle of swords, Theroun would have let the man wait. Watching Jornath's feet, his posture, his readiness. The first warrior to charge in a duel was often the first to become dismembered. But this was a duel waged inside their minds, a terrain not foreign to Theroun, only utilized in a different way. He knew how to judge a commander's will from a bloody field, and he could read Jornath's utterly at-ease posture. Every expression the man had was known, every grip of muscle in his lips and cheek, and at the corners of his subtly-creased eyes. Theroun could read the tense attention of Jornath's comrades as they watched – feigning indifference but too rigidly eager as they anticipated this duel.

A duel which was clearly off-tactic for the Kreth-Hakir. Jornath was stepping out on a thin blade, going after Theroun in personal vendetta and without the mind-support of his Brethren. But what Theroun didn't know, was why, and what Theroun also didn't know was just how this duel was supposed to begin.

Or what would happen once it did.

The heavy waiting would have broken most men by now, but it only pissed Theroun off, making him go still – to a place that knew only the strike. Theroun made no move, matching Jornath and doing him one emptier. A vast nothingness flowed between them. Theroun could almost feel it swirling around him; a place where emotion should have been. Where one man should have hated the other, snarling for his enemy's death.

17

Yet Theroun felt nothing. No animosity. No wrath. No brimstone and fire, though it burned on all around them. Here, facing this herringbone-clad commander, all he could see was his own posture before him. His own face, impassive upon the battlefield. His own arms crossed at his chest, a mirror to himself but taller, broader. Theroun's own empty-ready eyes staring back in a face with thick lips, cutting cheekbones, and heavy eyelids.

Shock snapped Theroun, cracked his ready equilibrium. He'd felt no mental attack, it was only the surprise of seeing his own self in this other commander. In that moment something ripped out from Theroun, lashing like a serpent's strike. Thrusting the barbed black spear he had previously imagined straight to Khorel Jornath – as if it was a real weapon and not just willful intent.

Jornath flinched. The man's big face twitched aside and opened in surprise, as if a snake had actually struck at him. The dominance dropped from his lips. A leaning press upon Theroun's psyche lifted in that moment, something Theroun had not even known was there. As if the weight of a mountain had evaporated from Theroun's shoulders – the solid strength of Jornath's own mind.

A subtle trick that Theroun had not known was there until he'd broken it. And now, somehow, the Black Viper of the Aphellian Way had bested Jornath for a second time in as many days, but it didn't last. Theroun could no more wield the black spear in his mind than he could control a wild snake, and when Khorel Jornath's expression of dominance returned, it came like a hurricane, his gaze cold as death.

"*Kneel, Theroun den'Vekir.*"

The force of his command hit Theroun like an avalanche. It wasn't a mountain, it was the upheaval of the earth. It was a pummeling of sand and stone, river and chasm, oceans and thunder. It was the sound of wreckage and the feel of ruin, of the plates of the earth grinding together and shaking everything into obliteration.

Theroun's resistance snapped. His black mind-spear was shattered beneath that utterly dominant force. Driven to his knees, one hand slapped the cobbles to keep himself from being plowed down altogether. His jaw snapped closed, teeth hitting each other so hard he clipped a piece from the side of his tongue. The iron tang of blood filled his mouth. Pain blossomed in red streamers from his old injury. Pain devoured him, a ripping agony that had no end, only the horror of the now. Head hanging, eyes tight, spasms ripped through Theroun's body.

"Fight him, Theroun!" Merra's roar cut the burning night.

Somewhere in his annihilation, Theroun felt Khorel Jornath take a knee before him. The big man whispered at his ear, "Fight me, Black Viper. Show me you are better than I am. Show me your willful defiance, and I will let your fighters go free."

Pain was no stranger to Theroun. For years he had lived with it, struggled with it – managed it. Daily, he had kept an arrangement with his war-maimed body, practicing the breathing and stretching that made his hours livable. He used that now, drawing slow breaths, sending it deep into his injured side, using his chest's bellows to work out the gripping agony. Gradually, he re-learned how to think. He remembered that he was a General among men. He remembered that he had killed over five hundred fighters in combat over the decades. He remembered that he was the Black Viper of the Aphellian Way, ruthless and utterly cold.

And he remembered that if he'd fucked Khorel Jornath twice, he could do it again.

Slowly, Theroun's spasms came under control. Fighting the weight of Khorel's enormous attack, Theroun's head came up. Cold rage filled him. A darkness so vast he couldn't even begin to see the edges of it. A darkness so terrible that a part of Theroun ran screaming, to see what lived inside himself. A cold uncaring that devoured the hearts of men.

The Scorpion had stung, but the Viper was far from beaten.

A bloody snarl split Theroun's lips. *"No matter how you send me to Halsos' Hells, I'll be waiting – for when you get here."*

And then Theroun laughed.

He laughed and laughed, his body bright with a sensation he didn't understand. It wasn't pain, more like a terrible pleasure. Something of heinous power searing every limb, it rushed through him, exhilarating; a hot fire like poison in his veins. A liberation that was part of his very core – a man who had nothing left to lose. It filled Theroun, taking him into madness and pushing back the pain, and with it came an image of searing red eyes in the center of his mind, willing him to take it in.

To take it in, and obliterate the world.

"Stop!" Khorel Jornath commanded, his grey eyes wide in horrified surprise. "*Cease!*"

But his commands had no effect. The bright poison that had taken Theroun was all-consuming, and the pressure of Khorel Jornath's mind evaporated like mist before a falling star. The burning eyes grew in Theroun's mind, wild, incalculable in their unimaginable horrors. Theroun doubled over, laughing, mad. And with it came freedom as those burning eyes rushed up to take him – to swallow him whole.

A boot kicked out, connecting with Theroun's face. He sprawled to the paving-stones, his vision blacking out. The red eyes were struck from his mind as his body seized. Theroun lost time, flicking through unconsciousness. Some part of him felt the Kreth-Hakir Brethren surge in, clamping manacles about his wrists, manacles that carried the thrusting weight of their combined minds. Pain lanced Theroun's body, tripled, quadrupled. Agony left him unable to think as he was cuffed and forced up, dragged over the cobbles with his knees scraping.

"*Theroun!*" Merra's shout behind him was raw. "Get off him, ye bastards!"

"Take your warriors and go, woman! *Now!*" Theroun heard Khorel Jornath roar. "*Take your lives and go!!*"

But Theroun could not even growl a response through his strangling throat. Screams rose inside him as another wave of spasms hit, as he choked them back with clenched teeth. Through the skirling ash he felt the mass of Elsthemi heel away, marked by the strangled roars of cats and the whinnies of horses yanked by hard hands. Theroun heard the groan of the palisade gates crank open, rattling their chains like bones of the damned.

A mass of cats fled out through the gates of Fhekran Palace as Theroun was dragged into the grounds. Cat-musk flowed by Theroun, the rank sweat of men and horses departing the palace like ghosts before the torch. Some sane part of him understood that Khorel Jornath had kept his word. That he'd allowed what was left of the Elsthemi and defected Menderians to go free. That Jornath wielded the Kreth-Hakir to urge the allied forces into departing without any further loss of life, even though they would have fought and died to the last man or woman.

There were no words. There was no resistance. Just the yowls of cats and the jingle of metal as the last of the Elsthemi army fled Lhen Fhekran – leaving only the roar of fire in the night.

CHAPTER 1 – ELOHL

The man with golden Inkings stared out at the dawn and had no remembrance of who he was.

The eastern sky brightened rose and then gold as the sun fought its way higher in the mist-wreathed dawn. A green countryside ripe with grain and early-autumn glory spread out below his vantage upon the high white balcony, to a barrier of purple mountains in the far distance. It was a vantage he remembered like a dream; standing upon a white spire that thrust into the dawn.

A dawn that was his to claim, with an ocean of blue around it.

Blue. Blue washed over his vision, a deep cerulean like mountain lakes penetrated by the first rays of morning. He remembered a woman in that lake-cool color. The soft curve of her throat, the feel of soft white hair whispering over his skin, the scents of tundra and pine. How she sighed his name in the glory of those first rays. Moving with her, breathing with her, knowing this was where he had to be. Everything he had suffered to be here – snowstorms, gales, climbing sheer walls of ice with hands gone frigid and numb.

To be in the white spire with her, creating that bliss with the rising dawn.

The man shivered in the chill wind, and it slipped away. He couldn't recall it. He couldn't even remember where he was or what exactly he was doing here, in this white tower rather than that one.

Gazing down at his hands where they rested upon the opalescent stone railing, he noted the golden marks curling over his arms. The backs of his scarred and weathered hands glinted in the lifting light, marked by a flowing language that breathed through his skin like fire. As dawn crept down the ethereal turret behind him, finally filling his eyes with its glory, he felt the marks come to life. Curling and shifting as if liquid sunlight flowed through them, the golden marks were a beautiful mystery.

The man gripped the cool agate of the balcony, flexing his hands. He knew their strength; knew they were capable; knew his body was so much more than it seemed. His gaze traveled over the near distance, seeing a sprawling palace below carven of the same white agate as his balcony. Milky in the dawn, the turrets, domes, and minarets seemed to glow with subtle veins as the light lifted. From this vantage, he could see the palace was carven to resemble a flowing forest, as if tree and river and vine could petrify into stone yet remain fluid. Even the railing he clutched ran with carven vines and milk-white flowers.

His gaze rested upon the verdant grounds. Far below, he marked the glossy late-summer foliage of olive groves: the dusky *Olea lithii*, the Peace Olive – a dark and succulent fruit. Something they'd had in his city as a boy.

There was something important about olives, something he was supposed to know, but he couldn't remember it. A small green lizard with a yellow throat and a red stripe down its back raced across the railing. The man was so still that the gecko raced over his fingers and paused upon his knuckles. Looking up, it regarded him with slit golden eyes, unafraid. The man stared down at it, recalling that this lizard was the *eloi*. The man took a long, slow breath. A single breath to steady himself, before he let it out in a whisper.

"Eloi…"

The lizard scampered away.

A sound came from the room behind him. Beyond the balcony doors with their gossamer veils hemmed in pearls, he heard a groan. Startled, the man spun, hands whipping to his hips. He should have had knives, long knives of keen function and a blade strapped to his back, but there was nothing: only the silk of sleep-trousers he'd donned from the bed when he'd woken naked in an unfamiliar room.

The room behind him was lush – an agate-stone bower with vaulted heights lost to an arching tree pattern. Copper summer braziers of nearly-dead coals smoked near a dark fireplace of the same agate-stone blocks as the rest. Sunlight flooded in the arching windows, gleaming upon lush carpets and gilded chaises. Red and gold silk accented the pale room, with enormous floor-pillows for lounging and tasseled rugs. A cold breakfast was laid out on a gilded white pine table. Crimson and gold ceramic censers choked the air with a hazy perfume – the reason the man had pushed out to the balcony when he'd woken, parched, with a thundering headache and a cottony mouth.

Through the latticed doors, the man's gaze fixed upon a naked fellow now struggling up from a mess of crimson pillows upon the floor. The room was clearing of its pestilence, and the man on the balcony saw that the fellow in the pillows was fit and lean, average in stature but somehow impressive. Corded sinew and lean muscle stood out upon every inch of him, cut in stark detail as he moved. His brush-cut auburn waves would have been unassuming had the slanting rays of sunlight not illuminated highlights of brilliant gold as he clutched his head, then rubbed his hands down his trimmed beard. His hands had the weathered look of a man who had climbed hard in bad ice – a detail the man on the balcony couldn't understand how he knew.

The fellow in the pillows coughed, tensing his closed eyelids against the flooding light. He inhaled, making a ferocious scowl as he tasted the air, then curried both hands through his short mane again. With a groan he shifted, only to find his lower body caught up in a crimson silk sheet half-pulled from the bed. The man fought the sheet as if enraged for a moment, then gave up and hung his head over his knees, rubbing the heels of his hands in his eye-sockets.

"Undoer's *hells*, that's bright!" His eyes opened and the man on the balcony saw his companion's eyes were a stunning color – a copper brown that would have been dull in the shade but which glowed with a golden ring in the sun. "Pull the drapes, will you, Elohl? But leave the balcony doors open. That fucking woman and her threllis! Shaper fuck me, we need to get out of here…"

The man on the balcony frowned. He supposed the man on the floor was addressing him, as there was no one else in the room. He knew then, why he had been fascinated with the *eloi* lizard; because it was his given name – Elohl.

Elohl drew a breath to speak. "Were you addressing me?"

"Seven fucks of Jeldhaia!" The man's eyes fired with alarm. Red flashed through those eyes, but it was just a trick of the morning light. Without a trace of the suffering he had evinced earlier, the man rose in a fluid wave and crossed the room. His hands grasped Elohl's face before Elohl could move. Holding him, he searched Elohl's eyes, then his gaze flicked to Elohl's golden Inkings, shimmering with the rising dawn.

"Shit!" He looked back up. "Elohl! Tell me who I am! Quickly."

Elohl knit his brows. Struggling through memories, he could recall the man's face, though it was cast in stark shadow as if from a fire. He remembered the man shouting at him, brandishing a polearm, riding atop a massive cat...

Elohl shook his head. "I know you. Don't I?"

The man before him gave a vicious growl. With a lithe movement, he reached out and picked up a ceramic censer from a nearby table and hurled it to the stone floor. It shattered, scattering coals into the fireplace, smoke curling up the drafting flue.

"Damn that bitch!"

Elohl thought he saw the man's eyes flash red again as he stormed the room, seizing censers and hurling them with impressive strength and accuracy into the dark fireplace. They shattered with a popping sound, delicate gold pottery reduced to so much trash.

Returning to Elohl, the man seized Elohl by his short-bearded face, shaking him. "Remember, damn you! Remember who I am! Remember who you are!!" With a quick hand, he delivered Elohl a stunning slap that rang his head and buzzed his ears. A copper river broke upon his tongue as Elohl's lower lip split. Upon the taste of blood and violence, something roared to life inside Elohl. With a quick up-strike, he threaded his arms between the other man's and broke them away.

"Unhand me!"

"*Please* remember!" The man's eyes were desperate, terrible.

"I don't know you, fellow," Elohl growled as he backed away. Cautious, his hands were up and relaxed – ready to fight. "Come at me again and get yourself broken for your trouble."

The man before him roared. He wasn't a big man, but somehow in that moment, he was terrifying. Elohl backed off, his heart pounding fast in his chest from alarm as he watched the man's eyes come to life. Where once there had been placid brown and stunning gold, there now bled a burning heat, a molten red that churned fire. Elohl realized with a shock that the fire in the man's eyes had been no trick of light.

With a rough growl, the wiry man strode past Elohl and out the balcony doors. He curried one hand through his short brown waves, a gesture of frustration that Elohl realized was familiar. The man stepped to the balcony rail, bracing his palms upon it and breathing deeply with eyes closed. A sudden roar spilled from his lips, and the man whirled about and threw a fist into one windowpane of the tower.

With a wrenching shriek, the twenty-foot pane shattered. Instinct tingled his limbs and Elohl leaped forward, yanking the fellow out of the way as shards of glass came ripping down, smashing to pieces and skittering over the balcony. The lean fellow roared again in Elohl's arms, his ribcage heaving like a bellows. For a moment Elohl thought the man had been pierced by glass. But the man balled his fists, smashing them into the turret's stone, shattering a massive agate block that spiderwebbed in cracks.

"She fucked us, Elohl – *dammit*!!!"

The sky above the balcony darkened, a maelstrom of clouds gathering from a bright blue sky. Pressure built upon Elohl's eardrums like an impending thunderstorm. He remembered storms like this, flash-furious maelstroms that came quickly in the mountain highpasses, up where the air was thin and seasons changed fast, but this was far more than those monstrosities, unnatural. Clouds thickened to columns above the tower, blue sky snuffed out in moments. Climbing cumulus swirled, darkening to a livid bruise over the palace. A wind picked up, rattling the windowpanes in their brackets. The olive grove whipped far below, a violent wind lashing hard enough now to drive moisture down in chill daggers. Sleet came, and a rattle of hail stung Elohl's skin.

Electricity triggered every hair on Elohl's body, lightning soon to strike, and Elohl knew this was no natural storm: this was pure power, the man's rage made manifest. A rage of such violent character that it could turn a summer's day black in moments. Elohl's heart pounded in his chest. Terrified for the man who struggled in his arms, for himself, for this horrifying ability. He watched the sky turn dark as death, swirling with obliteration as the wiry fellow screamed again and heaved against Elohl's iron grip.

Bolts of lightning lanced from bruise to bruise, slicing the green-tinged dawn with booms of thunder.

A quick flash struck the tower above them. With a deafening crack, the explosion hammered him and the raging man to the balcony, chips of agate-stone littering down around them. As Elohl landed atop the furious man, whorls of crimson and gold blossomed to life through the skin upon the man's bare back. Curling through his veins, spreading out upon the stark lines of his muscles into an ornate Inking of a wolf and dragon battling inside a ring of flame that seared as bright as the storm was dark.

Staring at the emblem, feeling it burn beneath his fingertips to the rage and crackle of the storm, Elohl suddenly remembered who this was: Fentleith Alodwine, the last Scion of House Alodwine, royal Kings of Khehem and bearer of the Wolf and Dragon *wyrria*. Elohl's mind focused with a snap so violent it cracked his head back, clear as the lightning that leaped through the blackened sky. A silver fog tinged with the tinkling of trapper's bells lingered in his thoughts, but it was distant.

"*Fenton!*" Elohl yelled against the storm, struggling to hold the raging man down. "Fenton, stop!"

But Fenton only roared like the beasts that fought within him. With a surge of tremendous strength, he bucked, trying to heave Elohl off, his wiry body far stronger than any man Elohl had ever grappled. Elohl's grip on his arms slipped. Fenton heaved a fast elbow back into Elohl's solar plexus, and Elohl huffed, gasping. Elohl threw his entire weight down to the balcony to pin the smaller man, but Fenton heaved him again. Lightning consumed the sky in endless rivers. Elohl's heart hit his throat and fear slit his veins; Fenton was building a storm that would tear the palace apart – and them along with it.

"Control yourself!"

Elohl's bellow was drowned out by a crack of thunder and another branch of lightning flashed. Striking the balcony, it exploded in a report that left Elohl's ears ringing and deaf. In that same moment, the golden Inkings upon his skin suddenly blazed to life; not an underwater luminescence, but searing bright as day under the storm's black belly.

"*Fentleith Alodwine – I command you to control yourself!*"

Elohl roared it, hardly able to hear his own voice. Fenton cried out as if in pain, but suddenly the naked man beneath him stilled. Thunder pummeled the air, but softer, lightning flashing up in the clouds rather than striking the tower. Gradually, the fury of the storm began to pull back. A few more flashes came as the seething mass roiled and the black clouds started to dissipate. Cumulus dispersed in cottony columns from the belly up as wind rattled the panes and died. The hail ceased and then the rain, leaving only a fresh autumnal scent behind.

Fenton breathed like a blown horse, pinned beneath Elohl. Limbs lax, his chest heaved from fury and exhaustion. Elohl gave the Scion of Khehem another moment, until he could see patches of blue sky, before he pushed up and out of Fenton's way.

"Are you calm?" Elohl stood, gasping for breath, fear still racing his veins.

"Yes." It was a dark reply, muffled from Fenton's face still pressed into the agate. Fenton lay facedown, unmoving, though his chest still heaved and his limbs trembled. The *wyrric* inking upon his back was still bright as fire, curling through its traces like lava on the move.

"Are you all right?" Elohl tried to not let on how relieved he was that Fenton's storm had abated.

"*No.*" In a fluid movement, Fenton set his palms to the balcony and pushed to standing. Brushing shards of colored glass and chips of agate off his body, he was cut in a dozen places but didn't seem to care. Flicking rain from his short-shorn waves, he grunted and looked down. A shard of red glass had lodged in the skin of his ribs. With a short growl, he braced the skin around the shard and drew it out, leaving an upwelling of blood to trickle down his abdomen. Looking up, he glared at Elohl with piercing, raw eyes, though they were their usual gold-brown once more. "Why did you do that to me?"

"Do what? Subdue you?" Elohl rubbed his chest from where the scaring of his Goldenmarks lingered, and from where Fenton had elbowed him in his solar plexus. "Because you were going batshit!"

"*Ordering* me, Elohl! Wake up, Aeon-dammit!" Fenton's gold eyes burned. He gestured angrily at the opulent room behind them, then set his fingertips to the weeping hole in his skin. "We've been trapped in this pouffed hell-hole for three weeks since we came through the portal-arch from Bhorlen's citadel to the Palace of the Vine – all because *you* keep abusing my Rennkavi's oath and ordering me to refrain from action!"

"You were out of control, Fenton! I did what I had to."

But uncertainty grasped Elohl. Memories washed back, as if Fenton's storm had sluiced the silver smoke of amnesia from his mind. His cheeks burned as he began to recall days of threllis-induced lassitude, and nights of largesse.

Three weeks trapped in the Falconry as willing prisoners of the Valenghian Vhinesse; her special little pets.

Elohl choked. He stepped to the balcony railing, sick. His arms shook as he gripped the stone, furious. Memories of the past three weeks hit him like forge-hammers: the Falconry. The Vhinesse's boudoir for her kept men. How easily the Vhinesse had snared him; all the times Fenton had tried to slap him out of it. Her luminous beauty, her tinkling laugh like a trapper's winter bells, her purring alto voice. All the clever ways Fenton had tried to sober Elohl up after the Vhinesse had visited. Her touch, commanding his body to obey with her silver vines and opiate-clouds twisting through his mind.

And after she had touched him… Elohl recalled what they'd done – so many nights, all night long. He recalled how he'd gotten his split lip, when she'd ordered Fenton and Elohl to fight one another bare-knuckled for her pleasure as she drank wine and lit censors before she took them both. Ghrenna's cerulean eyes rose in Elohl's vision. Elohl reached out to her with everything he had, screaming her name deep inside with the rising dawn.

"Three *weeks*." Elohl stared out over the olive groves, choking back wretchedness. It didn't even sound possible. That he had been duped so badly for so long. His emotions tumbled, and he let them come. Every devastating day after the Kingsmen Summons and his capture in Alrashesh; every night spent freezing and terrified in the highpasses indentured to the High Brigade; every time he'd stepped into battle upon a glacier, not knowing if his body had enough strength to fight one more opponent.

Abandoning his Queen and King. Not keeping Olea safe.

Losing Ghrenna.

"Couldn't you have tried a little harder to get us out of here?" Elohl growled over his shoulder. It felt good to unleash his rage. But besides himself, the only person to rage at was Fenton. "You could have blasted a hole in the wall, Fenton, or snuck us out! There are a thousand ways we could have left this palace by now. Did you try *none* of them?"

Fenton responded to Elohl's anger with his own fury, fire flashing in his eyes. "You think it's *my* fault we're still here? My blood-sworn oath will *kill me* if I lift a finger against you, my Rennkavi – which includes making decisions that supersede yours. I can only make a decision to *save your life*, Elohl! Fuck the Vhinesse and all she is, but she hasn't done a thing that puts your life at risk! We're her pets. *You're* the one who keeps ordering me to stand down! One touch of the Vhinesse's hands, and you fucking conveniently forget everything, except *my goddamn oath to your service!*" Fenton finished with a livid growl.

"She *does* something to me!" Elohl glared. Hurling the words at Fenton, their tempers were a good match now that they had both been unleashed. "Her touch! Fenton, when she touches me, I can think of nothing else! Believe me, if I'd had my wits, I would have strangled her skinny neck making me fuck her night after night when the only woman I want is—"

Elohl choked. His gut dropped through the stones and his chest clenched, his golden Inkings fading along with his rage. All of it had happened because Elohl was starved for the woman he really wanted. Starved for seasons, years, for a decade. Her cerulean eyes flared briefly in his mind, before they, too, snuffed out.

"Ghrenna." Fenton finished Elohl's sentence for him. "Say her name, Elohl. She deserves that much when you fuck another woman in her place. And force your liege-man to do the same."

"You enjoyed it." Elohl growled, bitter bile in his mouth.

"Sure." Fenton's gaze was hard, burning like firebrands. "The Vhinesse is a good lay. She fucks hard, and I'm able to take out my anger on her lily-white skin. But no more than I enjoy a prostitute, Elohl. Her *wyrria* doesn't affect me like it does you. I learned how to block mind-*wyrria* of many varieties over my ten centuries. No, *you* have been the one to put me in a compromised position these three weeks, not her."

"I'm sorry." Elohl murmured, spent, a terrible hollowness gripping his chest. He glanced into the room for something more to wear, but there was nothing. Just veils, gauze, silk, and that damned threllis lingering in the air.

"Sorry doesn't cover this," Fenton's gaze was still dark. Checking the wound beneath his fingertips, he paused, then removed them. The hole was closed, and though blood still marred his skin, the wound had healed just as quickly. "I couldn't *protect my Rennkavi* because of what he *ordered* me to do, Elohl. To follow the Vhinesse's every instruction. To stay and enjoy her *hospitality*. To fuck her, night after night, and not set a finger to her pretty white throat. Those orders still stand until you remove them. If I don't obey you, I'm damned by my own oaths…"

Fenton trailed off, gazing out over the rising morning with a lost look upon his face. Suddenly, Elohl realized what he'd done, the gravity of it. And it needed more than remedy: it needed undoing. Grasping Fenton's shoulder, Elohl turned him. Looking Fenton in the eyes, Elohl summoned command from his very essence.

"Follow *my* orders, Fentleith. Not anyone else. And from here on… I *order* you to act in my best interest. If you judge that I'm compromised, if I can't think for myself or protect myself or if something's wrong with me, then I need you to think and act for me. I *order* you to."

The Goldenmarks had lit again with a simmering glow, as if responding to Elohl's utterance. Elohl could feel them, a cascade of burning prickles over his skin. That slow luminescence seemed to twist in Fenton's eyes with the last of his wrathful fire, until finally, something in Fenton eased. Closing his eyes, he took a deep breath and let it out.

"Rennkavi. So you order. So shall I do."

The tension in the air cleared. With Elohl's command he had put Fenton's heart at ease, or perhaps his very soul. The day brightened to clear skies, sunlight glimmering in the raindrops upon the balcony and raising curls of steam. A cool breeze skimmed the olive grove far below, rustling the dark foliage.

Fenton stood very still, his eyes closed in the golden sunlight. Elohl watched the Scion of Khehem take slow, deep breaths in the rising dawn. Even though Fenton was becalmed, Elohl could feel a beast of unfathomable energy still trying to escape from his wire-tight frame. As if all his sinew and muscle was needed to rope in the power that seethed within – never ceasing, never sleeping.

Only dormant, because the man who contained it forced it to be.

Watching Fenton breathe on the balcony, Elohl found himself wondering at the power of the Wolf and Dragon *wyrria* that lived within Fenton, now yoked to the Rennkavi – to *his* command. Elohl pushed it from his mind. It was too enormous to think on. He had practical problems to deal with, most notably their current situation and how to get out of it. But the question of Fenton's power lingered in the back of his mind even as he shoved it there, like live coals raked under hearth ash.

A question that would rise again, and would need remedy.

CHAPTER 2 – ELYASIN

Queen Elyasin den'Ildrian Alramir woke with a gasp in the luminous darkness, brandishing her longknife.

Heaving deep breaths and rank with sweat in her bedroll, she waited, a woman's scream still ringing in her ears. All around the underground grotto the haunting sound of water flowed, cascading from rock walls and pouring into basins filled with phosphorescent moss. The expansive hush of the Heldim Alir, the Way Beneath the Mountains, breathed around Elyasin: ferns glowing moon-white in the water, luminous pink snowdrops pushing up through ice-blue moss beside her bedroll. Gradually, she realized that the scream had only been nightmare. Rummaging in a pocket of her undergarments, she retrieved a palm-sized stone. Producing a throaty hum, she watched the singing-stone brighten in her palm from a dull luminescence to a curling glow like moonlight through an ebbing tide, illuminating the grotto in a milky light.

At the edge of the light, Elyasin saw the sleeping mounds of Kingswoman Ghrenna den'Tanuk and Queen's Physician Luc den'Lhorissian in the bedroll they shared, nestled in a mossy alcove and surrounded by ferns. She could just see the blonde hair of the scribe Thaddeus den'Lhor where he was curled in his blankets against the perpetual chill. Elyasin gazed down at her own bedroll to see her King and husband Therel Alramir scowl at her light, then snuggle back down into the warmth so only his pale, unruly hair was visible.

All was silence in the grotto, save for the splash and burble of water cascading down the rock wall into a pool inset with gold and moonstone sigils. As Elyasin waited, willing her heart to slow, she heard an eerie sound from Luc and Ghrenna's bedroll. The sound of a woman singing – in a sinuous, rolling language Elyasin was beginning to know.

Giannyk, the language of the Giants.

Elyasin watched Ghrenna writhe in her blankets, then gasp as if in passion. She was asleep, but her long eyelashes flickered in dreams, lit by the grotto's unearthly glow. Luc stirred and sat up in the bedroll beside her, still fully clothed in his tan and fawn buckled leathers from the day before, his hands cupping the back of Ghrenna's neck. His eyes closed in a light trance, and Elyasin knew a soothing balm eased from his *wyrric* hands. Elyasin could almost feel that flow, seeping like warm milk into Ghrenna. She watched Ghrenna relax, breathing deep as her dream was banished.

With Ghrenna finally quiet, Luc let his hands slip away. The light from Elyasin's singing-stone started to fade and she hummed again. Resonance resounded within the stone, making the phosphorescent light whirl faster. All around, the grotto responded, veins of blue ore brightening until the space held an evening's gloaming that danced with the movement of galaxies.

They'd discovered these luminous alcove-gardens after escaping Lhen Fhekran. The first grotto they'd found in the dark tunnel beneath the Kingsmountains had illuminated to their speech. They'd chipped out ore to take with them these past three weeks, the stones a blessing in the expansive dark of the Giannyk tunnels. This dreaming was Ghrenna's tenth in the past three days alone, the episodes more frequent the deeper they plunged into the tunnels upon Morvein Vishke's ancient path. Ghrenna's seizures and headaches were a thing of the past, and though she grew more hale every day as Morvein's centuries-old memories trickled back, everyone else was getting worse from interrupted sleep.

Luc's green eyes were tight, his golden brows knit as he caught Elyasin's gaze. Therel made a low moan in his sleep and twisted in the bedroll, snuggling down into the soft carpet of moss. Gazing at her King and husband, Elyasin ran her fingers through his pale hair. His brows knit in dark dreams before his breathing steadied. She could see his pale eyelashes and strong, high cheeks, unearthly in the grotto's glow. His jaw was coarse, a beard showing the passing of their weeks underground. As Elyasin soothed her husband, she opened her senses. The dark tunnels held a resonance that rang in her mind and body. Like untapped streams, Elyasin felt a flow of power even more concentrated in the glowing grottoes than the tunnels themselves. Immersing herself in that flow, Elyasin felt an immaculate silence; the same as she'd felt since coming through the rose-crystal doorway beneath Fhekran Palace.

No one walked these ancient halls – and no one had in a very long time.

Therel growled in his sleep, and Elyasin resumed stroking his hair. He wasn't the only one having nightmares. Elyasin thought back over her own dark dreams and shivered: she could still feel the mind-warping power of the Kreth-Hakir the night they fled Lhen Fhekran, even though the Hakir had been trapped out of the tunnels. Elyasin and the others had waited two full days with weapons, ready to gut any Hakir who tried coming through the doorway – though no one had.

Elyasin could still feel her agony in the steam-hall of Fhekran Palace, pacing as sounds of battle drifted down from the hall's high window-slits. Ghrenna clad in black Kingsmen gear and snowhare furs, facing the portal in a trance with eyelids flickering. Her slender hands playing over rose-crystal and gold sigils, creating haunting music as shards of the doorway began shuffling back. Shouts, the ring of swords at the doors. Lhesher Khoum's booming roar in the corridor. Elyasin drawing her own sword fast, even lanky Thaddeus holding a blade in trembling hands, his green eyes enormous behind his spectacles. Therel and Luc standing their ground – Therel's lupine frame wire-tight, his wolf-blue eyes snarling for battle.

The doors kicking open. High Dremorande Adelaine Visck, Lhesher Khoum, and Jhonen Rebaldi had tumbled in, fighting like dervishes against thirty Menderian soldiers and nine Kreth-Hakir Brethren in herringbone black. Jhonen had fought like a keshar-cat, blood streaking her face as she roared for death. The mighty Lhesher's red beard and braids flew as he clashed with Kreth-Hakir and Menderian soldiers. Adelaine had fought like a tundra-wraith, her thin mouth set, her pale furs spattered with blood as she cut with sword and longknife – and battled back the minds of the Kreth-Hakir.

Even through the dampening of Elyasin's keshar-claw pendant, their golden sigils burning upon her skin during the fighting, Elyasin had felt the tremendous power of Adelaine. Against a raging tide of silver mind-weaves, Adelaine had stood like a beacon inside Elyasin's head, like a lighthouse in the harshest winter storm. Flooding their

35

allies, protecting them as fighting raged toward Elyasin and the others.

With a clash of swords, Elyasin had engaged. Her body had fought without her, everything Olea den'Alrahel had ever taught her rushing up as she'd spun in to hammer a Kreth-Hakir with her shoulder and rip her sword up through his armpit. Battle-fury had fired her veins and washed her vision red as she dodged a Menderian soldier and slit his sword-wrist. But the Kreth-Hakir had fought like professional war-makers. Sending waves of Menderian soldiers into the fray before them, the Hakir had hammered their group with a sundering *wyrric* power that swamped Elyasin's pendant and made it blister her skin.

Fall back, curs!

Elyasin had felt Adelaine's command rip through the Kreth-Hakir, staggering them. Lhesher had head-butted a Hakir and Therel gutted another. Elyasin had stabbed one in the eye and he fell; Luc sliced the throat of one more, grim.

But just as Adelaine's winter-white command rose again, Elyasin had felt the air around her choke. Like a shroud of silver despair, the Kreth-Hakir High Priest had joined the battle. A fist hammering the air, his mind had pummeled straight for Adelaine with the full force of his Brethren behind it. That power had hit Adelaine like a battering ram – slamming her thin frame against the wall, dashing her head against the stone. Furs careened as she'd collapsed in a heap, unmoving. Adelaine's beacon had failed, and it was only by the grace of Elyasin's pendant that she didn't go down writhing as pain assaulted her like a thousand silver lances shoved into her flesh.

Sagging against the wall, gasping, Elyasin had seen the rose-crystal portal singing with light, fully open at last. Therel had lurched close, the silver claw-pendant upon his breast blazing as he hauled her toward the portal.

"The Queen and King! Take them!" The High Priest had roared.

Elyasin's pendant had burst into white-gold *wyrric* flames as the High Priest's mind slammed through her. Lhesher and Jhonen, Thad and Luc, mind-taken by the man's massive power, had risen like resurrected puppets, lurching toward Elyasin and Therel.

When Adelaine's power had suddenly risen like a leviathan of winter. Smashing into the Kreth-Hakir, giving her all to break their hold. Snapping silver mind-weaves in their allies as she took all the Kreth-Hakir's warping – acting like a lodestone to draw them into herself.

It was only a moment, but it had been enough. Therel had tossed Elyasin through the dark crevasse, then seized Luc and Thad. As Ghrenna followed into the black, Therel had surged back to seize Lhesher and Jhonen. But the wall had closed before he could. The rose-crystal shards had sluiced back together with uncanny speed, sealing the tunnel and the fate of two nations at war. Cutting off a furious roar from the Kreth-Hakir High Priest – and a tortured scream from the Highlander King.

Elyasin reached up to massage tension from her brows, where a part of her still shrieked from experiencing even the smallest bit of the Kreth-Hakir's power. They were lucky Adelaine had sacrificed herself for them. Elyasin had seen the woman's heart in that moment, and known it was far stronger than anyone had guessed. Because of Adelaine, the Kreth-Hakir Brethren hadn't been able to follow them. Because of Adelaine, everyone in these tunnels was alive.

A debt Elyasin might never be able to repay.

Elyasin glanced at Luc. Retaining eye contact, he rose from his bedroll and padded over in bare feet, leaving dark imprints in the luminous moss. Crouching, he nodded at Therel. "Ghrenna's still dreaming. She'll be out for a while yet before we can move on for the day. How's he?"

"The same." Elyasin glanced at her husband. Therel's breathing was deep, asleep again.

"How are you?" Luc nodded his chin at her, his green eyes sober in the fey light.

"As well as can be." Elyasin gave a stolid smile, though feeling far from it. Her fingers stole out, brushing over corkscrew tendrils of blue moss, feeing its silken texture.

"Do you need more sleep?"

"No." Elyasin's fingers plucked a glowing white mushroom cap with fuchsia speckles. She'd feared they'd be without food beneath the mountains, but it hadn't been the case. They'd found flora, listed as edible in the ancient codices Thad had brought, and had it taste-tested by Luc. Other edibles had been discovered when Ghrenna would suddenly stop and nibble an herb, recalling Morvein's memories. Small luminous creatures they would catch for meat skittered through the grottoes, and a variety of greens were always available at these grottoes to add to their satchels as they walked, though some had slightly mind-altering properties.

This particular mushroom had stimulant effects, and Elyasin plucked it, breaking it in half and offering a part to Luc. He took it and popped it into his mouth with a nod. Elyasin's fingers lifted, plaiting her hair for the day. "I need to be up. I have to gather edibles for our next leg, fill everyone's satchels."

"You're running yourself ragged," Luc's green eyes searched Elyasin's in the wan light. He reached out, brushing his long fingers down Elyasin's golden braid. "Up before everyone else, last to sleep. Waking every time Ghrenna sings in her dreams or Therel screams in his. Always checking our supplies, foraging."

"You wake just as much as I do, Luc," Elyasin protested mildly, affixing her braid with a leather thong.

"I know." Luc murmured, his demeanor quiet. "But we've all lost it down here at least once, except you. I keep wondering when —"

"I can't afford to break, Luc," Elyasin admonished gently. "My King and husband needs me. He's lost everything from Lhaurent den'Karthus's vile machinations."

Elyasin's heart twisted. Dire memories poured through her, vivid and bleak. From her coronation and stabbing, to fleeing into the Highlands of Elsthemen – to becoming a new wife and a Queen. Only to lead her husband's soldiers in a war against her own country, and lose it all to flame and chaos. Therel's scream when the crystal door had closed had been the most wretched sound she had ever heard. Like the howl of a wolf losing his entire pack, the scream of a tundra-wight, and the roar of a man with nothing left to live for all seared into one.

"You've lost everything, too." Luc's green eyes were knowing. "Lhaurent didn't exactly spare you any courtesy these past months."

"I know." Elyasin spoke, holding his sorrowful gaze. "But I need to be strong like Adelaine was, the day we fled Lhen Fhekran.

She proved herself worthy of the title High Dremorande, even though those monsters have probably killed her for it. After I felt what she did for us… I promised myself I'd be like that – for me, for you, for my people, and for Therel's. That I'd be like the telmen-vines of the Highlands that survive through every snow and season. For all of us."

As if responding to the conversation, Therel shifted in his sleep and groaned again, his blonde brows knit as if his soul was being torn out from the inside. Elyasin stroked his hair again and he quieted. Too many nights, he would cry out in dreams – or worse, scream names of his countrymen. Elyasin would hold him, kiss him until he quieted, but there was no banishing Therel's torment.

"He's lost everything," she spoke, stroking his soft blonde hair. "His city, his people, his kingdom—"

"Everyone he ever held dear," Luc concurred.

An empty silence settled around them. Not wanting to wake her husband, Elyasin motioned to Luc as she slipped out of her bedroll. He caught her meaning and stood, nodding to the other side of the grotto where another cascade collected into a seepage-basin, one of many that punctuated the tunnels. Elyasin stepped over the moss, humming to brighten her singing-stone, and Luc followed.

A burbling stream flowed down the far wall in a trail of white-blue algae; the water pooled in a basin carved in the rock wall. Trails of wispy moss fine as cobwebs grew from the basin, glowing with phosphorescence. Luc leaned against the wall as Elyasin set her singing-stone in a niche, then tore a patch of draping moss from the basin. Dipping the moss in the water, she washed out her underarms.

Clad only in her silk battle-halter and underwear, she got an appreciative smile as Luc's gaze roved her, but he'd seen her nearly naked enough times. Elyasin had given up on privacy or clean garb weeks ago, though she kept up her daily routine of freshening. And it was becoming a pattern, Luc and Elyasin having a few low words before the rest of their party rose for the day. Luc had been a childhood friend, but he was gradually becoming a confidante as they traveled the darkness.

"Let me in at that?" Stripping off his tan buckled jerkin and white shirt, Luc beckoned for the moss. Finished, Elyasin handed it over. He doused it in the basin, scrubbing himself briskly. "Hand me the soap?"

"Soap," Elyasin snorted with a smile. "I'll hand over the soap if you hand over the boar meat."

"Like I'd share." Luc chuckled, dunking his head into the basin and scratching out his golden mane. He whipped his head back with a curse and a shiver, flicking water out of his hair. "Fuck, that's cold!" He turned to Elyasin with a roguish grin. "How do I look? Ready for the ladies?"

Elyasin gave his chest a light slap, though Luc's cheeky humor was welcome. It kept desolate thoughts at bay, and his healing hands were always there to push back despondency – which he did now, trapping Elyasin's hand to his chest as she started to pull away. Reaching out, he slid a hand up beneath her hair and pressed his fingers to her nape. Bliss rippled through Elyasin. Tension she'd not even known she'd carried melted away and she sighed, finding herself drawn into Luc's arms as he touched his healing into her neck.

"You're tense," Luc murmured.

"It's just all these memories," Elyasin frowned, "surfacing in these cursed tunnels."

"I know what you mean," Luc gave a wry, haunted smile. "I feel flooded with remembrances down here, things I haven't thought about since I was a boy at Roushenn. Very little of it is anything good. And damn if it doesn't make me want one helluva stiff hopt-ale."

"I've been dreaming of events that aren't even mine," Elyasin breathed, hearing the scream from her nightmare. "Therel and I's nightmares of the Brother Kings are getting more potent."

"Ghrenna's are, too," Luc murmured. "She's hard to wake sometimes, deep as she goes in her dreams of Morvein."

"I just wish I could be certain that we're any closer to our goal, Luc. Before—"

"Before this place tears us apart." Luc's hand slipped from Elyasin's neck and he glanced back at Therel, his face unreadable.

"Therel's changing," Elyasin spoke softly, following his gaze. "His nightmares are grinding him down."

"Like Ghrenna," Luc agreed, "though her dreams are winding

her up. She's stronger by the day, no matter how much she heaves at night and keeps the rest of us awake. Thad's fucking blessed that he sleeps as soundly as he does. Though even he's needing treatments from me now to keep strange thoughts at bay. Like some kind of change inside him is speeding up from being down here."

"I feel it inside me, too," Elyasin spoke quietly, letting herself be held as Luc's arms slipped around her waist. "I've got this heat in my body all the time now. I don't even wear my jacket or furs anymore. Something inside me is *sharper*, Luc. Hotter. More… volatile."

"From Hahled Ferrian." Luc searched Elyasin's eyes. "From your connection to him through your keshar pendant."

Elyasin reached up to touch the gilded keshar-claw that hung around her neck upon its fine chain. It was warm from the heat of Elyasin's body. The scar it had burned into her skin from the Kreth-Hakir battle had been healed by Luc, but her chest still felt tender, as if some things about the *wyrric* interaction could never be healed.

"It doesn't matter if Therel and I wear our pendants or not," Elyasin spoke. "We feel the Brother Kings all the time now. It's part of these dreams we're having – dreams of battle and bloodshed. My nightmares are Hahled's remembrances, and Therel's are Delman's. We're not having vertigo anymore, as if we're better able to integrate their minds – but that's just the problem, Luc. The Brother Kings *are* integrating into us. And Therel has become moody from Delman. Dark and taciturn in a way I've never seen him."

Luc was silent, his hands clasped at Elyasin's waist. "Can you hear Hahled Ferrian's thoughts?"

"No." Elyasin touched her pendant again. "And the memories are nothing I can explicitly recall. I've only the sense that Hahled's welling up inside me, and Delman's doing the same inside Therel. As if the pendants were only needed to make our connection, and once it was made—"

"You've become a lodestone. A channel for Hahled's *wyrria*. And it's getting stronger."

Elyasin nodded; shivered. Glancing to the faceted stones in the fey darkness, she frowned. "These tunnels, I feel like they're influencing whatever's happening. Like *wyrria's* breathing down our necks at every turn."

"I know what you mean," Luc shivered. "That creeping, vibrant feeling. Fucking maddening. My healing-*wyrria*'s gotten stronger down here, too. And Ghrenna's remembering Morvein faster, and her Brother Kings. She cries out in her sleep, saying Hahled and Delman's names like they're—"

Luc cut off, his eyes desolate. His hands fell from Elyasin's waist and he massaged his knuckles as if they pained him. Elyasin reached out, setting a hand to his chest, feeling the agony that twisted in Luc's heart. "I know. I see how you love her."

"Everyone but me." Luc's smile was awful as his green eyes burned with wrath. "Everyone else gets to love Ghrenna but me. She's changing, Elyasin. Morvein's taking her over. She's harder, stranger. As if Ghrenna could have gotten more strange, but there you go."

"Is she still dreaming of Elohl?" Elyasin murmured carefully.

"What do you think?" Luc's voice was hard. He crossed his arms and set his jaw at the mention of Elohl den'Alrahel, Ghrenna's first and only true love. "She sighs his name at night as much as her Brother Kings."

"Elohl's a good man, Luc," Elyasin chastised mildly.

"I know." Luc gave a sigh, then ran a hand through his unruly golden hair. Then made a fist and punched the mossy wall. "Fuck it, I know! But let me hate the guy. Mean thoughts of sucker-punching him if we ever see each other again make me walk longer hours down here."

Luc's gaze strayed to the grotto wall and Elyasin's followed. Covered in arcane script and sigildry that peeked through the mosses, the towering walls of the grottoes and tunnels came alive when one stared long enough. This section of wall had sigils and flowing whorls of precious ores inscribed in it. By the shifting incandescence, Elyasin saw writhing images flow across the wall – as if Hahled's *wyrria* could form pictures from the inscriptions.

Sometimes she saw fleets of mythic creatures taking wing. Once she'd thought she'd seen an army of fish-people battling beneath the ocean. This scene before her writhed with darkness, like a hillside city seen through a luminous mist but with an emptiness in the middle, like a night that ate the stars. The gaping hole in that brightness had a terrible feel to it – of battle and death. Elyasin had found the walls of the Heldim Alir to be a gruesome grimoire, telling stories of bloodshed and not much else. She blinked and the scene ceased, nothing but unintelligible whorls of gold, silver, and moonstone once more.

"Is Ghrenna remembering anything more of these tunnels," she asked Luc, tearing her eyes away from the tableau, "from Morvein?"

"Some." Luc rubbed his eye sockets with the heels of his hands as if he'd stared at the wall too long. "She says the ancient race of giants who built them, the Giannyk, were masters of sigildry and portal-making. They enchanted these images into the rock to remember important historical events. Morvein believed the tunnels were built intentionally, as a labyrinth. A place to walk in solitude and ponder the ancient past, the lessons to be learned from history."

"From his maps, Thaddeus thinks we should have reached some kind of exit near Lintesh by now," Elyasin glanced to the scribe's sleeping huddle.

"A nice thought," Luc chuckled, a wry smile lifting lips. "But I think this whole place is engineered to get lost in. We've been in these tunnels three weeks and still found no exit. All the branchings just turn back on themselves like some enormous underground glyph. We take branch-points, Thad marks them with chalk, and after a few days we wind up right back at the main tunnel. A true and maddening labyrinth."

"So it seems," Elyasin sighed. "Apparently, Morvein wandered down here like us, the first time. Seeking the Giannyk from her vision who could teach her how to create the Rennkavi's Goldenmarks. And the second time with her Brother Kings and the Rennkavi candidate to find the White Ring and work the Rennkavi's Ritual. But Ghrenna still can't remember Morvein's travels through these tunnels, not precisely."

"What happens if we find this place?" Luc held Elyasin's gaze. "The White Ring from Therel's seeing-dreams? Ghrenna wants us to perform the ritual to bring the Rennkavi and save our continent from war, but what if it doesn't work? What if it all goes wrong——"

"Like it did for Morvein?" Elyasin finished Luc's thought. He'd not been the only one thinking it. Fear moved in her deeply, a shadow of Hahled Ferrian's emotions, as Elyasin's gaze strayed to the wall's image with its gaping darkness.

"Thad's been learning Giannyk from the walls and his codices, and from when Ghrenna speaks it at night," Luc spoke as if picking up on Elyasin's thoughts. "He knows which sigils mark the main tunnel from branch-points now. We won't stay lost down here. All this has got to lead somewhere."

"How do you stay so hopeful?" Elyasin asked.

Luc gazed down from his lean height, a complicated look in his eyes. Sliding one hand up, he stroked her cheek. "You keep me hopeful. Your passion. Your dedication. You're a true Queen, Elyasin, and you lead us like one, even if we aren't much of a force to lead."

"Luc—" Elyasin flushed, flustered at Luc's closeness.

A grumpy growl came from across the grotto. And then, from the lump that was Therel, "*Fenrir rhakne!* Can't you both keep it down?"

"Time'ta wake?" Thaddeus peeked bleary eyes from his bedroll at Therel's growl, fishing for his spectacles on the verdant moss.

"No." Therel rucked back down in his blankets. "Go back to sleep, Thad."

"Luc," Elyasin stepped swiftly out of Luc's embrace, her cheeks hot. "I think my husband needs a morning treatment."

"No, *khrakane vishken*! I'm up. Kotar's balls..." With a groan, Therel pushed to sitting, his pale mane mussed from restless sleep. But as he set one hand to the moss, something scurried over his hand. As if water had legs and a tail, the three-foot translucent lizard could barely be seen by the grotto's fey light, but Therel's reflexes were fast. He snatched up the creature: longer than his forearm, it hissed as it whipped a barbed tail. With a snarl, Therel dashed the creature's head against a rock, but the barbed tail scored him. Almost instantly, the scratches began swelling with poisonous red lines.

Therel tossed the lizard aside with a growl and cupped a hand over his injured one. Luc was already striding over, catching up his King's poisoned hand. Slipping into a healing-trance with his chin lifted and eyes closed, Luc tended the wound as he'd done for the party countless times. As Elyasin watched, the red lines in Therel's flesh rolled back.

"Damn menaces." Therel cussed, remaining still for Luc's ministrations. Elyasin stepped over and picked up the dead lizard by its neck. In the dim light, she could see the opalescent heart and white blood slurrying its last through the creature's veins. Crimson poison streaked through the tail-barbs from a gland near its gonads.

"Well, at least we have breakfast." Elyasin quipped, trying to make light as she laid the lizard upon the luminous moss. With quick motions of her belt-knife, she soon had it disembowled, the poison sacs teased out from beneath the tail and the red-streaked underside cut away. Parceling what was left into five pieces, she handed them around. "We should be thankful. A little meat helps us stay strong down here."

"Tastes like chicken," Thad agreed, digging into his section with an amiable appetite. The scribe was always ravenously hungry, and something about that simplicity made Elyasin smile.

Ghrenna had risen at last, and accepted her portion from Elyasin, currying her white waves back from her face to eat. Though rumpled from sleep, her pale beauty seemed to shine by the grotto's light like the moon over a highmountain lake. The curling white sigils and script that poured over Ghrenna's collarbones and down beneath her shirtsleeves to her palms held a haunting glow. Her high cheeks were flushed and her lips full, an unnatural brightness in her cerulean eyes, framed by long lashes. Ghrenna's nights were full of sighing passions, but it was as if she gathered strength from every dream of Morvein's life. Her body was trim with muscle, her fingers strong when she reached out to take her meat. Curvaceous and fey, something about her seemed even more hale down in this place than when she had strode into Fhekran Palace so many weeks ago.

But it was a dangerous strength. As if something inside her moved too fast. Something that blew her where the dreams took her, like a fell wind – something that produced a feverish shine in her eyes. Elyasin's gaze connected with Ghrenna's as they ate and those cerulean depths bored into Elyasin, arresting. A chill wind rushed through Elyasin's flesh, or perhaps a wind of fire, burning her up inside. Elyasin had a roaring feeling in her body, like needing to lead an army into battle or leap into icy meltwaters to cool the burning in her chest.

She shivered and her gaze broke from Ghrenna's, the feeling

dissipating though not gone. Elyasin's gaze strayed to Ghrenna's white keshar-claw pendant, to the grey and red fire-opals, then to the sigils of amethyst set with onyx that ran through the white claw. Something about it arrested her, and it was only with a will that she hauled her gaze away, back to her meal.

Elyasin crunched through the delicate bones of her meat until only the lizard's skin-oil remained upon her fingers, which gave them a translucent sheen. She licked the lemony oils and the normal appearance of her skin returned. Finished with breakfast, all were rising – packing up bedrolls, stuffing them into rucksacks. Pulling on boots and buckling pelts on over down-padded jackets for another day of walking the underground halls.

The simmering feeling inside Elyasin did not diminish as she dressed in her buckled fawn leathers and pulled on her sable boots. Clasping her golden keshar-claw pendant, she found the inlaid sigils burning beneath her touch, as if they radiated her own inner fire – a *wyrric* fire that rose from the Brother Kings.

A fire which responded to the fell wind of Morvein's command.

CHAPTER 3 – ELOHL

Leaning upon the balcony rail, Elohl stared out over the alabaster Palace of the Vine and the olive groves. Fenton's storm was gone from the morning sky. Only a few wisps of cloud remained, scudding away on a high autumn wind. The seasons changed slower in the Valenghian lowlands, but Elohl could smell snow on the breeze from the heights of the Eleskis to the west. Summer was over, and as he gazed out over the ripe tilthlands of Velkennish Valley he saw oaks and white ash changing to autumn's golden tones.

Still entirely nude and not seeming to care, Fenton leaned his elbows on the balcony rail next to Elohl. Heat simmered from Fenton's wiry body like a smoldering volcano, as if he couldn't quite contain his Khehemni *wyrria*. Curling across Fenton's back muscles, Elohl watched his fire-red Wolf and Dragon inking slowly roil and fade. Elohl turned to face Fenton, leaning back against the railing with his arms crossed.

"Fenton. We need to talk. I'm finally remembering the events of the past weeks, but what I don't remember is *how* the Valenghian Vhinesse snares me. When I see her, when she touches me—"

"You're besotted." Fenton's eyes held a dark calm as he looked over, though he rubbed his fingers together out over the rail as if ridding them of a nasty sensation. "The Vhinesse has a powerful *wyrria*, Elohl, an ancient ability of the Oblitenne royal bloodline in Valenghia. It's a mind-*wyrria*, but propagated through the senses, and it makes people forget. Who they are, what they love – and why they should oppose her."

"Oblitenne. Like *obliterate*." The word fit as Elohl tasted it, raw.

"A drugged obliteration of both body and mind is their house gift." Fenton gave a harsh sigh. "It's rare, and the Vhinesse ascended to her position because she carries it in spades. She's got sensorial-weaves coming at you the moment you lock eyes with her. Once you touch her skin, you're hers – heart, head, and cock. The rest of your euphoria is all her fucking drugs…"

Elohl's cheeks flamed again, ashamed at the things he'd ordered Fenton to do. "She's fascinating, Fentleith. Her eyes, her voice – when she speaks, it tinkles with silver bells like a fur trapper's sleigh. It chimes through my head."

"Call me Fenton, Elohl," he corrected mildly. "We can't have you calling me something else around anyone who might know me. Thank all that's holy, you've only called me Fenton around the Vhinesse, and she hasn't known enough to ask for my true name."

"Do you change your name?"

"Every few decades." Fenton waved a hand idly. "I change my name and find a new area of the world to live in. But the Vhinesse's attributes – are they not affecting you right now?"

"Not right now." Elohl shook his head, rubbed the back of his neck. "I feel clear since your storm. But I woke this morning thinking of the white spire, Fenton. I couldn't recall it exactly, but I knew I was supposed to be there. It was as if I was looking through a set of filthy jeweler's lenses. And the sensation of being in the spire with Ghrenna helped clear me."

"Interesting." Fenton rubbed his chin, combing his short beard with his fingertips. "Your mind cleared from thoughts of Ghrenna and my exhibition of Khehemni *wyrria*. That's never happened before."

"You losing your shit or me thinking of Ghrenna?" Elohl gave a sidelong smile.

Fenton gave him a grin back, his brown-gold eyes finally lit with a natural humor. "Both, you irritating fuck. Is that any way to talk to your great-grandfather?"

"Is that any way to address your Rennkavi?"

Fenton laughed. Leaning against the railing, he gave Elohl a smile at last. "You know I consider you a friend, don't you? You may be my blood and Goldenmarked, but I'm not a father-figure to you. Not much of one to anybody, really…" Fenton trailed off. As if reading Elohl's earlier thoughts, his head turned, gazing down at the olive groves far below.

"I know." Elohl spoke at last, sober. "You were a friend to Olea in the same way, and I appreciate that."

Fenton faced the railing again, leaning on his elbows. He

sucked in a deep breath and let it out in a sigh, his gaze faraway. "Olea was the best thing in my world, Elohl. I knew she was my kin, of course, my bloodline, but I never felt like she was a daughter – more like a friend. I should have been teaching her about life, but… she taught me. She was the best friend I had found in many a long year, even among my own kin. Loyal, upright, honest, heartfelt…"

"She was my best friend, too," Elohl turned at the rail, settling into a similar posture. Together, they shared a gentle sadness, full of things spoken too late.

"Sometimes I wish my granddaughter Ennalea had never fallen in love with your father," Fenton's voice was soft in the curling breeze. "Lea was Alodwine, but I had to cut her loose when she wanted to become Alrashemni for your father Urloel. The Alrashemni could never have discovered what she really was, especially marrying a Rakhan. She was Khehemni blood, my blood. The Alrashemni would have killed her."

"I'm sorry." Elohl murmured.

"I'm not. Not anymore. She loved him, and it wasn't my place to interfere. I've done enough meddling in my family's affairs over the centuries." Fenton heaved a sigh, not explaining his cryptic words. He gave a shiver at the rail, and his shoulders dropped as he released the last of his tension, his red *wyrric* inking simmering out to nothing. He turned and gazed at the window he had shattered, a wry smile lifting his lips. "Haven't done something like that in centuries."

"Did it feel good?" Elohl eyed him with a slight smile.

"Felt fucking amazing actually." Fenton laughed, a good sound. Reaching up, he curried both hands through his gold-brown hair and laughed again. Turning, he clapped Elohl upon the shoulder, then gestured through the shattered window at a table laden with foodstuffs inside. "Anyway, we can't plan our escape without breakfast. Shall we?"

"Might as well."

Elohl stepped toward the open balcony doors, his stomach giving a fierce growl. He'd had nothing to eat during their grotesque endeavors of the night prior. He and Fenton stepped lithely to the table, Fenton picking up a bite of everything in his fingers and beginning to eat with his regular voracious appetite. Glancing over the spread, Elohl noted marinated kippers, green olives, sliced pear, quince, persimmon, and red currants with a pale salami. There was no flatware, but there were silver goblets and an ewer of water next to a ceramic crock. Elohl lifted the lid of the crock and sniffed, inhaling a bitter aroma from the hot, dark beverage within.

"We've not had this before. What—"

"Thank Shaper!" Fenton inhaled and his face opened in relief. "*Kaf-tesh*, a relative of the coffee plant, but native to Cennetia. Purges the system of poisons and intoxication." Fenton poured two ceramic cups, mixing in honey and cream. "And it's a muscle and mind-stimulant. But don't take it black. Black'll kill you."

"Poisonous?" Elohl accepted his cup, cradling the warm ceramic.

"No. Just damn bitter!" Fenton grinned, far more like his old self at last. They clinked mugs, and Elohl sipped. His chest quickly flooded with ease from the bittersweet brew, tasting like coffee with roasted chicory and dandelion root. A sharp clarity took him, lightening his mood; energy filled his muscles, far better than coffee. He sipped gratefully, feeling a dull headache from the threllis roll back. Elohl joined in picking through fruits and delicacies, as Fenton cleared more than half the platter in short order.

"So now we play the Vhinesse's game," Fenton sipped his beverage, devouring an golden autumn pear between sips and licking the juice from his wrist. "Until we create a chance to either kill her or escape. She's been asking a lot of questions, Elohl, night after night. I've hedged her off the best I can, but she's taken our gear and must have found our signet seals from Queen Elyasin and King Therel. I've mentioned we're ambassadors – there was no getting around that one – but she thinks we were on a diplomatic mission to rally the Elsthemi mountain-tribes and just got fucking lost on the glaciers. I told her we stumbled into a cave and found an old Alranstone inside, that it put us through here. Plausible enough. Those damn things are riddled throughout the Bhorlen Mountains, and unpredictable as hell."

"It merits asking," Elohl sipped as he picked through a bowl of sweet black telmen-berries, "why hasn't she killed us yet, if she thinks we're ambassadors from Elsthemen?"

"*Playing* with us is far more fun, I imagine," Fenton snorted, refilling his beverage. "And though she's at war with Alrou-Mendera, her peace treaty with Elsthemen under Therel's father has held, so far. But Vhinesse Aelennia Oblitenne has a fairly ruthless reputation, and it's warranted. Now that you're clear-minded, we need to pretend she still has a hold over us. From what I know of her these past twenty years she's sat the throne, her *wyrria* affects everyone, though men more so. I've been careful to act affected. Though I've been sullen in the sack, but she seems to like me sullen and slightly violent, which is interesting. Anyway, we need to discuss why Bhorlen's portal-arch sent us here. He said it would lead us to what we needed most. If we're here rather than in the Heathren Bog at Purloch's House, perhaps it means there's something in the Palace of the Vine that we need."

"Does her touch affect you?" Elohl asked, curious. "The Vhinesse?"

"I lose my concentration a bit." Fenton's eyes sparked with gold as he leaned his chair back on two legs and cradled his ceramic mug. "Enough to make my cock rise. But I don't let my *wyrria* flare in her presence, no matter how fucked I get on drugs and her sensorial pleasures, Elohl. She *cannot* know who or what we really are. She'd use us, snare us any way she can for her wars. Fortunately, you've not had cause for your Goldenmarks to spark while we're around her. And she knows nothing of what they are, thinking their origin only a pretty story you tell to impress her. Fortunately, she can't smash in and read our minds, not like a Kreth-Hakir, only influence our senses and—"

Fenton got no further. A click of the latch and a whoosh of air came as the pale ashwood doors were pushed inwards. In she strode, the Vine of Valenghia; dressed in a white gossamer gown of lace studded with tiny emeralds, she was pale perfection. Her silvery hair was swept over one shoulder in an ornate braid strung with bells that tinkled as she moved. A delicate silver circlet of pearls and emeralds rode her brow, her creamy collarbones bared to her décolletage. High cheeks and full lips held a flush like devil-berries in the snow, and her pale eyes with just a drop of blue sparkled as she swept forward. Elohl saw her dark-lashed gaze flick to the smashed censers in the fireplace, then to the shattered window, her silver brows rising. But the evidence of violence in their chamber did not break the

Vhinesse's stride as she moved to her kept men.

"My Brigadine falcons!"

Arms outstretched in welcome, she stepped to Elohl. Clasping his fingers and stretching up to give him a kiss, she stroked his Goldenmarked skin as her lips found his. Elohl was aware this time of the melting sensation that took him when they touched. One moment he was himself, and the next, he was water cascading down rocks. The perfume of her body wreathed Elohl, fresh like citrene and wintermint, exhaling from her skin and wrapping around him. It didn't even cross his mind to deny her. Silvery bells chimed in his mind, calling him to her sweet flesh. Stepping close, he wrapped his arms around her slender body, kissing her deep. His pulse raced with the taste of her. His hands drank in that exquisite skin. He'd never needed anything so desperately in his entire life – the fragrance upon her neck and her soft lips on his, her delicate tongue licking into his mouth.

When she pulled away, Elohl felt his heart scream. She gave a bright, tinkling laugh and placed a palm to his bearded cheek. He died when she turned to Fenton, full of hot jealousy. She pulled Fenton close, reveling in his wiry body. Their kiss was deep with a fierceness to it, anger tense in Fenton's jaw even as he placed a possessive hand behind her neck and devoured her. She pulled away with a laugh, breathless. Elohl raged, simmering.

But he would do anything for her – even if it was to watch while she devoured someone else.

Pulling away from Fenton, she placed a palm to both their bearded cheeks, gazing from one man to the other. "My falcons! One so proud and strong, with so much furious anger in his golden gaze, covered with placidity. And the other," she gazed at Elohl, and his heart actually jerked in his chest, "cool as a mountain lake, yet with a rushing river of ardor and sadness beneath. Both beautiful. Both mine."

"Yours." Elohl heard himself say.

"Yours." Fenton echoed, with bite.

"Their adornments, please." The Vhinesse motioned to a pair of guards dressed in the crimson jerkins of the Red Valor who waited patiently behind her. Elohl blinked, not recalling her ever coming to the Falconry with guards before, or ever in the morning.

But though he wondered what she wanted, he knew he would have worn anything for her. And then he saw the wrapped packet of rough white silk in the guards' hands – one for him, and one for Fenton.

"These are for you, my falcons!" The Vhinesse laughed, her eyes bright. "I've had them made especial for the both of you, gifts from my heart to yours. Know the vast honor you do me, to wear my gifts in pride today."

"Anything for you." Fenton spoke roughly.

"Anything." Elohl echoed.

But his eyes were watching the guard's hands, wondering what the thin silken packets could possibly contain that were garments. As the length of fabric was unwrapped, slim arm-torques of costly white palladian set with milky agates were revealed in the guard's hands. The torques rested upon the rough white silk, and falcon feathers cascaded from each torque by lengths of delicate palladian chain. There was a collar of palladian also, the kind that went not in front of the neck but behind it, with agates and falcon-talons tipped in palladian at each curled end, a delicate jewelry chain extending from them. The items were elegantly wrought, and the amount of rare palladian priceless. Suddenly, Elohl knew he could not accept such an exquisite gift – not when treachery lingered in his heart.

"Forgive me, my Living Vine." The words tumbled out of Elohl before he knew what he was saying.

"For what?" Her opalescent eyes held genuine worry as she raised her delicate brows. Elohl opened his mouth, compelled to tell her all about how he and Fenton had been plotting against her this morning. About how Fenton was immune to her charms. About how they were going to use that against her and escape.

But just as he began to speak, Fenton cut in. "Ghrenna. He apologizes because he remembers Ghrenna, a woman of tundra-pale beauty near to yours, but with blue eyes deep as mountain lakes. Eyes he could get lost in. Cerulean eyes that call a man's soul. Her touch, that electrifies every part of him. Her body, sweet under the dawn of a summer's morning, up in the white spires of the mountains. He apologizes for remembering this woman he once loved. He told me so this morning. We had an argument about it."

Fenton gestured to the broken window and the ceramics. As he moved, the side of Fenton's hand brushed Elohl, and a jolt of Fenton's *wyrria* leaped to Elohl's fingers, making him twitch. Elohl's mind came clear. He could suddenly feel the silver-white *wyrric* vines that breathed through his skin and netted his mind – but at Fenton's power, they shredded away like spiderwebs. Elohl could think again. The Vhinesse was not touching him, but gazing at Fenton. Elohl used the moment to breathe, firming Ghrenna's radiance from his dream atop the white spire firmly in his mind.

"Is it true?" The Vhinesse glanced to Elohl. "Do you think another woman more lovely than I?"

"My Vine." Elohl sank to one knee, imitating a besotted action. "I am aggrieved that I remembered this woman. The agony of my unfaithfulness tortures me. I bashed my fist through your window in my torment – forgive me."

The Vhinesse stepped close, eyeing him, but at last she smiled. "Your transgressions are forgiven. Windows and censers are easy to replace, but beautiful men are not. Be more careful of your body, and save it for my midnight pleasure."

"Yes, my Living Vine." Elohl lowered his eyes in a gesture of fealty and subservience.

"It is well!" The Vhinesse laughed, her voice ringing through the room. "Rise. I imagine my tempestuous men are weary of their Falconry, and need to stretch their wings. If you would do me the honor?"

"Of course, my Vine." Fenton played his part with a genteel bow.

"Yes, my Vine." Elohl echoed, though he had to bite back bile this time.

The Vhinesse motioned and the crimson-clad guards moved to Fenton and Elohl. Elohl stood, though he was clear now as the guards slipped the slender palladian torques around his biceps and clicked them into place, then set the matching torque around his neck. Fine chains dangled from the neck-torques. Their pearl-weighted ends were placed into the Vhinesse's hand, the same done for Fenton.

"My fleet falcon shows his plumage well, but we shall be discreet today." The Vhinesse smiled at Fenton, clicking her tongue thrice. "Though I adore your prowess, I do not enjoy sharing certain things. Guards – the rest, please."

Elohl's lips parted, realizing what she meant. The guards stepped close, their eyes downcast, their hands still holding the lengths of rough white silk. The Vhinesse moved to Fenton, receiving the first length of white silk. With precision and care, she wound the silk around Fenton's bare loins, tucking it in expertly to form a very scant, but workable, loincloth. Moving over to Elohl, she gave a lecherous eye at his silk trousers, then slipped her hands in. She gave him a fondle, stroking him until his cock surged. But Elohl held the cerulean of Ghrenna's eyes in his thoughts, and it pushed back the white mist that tried to take him. Even as the Vhinesse stripped away his clothing and bound the second length of silk around his loins, Elohl was able to breathe through her *wyrric* stranglehold.

Lecherously regarding both men for a moment, she said, "Now, my handsome falcons. Let's go show your beautiful plumage to the world."

The Vhinesse sashayed toward the door with her falcon's leads in her hand. The guards turned, opening the doors. Clearly, everyone believed Fenton and Elohl were docile. The torques and leads were fine as women's jewelry. They breathed with no *wyrric* power that Elohl could feel – inert decoration, but whose point was obvious.

Elohl stepped forward without glancing at Fenton. Fenton did the same at his side. On leashes, they moved out of their boudoir for the first time since they had arrived. Elohl caught his breath, gazing up and around, finally seeing the Palace of the Vine by day. Never in his life had he seen anything so beautiful, except the white spire. Roushenn was a rough-cut piece of coal next to this. Made entirely of opalescent white granite, agate, and marble, the palace caught the morning sunlight and reflected it, glowing with a luminousness that inspired the heart.

As Elohl followed the Vhinesse down a long flight of marble stairs from the Falconry tower, noting crimson-liveried guards with spears and swords at every door, it was the vistas that enchanted him. The inside of the palace soared, everything carven to enhance the natural elegance of the stone. Every white column and arch was pristine, with high windows of white glass. Oil-lanterns set in the walls and columns were encased in glass flutes with a coiled outlet that kept soot off the marble. White domes came to piercing pinnacles, cupolas were topped with elegant balustrades. Columns were adorned with impressions of vines and verge, faces of nymphs and satyrs peering out from the marble.

Reflected light rippled through the space, and looking down, Elohl saw an ingenious division of streams coursing along inset waterways, creating natural waterfalls and giving the constant echo of rushing water. Dripping mosses lined the waterways and myriad falls, choked with tiny white blossoms of glossy duckweed. Watercourses and cascading fountains with lily pads and purple-orange lotus burbled everywhere he looked. He gazed upward, seeing the tops of the columns branch into the vaulted ceiling like the inside of a towering forest. Balustrades of the upper floors could be seen to either side, carven with vines.

They wound down another wide staircase with a plush red velvet carpet, and thence to a red-carpeted foyer and a door of silvered birchwood flanked by guards. It was flung open to reveal an escort of guards in crimson. As the Vhinesse passed through with her falcons, Elohl heard murmuring voices and light music. Violins and harps sighed to a halt as the Vhinesse stepped into the receiving-hall with her men. Murmurs whispered, twining up into the vaults to join the sound of flowing water. Elohl's gaze flicked around as he entered, noting fine lords and ladies in crimson or vibrant silks flanking the edges of the opulent court – all staring at him.

Ignoring them, Elohl swept his gaze to the end of the bright hall. A tableau of a fighting wolf and dragon was carven into the alabaster behind the marble throne. Elohl was shocked to note how similar it was to the *wyrric* inkings upon Fenton's back, not to mention how it looked precisely like the same tableaux inside Roushenn – except this depiction had the beasts fighting around a blossoming vine, whereas inside Roushenn it had been a scepter. The throne, also carved with vines, sat upon a marble dais with ten broad steps to the receiving-hall floor. Checkered with opalescent agate and white marble, the floor was inlaid with vines of gold. Waterways ran through the floor, cut in channels and inset with flowering moss. Gold wreathed the pale marble columns, highlighting the carvings. Like the rest of the palace, the ceiling spread in a canopy of white trees, and far above Elohl could see the glimmer of gold running through it all.

The Vhinesse moved regally through her throne hall. Her smile was radiant, her manner impeccable. She ascended her dais, then motioned Elohl and Fenton to take up positions to either side of her throne. As they faced forward, she lowered into her seat and arranged her gown.

"Lands of the Living Vine, be welcome." The Vhinesse's melodious murmur carried effortlessly through the hall, and Elohl heard her subjects sigh to silence as if mesmerized. "Let us commence with the Commoner's Audience. Chancellor ven'Rhenni, if you would, please."

A man in red livery with a manicured silver mustache and pouffed silver hair bowed his way forward with a scroll. His pale gaze flicked to Elohl and Fenton, but settled upon his Queen. "My Living Vine. The first petition is of stonemason Heller ven'Osti opposing bridge architect Milo ven'Sachs, over the dispute of a collapsed bridge spanning the southern tributary of Fluss Helmenthal in the Province of Leddi."

"Bring them forward," the Vhinesse gave a welcoming smile and a genteel turn of her hand.

Suddenly, Elohl knew what today would be. Today, the Vhinesse's kept falcons were to stand at her side as she heard her common petitioners. As she showed off her newest men to her subjects, displayed for all the world to see and bound only in jewelry. Her conquests, the Falcons of the Vine, a testament to the world of her power. A statement for all to see, that she didn't have to conquer anyone – because everyone did what she wished willingly.

If Elohl had truly been under the Vhinesse's sway it wouldn't have been torture, but now it took everything he had to stand upon that dais. Setting his jaw, he tried breathing through the tension in his muscles, tried keeping calm and not letting his Goldenmarks flare in wrath as the Vhinesse held audience. As she orated judgements, Elohl and Fenton stood to either side of her marble throne like slaves – dehumanized, displayed, and degraded.

With her delicate torques around their necks that wouldn't have even held a falcon.

CHAPTER 4 – KHOUREN

Khouren Alodwine moved through the burned-out streets of Lintesh in the sunny afternoon, his dark hood up. The flat storm grey of his soft leather jerkin, roughsilk shirt and trousers matched the soot-smirched crowds meandering the rubble in the dwindling afternoon. His ancient garb was the color of the scorched avenue and the folk moving listlessly along it – the color of ashes.

Fires had consumed the city after the riots three weeks ago. A brisk wind teased Khouren's bluebottle braids where they escaped from his hood, his soft doeskin boots making no sound as he slipped through the despondent crowds leaving the King's City. Khouren had intended to evacuate also, as soon as he'd left King-Protectorate Temlin den'Ildrian's prize at the First Abbey, but found himself unable to depart.

A Ghost among the ruins, just like everyone else.

People coughed around Khouren, from the smoke that still clung in a haze to the city. Wisps of char lingered in the sooty sky, the fall breezes off the Kingsmount not strong enough to clear the air. Filthy cloths were held to chapped lips and noses, keeping out wafting ash, or holding in gags from the reek. Faces were smudged with soot; hands were seared from clawing loved ones out of burning dwellings. Blackened rubble lined the avenue, ancient timbers of the Abbey Quarter in ruin. Much of Lintesh's bones still stood, including the First Abbey, its bluestone granite carven directly from the Kingsmount. But the hovels and slums were in chaos, the shanties as Khouren crossed into the Tradesman Quarter little but charcoal and refuse.

Massive pumps commanded an impressive view as Khouren passed a grime-muddied fountain. During the burning, Khouren had joined the bucket-brigades, working pumps like this one that dredged up black water from the river beneath the city. Dousing structures, running into buildings to pull out screaming people trapped inside flaming wreckage. The smoke had been thick. No one had seen him move through walls, seizing citizens and heaving them over his shoulders like sacks of charred grain. They'd only seen a man in black ferrying out neighbors and loved ones from certain death, over and over.

Then disappearing like char on the wind.

Down here in the lower Tiers, filth in the city burgeoned, and disease. Excrement choked the gutters, crawling with rats and roaches. Normally palatable, the reek of the Tradesman Quarter had reached an unmatched atrocity. Tens of thousands had been dispossessed, and Khouren walked among them in the choked avenue, without belongings and without a home. People had flooded from the King's City for the past three weeks, just as they did now, passing wearily beneath the yawning portcullis of the Watercourse Gate. Giving up on their burned-out life, with wains, handcarts, and whatever was left to them – moving out to make camp upon the wide plain of the Elhambrian Valley.

Standing before the portcullis at the edge of the city now, Khouren paused, the mass of bodies breaking around him like minnows in a river. Staring up at the iron jaw of the gate, Khouren felt a tightening in his chest and a grip in his guts. Vertigo rushed through him, making his ears buzz and vision tunnel: this was leaving his city – his fortress. The place he'd haunted like a ghost, that had been his impenetrable vault for more than a hundred years. But now, he would be exposed. Leaving his protection – his place to be anonymous from a life of shame and guilt.

Thrice in as many weeks, he had approached the gate. And thrice, this same awful sensation had betrayed him.

Gazing up at the yawning portcullis, Khouren trembled. He was leaving one Rennkavi behind to search for another. A man who was as much a specter as Khouren had been in the dark halls of Roushenn. What if this other Rennkavi wasn't really Goldenmarked? What if it was just a clever Inking from some foreign land? A falsehood – and this Elohl den'Alrahel hadn't really been touched by an Alranstone at all?

What if Castellan Lhaurent den'Alrahel was the only Goldenmarked – the true Rennkavi to unite the nations in a high golden age?

Khouren shuddered. The portcullis grinned at him like a challenging foe – daring him to step forward. To break his oaths and be damned following a new Rennkavi by a wraith of a rumor. Gazing through the gate toward the rolling grasslands where a shanty-city had built up like a haphazard anthill, Khouren trembled. Even the thought of being out in the open set him shuddering: to be so exposed. No walls to run through. No oubliettes to wait in, away from threat, to think and plan. No weapons to take from ancient vaults when he needed one.

Not a Ghost anymore – only himself.

A shudder shook Khouren and heat flushed his face as his fingers became icy. Reaching up, he threw back his hood. He couldn't breathe. Gasping, he sank to his knees. One hand braced the earth while tears beaded in his eyes as he fought for air. As it had been the first three times he'd approached the city's egress, so it was now. A nightmare of desperation. A torrent of racing heartbeats and this fish-out-of-water feeling.

"Easy there, *ghendii*." A solid hand settled to Khouren's shoulder. "Breathe. The smoke of the city has affected us all. Here, inhale."

A vial was presented beneath Khouren's lips. His tunneling vision could see nothing but the shine of glass in the sun, and the amber color of some liquid inside the vial. A man's hard-weathered fingers held the glass.

A crisp musk like scorchgrass and essenac wafted up Khouren's nose and over his tongue. Suddenly, his lungs opened. His mind cleared; his vision widened. Sitting back upon his heels on the blackened stone, Khouren took great lungfuls of air, grateful, as people flowed around him and his savior in the filthy sunshine.

"Better?" The man capped the vial and slid it away in his jerkin. As his vision cleared, Khouren noted the man's garb was a decades-old fighting style, worn to Halsos' hells: a ranger's tawny brown like they wore in the Fleetrunners and High Brigade, his white shirtsleeves were rolled up to his elbows, scuffed leather bracers at his wrists and a ravaged climbing rucksack slung over one shoulder. His garb said Menderian military veteran, but his rolling accent sounded Elsthemi, while his slang hailed from the southeastern coasts near Ghrec.

"*Ghendii*. No one says that but Lefkani pirates. Are you a privateer from the border-coasts of Thuruman?" Khouren managed, blinking to clear his vision.

"Nah, kid. Just something I picked up. I did my time on the high seas, long ago."

The man's lilting voice held a laughing presence as he hunkered before Khouren. A wild mane of russet hair partially streaked with grey was pulled half-back with narrow Elsthemi braids, though his face showed the deeply bronzed skin of Cennetia. His cheekbones were high and strong, a reckless humor and weathered hardness in his green eyes, echoed in his grin of impeccable white teeth. Khouren blinked. Memories flooded in, as if they'd never spent over a hundred years apart.

Over a hundred years hating each other.

"Ihbram!" Khouren breathed, stunned to see Ihbram Alodwine den'Sennia, third son of Fentleith Alodwine, hunkering before him. The renegade Brigadier was Khouren's only remaining uncle out of the six treasured children Fentleith had spawned over the centuries. Ihbram's clever concoction had cleared Khouren's mind, but his presence befuddled Khouren's tongue, stunned as he was to see his uncle here in Lintesh.

The last place Ihbram would ever be.

"How—?" Khouren gaped.

Ihbram den'Sennia lifted one russet eyebrow. An amused but dire glint lit his lance-sharp green eyes. "We'll worry about the how of me being here later. Right now, let's get you up. Find somewhere better to rest."

Ihbram reached down, and with surprising strength in his weather-honed frame, seized Khouren and hauled him up. They faced the portcullis, dispossessed citizens flowing around them in a steady stream. Halting like a marionette in a Travelers' show, Khouren gazed at the golden plane beyond the shadows of the gate, then up into the arch's purple gloom.

He balked, that sinking, sliding sensation filling him again.

Trying to focus, Khouren watched the sea of grass upon the far side of the dusty highway. He focused upon the city of squalor that rose there, with its reclaimed stones and repurposed beams – a rickety mess of shanties and strung-up awnings. His salvation squatted amidst the plains spreading to the violet, mountainous horizon. Golden from the autumn chill, the grasses undulated like a sea in the sighing wind. They mocked Khouren: as if living could be simple, filled with new dawns like it had been when he was young. Khouren watched the grass curl and sway, forming eddies of color. Dark now beneath a towering swath of cumulus clouds; bright now under the sunshine.

But gaze as he might, Khouren couldn't approach. Couldn't set a single foot into the shadows beneath the gate.

"Come on, *ghendii*." Ihbram gripped Khouren by the collar and hauled him onward. Black iron and bluestone yawned above as they stepped into cold shadow. Khouren shuddered, his chest gripping, his feet stumbling, his breath coming in panicked sips. His knees turned to water and he sank down, gasping, heart thundering as if it would break his chest.

The weight of the portcullis pressed down, and he was sinking.

"For fuck's sake!" Ihbram's curse was disdainful. Seizing Khouren by the collar, he dragged him backwards – into the sunshine and out of the way of carts and people. Some spat in Khouren's direction for holding up traffic, and Ihbram made pacifying gestures. Khouren curled up in a ball in the dirt and soot, gasping, his vision blacking out.

The vial wafted beneath his nose and Khouren coughed, returning.

"Aeon dammitall," Ihbram cursed softly. He hauled Khouren to his feet and brushed smirch from Khouren's greys.

"I can't—!" Khouren doubled over, dry-retching.

"I know, I know," Ihbram chuckled, both amused and disgusted. "Welcome back to the wide fucking world. You've been stuck in that prison of a palace far too long. Come on. It's gonna be cold tonight, wind's got that snow-skirl bite. We need to find some fire."

Khouren's uncle pulled him toward a sprawling mess of new shanties along the inside of the First Tier and Khouren went without a fuss, defeated by the portcullis. Most of the lower Tiers had burned, and these extensive new shanty-villages were the response. Threading through impromptu alleys, Khouren and Ihbram maneuvered around tents and lean-to's, hastily cobbled apartments of slat-board, and hovels of repurposed bluestone. Wash-lines were strung in a hodgepodge, barely above them. Tired women hunkered against the wall of the First Tier, shushing mewling babes. Men with deadened eyes idled against slat-boards, smoking pipes and looking lost. Some were industrious, bustling around cook-fires as they roasted deer and boar, cauldrons of stew simmering over braziers, but most idled in the gloom, as ruined and bleak as their blackened clothes.

The sensation of pressing spaces and darkness was familiar, and Khouren breathed easier in the tight confines of the shanty-city. His belly cramped with hunger suddenly and Ihbram glanced at him as if he'd heard Khouren's thoughts. Khouren didn't know if his uncle had actually read his mind, but Ihbram sidled them into a crowd now forming around a crisp and blackened boar, nearly finished roasting.

Five brawny men corralled the amassing people, demanding coin for the meat. Determined to have the meat for free, the famished crowd had started to push. Through a slick maneuver, Ihbram slipped through the throng, close to the carcass on the spit. He threw a hard elbow into one profiteer's gut, so fast that the man stumbled – and so uncannily that the man thought it was a peon with black hair nearby that had done it.

The profiteer threw a fist. The man with black hair went down. The crowd surged, irate, and suddenly the men who protected the carcass had their hands full with a melee. Ihbram was smoke on the wind as he slid through it all, straight to the carcass. Khouren hardly saw the belt-knife flash in his uncle's hand. As the distraction raged, Ihbram's swift cut sliced off a generous hunk of meat, which he slipped into a pocket of his rucksack as he slid back through a gap in the ruckus.

"Come on," Ihbram murmured to Khouren, low. "I don't pay poachers."

Slick as specters, the Scions of Alodwine melted away through the seething crowd. Soon away through tight alleys, a deserted nook with a lit brazier welcomed them as the evening's shadows lengthened. Slinging his pack to a block of byrunstone next to the brazier, Ihbram sighed as if exhausted. Khouren noted that sigh – it was unusual for his uncle to show weariness. Settling to the block,

Ihbram fished out the crisped meat from his pack, sliced it with his razor-keen knife and handed half to Khouren.

"Here. Eat."

Khouren needed no second urging. His stomach roared as he dug his teeth into the roasted boar. It was heavenly; crispy with fat, dripping and hot. Khouren ripped into the meat, but a relentless thought made him speak even as he ate.

"Ihbram. How are you here? I thought you were in the mountains near the Elsee—"

"I was." Ihbram stretched his worn boots toward the brazier, tearing into his meat with more refined gusto than Khouren. "I was guarding a young Kingsman in the High Brigade these past ten years. Just after the Summons, your grandfather and I organized protection for some of the Kingskinder who showed *wyrric* promise, as many as we could. We couldn't let all the old bloodlines get killed off. No thanks to you."

Ihbram shot Khouren a severe look, hostility piercing through his emerald gaze. Khouren swallowed his bite of meat, feeling their ancient feud rise, renewed in blood and fire. Khouren lowered his dinner to his lap, watching his uncle. Shadows choked their alley and a wind picked up, making the firelight flicker across Ihbram's high cheekbones. Ihbram's emerald eyes flashed gold-red in the night, but Khouren knew it wasn't the firelight.

It never was, with the Scions of Alodwine.

"You swore you'd never return to Lintesh," Khouren spoke softly, "because I called it home. Have you returned only to resume berating me for my choices, uncle? If you have something to say – say it."

"You have a lot of balls, *ghendii*," Ihbram growled, his eyes flashing, "leaving your rat-hole."

"Unlike some rats," Khouren's tone was ice as his eyes flashed back, "who enter too many holes. Of other men's wives."

"Elemnia del'Letti came to me that night, not the other way around, you know that," Ihbram simmered. "Besides, she was never your wife, not officially."

"Nothing's ever official with you," Khouren growled. "No pledge of devotion could ever interrupt your eager loins or get through your thick skull."

"I'm not the one who became so freakishly zealous that I tried to light my own uncle on fire because my woman slept around on me!" Ihbram's eyes flashed fury in the fire's light. "Gods, Khouren! If it hadn't been for Lenuria's healing a hundred years ago, I'd be a disfigured lump of candlewax for the rest of my days!"

"Maybe you should be." Khouren's gaze was hard across the flames. "Maybe then that lump wouldn't fit in so many holes."

"And here I thought maybe you'd changed after all these years," Ihbram's gaze had gone from hot to glacially chill, "but you're still the same bitter, zealous asshole I recall."

A dark silence stretched across the flames, the two Scions of Alodwine eating up all the light in their simmering feud.

"How did you know where to find me?" Khouren asked at last.

"Come on." Ihbram gave him a snarling smile. "I'm not *that* bad at mind-tracking. If I can find silver weaves of the Kreth-Hakir five leagues away, I can find your tangled red strings, Khouren. Besides, I'm not here for you. I'm checking on information I heard in the mountains while I was tracking Kreth-Hakir. I came to talk to Lenuria."

"Figures that you're not here for me," Khouren snorted. "I suppose hate is thicker than blood."

"If you hadn't gone so insane over Elemnia way back when, we'd all be in a very different place right now." Ihbram gave Khouren a level look. "You and she were the reason things went sour between all of us. Aeon's balls! You and Lenuria and I, we *fought* together for over two centuries! Don't you remember any of that?"

"I remember confiding in you about how I was going to ask Elemnia to marry me," Khouren darkened as he stared at his uncle. "And having *you*, of all people, tell me to give it up."

"She was a bad kind of trouble, Khouren," Ihbram growled back. "Illianti poison and not much else. I wasn't her first liaison, nor her hundredth. You only turned a blind eye on it until you snapped. She was a woman of the fight, the fuck, and the kill."

"I *loved her*, Ihbram." Khouren continued, a darkness settling about him, though a hot wrath roiled in his gut. "And you know love only runs one way for me."

"Blind fucking devotion." Ihbram gave a hard sigh, running his finger over the stone upon which he sat. "You should have become a monk like Lenuria. Prayed that damn love of yours up to Aeon, for Fifth's sake. You've the zealousness for it."

"What I want to know," Khouren countered, bitter anger rising at their centuries-old dispute, "is how is Jennaia? Or Lemnitha? Or — what was her name with the golden hair? Oh, right. There were at least fifty of them with golden hair. Have you even kept count of the women you've left in the lurch over the centuries? Pining for you with a baby on their hip?"

"You know I loved every one of those women." Ihbram's words were soft, his emerald eyes wrathful in the darkness. "You're the one who had severe problems with love. Elemnia was a storm and you were unhinged around her. She was smart to leave when she saw you turn me into a human torch with pythian resin for sleeping with her. You terrified her, Khouren! She had seen so much killing in the dark that her veins ran bloody, yet your zealous shit terrified her. That's on you. Fuck you for trying to drag my ass through the mud when yours is just as full of crap. I'm going to sleep somewhere else. Have a nice fucking life."

Khouren watched Ihbram turn, rising from his perch and taking up his pack.

"Wait." Khouren reached out, fingers splayed to forestall his uncle's departure. "I shouldn't have said those things."

Ihbram's gaze could have seared flesh, but he settled back down to the stone block. He was silent so long that Khouren began to ease his fingers toward a hidden knife in his jerkin, wondering how this would go. At last, Ihbram gave a heavy sigh, scrubbed his short russet beard with his fingertips and took a deep inhalation. "Fuckitall. We're family, Khouren. Are we going to be at each other's throats forever? Because forever is a long time for Alodwine blood."

Khouren's fingertips eased away from his knife. "What I did to you... it kills me more than you know. That's why I left and came here."

Ihbram's russet eyebrows lifted in the flickering light. "Is that a fucking apology?"

Khouren was quiet a long moment, fighting to not rise to his uncle's bait. It was what he would have done yesterday or the day before, but today he was trying to be different. Inhaling a deep breath, he spoke again. "It was wrong. I knew as soon as I did it. But the feeling – the rage – it consumed me. I couldn't live among the real world for a while after that. Not with… the burning inside me."

"The burning." Ihbram snorted, then lifted a hand to his beard and rubbed it. He ended up scrubbing both hands over his face, as he let out a heavy sigh. Quiet finally, Ihbram stared at Khouren with eyes that were no longer wrathful, but strangely understanding. "Did it ever get quieter living down in the shadows beneath Roushenn?"

"Some." Khouren murmured. "Not enough."

"So to escape your ghosts you became one?"

"Except that ghosts can never be outrun." Violet eyes surfaced in Khouren's vision, and the impression of long sable hair, the last memory he had of Elemnia. Time had blurred her, and her face sighed away, replaced by Olea's.

Yet another woman who had never really been Khouren's.

"Love and ghosts," Ihbram spoke solemnly. "Both will track you down to the end of your days. Alodwine love is the worst of all: we desire it even though it kills us, but Alodwine love brings conflict, Khouren, and from conflict comes our power."

"*Werus et Khehem*," Khouren murmured, bleak. "I just – I broke, Ihbram. One moment, I was furious at what you and Elemnia had done, and the next… I was blank inside my mind with nothing but red fire."

"From your conflict of loving, your *wyrria* grows, Khouren," Ihbram admonished. "But you have to realize, that you and I are far more than dangerous blades when we're wrathful. We are the blood of the Wolf and Dragon. Every conflict we endure grows our magic. Makes it wild, stronger. And from the conflict of all those women I've loved and left, all those families I sired but never knew—"

"Your *wyrria* grows." Khouren blinked, understanding something about his uncle's history at last. His gaze swung up to meet Ihbram's, and he saw a dire truth in his uncle's eyes. "You leave the women you've bedded—"

"Because my magic strengthens when I leave something I love." Ihbram's eyes were haunted by the fire's light. "I am the mind-fighter that I am today because I've wrestled my emotions, year after year. And your love that you lost – that makes you stronger, too."

The air hung heavy between them with memories and regrets. Khouren let his gaze flicker away, watching the brazier. "I didn't think I would ever fall in love again, Ihbram. But I did love someone again, recently. One woman who outshone them all."

"Just one woman in all this time?" Ihbram raised his eyebrows. "Well, where is she?"

"She's dead. Lhaurent killed her. Just a few weeks ago."

"Aeon's fucking burn." Ihbram's voice was soft. "Though I can't say I'm surprised. Lhaurent's vicious bad news, Khouren. The longer you serve him, the worse it will go for you."

"The Rennkavi is not my problem anymore." Khouren held his uncle's gaze. "I left Lhaurent's service."

"Say what?" Ihbram sat up, interest prickling his demeanor as his simmering rage slid into astonishment. "Are you playing me, *ghendii?* Because you know I can break that mind of yours anytime I choose."

Khouren swallowed. He remembered Ihbram's formidable mind-reading talent. It would hurt, if Ihbram chose to find out any truths Khouren was hiding. Ihbram's *wyrria* wasn't as strong as the High Priest of the Kreth-Hakir, but it was damn close. The Brethren would have tried to recruit Ihbram had they known about such a vast talent, but Fentleith Alodwine had kept all his children and grandchildren a secret from Leith's Kreth-Hakir – as well as from Leith's Khehemni Lothren.

Until Khouren had decided to align himself with them over a hundred years ago, in his bitter wrath against his blood-family.

"I tell you no lies," Khouren murmured. "Lhaurent crossed too many lines."

"Well." Ihbram gave a snort. "Thought I'd never see the day. Was it the death of this woman that moved you out of Lhaurent's darkness? Because slaughtering thousands of Alrashemni Kingsmen didn't do it, as I recall."

Khouren ignored his uncle's barb, but the truth was hard to pull from his lips. Even now, it gripped his heart. He told himself it was Olea den'Alrahel, her beautiful face and terrible death that twisted him. He had loved her, worshipped her beauty and queenliness like he'd worshipped no one since Elemnia. Khouren had been devastated when Olea had died at Lhaurent's hands. She had possessed his heart these past ten years, scalded his loins, and poured through his mind.

But the hard truth, the one he hadn't been able to ignore, was that as much as he had obsessed over Olea, there was only one woman who could have ever made Khouren turn from darkness.

"Lhaurent killed Lenuria," Khouren whispered, his heart twisting in his chest.

"Undoer's curse!" Ihbram sat up, deathly still. "Your half-sister – she's *dead?*"

"She came to find me in Roushenn," Khouren's tone was hollow, trying not to relive it in his mind. "To tell me… that I could finally follow someone worthy of being followed."

"What do you mean?"

Khouren's fingers picked up a pebble and tossed it into the brazier. "Lhaurent's not the only Rennkavi. Another one's been Goldenmarked, this past summer."

"Another one—!" Ihbram's murmur was shocked. And then Khouren felt it, a burning sensation in his mind as Ihbram used his *wyrria* to search for the truth. In his mind's vision, Khouren could see threads of crimson flame seeping into his skull, diving into the darkest corners of his thoughts. Khouren clenched his jaw, swallowing down nausea before that touch rippled away. "You're telling the truth."

"I heard it from two different sources," Khouren confirmed. "Another Rennkavi has been Goldenmarked, near Highsummer. An ex-Brigadier named Elohl den'Alrahel."

"Elohl!" Ihbram's whisper was astonished, his eyes wide in the brazier's light. "Shaper and Undoer! Dammit! I should have never let him leave the High Brigade. Fentleith's going to give me Halsos' Hells for this…!"

A long silence filled the night, as Khouren let his uncle digest this astounding revelation – news that was against everything they'd been raised to believe. Flames simmered in the brazier, burned down to red coals. A wind picked up in the night, stirring sparks up into a star-shot sky.

"How can there be two Rennkavis?" Ihbram spoke again at last, hushed.

"I don't care how," Khouren gave a tired sigh, watching the sparks burn out to the backdrop of the stars high above. "But I'll take it. I can't follow Lhaurent anymore. Not after everything he's done. I *will* find Elohl, if it's the last thing I do."

"Once a cur, always a cur, aren't you? Always the servant, never the master." Ihbram's words were hard, but there was no malice in them now. It was simply an observation of Khouren's character – his need to follow, to believe in someone stronger than himself. At first, Khouren had believed in Fentleith, then he'd slavishly followed Elemnia until she'd fucked Ihbram. In the rancor that followed, Khouren had broken from his family, following the Khehemni Lothren and searching for the roots of Leith Alodwine's magic. When a Rennkavi had arisen, Khouren had followed – to his horror and regret. Khouren couldn't fault Ihbram this time. His uncle's words were true, and they stood, desiccating in the violet dusk.

"I am what I am." Khouren spoke to the shadows, as if it was any kind of excuse.

Silence devoured his comment. Khouren looked over to see his uncle had settled down upon the stone, his head on his rucksack and his hands clasped over his belly near his longknives. Ihbram had pulled his hood up over his eyes, drowning his face in shadow and making it all too clear that their conversation was over.

For now.

Dire thoughts churned in Khouren's mind, tingeing his thoughts red. With her final breath, Lenuria had bade him seek redemption. She had been Khouren's only light of reason this past century, stationing herself in the First Abbey to stay close to him, to steady him after his break with sanity. He'd been a madman after he'd tried to kill Ihbram. Red had consumed him, fire and darkness – and he'd run away from the Alodwine clan rather than face the horror of what he'd done.

Of them all, only Lenuria had stood by Khouren when he'd defied his grandfather and sought out the Lothren, needing answers to the rage that burned inside him. But Khouren might not get a chance to redeem himself in her dead eyes if he couldn't conquer his panic and leave the city.

Pushing off the bluestone block, Khouren settled his back against it. Breathing a sigh, he gazed up at a sky full of dead faces – sleep far away.

CHAPTER 5 – THEROUN

Theroun stared into the grey drizzle, manacled into a line of
Elsthemi warriors. Watching mist drift upon the chill dawn wind, he
and the others knelt upon a dais of white stone before the grand
entrance to an Elsthemi cathedral carven with sickles and wheat.
Beyond the cathedral, Theroun could see what was left of Fhekran
Palace. Consumed for two days by fire, its enormous red cendaric
timbers and towering gables had been devoured. Heat had exploded
its white foundation-stones in retorts that had split the night like
Ghreccan war-cannons. Vaults that had once been a marvel of
elegance had collapsed, massive timbers charred like kindling.
Nothing of the soaring roofline or supports remained, only charcoal
jutting into a grey sky like biting teeth.

Gazing into the drifting mist, Theroun took in charred
buildings doused by the heavy rainfall, houses of worship and hovels
sundered and ruined. Flames had towered into the crimson sky in
writhing columns the night of the invasion three weeks ago,
heatwaves boiling the avenues. Everything the Elsthemi held dear
had been reduced to so much ash. A slurried sludge ran through the
cobbled streets today, coating what was left of the ruins in mystic
shades of black and grey.

Theroun should have felt sorrow staring at the burned-out
buildings, but viewing a city lost and a people decimated, all he felt
was emptiness; used-up, like his innards had been scooped out and
cast away. He sat, numb to the fingers of autumn that trickled down
his skin with the chill drizzle. It was not ennui, and it was not defeat
that possessed him, nor was it rage or hopelessness. What it was, was
a roaring fire of hope that had been drowned when the Kreth-Hakir
Brethren had pummeled him into submission.

Hundreds of Elsthemi fighters were chained in the plaza before
the cathedral. The cathedral, once a tribute to some Elsthemi
goddess of grape and grain, was now the Kreth-Hakir's

headquarters. Theroun took in the cathedral steps, wondering if there was to be a show – if he and the other Elsthemi captains were going to be punished, but there was no scaffold for hanging, no rack of weapons, no implements of torture. There was nothing upon the stones before the cathedral, except for Theroun and the others chained on their knees.

Since they'd been taken captive, Theroun and the Elsthemi and what was left of his Menderian defectors had been kept in chain-gangs. Used night and day to douse smoldering wreckage with buckets, or haul debris from buildings the Menderian military now occupied. They'd rounded up itinerant livestock, erected mess-tents and dug latrines. Sleeping manacled in the lee of buildings at night, there was no roof for them, no refuge. A number of fighters had died from untended wounds, their corpses dragged around in their chains until someone came to release the body.

Theroun didn't know where the bodies went. He'd ceased caring after three weeks of living like an animal, but some part of Theroun's mind registered that today was unique. For the first time since he'd been broken, he was gaining a chance to see the entirety of the Elsthemi forces gathered in the plaza, even though they were ringed by a silent Menderian host.

General Merra was not among those captured, nor were her elite fighters. Khorel Jornath had kept his promise, but fierce, redheaded Captain Jhonen Rebaldi was in Theroun's chain upon the dais, staring despondently towards the burned-out palace in her ruined battle-leathers. Two men over from Jhonen, the massive beast of a Highsword Lhesher Khoum sat, glowering through the rain at everything and nothing, his braided red beard and hair sodden. Ever the survivor, Fleetrunner Captain Vitreal den'Bhorus sat nearby with his burning green eyes and hateful sneer. The Kingsman saw Theroun watching him and gave a solemn nod of support, one manacled hand reaching towards his heart.

Jhonen and Lhesher had been on the King and Queen's detail the night of the invasion. Theroun hadn't had an opportunity to speak with them. But from their defiant attitudes, he assumed the Queen of Alrou-Mendera and the King of Elsthemen had made it out of Fhekran Palace through the tunnels.

Theroun glanced at the six Kreth-Hakir patrolling the Elsthemi prisoners. They would stop occasionally, gazing at a warrior, narrowing their eyes when they felt unrest from someone. Two stopped before Vitreal den'Bhorus, staring him down. The Alrashemni Kingsman dropped his mean gaze to the slurried stones, teeth gritted, shivering.

Defiance didn't last long around the Kreth-Hakir, even from Kingsmen.

Theroun sat, waiting in the dripping rain for whatever was supposed to happen. Movement caught his eye from the side of the cathedral. Two men in herringbone leathers dragged a bird-frail woman toward the plaza. She was a wreck: her high cheekbones were purpled from beatings. Bruises stood out livid upon her china-white skin. Her pale lips were swollen and split, her white-blonde hair mangled with old blood, as if someone had ripped it out by the handful. Barefoot, she wore a thin silk underdress now ripped to shreds and stained with soot, hardly covering her nakedness. Theroun saw darker patches on her garb, like feces and blood. As she was thrust to her knees next to him, he saw vicious blade-cuts upon her delicate skin, some old and festering, some new and raw.

The haughty face of Adelaine Visek, High Dremorande of Elsthemen, burned with a righteous fury. Yet for all her fire, she winced as two Brethren set her tiny wrists into an empty set of manacles next to Theroun, abandoned five days ago when the soldier who occupied them had died.

One of the Kreth-Hakir with a row of Lefkani piercings up his left ear seized Adelaine beneath the chin, forcing her head up. Adelaine set her jaw and the man narrowed his dark eyes. The second Kreth-Hakir, a young man with short Valenghian-silver hair, paused, gazing at the first. He stepped close, laying a hand upon the first man's shoulder. The second Hakir added his gaze, pale and piercing, and together they stared the High Dremorande down. She began to shiver in her thin shift. The swarthy Lefkani lifted his lips in a leering snarl. Adelaine flinched, but did not look away.

With twin snorts, the two Hakir at last backed off. Therel could tell the battle of minds was over, though he couldn't tell who had won, until the Lefkani backhanded Adelaine across the face, hard. Her thin body wasn't meant for such treatment, and she sprawled into Theroun's lap. Theroun helped the Dremor sit up as the two

Hakir stepped back to their duties in the thin rain. She nodded her thanks, wincing as she took her lip into her mouth, sucking on a new split that dribbled blood.

"They're going to kill me." Adelaine spoke, her voice grim but steady as she watched the two Brethren disappear around the edge of the cathedral.

"I don't think they appreciate resistance." Clearing his throat, Theroun responded in a voice thick with the gravel of extended silence. "Though they enjoy the game. Seeing how long someone can last against their dominance."

"But where is the line between resistance that intrigues them, and resistance that is simply too tiresome?" Adelaine croaked too, her voice wretched. Theroun wondered how much torture she had endured these past weeks.

"Find that line and live, perhaps," Theroun responded.

"I can't." Adelaine said simply. "I have information to protect. They'll keep digging into me until they have it, one way or another."

Theroun found himself impressed. That the Dremor had protected vital information for three whole weeks from not just Khorel Jornath but the entirety of the nine Brethren stationed on this campaign. Something within him shifted, desiring a fight – a feeling he'd not had in weeks. "How do you keep them out of your mind?"

"I have a failsafe," Adelaine murmured. "I shut my mind and body down into coma before they reach that which is most secret. I've used it quite a few times now. I feel like I've barely been awake these past three weeks."

"Which infuriates Jornath, apparently," Theroun lifted his eyebrows at Adelaine's bruises.

Adelaine sneered, fierce, but tired. "Jornath never touches me. His curs carry out such things."

"What do they want? Information about the tunnels?"

"Your scribe Thaddeus has an incredible mind, Theroun." Adelaine gave a terse nod. "And yet, I fear he may be our undoing. I wish to Karthor I had not spied into his thoughts. It's a curse of mine, wanting to know too much. Sifting minds for information, looking for a way to wield it like a lance. But I fear this lance has speared me instead. They want information about those tunnels.

They want what Thad knew, everything he surmised from the information he gathered, and they'll get it. Eventually."

Theroun was silent. Thaddeus' hopeful face came to him. What would Thaddeus think of his General of Generals, sitting empty of heart in the mud, chained in a gang? The thought prickled Theroun, like a limb waking after a long sleep. "Did the King and Queen get away?"

"They did." Adelaine stared through the dripping rain toward the charred palace. "I bought them enough time to get through the crystal door. The tunnels have their own protection. Jornath and the other Kreth-Hakir have tried for weeks to re-open that gateway, but they can't breach it."

"They'll keep torturing you. For resisting them," Theroun spoke quietly.

Adelaine's icy blue eyes burned and her lips twisted like she sucked a sour cherry. She sat up tall in her ruined shift, though she shivered from the drizzle. "Physical pain is nothing. They can break my bones, take of my body that which they wish to take. I've mastered my mind long enough up on the tundras against cold, pain, and humiliation."

"There are twelve of them today." Theroun had counted the herringbone-clad men that patrolled the manacled warriors. "Their organization has delivered more Brethren as of yesterday. With Khorel Jornath, that makes thirteen."

"Some were killed in the fight under Fhekran Palace," Adelaine's breath sent up small puffs of steam in the drizzle. "But they've been replaced by new faces, and more. I don't have much time, Theroun. They've been waiting for reinforcements to fully break me. Nine of them, I could fight. Even with Jornath. But thirteen…" Adelaine took a deep breath, staring at the palisades. "But I knew this would be my fate when I saw you at Fhekran Palace, Black Viper."

Turning to Theroun, Adelaine held his gaze with steady eyes, nearly white in the grey morning. Reaching up a manacled hand, she touched Theroun's beard-roughened cheek. "For years, I have seen a black viper lingering outside the candlelight when I sleep at night. Coiled, waiting. For years, I wondered what it meant. I used to think it was Therel. But now I know it is you."

Adelaine straightened to attention. Lifting her spindly arms, she placed her palms upon Theroun's temples. Theroun felt a cool wind sweep into his mind like a storm breathing down from the tundra. In half a breath, his entire body went rigid, held in a vise beneath Adelaine's thin hands.

Hear me. Adelaine's voice boomed into Theroun like giants hurling boulders. *Your strength is in oblivion, Theroun den'Vekir. That place deep inside that cares nothing for the restraint of men. Only for freedom, for the bliss of the strike. For some men, their strength is love, or rage, or altruism. For you, it is the unblinking strike. Motion without emotion. The ability to laugh in the face of darkness, because you alone know true darkness. Be that, Theroun. Be your true strength now.*

Theroun breathed hard in the chill drizzle, Adelaine's words thundering through his mind. He sat rigid, remembering that place of bright madness he had recently touched. The place that had filled him before Khorel Jornath had booted him in the face during their duel. It had come so suddenly the night of his battle with Jornath – not a place of seething darkness like the Aphellian Way, but something else. A place where he had no mind.

Only the strike – and the bliss of it.

A memory of cold, red eyes filled Theroun. Four men in black Herringbone leathers suddenly rounded the cathedral at a swift run. Rage was in their faces, fury, and fear – their collective gazes locked to Adelaine, to whatever she was doing. Adelaine's fingers tightened upon Theroun's temples. Her white eyes blazed into him like diamonds under a winter sun.

Take this gift, Theroun. Of all the men I have ever felt, you press upon my mind with strength both ancient and powerful. I know now that the viper in my dreams was only waiting. Waiting for me to wake it. So take what is mine, Theroun. Take from me, and let it wake you!

A thundering blizzard built in Theroun's mind, like high seas frozen into ancient ice. The Kreth-Hakir ran for them full-tilt, joined now by the six Brethren from the plaza, the tide of their hive-mind screaming to drown out whatever Adelaine was doing. Suddenly, an enormous spear of energy thrust through Theroun from Adelaine. The Kreth-Hakir were smashed back, as if hit by a lightning strike.

And in that moment, Adelaine pressed her lips to Theroun's.

Theroun felt energy pour down his throat. Adelaine's energy, sluicing into his body and mind, into his very essence. Like wintermint and ice floes, she obliterated him, and all Theroun could do was drown. Something awoke in him. With a roar, it rose to what Adelaine offered. Eating her energy. Sucking that flow, drinking her down. Theroun reached out his manacled hands and crushed her to his chest, wanting to devour everything she offered.

Adelaine's head snapped back as she was jerked away by the hair. Her hands were wrestled from Theroun's head and she was smashed in the temple with the pommel of a shortsword. Ten Kreth-Hakir had arrived. Two of them punched Theroun in the gut and neck. He went down, his head ringing, his body spasming from the energy the Dremor had fed him. His cheek pressed to the rained-washed cobbles, his eyes met Adelaine's as she was pressed to the ground also, her manacles unlocked from the chain.

"Be the viper's strike!" Adelaine gasped. "*Taste their blood for me!*"

A boot smashed Adelaine in the mouth. Another found her gut and she rolled into a ball, keening. Four Kreth-Hakir hauled the Dremorande up. Gripping her by the hair and skinny arms, they hustled her away.

Twitching in spasms from whatever the Dremorande had done to him, Theroun could do nothing. It was all he could do to gasp in agony, his forehead upon the chill stone, grateful for the breeze licking his cheeks. Everything burned like ice and poison, and something writhed in the depths of Theroun's belly – cramping every muscle, sending him into a rigor. Pain devoured him, and he knew he had shit and pissed himself, his body unable to control whatever Adelaine had done.

What she had sparked in him.

Something massive moved inside Theroun. Something with an oilslick darkness that swallowed the edges of his vision. More than an echo of what he had touched the night he and Jornath had battled, it was as if that darkness had found a home inside his flesh and bones – and stretched beneath his skin, trying to find a way out.

Theroun couldn't control the scream that tore from his mouth. He felt a press of eyes, the attention of two armies wondering what was happening. Not because they were being controlled by Kreth-Hakir, but because their General was losing it. Hands were upon him. Herringbone-clad men unlocking him from the chain, holding him down. Khorel Jornath came rushing out the main doors of the cathedral, taking the steps at a run, down to where Theroun spasmed. Seizing Theroun's face in his large hands, Jornath forced Theroun to look into his eyes. Theroun's body spasmed again, but Jornath hauled his face back with a growl.

"*See me.*" Jornath rumbled. The sound of his voice and the silver power of his mind thundered through Theroun. "See me and be calm."

Theroun gasped for breath, twisting in annihilating pain, but where he'd have thought Jornath would have added to that agony, he found only a soothing calm issuing from Jornath's mind and body. Theroun inhaled that sanguine calm, devoured it from Jornath's hands. Like a moonlit balm it rushed through him, until he could breathe at last. His tremors shuddered out, leaving Theroun gasping upon the rain-slicked stones – the dark force inside him quiet.

"Easy. Be still and breathe." Khorel Jornath's level gaze held an emotion Theroun never thought to see from him: sympathy. He watched Theroun's eyes, one and then the other. "I cannot permit your *wyrria* to rise, General Theroun. Not just now. But we will speak of it later. For it is a thing that cannot be denied."

Still gasping for breath, Theroun could make no response, but he wrenched his face out of Jornath's grip and the big man let him go. Jornath stood. He locked eyes with Theroun in warning, though there was no press of mind behind it. Jornath then adopted his usual cold detachment, vacant of his previous humanity, and faced the cathedral doors.

Theroun's brows knit, confused.

And then his guts turned to ice as he saw a smooth shadow emerge into the drizzling day.

Lhaurent den'Karthus' presence was liquid as his steps whispered down the stairs. A robe of velvet slithered behind him, the tail of the eel. Not clad in grey today, but in a doublet and breeches of pure white silk chased with gold threads, his dark-opal eyes met Theroun's, glowing with pleasure. Lhaurent shone in the rain like a sea-pearl as he raised his hands to the heavy clouds. Gold starburst pins decorated his high collar, each with a ruby in their center and looped chains of gold, an insignia Theroun didn't recognize. As Lhaurent raised his arms, Theroun felt a wave of *wyrric* command, golden as a sunrise rather than silver like the Kreth-Hakir, surge over the Elsthemi captives and Menderian regiments.

"Elsthemen has fallen."

Lhaurent's words hit Theroun's eardrums like a surging sea. Amplified by Aeon-knew-what power roared out from Lhaurent's body, those words devoured Theroun's mind. They flowed through his skull with the force of belief, making him shudder. It was mind-games, he knew, and still he could not control it.

Slowly, Lhaurent den'Karthus began to unbuckle the high collar of his doublet. Letting his robe slip to his elbows, he opened his doublet, baring his collarbones and chest to the rain. Searing white light surged from his skin like a glowing tide, from a complex pattern of golden sigils engraved upon his body. Theroun felt a sublime power spread out into the grey day, like a shining net engulfing the armies in the shifting rain. And where the luminescence touched, seeping into hearts and eyes like a squid's tentacles, men were sundered. Theroun could only watch in horror as men of both armies cried out, falling to their knees in the mud, rapturous.

Soldier after soldier, succumbing to the vile *wyrria* issuing out from Lhaurent den'Karthus.

"The deviance of the northlands has been culled!" Lhaurent spoke, his hands upraised as his power poured out. "Alrou-Mendera has answered King Therel Alramir of Elsthemen, who murdered our beloved Queen. There will be no mercy. Know that you Elsthemi have been mastered. *Submit to Alrou-Mendera. Submit to the will of the Rennkavi your master, Lhaurent den'Alrahel of the Line of the Dawn. And to the Unity of all."*

Submit. It was the only word Theroun really heard from Lhaurent's treasonous speech. The word poured through Theroun's mind by the force of Lhaurent's terrible magics. Amplified by every Kreth-Hakir, including Khorel Jornath standing tall at Theroun's side, it was not a command he could fight. The mind of one man was a challenge; the mind of so many was impossible with that vile power of Lhaurent's behind it.

Theroun could taste the desire to submit upon his tongue like a cloying perfume. He could hear it washing through him like the ocean's roar. His vision bleached out like seafoam, and Theroun broke to that vast inundation, his head bowed even as he grit his teeth. Though others gazed upon Lhaurent with rapture, Theroun's face set in a rictus snarl, tasting only dark water and lies.

But he was alone in his defiance. As the entirety of the Elsthemi and the Menderian army went to their knees – even the stalwart Jhonen, the burly Lhesher, and the rabid Vitreal – Theroun finally understood what he had missed: that Lhaurent played a far deeper game than Theroun had ever known. And that Lhaurent's well-oiled subtlety had played them all – Uhlas and Alden, Elyasin and Therel, Theroun and even old weathered Evshein.

Had played them until the game was utterly, undeniably, his.

Rain sluiced the cold day. All went to their knees, submitting to the will of Lhaurent den'Alrahel, the Rennkavi. As Theroun sat there, manacled and understanding at last, he watched Lhaurent's soft-booted feet slip close over the stones and pause before him.

"Theroun den'Vekir," Lhaurent sighed with obvious pleasure. "Do you not know when your time to submit has come?"

"I submit only to my liege," Theroun growled through his teeth. "And that *is not you*. Eel."

The power pressing him lessened. Theroun was able to raise his head and meet Lhaurent's gaze. Lhaurent's grey orbs shone with vicious pleasure. Sweet cologne seeped from him, filling Theroun's nostrils with charnel stench. Unable to rise from the Kreth-Hakir and Lhaurent's combined power, Theroun could only kneel in the rain as Lhaurent held out his hand.

A ruby ring of dusky white star-metal fashioned with a wolf and dragon gleamed upon his right index finger. Suddenly, the full force of Lhaurent's power slammed Theroun. Lhaurent's ornate inkings seared like a falling star, and that terrible power came with a sundering ocean behind it. All Theroun could do was drown in the scent of eels. Suddenly, he understood: that he was a grain of sand on the ocean floor, a serpent drowning in the leviathan's coils. Everything had been taken from him, doused beneath this oily water.

His life, his purpose – even the battle in his soul.

Lhaurent stood before Theroun, his inkings burning white. He reached out, stroking Theroun's cheek, and delight shone in his eyes as he proffered the ruby ring. Power hammered Theroun, and with a strangled choke, Theroun's lips were made to touch the ruby. The ring of dusky white star-metal tasted of horror, that spoke in whispers as it burned. As it touched Theroun's skin, the power took him utterly and a paroxysm shook him. Before his men, his army, and the gaze of his bitterest enemy, General Theroun den'Vekir, Black Viper of the Aphellian Way, was finally brought low.

Crushed beneath an ocean of *wyrric* power.

The ring fell away. Lhaurent stared down with an endlessly pleased smile, his grey eyes shining with victory. Even as Theroun knew that he had been broken at last, something else shifted inside him: something made of unimaginable darkness and impossible might. It devoured the edges of his vision, stretched its immense oilslick blackness and inhaled. Except this force was not made of burning light, nor of hot or cold, nor silver mind-weaves. It was the absence of these things – of all things. A force as vast as the Void stretched and woke inside Theroun.

It was only readiness – and the strike.

CHAPTER 6 – DHERRAN

Delennia Oblitenne was, quite possibly, the most beautiful woman Dherran den'Lhust had ever seen. Tall of stature, she was muscled and curvaceous. Her waist was hardy, and from her athletic structure blossomed the hips of a goddess and full, ripe breasts. Long waves of silver hair were bound back in an ornate bun, her white eyes with their ring of pale blue glacially vicious. Thick muscle corded her thighs, and her ruby lips dripped blood to her chin and bare chest – because she was fighting stark naked, and had just bitten a man's ear off.

Her opponent, a thick fighter of enormous stature, roared in pain. The big man only struggled fruitlessly in Delennia's vise-tight grip while she choked him out from behind, one arm locked around his throat and the other behind his neck, on her back in the sand. He flailed, pummeling her as blood poured from his ear over her white throat and collarbones. His struggles weakened as she grinned, teeth red. Putting her lips close to his mangled hole, she whispered something as his eyes rolled up – and he passed out.

The crowd in the underground catacombs went wild as the fight ended. They roared so loudly that the soot-blackened stones far beneath the city of Velkennish vibrated with it. Torch-flares shivered in their iron brackets from the power of the din; lantern flames danced in vaulted stone niches. Gold exchanged hands and drinks slopped into mouths as Delennia Oblitenne roared in triumph. Slipping out from beneath the unconscious man with a deft twist, the Bitter part of the Bitterlance launched to her feet, sand cascading from her muscular ass as the crowd chanted her name. Stepping over the downed man, thighs rippling, she straddled him and gazed down upon her conquest. Setting a foot to his chest, she shook him with it, then put her foot to his face, smushing his lips and nose.

And then she squatted over him, and peed in his slack-open mouth.

The crowd cheered. The fighter was out, dead to the world and his own humiliation. Lingering in the shadows near a pillar at the top of the coliseum tiers, ten rings up from the fight-floor, Dherran, Khenria, and Grump watched the sordid yet exhilarating scene. Dherran and Khenria blended in tonight in black sneak-thief jerkins with leather hoods up, but Grump had come dressed in fine lord's attire – as his alter-ego, Grunnach den'Lhis – part of how he had secured their entrance to the fight this evening. Bristling with weapons, the trio were generally left alone up in the top tiers where there was less musk and piss-scent wafting through the gargantuan space.

From his vantage Dherran let out a slow breath, horrified as much as he was awed. Delennia Oblitenne, the Vicoute Arlen den'Selthir's once-lover, held power and glory in her every movement, and yet, she was also terrifying. Delennia came to her knees astride the fallen fighter, her well-muscled thighs gripping his hips. She mimed fucking him as her glacial gaze commanded the soot-stained fight-hall far beneath the city. The crowd exploded into frenzy yet again, as the magnificent woman got up and kicked her fallen opponent in the ribs.

"My friends!" She roared to the crowd. "Who is this lout that does not acknowledge a good night spent with Delennia Oblitenne?!"

Jeers exploded in the underground space, deafening Dherran.

"You've *got* to be joking!" Khenria hissed.

"Shush." Grump admonished, his eyes pinned to the fight-ring far below. "Watch. If all goes well, Dherran fights her next."

"I'm fighting *her?*" Dherran blinked. "Three weeks wandering around Velkennish and doing shady deals in order to gain access to these fights to show me off – you said I'd be facing the fiercest fighter in the city!"

"Delennia *is* the fiercest fighter in the city, Dherran, my boy," Grunnach chuckled. "She's why we're here. And *you* are our bargaining chip."

"Why don't I like the sound of that?" Dherran growled, wondering for the hundredth time if they'd made the right move to come to Velkennish in search of aid for Arlen den'Selthir.

"Trust in Grump, Dherran my lad." Grump chuckled, still

watching the sand-ring and the woman within. "He knows some things about love, loss, and warfare. Having you fight Delennia is just our opening gambit. Our fist in the door, so to speak."

"If Dherran's fight is only our opening gambit, then what is our closing one?" Khenria piped up, her dark brows knit in as much confusion as Dherran felt. Grump was full of secrets, and he'd been less than forthcoming about his past here in Velkennish or his overarching plan to secure Delennia's alliance for Arlen.

"You'll see, you'll see," Grump murmured distractedly. "For now, just watch."

As they turned back to the scene far below, Dherran heard a number of suggestions issue from the crowd, of what Delennia should do with the man she had conquered. Her head was cocked, listening to them all, until finally she raised her hand. "Friends! As my opponent has so thoroughly *embarrassed* himself in front of my guests," she made a sweeping gesture to the crowd, who cheered riotously, "I don't think he deserves my hospitality, do you?!"

They booed, shuddering the vast underground catacomb of blackened stone and slime-encrusted columns.

"I agree!" Delennia crowed. "So take him away, fellows, and string him up in the privy! Let a shit fighter be graced with the stuff of his make tonight, so he'll never forget what he is!"

At her pronouncement, the crowd surged forward, hauling the unconscious man up out of the blood-spattered sand to their shoulders and carting him away. His head fell slack, piss dribbling from his mouth as the centipede of unsavory humanity hauled him out above their heads. Moving through the crowd, the unconscious fighter was carted off through a hulking stone arch in the fifth tier into shadowy catacombs beyond.

"Where are they taking him?" Dherran hissed, watching them go.

"To the privy, Dherran my lad." Grump's chuckle was sour. "They'll put him in manacles there so everyone can shit and piss all over him until dawn. And then she'll let him stumble home."

"Halsos' hells!" Dherran gaze swung back to the sand-pit. "Will she do that to me if I lose?"

"The privy is the good spot, my boy. I have no idea where she'll put you." Grump gave another sour chuckle. "This is Delennia's domain, lad. This is the catacomb beneath *her* estate. She runs these fights. But she doesn't like men who lose on purpose, trying to curry favor with her, so she makes sure they don't want to lose."

Dherran's stomach churned. "How many fights does she perform a night?"

"These fights only happen once a season, and the days rotate so the Vhinesse's guards can't catch them. Delennia fights a few herself at the start of the night, then turns it over to more interesting bouts."

"The bouts get more interesting than this?" Dherran glanced over.

"Vastly." Grump's eyes were hard staring at the sand-ring. Though he lounged against the soot-blackened column in his hunter-green lord's finery, his doublet chased with golden thread and his breeches a fine russet leather, Dherran saw that Grump had set his fingertips to the gilded close-work knives at his belt, fingering them gently, then adjusting the long rapier at his hip.

"It's rare for men to live through a fight the later the hour gets," Grump murmured, his gaze hooded and dangerous. "Delennia's seasonal fights are famed throughout Cennetia, Praough, and Valenghia. They attract the best fighters in three lands, and the most brutal. Some come for sport, some for glory, some for the purse of gold that is ensured if they win a match. But some just come for blood. So you see, it's better that you're fighting Delennia herself, if we can get her to notice you. Thankfully, I've greased a few palms tonight with ample coin, which should have done the trick."

Taking out a blackened steel coin from inside his doublet, Grump began walking it over the backs of his knuckles. It was the talisman that had gained them entrance to the fights tonight, at the storm-grate behind the Weeping Sepulcher in the Cemetery of the Fallen. The damn thing featured a scorpion being strangled by a vine on one side, a blazing crown around a bleeding heart upon the other. Just the look of it gave Dherran jitters, as had the statue of the Weeping Woman before the sepulcher. A red verdigris had corrupted the statue's eyes, making the angelic figure seem like it wept blood as it gazed penitently up at the sky with prayerful hands.

Fitting, for the entrance to a fight-hall as vicious as this.

"Don't do it, Dherran." Khenria's grey eyes were fierce as she gripped his arm. "Don't fight her. She's insane!"

Dherran took a deep breath, gazing down upon his fierce little hawk. Ready for anything, lean and sinewy Khenria den'Bhaelen was everything a young Kingswoman could be – a vicious ferocity searing from her opal grey eyes, her tumble of short black curls shining with a nimbus of blue in the torchlight from a nearby bracket. Standing tall in her black leather thieves' corset purchased three days ago and absolutely bristling with knives, which weren't proscribed here in the fight-hall, she looked every bit the young killer – able to keep her own in a catacomb of thugs, thieves, and mercenaries.

"I'm afraid I have to, Khen," Dherran murmured, reaching out to stroke a lock of her short black curls out of her eyes. "We need Delennia. She was once allied with Arlen den'Selthir, and we need her standing army if we're going to have any hope of helping Arlen secure Vennet and the surrounding locale against Lhaurent's forces. I have to fight her. Or else our entire journey here, through the Heathren Bog and everything else, has been for nothing."

"Well said, Dherran my boy, well said," Grump grated, his gaze still pinned to the sand ring.

"I don't care!" Khenria's eyes flashed in the torchlight, her jaw set. "We'll find another way to approach her! There has to be some way to—"

"I hear we have fresh meat tonight!"

As if she had heard their conversation, Delennia's voice pierced through the jeering. She took a slow turn, her gaze sweeping the crowd and the high-vaulted tiers all around the fight ring. The crowd erupted in cheering, pumping fists and hollering. "I quite agree – Delennia wants to fuck another strong man, and a little bird has told me we have quite a treat this evening! A boar of a fighter who's entirely new to my domain! Where are you, fresh meat? Come to Delennia! Let's see if you have the strength to take a real woman down to her back!"

Jeers and wolf-whistles sounded, the double entendre not lost upon the crowd. Like a swallowing tide, the chant of *fresh meat* began rolling through the space. Grump gave Dherran a nudge. "That's us. Down you go. When you get there, strip. It's a bare-handed fight, no weapons."

"My Inkings?" Dherran glanced at Grump, suddenly worried about what fighting nude might expose in a foreign locale. "Will it be a riot if the crowd sees my Alrashemni Blackmark?"

"It'll just get you more hollers, boy," Grunnach smiled a little. "Even if the crowd is sour to your lineage. No one accosts the men Delennia fights – if you win."

"*If* I win?" Dherran snarled. "This is a fucking disaster, Grump!"

Dherran pulled free of Khenria, scrubbing both hands through his short blonde mane in a sudden fury. He'd never shrunk from a fight and he wasn't about to start now, even if the stakes were high. Khenria let him go, her grey eyes tracing his passage. Turning, Dherran began pushing through the crowd, his roaring temper preceding him as he descended tier after grime-slicked tier. The crowd was peevish, jostling him back, though some shrunk away from his raging fury. As he neared the ring, Delennia's white-blue eyes caught his descent. Her gaze locked upon Dherran, and he felt a shiver crest through his body.

In all that scandalous noise, a moment stretched between them like a thick molasses cord. Something unnatural eased out from her, which prickled Dherran's skin and plucked at his mind. Suddenly, Dherran began to doubt himself. Uncertainty crept into his head, made his limbs weak and cold. He found himself watching the incredible woman not with amazement, but the slow creep of fear. His guts tightened; a cold sweat washed his palms. Dherran stopped dead in his tracks at the third tier, the hollering dying out as the woman's unearthly white-blue eyes bored into him.

What the fuck was wrong with him? He'd never been afraid of a fight before. With a low growl, Dherran felt the hot snap of his infamous temper flash back. It roared up through his body, making his skin hot and his vision wash red. Dherran tightened a fist, impassioned, ready to hit the bitch.

Whatever *wyrric* magic she had, he'd be damned if he'd roll over and take it.

"Fuck you." Dherran snarled under his breath, as he resumed his steady approach.

"*Fresh meat!*" Delennia crowed, a wicked, knowing smile upon her perfect face. "Come on down and let me have a look at you!"

The crowd parted for Dherran, and he descended to the low stone berm around the sand-pit, then stepped over into the blood-spattered white expanse. Delennia pondered him, her hands on her bare hips, and Dherran saw a shrewd mind churning behind her impeccable, brutish beauty.

"You know the rules, fresh meat?" She lifted an eyebrow. He nodded. "Then strip. Let's see what you've got."

Delennia Oblitenne quirked an eager smile. Dherran began to remove his clothing, first his leather bracers, then unbuckling his hooded black jerkin to whistles and taunts, followed by his weapons and boots. All of it was carefully received into the hands of a very large, dark-eyed bald man with crimson Inkings all over his well-shined pate, whom Dherran had been briefed was Delennia's personal guard, Emeris ven'Khern.

"Your belongings will be stowed until the morning, sir," the guard murmured, "at which time you will receive them back with your compensatory winnings."

"You mean I get paid even if I lose?" Dherran blinked, ignoring the crowd's jeering.

"Of course," the guard chuckled. "A small… compensation. For the show. Good luck to you."

Dherran nodded, then turned back to Delennia, stripping his linen shirt off over his head. As it came off, he heard a hiss run through the crowd, then a series of low boos.

"A Kingsman." Delennia's white-blue gaze was frosty. "You have balls, Kingsman, showing your Blackmark here. Come on. Let's see those big balls of yours."

Dherran unbuckled his trousers and dropped them, unashamed. He'd never fought naked before, but it was strangely exhilarating. As he stood before this gorgeous woman, also immaculately naked, with the passion of a fight thrumming through his veins, his excitement showed.

"He wants Delennia to fuck him, gents!" She laughed, surprise in her white-blue eyes as she leered at his crotch. A riot of laughter went through the crowd. Delennia strode forward, sinuous and deadly. She could have been an empress, with that slow, sultry stride. When she neared Dherran, he found himself caught in her icy, dominant gaze. "Do you need me to fuck you, fresh meat? Because I will. If you ask nicely."

Reaching down, she stroked his cock with her fingertips, her commanding gaze never straying. Dherran felt those rippling tendrils come at him again, like a white mist in his thoughts, trying to take root like a thousand seeping leeches. The fight went out of Dherran suddenly. His passion guttered. Breathless, he could only stare down at her, feeling weak.

Her first punch, Dherran didn't even see. Delennia telegraphed nothing – not a lift of her shoulder, not a shift of her weight. Her muscled arm and solid fist just came straight at him, catching him hard on the angle of his jaw. Stars exploded in Dherran's vision. Her punch carried the weight of a mountain, and it was all Dherran could do to let the momentum drop him in a backwards roll. He came up on the other side of the ring, sand-coated, as the crowd erupted in drunken jeers.

"Gotcha, Kingsman." Delennia teased, her white eyes utterly dominant now.

Dherran cussed as he shook stars from his head and spit blood from a bitten lip, fresh crimson upon the sand. With the taste of iron and the radiating pain consuming his jaw, his heart to fight flared back: like a demon it roared through his body, making the world tinge bloody. Bristling with the power of a mad boar, Dherran snarled and raised his fists, pummeling back her seeping *wyrria* with a blistering fight of his own.

Delennia's silver-white eyebrows rose. She gave him a subtle nod, an eager smile lifting one edge of her ruby-stained lips.

Then the fight began.

They circled each other like keshar-cats. Dherran had long years of patience learned at the uncomfortable end of his rash temper, and like him, Delennia was graceful, stalking him and taking his measure. Dherran couldn't help but admire her as they moved in a lithe dance, his arms loose like the Vicoute Arlen den'Selthir had taught him. Their bodies were supple in their readiness, and Dherran had a sudden realization that the Bitter and the Lance had once trained together in the ring.

That was why they were here, after all: to see if Delennia could be convinced to come to Arlen's aid once more – reunifying their

Kingsmen and Khehemni forces into an army.

All thoughts were erased from Dherran's mind as Delennia struck. Even faster than Arlen den'Selthir, her sinewed strike was direct, again without any telegraphing, only a swift pivot of the hips. Dherran slipped it like Arlen had taught him, not contesting but allowing her to complete her strike. To feel as if she had won, rolling past and deflecting her fist off his chest laterally. Flowing up under her guard, Dherran struck at her ribs, but she curled her body around his punch like she had no bones at all. Deflecting his fist off her ribcage, she directed it back into Dherran. He slipped it, pivoting as she tried to land a punch on his spine, sliding it off his shoulder-blade.

It was fast, complicated. Neither opponent allowed punches to land, only slipped and slid like water around an oar. They used torsos, chests, ribs, and thighs to deflect. Delennia caught one of Dherran's punches with the instep of her foot and sent him rolling down into the sand, a move Arlen had never used. Dherran took one of her punches and let it flow past, slipping aside to get her in a headlock. Using the crown of her head, she rolled off him, up under his armpit and away.

Minutes passed of this tenebrous, complicated dance. Tens of minutes; the crowd utterly silent. Dherran and Delennia both breathed hard, sweat glistening as they separated for a moment, gazing at each other from across the ring. Delennia lifted an elbow, wiping sweat from her eyes. Dherran took the moment to do the same.

Delennia lifted her chin, and her white eyes flashed. "Knives!"

Her guardsman rushed forward, silver brows furrowed. He bent his massive bald head low in conversation, but Delennia shook her head, her white-blue eyes pinned to Dherran. "Knives, Emeris. Now."

The guardsman gave a guttural snarl, his gaze flicking to Dherran, but he obliged his mistress, producing one plain belt-knife for her and turning to hurl a matching knife into the blood-spattered sand at Dherran's feet. The guard shot a warning glower at Dherran from under his silver brows and crimson-tattooed head and stepped from the ring.

"Pick it up." Delennia Oblitenne nodded at the knife in the

sand. "There is only one rule, which I swear upon my house I'll not break. And you will not either, on pain of death under my house rules. No throwing your blade. I want to see what you can do with it in your hands."

"How do I know that an oath upon your house means anything?" Dherran hunkered, retrieving the knife, keeping his eyes on her.

She blinked, those white-blue eyes startled for just a moment. "Don't you know House Oblitenne of Valenghia, Kingsman?"

"Should I?" Dherran growled, nonplussed.

"No…" A slow, amused smile came to her face. "No, I suppose not. Shall we fight?"

Dherran nodded, and they began to circle again. Dherran let Delennia set the pace once more, in that slow, sinuous dance. When she rushed him, he was ready, sluicing like water around the deft thrust of her knife, rolling his shoulders and camming her hilt back towards her. She slipped out, bringing her center of gravity up to unseat Dherran's balance. He twisted, slipping the flat of her blade with his palm. She struck at his neck with her elbow. Dherran rolled under, his blade up in her ribs, and she arched like a cat to avoid it.

She landed a punch from her unarmed hand, right into Dherran's stomach. He huffed in surprise – and in that moment the heel of Delennia's palm came up under Dherran's chin, fast. Dherran was blasted backwards, landing flat on his back in a spray of sand, ears ringing and vision black.

Delennia was astride him. The steel of her knife was at his throat, leaving Dherran barely room to swallow, but he jiggled his own knife, snugged perfectly up under her left breast. The point of his blade was angled between her fifth and sixth ribs, poised to take her heart. Her blood trickled over his fingers as his knife-tip pierced her perfect white skin.

"You're quick, Kingsman," Delennia leaned in, whispering by Dherran's ear. "Hopefully not too quick…"

"Arlen says hello," Dherran retorted, unimpressed by her seduction.

Delennia jerked back as if she'd been struck. Her blade still up under Dherran's jaw and his dug into her ribs, she went perfectly still as if she'd turned to stone. Ignoring the raucousness all around them, her face settled into a hard mask. "If Arlen said hello, Kingsman... I'd have his guts strewn all over this cavern in half a heartbeat. Are you telling me you say hello on Arlen's behalf?"

"Maybe." Dherran gave a hard smirk. "End this charade and find out."

She smiled, ruthless, more a snarl than a smile. "This was no charade, Kingsman. If you hadn't fought so well, I would have killed you. But you've talent, with the flavor of Arlen's training, not to mention some resistance to my *wyrria*. So you've earned a talk, even if it is for that brazen bastard den'Selthir. But first—"

"First what?" Dherran growled.

"First, this." Delennia leaned down and slid her perfect lips over Dherran's, drawing him into the most luscious kiss he'd ever tasted, and the most bloody. Which didn't stop, for a long span of whistles and jeers.

CHAPTER 7 – ELESHEN

Moving like silk over water, Eleshen den'Fenrir parried and slipped, pivoted and cut. Bouting at swords with Temlin den'Ildrian in the dusty promenade inside the First Abbey, she glistened with sweat in the crisp autumn afternoon. Her breathing steady and deep, Eleshen's long limbs were corded with sinew that obeyed her every instinct. Her mind sighed out to the quacking of ducks in the pond nearby, to the crunch of a bare footstep upon gravel as someone passed, to the ring of steel as she slipped another down-stroke and spun, bringing her sword up to slice beneath Temlin's armpit. Gone was her lack of balance. Gone were hands that dropped things. Gone was fumbling and stumbling. After two hours, Eleshen was barely winded – her new body knowing the precise timing of every movement for battle.

"Halt!" Temlin finally barked. He stepped back, lowering his beautiful silver-white sword inset with runes down the blade and a massive ruby in the pommel. He gasped to catch his breath, drenched with sweat in his light linen shirt, tan breeches, boots, and the weapons-harness he'd found up in Mollia den'Lhorissian's vale atop the Kingsmount. The Jenner-turned-King-Protectorate of Alrou-Mendera had been handsomely aged when Eleshen had met him at Highsummer, but now, the wire-tight vigor of his prime was restored. Eleshen could feel the roar of a lion in Temlin's every movement, a true den'Ildrian royal. Palming sweat from his thick russet mane, Temlin wiped his bare forearm across his brow.

"Tired, old man?" Eleshen stepped back with a smirk.

"Hardly! Give me a breather and I'll take you for a second round!" Temlin barked a laugh, eyeballing her with piercing green eyes full of impish humor, devoid of spectacles now.

"I think you need a nap," Eleshen sassed.

"I only nap with beautiful women." Temlin lifted a red-gold eyebrow. "But bouting with them is far more fun."

Eleshen felt heat flush her pale cheeks, and not from the sword-practice. Temlin was a rake, the kind of man she would have hit with her frying-pan once upon a time. Destiny had brought them together these past three weeks. A dance of flirtation had sprung up between them as they practiced at swords day after day, but it was a thing of cheeky banter and little substance. Over the weeks, it had helped Eleshen heal from her ordeals under the old Abbott's cruel blades.

But fighting helped more. Though Eleshen had not earned Inkings, the Abbey's Kingsmen had seen her move and conferred upon her the honor of their garb. An ancient set of Greys had been gifted to her from the armory – a charcoal leather jerkin with a high collar and deep hood, tooled with Alrashemni symbols, with charcoal leggings and tall boots with longknife side-sheaths. Sliding the sword away over her shoulder in her weapons-harness as if she'd done it all her life, Eleshen pulled the longknives from her boots.

"Well if you want to bout, come at me, old man."

Eleshen's voice sighed through the air like midnight reeds as she settled into a fighting crouch. Sinews bunched in perfect coordination as her left foot slipped back in the dirt. Her hands were pale in the sun, her long cable of black hair cascading over her shoulder to her waist, sleek as an otter's pelt. Eleshen pierced Temlin with her eyes, now vibrant as violets in the rain.

Gone was the golden innocent she had been – replaced by something darker.

For a moment, she saw Temlin's breath catch. Saw him undone in a way Eleshen had never affected men before. She had always been able to read people, but since her ordeal with Lhem, she had a keener understanding of the world. Of how a person could be bent or broken by another. It was a dire knowing – the understanding that she could break a man with her beauty, ferocity, and passion.

Temlin gave a wry grin, then tossed his sword to the dust. "You slay me, woman. Enough. I've matters of war to attend today."

Eleshen slid her longknives back into their sheaths with an answering grin. As if he'd been waiting for them to finish up, brawny Brother Sebasos from the brewery approached, clad in his own well-worn Kingsmen gear from decades past. Sebasos' grey-shot beard was neatly trimmed to his boulder-cracking jaw, his iron-shot black curls pulled back into a tight tail streaked with grey. Sebasos set a palm to his chest in the Kingsman salute, one hand upon the longknife at his hip, a two-handed broadsword strapped to his back. Temlin's gaze flicked to Sebasos as he swiped his sword from the dirt and slid it away over his left shoulder. Sebasos gave Eleshen a nod next. Setting a palm to her chest, her other hand a longknife at her belt, Eleshen nodded back. She wasn't a Kingsman, but she would damn well do them honor like one.

"King-Protectorate," Sebasos turned to Temlin. "We've had an answer from Roushenn."

"Have we?" Temlin's grin was sour. "Lhaurent's decided to parlay at last, has he?"

"He has." Sebasos' dark gaze was brooding. "He wishes to talk terms. The city is in severe unrest from your order to close the Abbey and withhold ale from the masses, in addition to the war-fronts. The new *king* wishes the populace to enjoy their upcoming celebrations for Autumn Harvestfest in the manner they are accustomed. With ale."

"Thought so." Temlin flicked his fingers to Eleshen. "Milady. Accompany us?"

"Of course." Eleshen nodded, and they set out toward the paving-stone path near the byrunstone towers of the Abbey Annex. The trio received salutes from all around. Men in grey quadrant-split Kingsmen garb with blackened steel buckles and the tooled Mountain-and-Stars honored them near the arched gables of the Brewery with a palm to the heart. Women wearing black Jenner Penitent robes and picking herbs in the burgeoning gardens placed two fingers to the lips and stepped a foot back into a moderate bow before resuming their tasks. A company of Palace Guardsmen in cobalt actually bent a knee before their King-Protectorate as he passed, and Temlin gave them a sober nod back.

He was aware of their tenuous position, supporting him rather than Lhaurent.

The First Abbey had been mobilized in the past three weeks. As Eleshen glanced around, it seemed a hornet's hive, humming with activity. The verdant grounds were thick with uniforms of cobalt, grey, and cowls of black, all hustling about their appointed tasks. Jenners and Kingsmen and a full third of the Palace Guard had come together within these bluestone walls, in support of King-Protectorate Temlin den'Ildrian who had claimed the throne for his niece the Queen. Castellan Lhaurent den'Alrahel's powerful unveiling the day after the city burned sat sour in the bellies of those who crowded the Abbey. His proclamation, that he was some kind of god because of golden markings that moved the palace and swayed people to his will, sat bitter as gall in the hearts of the last Alrashemni Kingsmen.

Together, the trio stepped up the worn bluestone stairs of the Abbey Annex. Sebasos hauled one heavy ironbound door open with his muscled arm. Temlin paused, allowing Eleshen to enter first, and she smiled at his courtly habits. Temlin treated her like a lady in silks when they weren't bouting, no matter how much buckled leather she wore.

But Eleshen sobered as she moved into the gloom of the Annex hall, her gaze sweeping the shadows in the cupolas on instinct. She held a deep watchfulness that she was unable to shake now, since Lhem's torture. Though he commanded the Abbey from sunup to well past sundown like a lion, Temlin was broken in his own way. Eleshen spent some evenings in Temlin's company, when nightmares of Lhem assailed her. She would steal to his room, often finding him awake perusing documents, ready with a cup of ale and and a quiet sit at the hearth. Despite his heinous flirtation, Temlin understood things younger men didn't. He never said a word when she came for a reprieve of her awful nightmares; simply wrapped her in his arms, breathing softly without speaking. In their evening quietude, Eleshen could feel his aching grief for his beloved Mollia den'Lhorissian, now trapped within the Abbeystone.

Glancing along the shadowed corridor, Eleshen saw Temlin's cramped study lit with swirling dust motes filtering down through an ochre and cinnabar sunbeam. It seemed like ages since she had come here at Highsummer, moving in the fell tides of Elohl den'Alrahel. Elohl was further from her mind now, though his abandonment still stung. And Eleshen had found a new life, a new purpose here among the Alrashemni. The Abbey's Kingsmen had watched her bout Temlin that sweltering morning two weeks ago, the first day she'd been recovered enough to hold a blade. Feverish and still healing from her ordeals, Eleshen had taken Temlin down

fast that day – then Sebasos, then three more Kingsmen fighters who
came at her. Right there, it had been voted on and agreed that
Eleshen could test for her Alrashemni Seals.

And become a Kingsman.

Passing the vaulted worship hall, Eleshen followed Temlin and
Sebasos up a winding staircase, toward the wide circular hall with its
soaring facades that served as their war-rotunda. The ironbound
doors were already open and Temlin's skinny runner-lad Brandin
stood near the central bluestone dais, a scroll of vellum in hand. A
colored-glass window of a fighting lion poured golden and red
sunlight down upon the dais, as if marking this war-room for the
den'Ildrian reign. Temlin gestured as he came. Clad in a plain
brown leather jerkin with a bronze lion pin at his collar rather than
Jenner robes, the lad whisked forward and deposited the scroll into
Temlin's hand. Temlin spread the scroll out on the stout ironwood
map-table. Eleshen saw the sour twist of his lips as he noted the gold
wax seal imprinted with a crossed scepter and olive branch topped
by the Kingsmount and Stars.

"Lhaurent's using the seal of the King of Alrou-Mendera.
Whatever will be next?" Temlin gave a huff as his piercing eyes
flicked over the vellum, his palms flat on the desk. Reading on, he
gave a dark chuckle. He straightened and met Sebasos' gaze, raking
a hand through his unruly russet hair. "Well. His demands are not
unexpected."

"No, King-Protectorate." Sebasos set his jaw, his grey eyes
burning with fury and disdain.

Eleshen stepped to Temlin's side. Fingers settling to the stout
grey wood, she skimmed the document as Temlin crossed his arms,
making a growling sound. But like the two seasoned Kingsmen,
Eleshen found she was also unsurprised at the message.

"Lhaurent threatens retribution upon the Abbey if we do not
deliver ale for Harvest." She lifted her eyes to Temlin. "He'll send
the Roushenn Palace Guard against us."

"The Roushenn Guard don't worry me," Temlin snorted.
"They've not got enough men to break these walls. It's what
Lhaurent isn't saying that does concern me. What has he got in his
pockets that we don't?"

"Mind-benders. Those Kreth-Hakir fellows in herringbone-weave armor." Eleshen's answer was prompt. Already, they'd had to execute eight refugees from Lintesh who had attacked members of the resistance – including one who had nearly succeeded in assassinating Temlin. When interrogated, all nine had professed to loving King-Protectorate Temlin with tears in their eyes, even as they stood at the chopping block. They couldn't understand why they would have raised a knife against him; why their bodies had functioned without their permission.

"The mind-benders are a concern," Temlin nodded, scowling. "That was a nasty business these past weeks with the brainwashed refugees, but we've found the Hakir's effects to be distance-related. Our patrols atop the walls are being watched for signs of mind-infiltration, but so far, nothing. Mind-bending effects must not reach so high up, or penetrate well through stone, or else Lhaurent's curs would have caused far more fuss then they have. No, Lhaurent clearly believes he has something else that gives him an advantage over the Abbey."

"Control over the King's Army?" Eleshen quipped, crossing her arms and fiddling with the end of her stable braid.

Temlin gave a hand waggle. "Yes and no. The news in the city is that Lhen Fhekran has fallen and Lhaurent has laid claim to Elsthemen. Alrou-Mendera's army is busy with this two-front war Lhaurent so blatantly believes he can sustain. He'd be more than a fool to split his armies in three to attack us. Besides, the First Abbey is built to withstand tides of men hammering it. If we keep enough archers on the walls and in the death-holes above the gate, we have little to worry about."

"Then what does bother you?"

"Trebuchets." Temlin crossed his arms over his chest, scowling. "Lintesh has seven upon the outer wall of the First Tier, and five upon the wall of the Third Tier. Six of those are close enough to the First Abbey to be aimed in our direction. And if they hurl fire——"

"We'll be burned out." Sebasos returned Temlin's frown. "All our supplies, our gardens. Our storage and food."

"Not to mention exploding spirits from the distillery." Temlin lifted a russet eyebrow.

Sebasos let out a soft whistle. "That could blow a hole in the walls. The distillery sits too near the south towers."

"Indeed." Temlin gave a strained sigh. "Or Lhaurent could take a more diabolical tactic, hurling corpses from the shanty-cities over our walls and riddling us with disease. What we don't know is if he has an experienced General advising him, telling him how to siege a fortress without destroying the entire fucking capitol."

"Burn a city too far, and its people will abandon you," Sebasos growled in agreement.

"Unless his mind-benders can make the populace stay put," Eleshen mused.

"Starving men and women will leave Lintesh no matter Lhaurent's darkest influence," Temlin eyed Sebasos and Eleshen. "Some hungers go deeper than the mind. Which is why Lhaurent wishes to parlay about Harvestfest. He cannot have more riots over withheld ale. The city would destabilize too far, and his reign would crumble."

"But he's not negotiating from a place of weakness." Eleshen spoke again.

"Not by any means," Temlin's attention turned to her. "Which is why we must tread carefully. Sebasos. Write a missive. We accept a preliminary meeting. But it will be done in the open, in the fountain-plaza before the Abbey's main gate. Mind-benders are not to attend. If any of our people feel even a *hint* of interference, the negotiations will be considered void and will be ceased at once."

"King-Protectorate." Sebasos crossed his arms. "Lhaurent's demands include you rescinding your claim upon the throne for Queen Elyasin."

"I know." Temlin went silent, staring out the nearest bank of windows to the clear day beyond, his fingers fidgeting at the ruby in the pommel of his sword. A trickle of sweat slid down his temple in the suffering humidity, though the windows of the upper gallery were cast wide to the afternoon air.

"Are you seriously considering ceding the throne to Lhaurent?" Sebasos growled softly, iron and menace towards the false ruler in his tone.

"We no longer have any confirmation that my niece the Queen lives." Temlin blinked at last, and sighed. "From her Abbeystone, Mollia observed Elyasin and her Elsthemi King escaping by a tunnel from Lhen Fhekran, just before the palace fell, but it has been three weeks, and Molli has seen nothing more."

"Your niece lives," Sebasos gripped Temlin's shoulder with one battle-scarred hand. "I feel it."

Temlin drew a deep breath. "And if I end up destroying her capitol with my resistance in her name?"

"Much is risked in war," Sebasos grated.

Temlin's nostrils flared. His eyes went from misty to hawk-sharp. "Send the missive. Milady Eleshen, attend me. I have somewhat further to discuss with you."

"King-Protectorate." Sebasos gave his liege's shoulder a squeeze with his big hand, then turned on his heel with a quick Kingsman salute and marched from the wide rotunda.

Temlin wore a thoughtful frown as he gestured for Eleshen to follow. They retreated from the rotunda, down the winding staircase to Temlin's dusty study. Temlin led Eleshen inside and shut the heavy door, latching it. He sank to his stout ironwood chair with a hard sigh, his gaze raking the sagging bookshelves. They were even more choked now than Eleshen had first seen them. Temlin had strategically hidden within their hodgepodge all the books and arcane items the black-clad Ghost of Roushenn had liberated from Laurent's war-room the night Lintesh burned.

The Ghost of Roushenn. Eleshen's thoughts wandered back to him as she took a seat upon Temlin's overstuffed leather couch, sending up a puff of dust. A strong man with grey eyes like the sea, the Ghost had haunted Eleshen's dreams ever since he'd saved her. Saved her, betrayed his alliance with Lhaurent, then disappeared like smoke through the walls.

Inhaling, Eleshen banished her whimsy. She could muse on the mysterious Ghost later; right now, she had a King-Protectorate to deal with. Temlin was harrowed – Eleshen could tell by the way he scowled and steepled his fingers at his desk. She didn't press him. Temlin was loquacious when he wanted to be, but having rigorously eschewed his addiction of ale these past weeks, he was a more thoughtful man than the fiery bastard he'd once been.

"A worry grows in me," Temlin met Eleshen's gaze at last, "based on things Molli sees in the wider world from inside her Plinth."

"What do you mean?" Eleshen sat up. She knew Temlin

retreated to the Abbeystone in the catacombs beneath the Abbott's quarters to speak with his beloved Mollia, trapped inside the Stone. He'd rarely spoken of those conversations, unless they were of import to his war-stratagems.

"Molli has been watching movements of Menderian troops," Temlin began, tapping his steepled fingers together. "Not only has Lhaurent taken Lhen Fhekran, but he also shunts thousands of soldiers through Stones all over the nation to Ligenia, and he has ships coming into Ligenia at all hours, bringing slaves from the southwest."

"Slaves to supplement his armies?" Eleshen interrupted.

"So it seems." Temlin growled, setting his chin upon his steepled fingertips. "I believe Lhaurent prepares for a tremendous battle. To march out from Ligenia to the Aphellian Way, and launch a devastating campaign against Valenghia."

"To invade Valenghia?" Eleshen blinked. "To end the Valenghian-Menderian war?"

"Indeed." Temlin set his lips to his steepled fingers. "The maps the Ghost of Roushenn liberated for us include supply lines intended to support a massive force stationed near the Valenghian border. I've finally had word from Arlen den'Selthir, the leader of our Shemout Alrashemni: a hasty missive sent by hawk, saying that a Menderian force some thousands strong marched from Quelsis, sieging Vennet with Kreth-Hakir at their lead. That was three weeks ago, and I have heard nothing since. I fear the worst, though Arlen has a contingency plan he's been building these past years that should keep his Kingsmen safe – for a time."

"But that's not what eats at you," Eleshen murmured, watching him.

"No." Temlin snarled behind his fingertips, green eyes flashing. "What gnaws my gut is that Lhaurent makes no preparations in Lintesh. He amasses no military here. There's been no felling of trees in the King's Forest for siege-towers or battering rams to deal with the Abbey, and he's not hired more Palace Guard, who are decreased by a third since many of them defected to my banner."

"Lhaurent has something else that he believes could break the Abbey. Easily." The realization hit Eleshen like a black wave, raising the pulse at her throat.

"The Abbey is vulnerable," Temlin nodded, his brooding eyes meeting hers. "From something I cannot take into account. We have food against a siege. We have medicine for a conflict. We could even survive fire, though it would cost us, and we have discovered many of Lhaurent's mind-warped pawns. So what is it that I don't know?"

"Was there anything in the items the Ghost brought?" Eleshen's gaze perused the shelves.

Temlin leaned back in his chair; put his boots up on the corner of the stout desk. "Lists, ledgers, maps – plans of battle and records of how Lhaurent pays for it all with emeralds. Mercenaries from Thuruman, hired thugs from Ghree, Lefkani and Crassian pirates that raid the southwestern coasts to enslave Jadounian and Perthian men into fighting. His net has been woven wide in his four decades behind the throne. Much of it I have passed along by sea-hawk to King Arthe den'Tourmalin of the Isles, who has declared a cessation of the former peace agreement he held under King Uhlas."

"The Tourmaline Isles have declared for you?" Eleshen asked, eyebrows raising.

"As much as they can." Temlin combed his short red-gold beard with his fingers. "Lhaurent harries them night and day now with fleets of Lefkani pirates he's bribed to get his slave-ships through. But as for the arcane items the Ghost left us… they seem inert baubles, nothing more. A few are clockworks so ancient they belong in a Praoughian museum."

"And the books?" Eleshen ventured. "There must be something useful there."

"Would that were true!" Temlin snorted, gesturing expansively. "The books are unhelpful. Genealogies of royal lines from a nation to the far southeast, the Sun Tribes. Detailed descriptions of fanciful *wyrric* abilities, like transforming the physical body into a beast. Rubbish."

"So all of it was just a waste of time?" Eleshen's heart sank and she fidgeted with her braid.

"Actually." Temlin slung his boots off the desk and sat up. "Two of the volumes the Ghost brought were not rubbish. Not rubbish at all, in fact."

"Which ones?" Eleshen glanced around the cramped study. Temlin rose and pushed back his stout wooden chair. Eleshen watched him press a sophisticated catch in the floor with his fingertips. A false flagstone lifted from the floor beneath where his chair had been. Temlin pried it up and fished out two slender tomes of cobalt leather, and one far larger volume bound in plain brown leather, yet inscribed with a mad *tarentesh* of arcane symbols all across the cover.

He set all three upon his desk with reverence. Touching the slim cobalt volumes with a wry smile, Temlin spoke. "These volumes chronicle the Alrou-Menderan royal line, back to the founding of our nation nearly a thousand years ago. They speak of the royal line's *Alrashemni* origin, something I had always suspected but never knew for certain, part of why I pledged myself to the Shemout when I was young. These volumes state that House den'Ildrian is actually an Alrashemni house, though our nation was founded by a different Alrashemni house – the Alrahel. *Den'Alrahel*, in the tongue of the native Menderian tribes. The Line of the Dawn."

"Lhaurent's surname – and Elohl's!" Eleshen breathed, astonished. Moving close, Eleshen reached her fingertips out to touch the cobalt volumes, each with a blazing sun imprinted upon the cover. "These establish Lhaurent's legitimacy as King of Alrou-Mendera."

"Unfortunately, yes." Temlin snorted. "And I'm sure he wants them back. Without these volumes, Lhaurent will never be able to assert his legitimacy to the monarchs of other nations. They'll only ever see him as a warlord, and treat him as such, blocking his negotiations and causing him to engage in wars to smash his way through the continent, rather than win allies through diplomacy. Interesting to note that your friend Elohl also could stake a claim upon the throne if these volumes ever came to light."

"What stops Lhaurent, then? From using whatever he thinks he's got against the Abbey?"

"These." Temlin gestured to the slim volumes. "I wrote him and told him I had something he needs. Something that I'm sure he wants back. The only thing stopping him from making a move against us right now is that he's trying to find out what I have and where it's hidden. Hence, all the brainwashed spies we've had to execute recently."

"What does that mean for us?" Eleshen turned to face Temlin.

"What if he finds these volumes?"

Temlin gripped her shoulders kindly with his sword-calloused hands. "Then we're screwed, my dear. He'll use his mystery leverage upon the Abbey as soon as he has the chance. Laurent's not the kind of man to wait for his enemies to play nice. He'll not wait for any parlay, and *that's* what keeps me up at night. Any day, any *moment*, one of his mind-sundered spies could find these volumes. And when they do, the game is up."

"Then we have to leave," Eleshen spoke decisively. "All of us – the Kingsmen, the Jenners. We have to escape through Molli's Abbeystone. Have her put us through somewhere safe, far from Lintesh."

"I can't leave Lintesh." Temlin thrust a fist down to the ironwood table, his face set. "I am King-Protectorate. I am the representation of everything that resists Lhaurent's atrocity in Alrou-Mendera."

"But if you stay, you'll play right into whatever trap Lhaurent has set for us!"

Temlin's emerald eyes were fierce, but calm suffused them suddenly. A small smile lifted his lips and he reached out, cupping Eleshen's face tenderly.

"I am an old man, Eleshen my dear," he chuckled. "I may look young again, but I have lived more winters full of ale and hate than any man has a right to. Living the wreck of a life that I have has taught me about defiance – the strongest defiance is the one which faces the great maw of the Void."

"But Lhaurent could kill you," Eleshen whispered.

"Death doesn't scare me," Temlin murmured. "But the death of all our Kingsmen – that terrifies me. With Lhaurent's threat against the Abbey and his move against Vicoute Arlen den'Selthir, the Kingsmen have got no strongholds left. If we fall, the Alrashemni will be wiped out. I never listened to my father much. He was a cold spar of iron and dry as sour cider; but one thing he never failed to tell Uhlas and I was that the Alrashemni Kingsmen are the backbone of this land. That I could always depend on them. If they fall – who will our nation turn to? Who will defend us as a tyrant like Lhaurent rises?"

"If the Alrashemni Kingsmen die," Eleshen spoke, "so too does the heart of Alrou-Mendera."

"Indeed." Temlin brushed a wisp of hair from Eleshen's face. Something sad suffused his eyes, and Eleshen's eyes filled with fierce tears in return. She stared up at him, defiance rushing through her as she understood everything he was trying to tell her. "You want me to leave the Abbey. Take the remaining Kingsmen and flee, leaving you here to play Lhaurent's game."

"I want you to shepherd the Alrashemni Kingsmen," Temlin murmured kindly. "To wrest from Lhaurent that which he wants from under his very nose, while I make a show of defiance and negotiation. I know you can do this. Whatever happened to you," he stroked her sleek hair back from her face, marveling at it, "changed you in ways I cannot begin to describe. From a hot-tempered innkeeper has sprung a sword of cold wrath, full of unknown elements. Perhaps something you had all along. But in you, I feel a fighter with unsurpassable tenacity. You are utterly dedicated to the Kingsmen, to preserving our legacy. And *that* is who I need to lead this mission. The Abbey's Kingsmen are too old. We need someone young, someone with fire in her heart and unshakeable belief in our legacy. And that, my dear, is you."

"And this missive?" Eleshen took a deep breath, steadying herself to be chosen for such an important endeavor.

Lifting the large tome of sigil-scrawled brown leather from the desk, Temlin placed it reverently in Eleshen's hands. Gazing at it, he touched the cover softly, his gaze pained even as much as it was sweet.

"This is Molli's last journal." Temlin murmured, his gaze lifting to Eleshen's. "It is my most precious possession, besides the garb she made for me while I was in her company. I would like you to take it out of the Abbey. Shepherd all our treasures and people out of the Abbey, all but a few elders who will keep up a mockery of resistance here. Escort them through the Abbeystone to a valley in the mountains called Gerrov-Tel, protected from Kreth-Hakir notice by a powerful Alranstone Molli knows. Once that's done, make contact with the Shemout Rakhan, Vicoute Arlen den'Selthir of Vennet, if he lives. Sebasos knows where his contingency location is. Regroup the Kingsmen into a unified force. Keep us, Eleshen. Keep us alive, and keep Lhaurent in the dark."

"You would truly sacrifice yourself to Lhaurent?" Tears prickled Eleshen's eyes as she cradled the leather tome to her chest, ready to guard it to the end.

"I will do what I must to protect our people," Temlin spoke, hard fire in his emerald eyes. "That is what a King-Protectorate does. Please. Help me save our Kingsmen from annihilation. For Queen Elyasin."

Eleshen bowed her head. With a heavy sigh, Temlin pressed his forehead to hers. They breathed together for a long moment, and Eleshen could almost feel Temlin's heart as their breaths intertwined in the fading sunlight. So strong. So determined to raise his roar to the world, that his reign as a den'Ildrian King would not be forgotten, even if it was short. Eleshen hitched a breath and straightened her shoulders, still clutching the leather tome tight. Blinking away tears, she gazed up at her King-Protectorate, a man she had come to respect sooner than anyone she had ever known.

A friend she had come to know too late.

"I'll do it, but not for Elyasin. For you," Eleshen spoke. "And for our Kingsmen. Tell me where we begin."

CHAPTER 8 – JHERRICK

Jherrick den'Tharn sat by the raised bier in the vaulted atrium of opalescent stone and falling leaves. It was always autumn here, in the Sanctuary of the Great Void. Stone archways surrounded him carven into ornate filigree, vaulted into a dome with an oculus that never saw rain. The light was soft, never the harsh light of true day, filtering in through the oculus and the milk-river walls around him. This place did have day and night, but the day was curled with mist and the nights endless with stars. Deep midnights devoured each evening, colored in auroras and constellations Jherrick had never seen.

Wherever he was, this wasn't his world.

Like a dream, his life before the Sanctuary of the Great Void had become muted, distant. The horrid events of the past few months in Lintesh and Ghellen flowed from his thoughts, untenable here in the quietude. The walls of the agate-stone dome emitted a soft-hued light, twisting vines and tree roots climbing the sides, until the space seemed like a wild forest devouring all civilization. Boughs trained into candelabra surrounded the space, white oil lamps flickering like tiny flowers in a sighing breeze through the filigreed walls. Otherworldly, the lamps licked with flames that twisted through every color, but in those flames waited specters that darkened the edges of Jherrick's vision. He knew that despite the solace he'd found in the gentle care of the Noldarum, he'd have to face his demons eventually.

Music rippled through the space, like harps or voices, far away. A solid rhythm like drums came as Jherrick's gaze fell again to Second-Lieutenant Aldris den'Farahan's body. The man looked so alive laid out upon the agate-stone bier. Jherrick reached out, touching Aldris' hand: it was cold, just like every other day Jherrick had come to this beautiful tomb. Ripples expanded from a falling leaf as it wisped to the surface of the rectangular pool around the stone bier. Jherrick watched the ripples pass, silver and golden light glimmering the surface until the pool was once again silent.

Aldris was dead. His Essence Scattered, whatever the fuck that meant, from traveling through the blood-Plinth at the cave near Oasis Khehem. The Noldarum had dressed Aldris in state, before Jherrick had woken from his ordeals. A dark emerald doublet of soft velvet clad Aldris' tall frame, embroidered with silver thread fine enough for any king. Black trousers of rough silk fit close to his long legs. His hands were clasped over a sword with a hilt of black crystal and a blade of milk-pale glass inset with silver runes. His golden beard and hair had been carefully trimmed and oiled, until they shone in the soft light of never-day. Color suffused the Guardsman's cheeks, as if he might rise at any moment – as if life yet breathed within him, his heart still beating blood through his veins.

But he was cold – cold and gone.

Jherrick steepled his hands under his chin, elbows upon his knees where he sat upon the stone viewing-bench by the bier. Within the rippling waters of the pool, the bier and bench left Jherrick alone with the dead Guardsman, an enemy he'd come to call friend. Once more, Jherrick was alone. The story of his short life was only loss. Losing his Khehemni parents during the raids on Quelsis. Trusting in the Lothren to harbor him only to lose his integrity. Watching life after life be snuffed out by Lhaurent den'Karthus behind the walls of Roushenn.

Walking the night forest alone to throw bodies into the wolf-hollow.

Jherrick scrubbed fingers through his short blonde hair, then laced them together again. Another leaf went falling into the still pool from a gnarled vine-maple writhing its way up a column by the oculus. The leaf floated in the pool, crimson with tones of autumn; crimson, like blood. Olea's face rose in Jherrick's mind, as blood poured from the deep slash that had severed her throat. Her death, lit by the brilliance of Khehem's Alranstone in a pool of her own crimson gore, surrounded by the slain Kingsmen, stacked like cordwood to rot beneath the desert sands. Plus the only man Jherrick had ever called friend, now laying dead in this nowhere realm.

"Aldris," Jherrick choked, tears stinging his eyes. "Why did you leave me?"

"He cannot hear you."

Jherrick startled. Surging to his feet, he resisted the urge to snatch the sword from the dead man and level it at the intruder, but it was only the calm presence of Noldrones Flavian, standing with hands clasped in his pale starlight robe by the colonnaded entrance to the Memorarium.

The Herald of the Noldarum's monastic order, Noldrones Flavian had been a presence during Jherrick's recovery under the kind care of Noldra Ethirae. Standing quietly near the pool, hands loosely clasped behind his back, Flavian was cowled in his usual flowing robe of pale silk. Strength emanated from him; sharp eyes full of intelligence and dark with starlight watched Jherrick. Slender but muscled beneath his robe, his ageless presence held the whisper of eons, not a line marring his smooth skin. His long silver hair was braided over one shoulder, his profile masculine but graceful, lips full and nose aquiline. Jherrick shivered, then sank back to his seat upon the bench, his startled energy leaving him like a departing specter.

"I know Aldris can't hear me." Jherrick clasped his hands together once more, rubbing his knuckles.

"But it calms you to speak to the dead." Noldrones Flavian moved in upon feet so silent Jherrick heard only the slip of his silken garb over the opalescent stone floor. Having a seat upon the bench, Flavian gazed upon the dead man with an unreadable expression. Flavian's expressions were often unreadable, as if he had seen ages turn and neither life nor death surprised him anymore.

Jherrick knew he was ancient, but had no notion of the man's age. Noldrones Flavian simply *was*, like a river or an ocean – silent and calm, endless and timeless. His long silver hair, braided ornately, framed a high-cheeked face that might have been austere had it not been so impeccably calm. Straight silver brows made no expression over eyes swallowed by black and endless with tiny flecks like stars in the cosmos. His lean body was still as time under his fitted silk robe, his long, pale hands resting in a folded position in his lap.

As Jherrick watched him, the man made an expression at last. The most ageless smile curled the edges of his mouth, and he lifted his strange eyes to the high dome at the center of the atrium. "It calms us all to speak with the dead. Just as it calms you. Because you know somewhere, out there… your friend still exists, and his essence still hears your words."

A shiver lifted the hairs upon Jherrick's neck. The Herald of the Noldarum was often cryptic, but at times the things he said resonated so strongly with Jherrick that he felt the man had seeped into his very being and learned all there was to know.

Learned that Jherrick was nothing but death – death and loss and a life of wrong choices.

"I feel like I need to do right by him," Jherrick spoke, wringing his hands. "First Vargen, then Olea – then him. If I never left Roushenn, they might all still be alive. I was the one who cursed our mission. The Alranstone told me, when I came through from Lintesh to Oasis Ghellen: it said I would learn to shed tears when everything I loved was taken from me. It was right."

"Heavy words and a heavy sorrow," Flavian sighed, bringing his star-scape eyes back to Jherrick, holding his gaze with steady intensity. "But you can still do right by them."

"How?" Jherrick's brows knit in a frown.

"By doing what you came here to do. It has been twenty days since you came to us. You have slept, eaten, wandered our vast Sanctuary, mended your body and your strength. Yet, still you linger in the shadowlands. You have no curiosity for our hallowed libraries, full of more treasure in knowledge than your people have ever seen. You raise no eagerness towards the incredible feats of *wyrria* you witness others doing in our realm. You speak not with those here who have vast knowledge and would freely give it to you. You only sit, and stare into silent water and up to the endless stars – and into the face of death. You wait, like wraiths in the mists of evening. What are you waiting for, Jherrick den'Tharn? Why have you not sought to begin your journey?"

"My journey?" Jherrick gave a hard laugh. "You mean finding Olea – *resurrection*? I don't even know what that means."

"You have not even tried." Flavian's visage was unreadable.

"I have to go home," Jherrick sighed. "I have to avenge Olea's death. To do what I swore I would do."

"Oaths without the alignment of your will are but empty words," Flavian countered, "as is your vengeance without any fire to fuel it. For you know as well as I, that you have nothing – and no-one

– left to return to."

Brother Flavian's statement hit Jherrick like a punch in the gut. His lips dropped open, but there was nothing he could say. Pain tore through his heart, a hollow loneliness that none of the wonders in this place could possibly fill.

"Aldris was all that—" Jherrick rasped.

"He was all that was left." Brother Flavian reached out, touching Aldris' body gently upon the shoulder. "All that remained of home. All that remained of your once-self. Of the man you thought you had to be, who once wore strong leather of cobalt but had lies in his heart."

Lies in his heart. It was far too close to Jherrick's reality, and he sat silent, not wanting it to be the truth.

"And when your comrade departed," Flavian continued, "as so many others have before him, you were left with no tether, no course and no compass. You are a no-man. You have no family, no home, no loyalty. You have no lover, no heart's purpose, no bliss in your life. You are a hollow shell of a wraith – searching. You watch the stars and water and death, hoping to find some comfort in emptiness, but find only emptiness, inside it all."

Jherrick swallowed, blinking back a sting of tears. Staring at Aldris, he could say nothing, his fingers laced so hard his knuckles turned white. Something sang in his veins, something awful, twisting at Flavian's honest words. "Am I that transparent?"

Flavian gave a soft sigh. His midnight-star eyes were full of an emotion Jherrick could not name. With a swish of fabric, he rose and came to stand behind Jherrick, his hands upon Jherrick's shoulders. "Close your eyes, wanderer. Close your eyes and picture her, your deceased beloved. Describe her for me. Her essence."

Jherrick shuddered. Closing his aching eyelids was a relief, and tears leaked from beneath them. His heart was so full and so hollow at the same time. Olea's face rose in his mind. Not her dead face, but her living one. Laughing in the guardhouse, her white throat flashing. Snarling at an insult, her grey eyes fierce. Scowling at ledgers, her black brows pinched as she drummed her fingers on the stout desk. Smiling for him, all for him, when he dropped his spectacles for the umpteenth time and she swiped them up off the floor and handed them back.

Sometimes Jherrick had bumbled his fake spectacles on purpose, just so she would return them – with that incredible smile.

"Olea was like light," Jherrick spoke at last. "The dawn that shines with truth. Honesty poured from her every movement. Generosity. Love. She loved life, even though it had done her so many wrongs. She loved the warrior's way. Sometimes she was tempestuous, but she was never mean – never without righteousness. Her blood sang for justice in the world, and peace."

"Feel these qualities surrounding you," Flavian intoned in his solemn voice that surged through the vaulted space like a quiet sea. "Feel all those things gathering around you, coming into this space. Feel them touching your skin, breathing in through your nose. Feel them sliding across your tongue and diving down your throat – touching every fingertip and caressing every rib. Feel them moving into you, like a lover. Feel her now, still here, still with you."

Jherrick gasped. He could feel Olea's essence, her light and goodness, like mist diving in through his throat and seeping into his chest. Caressing like a zephyr with ethereal fingertips that made his flesh sing with bliss. He shuddered, astounded – regret and need combining with an ache so horrible his heart spasmed.

Jherrick sobbed. Noldrones Flavian's arms wound around him as Jherrick doubled over with a primal scream, gripping the stone bench with both hands. Flavian was a solid presence at his back, holding, strong. Jherrick screamed again, releasing the ache, the misery. Of failing Olea, of not being able to avenge her death, of not belonging anywhere in his life, and not having anyone to come home to.

Of having no purpose – nothing but death and emptiness.

"Feel oblivion enter you," Flavian murmured in Jherrick's ear. "Feel the space that opens when we have nothing left. When we are nothing to the world we knew. Feel the space that opens inside of you when you are no longer the man you thought you were. When you are nothing, and have nothing. Feel the space that takes you, deep within. Feel it fill you. Expanding everything. You are it. It is you. You are the space and the nothing all at once. You are… the Void itself."

Jherrick could feel it, everything Flavian described. Every torturous wrench of it, every hollow nothingness of it. Suddenly, everything within Jherrick expanded; like the primal nature of some ancient god filled him, his sobs halted, his breath paused. His sense of self was annihilated, and all he felt was the world breathing, through his every pore and sinew. A space as massive as the night sky opened up inside him, pushing his mind, body, and essence out to the ends of the world, and further – to nothingness.

Jherrick stared at a golden leaf, quiet in the pool. "I am nothing," he breathed.

"You. Are. *Everything*." Flavian's voice was soft by his ear.

Suddenly, Jherrick felt presence in the nothingness. Something massive, unknowable. Something intelligent that watched him, yet cared not how he chose, nor what he chose to do next. Something that loved, unconditionally. Its presence filled the emptiness, soft and quiet. Touchable, limitless, warm with love and creation and bliss. Jherrick came to absolute stillness, breathing with eyes open, marveling at the presence inside the nothing. The presence that filled everything around him, even his very body.

"Now you see." Flavian spoke by his ear. "There is a reason you came to us. Your exposure to death and suffering have honed you, prepared you for your journey. Come with me now. It is time you began the Path of the Dead."

Jherrick's breath stilled. A dead boy's glassy eyes rose in his thoughts. "The Path of the Dead?"

"For only when one walks the Path of the Dead, can one find the souls who wish to return."

Jherrick's eyes snapped up to the oculus. "Resurrection. You'll teach me how to bring Olea back."

"Perhaps." Noldrones Flavian moved around Jherrick and knelt, his starlight eyes infinite. "But I must warn you. Those who have truly completed their journey cannot be brought back. If their Essence deems its mission upon this world complete… they will not come to your call. If they have left things unfinished, though, their Essence can be found and returned to their flesh. In order to learn this, you must allow all that you have been to die, so you can be reborn into what you are becoming."

"How do I do that?" Jherrick breathed.

"By dying. Come. It is time we prepared you for your death." Brother Flavian stood. He held out his long-fingered hand.

Jherrick paused, then slowly rose. "Are you going to kill me?"

"No." Noldrones Flavian's smile was ancient, unknowable. "You are going to kill *yourself*. Then you will make a choice; to become what you are meant to be, or to sigh away into the breath of the Void. Come. It is time to fast and prepare."

Jherrick glanced back at Aldris. Flavian followed his gaze. "It may be that you can gather him back together again, but it may be not. If his purpose has been fulfilled with his death… he will remain as he is. Forever."

"In this tomb," Jherrick murmured. "A beautiful corpse."

"Where eternity will see him as he is," Flavian murmured. "Noble. Righteous. A true warrior with a kingly heart. Come – you shall not be allowed to return here until you are ready. It would be too much of a temptation, so say your goodbyes."

Jherrick sank to one knee, a palm to his chest. He gazed at Aldris' corpse for a long moment, feeling the emptiness of eternity. The man was at peace; he was peaceful, laying as he was. Who was Jherrick to disturb the dead from their rest? To pull them from the maw of the Void and thrust their souls back into their bodies? Yet, that was exactly what Brother Flavian was insinuating Jherrick might be able to do. Rising, Jherrick gazed down upon his dead Second-Lieutenant once more, and wondered: if the time came, could he do that to a friend? Could he take away that eternal peace and make a man – or a woman – resume a life of misery?

Jherrick took a long breath, then turned, following Brother Flavian's silent steps out through the opalescent colonnades.

* * *

Jherrick stood in the open air, shivering in the lingering chill of dusk. Naked but for a loincloth of white silk in the mist-wreathed evening, he stood in an ancient place of learning. A semi-circular amphitheater of opalescent stone rose up behind him, on the last vestiges of the Sanctuary's citadel. In every direction beyond the amphitheater roiled a thick, impenetrable mist. Endless, as if whatever world this was had forgotten everything else, besides the staircase that wound back up through that mist to the citadel.

There were no stars high above, the dusky evening sky lost to the shifting mist. Before Jherrick stood a towering cliff of white stone thrust up out of the vast nowhere. Carven with the effigy of a winged bird-woman lifting hands in prayer above her head, her eyes were rolled back in ecstatic trance. Thirteen breasts decorated her chest. Feathers flowed down her body and opened from her figure in enormous wings, blending her into the mist all around. She had not one set of wings, but seven, from the smallest at her neck down to the longest at her hips, even a tiny set of wings opening from the inner eye between her brows. Demonic creatures writhed around her ankles. One clawed foot crushed a demon that snarled with a dragon's head, tearing at her feathered ankle with fangs.

Between her clawed feet lay the tomb. It yawned before Jherrick, black, a natural crevasse riven between the bird-woman's strong legs. The entryway had no carving, no decoration. This was a place of trial, and the barrenness of the rip in the rock told him as much. Noldrones Flavian stood before that void, wearing his usual fitted robe of starlight silk, though today he had painted sigils in a white shell-paint over his high cheekbones and the backs of his hands. It was the same paint he cupped in an agate-stone bowl as he stood before Jherrick, daubing a fine-tipped brush into the white slurry and beginning to inscribe similar sigils upon Jherrick's naked chest.

"To the Dusk we send you."

The death-ritual had been explained to Jherrick, and the wet touch of Flavian's brush with its white shell-paint was chill but not unexpected. Painting sigils that Jherrick didn't understand, Flavian worked his way with his stylus over Jherrick's collarbones, his chest, in a line down his abdomen, then moved around to his back. And then, he focused upon the left side of Jherrick's neck, painting with careful precision.

"To the Dusk we intend you."

The sigil Flavian had writ upon Jherrick's neck burned like fire, and as this last piece was committed to his flesh, the rest of the sigils began to itch and sear also. Jherrick shivered, enduring the sensation, but it was not unexpected: the shell-paint used for this ritual contained poison. A poison that would send him far, out past his own mind and into the emptiness of the Void. A hallucinogen and system depressant, it would bring Jherrick visions, then cessation of heart and breath. If he came to an understanding of what he was and wished to come back, he would return to life.

Theoretically.

"To the Dusk we commend you. Break, Child of She Who Made Us. Break, and be re-formed by the hand of the World Shaper."

At last, it was finished. Flavian stepped back, then nodded toward the tomb's riven entrance. "Are you ready, Acolyte of the Noldarum?"

"Yes. I am ready." Jherrick's voice was hollow to his ears.

"Then enter the Tomb of the World Shaper and see what you will see."

Jherrick stepped forward, chill curls of mist crawling over his skin in a counterpoint to the burn of the paint, now smoothing out to a dull throb in his flesh. A lit orb-candle was placed in his hands by Noldrones Flavian. "Place the candle in the niche as you situate yourself. Have a few dippers of water, then lay down in the grave. Once you are situated, blow the candle out. And then you will travel to the Void. If you decide to come back, you will."

"Thank you." Jherrick accepted the candle in his cupped hands. His eyes locked with Flavian's, but there was nothing more to say. Flavian nodded, and turning to face the black crevasse, Jherrick stood tall. Whatever happened, he would be a changed man. Tomorrow, or the next day, or sometimes up to seven days. The Noldarum would wait a week before they came to get Jherrick's body from the tomb; sometimes it took a while for a man to rise from his grave.

Sometimes they never did.

Jherrick stepped forward, his bare feet chill upon the white stone of the amphitheater. Moving into the crevasse, he entered a shadowed space so dark he was thankful for the candle's meager light. Jherrick could see no more than three feet ahead as he moved slowly forward. Twenty paces in, he came to a set of descending stairs and stepped down. Down and further down they went, until the last glow of the crevasse's outlet behind him was utterly lost in the darkness.

Then he arrived. A small dead-end space, it had an alcove carven with the bird-woman again, but smaller: only human height.

Decorated in luminous paints, she glowed ochre and umber, jade and turquoise, and a vibrant royal purple by the light of Jherrick's candle. Every set of wings glowed in jewel tones. Her gaze was fierce, uncompromising. Spying the candle-niche at her clawed feet, Jherrick nestled his flame in amongst a thousand orbs of melted wax. The goddess' face came alive in the light, hideous, beautiful, her wings stretching out as if they would encompass the world.

A narrow tomb lay at her feet, carven two feet down into the opalescent bedrock. Gazing in, Jherrick saw a concavity of stone for his head, situated beneath the goddess so she would be the last thing he gazed upon as he dwindled to the poisons. To one side of the room was a circular well, with a winch and a stone bucket. Jherrick moved to it, recalling Flavian's instruction to take water before he lay down. He let the bucket fall, heard it splash, turned the crank. It came up full, the water black within, clean and cool.

Jherrick doused his hair, then brought water to his mouth and drank. His body was beginning to sweat from the poisons in the paint, chill yet strangely warm and pulsing, as if with fever. He shivered, though his neck and chest felt hot, flushed. He'd been through trials of poison before to earn his Khehemni Bloodmark through fever-dreams, but never one that was supposed to actually kill him – and this poison was working quickly, making him feel faint, his head reeling.

Jherrick swallowed bile, arresting himself from vomiting. He took one last mouthful of water, then stepped to the grave. It yawned at him, waiting. He looked up at the goddess, lit fierce and horrible by the candle's light.

"I will die and return," Jherrick murmured, readying himself for his journey. "I will learn resurrection magics. Then I will find Olea and I will bring her back to this world – to me."

Jherrick den'Tharn stepped into the grave. Within its dark confines he sat upon cold stone, staring up at the goddess with her wide jeweled wings. Turning his head, he blew out the candle, and was doused in an intimate, crushing darkness. Closing his eyes, he lay back. Settling his hands upon his chest as he'd been instructed, he cupped his bare, beating heart.

Then the poison took him – straight to the Void.

CHAPTER 9 – ELYASIN

The darkness of the Heldim Alir was absolute beyond the group's lofted singing-stones. Elyasin's mind drifted as she gazed from one ghostly tableau upon the tunnel walls to the next. Battle raged around them in the fey light: images of war wrought so long ago that none who had inscribed these runes of precious ore yet lived. Lost in thought as she paced behind Therel and followed by Luc, she hardly noticed that Ghrenna and Thaddeus had halted at yet another branch-point before them – the fourth one they'd come to in as many hours since their morning meal.

Squinting at a series of way-marker runes running through a recessed alcove to their left above an ornate seepage-basin covered in sigils and draping white moss, Thad suddenly cursed and halted. The scribe's uncommon response to a branch-point caused Therel to run right into him.

"Move on, Thad!" Therel chastised with a jostle. "Read the way-markers and let's get going!"

But Thad was rooted, staring at the lefthand wall of the Y-split. Gaping, he stepped to the recessed wall and basin, and Elyasin's heart sank, realizing why the scribe had stopped. There was Thad's white chalk mark upon the wall – the same mark he'd made just an hour ago. They had come full circle, the tunnel looping back upon itself to join up with where they'd been.

"Dammit!" Therel cursed as he realized it also. Lifting a hand to touch Thad's mark, he gave an exasperated growl. "I thought you were leading us along the main thoroughfare, Thad! Not another Kotar-fucked side-branch."

"I was! I mean, I am!" The scribe was flustered, taking his wired spectacles off and lipping at the ends. He gestured one lanky arm at the moonstone and silver sigils flowing above the basin and its wealth of luminous moss. "These are the same sigils as before! They mark the main tunnel I've been keeping us to. We've just come full-circle."

"The main tunnel of the Heldim Alir led us in a circle?" Elyasin asked. "Well, that's never happened before."

"No," Thad spoke breathlessly, "it hasn't! The sigils of the full moon and the *kruk-tan*, the Giannyk scythe, that signify the main tunnel have always led us onward – not around to a point we've been before."

"So the main tunnel's ended in a loop?" Therel's brows knit, and he set his hands on his hips, gazing at the sigils above the basin. "Well, where's the fucking exit?"

But Thad's eyes were unfocused, his lips fallen open as he gazed at the alcove above the basin. "Of course! Why didn't I see this earlier?!"

"What is it?" Elyasin moved close, easing her eyes into a light trance to see the picture upon the wall. Luc stepped to her side lofting his singing-stone, as did Therel. Elyasin saw the same picture she had seen numerous times in the past three days since her and Luc's talk in the grotto. It was an image of that hillside city with the cavernous darkness again. Obscure and too bright, the image looked like the city was swaddled in fog lit by a hundred lighthouses, yet with a cavernous emptiness in the center.

"We've seen this," Elyasin murmured. "I've seen it at least twenty times on the left-hand wall in the last hour alone."

"Since we took the last branch," Thad nodded, turning eager green eyes to Elyasin. "Yes! And always upon the left-hand wall. Don't you see? The main tunnel took us in a left-hand loop, marking *this image* upon the left the entire time. We've just come around something. Something massive. And I would wager, important."

"But there's been no doors!" Luc scoffed, stubbing his boot in the grit upon the stone floor. "We went all the way around a dead-end."

"Or is it?" Thad murmured cryptically, peering at the wall.

"What are you looking at, Thad?" Therel sidled close, leaning forward to peer at the image.

"It's Ghrenna!" He turned enormous eyes to Ghrenna now, who was hovering back a few paces and gazing up at the sigils that crowned the recessed juncture. "Or Morvein, at least. There, standing on a high lip of stone just beyond the picture to the left!"

Moving forward with the grace of a wraith, Ghrenna stepped close to inspect the wall. Elyasin stepped in also, looking at the left margin of the image. She could still see the mist, and the town on the hillside, but now, she saw what Thad had seen – a woman standing upon an overlook. With long white hair done in an ornate braid over one shoulder, she was pale and dressed for battle, with a white keshar-claw pendant depicted around her neck.

Glancing at Ghrenna, Elyasin was shocked: Ghrenna was the spitting image of the woman in the picture. Dressed in charcoal-black buckled garb something between the wild Elsthemi style and Kingsman gear, Ghrenna had a snowhare pelt around her shoulders. Her lush white waves were woven into the exact same ornate braid as the woman in the picture, and Morvein's white keshar-claw pendant glinted in the blue light of the singing-stones upon Ghrenna's bared chest, set through with fiery opals and veins of amethyst and onyx.

"What in Halsos' Hells?" Therel leaned forward, blinking at the wall. "Is that Morvein? And is this a town?"

"It seems like it's a cavern," Thad spoke fast. "See the vastness of the dark edges? Like it's not the black of night, but inside the mountains here. The buildings seem odd – I can't make out windows or doors."

"Like a cavern large enough to walk around in an hour?" Therel's deductive logic was keen as he hummed to brighten his singing-stone. "One whose entrance is hidden by *wyrria*?"

"The Giannyk were masters of portal-*wyrria*," Ghrenna interjected. "I don't remember a chamber like this, but it could be a place I – *Morvein* – found."

Ghrenna's slip of pronoun was noted by Elyasin. Therel and Luc's glances were sharp also. No one had missed it, but everyone held their tongues. Ghrenna had been referring to herself as Morvein more and more lately – it was all too obvious that Morvein's memories were seeping into Ghrenna's everyday awareness. In addition to singing in other languages at night, Ghrenna had started to murmur Giannyk phrases by day. As she did now, her cerulean eyes going distant and her lips speaking the rolling vowels and clipped consonants of the Giannyk as her hands smoothed over the stone of the alcove.

"There's more." Thad frowned, watching Ghrenna and pushing his spectacles up his nose. "Glyphs form around the edges of the picture as the mist curls. I've seen them in other tableaux down here, like someone imprinted the walls not only with scenes of memory but overlaid pictographs. Many glyphs repeat. Not just directions through the tunnels like the way-markers, but like descriptions of the pictures themselves."

Elyasin shared a look with Therel as Ghrenna wandered away to smooth her hands over a different section of wall. "Are the glyphs anything you recognize from the maps of the Brother Kings, Thad? Or Metholas' codices that you found down in his crypt under Fhekran Palace?"

Thad peered harder at the wall. He slung his pack to the ground without letting his focus break, digging out a piece of parchment and a charcoal nib. Without letting his eyes wander, Thad placed the parchment upon the tunnel floor. Drawing without looking, he set down twenty symbols, then thirteen more, then wrote numbers below each glyph. At last, he allowed his trance to break. Blinking behind his spectacles, he glanced down at the parchment.

"That's all of them in this image. The numbers are how many times I've seen each glyph on the walls these past weeks. Though there are far more glyphs than the ones just in this image. I've chronicled five hundred and thirty glyphs so far in my journal as we've walked, which I believe make up the pictographic Giannyk language. I'm starting to put sounds to them when Ghrenna speaks Giannyk while looking at a wall."

Elyasin stood over Thad's shoulder, gazing at the paper. "You've seen that first glyph *three thousand and six* times?! Sweet Aeon, and you kept track?"

"They're fixed in my mind." Thad's gaze was level behind his spectacles as he regarded his Queen. "So are the tableaux each came from. My memory's even sharper since we've been walking these tunnels. This glyph," he pointed to most common one, like a sickle slicing stalks of wheat beneath a full moon, "I think it means *harvest*, or *reaping*, and I believe it's pronounced *kruk-heyya*. I see that one in images of battle and destruction – images with a lot of death. It's the primary glyph of the way-markers for the main tunnel. This glyph," he pointed to the next one, a curling sigil like whispering wind, "I

121

think means *spirit, essence,* or *wyrria,* and is pronounced *wyrrdani.* I see it in tableaux with people performing incredible feats – things impossible in the normal world."

"Like?" Therel interrupted, a thoughtful frown upon his features.

"Like throwing lances of fire from their bare hands." Thad glanced at him. "Like moving a mountain by slamming their fists into the ground. Like swimming through an ocean without needing air. Like sculpting ore-veins in stone to form these memory-vaults we're wandering."

"Memory-vaults?" Elysian looked at him.

"My word for the phrase Heldim Alir. One of the glyphs on the map, here," Thad retrieved the map of the tunnels and pointed at one that looked like a stylized hand grasping a sinuous thread, "I think this means *memory* or *remember,* and is pronounced *heldi.* This other one, the radiant sun around the hand, this one is pronounced *aliri* and means *light* or *enlightenment.* I saw this upon the rose-crystal door. Memory pictures that show the artist laying down the image, they all have that glyph – *heldi aliri,* or Heldim Alir, the Place of Enlightened Memory."

"Enlightened memory." Ghrenna's haunting voice dropped like a stone into a still pool, making Elyasin jump as she emerged from the shadows beside them. "A living hall of memory, to wander at your leisure and become enlightened."

"Or a bloody tomb to get depressed in," Luc grumped sourly, crossing his arms and gazing up at the heights of the tableau above the basin, easily twice as tall as any of them. "All the images are of battle and destruction."

Thad nodded. "In this picture, Morvein stands in the same position as the other artists, in the foreground but off to one side. But it's strange. She's not as crisp as the image, as if her representation was an after-thought, not laid down by the original artist."

"As if the image of Morvein is her own memory. Laid down by her less accomplished *wyrria.*" Ghrenna blinked, a thoughtful frown upon her face. She reached up, sliding her fingers over the luminous spot that was the ancient Gerunthane.

"Exactly." Thad drummed his fingers upon the ground, then

rose. "But to mark what? I saw an image of her at the tunnel entrance behind the rose-crystal doorway, though I thought nothing of it at the time. And I've seen one a day as we've traveled. But this is the first one where I can see her face, and it's clearly Ghrenna. I mean, Morvein."

"One a day." Ghrenna's pale brows were drawn into a line, her blue eyes dark. "Morvein marked the walls to count the days it would take to travel here. Why don't I remember any of this?"

"There's something else." Thad nodded at the portrait. "Each image of her was scribed with her cupping a moon in each hand. But while one progressed through the phases, the other stayed stagnant, a full moon. Until yesterday, where the two were nearly matching. And in this image, there is only one moon – and it's full. Right above her head."

"We've arrived at whatever destination Morvein marked." Elyasin ran one hand along the image, then looked to Ghrenna. "What if this location she marked is behind this wall as Thad surmises, and the portal is obscured by *wyrria*? Could you work the vibrational music that got us into the tunnels to open this wall?"

"Perhaps." Ghrenna stepped forward to examine the alcove. Moving her hands over curling sigils of gold and silver, moonstone and jet, she slipped into trance. Elyasin watched her feel the picture, tracing it. Issuing a hum while lofting his singing-stone, Thad brightened the passage to the fullness of daylight. Ghrenna hummed a low tone, then began to sing: a haunting, lilting melody in the rippling Giannyk language. The mist in the picture began to glow beneath Ghrenna's fingertips. As if the ores and crystals awakened to her touch and song – simmering with phosphorescence. Ghrenna's voice echoed in the tunnel, caught in an endless loop inside the alcove. Cascading into the basin, the Giannyk syllables were reflected to the walls behind them and thundered back, amplified, shuddering Elyasin's bones and pummeling her ears.

When the sound was so explosive Elyasin thought she'd go mad, the walls behind them illuminated in a vast series of arched porticos. The basin became the focal-point of that luminous power, a searing brightness reflecting off the water into the alcove. A vaulted portico with intricate runes and glyphs was suddenly illuminated within the high alcove, and the image of the hill-city beneath that towering archway brightened a hundredfold. The scorching mist seared Elyasin's eyes and she held up a hand with a cry, but the darkness in the center of the tableau devoured all light.

Consuming it – in, and in, and in.

Elyasin stumbled in. She fell to her hands and knees upon smooth floes of obsidian glass, and realized with a belated vertigo that she had been sucked right through the wall. Therel and Luc had fallen in upon her left, Thad and Ghrenna to her right. The tunnel was gone; a vast underground cavern opening up now before them. Behind them glowed their doorway, though the rock was solid at their backs and the glow of the archway fading. As Elyasin's eyes adjusted, she spied not one glowing arch but hundreds ringing the gargantuan space, spreading out from their location and continuing far off through a low-lying mist.

It was the center of the chamber that arrested Elyasin. As Luc and Therel rose to their feet, humming their singing-stones brighter, she could see the flows of obsidian glass upwelling into a low peak in the creeping mist. Dotted up that hill were the strange, squat buildings she had seen in the tableau. Some were spaced far apart, some crowded together as if in family groupings.

"This is it," Thaddeus spoke in hushed awe. "This is the place Morvein notated for us. The place we walked all the way around in our loop."

"Morvein didn't tell *us* anything, kid," Luc murmured, his eyes narrowed upon the strange city. "She was leaving a message for herself about this place."

"A warning." Therel growled, his hackles as high as Elyasin had ever seen them.

Luc and Therel exchanged a glance, both men of the same accord. Both had a hand upon the hilts of their weapons, and as Elyasin watched, they drew steel. It was more than a gesture for comfort. Both men expected trouble in this mist-shrouded place, and Elyasin was not going to gainsay their instinct: something about the hillside city wasn't right. Too strange through the mist, too irregular. Elyasin pulled longknives from her boot-sheaths, and Ghrenna was no less agile, ready with her own weapons as they advanced into the underground vault over the smooth obsidian floes.

Mist breathed around their ankles, a deep chill that Elyasin couldn't shake. It held to the ground as they paced forward and began to ascend the gradual incline, stepping upon slick obsidian glass. The mist held a grey opalescence unlike anything Elyasin had ever seen. It curled with currents to lick at their knees, but no higher.

"Some kind of *wyrric* vapor…" Thad mused.

"Keep alert." Therel growled, eyes narrowed as he skimmed the grey mist.

Stepping forward in a ready arc, they moved as a group. Elyasin's sights were fixed upon the nearest building: a long, squat rectangle of carven obsidian looming up out of the mist twenty paces ahead. Covered in sigils of some strange, ghost-white ore, the building was an odd height – not quite as tall as Elyasin and long like a lodge-house. As she neared, Elyasin lifted her fingertips to trace the sigils of odd phosphoric ore. They flared with blue light like the sighs of the dead when she touched them, and suddenly she knew what the obsidian vestibule was.

"These are Giannyk tombs," Elyasin's utterance slit the silence.

"Tombs!" Thaddeus echoed, gazing around the massive chamber at the hundreds of obsidian edifices. Lifting his fingers, he tentatively touched the bier. The blue phosphorescence flared beneath his touch, then died.

"Makes fucking sense," Luc commented, stroking the stone also. "Halls of memory, connected to a house of the dead. All the battles on the walls – maybe these are their fallen heroes."

"Giannyk were long-lived," Ghrenna spoke, a hollow note to her voice that was the hallmark of Morvein's memories. "It was considered normal for a Giannyk to achieve two thousand winters, unless something killed them."

"Two thousand years! Aeon's prick." Luc whistled low.

Therel frowned at the obsidian bier, then around the cavern. "The tunnels were full of battle and bloodshed. Are these tombs here because they are heroes, or because they were usurpers cursed to forever remember their atrocities?"

"It doesn't seem a friendly place, that's for sure," Luc harrumphed.

"When we entered, the place made my skin crawl." Therel glanced around. "I expected *wyrric* warnings against intruders. But there's been nothing so far. Just this horrible feeling in my gut like we're being watched."

"Perhaps Morvein disarmed any wards when she passed through here," Thad quipped.

"Only one way to find out." Luc jumped up to a natural upwelling of stone next to the massive bier. Perusing the sarcophagus with his fingers, Elyasin saw him smile as he located a seam that distinguished the lid. Leaning in, he shoved at the lid with his shoulder, then grunted when it didn't budge. "Fucking heavy."

"That's tonnes of stone, healer. You'll not move it alone." Therel vaulted up next to Luc. Together, the men set their shoulders to it, but still nothing happened.

"Maybe it's like the alcove," Ghrenna's fingers began tracing the phosphorescent sigils. Swaying, she deepened into a trance again, singing in Giannyk. But when nothing happened but a pattern of fading light, she ceased, stepping back. It was Thad whose perusing fingers caused a sigil to glow bright white suddenly. Pressing in, there came a click and a hollow groan, and the lid of the massive sarcophagus divided in the center from a complex locking mechanism, then shuffled away from its own parts – a *wyrric* clockwork. Therel and Luc jumped back upon the obsidian outcropping as the two sides of the lid retracted, exposing the center of the tomb.

Elyasin glanced at Thad, her eyebrows lifted. He shrugged, pointing at the phosphorescent sigil he'd touched. Elyasin saw now it was the *reaping* sigil Thad had described earlier, cleverly combined into a seamless unit with the *spirit* or *wyrria* sigil.

"It just made sense," the lad apologized, though his eyes glowed with eagerness at the discovery.

"Get your butts up here and come see this!" Luc called down. Elyasin looked up to see that Luc and Therel had leaped to the rim of the obsidian sarcophagus and were viewing the contents. Elyasin vaulted up the outcropping, some part of her eager at the mystery, brushing obsidian shards from her hands. Ghrenna was agile at her side as Thaddeus scrabbled up after, all knees and elbows.

Gazing down, Elyasin saw a massive person laying within the cradle of the tomb, dressed for battle with hands folded over an enormous longsword. Viewing the body, a sensation of loss engulfed Elyasin, and awe.

The body of the giant within the obsidian bier was pristine. A myth come to life, and in immaculate condition. Whatever else they had been, the Giannyk had been masters of mummification; the body had not been mutilated. No organs had been cut from its flesh, and the brains had not been rattled from its nose. The skin was hard and lustrous, not pink but a pale blue-grey. A woman, she had thick dark hair braided back from the crown of her head in the Elsthemi fashion, and wore leather battle-armor and furs the twin of Therel's. But while Therel's were black leather, this woman had armor of a blue so dark it shone like the midnight sky against the white keshar-pelt slung around her shoulders.

Her face was haunting. Austere from a life of battle, she had little fat upon her. Proud cheekbones cut high, her thick lips were set in a ready snarl, but her skin was what intrigued Elyasin. Writ upon every inch of her exposed flesh were white tattoos of the same phosphorescent ore as the tomb. Whorls of light shimmered with a slow movement, like sunlight underwater. As Elyasin stared down at those markings, she suddenly recalled where she had seen them before.

"These markings look exactly like Elohl's Goldenmarks. Except they aren't in gold."

"*Fenrir rakhne*, you're right!" Therel exclaimed. "The pattern is the same, and Merra said Elohl's markings flared with light when his *wyrria* interrupted their clan-feud on the road. A light like the sun underwater."

"The same hand that created these must have helped design the Rennkavi's bindings," Ghrenna's voice haunted Elyasin, to her very bones. "Bhorlen…"

"Bhorlen?" Thad perked, taking off his spectacles and lipping at them. "Like the Bhorlen mountain range that borders between Elsthemen and Valenghia?"

"Actually," Therel interrupted, "all the mountains that surround Elsthemen were once called the Bhorlen Mountains. More properly, *Bhorlen's Ring*. In the oldest tales of the Dremors, they recall the name as *Bhorlen's Barrier*. They remember an ancient battle involving a race of giant men who co-existed five thousand years ago with the tundra-tribes. Some say us Elsthemi are descended from interbreeding of the tundra-men with giants." He shrugged. "I don't see how anyone would be able to mate with a woman like this, though."

"Use your imagination," Luc murmured, staring in awe at the giantess.

Elyasin reached out, gently touching the skin of the long-deceased warrior. It was cold as stone, but held a healthy texture: firm and resilient.

"It's as if she still lives," Elyasin commented.

"Something like that." Ghrenna frowned, rubbing her chest over her heart. Her collar unbuckled, Elyasin could see the white sigils of Morvein flowing with a ripple of light not unlike Elohl's Goldenmarks. Elyasin stared and the others glanced over. At last, Ghrenna dredged a deep breath, her gaze flicking to Elyasin. "Morvein bound herself with sigils like these – beyond death, forcing her soul to return when the time of the Rennkavi was nigh. The Rennkavi's marks and Morvein's and the ones she gave the Brother Kings – she learned them from a Giannyk named Bhorlen…to bind souls to her purpose."

"But these seem to bind the body," Elyasin touched a whorl upon the giantess' cheek.

"Like an enchanted sleep," Thaddeus spoke eagerly. "Like the story of King Trevius!"

"King who?" Luc looked over at Thad.

"King Trevius' Sleep is an ancient Elsthemi tale," Therel's voice ran with legend as he spoke an answer, touching the sleek hair of the giantess. "Even Dremors don't know how far back that fable goes. A warrior king, Trevius was enchanted by his *Helta Wyrrin,* or High Magus, to sleep five thousand years after he faced a great evil. The evil that Highland legends call *Utrus,* a demon with red eyes who destroys heaven and earth. But those tales are old hearth-fable."

"What if it's real?" Thad gazed around at the hundreds of biers in the massive underground space. "What if *Bhorlen's Barrier* is this? Tunnels that ring Elsthemen, stocked with King Trevius – not an Elsthemi king but a *Giannyk* king – and his sleeping warriors. Bound by this Bhorlen fellow, whom the mountains were eventually named after, and whom Morvein met to learn binding-arts. Perhaps these tunnels act as a barrier to contain… something evil. Perhaps this red-eyed demon from Highland legend, the *Utrus.*"

"Aeon preserve us." Luc's voice slit the mist. "You have a diabolical imagination, kid."

"Fables hold truths." Thad countered, giving Luc a sharp glance. "One just has to dig deep enough, back far enough, to find it."

Staring down at the giantess, Ghrenna spoke. "I feel like I have to – like Morvein had to prevent something awful, for which she sacrificed everything. She traveled under these mountains to learn the Rennkavi's bindings and ritual from Bhorlen. And when the ritual failed, she banished her Brother Kings into Plinths for eons in order to try again. To create a hero who could battle a great foe which she had Seen would rise, renewed from the times of the Giannyk: the Red-Eyed Demon."

A shiver passed through Elyasin as Ghrenna's words rang in her ears like death-knells. Suddenly, the tattoos upon the ancient Giannyk warrior flared. Bright as day, they roiled so furiously that Elyasin had to shield her eyes. The sigils on the sarcophagus flared also, a dazzling diamond that smote the darkness.

Thaddeus shouted in alarm and jumped off the bier with Luc, back to the outcropping, but Elyasin was riveted, that brightness swallowing her. Like a frigid wind, a presence roared out from the warrior, freezing Elyasin in a vise-like grip. Elyasin heard Therel scream her name. Still upon the bier, he reached for her – when he cried out also, freezing in agony in the diamond-bright mist.

Elyasin's body was on fire. Her keshar-claw pendant burned with golden *wyrric* flames, searing her chest. Eyes clenched, Elyasin screamed in torment and heard an answering scream from Ghrenna and a roar from Therel, both transfixed beside her. Terrible within the bright wind, the presence smashed into Elyasin's mind, forcing her to open her eyes and behold its glory.

At the center of the raging mist, she saw a diamond-haloed outline. A woman, black emptiness inside the scorching white – though the corpse inside the bier had moved not at all. Enormous, the wight's ice-blue gaze was endless, her voice unintelligible inside Elyasin's mind. Swirling and cold like a thousand stars in the Void, it was a cacophony of discordance. Like the scream of chalk over slate, she spoke languages of death and destruction. The fabric of Elyasin's essence was shredded by that voice and she screamed, writing in an agony with no end.

The whirling brightness was cold, as the wight inside that terrible light stared, devouring Elyasin with its eyes. Talons of wind ripped down her back, raking her, and Elyasin shrieked, knowing that it wanted her to suffer. It wanted her to scream, until all the ages died and the world came to annihilation. As it ripped her, Elyasin realized it was toying with her. Screams came from Therel and Ghrenna, and she knew the creature in that terrible light played with them the same way.

Suddenly, Elyasin was furious. She didn't know where it came from, but a righteous wrath surged through her, making her mind rage. Something rushed into her from the golden pendant upon her chest, flooding her limbs, and Elyasin let out a vicious battle-roar. Like a flow of fire with a roll of exuberance, it surged into Elyasin, wild and gleeful. With that rush of power, something concussed out from her. Full of flame and fury, it raced from Elyasin's veins, ready for a fight. Hammering into the ancient wight's presence, it concussed like a thunderclap. Roaring with Elyasin, it attacked as she made a slashing movement with her hands like longknives. This energy that consumed her was fire and fury – and it was ready to fight.

The bright wind howled. Elyasin felt its surprise – and pain. She slashed again with her hands, whirled as if gathering ether, then slammed a shoulder into the wind. She felt her body hammer the wind, hurting it. The wight flinched back with a shriek, releasing them. Elyasin felt Therel move then, in a fast, flowing strike similar to hers but with smooth power and deadly grace. With the brutal force of a breaking wave, Therel's movement surged into the creature, and Elyasin felt it slap their foe back, hard.

As their foe was concussed backward, its grip upon Ghrenna was released. A maelstrom of silver and white weaves blossomed out from Ghrenna suddenly. Elyasin could see them in her mind, shooting from Ghrenna and enveloping the wight. The wight howled in the net, spectral talons shredding at Ghrenna's intricate weave, trapped.

Elyasin and Therel moved in, full of rage and twinned power. Innate, they were dancing – a coordinated battle-dance of flow and slice, cut and hammer. They had drawn no weapons – they *were* the weapons, wielding flows of white, crimson, and indigo ether that were visible to Elyasin's mind, racing through their bodies and out their hands, blasting the trapped wight. As tremendous heat flooded Elyasin, inkings of red and white searing to life over her hands and arms as she fought. As if wielding Hahled Ferrian's ancient *wyrria* bound her to him, his markings flaring to life upon her flesh in a wash of molten glory.

She roared as she hammered the wight again. Therel roared at her side as inkings of white and purple erupted upon his flesh, a wash of cool power twisting into Elyasin's fire in a twinned bond. The wight shrieked in desperation, shredding free of Ghrenna's mind-net, but even as the last threads were raked away, it was commanded back – by the power of the Brother Kings.

The bright wind howled, rushing away from them. It fled, flowing up to the pinnacle of the obsidian mound in a swirl of blistering light, and then flashed out – leaving Elyasin, Therel, and Ghrenna breathing hard in utter darkness.

CHAPTER 10 – DHERRAN

Delennia Oblitenne was clean and dressed, her magnificent body obscured by a peacock-blue robe of elegant silk. Settling into a chair at a heavy white pearlwood table, she picked through a silver tray of grapes and popped a few into her mouth. The manor's ready room above the catacombs was richly appointed with a crimson velvet chaise and thick Perthian rugs, the walls of the room snarling with banners of Valenghian royal houses. A fire roared in the massive hearth, pushing back the subterranean chill of the catacombs below. As she chewed, Delennia signaled to her bald servingman Emeris who moved forward, handing Dherran his things plus a leather purse heavy with coin. Dherran accepted his winnings, then hauled on his trousers. Delennia gestured at a nearby chair as she ate, entirely business, nothing remaining of her sexual manner in the fight-ring.

"So is it all a show, then?" Dherran spoke, stepping to the table and setting his things in the chair.

"You mean, am I as sexually deviant as I pretend to be in the ring?" Delennia eyeballed him, popping another grape in her mouth as the thick pearlwood door at the top of staircase clicked shut behind the retreating Emeris.

"Something like that."

"Live a little longer, boy, and learn how to win alliances." Delennia spoke archly, very much like Arlen. "A woman who fights has to show her men certain attributes."

"Sexuality. Ruthlessness," Dherran commented.

"Bravado. Domination." Delennia stripped a few grapes off the vine, her long fingers brusque. "Now, sit. And tell me," she reached out to a carafe, pouring two goblets of red wine. "Why the fuck is Grunnach den'Lhis in my city?"

Delennia slid one goblet out to Dherran. He stood by the table, gaping like a fish on the line. She threw back her magnificent silver head, her long mane brushed out over one shoulder in a cascade of waves, and laughed. "Don't look so dumb, boy! I have spies. Some of them know Grunnach on sight, no matter how he perfumes himself. He's a gutter-rat. Don't let him tell you any different."

"Grump's a good man." Dherran set his jaw, feeling his anger rise.

"For Aeon's sake, sit." Delennia gestured to the chair. "Grunnach's a sneaky squeaker. What does he want?"

Dherran decided on the truth. "To reunite you with Arlen. To wake the Bitterlance again. Alrou-Mendera is facing trouble from within, and Arlen's forces are under attack. He needs you."

"*Arlen* needs to stuff his cock up his ass." Delennia's luscious mouth set in a hard line and Dherran saw again why her nickname was *bitter*.

"Please." He tried a different tactic, lowering into the chair. "Grump believes there's someone behind the recent assassination of Alrou-Mendera's Queen, and that those same people are behind the Valenghian Vhinesse, pushing our nations to war. All of it is connected to the forces now moving against Arlen and the last remaining Alrashemni Kingsmen."

"And what am I supposed to do about my sister's dire activities?" Delennia commented brusquely.

"Excuse me?" Dherran blinked.

"My sister." Delennia swigged her wine. "The Vhinesse. Aelennia Oblitenne. Oh, that's right. You've come to bargain with House Oblitenne not knowing *whom the fuck* you're speaking to."

"You're *sisters* with the Vhinesse?"

"Twins." Delennia sneered, her white eyes flashing bloody murder. "She's born three fucking minutes earlier with special abilities thrice what I've got and worms her way up the ladder until she has the throne. And what do I receive once she's Queen? One fuckhole of a manor with dirty sewers beneath it and a chip on my shoulder."

"You have… charisma. What you did when you touched me – how you control the crowd." Dherran was at a loss trying to describe the seeping sensation he'd felt when Delennia had touched him, some kind of *wyrric* ability.

"Charisma! Ha!" Delennia spread her arms, mocking. "Men

come to see a woman fight naked, you halfwit! And fill my coffers with their admission fees and the clever betting of my spies. Charisma is *nothing* compared to what my sister can do."

"What can she do?"

"Did you enjoy what I did to you in the ring?" Delennia eyeballed him.

"Not particularly." Dherran leaned back. "You sent some kind of energy into me that sapped my will to fight you. That made me want to fuck you instead."

"Look at me, boy." Delennia set her goblet down, holding his gaze. "Aelennia makes what I do look like juggler's tricks. She's dangerous. And she'll never consent to aiding anything you might want for either me or Arlen den'Selthir. Leave it and go home."

"But you're the Vhinesse's kin. You could talk to her. Reason with her to stop this war—"

"*Reason?* With Aelennia?" She snorted, swigged more wine, then set it down. "Look, boy. I'm tired. Go back down and tell Grunnach and your little friend that you all can stay the night, but that's it. In the morning, you leave. My real fighting days are done."

Delennia Oblitenne stood. Turning her back, she moved toward a set of ascending stairs.

"That's it?" Dherran snarled, incredulous. "The woman I heard about wouldn't have been so fucking *weak.*"

Fast as a demon, Delennia turned. In a series of moves Dherran hardly saw, she seized his wrist, kicked his knee, slapped his thigh – and he was suddenly broken, falling to the floor like a limp noodle. He stared up at her as she straddled him, sitting upon his hips.

"Look, you Kingsman fuck." Delennia stuck a finger in his chest. "You think you know me? You think you know Arlen? Or Grunnach? You don't know *shit*. This death-song goes back before you were *born*. You want to try to break me? Go ahead. I'm not going back to Arlen. Ever."

"What the fuck did he do to you?" Dherran snarled, his rage rising.

"He abandoned our campaign to overthrow my sister, then he slept with her." Delennia's white eyes seethed, her luscious mouth set in a bitter line. She rose from her straddle and paced to the upper stairs. "Get dressed. Emeris will find your friends and show you to guest rooms. Enjoy my hospitality for the night, then get the fuck out of my house."

She turned and strode up the stairs, leaving Dherran alone in the well-appointed room. He was halfway through donning his clothing and weapons when the door to the descending stairwell opened and crimson-tattooed Emeris returned, Khenria and Grump following. Rushing forward, Khenria caught Dherran in a fast embrace and he held her close, inhaling her anxious musk.

"Are you alright?" She pulled back, reaching up to touch his face, her grey eyes wide.

"I'm fine." Dherran kissed her brow, feeling tenderness stretch between them.

"Well done, Dherran my boy!" Grump crowed, patting Dherran upon the shoulder with a fluttering hand. "An excellent fight!"

But before they could say anything more, big baldy stepped forward, gesturing to the upper staircase. "My mistress bids the three of you to enjoy her hospitality for the night. If you would follow me."

Dherran noticed the sour twist of Emeris' lips as his gaze met Grump's. The two shared a prickly moment, and Dherran was suddenly unsure if they were about to draw weapons. Khenria noted it, too, moving to Dherran's side with her hands near the fly-blades upon her harness. With a dark snort, the bald guard relented, veiling his eyes and turning to lead them upward. The tension in his big shoulders didn't leave, however, as Dherran and the others followed him up the corkscrewing stairwell.

From the ready-chamber under Velkennish, they ascended through an ironbound door, emerging into a short alcove and then into the manor proper. They walked vaulted halls, ornate with banners and tapestries in hunting scenes. Elegant niches were set with busts of men long dead, gilded furniture, and candelabra. Dherran found himself impressed by the wealth of House Oblitenne, realizing that the manor was more a palace than a home. Martial history greeted him upon every side, racks of spears elegantly presented, ornately etched shields, gilded swords, and dummies of armor. A creeping feeling assaulted Dherran of being

135

watched – as if all those racks and dummies had guards behind them, just waiting to seize those honed blades and charge to war. Yet, other than Emeris walking with them, the long halls held not a single breath of humanity.

At last, they were led up a stone staircase with royal crimson carpeting, the pearlwood banister carven with trailing ivy. At the top of the stairs, Emeris gestured to three open doors upon the left, spaced far apart. "Your rooms. Meals are within and baths await you. Fresh linens are in the armoires. Breakfast will arrive at sunup and should you need anything during the night, each room is equipped with a bell-pull. Milady has *insisted* you not wander about the manor."

"And what are we going to do, Emeris?" Grump chortled, though his eyes were narrowed. "Steal all the silver?"

"I wouldn't put it past you, Grunnach." A flicker of personality lit the guard's eyes. His bristling manner around Grump had not lessened, and Dherran wondered at it. The two had a past, it was plain.

"Is she setting a watch upon us?" Grump cocked his head, something about that movement dangerous in the extreme.

"She wouldn't insult you so. She knows you can slip any guard any time you like, and strangle a man in his sleep." Emeris' dark eyes hardened, his intense dislike of Grump amplified, leaving Dherran wondering if Grump had pulled a fast one on the big guard sometime in the past – maybe a few times. Perhaps resulting in someone's death. "In any case, you'll not have a guard on your doors, but my mistress will show you all her *distinct* displeasure if you wander tonight. Starting with the little Alrashemni bird." He nodded at Khenria.

"Did you just *threaten* me?" Khenria's eyes blinked wide.

"No." Emeris' dark eyes were back to being veiled. "My mistress did. She knows the weakest link in a chain when she sees it. Goodnight, gentlemen. And lady." With that, he turned his broad back and strode off down the long hall.

"That didn't go very well." Grump watched Emeris go, a thoughtful scowl on his face. His hands lingered near his close-work knives, tapping a hilt with one finger.

"How do you and Emeris know each other?" Dherran asked,

watching Grump carefully.

Grump took a deep breath and sighed. "Ancient history and old wounds, Dherran my lad. I once liberated something from this house that Emeris believes I did not have permission to take, and someone got killed in the process, someone who was important to him. He's probably wondering why Delennia hasn't ordered him to slit my throat yet."

"Holy Halsos, Grump!" Khenria spoke, her dark brows narrowed, arms crossed. "How many more surprises are we going to find out about you here in Velkennish?"

"At least a few more," Grump sighed, then gestured effetely to the open doors. "I'll take the center room. You two take the one nearest the stairs, and we'll leave the third empty. These two have the least amount of secret entrances."

"The least amount?" Dherran balked, gazing at the open doorways with a sudden worry.

"Ask why you feel a creeping unease in this house." Grump spoke darkly, glancing at the niches of armor and a large tapestry upon the wall, of a woman in crimson sitting on a gilded chair and feeding a wire-haired hound. "Delennia has a large force of retainers, and she hasn't a separate house for her garrison anywhere else upon the property. She's been banned these past eighteen years from having her standing army, by order of the Vhinesse, but don't let the emptiness of these halls fool you. I sincerely doubt she would have given them up."

Grump led them toward the room nearest the staircase, peering in with one hand upon the rapier at his side rather than his knives. His eyes darted through the room and he nodded. As everyone entered, Grump moved right, opening a through-door to the next apartment and repeating his check. Dherran heard the door to that suite lock. Grump returned with an ample tray of food and a pitcher of wine from the far rooms, settling it upon the broad table in Dherran's room, already laden with a good spread. Moving around, Grump eyeballed the tapestries and the gilded wainscoting decorated with angeli and trailing ivy. Taking up a few lit candelabra, he placed them before the tapestries. Heaving pieces of furniture, Grump backed them up against the panels he'd eyed, until the room's decor was largely re-arranged.

"Redecorating?" Dherran quipped, though it was easy to see what Grump was up to.

"Just insurance, Dherran my boy." Grump's eyes were lit with a twinkle as he looked around. "This way, you'll hear anyone who enters in the dark of night."

Dherran moved over to shut the through-door as Grump finished up, the small lord moving to the table and putting his boots up on a gilded chair as he started to pick through the trays.

"Should you be eating that?" Dherran eyed the food suspiciously.

Grump popped some roast pheasant with a pink berry chutney in his mouth and gestured to the spread. "Poison isn't Delennia's style. Besides. She's wondering why I'm here. And why I brought the two of you. And how in the world I'm allied with Arlen again. She'll make contact before dawn. I bet my sack on it."

Khenria stepped towards the fire, adding another log to push back the autumn chill, then moved toward a copper tub of steaming water by a gilded dressing-screen. Sticking her fingers in, she glanced back at the men. "It's hot. Do you two mind if I—?"

"Go ahead." Grump waved one hand idly, not looking over from his meal. "Nothing I haven't seen before when you were little."

"Enjoy," Dherran smiled.

Khenria began to strip before Dherran had turned away, and he thought again of what the servingman had said. Khenria was learning Alrashemni arts fast, but she was still scrawny, despite her curves. Dherran thought about all that honed, fit muscle of Delennia Oblitenne, a woman of forty-plus years – how strong she was, how fast. Thirty years of training or more, to become that ruthless. Khenria's young muscles would break like a populus branch to Delennia's blows. Dherran steeled himself, that he would do nothing amiss tonight in Delennia's home – nothing to put Khenria's life at risk. Nearby, Khenria slipped into the bath with a sigh, her head falling back upon the copper tub's rolled edge.

"So what now?" Dherran sat at the table, taking up some crispy boar-belly and devouring it, ravenous from his fight.

"Now we wait, boy," Grump spoke between mouthfuls. "Delennia knows what we came here to tell her: that Arlen needs her. Now we see how curious she gets."

"About what we brought to bargain with." Khenria's dark eyes glimmered as she spoke up from the tub. "When are you going to tell us what exactly that is, Grump?"

Grump shrugged, but his clever smile told all. He knew exactly what he'd brought to bargain with, but wasn't telling.

"Even if you have the strongest Ghenje strategy ever, Grump, I doubt she'll come back to aid Arlen." Dherran spoke. "Delennia seemed certain she wants nothing to do with him, or us."

"You underestimate the power of the past, Dherran, and of the future." Grump popped a blush cherry into his mouth and chewed, his gaze gone thoughtful. "Arlen's an old fighter. He's looking for someone to take his place, to defend the Alrashemni. He's training you for a reason – as his *replacement*. But the past never dies, and us old fighters have more of it than most. The strings that connect the past to the future gather in our hands tonight, and Delennia knows that. Thus, she's curious."

"Curious about what life could look like if the war ended?" Khenria swished water over her shoulders with a cloth. "If we had peace between Alrou-Mendera and Valenghia?"

"Indeed," Grump nodded, his dark eyes sharp. "But it's a peace we can't get without a fight. Especially with Lhaurent den'Karthus now commanding the game, along with the Valenghian Vhinesse. Two rotten peas in a pod; one of which, Delennia hates with a passion, and the other, that she could be convinced to hate also – with the right motivation."

Dherran bristled, his rage rising to the surface. "I want peace as much as the next man, and I'm willing to fight for that, but where does it end? I'll be Arlen's new commander for the Alrashemni if that's what he believes I can be – but even so, I'll be *damn* careful what I'm fighting for."

"And what are you fighting for, Dherran?" Grump's gaze was keen, something knowing sliding through it. A long moment stretched in the fire-lit room. Khenria dunked under the water again and Dherran looked around, seeing her rise to scrub water from her face by the firelight. She was beautiful: fierce, intense, and everything in Dherran's life that was worth fighting for.

"Once, I would have said revenge," Dherran murmured, watching her. "But now..."

A slow smile spread over Grump's face. Reaching out, he set a hand to Dherran's shoulder and squeezed. "Dherran, my boy, you are wiser than any of us old men. Only the old and brittle fight for revenge – the idealists of the world fight with what you've got: heart." With a deep sigh, Grump continued, "I need to retire. We have a big day ahead. Khenria!"

"Hmm?" She looked around from the tub, eyebrows raised.

"I need to speak with you a bit before we retire."

"I'll be right there."

"Indeed." Grump rose from the table with a long stretch.

"What about Delennia?" Dherran eyed him. "Do you really think she'll make contact again before morning?"

"I know she will." Grump's eyes twinkled mischievously as he turned toward the pass-through, then stepped out, closing the door behind him. Dherran heard the sound of Khenria rising from the bath, splattering the hearth-stones with wet as she stepped out. He turned to look just as she slipped into a soft crimson robe from a stand near the tub and cinched the sash. Dherran stood and went to her; netted her loosely in his arms, but she was strangely rigid tonight, her muscles taught and her pretty mouth in a line.

"Are you alright?" Dherran asked, bending to kiss her.

"I just feel… strange here." Khenria's dark gaze pierced like talons as she gazed around the room. "Like I know this place. I thought it was just the sensation of being watched from the walls, but it's not that. It's like – I've been here before, and that feeling I have inside me, Dherran. The simmering heat, the crawling prickling that snapped out from me when I was captive as a young girl. It's been rippling all over my skin since we arrived in the catacombs, but when we came into the manor proper, it's like fire-ants under my skin. Like… flames. Breathing through me, just under the surface." Taking a deep breath, she forced a small smile. "But that's crazy. Maybe I'm just tired. I need to go talk with Grump. I'll be back in a little while."

Standing on her tiptoes, she stretched up and kissed Dherran on the mouth, letting it linger. He drew in her scent, in the smoothness of her body under his hands, gripping the silk over her hips. She made a little sound, then pulled away, a dark light in her eyes that promised more. Turning, she moved to the pass-through and slipped out, shutting it softly behind her.

Simmering with lust, a small smile upon his lips, Dherran stepped to the bath. Sticking his fingers in, he found the water still hot enough for soaking. Stripping away his garments, he slid in, currying water through his hair and sighing back against the angled rim. The water was perfumed with jasoune bloom and sandalwood, and it made his mind drift. Old memories surfaced behind his closed eyelids: Suchinne sparring with him at staves, her dark eyes round as saucers when he stepped in to kiss her for the first time. How her tiny body yielded to his, his hands palming her waist and wrapping around her bird-fine ribs. Her lips so gentle…

Dherran startled at a press of lips upon his. But he smiled beneath those lips, knowing whom they belonged to. Not Suchinne, but a lithe hawk of a woman who'd captured his heart in her talons. Opening his mouth, Dherran deepened their kiss, breathing in Khenria's honey-sweet musk by the crackle of the fire. She kissed him back, slow and deep. Not touching him, just the linger of lips, sliding her tongue into his ready mouth. It was deep, satisfying, and when at last he pulled back with a sigh, he heard a low sound of delight issue from her throat.

"That was nice, Kingsman. You kiss almost as well as you fight."

Dherran's hand shot out from beneath the water as he growled, seizing the woman who had kissed him by the throat. Blinking his eyes open, he stared into the clear gaze of Delennia Oblitenne rather than Khenria, wearing her peacock blue robe where she leaned over the tub, her hands upon the sides.

"Have a care whom you steal kisses from, woman!" Dherran growled, seething. His hand squeezed her neck so hard her face mottled. A small smile curled her lips, not cruel, but knowing. Seeing that she made no move for a blade under her silk, her hands quiet upon the edges of the tub, Dherran gradually released his grip.

"You have some strength in you." Delennia kept her smile, reaching up to rub her neck.

"Careful how you test it," Dherran growled.

"Do you find me so unenjoyable?"

"I've seen everything I need to see."

The smile was wiped from her exquisite face, her silver brows pinching into a line. "I've heard tales from my spies in Alrou-Mendera about a golden-maned Kingsman, you know. Stout as a boar, who fights with a glorious passion in the summer-rings. He wins and wins, despite his temper and an untamable death-wish, inciting riots wherever he goes. Do you wish to incite my ire, too?"

"Fuck off." Dherran rose and stepped from the bath, claiming a towel from the wrought-iron rack.

"But I've come to negotiate, Kingsman. Isn't that what you and Grunnach want? My help with Arlen's predicament?" Delennia stepped behind Dherran, her hands sliding over his hipbones as he tucked the towel in around them.

"Don't touch me," Dherran growled. Under those clever, knowing hands, he felt that seeping pleasure again; like a white mist curling through his body, down into his groin and up into his heart. He found himself stalled, unable to push her away. Delennia stepped close, kissing his well-muscled back, her lips smoothing over every rope and furrow as her hands slid over his abdomen.

"I'll not trade sex for an army," Dherran strangled.

"Are you sure?" Delennia's hands slid lower, beneath the towel. Dherran's breath was fast. His head tipped back at her expert touch. He shivered as he felt his rage try to rise and found it sluiced back. That white mist surged through him again – washing away his will to fight her offer. His breath caught as her hands slid in, grasping him. Dherran's fingers let the towel fall and she stepped close, brushing her delicious curves over his back as she stroked him, slow and firm.

"Fuck Aeon—!" Dherran strangled, his voice husky.

"I would like to negotiate my return to the Bitterlance. I have three demands," Delennia whispered in Dherran's ear.

"Define your terms." Dherran grit his teeth, fighting her touch with thoughts of cold snowbanks and ugly hags.

"First, you will secure an audience with my sister the Vhinesse, on my behalf."

"How – do we get an audience with the Vhinesse?" Dherran let out an involuntary groan.

"You've got a clever little rat for a friend," Delennia cooed in Dherran's ear. "Figure it out."

Delennia was firming her speed, coaxing him, flooding him with her white waves. She released her grip and Dherran spasmed.

Clamping her hands over his hip-creases, she held firm, feeling him gasp before she chuckled in his ear, her hands resuming their play. "Second, at this audience, you will bargain for me to officially resume House Oblitenne's standing army. As well as the standing armies of House Jhudisse, House Fhouriquet, and House Salvea, my strongest allies, so I may bring them to mass in force for Arlen's support."

"And third?" Dherran choked, her hands working him just fast enough that he couldn't catch his breath.

"Fuck me. Now."

Delennia's hands released Dherran as she stepped to his front. Sliding up her silk robe, she moved back, her bare ass to his groin. Bracing one hand on his hips and one on the tub's rim, she pressed back. Suddenly, every control that Dherran had worked so hard for over decades was on the brink of shattering. He fought to think. Fought to become utter stillness, ultimate control – and not shove himself to the hilt in Delennia's firm flesh. He could feel her mist-wreathed magic, pulling him. Moving through his body like an evil rip tide, demanding that he consummate his promise to her. Suddenly, with a ragged in-breath, Dherran knew it was wrong.

"No." Dherran's voice was a low growl as he placed his hands firmly on her hips and pushed himself away. "No one controls my passions, nor their outcome. No one but me."

Something snapped. As if Dherran had ripped apart Delennia's white seductions with his pronouncement, he was suddenly hit with a physical recoil. Stumbling backward, he ended up sitting upon his bare ass on the hearth-stones near the tub. With a quick breath, Delennia looked around, her eyes wide. Rising and letting her robe fall back into place, she turned, staring down at him, her pale eyes incredulous.

"So that's what Grunnach came to bargain with... *jinne wyrdi!*"

Regaining his breath, Dherran pushed to standing, swiping his towel off the floor and tucking it around his hips, securely. "I'm not your fuck-boy. I don't care who you are, or how many armies you can muster, or what kind of vile *wyrria* you have. If Grump thinks I'll sell my body for your help, he's dead wrong. You can show yourself out."

Dherran turned away, breathing hard. He could still feel her vile mist flowing over him, trying to get in, but he'd closed that door – his heart unassailable stone now. He heard Delennia give a low chuckle, then begin to laugh. Rather than seduction, her laugh held astonishment, as if she found something vastly funny. As Dherran turned to eyeball her, he found she had taken up a seat at the dining table.

"Well, Kingsman!" Delennia wiped a tear of mirth from her eye as she poured herself a goblet of wine. "You certainly know how to surprise a woman!"

"What's so funny?" Dherran snarled, one hand over the fold of his towel.

"Sit." She waved at an empty chair. "I won't molest you again. I swear upon my House. You and I have much to discuss."

"Negotiations are over." Dherran didn't budge.

"On the contrary. They've just begun." Delennia eyed him, not lecherously this time, but like Arlen often eyed Dherran – with shrewd thoughtfulness. "I was wondering what it was that I felt from you in the fight-ring, and now I know. So. Arlen is training you, is he? Grooming you as his replacement to lead the Alrashemni, no doubt."

"What are you talking about?" Dherran growled. Grump had shocked him once already tonight with his talk of Arlen grooming Dherran to lead, and this was another piece of the puzzle. One he knew nothing about, but which needed filling in.

Delennia poured another goblet of wine, slid it over to the waiting space at the table, and lifted her silver eyebrows. Dherran gave a harsh sigh then acquiesced, moving forward to don a crimson robe from the stand rather than just a towel, cinching it well closed before sitting. "The thing you said Grump came to bargain with – *jinne wyrdi* – what is that? And what does it have to do with me?"

Delennia chuckled again, sounding very like Arlen. "You're a boorish brute, but I know it when I feel it. Tell me, do you know what *Children of the Sands* are?"

Dherran lifted an eyebrow. Taking a swig of his wine, he said nothing.

"Passionate." Delennia gestured with her goblet at him. "They have a strength not of the body, though you have that, nor necessarily strength of will. It's strength of heart that they possess.

That *you* possess. Arlen knows this. Somehow, he figured it out about you, and that's why he chose to train such a callous lout as yourself to become his champion."

"What do you mean?" Dherran was listening now, the wine and his interest in the conversation calming his fury.

"You know that Arlen couldn't resist my sister the Vhinesse, when she came for him," Delennia eyed Dherran acutely. "He betrayed our forces in the very moment we had that bitch surrounded, penned in her throne room during our coup on the White Palace eighteen years ago. With her magic, she called him close enough to touch him – and when she did, it was all over. Arlen turned on his allies to protect the Vhinesse. He was a demon, fighting against our own soldiers, and against me. We lost that day because of it – Purloch, Grunnach, myself – all of us sent running for our lives for the next eighteen years. After my sister grew bored with Arlen's punishment and he was finally released from her *falconry*, he retreated back to Alrou-Mendera in shame. He's been there, *hiding*, ever since."

Dherran watched Delennia, seeing something new in the woman: a stalwart commander, recounting her tale of hardship with calm strength. A vicious bitch but a strong leader. Her pale eyes burned, not because her beloved had fucked her sister, but because he had broken during battle.

Delennia took a deep breath and let it out slowly. Dherran lifted his eyebrows, surprised that her Khehemni training held the same practice for emotional control as his Alrashemni training. She set her fingers to the table-top. "Dherran. We have a weighted dice in the pocket. Grunnach knew it, that's why he brought you to me. He knew, as did Arlen, that *you* have a strong enough *wyrria* to resist my sister the Vhinesse. To bring her down."

"What are you talking about?" Dherran breathed, though something inside him stirred.

"I'm talking about *heart magic*, Dherran," Delennia held his gaze with impeccable strength. "*Jinne wyrdi*. The magic of the ancient Djinni of the southern deserts. Elemental beings who long ago would take women who wandered out into the dunes, blessing upon them children who could change the outcome of events. Children of the Sands. Who held *jinne wyrdi* and passed it down their bloodlines through the ages."

"You're saying that I'm one of these… children?" Dherran murmured, incredulous, his wine forgotten.

A small smile lifted Delennia's lips, though her eyes were hard. "I'm saying that someone far back down your bloodline was taken by a Djinn, and bore a child who had the power to change any future. *Jinne wyrdi*, or *jinnic wyrria*, is the magic of the pure heart. A heart that knows what it wants, a heart so passionate that it will hold onto its convictions and desires during any circumstance. And *change* that outcome. Have you ever asked yourself why you win, fight after fight, when the populace hate you? When they'd rather see you fall and run you out of town? It's not your will, Dherran, and it's not impeccable battle-skills: it's your heart. Your passion. When you use it – it undoes all opposition to your desire. I didn't let you win against me in the ring, Dherran. I never let a man win. Once I touch my opponents, they loose their will to fight me and become sloppy, but you resisted that. And just now, you resisted my sex, which no one has *ever* done. Arlen and Grunnach sent you to me, because they know your magic is one of the only things that can truly counter the *wyrria* my ancient line possesses. Heart magic is one of the few things that can bring my sister the Vhinesse down."

Delennia Oblitenne sat back, swirling her wine and staring at him. And for his part, Dherran gaped at her, knowing he looked the fool and unable to do anything about it.

CHAPTER 11 – ELOHL

Elohl kept his ears open during the Vhinesse's war-conference and
his mouth shut – Fenton doing the same upon the other side of the
Vhinesse's gilded chair.

Vhinesse Aelennia Oblitenne sat in a modest throne of gilded
vines today, at a round table of white marble cluttered with
documents in the center of the lofty war-room. The sun had long
since set, and only stars could be seen through the vaulted windows
that circled the round hall on one side. Glass flutes flickered with
burning oil at every column, Generals and Captains in the crimson
and black livery of the Red Valor giving reports by turns. The war-
council tonight included not only Valenghians with their silver hair
and handsomely arrogant features, but also sword-slim Cennetians
with russet-blonde manes and fiery green eyes, and tall Praoughians
with sleek flaxen locks, their cobalt gazes pinched in frowns.

Elohl took in the conversation with an impassive face,
committing names and stations to memory as information came
tumbling out about the Valenghian-Menderian war. His mind was
clear. Day by day, Elohl's thoughts had become less enslaved to the
Vhinesse's white mist – Fenton sparking Elohl's will with talk of
Ghrenna and shocks of *wyrria* each night for the past three days.

Now, Elohl was able to hold onto his memories in the
Vhinesse's presence, her touch producing no effect. Elohl had given
Fenton a signal they'd arranged, touching his pinky to his thumb to
let Fenton know he was in control of his faculties as they'd moved
out of the Falconry this morning. Fenton's mouth had quirked,
though he kept looking straight ahead as they'd stepped into the
corridor.

Acting docile upon his palladian chain, Elohl found it was
actually somewhat freeing to bare his Goldenmarks to the world. To
the Vhinesse's people, Elohl was a lovely ornament, a captured
Alrashemni Kingsman with a pretty mystery of intricate gold upon

his skin, but Elohl was able to control his Goldenmarks from flaring and declaring him further. Though he scanned their faces, he saw no shrewd looks of any who might have known what his markings truly were.

Elohl was listening to a recounting of the healing herb supply in the eastern Provinces, when the gilded doors to the war-hall suddenly boomed open. A man strode in, his bronze Cennetian skin well-tanned, his dark hair streaked with copper and also a lustrous silver-grey. The man's shrewd eyes were copper-tinged, and he moved forward with a battered scroll in one ruby-ringed hand. His cloak was a swath of elegant orange and saffron velvet, though the uniform beneath was the crimson of the Red Valor.

Silver pins of a flowering vine with five blossoms – the insignia of the High General of Valenghia – were tacked to the Cennetian's collar. As he stood there, strangely defiant in the presence of the Vhinesse, Elohl saw his physique was that of a good sword, his manner holding no infirmity despite his silvering hair and the lines at his eyes and mouth.

Flourishing a low bow in Cennetian fashion with a swirl of his cloak, he clacked his bootheels.

"My Living Vine. Forgive my lateness. I have arrived just this hour from the Aphellian Way with news of import." His voice was low and melodious, with a rolling Cennetian accent. His copper eyes roved over Fenton, then blinked when he came to Elohl.

And widened. For a moment he could not look away.

"High General Merkhenos del'Ilio." The Vhinesse's voice was tart and her blue eyes cold, though Elohl could tell she attempted to be her usual graceful self. "I am surprised to see you return so soon from your post upon the Aphellian Way. Were you not instructed to remain at the passage until six months hence, securing my borders?"

"My Living Vine." General Merkhenos swept a very low bow, dropping his gaze this time. "As I was bid by your Eminence, so have I done, but a message has come from my spies in Ligenia Bay. I thought it of the utmost importance to deliver it to you with haste, personally."

Elohl took in the words between the Vhinesse and her High General, understanding that the Cennetian had been sent to the Aphellian Way as punishment – a punishment which was not over.

Elohl filed this information away as the Vhinesse extended one perfect hand and the High General placed the scroll into it with a brisk gesture, though he did not touch her skin. The Vhinesse read through the scroll, her visage darkening as her silver brows drew together in a line.

"Lhaurent den'Alrahel has done *what*?!"

Men all around the table shuddered to hear her tone, and Elohl and Fenton imitated it as if affected by her *wyrria*. But Merkhenos merely held her gaze. The Vhinesse's eyes were frosty as she spoke with a regal wave. "All of you. Leave us."

Her other Captains and Generals went with smart salutes. But the copper-haired Cennetians nodded at Merkhenos as if in solidarity, before filing out of the war-room. At last, all were gone. Not even guards remained in the chamber, though Elohl and Fenton still stood by the Vhinesse's chair, undismissed.

"Speak." The Vhinesse's tone was chill, her arms crossed as she stared down her High General.

"Lhaurent den'Alrahel gathers a support-army in Ligenia Harbor." The Cennetian's narrow lips held a quirk, as if he was trying not to gloat. "Tens of thousands strong. Our spies have been watching them come through the Alranstone at Ligenia, others arriving by ship. Regiments of Menderian troops, Southron indentured warriors. This army is to join his main host and press along the Aphellian Way, imminently. He also has Kreth-Hakir at their lead. Twenty, or more."

"Twenty!" The bloom of color left the Vhinesse's cheeks, before her face set into stone-cold fury. Her pale eyes flashed in the light of the fluted glass lamps that studded the columns. "How *dare* he! We had an alliance!"

"That alliance is unquestionably over." Merkhenos could not keep the smile from his face now, though it quickly flashed away. "He intends to wreck war upon Valenghia. *Real* war, not this stymied sham that the Khehemni Lothren in both nations have engineered these past many years."

Elohl perked, hearing the high council of the Khehemni mentioned, wondering what the Lothren had to do with the war. Merkhenos' copper eyes flicked to Elohl again. Elohl banished all life from his face and the High General's gaze moved back to his liege.

She was stewing. Fuming. Elohl had never seen the Vhinesse so flushed, even during the height of passion. With a hard set to her jaw, she rose, setting her fingertips to the marble tabletop.

"Lhaurent *den'Alrahel* oversteps his bonds." Her voice was icy, her silvered demeanor cold. "His coup upon the Khehemni Lothren in his own nation was forgivable, understandable even. Long were his aspirations choked by that insufferable Evshein den'Lhamann and his cronies. Lhaurent was the inspiration behind the Kingsmen Summons, and the hand of that triumph. But even after, Evshein did not allow him his rightful place. But now, Lhaurent believes himself clever in the game of nations. A game in the sun, rather than shadows. A mistake."

"Grievous and blatant," Merkhenos interrupted, "to move against the Valenghian Lothren. Once, his supply of indentured fighters to both sides of our border served purpose for the Lothren in both nations. To eliminate Alrashemni fighters by continued warfare. But now, he moves upon your tilthlands, Vhinesse. With Kreth-Hakir Brethren under his banner like they were at the Kingsmen Summons—"

Her pale eyes flicked to his. "Lhaurent had Kreth-Hakir involved in the Kingsmen Summons? And you *withheld* this information from me?!"

Merkhenos' copper eyelashes flickered, but he did not lower his gaze. "My Vine. There were rumors, unconfirmed. The rumors cited that three Kreth-Hakir Brethren were involved in the capturing of the Alrashemni Kingskinder – to take many of them back to the Unaligned Lands and induct into their order."

"Where there is one Scorpion, there are *dozens!*" The Vhinesse leaned over the table, wrath in her beautiful eyes. "Were you not who you are, Merkhenos, I would have your head for this!"

The man settled back onto his heels, a subtle swordsman's stance. Merkhenos del'Ilio set his fingertips to his weapons, staring her down. "Take my head and start a rebellion, woman. Cennetia follows you because I will it. Because being adjunct to your nation was beneficial to our city-states, ever at war from within. My Cennetian Lothren favor it for Cennetia's solidarity, and to our oaths I stand loyal. But test me, *putistena*, and I will burn you down. Nothing unites Cennetian city-states more than fighting an enemy who has betrayed the Sons of Illium."

The Vhinesse paused, watching the Cennetian with wary attention, as if he was something utterly deadly that she'd learned to not try and dupe. Then, her demeanor softened, her voice sweetening with the chime of bells as she reached out a hand toward his wrist. "My dear Merkhenos. Must we be so at odds?"

"Touch me not, woman." Merkhenos slid a step backward. "I've had six months free of your odious personage, and I'll not be swept into your snares again."

"You know nothing of the torment I can bring you." Her voice was cold, bitter.

"I know your variety of torment," he spoke back, copper eyes flashing, "and I'll have none of it."

"Cur." Her tone was frosty, but her lips held a little smile, as if enjoying his defiance.

"*Puta.*" He gave a hard smile back. His gaze flicked again to Elohl and stayed. He motioned at her kept falcons. "You waste your *wyrric* hold over your Generals, keeping your pretty prizes near during a war-council. Some might call it rash."

Elohl tried to show nothing, but again, the Cennetian had given him interesting news – that the Vhinesse's talents had a limit.

"The only one who has made a rash move here is Lhaurent den'Alrahel." The Vhinesse's pale eyes were frosty. "He calls himself a god, all because he has bloodlines that supposedly fulfill some ancient *prophecy* that he's supposed to unite our continent in a golden age. Trash."

"And a unique *wyrria* that has convinced the Kreth-Hakir to ally with him." Merkhenos lifted a russet eyebrow as he put his fists to the table. "Not a small thing. Lhaurent has convinced the Kreth-Hakir of his power. Of his ability to be the most dominant force of our age. Clearly, they believe him, and thus, they support him."

"So the Scorpions have chosen a side," the Vhinesse mused, her fingers drumming upon the table. "And where does that leave my Valenghian Lothren? Or your Cennetian Lothren, for that matter? Lhaurent annihilated his own Lothren in Alrou-Mendera. Would he send the Scorpions against us?"

"My Lothren fear so." The Cennetian straightened. "Where a rabid cur bites once, he will likely bite again. My Lothren have asked me to keep our aims unified, and as you are head of the Lothren here in Valenghia, I will honor that alliance. But don't push me, woman. Or find two wars on your borders, and half your naval support gone."

"You drive a hard bargain, King of Poisoners." The Vhinesse's eyes were frosty.

"Cennetia hasn't had a king in ages." Merkhenos del'Ilio's copper eyes were amused. "But test me again and I will unite the city-states against you. They will follow a strong *Generalisso d'Iscurro*, with knives in the night and dark draughts in your wine."

"A bitter brew." The Vhinesse crossed her arms, her face impassive.

"Indeed." The Cennetian swept a low bow. "I must retire. The ride from the border was long and dusty. I will be in my chambers. Know that should you even *attempt* to cross my threshold, I will put a knife in you. Coated in a very slow poison of my own devising. To which there is no antidote."

The Vhinesse finally smiled. It went with a laugh, free and throaty, though no bells tinkled inside Elohl's mind now. "You are a vicious cur! Go, then. Have your leisure, but you will come when I summon you, Son of Illium."

"As long my audience is in the war-hall and not your bedchamber." The Cennetian's gaze flicked to Elohl one last time. "I would interrogate your new falcons, my Living Vine."

She lifted one eyebrow, then glanced back at Fenton and Elohl, both impressively quiet beside her chair. "They have given me no trouble. You believe they are not mine?" Reaching out, she stroked Fenton's face, then Elohl's. Elohl made no movement other than to give the Vhinesse an idolatrous smile as she stroked down his chest. Elohl felt her twining snares, but thoughts of Ghrenna pushed them back. The Vhinesse gave him a lovely smile — she didn't know she was being pushed out of his mind, or Fenton's.

She turned back to the Cennetian. "Interrogate them as you will. I'll bring them to you this afternoon, but you may not harm a hair upon their heads. I want them intact."

"Indeed." Merkhenos bowed again, snapping the heels of his boots together, then turned and pushed out the doors. The Vhinesse gave a sigh, scanning the documents upon the table. At last, she turned to her men, taking up their fine palladian chains.

"Let us retire, my falcons."

"Yes, my Vine," Elohl and Fenton murmured.

With a weary smile, the Vhinesse took up Elohl and Fenton's chains and led them through the arched doorway. They took a winding route, following a burbling stream that ran through the floor until they were in a section of the palace Elohl hadn't seen. This wing had the same columns carven like trees and rivulets of cascading water. But where other areas sported demure carvings, this area cavorted with nymphs and satyrs in coitus, writhing in wanton delight. It was so excessive as to be lewd, and Elohl fought to make his face impassive as they continued through the airy hall.

At last, the Vhinesse came to a door flanked by two liveried men in the crimson jerkins of the Red Valor. The men were Cennetian, and their hooded eyes, complemented by deeply bronzed skin and bright copper hair, were so alert they prickled Elohl's spine – even though the men leaned against the wall in a lazy fashion. The guards didn't exactly bar the Vhinesse from knocking on the door, but one with a silver bar pinned to his collar stepped before her with a rakish smile that didn't quite touch his eyes.

"My Living Vine," he murmured. "I will alert the *Generalisso* that you have arrived."

The Vhinesse's eyes were frosty, but she didn't rebuke him, which Elohl thought odd. The Red Valor were her fighters, after all, but these Cennetians acted as if they were loyal to their country of origin rather than their oaths.

For some reason, the Vhinesse let it pass. Waving one regal hand, she said, "As you will. I shall not trouble your master. I only leave him these two for his exquisite perusal. He may send a runner to my chambers when he is finished with them. That is all."

The guard snapped his bootheels with a genteel nod. The Vhinesse turned to her kept men. With solemnity, she lifted Elohl's hand and then placed his palladian chain in his palm. Turning to Fenton, she did the same. Stepping between them, she set a palm to each of their cheeks.

"Now, my falcons. You are to enter this chamber. You will speak with my High General inside, and tell him everything he wishes to know. If he wishes for any kind of demonstration, you will do it. You will be pleasant, and answer him thoroughly. When you are finished, you will be escorted back to the Falconry, and will remain docile all the while. When I come to you later, you will recount to me *everything* that transpired, down to the smallest detail. Yes, my loves?"

Elohl could feel the Vhinesse's cloud of poison trying to choke his mind. He could feel that slippery, suffocating sensation of losing himself again. The command of her touch was so potent, so specific, that he found himself wanting to do as she said. It was a struggle to maintain the image of Ghrenna in his mind; deep cerulean washed out the entwining vapors of the Vhinesse, until Elohl could fake a smile.

"Yes, my Vine," Elohl murmured.

"As you wish," Fenton responded.

The Vhinesse beamed at them, and what Elohl saw smiling at him was merely an elegant woman, nothing more. The Vhinesse kissed him upon the lips, then gave one to Fenton. "Now, go. Do my bidding."

As she turned back down the airy hall, Fenton and Elohl faced the door. With a swift bow and a clacking of bootheels, the Cennetian Red Valor soldiers pushed the lewdly-carven door inward. Elohl and Fenton stepped inside, the Valorman with the silver bar upon his collar with them. The inner suite was just as disgustingly carven as the hall, phalluses in gargantuan representation upon every column. Elohl fought to not set his jaw. The entire room writhed – a place where sex and innuendo could never be escaped. Some might have found it arousing, but Elohl could only gaze at it with disgust – rutting surrounding him rather than lovemaking.

The Valenghian High General sat at a white-ash writing desk by the bay windows, and noted Elohl's disgust with a quirk of his lips. Tossing spectacles to his desk, he set a hawk-feather quill in its holder from a document he'd been writing. Putting his russet Cennetian-leather boots up on the corner of his desk, he leaned his sword-thin frame back in his chair and steepled his fingers with a shrewd narrowing of his copper eyes.

"The Vhinesse's falcons, *Generalisso*," the guard with the silver bar at his collar spoke, with a clack of bootheels.

"Thank you, Ghirano." Merkhenos del'Ilio's voice flowed with the liquid patter of his homeland, deep with an authority that wasn't bred into a person, but born. "And do refrain from using the term *falcon* in my presence."

"Forgive me!" The guard reddened under his short shock of copper hair, his gaze dropping. But his eyes came back up. "*Generalisso,* would you like me to remain here to—"

"Please wait in the foyer until my business is concluded, Ghirano. You may go."

"But sir—" Ghirano's dark eyes flicked nervously to the Brigadiers. He was clearly uneasy, and Elohl wondered if the man feared the falcons had been sent as assassins. Elohl wondered if such a thing had happened before. He wouldn't put it past the conniving Vhinesse.

"Thank you, Ghirano," Merkhenos repeated, his words very soft. "You may go."

Ghirano stiffened like he'd been whipped, his dark eyes flashing though he kept silent. Turning on his heel, he retreated from the room; the doors closed with a marked boom. As the sound died, the *Generalisso* met Elohl's eyes, and Elohl saw questions there, but also a vastly patient man. Merkhenos turned his copper gaze to Fenton, then gestured to two carven chairs at a white-ash dining table laden with food.

"Gentlemen. Please join me for refreshment."

Merkhenos rose from his desk and moved to the dining table, then sat in an ornate white-ash chair. Reaching to a wine carafe, he poured two gilded goblets before filling his own. He removed all of his rings, then sipped from each goblet – a Cennetian gesture of peacemaking – then set two of the goblets upon the other side of the table for his guests. Pushing forward a tray of bread, cured meats, olives, and cheeses, he waited as Elohl and Fenton each took a chair.

"So," the Cennetian began, his copper eyes amused. "Two Brigadiers of Alrou-Mendera, strangled in the Vhinesse's vines. I heard how she found you, come through the Alranstone below the palace, but what I want to know is: how is it that my Living Vine was able to snare two *wyrrics* of such impressive power – my lord of the Wolf and Dragon, and my Rennkavi?"

Elohl's lips dropped open. Merkhenos' laughing copper-dark

eyes took delight in his surprise, as he threw back his head and gave a great roaring laugh. He met Elohl's eyes and held them, something ruthless in their depths, though they also held an awed kind of respect.

"Yes. I know what you are, but our esteemed Vhinesse doesn't. She believes she has caught a duo of falcons. But what she has caught, in my estimation, are a pair of *dragons* – or perhaps, a wolf and a dragon. Most Khehemni Lothren don't know the truth of the Rennkavi, and my esteemed Vhinesse has not seen the Goldenmarks in action yet upon any front. My tribe remember the Rennkavi legend, in the darkest houses of our sweating city-states."

At this revelation, Fenton's posture shifted subtly, settling back in his chair and crossing one ankle over his knee. He didn't seem surprised at the Cennetian's revelation, and sat with an air of command, as if he was utterly comfortable in just his loincloth and jewelry. His posture, Elohl realized, was a challenge – one that came with a glower and a flash of red-gold from Fenton's normally placid eyes.

"Play us no games, Son of Illium," Fenton's simmering growl brought the hairs upon Elohl's neck up straight as a prickle of electricity shivered through the room. "As I recall, your tribe has a long memory. Surely, you know just *exactly* who I am and the honor you owe me."

Elohl glanced to Fenton, his eyebrows lifting to see Fenton gazing upon the Cennetian with regal austerity, a slow red-gold fire twisting through Fenton's eyes. Elohl felt another trickle of Fenton's power simmer through the room, and with a smooth movement, Fenton rose. Turning, the crimson and gold *wyrric* Inking of Fenton's line blossomed upon his skin, curling through his sinews and spreading out upon his back like burning blood. Wisps of crimson and gold etheric fire simmered around him, and Elohl heard Merkhenos draw a swift breath.

"Behold your Living Dragon, servant of Alodwine. The last fountainhead of Khehem's *wyrria*." Fenton's words were soft. Dangerous. Regal, as he turned and gazed at Merkhenos del'Ilio.

The Cennetian watched with awe in his copper eyes, as if witnessing the glory of a fallen god. It was then that Elohl understood true power, watching Fenton as the Cennetian saw him.

Ancient, strong; a being that had walked this earth for a thousand years – traveling, learning, seeking, serving. Fighting. Elohl saw it now, in every line of Fenton's honed body. Glorious, Fenton turned back with a slow fire surging in his eyes – hinting at what terrible storms he could wield, should this man oppose him.

With a wry smile, Merkhenos pushed out of his chair and sank to one knee upon the plush Perthian carpet. With two fingers to his brow, he bent his head and spoke. "I am no fool, milord Fentleith Alodwine, Last Scion of the Wolf and Dragon. I know you for who you are. Long are the memories of the Illianti. It is my honor to serve Leith's line, as my grandfathers did of old. As it is my honor to serve our foretold Rennkavi against the Red-Eyed Demon's Rise. I am your servant. I am *Leithren*, a true servant of Leith's line."

Silence filled the room. Elohl stared at the Cennetian, still kneeling upon the carpet but watching Fenton carefully.

"Tell me of my Leithren, Son of Illium." Fenton's words were gentler in his sonorous baritone as he stared down upon the Cennetian, his eyes bled out to gold-brown now. "How many still know of my existence, and how many yet serve me – allied against the Kreth-Hakir Brethren?"

"It is a complicated question, milord, for which there is a long and complicated answer. If I may?" The Cennetian lifted an eyebrow at his chair and Fenton beckoned him to rise. Reclaiming his seat as Fenton reclaimed his, the Cennetian refilled each of their wine goblets. Fenton sipped his wine, though his presence still commanded the room, prickles of energy biting at Elohl's skin in diminishing surges.

Elohl noticed that Merkhenos took a large swallow of wine, as if fortifying himself. Setting his goblet down, he smoothed his fingers around the rim with a deft touch, his copper gaze frank as he took up the conversation again. "Let me start at the beginning. Eight hundred years ago, just after the War of the North, there was also a shadow-war within your Leithren, milord Alodwine. An internal schism. It was bloody—"

"I know about the shadow-war," Fenton held up a hand, as if exhausted. "I know most of the Leithren who knew me were killed in a massive coup aided by the Kreth-Hakir, acting for their own preservation against my edicts. I know that those who remained were seeded with doubt – that I was real, that I was truly Leith's grandson. I know that the Leithren re-named themselves the *Lothren* at the Kreth-Hakir's urging, and that their forces have been allied ever since. What I'm asking, Merkhenos, is how many of my original supporters remain?"

"In Cennetia, we believe." Merkhenos gave a subtle chuckle. "The Illianti had plenty of contact with you in days of old, and with your children – particularly one by the name of Ihbram. Our poisons have long been crafted against Kreth-Hakir mind-bending. Among my clan, we remember not only that we must support the Goldenmarked when he comes, but respect your warnings about the Kreth-Hakir Brethren, about the danger they pose to all of humanity. My Illianti clan have never forgotten whom we serve. Though we have gone very deep underground, inside the Lothren itself."

"Do your people know why I was given these marks?" Elohl murmured, wondering if the Cennetian could tell him anything.

The Cennetian gave a cunning smile as he sipped his wine, his gaze flicking to the Goldenmarks curling over Elohl's torso, arms and legs. "Why were you chosen for this honor? I know not. Leith Alodwine himself created the marks you wear. My people only know that the Rennkavi was to be Leith's focus of power against the Red-Eyed Demon: a weapon for Leith to wield. Now that I see you, I wonder. Your presence is proof that we live in dire times – the age of the Demon's Rise, as Leith supposed."

"You believe my grandfather was a hero," Fenton snorted derisively.

"I do." The Cennetian's eyes flashed. "My kin remember a courageous man who stood up against a future so frightening that he enacted terrible measures to control the outcome. A man who did what he had to, to prevent worse."

"My mother's spear-maidens remembered a tyrant who devastated the Thirteen Tribes," Fenton's voice was cold. "Who brought *wyrria* to a grinding standstill, killing off thousands of *wyrric* adepts in an instant. Making *wyrria* vanish from our world, except for the barest trickle."

Elohl attended the conversation with rapt attention. The Cennetian leaned forward, his eyes flashing at Fenton. "*Wyrria* that you and your bloodline got in spades. So did the Kreth-Hakir, and the Rennkavi – while everyone else was essentially abandoned except for small tricks. Why? We can only assume because Leith foresaw that these *wyrric* lines would be instrumental in bringing down the Red-Eyed Demon."

"Any news of that?" Fenton's fingers perused his lips.

"No." Merkhenos shook his head, sitting back. "I have heard nothing of the Demon's Rise. My allies report that the Kreth-Hakir watch a handful of people, including our Vhinesse. Though Lhaurent den'Alrahel is the one they watch most, and whom they have chosen to serve. However, I imagine——"

"You imagine what?" Fenton commanded.

"The Kreth-Hakir would follow you, if they knew you lived." Merkhenos held Fenton's gaze. "Like the Leithren, the Kreth-Hakir still believe in the Rennkavi legend. They were sworn to Leith's bloodline, the same as we were."

"The Kreth-Hakir won't follow me." Fenton's voice was suffused with a hard darkness. "We had a difference of opinion, long ago. It was what led to my edict with the Leithren, and why the Kreth-Hakir became involved, cutting them out from underneath me. I should have destroyed those mind-bending bastards when I had the chance."

Fenton fell into a deep silence, and though Elohl waited for more of the story, it didn't come.

"They would have resisted your destruction," Merkhenos spoke at last, swirling his goblet. "They are the Scorpions. Where there is one, there are many. Such a vast and coordinated mind is not an easy thing to kill. Leith Alodwine saw an opportunity to bind the strongest forces in the continent to his aims and he took it. Odious as they may be."

"Who are these Kreth-Hakir?" Elohl asked, not comprehending this piece of conversation.

Fenton's eyes were desolate as he turned to Elohl. "Do you remember men dressed in herringbone leathers, who came to collect the Kingskinder after the Kingsman Summons?"

"*Them?*" Elohl bristled, rage rising within him as he remembered the scorpion-rider who had nearly killed him in the Elhambrian Forest near Lintesh, and who had captured them at

159

Alrashesh. "They were sworn to your line? And to the Rennkavi?"

Fenton drew in a breath, his eyes closing. When they opened again, they were bright with golden flame. "Ask me again why I think my grandfather was evil, Elohl – the Kreth-Hakir are the proof. Leith bound them, then entrusted them to find and follow the Rennkavi. Or if that failed, get close to anyone who showed signs of harboring the Demon – an ancient evil that is supposed to usher in dark days when it arrives."

"So what do the Goldenmarks actually do?" Elohl gave Fenton a hard glance. "What else have you not been telling me about all this?"

"The Kreth-Hakir and the Leithren," Fenton sighed, "believe my grandfather was a visionary. That Leith created the Rennkavi's Goldenmarks to unite the world in an indestructible system of *wyrria* against the Demon's Rise. So the Rennkavi could be Leith's champion and conduit – a weapon channeling all the world's *wyrria* for Leith's use, who would then use it to vanquish the Demon."

"But Leith," Elohl settled back, his mind spinning, "isn't he dead? Who fights this Red-Eyed Demon if Leith's not at the pinnacle of the magic? And is this Demon even real?"

"You're the pinnacle of the magic now, Elohl." Fenton gave a tired sigh. "And as to the reality of the Red-Eyed Demon... oh, it's very real. Don't ask me how I know, just know that it is. My grandfather wrought terrible crimes, Elohl, so zealous was he in believing he was the man to bring it down."

"By uniting the world." Elohl touched his neck, feeling the shifting prickle in his golden Inkings. "Is that a good thing or bad?"

"It depends." Merkhenos' copper eyes were sly as he cut in. "Would you see the world united in love and peace? Or in destruction?"

"Are you saying that my intention determines the outcome of the Goldenmarks?"

"I'm saying that at one time," Merkhenos eyed him, "Leith Alodwine would have been the mind behind the Marks. They were bound to him as their master and creator, but now they are bound to no-one. Now, it is only you. I can only suppose that in the absence of his will, yours reigns supreme. Your ideas about unity... may determine how the Goldenmarks behave."

"Elohl." Fenton's voice was low, and so somber that Elohl turned, watching him. Rubbing both hands over his face, Fenton closed his eyes and took a long inhalation, then met Elohl's gaze. "You need to know. You have a rival. There is one other who carries the marks you bear. The one the Kreth-Hakir have chosen to serve: Lhaurent den'Alrahel, who used to be the Queen's Castellan."

Shock raced through Elohl's veins as his Goldenmarks lit with a simmering recoil. Not just because Fenton's revelation was a jolt, but also because Elohl recalled Lhaurent. That moment of connection they'd had in the Small Hall of Roushenn, after the attempt on the Queen's life. He could still feel that smooth lack of care in the Castellan's gaze, sliding through his body like deepwater eels. Elohl had felt a resonance then, and he felt it again, slipping through his body like he'd swallowed leeches. It made Elohl feel sick, and he choked down bile with a grimace.

"And you didn't think to tell me that sooner?" Elohl rasped, furious and barely containing himself.

"I can see you have personal experience of our dear Castellan." Merkhenos wore a dark smile as he watched Elohl. "Your expression is priceless."

"I didn't want you to mistrust the magic," Fenton spoke softly, gazing into Elohl's eyes and ignoring the Cennetian. "I didn't want you to think it was evil because Lhaurent also wields it, and because it was created by my grandfather. Whatever the Goldenmarks are, Elohl, they have a tremendous possibility, if wielded by the right man. I believe you are that man. Down to my very bones, I believe it. My mother believed it, too. Her Prophecy was very clear on the vast benefit of the Goldenmarks, even though she never mentioned two people having them."

Elohl sat back, digesting all that had been said, his gaze still pinned to Fenton. "What else? What else do I need to know about these marks that you've conveniently avoided telling me?"

"That the marks grow stronger through trust, through touch." Fenton spoke plainly, holding Elohl's gaze and ignoring his barb. "Your Rennkavi's power grows by having those around you that you trust, those who bring you peace of mind and heart. But you're a lone wolf, Elohl. I've picked your brain these past months trying to find out whom you love and trust, and found almost no-one. You don't even trust me, not really."

"You've not given me a lot of reasons to." Elohl's gaze was hard, cold, something dark writhing in his gut at how long Fenton had kept this information from him. As he watched Fenton, he realized that although part of him did trust him, something about Fenton bothered him. He roiled with an ancient pain that sent shivers of *wyrria* curling off him constantly, his core full of power and conflict. Elohl trusted Fenton to have his back in a fight, but he found he did not feel peaceful around Fenton. The man had a bad habit of lying, of withholding the truth to cover his own ass, and it burned Elohl so deep inside that his Goldenmarks simmered to life in a rippling wave.

The Cennetian's eyes flashed as he straightened in his seat, watching Elohl's marks simmer, but Elohl cared nothing for Merkhenos as he held Fenton's dark gaze with power and fury. "Lie to me again, Fentleith Alodwine," Elohl rumbled, command pouring through him upon the tide of his marks, "or withhold vital truths in *any way*, and know that I will banish you from my service. For good or for ill."

Fenton's gaze was riveted to the marks. He breathed a soft sigh, his face strangely drawn. "I've tried to tell you the truth, Elohl. Shaper knows I have. But I debated with myself, over and over until it ate me up inside with indecision, worried about the outcome of my actions. The curse of my *wyrria* is conflict, Elohl. And in this way, my inaction made it all the worse. I swear to you. From now on, I will tell you every truth I know about who and what you are."

It was as good an oath as Elohl could have asked for, and yet watching Fenton, he found himself concerned that there was far more Fenton hadn't told him, or might not even know to tell him. The man sitting before him with the burning firebrand all across his back was ten centuries old. He had seen more of life and *wyrria* and battle than Elohl could ever dream – forgotten more lore and legend than Elohl could ever learn, but all that was neither here nor there until they could get out from beneath the Vhinesse's sway.

Turning to Merkhenos, Elohl spoke. "High General. How many men do you command upon the Aphellian Way?"

Merkhenos paused, with a knowing glint in his copper eyes. "Rennkavi. How many men can you control with your *wyrria*?"

"I've not tested it widely." Elohl held his gaze, undaunted. "The most was a small skirmish."

The Cennetian drummed his fingertips upon the table as silence took the room. At last, he steepled his fingers beneath his chin and cleared his throat. "I am of a mind to support you gentlemen, to offer you everything you need. One – escape from this palace and the Vhinesse's ugly charms, which is easily accomplished by liberating you quietly, disguised among my Red Valor when I return to the war-front in two week's time. Two – helping you figure out just how many men you can command when we reach the Aphellian Way. And three – helping you use your powers against Lhaurent den'Alrahel and the Vhinesse both, when the time comes."

"You would rebel against your liege?" Fenton eyed Merkhenos thoughtfully. "Take her army from her for our use?"

"I was once upon a palladian chain, gentlemen, not so very long ago." Merkhenos' copper eyes flashed as he met Fenton's gaze, then Elohl's. "I have tolerated our alliance because my Leithren ordered me to remain close to the Vhinesse, since the Kreth-Hakir wouldn't. But believe me when I tell you – it has been the most unpleasant duty of my entire life."

With that, Merkhenos stood, setting his fingers to the tabletop. "Gentlemen. The Vhinesse will be expecting you back in your Falconry. Bide your time upon her chains. We will find our moment to break you free. I swear it. Then we will strike down against tyrants, and when we do, our wrath will know no boundary."

Fenton and Elohl both stood. Elohl saluted Merkhenos with a palm to his chest as Fenton did the same. With a wary glance at Fenton and reluctance in his heart, Elohl steeled himself to return to the Vhinesse's Falconry once more.

CHAPTER 12 – THEROUN

It had been a week since the Brethren of the Kreth-Hakir had taken Adelaine Visek away. A week since she had breathed her glacial power down Theroun's throat. A week that he had twisted in agony, something writhing within him that he couldn't possibly name.

He'd been taken out of the chain gang. Four Kreth-Hakir had hauled him off around the palisade to one of the remaining cat-cradles inside the grounds of Fhekran Palace. The enormous barn of a building reeked of cat-piss and vinegar, with the tinge of dead flesh, but the pile of straw they'd thrown him in had been clean as they re-set his manacles to an iron ring in the wall, with room so he could sleep.

He hadn't done much of that. Something seared inside Theroun from what Adelaine had done. At once icy and hot like a poison, it twisted his guts and gave him no peace, stabbed him until his body was a writhing mass of torment. He didn't believe Adelaine had meant him harm, and yet, that was the outcome. For the past week Theroun had endured moment after endless moment of shredding within his guts and venom surging through his veins – like some vast creature made of oilslick darkness stabbing him incessantly from within.

Theroun was doing the only thing he could about it; breathing. Night and day he sat, legs crossed, drawing in slow breaths through his nose and releasing them. When the pain became too unbearable, he did a fire-breath he'd learned for his old wound, a bellow-fast pant with a hold at the end followed by deep inhalation that induced euphoria.

Or at least, whatever euphoria he could generate right now – only enough to keep him from going completely insane.

Kreth-Hakir had come and gone these past seven days, watching him. He'd eaten nothing they brought him – neither gruel, cured meats, nor late-summer pears – letting it all rot upon the plate until they took it away. He slept not at all and took only mouthfuls of water, letting it absorb in his mouth rather than swallow and risk retching.

He felt two Hakir arrive today, setting a dish of something that smelled like roast guinea-fowl within reach. Theroun could have lashed out, struck them, but he could not even open his eyes to confront them, much less tell them to leave him be. He couldn't break his concentration for even a moment, so focused was he upon merely holding to sanity through his diabolical oilslick pain.

More Kreth-Hakir arrived. Before long, the space of his cat-stall was crowded with Brethren idling against the wooden walls or sitting silently in the straw. Theroun could feel them, the silver threads of their minds dancing around him. Talking amongst themselves, seeking Theroun's boundaries, testing the edge of the thing that consumed him. Every time they dipped in, his pain would rise like a black leviathan and they would be thrust back – their minds cast out from ruin with no end.

"He'll waste." A burly baritone spoke aloud, something the Kreth-Hakir never did. "No one can survive this."

"It's like what High Master Yesh did to Sage Pierce," a younger voice murmured, "when Pierce betrayed the Brethren at Darkwinter six years ago."

"Awakening a latent *wyrria* without warning," the grim baritone growled again. "There's a reason such an action is forbidden in our Order, Brother Antonius, unless you challenge another Brother to the Kiani-Hithrai. To force a latent *wyrria* as brutal as this one into awakening is often a death sentence, but the tundra-witch did not know that. Will the Menderian General live or die? All we can do is wait."

"It's more than that," an ancient voice spoke, a soft step swishing through the straw near the stall's open gate. The wheeze of time was strong in this new voice, though he spoke with a melodious, almost comforting tone. "The brave General is wrestling the Beast's Awakening – something I've not seen for six hundred years. None without awareness of their *wyrria* has survived such a spontaneous Awakening since the time of Leith, when Agni roamed the skies. Give this man your honor, Brothers. It's incredible that he's lasted this long. Especially without any training."

165

"Brother Kiiar." Voices murmured respectfully in near-unison, as Theroun shifted into his fast breathing to handle a sudden surge of venomous agony.

"It's time to take him to Brother Jornath. He's the closest thing we have to a Sage out here in these wretched wildlands." Old Brother Kiiar spoke again. Theroun felt someone reach out to touch him, and in his mind's eye he could see unseen fingers of silver hovering over his face. As those silver fingers wisped over his energy, sensing his torment but not touching it, he saw a man's shape materialize in his mind. Woven out of liquid silver threads, the *wyrric* body of the man leaned in, black eyes shining through that mercurial light as the Brother perused Theroun's condition.

"Brother Jornath said to let him stew." The baritone voice said, burly and aggressive.

"And I'm saying that time is over. He's had far more than the required three days for his Adept's Proving." Kiiar's wheezing voice had an edge to it, and the silver man-shape pulled back, gone from Theroun's inner vision. "Would you defy me, Brother Caldrian?"

"No, Brother Kiiar." Brother Caldrian's big voice surrendered with a growl.

Two men in herringbone leathers knelt by Theroun, unlocking his manacles. Theroun's head reeled as another wave of slick-dark pain came. They grasped him beneath his arms and hustled him up. Dizzy, his equilibrium tilted and the pain surged; Theroun's knees collapsed. Sweat stood out in a hard flush upon his brow, and the reek of seven days soaked his filthy tunic.

"Carry him," Brother Kiiar commanded. "He can't walk. It's a miracle he's still conscious."

Theroun felt himself hauled up by surprisingly gentle hands and slung into a stretcher of arms. Moving in perfect coordination, Theroun felt the Brethren carry him out of the cat-cradle. A thin drizzle hit his face, cooling his wretched fever. Theroun risked opening his eyes, though even the weak dawn light hit him like a sledgehammer.

The force within him roiled, but Theroun wrestled it back in order to take stock of the Brethren who carried him around the side of the ruined palace. One was young, barely in his twenties, his pale scruff of beard and short shock of hair Valenghian silver, though his eyes were the drowning orchid-blue of the Lhemvian Isles. Another man was swarthy, as large as Khorel Jornath, though more lean. A ragged scar tore down his right temple, that ear missing, a long black mohawk braided back in Thurumani fashion and bedecked with fetishes of feathers, shells, and human teeth. Gold hoops were pierced through his remaining ear, badges of Lefkani pirating prowess – each hoop indicating ten men killed in battle. Theroun supposed he knew to whom the belligerent baritone voice belonged.

The other man in his sightline was small, a frizz of white hair haloing his head. Thin as a bird and twice as frail, he was nonetheless upright as he walked alongside those who carried Theroun. He glanced over, as if feeling Theroun's delirious regard, and gave a comforting smile with his bushy white brows and sparkling black-on-black eyes. The same eyes Theroun had spied conjured out of *wyrria* just moments ago. The old man exuded a calm yet fierce nature, though only half his face smiled. The other half was burned beyond recognition, a mask of dripping candlewax.

Theroun had no more time to wonder as he was taken around the edge of the charred palisade to a soaring cathedral. The same building where he'd sworn allegiance to Lhaurent, the Elsthemi house of worship the Kreth-Hakir kept as their headquarters. As the pain roared back in a furious wave and he had to shut his eyes and deepen his breath, Theroun felt himself taken up the wide stone stairs. He heard men haul back the massive white-pine doors. Inside, the building had a sanctuary feel, all vaulted halls and soaring space. Theroun risked another glance. Elsthemi pearled-glass illuminated white timbers bent into elegant curves reminiscent of whale ribs throughout the buttressed space. White marble colonnades were topped by soaring arches, giving an overall impression of peace and solace.

The hall had not been sacked nor looted. Prayer-benches had been pushed back to the walls to make room in the center for a stout ironpine war-table and chairs. The white wool banners at the front of the nave had an image of a winged Madonna upon her knees in supplication, hands in prayer above her head with sheafs of wheat all around her. Even the table of white candles at the front of the hall was undisturbed, only pushed back to make more room in the middle of the space.

167

Khorel Jornath sat at the heavy ironpine table that occupied the center of the hall, taking a cup of wine and a plate of food. Graceful tapers burned in floor-stand candelabrum nearby. He sat with a thoughtful frown, studying a map as he ate. He glanced up as Theroun was hauled in, then beckoned his Brethren forward.

Theroun saw no more, shutting his eyes as his pain rioted. Taken to the middle of the hall, the cold stone floor was a relief as he was lowered to it. Theroun felt the Kreth-Hakir step away. He heard creaks of leather and the whisper of silk as the Brethren bowed, then the soft whisk of boots over stone as they retreated from the hall. The heavy doors of the hall boomed shut, leaving only two impressions of silver upon Theroun's suffering mind.

"Please forgive my intrusion, Brother Jornath, but the Initiate needs to see you," Brother Kiiar's wheezy voice spoke. "The *wyrria* within him still tries to change, going on a full seven days now. It's tearing his body apart... I'm afraid he doesn't have much time."

Theroun heard the scrape of Khorel Jornath's chair as the man rose, then a massive sigh like wind through a cavern. "You did well, Brother Kiiar. His First Rite of Proving has passed. Indeed, it passed the first time he faced me in single combat. I did but wish to know his stamina, and now we have all seen it. Leave us, please. General Theroun and I have much to discuss."

Khorel Jornath's smooth baritone would not be gainsaid, and Theroun heard the soft step of Brother Kiiar departing, the doors booming shut. A massive presence approached, limned in quicksilver within Theroun's mind. Khorel Jornath came to one knee beside Theroun, and Theroun felt as much as saw an enormous hand laid gently to his brow. The big man placed his other hand beneath Theroun's neck, cradling his head. Suddenly, thousands of silver threads blossomed out from Jornath's mind-persona, weaving an enormous net of quicksilver around Theroun's body. Like water pouring through a funnel, they slipped into Theroun from the presence of Jornath's hands, sinking that tremendous net into Theroun's flesh – around the massive oilslick darkness that had woken inside Theroun.

"*Be still.*" Jornath's command was so strong, it thickened the air in the room. Theroun's breaths were harder to claim, his body heavy, his limbs dense. He sank into the stone floor as the net thickened though his body like a quicksilver flow. Enveloping whatever it was that tore Theroun apart, the net settled around every aspect of the darkness – and then cinched it all up like catching rats in a bag.

The pain snuffed out. Theroun spasmed with a cry of relief. His next breaths came in grateful gasps. His body felt lighter and he was able to open his eyes. Khorel Jornath stared down from above, a mixture of emotions upon his face. Respect and awe shone in those dark grey eyes, mixed with concern, sorrow – even a wry twist of humor upon that full mouth.

"Can you stand?" Jornath eased his hands away from Theroun's skull.

Theroun lifted an eyebrow. Inside, he felt the darkness writhe, but it was trussed up neatly in the quicksilver net, and did little harm but for a fleeting grip in Theroun's guts.

"Some trick of yours." Theroun commented wryly, pushing up to a seat.

"Indeed." Jornath's smile was mysterious as he rose and turned away.

Holding his ribs at his old wound, Theroun pushed to standing. When he felt no more than a casual roll of pain, he glanced to Jornath, intrigued. Khorel Jornath had resumed his seat at the table, picking up eating where he'd left off. He took a sip of blood red wine from an agate chalice, with impeccable manners. Jornath did not slop his food, nor drink while chewing, and did not spill even a crumb of crusty bread as he spread butter upon it. Of a gigantic size, the man had hands like a mason, but Theroun watched the sensitivity of those hands as the man ate, rather like an accomplished duelist than a laborer.

Khorel Jornath looked up as if he could feel Theroun's thoughts, his dark gaze level. He wiped his mouth with a linen napkin, then turned in his chair, regarding Theroun with one hand skimming the rim of his chalice. Khorel Jornath wore three rings of silver, Theroun saw. One a scorpion with a sapphire in its pincers, one a dragon with a ruby in its jaws. And the third bore a simple onyx pyramid, etched in tiny runes and set at the apex with a cap of dusky white star-metal.

"What did you do to me just now?" Theroun barked casually. He clasped his hands behind his back in a military at-ease, ready to engage his enemy even though his body still felt weak, trembling with hunger and lightheaded with thirst.

"I did what needed be done. The tundra-witch's little stunt, awakening your latent *wyrria* with brute force, would have torn you apart." Khorel Jornath's accented baritone echoed through the vaulted space. "So I arrested your *wyrria*. For a time."

"And yet, your Brethren seem impressed that I managed to last seven days."

"You are formidable, General." Jornath gave a soft smile, containing little of his domineering persona, all things considered. "With a bit of training, you might become one of our best. A Sage, perhaps. Even a High Master."

"Recruiting me into your Order?"

"We'll see." Jornath said it without any intrigue; it was simply a statement, as if the man actually was thinking about recruiting Theroun into the Kreth-Hakir. Those simple words shook Theroun more than anything else the man could have said. Jornath beckoned, indicating a chair to his right. "Come, sit. Eat. Before you fall over."

Theroun saw a plate and chalice before the chair, with ample food upon the table. It was a negotiation tactic, but his stomach gurgled, ravenous, his limbs trembling from too many days without sustenance. Theroun moved forward at a brisk clip, hauled out the chair and sat decisively, without removing his eyes from Jornath. The leader of the Kreth-Hakir took up Theroun's plate and served him a sizable portion of roast guinea-fowl, a vine of grapes and a portion of wine-roasted pears. Pickled beet chutney went over the fowl before he set it in front of Theroun. Pouring a long measure of red wine from a ceramic pitcher, Jornath removed his rings before tasting it, then set it near Theroun's hand in an oddly Cennetian gesture of peacemaking.

"Please." Jornath spoke with a genial smile. "You have my word that nothing is tainted."

"Your word?" Theroun growled. "Does the word of Kreth-Hakir stand for much?"

All smile dropped from Jornath's eyes. "The word of a Kreth-Hakir is his *everything*."

Something about the way it was said pulled Theroun up short. He believed the man. What's more, he felt no mucking about in his brain other than the silver weave Jornath had created earlier, which was quiet.

"You let General Merra and her contingent go," Theroun spoke, intrigued. "Why?"

"Because I gave you my word." Jornath's eyes were level, their intensity a match to Theroun's. "If you could best me in single combat, she and her fighters would be preserved. And they were."

"Yet I ended up with a boot in my face, cast into chains," Theroun gave a hard-humor smile. "Do you count that a win from our duel?"

"I do." Jornath's gaze searched Theroun's. "Thrice you and I have faced each other. And thrice, you managed to surprise me – once very nearly fatal to me, once nearly fatal to everyone in your vicinity. You do not know what you are, do you, Black Viper?"

"I am what I have trained to be," Theroun spoke. "A General of war. Nothing more."

"And yet, you *are* so much more." Jornath nodded to Theroun's plate. "You see yourself as a meal of but a single crumb. I see you as a meal of endless bounty."

"Not a very good metaphor."

"Quite the opposite," Jornath reached out and took a sip of his wine. "A very good metaphor, I'm afraid. For you see, we are all a meal, to our Beast."

"Beast?" Theroun shifted. Something about that word made the disturbance within Theroun roil as if restless. His guts gripped in a brief spasm, and he felt it flicker through his face before he controlled his visage.

Jornath leaned in, searching Theroun's eyes. "Long ago, when the first ancients walked this land, *wyrria* was called the Beast. An immense power that once raged wild in the very earth itself, and everything upon it. Due to a restriction a thousand years ago, few men feel the strange call of their *wyrria* these days. Fewer still, hold it latent, slumbering in their body but never awakened, though sometimes used on instinct. Very few indeed, survive the sudden waking of a powerful *wyrria* late in life – but you did. Your natural *wyrria*, once latent but now awoken because of what that tundra-witch did, has been raging for seven whole days. Lesser men would have died in the first minute of such torment, especially with a *wyrria* as vast as yours. I let you suffer its wrath not because I was curious how long you would last, but because the First Rite of Proving among our Order requires it. For the practitioner to be left alone to manage his *wyrria* or die after it has been awakened, for the duration of three days."

"You put me through some ungodly Kreth-Hakir rite of passage?" Theroun crossed his arms.

"Our first level of testing, yes." Jornath gave a quiet laugh. "To those who are suddenly awakened to a latent *wyrria*, we give this test. Those who are born with their *wyrria* awake receive other challenges to gain the Path of Initiate. I did not start you on our Path, Theroun. The tundra-witch knew nothing of what she was doing, and yet, she was successful at giving you a Kreth-Hakir Initiation all the same. For which, I must give her credit."

"Adelaine withstood nine of your Brethren for three weeks," Theroun snarled, "and kept our Queen and King from your clutches. Perhaps she deserves more credit than you think."

Jornath sat back, his gaze veiled. He swirled his wine goblet in one hand with his fingers upon the rim. "You care for the woman?"

"Not at all," Theroun returned. "She's a bitch. But she's a powerful bitch, and that I can respect."

"As can I," Jornath responded. "But the tenets of my faith cannot suffer an Outsider with such talents as ours to live. She will be killed, General. And before she is, I will focus my Brethren and break her for the information I need."

"No less would I expect." Theroun took a sip of his wine.

"You're not going to bargain for her life?"

"I am your captive. What position am I in to bargain with?" Theroun retorted. "Your silver net is already in my body. I'm sure you can do whatever you want with it, including killing me."

Jornath waved one hand dismissively. "The net will merely contain your *wyrria*. For a time. It will fail eventually, and I hope to have you ready before it does."

"Ready for what?"

"Ready for the pain to return. Ready to make a choice as to what you want to do with your *wyrric* blessing." Jornath set his goblet down. Theroun hated that the man watched him so carefully, for he saw Jornath note the quail of fear that flashed through Theroun before he squelched it.

"Everyone fears their Beast," Jornath murmured, as if consoling. "People do not fear how small and wretched they can be. Only how tremendous they can become."

"Platitudes?"

"Fact." Jornath swirled his wine, eyeing Theroun. "What would you be, General? If you could not only take the name Black Viper, but if you could *be* that? What if it is not merely a title, but an energy that lives within you – an energy of true purpose? Something that breathes, that *writhes* with *wyrria*, trying to escape from your very flesh and sinew? What if it could be awoken, trained, harnessed to your conscious will? What then?"

Something roiled inside Theroun. As Khorel Jornath spoke, that black energy within the silver net rippled, trying to fight its way free. Even as Theroun pondered the Kreth-Hakir's words, he felt a silver thread within his mind snap.

And then another.

"I can feel it, Theroun," Jornath leaned forward, "fighting my weave. You have been given something only the highest echelons of Kreth-Hakir Brethren ever hope to receive; an Initiation which awakens the deepest nature. For our everyday selves are but shells for that which lies within. Even the talents of many who hold *wyrria* cannot match the full force of the sleeping leviathan that fights to get out of you now, awake and aware. It has a form, Theroun, and it has a need. It will tear you apart to get what it needs."

Theroun let out a slow breath. He could feel the truth of Jornath's every word. The enormous force within him fought, sliced, stung. More silvered threads snapped to its raging. "I'm not Alrashemni. I don't have *wyrria*."

"Delude yourself like that, dear General, and you will soon have no *life*." Jornath's smile was gone. "You may not be Alrashemni, but you have a *wyrric* talent stronger than any I've seen in a god's age. You have a *wyrria* to match the Scions of the Wolf and Dragon. But yours—"

Jornath ceased speaking suddenly. A tiny smile held the corners of his lips. He pushed his bulk to standing, and Theroun pushed back his chair and rose also – though for what, he didn't rightly know. Jornath towered a head higher than Theroun. As he stepped closer, Theroun was forced to look up to meet the man's gaze. Stepping into Theroun's personal space, the man halted. Lifting a hand, he settled it to Theroun's shoulder. His hand was solid, but with a lightness that spoke of dynamic strength.

"I will not press you, Theroun, to take up our mantle," Jornath's words were almost kind. "But I can tell you that within my Order are the only people who can save you from the force that fights inside you. For thousands of years, we have honed ourselves to survive the venom of our own will. Until *we* control our *wyrria*, not the other way around, and from it, we harness power. A power greater than any mortal man. You have two choices – embrace the venom and learn our ways, to control it – or succumb."

Theroun shivered. He shrugged off Jornath's hand, and the man let him go. "I will never become one of you. No matter what salvation you promise."

Jornath's eyes faded to a sorrowful place. "That's what I said, too, once, when my latent *wyrria* was awoken. By the touch of a man with fire in his veins, the hand of our God, Leith Alodwine. I was just seventeen at the time. Leith seized my wrist when I tried to slip a ruby ring from his finger during a distraction my urchin friends had concocted…" Jornath's smile was wry. "Destiny comes when it comes. Embrace yours. Only the Brethren could save me then, and only the Brethren can save you now. Learn what we have to teach. Become so much more than a mere mortal."

Uncertainty roiled within Theroun. He knew he could never take such an offer, and yet. "You met your god in the flesh?"

"Our god was only a man." Jornath's smile was mysterious. "We revere Leith Alodwine because of everything he brought into being, and everything he came to be."

With that, Jornath stepped backward, giving Theroun space. "I have duties to attend. Please, enjoy your meal. When you are finished, Brethren will escort you to new rooms, for a bath and a bed. You hold status as Initiate among us now. One who has awakened Scorpion-*wyrria* but has no formal training. One who shall be treated with respect until his decision is made to join us."

"No more shackles?" Theroun lifted an eyebrow.

"You may escape if you like, General." Jornath's lips twisted into cleverness. "But know that wherever you go, I go. That silver weave in your body remains, until your *wyrria* shreds it to nothingness. And when that happens… I doubt you'll be running much longer."

"How long do I have?" Theroun felt the pain just on the other side of Jornath's silver web – how dark it could be.

"Not as much time as you would like." Jornath's eyes lost their humor. "Not with a *wyrria* suddenly woken so strong within you, with no markings or bindings to contain it."

"What is it?" Theroun asked, needing to know. "Scorpion-*wyrria?*"

"It is the essence of willpower." Jornath's gaze was frank. "That force of mind and matter that can turn the universe to your own intentions, to the power of your focus and intent in the world. It is the very manifestation of your will. In every way."

"What can a man do with it?"

"Whatever he wills," Jornath's eyes were uncompromising in their intention and strength. "If he wills it hard enough, and with enough impeccable focus."

"And my will?" Theroun took a breath. "Why is it trying to tear me apart?"

Jornath's eyes became sad, penetrating. "Only your own will knows why it is trying to kill you. Why, in the deepest part of your essence, you do not wish to live. Why the sting of the scorpion and the strike of the viper's poison are taking you down from the inside. I might have said your *wyrria* was Wolf and Dragon, so deep does conflict writhe within you, except that I know the flavor of the Scorpion's poison. Have a meal while you can, Theroun. Build your strength. For your darkest battle is not far ahead, I'm afraid."

With that, Khorel Jornath turned on his heel and strode from the room to shadowed halls beyond. The doors shut with a low boom and Theroun was left alone in the white hall, pondering all that had been said. He could feel the enormous power of his *wyrria*, stretching, trying to find the weaknesses of its prison. He felt a few more silver threads break – snap, snap, snap.

Without a word, Theroun sat back down at the table. He began to eat, his mind racing through strategy after strategy.

Only to find that against this foe, he knew nothing.

CHAPTER 13 – KHOUREN

Khouren stood at the edge of the shanty-camp inside the deep pre-dawn shadows of the First Tier. Blending into the darkness, he'd lingered there most of the night. Facing the black portcullis of the Watercourse Gate, he stared at the dim line of the Elhambria grasslands, just beginning to brighten in the quiet autumn chill. Dawn suffused the eastern peaks of the Eleskis with an amber glow, wispy clouds moving through the rose sky.

Guardsmen in cobalt moved about the quiet gate, extinguishing the night's torches and hailing each other with sleepy grumbles and quiet jests. Five hundred paces distant, the waving grasslands beckoned. Rousing himself, Khouren shifted, ready to step forward. Away from the shantytown and through that yawning portal, into the vastness beyond. He'd lived out in the world before. It wasn't so far to the gate.

As Khouren tried to twitch a foot forward, however, weakness overcame him. A sliding feeling like he was falling into deep water. Drowning. Choking. Breathless, Khouren collapsed to his knees. Head hanging, he fought for air as his vision tunneled. Closing his eyes, he fought for calm.

At last, the vertigo passed. Opening his eyes, he saw more light lifting the sky. True dawn had arrived, and as Khouren mused upon its hateful loveliness, he heard a quiet figure step to his side. Looking over, he was not surprised to see Ihbram gazing at him with a savvy frown. Khouren's uncle hunkered, nodding his trim russet beard at Khouren.

"Need the vial?"

"No."

"How many hours have you been doing this?" Ihbram gazed at the gate.

"Too many." Despair filled Khouren as he stared despondently at the grasslands. "I have to go to Elsthemen, Ihbram. The true

Rennkavi – I have to find him."

"You're not getting far, *ghendii*," Ihbram snorted. "It takes time to conquer battle-panic as bad as you've got. I've seen it before: it cripples men. Takes them years to recover, if ever."

"I don't have years." Khouren's tone was dead, though deep inside, a tumbling wrath of emotions flooded him. He rose to his feet and seized his uncle by the jerkin, abrupt. "I have to get to Elohl. Don't you understand? If I don't, than I have to follow—"

"Lhaurent." Ihbram's words were soft. "I know."

"I can't do it, Ihbram!" Khouren gasped, giving in suddenly to the torture that flooded him. "Shaper!"

Khouren hadn't felt such twisting agony in decades. It wasn't like him to have strong emotions, but this desperation was so terrible it made him shudder. The conflict of the Alodwine *wyrric* bloodline rose in him, and he felt it again – just as strong as it had been a hundred years ago, when he'd left the world behind to crawl into the darkness and try to live the deadened life of a Ghost. Fire seared his gut as he sank to his knees in the packed dirt, staring listlessly at the gate. Raging, yet empty inside as fire burned up all his emotion and left purposelessness in its place.

In that despondency, he could suddenly feel his uncle's presence. Solid, steady at his side. They hunkered together, for a long moment.

"Maybe we can get you past this," Ihbram spoke at last, his voice surprisingly absent of scorn.

"You mean just drag me through the gate?" Khouren's voice was cold with self-loathing. "You tried that already."

"No, I mean rehabilitate you, *ghendii*." Ihbram spoke, patient.

"Why would you help me?" Khouren spoke to his uncle, despairing. "Take your missions and your potions and go find the Kreth-Hakir, Ihbram. Go be the hero grandfather always wanted out of you. I'll find my way."

Ihbram gave a tired sigh. Khouren saw his uncle take out a faded charcoal wrap of the fine weave silks that only came from the far southeast, running the charcoal silk through his hands. A *shouf* just like the gift from Fentleith that Khouren had bound his grandfather's wounds with when they had parted ways.

"Come on, *ghendii*," Ihbram stood, tucking the swath of silk away and motioning with his chin for Khouren. "How about a drink? It's not too early for a good shit-facing. I'd say we both need it."

"Why are you doing this?" Khouren paused. "Playing like you give a damn?"

Ihbram put his hands on his hips and scuffed the dirt with one worn boot, his russet brows knit in the rising light. "Because I believe in second chances, Khouren. Fentleith wasn't always the man he is now. Once he was an unholy terror, before he learned how to control his *wyrria*. I remember those days, but he and I reconciled after I cracked his mind open once and saw what was in there. He's a storm, Khouren. Of all of our clan, his magic is the closest to tales of Leith – a true madness of rage and conflict. Fentleith always persevered with you and your troubles because he saw himself in you. Of all us surviving Alodwines, you are the only one with ability to match Fentleith's, and he still believes in you, that you can be better then your past. Lenuria believed it, too, Shaper rest her soul. So I'm giving you a chance to make us believe, Khouren – that you can be a better man."

Still in his crouch, Khouren breathed out in the wakening morning. Something trembled within him to hear his uncle's words – as if hope was a palpable thing, he felt it shiver across his skin on the fresh wind. With it came an ocean of doubt, threatening to swallow him as he gazed at the black gates of the city.

"Choose, Khouren," Ihbram's voice cut the rising morning. "Now's the time. Stand up and be a better man. Or grovel like a cur and crawl back to your master's shithole. Forever."

A tremor rocked Khouren, as if a bell had been struck inside his soul. Something rose inside him as he realized his moment, a dark leviathan with edges of flame. It came with power, a devouring belief that some things were wrong and some were right. A furious knowing, that Khouren's life had purpose – that it hadn't ended when he'd left Lhaurent. As that burning darkness rose in Khouren, like a shroud of ghosts aflame in the scarlet morning, he suddenly felt strength.

Knowing that no matter how he ruined his life, there was still something he had yet to do. Some purpose he had yet to fulfill.

With a slow breath, Khouren rose to his feet. Standing strong, he gazed at the black jaws of the portcullis without trembling. "Lead the way, then. Show me the path to becoming a better man."

He would have thought Ihbram would chastise him again for being a zealot, but it wasn't so. Ihbram led and Khouren followed as they moved up the soot-charred avenue into the city. Meandering in silence, the Scions of Alodwine moved like shadows in the waking day. People had begun to stir from hovels and rubble, and an impromptu trade market had begun in the broad plaza before the First Abbey. The Jenners had their gates open this morning, as they did for a brief period every morning, distributing autumn vegetables and fruits from their gardens to the hollow-eyed throng. Their ban on ale still held. Khouren saw no wains or barrels among the charity they distributed. Eagle-eyed Brothers and Palace Guardsmen gazed down from the walls, hoods up. By the way they stood, Khouren knew they had bows, invisible below the ramparts. The Jenners and defected Guardsmen didn't like this new city under rule of Lhaurent, and Khouren didn't blame them.

At last, Khouren and Ihbram came into a wealthier section of the Abbey Quarter, towering bluestone buildings only slightly blackened from the fires. Ihbram nodded at a tavern and they mounted the bluestone steps and pushed inside. It was crowded despite the early morning, smelling of stew and vinegar, the sharp-sour tang barely masked a heavy reek of sweat and char.

They pushed inside, ignoring casual glances. Khouren eyed his uncle's worn Brigadier garb, then his own roughsilk greys. The both of them were filthy with soot, but no one in the tavern seemed to give two coins; indeed, they were cleaner than most of the patrons in this dim shithole. It had probably been a nice tavern once, but it was filled with filthy customers now, the floor strewn with straw to try and soak up the tracked-in soot, the straw littered with hulls of bitel nuts. Barmaids moved quickly through the tables with hard scowls and trenchers of stew and eggs, demanding coin before they placed down a plate. As Ihbram and Khouren settled at the chipped ironwood bar, Ihbram pulled out a beaten leather purse from an inner breast pocket of his jerkin and immediately tossed down two five-rou coins, far more than they needed to get a drink. The greasy proprietor barely glanced their way, coming over and swiping it off the table and replacing the coins with two pewter tankards of thin, odiferous ale.

"That's the lot." The man grumbled, wiping pudgy hands on his filthy apron. "Show me more coin and get another round."

"Steep." Ihbram grumbled as the man whisked away. "Fucker's charging five times what his piss-poor home-brew is worth."

"It's the best a man can get in the city right now," Khouren commented mildly, "with the First Abbey boycotting Lhaurent's takeover and trade stalled on every front due to war."

"So I noticed. Ale's been shit everyplace I've tried. Not a trace of mellon-blume wine or a nice spicy Yegovian cider in sight." Ihbram took a swallow of his brew, grimaced, then drank a number of swallows with stolid determination.

Khouren contemplated his flagon; tipped it back. It was Aeon-awful, like a rotten potato mixed with sour peaches and the musk of fish. He gagged, then drank the entire thing off fast like his uncle. Ihbram threw more money on the counter and the barman returned, eyeing them before swiping the coins away and replacing it with another round of horrid drinks.

Which weren't as bad, now that Khouren's tongue was numb.

"You need a bath, *ghendii*," Ihbram snorted over his flagon as they finished up the second round and went for a third.

"So do you." Khouren retorted sourly, already drunk and not giving a shit. His lips were tingling nicely, his head flush with a good buzz. It was the first time he'd had a drink in recent memory, seldom having imbibed while in Lhaurent's service. "How's your drink?"

"Not as good as sex," Ihbram scowled at his brew, but sipped again anyway.

"Apparently." The vapors of Khouren's ale wafted up his nose and he coughed.

"How long has it been since you've gotten laid, Khouren? Since this woman Lhaurent killed?" Ihbram's gaze was drunk but keen in the filthy translucence from the grimy windows.

"Not your business." Khouren drained his ale and signaled the barkeep. The man arrived with another tankard, palming perspiration from his brown hair. Khouren mimicked the gesture, unconsciously. His black curls were longer: even in braids, they touched his shoulders, longer than he would have allowed at Roushenn, but life was different now. Khouren brushed sweat from a stubble he'd not realized he'd grown.

"Why are you in the city?" The question left Khouren's lips suddenly. "What was it that you needed to talk to Lenuria about?"

"I have news of Kreth-Hakir movements," Ihbram's gaze pierced him. "And I wanted to know if she'd seen Fentleith recently."

"Can't you mind-track grandfather?"

"Not lately," Ihbram's gaze slipped to the grimy windows. "Fentleith's *wyrric* imprint dropped out of my mind near Highsummer. He's gone off my mind-sight before, but never this long."

Khouren cocked his head, his interest piqued. "You said you're hunting Kreth-Hakir? How? Can't they break you?"

"Not the lesser Brethren, not anymore." Ihbram gave Khouren a sidelong gaze.

"Your powers have grown."

"Indeed," Ihbram nodded. "I first felt them jump forty years ago, when your bastard Rennkavi Lhaurent was Goldenmarked. Fentleith's abilities got stronger, too, then. Harder to control. Since this summer, my abilities jumped far higher. Triple what they were, maybe more."

"You decided to try them out," Khouren leaned forward, intrigued. "You killed one of the Kreth-Hakir, didn't you?"

"I killed four. Just a few weeks ago." Ihbram gave a hard smile, his green eyes glinting with pride. "After my duties in the High Brigade were up, I tracked of a party of Hakir near the Elsee. That's when I felt my abilities jump one night. So I said, *the fuck with tracking, let's try some action.* I captured them one-by-one, prevented them from communicating back to the group. Kept my mind nice and hale while I slit their ever-loving throats. I mind-fucked the last one for information. He told me their Brethren were forming a pact with the Castellan. So I came here. They're here, aren't they? In the city."

"Some are. But a handful went north with the military," Khouren confirmed. "The strongest ones, including their High Priest, went to the Elsthemi war front, but that was months ago. They were supposed to break the minds of the keshari riders, to rout Elsthemen's forces. They've done so. Lhaurent boasted of his sovereignty three weeks ago; that Lhen Fhekran had fallen, but he said nothing of the Elsthemi King, nor of Queen Elyasin."

"I heard as much these past two days in the city," Ihbram murmured. "So Queen Elyasin may have escaped Lhaurent's coils. And what about a tall Hakir with dark grey eyes, who rides a black scorpion?" Ihbram's green eyes were piercing.

"Khorel Jornath." Khouren's gaze met Ihbram's. "He's the High Priest with the Brethren. He went with the main army to Elsthemen."

Ihbram's scowl was ruthless. "He was the one who broke the Kingskinder ten years ago. I've tracked him a few times, but he's slippery. Strong. You say he's up north?"

"Search my mind if you have to," Khouren spoke. "I'm not lying."

Ihbram cocked his head, but Khouren didn't feel any search through his mind. Though his uncle's knit brows told him that Ihbram knew Khouren wasn't telling Aeon's honest truth. "What are you hiding, *ghendii*? There's something you don't want to tell me that you're putting off. I can feel it rattling around in that mind of yours. Something big. Spill it."

Khouren shifted on his barstool, but knew he had to speak. If he didn't, Ihbram would simply invade his mind and find out what he was hiding, and it would be far worse between them. Even so, Khouren didn't imagine his uncle was going to take this news well. Vapors curled through the rank air from the grimy sunlight heating up the day outside. Patronage in the bar was clearing out as city-workers finished their breakfasts and left. Only a few people lingered, playing a hand of cards in carven wooden booths or drinking listlessly at the bar in besmirched finery. Two Guardsmen in clean cobalt jerkins pushed in and hailed the bartender with coin. They gave Khouren and Ihbram a casual but searching glance as they leaned at the bar, before their attention was drawn by an aging oube-player beginning to tune his stringed gourd in one corner for a morning diversion.

Khouren looked away, back to his ale. He drew a deep breath, then spoke. "Lhaurent's machinations at Highsummer got grandfather hurt. Badly."

"Fentleith—!" Ihbram exclaimed, one hand flashing toward his longknife.

"Is recovered." Khouren spoke quickly, not missing his uncle's deadly gesture. "He went north with the Queen's party at Highsummer, protecting her and the Rennkavi, Elohl den'Alrahel."

Ihbram's eyes narrowed. Khouren felt his uncle's touch sear through his mind; like fingers of fire, they charred through Khouren's skull more deftly and painfully than Khouren remembered his uncle's *wyrria*. The invasion churned Khouren's stomach, and his ale threatened to rise. He fought retching as images of his and Fentleith's battle with the Khets al'Roch surfaced. Then Fentleith's dire injury. Then Khouren running him through the bowels of Roushenn to Leith's ancient talisman, and slapping Fentleith's bloody hand to that cursed object.

"See everything you needed?" Khouren gasped. The searing lines exited Khouren's mind, and he glanced up, to find Ihbram furious with shivering tension.

"I should *kill* you! Putting Fentleith's hand upon Leith's talisman! Feeding it Alodwine blood!" Ihbram's eyes flashed with golden Alodwine fire. "Fentleith should have killed you long ago, whelp, for all the destruction you cause with your bad and worse decisions."

"Fentleith was dying!" Khouren retorted in anger, not backing down. "Putting Fentleith's hand on Leith's talisman at the center of Roushenn saved him! I should have done the same with Lenuria, but I didn't have time."

"You exposed Fentleith to Leith's *wyrria*! And you would have done it to your own half-sister?" Ihbram's tone was scalding. His eyes flashed fire. "You let the tyrant's magic touch him, Khouren! *How could you?* You know what Fentleith is capable of! You know that his careful and hard-won control is all he has from becoming a monster!"

"It was the only way to keep him alive," Khouren protested.

"No. It was the way you *chose*." Ihbram's voice pounded Khouren like the hammer upon the blade. "Just like all the choices you've made in your despicable life. It was a good thing you had Lenuria to defend you over the years, because I don't think anyone else could. Not with the evil you've created in your zealous righteousness."

His uncle's words struck Khouren like a blow, the realization that he might be evil. And just like that, Khouren snapped. His longknife was out of its sheath fast – pressed to Ihbram's throat even faster. "I'm no zealot!"

Ihbram didn't flinch. Just stared Khouren down with his furious green eyes in the grimy sunlight. The Guardsmen at the end of the bar perked, watching their argument intently, hands off their ales and upon their longknives. Like two hawks, they began to advance. Ihbram's gaze pierced Khouren, asking Khouren what he was going to do.

With a growl of anguish, Khouren put away his knife. If he wasn't going to use it, it was just an empty threat, and making such a threat in broad daylight in front of two Palace Guardsmen was worse than stupid. As soon as his knife disappeared, the Guardsmen eased, but they still approached, their eyes flicking between Ihbram and Khouren.

"Problem here, Brigadier?" One of them spoke, aiming his question at Ihbram.

"No." Ihbram was still looking at Khouren. "Just a spat with my nephew. It's nothing."

With his mind-sight, Khouren was vaguely aware of strings of red fire easing out from his uncle's lips. They lanced in through the ears of the two Guardsmen, and Khouren saw both startle as if they'd been bit by ants. They looked confused, then gave twin smiles.

"Well, then," the one spoke again. "I suppose it's nothing."

Deep under the influence of Ihbram's mind-*wyrria*, they turned and strode out of the bar without so much as finishing their ale. The barkeep claimed the abandoned tankards and drained them into a wooden bucket, no doubt to serve later. Khouren stared at his uncle, fear driving into his heart for the first time around Ihbram.

"That's new," Khouren spoke, shakily, both from rage and astonishment.

"Be glad I don't puppet you around," Ihbram growled. "Though perhaps I should. Might save us all from your inanity."

Khouren lifted his ale, taking a deep swig. He needed to be drunk, rather than feel his heart eating through his chest from fear and tumult. A tense silence settled between the two Scions of Alodwine in the grimy bar. They watched each other, the renegade and the sneak-thief, blood and mistrust thick as tar between them. Few patrons came and went now, the clinking of tankards and the murmur of tired men occupying the morning. Khouren held their standoff, feeling sweat trickle into his stubble as his own conflict twisted deep inside him, ready to be unleashed. Swirling like a vortex, a movement of dark power and horrible depth.

A grin cracked the edges of Ihbram's lips at last. "You've unleashed all of Halsos' hells, *ghendii*, you know that?"

"How so?" Khouren frowned.

"I can feel it." Ihbram leaned in, his gaze intense. "All around me. This whole place – Halsos, I felt it ten leagues out, before I even saw the city's walls on the horizon. What you did – allowing that artifact of Leith's to drink Fentleith's blood – it woke the bowels of hell. My skin has been crawling with *wyrria* from the moment I stepped foot inside the city. You woke the beast, Khouren. And the beast has fangs."

Khouren was quiet, feeling his way through this revelation. He didn't need to think about it. He knew. Ever since that moment, he'd been able to feel it. The press and power of *wyrria* in his ears at night. The feel of it, rippling across his skin as he moved through a wall. The entire city of Lintesh was breathing down his neck at every turn, breathing with *wyrric* power. It was a fountainhead, partly unleashed by what Khouren had done.

"It's like a dragon," Khouren spoke softly, "breathing down my neck. Making my skin crawl. I can't even count how many times I've fallen through the streets unintentionally in the past three weeks, Ihbram. I can't focus. The power – it's waking…"

Ihbram gave a slow nod, then let out a breath through pursed lips. "You woke a demon, Khouren. Even if it's only partially awake, it's enough to wreck havoc through those who know how to use it. Fentleith always told us that Leith trapped all *wyrria* inside the earth for his own vile control, but what I feel right now – it's like lightning burning over my skin, Khouren. If it's like this for us, then other *wyrrics* must be able to feel it, too. And if it makes our power jump, then Lhaurent and the Kreth-Hakir are far more dangerous while here in Lintesh than even Fentleith could imagine. The marking of the Rennkavis was a small opening of power compared to this. This… this is big. And Lhaurent's made his home right smack in the middle of it, drinking it in, every damn day."

"It's worse than you know, Ihbram. Lhaurent has Leith's ring."

Khouren wiped a hand over his face, feeling tears prickle in his eyes, despairing.

"*What?!*" Ihbram's eyes had bled to hot green-gold fire, his lips fallen open and his ale paused mid-drink.

"I gave it to him," Khouren continued, his heart twisting. "A while back. I took it from Leith's hiding-spot and gave it to Lhaurent, when I first saw his Goldenmarks decades ago. He's got Leith's ring and he's harnessing the *wyrria* opening in the city. Learning to use it, to control the dome, to view far. A part of me has been waiting these past weeks in terror, wondering if he'd use it to hunt me down. I stole artifacts from him, and documents, back when I left his service. Took them to Temlin den'Ildrian of the Jenners, who has been nominated King-Protectorate against Lhaurent. Among them were tomes that state Lhaurent's legitimacy as a den'Alrahel King. But what if… what if Lhaurent can feel where they went, can see them? Can track them now that the city is awake, with *wyrria* that he's learning to wield?"

Ihbram let out a slow whistle, his gaze incredulous. "You sentenced the whole damn First Abbey to death, *ghendii*."

Khouren's eyes were wide. His breath clenched into tight sips; his vision tunneled. But suddenly, he felt Ihbram slide off his barstool, hauling Khouren into a strong embrace. Khouren's breath eased. The feeling of touch, of family, overwhelmed him, and he was able to draw breath. Pulling back, Ihbram rested their foreheads together for a long moment. Calm eased into Khouren's mind. A slow fire, a feeling of safety and solidarity, emanating from Ihbram's *wyrria*.

"We have to fix this," Ihbram murmured.

"How?" Khouren choked.

With a hard breath, Ihbram stepped back. Picking up his flagon and tossing its contents back, he set it to the chipped ironwood bar. Taking up his pack from the barstool beside him, Ihbram gestured to the door, masking his former revelations. "Come on. Time to get to the Abbey. We need to tell them they're in danger."

Together, they stumbled out into the dirty sunshine. The Abbey Quarter was abustle, though cool breaths of autumn curled the streets. Khouren's mind was in tumult as they traversed the dusty avenue, hardly aware of his surroundings in the bright day. As they crossed a fountain-plaza, he suddenly felt his senses tingle, and saw Ihbram give a quick glance back over his shoulder.

"We're being followed." Ihbram deftly loosened the straps of his pack as he slipped longknives into his hands, hiding them along his body as he paced toward an alley. "Six men. Ready?"

Khouren's knives were already in his hands when Ihbram ducked into the alley. The suddenness of an oncoming fight banished Khouren's worry and drunkenness. Khouren was fast on his uncle's heels as they played into the thugs' hands. As anticipated, the thieves spanned the alley mouth, leaving no exit, the alley's end blocked by a tumble of stone from a toppled mansion and stacks of empty crates. As Ihbram slung down his belongings and he and Khouren turned with knives at the ready, they saw the coarse thugs grin.

Until the Scions of Alodwine dropped into fighting crouches.

"Stand firm." A smooth voice rippled the air. A lean fellow in black herringbone leathers moved out from the shadows. His black mane was braided back at the crown, the sides shaved like the Unaligned north-sea pirates wore, tattooed with stark white inkings. A ravaged scar lifted the corner of his lip, giving him a sneer.

State your business in the city. The command sliced Khouren's mind like a silver knife. He was already opening his mouth, when Ihbram's hand stopped him. In his mind-sight, Khouren saw a net of red fire sweep out from his uncle, swatting the silvered command of the Kreth-Hakir away.

"Our business is none of yours," Ihbram grinned, his green eyes cold.

The Kreth-Hakir's eyes went wide that his mind-command had been so easily rebuffed. A ferocious scowl knit his black brows. Khouren felt the man's next command hit him like a charging bull. Khouren stumbled to one knee in pain, barely able to hold onto his weapons. But Ihbram withstood that gale, though he jolted – his eyes flashing green-gold fire. "My turn."

To Khouren, it only looked as if his uncle pivoted, stepping swiftly toward the Kreth-Hakir. But that movement held a hard wave of burning power that surged out from Ihbram, slamming into the Hakir brother. The man cried out, stumbling. Blood gushed from his

187

nose as if he'd been punched in the face. In that moment, Ihbram rushed in, gutting the man one-two with his blades.

Khouren wasted no time. He was up, spinning into the mercenaries in a liquid dance. Slicing throats, stabbing eyes, rolling and cutting hamstrings, disembowling. The fight lasted ten seconds, and the final two mercenaries ran, piss darkening their trousers. Khouren stood, breathing smoothly, letting them go. Ihbram stepped aside, wiping his knives on a bale of straw.

"Cunt." Ihbram kicked the fallen Kreth-Hakir. Blood spurted from Ihbram's finishing slice to the man's carotid artery, as the man's eyes dimmed out.

"We need to move." Khouren glanced to the avenue as he wiped his blades on the bale and slid them away. "The others will have felt that. This way."

Khouren took off toward the blocked end of the alley, Ihbram swiping up his pack and fast on his heels. As Khouren stepped to the blockade of stones and crates, he held out his hand. Ihbram knew the drill, and grasped it tight. Khouren took a breath, letting his body relax from the tension he always held, that kept him from falling through structures. And like a sluice of water, he breathed into oneness with the stone and wood, pulling his uncle through behind him.

Together, they poured through the walls of the city like water through a sieve. Upsetting a weaver at her loom, making a cat hiss in a larder, passing through heaps of burned-out rubble. With one final dart across the avenue that ringed the First Abbey, Khouren led his uncle through the Abbey wall, emerging at a stone bench near the ponds in a copse of sighing willows.

"*Imendhe nethii hakkane!*" Ihbram cussed, ducking behind the thick branches of the willows. "Someone's going to see us standing here with our thumbs up our assholes! Dammit, haven't you ever heard of using a front door?"

"We need to get to a basement," Khouren bit back, feeling out with his *wyrria* for sub-basements or larders and finding nothing but earth and solid rock nearby. "Somewhere we can hide until we make our presence known to the King-Protectorate."

"Fine. Fuck it. I'll camouflage us as much as I can." Ihbram exhaled, his eyes void of drink now and sharp with concentration.

Peering through trailing branches, Khouren saw that monks, cobalt-clad Palace Guardsmen, and Kingsmen in ancient battle-Greys came and went upon the gravel paths in the bright morning. Before they were noticed, Khouren saw in his mind-sight a shimmering red-gold net blossom from his uncle's body, knitting around them both. Khouren's brows rose, impressed. Ihbram had been able to camouflage himself before, but never two people.

"That's also new," Khouren marveled, reaching out a hand to touch the shimmering mind-strings that wreathed him in the willow-bower.

"Don't fuck with it," Ihbram admonished as he took the lead out of the greenery. "Let's move."

CHAPTER 14 – ELESHEN

The Rare Tomes Room below the Abbey Annex was a delight for any scholar, but Eleshen had no time to explore it. Tall stacks of carefully-catalogued tomes and scrolls loomed around her in the shadowed vaults as she hastily packed items into crates atop one stout cendarie table. Full of arcane writings and genealogies, herbal compendiums and collections of ancient lore, the Rare Tomes Room was a treasure-trove. Placed in charge of the Abbey's emptying and relocation to Gerrov-Tel, Eleshen had put everyone to task in a diabolical schedule, and hadn't had a moment to read even a single word of the knowledge contained here.

Up all night, busy all day, Eleshen directed her army of Jenners and Kingsmen from sunup to sundown. Collecting books from the libraries, rounding up supplies and necessities. Harvesting everything that could be harvested and breaking down brewing equipment. Shuttling it all and everyone who could be spared through Mollia's Abbeystone to the ruined fortress of Gerrov-Tel in the northern Kingsmountains.

And though the avenues of the First Abbey were abustle above, it was all silence and seeping shadows down here. Only a few lamps were lit in the sconces, causing Eleshen to nearly blend into the shadows in her new Kingsman Greys. No hands were available to help her right now in the late morning, everyone using the daylight to harvest as much as possible from the gardens for transport. Eleshen found she enjoyed the quietude, though. Keeping an inn for so long by herself in the Kingsmountains had adjusted her to being alone, and it gave her time to think.

About everything that had happened these past few months. About how she had changed. Pausing as she set a leather-bound volume into the crate, she lifted her hand. Gazing at her pale skin, seeing blue veins beneath her long, slender fingers. Rubbing her fingertips together, it was almost as if she could feel a buzzing sensation in them, like some strange energy poured through her now – something more than excitement; more than alertness.

Suddenly, she felt a breath of wind stir the catacomb. The hard thump of boots hitting stone came, as if two someones had fallen from the ceiling. Every hair upon Eleshen's body was instantly alert. Dressed in her Kingsman garb, she shifted immediately into the deep shadows behind a stout cendarie stack, both longknives from her belt drawn. Crouched in a fighter's stance, she waited. Invisible, ready. Waves of thrilling energy poured through her – eager for a fight, to battle whatever intruder had surprised her.

She held it in check. It wouldn't do to accidentally skewer a Jenner monk who was here to help her – though how anyone could have fallen from a ceiling of solid stone was unfathomable. The smooth voices beyond the sconce-lights at the end of the stack were not anyone she knew.

"No one's here. Let's move." A medium baritone spoke, smooth like ghosts on a dark wind.

"Dammit, Khouren! You could have warned me we were going to drop thirty feet!" A man's tenor voice held a rough growl, but also a laugh of humor in it.

"I didn't know it was so deep," the first retorted. "We can get to the larders from here, fetch something to eat."

The speaker slid from the shadows, and Eleshen beheld a man of slender muscles and medium-tall build, dressed in silken charcoal garb that ate the light. The hood of his grey gear was down, braids pulled half-back from his face, their incredible bluebottle color glinting in the light of the glass lamps. His pale grey eyes flicked around, arresting Eleshen from a chiseled, handsome face – though he didn't spy her in the shadows at the end of the stacks.

And suddenly, Eleshen knew him.

The Ghost of Roushenn.

Elohl had been beautiful in a rugged sort of way, but the Ghost was disarming, a haunting kind of masculine perfection. Those eyes stared at her, not in apology, not with any kind of emotion except a possessing fervency that she could almost feel radiating out from his silent being. It was almost as if he could see her in the shadows, but then his gaze slipped past, surveying the rest of the room. Tingles rioted through Eleshen, like she'd been struck by live lightning.

The Ghost seized his taller, red-haired companion by the arm and urged them forward, one hand to the hilt of his longknife. Suddenly, Eleshen knew she had to make herself known or they might move on and be gone, and she would never see her savior again.

"There's no path to the larders from here. Besides, if you've come to raid them, you'll find them disappointingly empty at present." Eleshen's voice rang through the darkness from between the deep stacks. Hard yet sultry, her voice was almost unrecognizable even to herself: it was a voice of command, of battle. A voice of challenge and righteousness. The Ghost of Roushenn startled so badly he jolted, one foot falling down through the stone floor before he righted himself. The red-haired man with the long Elsthemi braids spun to face their unseen foe with both longknives drawn.

"Who are you?" The redhead demanded. "Show yourself!"

"I might just ask, who are the both of *you*? And how *did* you get in here?" Eleshen demanded from the shadows. She slid forward showing herself in the light of the glass lamps, knives still ready, and saw both men arrested by her appearance – undone by what she was now.

Eleshen had been golden-haired and pretty the last time the Ghost had seen her, but now she wondered if he even recognized her. Her heart-shaped face was similar now that she'd gained some meat back, but she was still far more lean than she'd been. Her cheeks were high and full, her jaw strong and defiant, and she set that jaw now, giving the intruders a stern eyeball. With a toss of her head, she flicked her long cable of otter-sleek black hair back over her shoulder – her longknives still ready in her hands.

But as the Ghost of Roushenn stared in shock, she realized that he did know her. His dark eyelashes flickered, his lips fallen open. "Eleshen den'Fenrir!"

"You know this woman? Sweet Aeon! Why don't you introduce us instead of standing there with your tongue falling out all over the floor while we're in danger of being gutted?" The red-haired fellow was a rogue, Eleshen could smell it. In a sweep of courtly but renegade glory, he slid his longknives away, then executed a perfect bow – his laughing green eyes not leaving her violet ones for a moment.

"My name is Ihbram den'Sennia, milady Eleshen. Forgive my nephew and I's rash intrusion on your—" His gaze flicked to the crate of tomes. "Cataloguing."

"Give me one reason to not cut your glib tongue from your mouth, rascal," Eleshen lifted a dark eyebrow, pointing one longknife at him. "And I may think about it. State your business in the First Abbey."

The redhead, Ihbram, coughed in a spasm, covering a laugh. His green eyes were piercing, challenging and sexual. "Well, milady, with such beauty and ferocity hiding among the Jenners, how could I have possibly—"

"Enough, Ihbram." The Ghost of Roushenn slid forward in front of his comrade, and did far more than a courtly bow. He sank to one knee before Eleshen, his hands far from his weapons, lifting his amazing pale grey eyes up to hers.

"My pardons. My uncle's tongue wags inappropriately with women. We've come to the Abbey upon a mission of dire importance, and perhaps you can help. We need to meet with King-Protectorate Temlin den'Ildrian. At once. It concerns the safety of the Abbey against Lhaurent den'Alrahel."

Eleshen's brows climbed her forehead. She knew the Ghost had dumped a veritable treasure-trove of Lhaurent's documents upon Temlin's desk, but from the way Temlin had described that interaction, she'd thought the Ghost long gone from the city. Yet, here he was – not an actual ghost, but a man of flesh and bone, gazing up at her, imploring her for help.

"I—" Eleshen was undone a moment, as the Ghost watched her with his uncanny grey eyes. A pale, luminous color, they reminded Eleshen of Elohl's. But where Elohl's eyes had held unceasing storms, the Ghost's gaze was both brighter and far more ruined. Something ancient held court in those eyes. Something that had seen so much darkness, it was almost startled to come back to the light.

Eleshen paused, arrested, the knives in her hands forgotten. This man was her savior. He'd spied upon Abbot Lhem's torture of her and come to her rescue. He was an enigma wrapped in a mystery, wrapped in a conundrum, and Eleshen quite suddenly wanted to figure him out. Gazing at him now, she still couldn't tell if those grey eyes were sorrowful or menacing, but the shine in them spoke of a fervency she couldn't deny. It pulled at something deep within her newly awakened self.

"I can take you to see the King-Protectorate," she spoke at last, mastering herself. "On two conditions."

"Name them." The Ghost was fervent, rapt with attention.

"One. No one inside the Abbey's walls is injured by either of you in any way."

"Done." The Ghost promised. "And two?"

A slight smile lifted Eleshen's lips. "Tell me your name. I assume you're not called the Ghost of Roushenn by your *uncle* here. What name do you go by, and what can I call you?"

Suddenly, all the darkness cleared from the Ghost's haunting eyes. They shone, luminous, and he smiled as if startled to be seen. "Khouren." He said at last. "You would do me a great honor, to call me by my given name. Khouren Alodwine."

"Get up, Khouren." The redheaded man scoffed, rolling his eyes and palming a hand over his short-trimmed beard. "She's not the bloody World Shaper."

But the Ghost, Khouren Alodwine, remained kneeling. Watching Eleshen, waiting for her as if she would bless him like a Queen. Slowly, Eleshen slid her longknives away. He'd promised her no harm, and in this moment, something inside her resonated with him like a plucked harp-string. Standing here, feeling intensity surging from him as he stared her down, she felt an answering fervency rise in her.

She shivered, a rush of heat sweeping her as she stared into his eyes. Moving forward with a dreamlike intensity, she reached out. As her fingers neared his hand where it rested upon his knee, he turned his palm up. And then their fingertips met – shivering Eleshen to the depths of her soul.

Her lips fell open; so did his. Eleshen couldn't help it; she blushed furiously, and saw an answering flush rise upon his handsome cheeks. His eyes were wide, their pale grey almost burning with the heat of the current that passed between them. He hesitated, then lifted his other hand to cup hers, interlacing their fingers together. His touch was scalding. Eleshen shivered, feeling like she burned inside as his thumb brushed her knuckles.

"Khouren Alodwine…" Eleshen breathed, hardly knowing her own words.

"Milady Eleshen…" He answered, riveted.

"All right, lovers." Ihbram moved forward, a curious yet wary expression upon his face. "We've got to speak to the King-Protectorate, remember?"

Eleshen blinked, her trance breaking. A rush of color flushed Khouren's cheeks as he released Eleshen's hand suddenly. Placing his hands on his knee, he heaved up from the stone floor in an outrageously fluid movement. Eleshen remembered how effortlessly he had carried her when she was wounded, as if heavy burdens weighed nothing. She'd learned that much about the Ghost – that his lean frame held more strength than any man she'd ever met.

But the rest was a mystery yet to be discovered.

"After you, milady," Khouren murmured, gesturing for her to precede him through the catacomb toward the far end of the vault. Eleshen dipped her chin in a quick nod, then paced toward the stairs, leaving the glass lamps behind. Though her heart hammered her chest to feel the Ghost following her up the dark spiral staircase, she kept her hands near her longknife hilts. Attraction meant nothing – he was her savior, but who was he really?

Her mind churned as she led the Ghost and his uncle up to the bright day and shut the wrought-iron grate behind them. Beckoning in the midday sunshine, she moved along the gravel path that flanked the Annex to a side-door. Khouren stepped up, hauling the heavy ironbound door open like a gentleman before she could. Eleshen gave a brisk nod, meeting his eyes before proceeding in.

The pressure of his attention upon her back as she jogged up the stairs to the upper gallery was electric. She was out of breath when she hit the upper landing, but not from exercise. Eleshen moved on with fast strides so the Ghost could not catch her eye again. Nodding to the four Kingsmen guards that stood at attention beside the double-doors of Temlin's war-rotunda, she pushed in with no announcement. Temlin was there, just as she knew he would be. He hardly left this hall now, the myriad ironwood tables upon the dais cluttered with Lhaurent's missing scrolls and ledgers, now guarded at all hours. Glancing up as she barged in, Temlin was thankfully alone in the vaulted space, lit bright in the rays of the lion pearled-glass window that captured the high afternoon sun.

"The Ghost!" Temlin's mouth dropped open, his green eyes bulging at their entry.

"His name is Khouren Alodwine, he's very real, and he's here to see you."

Eleshen gave an efficient summary as she marched to the dais and sprang up beside Temlin. One hand settled to her longknife hilt as she turned, eyeballing the two men who approached more slowly. The redhead shut the doors, and the two moved forward in a synergy that reminded Eleshen of brothers rather than an uncle-nephew pair.

"Well." Temlin rolled up a scroll he'd been perusing and set it aside. "I suppose I should thank you, Khouren Alodwine, for the bounty of information on Lhaurent's operations that you delivered us. The Ghost of Spies, I think, would be a better title for you than Ghost of Roushenn."

"King-Protectorate." Khouren sank to one knee, and Ihbram did the same beside him.

"Get up!" Temlin barked irritably. "Kneeling wastes your time and mine. I don't have to ask how you got in here when the Abbey's gates are locked and barricaded, do I? So what do you want?"

"We'll not waste your time." Khouren's gaze was intense. "My uncle and I have come to give you a warning."

"A warning?" Temlin's red eyebrows climbed his face as he set a fist to the table. "Does Lhaurent issue threats that you deliver as errand-boy?"

"Dammit, Khouren! Learn a little diplomacy in all your cons, will you?" Ihbram stepped forward with an exasperated growl for his nephew, then gave a genteel bow to Temlin. "King-Protectorate. My name is Ihbram Alodwine, though I go by the surname den'Sennia, and this is my nephew, Khouren Alodwine. What my nephew with his poor choice of words intended to say is that the Abbey is in danger. We have news of it, and have come to make sure you know."

"Ah." Temlin straightened, but set his fist on his hip instead. His hawkish green eyes pierced one man, then the other. "So?"

Ihbram gave a smile at Temlin's brusqueness. "I'm afraid that my nephew, when he delivered Lhaurent's more precious items into your care, did not think his plan through."

"Explain." Temlin's eyes narrowed.

"As you may have surmised, my nephew has *wyrria*."

"Obvious." Temlin snorted, but a grin stole over his lips now. "What are you getting at, Brigadier?"

"*Wyrria*, as you most likely also know, tends to run in families."

"So you also have some, is that it? Also walk through walls like smoke, can you?"

"Yes. And no. I can block minds." Ihbram gave a renegade smile, and Eleshen sensed that he and Temlin would get along famously.

"Impressive." Temlin lifted an eyebrow, shrewd. "Something like the Kreth-Hakir Brethren?"

"I am *nothing* like the Kreth-Hakir." Ihbram's voice was suddenly cold, as his green eyes flashed with a subtle temper. "In any case, you can trust my information."

"Oh I can, can I?" Temlin countered, his head cocked with interest.

Ihbram lifted his hands, slowly, making sure Temlin knew he wasn't going for a knife. Unbuckling his worn brown High Brigade jerkin at its crossover collar, he opened it wide, then pulled open the laces of his white shirt. Baring his chest, he slowly grasped a rope-knife at his belt. Lifting it pinched in the web of his thumb with his hand still open as if in surrender, he used the small knife to nick the center of his chest. Blood flowed in a long, thick trickle, and upon his chest, curling out crimson like smoke in burning water, the Shemout Alrashemni Bloodmark of Kingsmount-and-Stars appeared. Though in a strange, highly stylized version than what Eleshen had seen upon Temlin's chest.

Temlin blinked, then inhaled a long breath. "Those are strangely done. Not a style I recognize."

"That's because it was done in Cennetia, six hundred years before you were born."

Ihbram's gaze was utterly level; no lie was in his eyes. Eleshen startled, and she saw Temlin ripple with astonishment at her side. Her mind reeled, face-to-face with a man who purported to be an ancient Shemout Alrashemni.

"Is that the truth?" Eleshen's gaze flicked to Khouren.

He gave a quiet nod. "I myself am over four hundred years old.

How do you think the tales of the Ghost of Roushenn haunting the palace have lived for so long? Because I have. My uncle is no different. Our clan is gifted with *wyrria* and immensely long-lived."

"There are others of you?" Temlin's gaze was sharp. Eleshen could practically see his mind calculating exactly how these two could be used to his aims.

"They live in secret." Khouren was very quiet. "It is not our place to expose them, for it could do them harm. Just as you understand the secrecy in the cells of the Shemout, King-Protectorate, so our clan maintains secrecy of our identities, for safety."

"Only because of recent events do we take such a risk and make ourselves known to you," Ihbram continued. "And only because a Rennkavi has been Goldenmarked, the Prophecy of the Uniter come alive since Highsummer."

"Elohl den'Alrahel." Temlin crossed his arms over his wiry chest. "You mean him, don't you? Not Lhaurent."

"Indeed." Khouren answered, almost too fast.

"However," Ihbram glanced at Khouren with an almost exasperated look, then back to Temlin, "Lhaurent is not to be underestimated. He has a tremendous amount of power, both from his own natural *wyrria*, the power to persuade and dominate, and what he has been blessed with by the Goldenmarks. And he has talismans, ancient artifacts stolen from the Alodwine line, that focus his power." Ihbram gave Khouren an accusing glance, as if Khouren had something to do with that.

"Because of an accident... after the Queen's coronation," Khouren spoke, avoiding his uncle's gaze, "Lhaurent has wakened a vast *wyrria* throughout the city. One that he can resonate with, and harness. He's able to track things, people. Spy without having any eyes in a location, if he focuses enough. He is still learning his power, but I made a regrettable mistake, delivering to you items he could summon to his mind, items he was familiar with."

Temlin blinked hard. He rubbed a hand down his short beard. "Fuckitall. You're saying that Lhaurent knows exactly what you delivered to me, where they're stashed, and who's been reading them?"

Khouren flushed. He looked down, unable to meet Temlin's

gaze.

"Most likely." Ihbram's voice was hard. He stared Khouren down like a dog that had piddled on the rug.

"We have no time. The negotiation is in three days." Temlin murmured it to himself, though Eleshen heard. A tremor shook Temlin's hand as he reached up and rubbed at his beard again. He suddenly looked old, as if his years had come tumbling back, even though his body was young. His gaze met Eleshen's, and she read there everything he feared: that if Lhaurent knew about the cobalt tomes, he'd come get them. By any means necessary, with whatever secret force he was hiding.

"Can we even wait for the negotiation?" Eleshen spoke, watching Temlin carefully.

He drew a deep breath. "If this information is true," he spoke, loud enough for the two men at the foot of the dais to hear, "than we have to clear the Abbey. Now. Forget the rest of the books. Forget the breweries, forget the vaults. If Lhaurent knows we have his books and ledgers, *those* books, he will come for them. Men like Lhaurent don't wait to pummel their foes."

"He's right." Khouren's gaze was infinitely sad. "Lhaurent is not forgiving with his enemies. You need to evacuate. Right now. Which is why we've come – to help you."

"Give me a straight answer, Ghost," Temlin eyeballed Khouren. "You were Lhaurent's lackey for some time, privy to his private information. What does he have that could destroy my Abbey without an army to back him?"

"Awakening *wyrria*," Khouren's speech was soft as shrouds. "My grandfather's grandfather, Leith Alodwine, Last King of Khehem, was a tyrant. In his time, he devised a tremendous evil – to trap all the earth's natural *wyrria* in its core, effectively arresting the use of magic everywhere. Only the strongest bloodlines, and those blessed by Leith, maintained a fraction of what was once possible."

"Your line," Temlin cut in, keen. "And the Khehemni Lothren, and the Kreth-Hakir Brethren. All blessed by Leith, I suppose?"

Khouren nodded, his gaze level. "And the greatest work of Leith Alodwine was the creation of the Rennkavi – the creation of the Goldenmarked bindings that grace the flesh of both Lhaurent and Elohl. I don't know exactly what Lhaurent will be able to do with the *wyrria* beginning to fountain up below Roushenn Palace since the accident at Highsummer. He's shown diverse gifts; able to use many of the ancient systems Leith built here, albeit crudely so far. But Lhaurent is a dedicated study – he will learn. And you do not wish to be here, sitting in the fountainhead of magic, when he does."

"We must leave, then," Eleshen quipped firmly. "At once. Any more time might mean Lhaurent getting the drop on the Abbey."

"Yes, indeed." Temlin agreed, rubbing his red beard as he watched the two men before him with an evaluating eye. "But we will not go empty-handed."

"King-Protectorate?" Ihbram cocked his head, his brows knit.

Temlin straightened, a dire gleam in his eyes. "I see a singular opportunity, gentlemen, with your coming to me."

"What opportunity?" Khouren frowned.

A slight smile played about Ihbram's lips. "Why do I get the sense that you want to fuck Lhaurent in the ass before you abandon the Abbey?"

"Because I do." Temlin growled, with an answering smile. "Because no one steals the throne of a lion, gentlemen, without getting bit. And I see an uncanny opportunity to bite Lhaurent in the balls. Or bite out his throat. Whichever works best."

"Assassination?" Ihbram's lips had turned up into a pleased, dark smile.

"Indeed." Temlin growled. "If Lhaurent's powers are growing, there will come a day, soon, when we will no longer be able to touch him. If everything you say is true, and I feel in my bones that it is, Lhaurent is doing everything he can to hasten that day, and let us kill ourselves in our bid for more time. More time is exactly what he wants. So we'll not give it to him."

"What do you have in mind?" Ihbram asked with a sly grin.

"Lhaurent and I have a meeting in three day's time," Temlin continued, "out in the fountain plaza before the Abbey gates. Technically, it was to negotiate the return of ale to the masses, but we all know that's a sham. He has called for my step-down as King-Protectorate. I possess his den'Alrahel genealogies that prove his royal blood, and I was intending to use them as bait to buy us more time to evacuate the Abbey – but perhaps we have a different option now. How good is your mind-blocking?" This last was addressed to Ihbram.

Ihbram lifted one russet eyebrow. "I can feel the silver mind-threads of the Kreth-Hakir at a five-league radius. I can block at least four at a time within that distance, keep them ignorant of me and a few companions, as long as they have no High Priest. I can shield people other than myself, make them unseen to normal eyes. I can bend minds to my will and convince people, or cause them to paralyze, but Kreth-Hakir train in mind-attacks, like throwing a spear or cutting with a sword. In those arts, I am unfortunately lacking."

"Fascinating." Temlin's lips lifted in a fierce grin. "A demonstration, if you would. On me."

Ihbram's lips smiled, though his eyes were warning. "I've given an oath to yon lady Eleshen, not to harm anyone inside these walls."

"You have my blessing," Temlin's raze was rash, piercing.

"Mind-invasion is just that," Ihbram countered, "invasion. It removes a man's free will. You don't know what you're asking."

"If I am to gauge the strength of potential allies against Lhaurent," Temlin's smile was hard, "then I must know."

Without warning, Temlin was on the move. He'd vaulted down from the dais faster than Eleshen could blink, his sword out from across his back even faster. He was barreling down upon Ihbram, fast as a lion in the leap, with a roar to match.

Ihbram raised no weapon. He simply fell back into a fighter's stance and set the knuckle of his thumb fast to his brow, eyes closed. Eleshen felt an enormous energy blast out from the Alodwine man, hot as forge-fires. She could almost see a net of living flame flung out from the center of the man's forehead, directly at Temlin and his swiping cut. Temlin was arrested. In mid-arc, he toppled, crashing to his side – so rigid with paralysis that he landed in the same form, only his eyeballs able to roll up and meet Ihbram's opening eyes.

Without thought, Eleshen was in motion, leaping in to protect Temlin. But a second blast of that incredible forge-hot energy was turned upon her, seizing her entire body in a vise-grip. She toppled also. The guards heard the commotion and the doors to the hall boomed inward, four Kingsmen barreling in – all paralyzed before they could take so much as a single step.

Ihbram lowered his knuckle from his forehead. His gaze found Temlin's, still bound upon the floor. "I could do this all day with normal men, if they come at me in small groups. Especially here in Lintesh, where the *wyrria* unleashed at Highsummer awakens. If I can use it, so can Lhaurent and the Kreth-Hakir. But if Lhaurent has four Hakir or less attending him, I can hold them off. I've trained for seven hundred years in my art. I know my limits."

Suddenly, the searing binds around Eleshen slipped away like sparks on the wind. They left her shivering with a chill, brushing at her skin with a sensation of burning cobwebs still clinging to her. She rose and Temlin pushed to his feet beside her. The Kingsmen at the door rushed forward, but Temlin arrested their charge with an upraised hand.

"Halt. I'll not have our allies molested."

The Kingsmen halted, though incredulous eyes gazed over Ihbram and the nearby Khouren.

"So." An eager smile lifted Temlin's lips. "Let's talk assassination, gentlemen. And lady."

CHAPTER 15 – JHERRICK

Jherrick was nowhere. And he was everywhere.

Some part of him knew he was dead, that his heart had stopped from the shell-poison's work. His breath had ceased, his veins were cold, and his body had no more sensation to give him, no more life. Some part of him knew this was what death felt like, this expansive emptiness of space. Looking down, he could see his body in the darkened hole inside the goddess' cave. Her effigy kept watch over him, wings spread wide as if to welcome a weary traveler to his death. A weary warrior with nothing left to fight for.

Turning from his supine body, Jherrick found his way up and out. Floating, or perhaps flying, he found that wherever he looked, he could go. He could focus on the blue mountains in the far distance above Khehem, and there he went. He could search for his birth-home outside of Quelsis, abandoned when his Khehemni family had burned to death, and there he went also. He could dig deep into the bowels of Roushenn Palace, those dire blue-lit byways, and there his consciousness would also go.

All of it was empty. In all his traveling, there was no one else; he was alone in this universe —no one was searching for him. No one was looking for Corporal Jherrick den'Tharn of the Roushenn Palace Guard, a fallen Khehemni warrior who had died from poison in some unknown realm. A realm where it was never really night or day, surrounded by people who weren't precisely human, who worshipped ancient gods that weren't exactly his. Now he was dead at the foot of their goddess, who didn't even care enough about him to show her face.

Jherrick drifted, out over Alrou-Mendera, over oceans, over deserts and barren tundras. Wherever he looked, it was the same: emptiness. No other souls, just him – alone. Further he pushed on. Beyond his continent, beyond his comfort zone, beyond his life. To other worlds, other places, barely glimpsed through an incandescent mist upon every horizon, a mist filled with ancient stars and darkness.

Where are you?! Jherrick's soul called out to the dead-realms.

But I'm here. Came an answer back. It stopped him in mid-float. Jherrick was arrested, solid in space yet not solid at all, fixed yet everywhere. Listening.

Show yourself. He called again, words without language, thought with no voice.

Here. The mind-thought coalesced, walking toward him from the ancient emptiness. He saw it approach, indistinct, a halo of light around a human-like shadow – or perhaps a halo of darkness around the light. It seemed to be both, and as it approached, it solidified into something human, though Jherrick knew it was not. It looked at him with unfathomable eyes, ancient, head cocked as if searching for something deep within him.

Then it smiled. Its radiance lit the emptiness, violet on white, white on black, all the colors that have ever been or would be. It looked at him with its expansive, subtle smile, and its eyes changed to a livid violet. Smiling with all the kindness of a mother or a father, or a best comrade, it spoke again.

I've been waiting for you, Jherrick. It's good you've found your way here at last.

Waiting for me? Jherrick cocked his head that was not. *What do you mean?*

It is for you alone, that I wait. To be your Strength in this Endeavor you now engage in.

And what is it that you think I engage in? Jherrick asked, curiosity jangling his soul-form.

Dusk magic. Its whisper was everywhere. Jherrick felt that resonance lift him – causing him to soar out over open fields, ripe with grain beneath a drowning violet evening. And now, the world was filled with people. Soaring high over Alrou-Mendera, Jherrick saw them all, and felt their pain. Every love or fear or annihilation of every person upon his world. Every hope that had died, every connection sundered, every babe that had lost the conquest of life. Like a forge-hammer, it rocked Jherrick, punched his gut. He found himself sobbing for them, shuddering in despair as his soul howled – because they could not even perceive the vast nature of their suffering.

How can I help them? The thought cried out from Jherrick, the only thing he could ever want, the only thing left to wish for in all the world.

By taking this. The presence turned and thrust a hand of violet light through Jherrick's chest. Through his skin, through his sternum. Right to his very core, it twisted and burned, expanded and churned. Filling him, eating him alive, devouring him and spitting him out – transforming him.

A scream burned Jherrick's throat, flooding the dark cavern as he sat bolt-upright from his deathbed. His living pulse thundered in his body where there had only been silence before. Panting in the darkness from a lack of breath, Jherrick clutched his burning chest, keening in revulsion and elation. Something had been pressed into him, some knowing, some *otherness* he'd never had before; the darkness around him felt alive. With every breath, his heart raced frantically in his chest. One shaky hand reached out, fumbling for the candle: it was out, the wick gone. The others he touched were the same. All out, all dark – all flame and light gone.

But his sight. The things he could *feel* now in the darkness. They pressed in with velvet hands; they touched and caressed; they sought him, eased over him like spiderwebs in the darkness. Jherrick felt himself begin to panic and his pulse sped to unnatural dimensions, his breath shallow. Shrieking burned in his throat. As the scream was nearly out, flung full into panic, he suddenly felt a heavy hand settle to his shoulder.

Easy, kid. A voice said in his ear. *Breathe. C'mon, I know you can.*

Jherrick blinked as he gulped air, hiccoughed, dry-retched. He fought to remain conscious and control his thundering heart as his body tried rejecting this newness, this *otherworldly* dimension he now possessed. He also knew it was only himself he fought, some part of his being that had always been there – not new, only *awakened*.

The touch came again at his shoulder, heavier. Soon a hand was at either shoulder, a presence lifting tall in the darkness behind him, uncompromising, protective. His body sobered. The presence spoke again, with Aldris' chuckle. *Nah, kid. I'm not really him. I'm a part of you, actually, but it just so happens that you listen when I talk like him.*

Jherrick blinked. The presence in the darkness was giving him sass, just like Aldris. Something about it caused the corner of Jherrick's mouth to twitch, even though he still felt like he was going to vomit. A dead boy's glassy eyes surfaced in Jherrick's mind, and then Olea's face, her blue-black curls shining in the sunlight, her effortless smile, luminous and heroic. Jherrick's heart expanded, filling the darkness: he knew what he'd come here to do. Olea was the savior this world needed, to end the suffering he'd felt in his death-vision. He would find her, and pull her back from the Void to right the wrongs of this world. Jherrick felt that passion fill him, resonate like a thousand lute-strings plucked at once.

Then get your ass out of this shithole and pay some fucking attention, the thing in the darkness growled.

Jherrick pushed to standing from his death-hole, resolute. He could see nothing, the darkness infinite with a touchable quality Jherrick had never known before. Inside his mind, space opened up – a realm *through* the real where he could see a million stars in the dark, all strung together in a vast network like a spider's web. He was now in two places simultaneously: here in the cavern, experiencing the velvet dark and cold, wracked with shivers and gut-wrenching cramps, but also in another realm; awakened to a space that transcended darkness and light into a unity of sensation and vibration.

The Void.

A space that Jherrick suddenly understood surrounded everything, wove *through* everything. The true fabric of the cosmos, a gossamer emptiness and fullness that Jherrick could now feel. He found he knew where the cavern's entrance was, where the well was. With weak limbs still flushed and shaking, slick from poison, Jherrick staggered to the water bucket and stuck his face in, drinking like an animal. When he'd had his fill, he wiped his mouth with one arm, tasting the acridity of the killing poison in his sweat as he cleared it.

Movement suddenly breathed around the room – from everywhere and nowhere. It was so full and pressing that Jherrick startled, dropping the water bucket and spilling its contents over the stone floor. Water dripped in the darkness as he hunkered in a ready posture, perfectly still.

Touches came, gossamer hands playing along Jherrick's skin. He shivered, eyes wide, seeing nothing yet everything. All around him in the Void, etheric tendrils manifested, seeking him. To take or corrupt, he didn't know, and it wasn't an enemy he could fight with hand or knife. Jherrick panicked all over again, flailing in the dark backwards over the wet stone. A subtle laugh came, assaulting his ears with seductive languor. Not his own soul's manifestation now, but a woman's voice. A woman's breath, hot on his skin.

Olea's chuckle in his ears, a sound of darkness and flesh.

"Olea!" Jherrick gasped.

Feeling the siren touch again, sliding along his forearm, he shuddered. As that touch slid up his shoulder, her face swam out of the darkness. Jherrick's breath caught in his throat. She was there – so frighteningly beautiful with those perfect features and regal bearing. Moving close, her breasts and figure were exquisite, just as Jherrick had always imagined. Sex rolled through the darkness as sighs echoed in his ears. Olea chuckled in a bravado as her breath found his lips. Jherrick's heart thundered as her touch slipped over his chest, pressing in, finding the racing of his heart under his ribs. Need coiled out from her, seeping into Jherrick with a pulling sensation like leviathans under the black. His breath came fast as her opal-grey eyes bored into his soul – wanting him.

Possessing him. Draining him.

Jherrick could feel Olea's need coiling into him, licking through his flesh like tentacles of evil. The thought hit Jherrick like a sledgehammer: this thing, whatever it was, would take his body, his mind, and his very essence until nothing was left. Terror flooded Jherrick, making his pulse rage. His breath came hard as his body roiled with the worst kind of chill – the kind that takes a man down. His heart jolted in his chest as if it might quit again, and he saw it was shot through with darkness, wormed into his very fabric. With a deep and wretched instinct, he knew that only darkness filled the presence that showed itself as Olea.

Only darkness and the emptiest kind of destruction.

Red eyes flashed in the Void. Olea's grey gaze was consumed by a burning destruction the likes of which Jherrick had never seen: it was pure malice. As if stars could implode with the chill of a dark and uncaring universe, the being that flowed into this manifestation had no understanding of creation. All it wanted, all it was built for, was to destroy – until the end of time.

With a cry, Jherrick jolted backwards, his spine smacking up against the lip of the well. Sprawling, he ripped his essence away from that annihilating touch, but it had snared so much of him, seduced its way into far more of him than he'd known. Jherrick felt those evil tentacles pull like taffy in his flesh – stretching, sticking, winding in deeper even as he hauled himself away. For it had a will, and a need: its need was to possess him, to take those vile appendages and sink them into everything that Jherrick was, and use him for its own aims.

Destruction. Annihilation.

Undoing.

With a scream that was part roar and part howl, Jherrick focused himself in the Void. A pure instinct, his own form suddenly flared in the Void like a falling star. Jherrick roared into being, as a sigil flared in his mind. Violet like the endless dusk, it was made of stars woven together, sharing energy in a curling, complex formation that seared outward. Luminous, made of a substance as ephemeral and star-shot as Flavian's eyes, the sigil flared – and the tendrils of the devourer were not expelled from Jherrick, but *consumed*. Jherrick felt the formation he battled scream in the vast night of time, furious. Then it gave up pursuit, its red-eyed presence misting into the Void as the vision of Olea dissipated upon a chill wind.

"What in Halsos?!" Jherrick gasped, shaking with the horror of the encounter, and the terror of his own sudden power in the Void.

Beware what you ask for, kid. Aldris' voice was solemn in the darkness, the magnificent presence still standing tall behind Jherrick. *You wished for Olea, well you got her. The manifestation you wanted – of your darkest desires. But learn this about desire, and learn it well: there are a million things out there that will use your desires against you.*

"But that thing – that thing is worse than all of them, isn't it?" Jherrick rasped. Clutching his chest, he felt true pain where the thing had woven its substance through him – as if it had actually damaged his terror-stricken heart.

Bingo. Not-Aldris chuckled in the dark. *You asked to awaken, and you got it. You want truth? Here's the hardest truth of all. Your wyrria knows the Void, kid. It can feel death, and creatures that have suffered worse fates. There's light out there, too, but fresh meat is fresh meat. And the things that linger out there will want you, before you know what the fuck you're doing. Before you learn how to protect yourself and make your intentions truly manifest.*

"What do you mean?" Jherrick's loins crawled, the evil's touch tingling through his body. Jherrick turned his head in the dark, though he could only see the presence that spoke to him as a glimmer of violet light on the edge of a moon-dark vastness. The being that guided him had Aldris' sass, but Jherrick knew it was a part of his own consciousness, this edged shadow spread out behind him in the otherworld.

In the dark, he felt it smile. *You'll figure it all out. You'll have to, and quickly. Stay open, learn what you can from the teachers you are blessed to be around. Your journey will take you into the depths of the dark, for only then can you understand your true power. You're right: that thing is worse than everything else, but then again, it's not. It's in all of us, a part of us – just like it was in Olea, too. When the right moment rests in your palms, you'll open them to find you know more than you ever thought you would, and can do more, than you could ever imagine.*

A light touch came upon Jherrick's left shoulder, encouraging him to stand. With it came a searing pain as if something had cut him, though the pain soon passed. With shaky limbs, Jherrick rose to his feet, a shiver passing through him. His consciousness' words were mystery, a labyrinth for him to walk, but where Jherrick had only been alone in his life, he suddenly felt held. Held fast by the shoulders, his steps encouraged – to begin what he was here to do.

With that understanding, Jherrick knew his trial had come to an end. Moving back toward the stone stairs, the climb back up was wrenching in his current state. Gasping, he struggled up stair after stair, his stomach heaving bile at its insistence that he do anything but try to move. Jherrick was nothing if not stubborn, fighting his way up. Bracing upon the wall, he slid along it, lifting his leaden legs to the top landing.

Arriving at the tomb's entrance, all his woes vanished as he blinked up at the luminous dusk. The world opened to a velvet violet above and all around. Standing in the open air, in the beauty of the living world once more, Jherrick felt an enormous expansion through himself and all around, like the spread of the goddess' massive wings in the thrilling evening.

He'd made it. He'd gone to death's door and come back. To the realms of the Void where all things are non-distinct, where one is everything and everywhere.

As Jherrick leaned in the sepulcher's entrance, he experienced the world anew. No longer did the realm of the Noldarum feel flat and lifeless. No longer was it filled with an impenetrable mist. The entire realm was now translucent like flawless crystal, shimmering with facets that caused the cosmos to be magnified a thousandfold. Everywhere he looked, the dusk was alight with color, with sound, with the breath of a thousand galaxies and a million worlds. From the Noldarum's realm, Jherrick could see the universe, with depth and prescience. Around him shimmered diamonds of life in the pearl-violet sigh of evening's dying, and it smote Jherrick's soul.

Crystalline. Perfect.

Jherrick collapsed to his knees in the egress of the cave, obliterated by beauty, marveling at how sightless he had been before, to have thought this sacred realm filled with only autumnal color and lifeless mist. He barely noticed that Noldrones Flavian had approached and was now kneeling before him, peering into Jherrick's eyes with his infinite starlight ones. Jherrick could see now that Flavian's eyes reflected the entirety of the magnificence that surrounded the Sanctuary's realm. As if they were one, the Void and Flavian's inner self, radiating out through his eyes as he stared upon the vastness of all that is.

As Jherrick hitched a sob, the Herald of the Noldarum cupped Jherrick's face in his kind warm palms. "Now, Jherrick den'Tharn, do you see? Now do you understand the fullness of the Void and everything that lies beyond death, beyond time, and beyond the body? Are you reborn, resurrected, a babe seeing the Void anew in all its glory?"

"Yes." Jherrick could barely breathe it. Tears slid down his cheeks, shimmering like drops of crystal as they tracked down his skin. "It's beautiful—!"

Brother Flavian gave a nod, a smile upon his perfect lips. "Then welcome, Noldrones Jherrick of the Noldarum – to the Way of the Dusk, the Path of the Dead, and the fullness of the Void."

With easy grace, Flavian slid an arm underneath Jherrick's shoulder and hauled him up. Flavian helped Jherrick stumble back the way they'd come yesterday, toward the amphitheater and the ascending staircase, as the entire citadel of luminous domes and spires reflected the magnitude of the blissful universe – not a trace of mist in sight.

Jherrick was still vastly weak as they ascended through the galactic night, leaning heavily on Flavian. Gradually, he became aware of a dull, throbbing pain upon his left shoulder, and recalled the sensation of having been cut during his death-journey. Glancing down, he saw there was indeed a long, shallow cut upon his skin, weeping slow runnels of blood as it flared his Khehemni Bloodmark – the Broken Circle he'd been given upon swearing his allegiances far too young.

The slow runnels of blood fascinated Jherrick's mind, absorbing his thoughts as Flavian walked him up another set of stairs. He hardly noticed when they arrived at Flavian's sanctuary with the gazing-pool and the oculus of woven vines high above. Living green whispered around Jherrick in the night, little white flowers breathing a heady jasoune scent through the world. The scents of iron blood, rancid fever-sweat, and heady perfume disoriented Jherrick, sending him spiraling out to all those galaxies far above the oculus.

He hadn't even noticed that Flavian had helped him step into the oculus-pool. He hadn't felt it when Flavian brought him down gently to his knees in the luminous water – reflecting the dark infinity above – and began sluicing Jherrick's wound. Ecstasy shivered through Jherrick, at the water's touch upon his cut. He fell back, caught by Flavian, and was lowered to his back in the shallow pool.

Breathing deeply, Jherrick stared up at the sky, watching the night whirl. Pain seeped out of his shoulder as Flavian let him be, moving to the side of the pool and no longer touching Jherrick. His back on stone, his chest and abdomen bared to the air, Jherrick breathed in the slow tides of the universe, and it breathed with him, around him – through the water, through the stone. He felt the poison of his life easing away to the vastness. As he looked to his shoulder, he saw the crimson of his allegiance slipping out of his skin upon spreading blossoms of blood. Where his Khehemni Ink flowed out, the water flared briefly in a luminous, shifting violet, then sighed away.

At last, it was gone. Deep peacefulness engulfed Jherrick and he heaved a sigh; content. Staring back to the midnight sky, he watched all of life and time, and wondered what was to be found out there – and how many universes he might have to travel to find it.

CHAPTER 16 – DHERRAN

The night was deep, Dherran's room in Delennia's manor silent but for the crackle of flames in the ample fireplace. He sat in his crimson silk robe, staring at her dumbly as she poured another round of wine into their goblets. She had just told him that he quite possibly had the power to bring down her sister the Vhinesse, and to change futures. By heart magic – *jinne wyrdi* – something so ancient that Dherran had never even heard of it.

"You want *me* to bring the Vhinesse down?" Dherran felt utterly confused, and it made him irate. "What about the Bitterlance?"

"If Arlen needs help I'll go save his ass, but Arlen didn't have what it took to resist my sister. He could resist my advances to some degree, so I thought he'd be safe in that throne hall. But if you can resist me," a smile lifted the edges of Delennia's lips, "your heart magic may be strong enough to resist Aelennia. Which would be a *tremendously* rare thing."

"You want me to take up your failed coup on the Vhinesse?"

Sitting with her legs crossed in her peacock-blue dressing-gown, Delennia swirled her goblet, her pale gaze thoughtful upon Dherran. "Grunnach is a sneaky sewer-rat, but he knows when the tides of nations turn – just like rats run from fire sweeping through a ship. If he's betting on you and Arlen, I would be a fool not to listen."

Dherran paused, uncertain, but before he could say anything else, the latch to the through-door lifted. Still in his lord's attire of the night, Grump hauled it open from the other side, his grey eyes a-twinkle. "O-ho! I thought so. But it's not just Dherran and Arlen I'm betting on, Delennia. It's also yourself. And Khenria here."

Grump moved into the room, Khenria on his heels in her crimson bath-robe and looking strangely flustered. Dherran rose to face them, but as he pulled Khenria into his arms, she peeped irritably, twisting away.

"You're squishing me, Dherran."

"Sorry." He eased back, loosening his arms, concerned that maybe she had heard something of his earlier encounter with Delennia. Khenria was looking past Dherran to Delennia, her gaze riveted upon the woman at the dining table – not angry like Dherran might have thought, but with a mixture of scrutiny and trepidation.

"Let us all sit and have some wine, and talk about things to come." Grump beckoned to chairs, pouring wines all around with a cat-got-the-cream grin on his face, smug as thugs. Delennia declined a chalice, already sipping her own wine.

Dherran lifted an eyebrow as he sat beside Khenria. "You knew something like this would happen, didn't you, Grump?"

"No man can see the fates, Dherran," Grump chuckled. "Only linger upon their ephemeral tails. But much, I do believe, will come out tonight. Khenria, it's your turn to have a revelation. Or give one, really."

"What's this?" Delennia looked sharply to Grump, then Khenria.

Khenria's gaze rested upon Delennia for a long moment. Her brows knit. She cocked her head and opened her lips, then paused. A moment seemed to stretch between them, Delennia narrowing her eyes now, perusing every inch of Khenria's face and form. Suddenly, Dherran realized that the two looked incredibly alike. Though one had the silver mane of Valenghia and solid muscle while the other was wan and black-curled, they both had the same sharp chin, exquisite neck and collarbones, the same cutting cheeks and almond eyes.

"Tell me, girl. Where were you born?" Delennia spoke at last, something soft in her voice.

"You can trust her, Khenria," Grump prattled gently, "as well as you could Arlen. In fact, you might find your story has an interesting connection. Quite."

Grump was still smiling his cheshire grin. Sensing something tremendous was amiss, but not knowing what, Dherran reached out to clasp Khenria's hand. She stared down at it, then took the deep breath of her Alrashemni training, her eyes flicking up to Delennia as she squared her shoulders.

"I was born to a royal house of Valenghia," Khenria began,

holding Delennia's gaze, "spirited away as a baby and raised among the Menderian Alrashemni at the Court of Dhemman. I don't know why, only that my Valenghian mother would have been persecuted as an Alrashemni sympathizer because her baby was born with Alrashemni coloring, rather than the silver hair of Valenghian royalty. I never knew my parents, but Grump knew them," she nodded to him, "and says he stole me away when I was an infant. At the mother's request, whom she told no-one. Though Grump took it upon himself to inform the father. Arlen den'Selthir."

Shock smote Dherran as he gaped at Khenria, not having known that part about Arlen. She'd told Dherran her history when they'd been in the Heathren Bog, but this was a piece he wasn't even sure she had known until recently. Certainly, she would have shared it with him. But as Dherran's gaze flicked to Grump, watching the man grin with pleasure, Dherran suddenly knew that this was Grump's second ace. The secret that he'd known would throw Delennia right into the fighting ring for them, a second secret she couldn't possibly resist.

A secret he'd not even told Khenria until tonight.

Delennia's goblet had come to rest upon the table. She was very still. So still that she looked carven out of marble, her eyes wide in the firelight. Slowly, that brutal, astounded gaze moved over Khenria – over every inch of her.

"Lovely, isn't she?" Grump's murmur held amusement, but also tenderness. "Your daughter turned out to be a fighter, Delennia, just like both her parents. And full of surprises that I'm sure you'd be proud to hear of."

Delennia's pale eyes filled with a luminous shine. Slowly, she rose from the table. Walking around to Khenria, she knelt by the young woman's chair. Reaching out, she touched Khenria's face. Her lips had fallen open, her eyes filled with pain, and joy. "Kaelennia! Daughter of my loins! I knew there was something about you from the moment I saw you in the crowd!"

Khenria swallowed. Her eyes flicked to Grump, and he nodded solemnly in confirmation, his hands clasped upon the tabletop. "Khenria. When you were very small, I was tasked with a singular duty. To take a little royal baby born out of Alrashemni-Khehemni wedlock away from Valenghia where she would be killed, to Alrou-

Mendera, and there surrender her into an Alrashemni family of Delennia Oblitenne's trust. Your mother couldn't keep you. Her sister the Vhinesse had heard of the birth and was hunting you to punish Delennia for her part in the almost-coup eighteen years ago. So I took you, to aid your father and mother, and when the Kingsmen Summons happened and you disappeared, I spent every grey hair I had hunting for you. To find you and bring you back home. Back to the great warriors whose lineage you bear. You are a Vhiniti, a *tendril of the vine*. A royal princess of Valenghia, in competition for the throne."

Khenria's eyes were enormous, but the way she held perfectly still told Dherran that Grump had informed her of this tale already, during their confidence earlier. Khenria's gaze flicked to Delennia, still kneeling by her chair, then back to Grump. "And Arlen? Did he know me while I was there, training with him? Did he know us back at the inn in Vennet?"

"Arlen knew." Grump murmured, tenderness in his gaze as he reached out to take her hand. Khenria pulled her hand away, though, and Grump settled his back upon the table. "Not at first, but after he caught me, I told him. He'd suspected it, though, seeing us traveling together, knowing your age, seeing your profile, so like Delennia's. That you were being trained to fight by a Kingsman. Which is why he took such an interest in you in Vennet."

"But Arlen wanted you caught." Dherran stared at Grump now, incredulous. "Punished for your crimes against the Alrashemni. Why would he want to punish you if you saved his daughter?"

"Did I?" Grump's gaze was dire, an ancient woe lining his face. "What worse crime is there, Dherran my lad, than losing a royal child you were oath-sworn to protect? Born of both nations, who could have united two countries torn by war? Letting her be kidnapped and suffer cruelty and wander the wilds? I have much to atone for. Arlen was right to be furious with me."

Dherran stared at Khenria. He couldn't quite wrap his head around it, but looking at her now, at that fierce profile and that stern, hawkish gaze, he suddenly saw the woman she would grow into. A combination of the woman who kneeled beside her and the impeccably righteous Alrashemni Vicoute – Arlen den'Selthir.

"Why did you let me go?" Khenria's eyes gathered tears,

shining in the firelight. "Why didn't you keep me?"

"If you had stayed, Aelennia would have killed you," Delennia murmured, her eyes shining fiercely as she reached up to stroke Khenria's cheek. "She had disbanded my House's army – I could do nothing to protect you. Fratricide is forbidden in the royal families of Valenghia, but killing a child born out of wedlock is due course. Such children are seen as *impure*, especially ones that do not hold the royal coloring. Aelennia would have been justified in the courts, to seize you and murder you as her revenge upon me. My only option was to send you with Grunnach, the only man I knew who could escape all notice – and thence to a family in Alrou-Mendera."

"Why didn't Arlen keep me?" Khenria's eyes were full of tears. She blinked and they shed down her flushed cheeks.

"He didn't know." Grump cut in, his voice low and sad. "Not until I told him later. And then he did what he could behind the scenes, keeping a watch on you in Dhemman as you grew up among the Alrashemni."

"He was a *fool*," Delennia spat from a vicious tongue, "not claiming her when he found out!"

"A man's heart is a tender thing, Delennia." Grump's words were very soft.

"A man's heart is *nothing*." Rising from her crouch by Khenria's chair, she rounded upon Grump. "He could have protected her in my stead!"

"Arlen is a good man," Khenria bristled. "He may not have been there for me growing up, but he's made up for it in recent months. Training me. Teaching me of war, and ruling a nation with fairness and balance."

Dherran's eyebrows rose. He'd not known Khenria was taking private lessons with Arlen, studying such things, and yet, it made sense. She had grown more commanding, more calm and weighing of situations under Arlen's care, rather than jumping into her rash temper. Khenria had grown into a woman in the weeks they had trained under Arlen den'Selthir – and apparently, had been groomed to rule as much as Dherran had been groomed to lead an army.

He stared at her, suddenly wondering about the young hawk before him. "So what now?"

"Now," Delennia stared down at her daughter. "We have two

aces. But you knew that, didn't you, Grunnach?"

"What does an old sewer-rat know?" Grump chuckled, sipping from his goblet.

"Much." Delennia's gaze pinned Grump. "You knew only a Child of the Sands could truly command the touch of an Oblitenne."

Grump lifted his goblet, saluting Delennia before drinking.

"Excuse me?" Dherran spoke, feeling this discussion involved him again.

"*Wyrria*, Dherran," Grump chuckled. "Oblitenne magic – the ability to seduce a man's heart with a touch or a glance or a laugh. Oblitenne magic is an odd variation of Scorpion *wyrria*, the magic of the Kreth-Hakir Brethren – though they tend to not conscript Oblitennes into their order, as it has gone disastrously wrong for them in the past. Khenria has Oblitenne magic, from her mother's line, but interestingly enough, Khenria carries two ancient strains of *wyrria*. From her father, she has acquired Werus et Khehem *wyrria*, the battle-magic of the ancient Kings of Khehem. Arlen hates to admit it, but he has a Khehemni ancestor far down his line somewhere. Though his *wyrria* is latent, it's still palpable – still enough to make him a demon in battle."

"Arlen has Khehemni *wyrria*?" Dherran blinked. It made sense, suddenly. Why the man would have the Khehemni wolf and dragon emblem carven into his training-room wall, even though he was Alrashemni. Why he was sympathetic to bringing his and Delennia's forces together as the Bitterlance. To unite two sides of an ancient war – that had borne misbegotten children over the ages. Bloodlines no longer pure on any side, but a hatred that still reigned culturally, depending on where one was raised.

Grump gave a small smile, watching Dherran think. "Khenria has both strains of *wyrria*, Dherran, though she hasn't learned how to use either one yet, due to a lack of available teachers. And you have the ability to resist her dynamic pull. Strong enough in your *jinnic wyrria* to choose your destiny around not only Oblitennes, but also around a Wolf and Dragon *wyrric*, like Arlen. To be the Great Boar among lesser swine. Now you will face the Vhinesse, and for all our sakes, I hope your love for Khenria is strong enough to bring that pale bitch down from her ivory throne."

"How—" Dherran blinked from Khenria to Grump. "How do you know all this, Grump? How do you know so much about *wyrria* and who carries it?"

Grump's smile was subtle, and something veiled came down behind his eyes. "I have my sources, Dherran. And you are not high up enough in the game to understand why I must hide my reasons from you. Only know that I have been trained, long ago, to sense such things."

Dherran's gaze narrowed upon Grump. "Does this have something to with how you were able to hide Khenria and I from those Kreth-Hakir on the road near Vennet?"

"Something like that." The smile had dropped from Grump's face now, and his gaze pressed Dherran, his next words soft. "The less you know right now, Dherran, the safer you are. If my enemies captured you… they would rip your mind apart, searching for my secrets. Please. Ask me no more questions just now. You and Khenria are safer, if you know as little about me as possible."

"Are you still being hunted by the Khehemni?" Dherran blinked, concerned.

Grump's gaze was penetrating. "I am *always* being hunted Dherran. And the out-riders of the Khehemni Lothren are the least of my worries."

Dherran sat back, something cold roiling in his gut. Holding Grump's gaze, he could feel truth in the man's words, and yet, he still couldn't trust someone that held so many secrets from him. Dherran bit back a growl, crossing his arms, processing. Khenria reached out, setting a hand to his arm. Dherran took a breath. It was almost as if he could feel it, a soothing balm pouring from her, like something she didn't even know she was using. Sometimes it was roaring for a fight, and Dherran realized that that part of Khenria affected him, too. But different from Delennia, he didn't see any threads or *wyrric* mist curling out from Khenria in his mind's eye.

As if she was something different, even from the two ancient strains of magic that ran through her veins.

Khenria's lovely dark eyes searched his, and at last, Dherran sighed. "You just embrace all this? Like it's the most normal thing in the world?"

"To me, it is," she stated simply, her dark eyes honest. "I feel all these dynamics inside me, Dherran, all the time. I know when I'm able to seduce someone, or wind them up and make them strike. But I just don't know… how to control it. Even Arlen couldn't help me there, though he taught me how to think clearly through it, and you did also. I don't have to be at the mercy of the magics that ride my veins, Dherran. But I still don't know how to use them."

"And she won't," Grump chimed in, with a glance to Delennia, "until she has a proper teacher."

"I can only teach my daughter how to use Oblitenne *wyrria*," Delennia spoke, tapping the table with one finger. "She'll need to find someone else to teach her how to corral Khehemni conflict *wyrria* into something useful. It's very rare now, even to the Lothren's knowledge."

Delennia and Grump shared a long look. At last, Grump sighed. "In any case, Dherran my lad, we must move our own plans forward without the help of magics, for now. Except, apparently, yours."

"But," Dherran paused, trying to take it all in. "How am I supposed to bring down the Vhinesse? Do we even have a plan? What do I do? I didn't even know I had *wyrria*, really, and I certainly don't know how to direct it."

"One move at a time." Delennia's words were calm. She returned to her seat, regarding them all with a very commanding, Arlen-esque look. "*Jinnic wyrria* is a spontaneous thing. It rises when it is needed, when it is tested. Aelennia will test Dherran, we can count on it. First, we will bring you before the throne, in disguise. Dherran needs to be in the same room as my sister, disguised as a petitioner airing a dispute for the Commoner's Audience. She does not touch commoners, and will not touch him, but we will get a feel for his ability to resist her charms. If he is strong enough, we will formulate a more thorough plan – to get Dherran close enough to assassinate her. Privately. Dherran, how do you feel about becoming a kept man, for a while?"

"For you?" He eyeballed Delennia.

"No, not for me," she chuckled. "The Vhinesse allows the men she keeps, her Falcons, close to her person with minimal security. It's the only way to get close enough to assassinate her – but you'd have to play besotted with her, and you would have to acquiesce to…

sleeping with her. To gain her trust, before we make our move."

Dherran took a breath. His gaze flicked to Khenria, saw her square her shoulders. "You have to take this chance, Dherran. If we could assassinate the Vhinesse, we could end the war, and bring the fullness of Valenghia's armies against Lhaurent. We could protect Arlen with the might of the Valenghian Red Valor. Protect my father."

Clasping her hands, Dherran found his eyes stung with tears. "I don't want to hurt you like that, Khen. It just... it feels so wrong."

"Destiny comes for us all, Dherran." Khenria's words were soft, strained. "Whether we like it or not. I knew it, when Elyria gave us our readings at Purloch's House. I knew then, that we would face challenges: testing from our fates. But if this is what needs to happen, to unite our world, my bloodlines, my family——" Khenria choked off, with a glance to her mother. "I have to do it."

Leaning in, Dherran set his forehead to hers. They shared a breath in the lowering firelight, then a gentle press of lips. "I love you," Dherran murmured.

"I know," Khenria murmured back. "But we have to take this chance. We can save countless lives, Dherran."

"What about our love?"

"Our love will heal. It has to." Khenria's words were firm, and in them, Dherran heard the echo of Arlen and Delennia both. Fighters who had risked everything for peace – and whose love had paid the price. If Delennia was willing to fight again, for her daughter and for unity between Valenghia and Alrou-Mendera – who was he to say no?

Slinging an arm around Khenria, he turned to Delennia. "I'll do it. Put me in the ring with the tyrant. I'll go toe-to-toe with her, and show her who wins when I fight."

"Great Boar," Delennia's smile was ruthless. "*Charge.*"

A shiver rippled up Dherran's spine, hearing the soothsayer Elyria's words fall from Delennia's lips. His mind was taken back to Purloch's House in the Heathren Bog, to that strange reading of fates he and Khenria had had at Elyria's subtle hands and blind-seeing eyes. He and Delennia regarded each other a long moment. At last, Delennia set her palm to her chest in a Kingsman salute, and for a moment, Dherran thought he felt the bristles of a boar's spine raise upon his neck, rippling with the charge of fate and destiny, and with his own livid passion.

His own magic of the heart.

CHAPTER 17 – KHOUREN

Khouren Alodwine was watching from the walls.

Or rather, from within a fountain.

The day of the Abbey's negotiation with Lhaurent den'Alrahel
had come. A sprawling silk pavilion had been erected before the
fountain in which Khouren waited, in the plaza near the Abbey's
main gates. Gold and white striped, the pavilion was a symbol of
Lhaurent's den'Alrahel reign rather than the cobalt and white of
den'Ildrian. With open-air sides, it allowed Khouren to watch the
negotiations from within the central fount of a buxom stone woman
riding the back of a lion.

Lhaurent sat in a gilded throne under the pavilion's noontime
shadow, gold and white Perthian rugs cast beneath the throne's legs.
Four Kreth-Hakir Brethren stood flanking him, faces shrouded in
the depths of their herringbone hoods. Having Brethren present
wasn't part of the deal, but Khouren saw King-Protectorate Temlin
den'Ildrian's retinue approach up the Abbey's causeway, cool and
unimpressed, as Temlin claimed a seat in a modest chair beneath the
awning.

Standing at Temlin's right with his hands laid gently on the
hilts of his longknives, Ihbram wore an impenetrable expression.
Dressed in a set of Greys today, Ihbram stood at attention with three
other Kingsmen, flanking Temlin's chair. Hands at their longknife
hilts and swords across their backs, the other Kingsmen had wisps of
white hair beneath their charcoal hoods. Expendable. Volunteered
for their positions today understanding that they would likely not
survive, and among them, only Ihbram had *wyrria*, easing out,
raising shields that would protect the King-Protectorate's retinue
from Kreth-Hakir treachery. Ihbram's ability had more than tripled
in the past months, and Khouren staggered from the weight of
Ihbram's fire-tinged weave in his mind. His uncle could have been a
Scorpion, had he not been shrouded from the Brethren by Fentleith

long ago.

Khouren saw one of the Kreth-Hakir raise dark eyebrows, aware of Ihbram's mind-blocking, while another fidgeted with a hand to his knife-hilt. They could feel Ihbram's weaves, screening off valuable information, but Ihbram was a clever mind-smith, sending threads of fire in every direction to keep the Kreth-Hakir guessing about what he concealed.

No eyes moved to Khouren, inside the fountain. Settling in, he judged the distance to the pavilion, knowing he was far closer to the throne than the Palace Guardsmen who held back the common rabble from the plaza. Atop the Abbey's walls, archers in grey stood at attention, looking down upon the scene below, longbows to hand and quivers full. It was a show of strength, yet it was also a farce – as much as the three ancient Kingsmen who attended the negotiations were. Though good fighters, those atop the walls were aged and ready to die, like Temlin's retinue – elders who had seen enough of time. The Abbey stood nearly empty behind those gates: Jenners, Kingsmen, and defected Palace Guard shunted through to the fortress at Gerrov-Tel only hours before, along with any last supplies they could carry. Much had been left behind, only the most necessary items shunted through to the mountain fortress.

Cool and composed beneath the pavilion, Lhaurent was clad not in grey anymore but gold and white robes that cascaded over his gilded throne. He wore the gilded ruby starburst pins of the ancient den'Alrahel line at his collar, his iron-shot dark hair oiled back from his high forehead, his beard neatly trimmed. There were no refreshments, no wine, no sham of civility. Lhaurent merely smiled his loathsome smirk as he waved a regal hand to begin the proceedings.

"Temlin den'Ildrian." Lhaurent raised his voice to be heard beneath the snap of the pavilion's silk in the light autumn wind, his grey eyes glittering with subtle amusement. "I would have brought wine today, but I hear it is your weakness. How I would hate to send these negotiations awry with such temptation."

"How kind of you, Lhaurent, looking out for my welfare."

Temlin's words held a witty bite, his eyes glinting like chips of emerald flint in the pavilion's shade. Temlin was clad per his kingly station today, no black Jenner-robe or even Kingsmen Greys. He wore a smartly-fitted longjacket of black wool with a high collar and deep hood, reminiscent of Alrashemni garb but different, though his leather belt and boots were tooled with Kingsmen symbols. Over that, Temlin wore a suit of lightweight armor that shone a silvered white in the shade, made of a metal Khouren had never seen. The curious metal flowed over his longjacket and fit his body like chain links, though it was solid plate. Temlin wore a matching set of weapons to the parlay, and Lhaurent eyed them with critical disdain. A longsword with a ruby set in the pommel, made of the same metal as Temlin's armor, was slung across his back in a leather harness, matched with two longknives of an odd sickled variety that rode Temlin's hips.

The overall impression Khouren had was of a lion. Ready to pounce and bite off the eel's head.

"Have you received my terms?" Lhaurent gestured for a document with his right hand, the ruby of Leith's dusky white star-metal ring glinted upon his index finger. A heavy sheet of vellum was handed over by a noble dressed in grey silk with white and gold threads.

"I have." Temlin held out his hand, and Ihbram produced a tri-folded parchment for him from an inner breast pocket of his Greys. "And to your demands I have made answer, as succinctly as I may."

"And?" Lhaurent waved a hand. His noble stepped forward to retrieve Temlin's parchment, then handed Lhaurent the document.

"No." Temlin crossed his arms over his chest, his green gaze hard and humorous.

"No?" Lhaurent's grey eyes glittered, dangerous.

"No."

"To what part?"

"All of it." Temlin gave a growling grin. "Your terms are shit. And as you'll see, I've drafted up counter-terms just there."

Lhaurent opened Temlin's parchment. A scowl ate his long face. "You demand that I cede Alrou-Mendera to you. That I hand over the nation's military and cease all campaigns. That I turn over my emerald mines and hand over my mercenaries to be *processed* by your Kingsmen. That I abandon my alliance with the Kreth-Hakir Brethren and send them *packing along home.* That I cease *hunting*

Kingsmen and *put myself in chains.* Well. I can see to whom Khouren passed all my missing documents."

"You should find the terms agreeable." Temlin's grin was feral. "I've not called for your head. Though it is within my rights as the last surviving den'Ildrian, other than my niece the Queen."

Lhaurent's eyes flashed as he handed Temlin's parchment to his lackey. The Kreth-Hakir at his flanks shifted, sensing the tension rise under the silk awning. The wind whipped, making the awning crack and buckle, bringing the scent of snow down off the mountains. Inside the stone of his fountain, Khouren held immaculately still. Lhaurent settled back. His face eased from a scowl to a slight smile. Pleasure flashed in his grey eyes, and Khouren knew that look: that was the look Lhaurent enjoyed when he was about to kill.

"Temlin," Lhaurent's words were smooth. "I'm afraid I cannot agree to your terms. You should know better, Scion of den'Ildrian. A man who is god-marked is not to be trifled with, especially not one descended through the blood of the ancient kings that founded this land. *Two* lineages, far older than yours."

"Oh?" Temlin quipped. "Produce these documents, then, that name you to such a kingly station. I don't see them. Did you leave them at home in your dark torture-chambers?"

It was only the third time that Khouren had seen Lhaurent lose his temper – once with Khorel Jornath and the second time when Khouren had defied him after Lenuria's death. Still, it was a subtle thing: a flicker of sneer crossed Lhaurent's lips, as his face set into a drowning chill.

"If you don't like my terms," Temlin continued archly, "then we can have another arrangement, Lhaurent. One that will take some months and waste quite a lot of your men. A third of your Guardsmen defected from your *kingly* rule, after all. I'm sure they'll be quite helpful keeping my Abbey fortified for some time. And keeping the city dry as a bone of ale."

"Dry bones we shall have," Lhaurent shot back, "but not before yours bleed."

"Threatening me?" Temlin growled, grinning.

"Threats?" Lhaurent gave a subtle chuckle, but his eyes were dark as the ocean's floor. "I hardly need to threaten your *ancient* forces. No, I believe *persuasion* is in order. And then we may resume our negotiations for the welfare of our great nation."

Rising from his throne, Lhaurent lifted his hands. Suddenly, the sham of negotiation was over. Khouren saw Lhaurent's hands tense, saw him focus upon the Abbey walls two hundred paces distant. Temlin noted it, too, a fast wariness crossing his features. With a quick hand, he reached in the open collar of his longjacket and whisked out two thin cobalt volumes, holding them up. Lhaurent paused, a look of eagerness sliding across his features before he stowed it carefully away.

"Destroy my Abbey, asshole, and you'll never be legitimate." Temlin's growl ate the afternoon beneath the crack of the silk awning.

"I don't need books to prove my legitimacy," Lhaurent spoke dismissively.

"Oh, but you do," Temlin snarled. "You know it and I know it. No matter how much magic you have, you'll have to fight ten times harder for what you want if our neighboring nations think you're a piece of lowborn sheep-shit. Now. Let's negotiate."

Lhaurent went immaculately still. As if he'd disappeared, Khouren could barely feel the man beneath the pavilion. Only chill waters that knew their purpose – to drown the resistant. Anyone and anything that opposed them, or insulted them.

"You have no clue as to the circumstances of my birth." Lhaurent's words were dead ice.

Temlin's lips twisted in a mean smirk. "Oh, but I do. Alranstones talk, Lhaurent. Did you know that? You may be able to step inside them and bend them into traveling where you wish, but there are those who resist you. And guess what? My beloved Mollia den'Lhorissian – you remember Molli, surely – is trapped inside a Stone now. And she likes to talk to a very particular Alranstone. One who gave you those markings you bear."

Khouren perked within the fountain, on high alert. Baiting Lhaurent was never wise, especially in regards to his murky past. Even Khouren did not know about Lhaurent's life before he came to Roushenn as a young man already Goldenmarked. Lhaurent had never spoken to Khouren of his early life, nor his birth. And now, Lhaurent was as deadly as Khouren had ever seen him.

"Go on," Lhaurent murmured softly, "tell me about my origin, son of Kings."

Temlin was missing all the signs. Warning screamed through Khouren's every sinew. Lhaurent was so still it was as if he'd turned into the ocean itself, standing immaculately calm before his throne – right before the storm.

Still, the King-Protectorate had to open his rash, snarky mouth. Khouren's heart screamed, as Temlin's green eyes flashed fire. "You were born in the Kingsmountains, in a small valley not far from the Elsee. Your mother was Alrashemni Kingsman, a fighter of the den'Alrahel lineage stationed up in the mountains on patrol. She met a ranger in those lonely wildlands, a Khehemnas, a warrior tall of stature with blind eyes and a war-axe across his back. He told her his surname was Alodwine. He told her he carried the ancient royal blood of Khehem, and from their union would be born a child of *twinned blood*, a savior to rule the worlds of men – the Rennkavi. He convinced her, and took her, and left her in the lurch. She retreated to a cabin in that mountain vale, mind-broken and wild, and gave birth to twins – a little girl and a baby boy. A boy, who had strangled his twin sister in the womb with his umbilicus. Wrapped it around her neck three times and throttled her with it until she came out blue like she'd been drowned in the sea. Just like the eel you are. And do you know what else?"

Lhaurent said nothing, his grey gaze glittering with stoic chill.

"This Alranstone told Molli another tidbit," Temlin continued with a growl. "That this youth it had marked so long ago, this murderer from the womb, had *failed his naming*. That the Alranstone had been tricked, by the force that young man's belief in who and what he was, to impart the Goldenmarks. As that young man grew into a cruel and coldhearted bastard, the Alranstone knew its mistake: that the bloodlines the man carried were Alrahel, surely, but not twinned with the ancient Kings of Khehem. Lowborn. Common. Begat of a father who lied to this mother and seduced her for his own aims, before he disappeared like smoke into the wind. So who is your father, Lhaurent, truly? Tell me again that you don't need these tomes I hold."

Khouren's heart sickened into despair, as shock hammered through him. Could any of this be true? What if Lhaurent wasn't a Scion of Khehem, but had only been raised from birth believing it so? Khouren thought back, to all his conflicts with the Rennkavi. To the times he'd walked away, disobeyed – and not been braised into smoldering ashes from his ancient oath. Lhaurent's force of will was tremendous, a part of his own innate *wyrria* that had nothing to do with being the Rennkavi. But what if he wasn't actually Alodwine blood, only *believed* himself to be so strongly that it had tricked an Alranstone – and tricked a High Priest of the Kreth-Hakir as well.

Into believing he was the *twinned blood* of the true Rennkavi – when he was actually something else entirely.

The Kreth-Hakir flanking Lhaurent's throne shifted, their eyes tracking to Lhaurent, narrowing. Lhaurent stood very still. His emptiness was precise as his grey eyes stared Temlin down. "Keep your books and stories, scion of Kings past," he spoke at last. "For *my story* is yet to be made."

Suddenly, it was as if the floodgates of hell opened, the rage of the entire ocean swallowing the day. A rigid tremor shook Lhaurent as he gathered a tremendous *wyrria*. Khouren felt his ears pop, even from inside the fountain, as if a tidal wave barreled down from the top of the Kingsmount. The Goldenmarks at the collar of Lhaurent's garb seared, blinding. Temlin's retinue moved fast into fighting crouches, but they were too late.

Lhaurent gave a tremendous stretch as if gathering the entire city into himself. Then gripped the air and hauled all that rippling power right from the foundations of the Abbey.

A rumbling roar consumed the avenue. Clockworks long-unused shrieked in Khouren's ears. Stones began to heave, causing a crevasse to rip open in the avenue. The roaring shuddered the city, Guardsmen and civilians stumbling back with shouts of horror as the avenue peeled away from daylight into blackness. City-folk scrambled, shouting, trying to clamber over one another to escape the fast-widening crevasse. Folk fell into the black of the Unterhaft with terrible screams – as the crevasse lanced straight to the Abbey's gate.

Risen to his feet, Temlin stared in horror, shock opening his face as Khouren quailed inside the fountain. He'd never seen Lhaurent's powers unfold with this kind of fury. Lhaurent had caused walls inside Roushenn to move, but this was fifty times that ability. With a grinding roar and a deafening sound, the Abbey's main turrets began to shuffle and re-shape. Walls pulled from walls, rooftops slid back and descended, solid parapets opened, dumping those upon the walls to their deaths with horrific screams. Grindings and crunchings accompanied the shrieks of terrified people, as bones were churned in gears by an ancient, terrible magic.

Leith Alodwine's legacy – a city built to crush any invader. Except this city wasn't devouring invaders, it was eating its own people.

Lhaurent's grey gaze shone with sick pleasure, occupied with his horrorshow. With the lesson he waged upon an entire city, to strike back at the heart of their King-Protectorate who dared challenge his validity, but the moment of Lhaurent's obsession was the allies' moment. Khouren saw Ihbram's focus triple, his red weaves brightening like volcano-flame. Ihbram's gaze flicked from the carnage, boring into the Kreth-Hakir Brother to Lhaurent's right, one with a ripping scar across his throat. The Hakir's leader here, their lynch-pin – smothering the man in blinding mind-weaves.

Khouren launched from the fountain's center like a wraith on the wind, longknives out. In three strides he was under the pavilion. Kreth-Hakir were turning; seeing him – too late. Khouren's blades lashed out. Glorifying in his destruction, Lhaurent's turn was slow. One of Khouren's blades pierced deep into his guts, but the other missed Lhaurent's throat as Lhaurent jerked away, his grey eyes wide. Khouren whipped his blades for Lhaurent's flesh again, but was arrested by a silver lance in his mind. Escaped from Ihbram, the Kreth-Hakir with the mangled throat had rallied, freezing Khouren in a vise-grip.

A knife thrust deep into Khouren's side and he staggered. Lhaurent's blade was vicious, shivving Khouren over and over in the flank. Ihbram roared as Khouren sagged with a gasp, his insides in ribbons as Lhaurent shivved him yet again. His red weave surging to arrest all the Hakir, Ihbram whipped a blade across Kreth-Hakir leader's throat – releasing Khouren from the mind-bind only to fall limp upon the plaza's flagstones at Lhaurent's boots.

"Cur! You should have stayed away."

Looming over Khouren with his right hand covering his own wound, Leith's ruby shone upon Lhaurent's index finger as if drinking the Alodwine blood that spattered it. The scent of shit wafted up Khouren's nose. His vision swam red from Ihbram's nearby battle with the remaining Kreth-Hakir. Fierce parries of red, vicious silver strikes. All Khouren could see were Lhaurent's eyes, shining with pleasure as he readied his knife to strike out and slice Khouren a new throat.

In that moment, it was Temlin who swept up behind Lhaurent. With a roar, the lion of den'Ildrian swiped his silvered white sword down – the ruby in the hilt and the runes along the blade flashing unnaturally as they matched the power of Lhaurent's searing Goldenmarks. Slicing flesh like silk, the sword severed Lhaurent's left arm at his shoulder. Lhaurent's knife-hand thudded to the stones, spasming like a spider as his blade skittered away through Khouren's blood.

Lhaurent screamed. Clutching his gushing shoulder, his entire body vibrated. A terrible energy poured from him as his blood fountained out, like a hurricane over a raging ocean. The Goldenmarks at his collar blazed, obliterating Khouren's vision as Temlin stumbled back with a cry.

The flagstones of the plaza erupted in a seething tide – buckling the pavilion, white silk shredding like wolves eating doves. Khouren was blind as the blaze of the Goldenmarks devoured his mind, but somewhere in that obliteration, he found a thread of crimson. One thread, all that remained of Ihbram's mind-protection in whatever terrible magic was igniting all around them from Lhaurent. Gritting his teeth against the hurricane of *wyrria*, Khouren clamped a hand on his wounds and hurled himself toward the red thread. His bloody hands found men where the thread ended and he seized them. Dropping them down into darkness, away from that sundering power, they splashed into a sewer far below the city.

Khouren landed with a scream of pain, Ihbram's hard grunt beside him. The florid curse was Temlin's and Khouren's heart surged to have found them both. His wounds roared as he hauled them up, but even though his decimated side seeped shit and blood, his flesh had already begun to knit.

"What the fuck did you do?!" Ihbram rounded upon Temlin, his green eyes on fire as the foundations of the city roared above them.

"I—" Temlin stared in horror at the sword in his hand. The

runes upon it seared, Lhaurent's blood making them glow red, but they had no more time as the ceiling of the sewers opened up to that obliterating power above.

"With me!" Khouren gasped, hauling both men by their wrists.

As Lhaurent's rage enveloped them, flagstones rumbled and split. Fighting to stay conscious, Khouren had a death-grip on Temlin and Ihbram, running them through the sewers far beneath the city. Stars flared in his vision, but his *wyrric* sense of direction never failed. He could feel life beneath the earth ahead. The bright, solid sensation of Eleshen and Sebasos holding the Abbeystone grotto for them with a small group of Kingsmen.

Men and women who would hold that position until death for their liege.

Stone peeled away from Khouren's feet and above his head as they ran. Chaos consumed the Unterhaft and the sewers, shit-choked greywater heaving around them. Up above, Lhaurent churned the milk and honey of the Abbey grounds into whipped butter as Khouren dashed through walls, gears, ancient furniture. The Abbey gate and its stolid walls crumbled down into the sewers, and Khouren dashed them through it. The oldest parts of the city groaned, churning and devouring souls. Blocks of stone came at them, walls moving and reeling. Vines and dirt collapsed as Khouren ran them beneath the Abbey's grape arbors, through churning hole after hole. Lhaurent threw everything he had into that meat-grinder – pursuing his rebellious cur, the man who had bested his Kreth-Hakir, and the King who had maimed him, but the trio were fleet, sprinting until their lungs burned fire. Shifting his focus, Khouren dissipated them through churning walls, tumbling furniture, and cellars erupting into so much rubble.

Suddenly, they arrived in the Abbeystone grotto, glowing in all its glory. Relief flooded Khouren to see the shocked faces of Eleshen, Sebasos, and their Kingsman retinue. With a hard gasp, Khouren released Ihbram and Temlin. Eleshen sheathed her weapons as Sebasos and the others raced forward to catch the trio from falling to their knees.

"Quickly!" Khouren gasped as he gestured to the Abbeystone.

Roaring smote their ears as the upper parts of the Abbey churned. The Kingsmen needed no second urging; hauling Ihbram and Temlin up, Sebasos and the others ran them toward the Abbeystone. Getting under Khouren's shoulder, Eleshen dashed them just after. Sebasos and Ihbram slapped their palms to the Abbeystone, but just as Khouren and Eleshen dashed up, a terrible sundering consumed the grotto. Stones careened down as the floor above peeled back. The only one left, Temlin darted forward to haul Eleshen and Khouren toward the Abbeystone.

But a byrunstone block ripped free from the level above, hurtling down just as he shoved them on. Khouren shot a hand toward Temlin. But the stone fell with the weight of promise, striking Temlin on the neck above his *wyrric* armor. Khouren touched him, too late. Their contact evaporated Temlin through the block, but the damage was done. Blood poured from Temlin's mouth, his body crushed, his neck broken.

Even as Khouren watched, the man's fierce green eyes dimmed.

A sound like an exploding gong hit Khouren's ears. Like a thousand war-hammers striking copper, the peal came straight from the Abbeystone. Brightening in a terrible flash, the Stone was hued with every color of creation as Khouren seized Temlin's hand, desperately slapping it to the Stone before the fierce King's eyes could close. Rumbling devoured the chamber. An enormous crack split the ancient Plinth, opening it from within. The pealing sound overtook the grotto, pouring back again and again from the sundering stones to the collapsing walls. Khouren knew that the Abbeystone was vibrating itself to pieces. Not because the building collapsed, but because the woman inside it had made a decision – to sunder the Alranstone.

Seizing Eleshen, Khouren ran them into the Stone without a moment to lose – and felt it shatter as they crossed over.

* * *

Temlin den'Ildrian had not made it through.

And the way back was shut.

Khouren knelt in the grass-choked amphitheater before the Alranstone in Gerrov-Tel, gasping for breath, one blood-slick hand bracing himself on the cracked flagstones. A vision of shattered shards consumed his mind, seen just before he crossed over, and Khouren knew that the Abbeystone had sundered. The brave woman who had occupied it, Mollia den'Lhorissian, had been released from her worldly torment at last – taking the soul of her beloved with her.

Khouren choked. Tears sprung to his eyes. Pushing to standing and ignoring his wounds, he struck bloody fists to the Alranstone in the high mountain vale, screaming out his anguish. A midnight-black rage consumed him and he screamed again in torment. He could feel his wounds searing closed fast with the terrible depth of his conflict, but it wasn't their pain that gripped him.

It was a pain of the soul. That he had caused so much devastation by having believed Lhaurent. By having trusted Lhaurent's conviction that he was a Scion of Khehem. That Khouren had ever given Lhaurent such powerful talismans as Leith's ruby ring, and Fentleith's blood upon Leith's object at the heart of Roushenn. A power Lhaurent wielded, not because he was Wolf and Dragon – but because he had convinced everyone and *everything* that he was.

Changing the course of history by convincing an Alranstone to give him the Goldenmarks.

Khouren's world went black and red, his vision searing blind with tears. It was a long while before he realized that Ihbram stood behind him, pinning his arms as he struggled and screamed. Eleshen had stepped to his front, holding his face in her hands and kissing his lips, her tears mingling with his.

"It should have been me!" Khouren roared, struggling against Ihbram's grip. "Not him – not him!"

"Temlin knew the risk," Eleshen kissed Khouren again. "Please! Please, Khouren! You did everything you could have—!"

"No! I could have kept his hand in the grotto! I could have run him faster! I could have thrown him into the Stone! I—"

"NO!" Eleshen gripped his face and shook him like a wayward puppy, her violet eyes full of tears. "No! What's done is done. Because of you, because of everything you told us, the Kingsmen live, Khouren! Look around you! See the faces that have survived today because Temlin sacrificed as he did, and because you stepped into the light and brought us some hope against Lhaurent! See all the faces you've saved, Khouren! Not just the ones who didn't make it."

Khouren fell still. His heart thundered in his chest, but now he saw the decrepit amphitheater full of faces in the glowing afternoon light through the pines. Old and young, woman and man, Jenner and Kingsman and Palace Guard. The Abbey had been emptied prior to the calamity and a few thousand people ringed him, staring in silent shock down the broad sweep of the amphitheater.

They sank to their knees, throwing cowls back or setting a palm to their hearts and sword. Brother Sebasos took a knee nearby. His dark brows knit as tears fell from his red-rimmed eyes. They all knelt. For death, for today, for the Abbey. For the last sacrifice of King-Protectorate Temlin den'Ildrian, saving his people from a destroyer's terrible wrath.

Tears washed down Khouren's face. His struggles passed and Ihbram let him go.

"See them, Khouren." Ihbram's voice was rough, but proud. "See our people. They live because of your bravery today."

"I'm not Alrashemni. They're not my people," Khouren gasped.

"They are." Ihbram gripped his shoulder, turned Khouren to face him. "A true Rennkavi lives. You've seen him. Elohl den'Alrahel. And if a true Rennkavi has come, rather than this false *thing* Lhaurent is, then it is time for Khehemni and Alrashemni to unite. The Rennkavi's dawn is more than just a symbol. The Rennkavi's dawn is hope for all of us, that we can be better than these old wounds that divide us. So put yours down now, as I put down mine – as we all laid down our lives today to make a better future. For that's what we have now, because of you. Because of Temlin's bravery, and because he exposed what Lhaurent really is, we have a future. And we *will* use it to tear that bastard down and unite our people. Against him – for our true Rennkavi."

A lump rose in Khouren's throat. He tried to swallow it, but it wouldn't go. "She shattered the Abbeystone! Molli, she gave her life—!"

"All the better." Eleshen stepped up next to Khouren, reached out to cup his face. "Molli was a warrior. She suffered torment all her life at Lhaurent's hands, and now she's free. No one from

Lintesh can follow us because of what she did. No one will know where we've gone. She saved us."

"But I never got to tell her... I'm sorry!" Khouren choked. "For everything he did—!"

"I know." Eleshen's violet eyes were gentle as she gazed up at him, though tears stained her cheeks. "We don't always get to say the things we want to, to the people who matter. But life moves on, Khouren. Life moves on and so must we."

Khouren choked, another tear slipping down his face. He drew Eleshen into his arms, burying his face in her sleek sable braid and screaming out his heart into her shoulder.

CHAPTER 18 – ELESHEN

Thunder smote the dawn. Bleary, Eleshen glanced up to the top of the ancient Alranstone at the center of the amphitheater at Gerrov-Tel, watching the storm gather. Wind stirred, sending long wisps of her black hair around her face as they escaped her braid. Clouds roiled above, twining the Highmountains, heavy with rain.

Even the sky would shed tears for the great man they mourned today.

Sitting with her back up against the Alranstone at the amphitheater's center, Eleshen blinked away her long night of vigil and of visions. A pyre of unlit timbers stood nearby, ready for the day ahead. There was no body to burn, though the pyre had been draped in cobalt and white fabric as if Temlin's corpse lay beneath. Tears crept from Eleshen's eyes, stinging in the fresh wind, and she blinked them away in the red dawn. Visions from the ancient King within the Alranstone rifled through Eleshen's mind, fleeting things. Visions of Molli and Temlin: two old lovers sharing a last moment of bliss, a reunion of love, before the Abbeystone's decimation.

Before being released together into the great Void.

Tears slipped heavy down Eleshen's cheeks. She didn't reach up to wipe them away, only when the light lifted into a suffering grey cast did she see that she was not alone. Khouren Alodwine stood just beyond the Alranstone. Silent as shrouds, his body held an unearthly quiet in the lifting dawn, the grey-gold morning shining in his eyes as he watched her. He said nothing, only stepped from the shadow of the Stone, sinking to a cross-legged seat beside her. Awakening sunbeams found the highlights in his braids, and their color dazzled for a moment like a dragonfly's wing before the oncoming storm swallowed the sun away.

"Did you sleep?" Khouren asked in his low, melodious voice.

"No," Eleshen breathed. "And if I did, it was with the dead, without dreams."

"Sometimes death is better." Leaning back to share her Plinth, Khouren extended his boots before him. Without a word, he pulled a breakfast of autumn peaches, hard cheese, and a pewter flask from a burlap sack in his hand. His somber gaze met hers as he offered a peach. Their fingers touched as she retrieved it – a blaze of electricity shivering through Eleshen as their fingertips connected.

Khouren's eyes twisted gold in their sky-grey depths, but he said nothing as they shared breakfast in a solemn silence. He'd gone off by himself after his breakdown the day before, and though Eleshen had seen Ihbram involved in the building of Temlin's bier, she'd not seen Khouren again until just now. It was kind of him to have brought her food, and she managed a few bites of cheese and a few of peach, but it was more than her grieving stomach could bear so she set the peach aside. "When is it to be?"

"Soon." Khouren glanced over to the bier, his own breakfast untouched as he took a pull from the flask. Eleshen extended a hand for it and he gave it over, watching her take a long drink of a searing Highland-style whiskey.

"Is everything decided?" Eleshen coughed, wiping her lips with her sleeve as she handed the flask back. She had been present for the discussions of Temlin's last rites earlier in the night, but as the debates between factions had raged on about what kind of funeral a royal-turned-Kingsman-turned-Jenner should have, she'd lost her appetite for the proceedings and come out here to be quiet and to mourn.

"Everything's decided." Khouren spoke, his voice haunting like a mourning dove in the suffering light. "Temlin's to be awarded the King's Rights of Alrou-Mendera. They don't have the correct supplies to conduct such a ceremony, nor official seals of Roushenn or den'Ildrian coats of armor, but I found enough correct pieces for the ritual in the fortress' vault. They're ancient, but they'll do for a ceremony of state. Especially in the old ways, since there's no tomb available here."

Eleshen glanced at him. Khouren stared at the pyre, but turned back to her, watching her with steady eyes.

"You found death-ceremony items for a royal in the vaults?"

Khouren gave a somber lift of lips. "I found a lion banner. It's not cobalt. It's red, threaded with gold, and it has the twin crowns of the Brother Kings of Elsthemen on it. It was King Hahled Ferrian's standard, long ago."

Eleshen looked back to the waiting pyre. A picture eased through her mind from the Alranstone, of that banner held high in a terrible battle over a bloody field. A wiry man with bared chest, wild red braids, and white and crimson tattoos roared to his army from a chariot pulled by two massive white keshari. Wielding fiery blasts of *wyrria* from his bare hands, his inkings alight like lava, he charged down a sea of foes beneath a blackened sky. The vision sighed away, but Eleshen was left with the feeling that the ancient King within the Alranstone approved of Khouren's decision.

That Temlin, in all his fire and fury, was worthy of the Brother Kings' ancient banner.

"Who will conduct the ceremony?" Eleshen spoke again.

"Sebasos," Khouren murmured. "Everyone agreed that he held a bridge position between the factions, as Temlin's right-hand officer. I led him through the proper steps of King's Rights, about an hour ago. He'll do fine."

"You led him through King's Rights? You've interred a King before?" A curl of curiosity eased through Eleshen, pushing back some of her grief.

"Yes." Khouren paused, as if he wouldn't say more. But then added. "Unofficially."

Eleshen let it be. It wasn't like her to not pry, but it was a solemn day, and her heart hurt too much to pick into Khouren's secrets.

He surprised her by speaking again. "The Jenners and Kingsmen have undertaken ritual fasting for the day. It's the ancient Menderian way, a seven-day fast for the death of the King, though Sebasos decided that all must break their fast tonight, as we are at war. He's ordered a feast at sundown to celebrate Temlin's memory. Preparation moves within the walls."

"A feast." Eleshen gave a soft snort. "With ample drinking, I suppose. Temlin would approve."

"So Sebasos said as well." At her side, the Ghost gave a soft smile. "You loved him? Temlin?"

Eleshen blinked at the Ghost's frankness, inhaling. "What is love? How can you love a man you barely knew? I met him too late.

Maybe in another lifetime, we might have been something, but he loved elsewhere. And me... I'm too broken in love, I suppose. Unlucky."

Leaning her head back upon the Alranstone, Eleshen regarded its heights. Black clouds choked the valley, just beyond the Stone's pinnacle. Gazing up at that great height, she thought of Elohl – of her slapping the Stone, urging him to come down from his midnight sojourn only to find him changed that dawn.

As surely as she was changed now with this one.

"Do you have something to burn?"

"What?" Eleshen blinked, surfacing from her reverie.

"On the pyre." Khouren nodded at the waiting structure of cut saplings stuffed with dry wood and bales of straw underneath. "We'll each have the opportunity to burn something in Temlin's memory, as per the old ways."

Eleshen fell silent. It was almost barbaric, thinking of burning a token of someone she had cared about rather than keeping it, but as she pondered, she realized that she did have something. Eleshen rose and Khouren stood at her side. When she turned to leave, stepping up the first stair toward the fort he moved also, like a shadow. Eleshen turned and stopped him with a hand to his chest. His hand rose to cup hers, cradling it. She could feel the steady beat of his heart beneath his quilted silk jerkin.

"I have to do this alone," Eleshen breathed, though some magnetism held her fast. Reaching out with his free hand, Khouren cupped her cheek. Eleshen's breath caught and she blinked, gazing into his steady grey eyes.

"I'll be here. Anything you need. You have but to ask."

She stood, riveted. Undone by Khouren's honesty, by his fervency. By the feel of him, so warm and close. They barely knew each other, and yet, she felt his strange dedication; as if he would follow her, the moon behind the sun, every step of her every day. It was unnerving, and also thrilling, and Eleshen found herself caught – wanting to trust it, yet frightened to.

With a will, she pulled away. He watched with luminous eyes, but let her go. Hauling in a steady breath, Eleshen shivered off their connection, but she could still feel it as she paced quickly up the tiers of the amphitheater toward the fortress above.

The Northeast Tower of Gerrov-Tel loomed, set with burning torches in the grey morning. Eight guards stood at the portcullis in the outer wall – four in Kingsmen gear, four in Guardsman cobalt. All had hands at attention upon their sword-hilts or longknives. Eleshen stepped up to the restoration in progress, beset with scaffolding, winches, and pulleys. As she approached, the guard in charge, Sister Nennia den'Thule, saluted her in Kingsman fashion.

Eleshen moved under the open portcullis, into the fortress' bluestone courtyard. Blossoming with raised boxes of herbs and edibles, the courtyard was a labyrinth. Barrels of ale, sacks of grain, stacked crates of clucking chickens and other sundries choked the flagstones beneath oiled canvas awnings erected against autumnal rain.

Kingsmen and Palace Guard choked the courtyard, splitting the last saplings into faggots for the pyre or bundling pitch and straw into torches for the ceremony. One corner had become the feast's abattoir, where hogs and chickens were being slaughtered and trussed up to drain from ancient archways. Sprawling bluestone steps led to a massive set of newly-wrought red cendarie doors, ironbound and solid, the entrance to the main fortress. Eight more Kingsmen saluted her at the doors, though they already stood wide, the heavy beam that braced the door aloft on restored Praoughian clockworks inside the hall.

Eleshen made a salute and moved past, into the ancient fortress. Ample like the throne hall of Roushenn, eight massive hearths stood sentinel upon either side. Two blazed, lighting a jumble of commotion. Every available corner overflowed with supplies, all the way back to the vaulted doorways that led down to barracks, and beyond to recessed alcoves that led to the kitchens and storehouses. Monks bustled through the columns, readying kegs of ale and barrels of wine.

Eleshen moved through it all like a ghost. She slid around bodies, avoiding eyes, working her way to the rear of the commotion. Heading past newly-wrought trestle tables, she took the leftmost portal and trotted down spiral stairs into darkness. A single torch illuminated the bottom landing, set before an ornate blackiron grate, locked by a complicated clockwork of flowers and vines.

Eleshen moved her fingers over the grate's mechanism, in a

pattern Molli had showed her over a week ago. Touching a florette here, moving a leaf there. Pressing a thorn, clicking a petal. Latches and gears moved as she worked the pattern, until the entirety of the mechanism shuffled into place and caused iron bolts to jump back. With a *chunk*, the ancient grate sighed open on newly-oiled hinges.

Moving inside the vault, Eleshen slipped through shadows of the ages. Between the stone columns and catacomb arches, a treasure-trove which spanned the entire underground beneath the main hall above was housed. It was a mystery Eleshen hadn't had time to peruse or catalogue in her haste to empty the Abbey. Strange items of forgotten times lingered in the shadows, coated in bluestone dust and cobwebs. Looming contraptions of precious ore set with jeweled stones, whose function she couldn't even begin to understand, rose up like leviathans in the aisles. Crates of tomes and arcane items from the Abbey's vaults occupied every corner and spilled into the aisles, stuffing the catacomb to the brim.

Most of the dust-choked items upon the sagging timber shelves had already been here when they'd excavated access into the main fortress. They were inert; dead oddities that did little to claim Eleshen's attention as she stepped to a corner where they'd stacked the books and scrolls from Temlin's study. Her eyes didn't need to search the gloom – the item she sought called to her like a siren song.

Stuffed in a crate and bound in plain brown leather, the volume held a jumbled mess of runes pressed into the spine and over the cover. Reaching out, Eleshen slid her fingers over the volume, the leather chill as the vault in which it sat. Claiming it, Eleshen moved back through the dim catacomb, closing the complex gate behind her. By the time she reached the top of the spiral staircase, men flowed like minnows in the sea, toward the open fortress doors. Heads were bared, Jenner cowls and Alrashemni hoods down as all took up torches and began to light them in the blazing fireplaces.

Ihbram den'Sennia and Brother Sebasos were in the main hall. As Eleshen neared, Sebasos handed her an unlit torch with a quiet nod. His dark eyes were somber as she took it, the gold and red cloth of Hahled Ferrian's banner draped over his arm in smooth folds. Claiming her torch, Eleshen let it take up the fire that would kindle Temlin's bier today. As if her torch's light were the signal, the mass of warriors and monks and Guardsmen was suddenly moving like a serpent ridged with spines of flame, coiling out into the grey day.

Setting out in solemn procession, there was no sound but the shuffle of bare feet upon stone, the soft step of leather boots, and the crackle of flame. As the procession gained the courtyard, the sky at last began to mourn. A fat drop hit the crown of Eleshen's head, then the rain began in earnest, releasing the ever-cool smell of autumn. Pattering to the dry stones, it spattered the grey byrunstone until the dust darkened, showing the blue for which the Kingsmountains were famed. Like an evening sky opened up beneath their feet, the heavy clouds caused the courtyard to turn cerulean – until Eleshen thought that the mourners walked upon the heavens as they went to commit their King-Protectorate to the earth.

Proceeding out of the fortress, the procession wound down into the vast bowl of the grassy amphitheater to the steady drive of rain. The amphitheater was vivid beneath the simmering storm, and Eleshen could feel vibrations rippling from the Alranstone like the slow pulse of a heartbeat as the amphitheater filled to the brim with men and women, warriors and monks. Sebasos, four Kingsmen, and Temlin's captains moved forward to kindle the pyre. Jenners stepped one foot behind the other, bowing in a formal wave with two fingers to their lips. Kingsmen set palms to their hearts and one to their blades. Palace Guardsmen snapped their boots and gave a salute, as all watched fire take root in the structure. The pyre caught quickly, bales of straw and kindling dry below. Flames spiraled high as saplings sizzled and split. Devouring the construct, fire twisted twenty feet up through the open clearing, making the oceanic blue of the amphitheater blaze gold.

Gold, for the Lion of den'Ildrian.

Sebasos fed the pyre, tossing bowls of ceremonial oil sweetened with wild rose petals and highmountain sage onto the burgeoning blaze. His words of royal dedication had come and gone. Eleshen hadn't even heard them. He unfurled the red and gold lion standard of Hahled Ferrian, Brother King of the Highlands, blazing with glory beneath the bruised sky. The world wavered and Eleshen blinked tears. The standard was already upon the pyre. Already blazing with a ferocity as bright as Temlin's heart – she had missed it. She had missed the moment of its dedication, but she found it didn't matter, as people moved forward, each dropping an item upon the pyre now, something that reminded them of Temlin den'Ildrian.

A strip of colorful fabric, a pair of wire-rimmed spectacles, a mug of ale. One old Jenner tossed a hawk's wing into the writhing flames, and Eleshen choked at that, even as she smiled. Temlin had been a hawk, and a lion, and a cur, full of piss and vinegar. Eleshen choked a laugh, wondering if she should just piss on the flames or dump a jar of vinegar upon it for her dedication, knowing that Temlin would probably snort from his grave.

Her smile dropped as she clutched the book to her chest. Temlin would have no grave – no marker, no headstone. He had been cut from the den'Ildrian line, cast out from history. All the tomes in the palace rewritten, all official records changed to erase his memory. Nothing would remain to show the world such a blazing, righteous man had lived.

Nothing but those who stood here.

Eleshen glanced at Brother Sebasos with his stern frown and black brows, motioning up others to toss their memorial items into the blaze. As she watched, a tear slid down the rugged man's cheek. Sebasos did not wipe his grief away, one hand resting upon the hilt of his longknife, his other palm to his heart over bared black Inkings, his Kingsman sword strapped across his back.

Eleshen's eyes strayed to Ihbram den'Sennia with his fiery mane of Elsthemi braids. Dry-eyed, he watched the ceremony with an expression of emptiness upon his roguish features. As if he'd seen ages pass, one more coming to a close with nothing left to show for it but ashes. Ihbram had only a touch of grey in his braids, but his climb-weathered face seemed more lined today. A man who had lived too many lives with too much sorrow, his eyes were haunted as he stared at the pyre.

Her gaze came to Khouren, standing quiet beside her in the charcoal greys of the Ghost. She'd not noticed when he'd come to her side, or if he'd always been there. As if sensing her, he glanced over, his head uncovered. Blue-black, his braids were hilighted by the roiling flame, his grey eyes like fire opals in the turbulent light. There was no comfort there, yet Eleshen found that she knew that gaze. It was a gaze one warrior gives another when their General falls in battle. Eleshen responded to it, hardening, understanding that now was the time.

To fight – to show their mettle or be damned to all of Halsos' hells.

Eleshen squared her shoulders. Standing tall, she narrowed her violet eyes. Sebasos' gesture arrived at her, and with a deep breath she stepped towards the pyre. Holding the leather-bound volume to her chest, her hands did not tremble. Her feet did not stumble as she moved over broken blue flagstones and trampled stalks of golden grass. Hard rain slicked down her hair, making their sable strands shine and running down her cheeks, sluicing away tears.

The pyre roared, the items within already blackened to char. With a deep breath near the roaring flames, just out of the blistering heat, Eleshen eased the tome from her chest. Gazing down at the worn leather cover, she gave a smile. It contained a madwoman's ravings, but neither her journal nor Mollia den'Lhorissian herself had been mad. The paramour of a King, banished to live in secret atop the Kingsmount, and Temlin, her true beloved, keeping her last journal close for so many years – his most precious possession.

Somehow it felt right to Eleshen, to sacrifice this for Temlin. Looking down, she saw rain spattered the old tome like lover's tears. She raised it and with a perfect throw, tossed it into the pyre. It lodged among snapping branches, sending up a flurry of sparks into the driving rain. Eleshen stood, rain running down her cheeks as she watched the last remembrance of Temlin and Mollia's love burn.

An emptiness of time spread out around Eleshen. Rain slicked the amphitheater, drove down into puddles that drowned the broken grass. Hours passed like moments. Torches couldn't keep up with the downpour, sizzling out to sodden stumps. Without oilcloaks to keep dry, the vigilant gradually gave up, turning and moving slowly toward the fortress like drifting ghosts. In the autumnal mountain gloom the underbelly of the sky burned, reflecting Eleshen's vigil. She shivered as darkness settled, chilled to her bones despite how close she stood to the sizzling flames of the pyre. Alone now in the empty night, she was still unable to come in from the rain.

Gentle hands settled to her shoulders. Eleshen jumped, startled, but she knew the feel of Khouren's cavern-deep energy behind her. His body was warm as he wrapped his arms around her and moved close, in a way Eleshen found she didn't mind.

"Will you remain out here all night?" Khouren breathed.

"I don't know."

Eleshen honestly didn't know. Something called her to remain, and yet, it was anathema to life and health to stand vigil through the dark hours out in the rain. Temlin would have scoffed at her for being idiotic. The thought brought a small smile, though it choked her.

"Feasting has begun. Inside the fortress." Khouren did not console nor push, simply stated certain facts with a hollow calm.

"I don't know if I can eat." Rain washed through the grey evening, a driving counterpoint to the pyre's endless roar. Khouren was silent a long moment, but then wound his arms closer about her. With a soft breath he set his lips to her temple. Something in Eleshen released and she shuddered, sagging into Khouren's arms as he cradled her.

"Come in." He murmured by her cheek. "The cold will deepen as the night drowns out."

"We should drown the night, one ale after another. Like Temlin would have."

"Perhaps we should." Eleshen felt the smallest smile at Khouren's lips. "The Jenners have already begun. Lushes, one and all."

"They'll drink it all before we even get to the fort," Eleshen snorted. "Holy men."

Khouren gave a soft laugh. Something about it made Eleshen shiver, but not from cold. "Come inside with me. Please."

Eleshen turned in Khouren's arms. The Ghost's grey eyes shone with a twist of gold in the fire's light. Honor was in those eyes, ancientness – and need. A need that rose in Eleshen also. A need for life, for love, for companionship. Lowering his chin, Khouren offered her his need, and lifting up, Eleshen offered hers back.

Their kiss was a silent thing in the night rain. Eleshen's mind left her. All she could feel was Khouren holding her, firm and close. His hands at her back. His lips, pressing and slow. His tongue finding hers and his breath in her mouth, sweet with spices and that strange scent of death. A slow eternity passed before he pulled back. As Eleshen gazed up into his eyes, she found them shining with something so fierce that her breath caught.

But just as Khouren was about to meet her lips again, his eyes shifted. He went utterly still. Then whisked Eleshen around behind him, his longknives out faster than thought. He bristled in the driving darkness, the fire's roar highlighting his sudden tense ferocity.

"Show yourself!" Khouren demanded, brandishing one longknife toward the darkness at the edge of the amphitheater.

There was nothing for a long moment. As if Khouren had called out to ghosts that only he could see at the amphitheater's rim. Then, an enormous white keshar-cat slid out from the darkness. Eleshen startled, whipping out her own longknives, but then she saw the wildcat had a bridle over its blocky head and ears, and a high-cantled saddle upon its back. A woman rode atop it in the darkness, dressed in a wildness of buckled brown leathers and thick furs that shed the rain. Her red-blonde hair was braided back and slick with wet, and as she stepped her mount slowly down the tiers of the amphitheater, Eleshen could see ice-blue eyes over fierce high cheekbones. She held a polearm in the night, the keen blade dazzling in the fire's flare as her cat stepped down the tiers with somber presence.

Khouren stiffened and Eleshen did the same, but he made no move to attack, watching the regal woman approach. Eleshen followed his lead, sensing no threat, just a calculating curiosity.

As the rider approached, the rim of the amphitheater suddenly teemed with eyes in the rain. Glowing eyes that slid forward into the light's distant ebb. Keshar-cats; tawny and black, speckled and roan, with blocky heads and enormous fangs. They moved into the light, and Eleshen saw each was ridden by a fierce warrior, all of them carrying polearms for battle. Dressed in gear of the Highlands, they were tattooed and pierced, hair braided back and set with fetishes of bone and feather, some with sides shaven. A motley crew of rough and ready riders, warriors in furs and leather filled the night, over two hundred strong. They sat astride their enormous mounts, watching, as the woman who was clearly their leader padded steadily down to Eleshen and Khouren.

"A right proper pyre." A rolling Elsthemi accent came from the cat-rider as she approached, a hard woefulness on her lovely face. Though imperious, her clear blue eyes shone with intelligence. "The gods'll bless yer departed. But I wonder – who are ye ta be givin' a royal send-off as per the ancient ways?"

The woman's gaze flicked back behind Eleshen's shoulder. Ihbram walked down the tiers from the fortress, his gaze without humor as he came, one hand lingering upon his undrawn sword. Though classically aloof, Ihbram's gaze roved the well-built woman's muscles and Elsthemi battle-braids appreciatively as he stepped to Khouren's side. The woman cocked her head, taking in Ihbram also, and gave a smile that didn't touch her ice-blue eyes.

"You've been watching us." Khouren had lowered his chin, his eyes lost to shadows, dangerous.

"Watching, aye," the woman's lips smiled but her eyes did not. "Cats smelled yer smoke five leagues off. Who are ye? An' why are ye giving Elsthemi royal rites to yer dead?"

Ihbram gave a winning grin that likewise did not touch his eyes. "Not Elsthemi rites, Menderian. Ancient, but well, fire seems as good a way as any to relieve our dead of their burdens."

"Our death-rites are none of your business," Khouren added coldly.

Eleshen glanced at Khouren. He'd not put his weapons away, still in a protective stance before her. He glowered at the lead warrior, and the cat-rider gave him a level gaze back.

"There was a time I'd cut out a tongue fer sassin' me like that," the warrior-woman gave Khouren a dangerous glance. "I'll no ask again. Who are ye, and what is yer will here?"

"Forgive me, lady of cats." Ihbram scuffed one boot on the sodden flagstones, his gaze hard. "But I could very well ask what you, a pard of General Merra Alramir's most elite keshari riders, are doing south of the Elsee?"

The warrior narrowed her gaze upon Ihbram and her white cat gave a growl. "Insult us, an' live no long enough ta see mornin', Brigadier. My cat's hungry, an' she likes ta bite the heads off insulting curs. Ye know our marks?"

"I see the Elsthemi High General's White Claw and Split Fangs emblems tooled into your saddles and weapons sheaths," Ihbram spoke, deadly. "But I don't see anyone in General Alramir's white armor."

"If ye know our marks, then ye would know Merra rides a snowy cat into battle," the woman spoke back coldly. "An' I'm losing my patience in all this rain."

Around the amphitheater, the cat-riders leveled polearms. A number of cats snarled as if sensing their cue to charge. Ihbram put hands on his hips and gave a chuckle, his green eyes holding a pleased awe. "Well, well. High General Merra Alramir of Elsthemen, in the fur."

"So. A defected Brigadier, an' Kingsmen, an' whatever else ye are, hidin' in the Highmountains." General Merra set the butt of her polearm to the stones with deceptive casualness, stroking snarls out of her wet beast's fur. "Cagey. Lying. Why should I not kill ye if ye will no tell me whom ye serve?"

"Because our aims are aligned." Eleshen cut in. Stepping in front of Khouren, she palmed strands of dripping hair from her face. "And the King-Protectorate for Elyasin den'Ildrian Alramir, the man we served, is dead." Ihbram was digging them into a conflict with all his defiant flirtation, and Khouren's standoffishness was no better. A conflict against two hundred warriors with battle-cats was not what they needed right now.

The woman's gaze sharpened on Eleshen. "Do say more if ye'd like ta keep yer hides."

"Lhaurent den'Alrahel is no friend to this fortress," Eleshen spoke, loud enough for all to hear. "And if you are who you say you are, then he's no friend to you! He's invaded your nation, sacked Lhen Fhekran, enslaved your people. If my guess is right, you're hiding out with whomever managed to escape, planning to attack him."

The woman's eyelids flickered, but she stared Eleshen down. "He'll no live a fortnight."

"He'll break you if you ride to Lintesh." Khouren interrupted as he stepped to Eleshen's side. "I'm guessing you faced Kreth-Hakir in Lhen Fhekran. He has more."

"Ye speak a dangerous game." The Elsthemi General's icy gaze pierced Khouren before she glanced back to Eleshen. "Who are ye, then? Speak plain."

"We're a faction of Alrashemni Kingsmen, Jenner monks, and Roushenn Palace Guard who have recently escaped Lhaurent's atrocities in Lintesh." Eleshen spoke up through the hiss of the rain. "And if you are no friend to Lhaurent, then we are allies."

"Alrashemni? Kingsmen?" The General's fingertips stroked her snowy cat's bedraggled fur.

"Some of us." Eleshen held her gaze. "Hidden in the Jenner Abbey for ten years, but Lhaurent destroyed the First Abbey. We had to flee."

Eleshen didn't trust the Elsthemi High General yet, and wasn't about to tell her everything, but the woman was listening – her face had lost its sneer, opening in surprise. "Do ye know the ronin General Theroun den'Vekir, then? Are ye allied with him?"

"I know the General," Khouren broke in, "and though he does not know me, our aims are aligned."

"Ye have a dark-devil way about ye." General Merra narrowed her eyes upon Khouren again.

"Trust us or do not," Ihbram spoke up, "but we've told you no lies tonight."

The woman tapped a finger on her weapons-belt, then palmed wet braids back from her forehead. Frowning, she finally spoke. "Lhen Fhekran has been emptied. All my people taken through an Alranstone. My riders have been watching from afar. A spy in the ruckus a few days past heard the Port of Ligenia mentioned. That everyone was ta be taken there, ta fight in a drive Lhaurent den'Karthus amasses upon the Aphellian Way against Valenghia. My riders head south, ta liberate our people."

"You'll die." Ihbram spoke up, his green eyes sharp. "Without anyone to bend the minds of the Kreth-Hakir, you'll be enslaved into Lhaurent's forces, just like all your kin."

"An' I suppose ye have an accomplished mind-bender among ye?" General Merra scoffed.

"We do." Eleshen spoke up again, feeling a need to convince the Elsthemi General. "Ihbram here held off four Kreth-Hakir during our attempt to assassinate Lhaurent den'Alrahel just a day ago."

"And if you'd like to hunt Kreth-Hakir, General," Khouren cut in, nodding to Ihbram, "there's only one man who can hold them long enough for your blade to find herringbone throats."

"Ronins with surprises," Merra's blue eyes were knife-keen, staring them each down in turn through the pummeling rain, before settling upon Eleshen.

"Indeed." Eleshen spoke again, raising her chin. "Before he

died, King-Protectorate Temlin den'Ildrian charged our faction to aid a siege that Lhaurent wages upon the last of the Alrashemni Kingsmen, near Vennet. There will be opportunity to kill Kreth-Hakir there. And reinforcements for you, if we win, to travel further south and free your kin."

Merra's blue eyes twinkled at last through the sluicing rain. A fierce smile rose to her lips as she shouted back over her shoulder, "Hear that, riders? Ye want sommat ta sink our fangs into? Fer Elsthemen?" A wicked roar went up through the rain behind her, and her smile was vicious as she turned back to face Eleshen's group. "We'll kill fer ye. And then ye'll kill fer us. Deal?"

"Deal." Eleshen's smile was just as keen. "But it's not a deal you can make just with me. You need to parlay with all the Kingsmen, allow them to vote, as is their way. The rest are up in the fort."

"Then lead on, and the keshari riders will follow. Miri!" Merra Alramir gestured with her polearm. A brawny woman with long cinnamon-red braids rode down on a grey-dappled cat. "Fall back to the main force. Tell them I've gone ta parlay with Kingsmen fer the night. If I'm not back by mid-morning, return here. Slaughter anyone ye find if they play me false."

"Yes, General." The rider snapped a quick salute and turned her cat. They flashed up the amphitheater, lost to darkness. General Merra called two more of her riders by name, Rhone and Rhennon, and two burly twins with wild wet braids padded down the amphitheater upon brawny tabby cats to flank their High General. Ready, General Merra gave a nod to Eleshen.

"Lead on, commander. Wolf's Child, was it?"

"Den'Fenrir, yes. Eleshen den'Fenrir, daughter to the Dhepan of Quelsis. Follow me." Straightening tall, Eleshen turned, walking swiftly up the slick tiers toward the fortress.

CHAPTER 19 – ELYASIN

They'd lingered in the cavern of the Giannyk for four days. The wight hadn't returned after Elyasin, Therel, and Ghrenna's display of *wyrria*, but after four days of trying Ghrenna's magic on every arch that ringed the space, they could still find no way out – every arch leading right back to the tunnel they had come in by.

Elyasin wandered the obsidian tombs, brushing them with her fingertips and making their sigils glow. They had opened three more in the past days, only to discover more preserved Giannyk warriors. Her step was soft upon the luminous mosses that coated the glassy obsidian floes, her boots stirring the creeping mist. Creatures scurried through the underground – insects and silverfish, translucent lizards, long white centipedes that would ripple from beneath the moss to her footfall. Elyasin took a deep breath of the misty air, but the chill didn't bother her, despite walking in her jerkin with her shirtsleeves rolled up.

Staring down at her hands, Elyasin watched a ripple of fire move through the awakened red and white markings upon her skin, but it went deeper than that: the bindings were written through her flesh to her deepest core. Exhilaration filled Elyasin, feeling Hahled Ferrian's awakened *wyrria* flowing through her veins. Reflecting upon how she and Therel and Ghrenna had banished the wight by the power of the Brother Kings and Morvein, she found herself still boiling with a power so great that it made the newly awakened inkings ripple upon her skin.

Hahled's *wyrria* was in her now, come what may.

Humming to brighten her singing-stone, Elyasin examined the glossy black tombs as she walked. All were carved with the flowing white Giannyk runes. Moving to a group she hadn't explored, she stepped to an obsidian obelisk central to the cluster, thrust up from the bedrock. Cleverly fashioned, the obelisks in each grouping of tombs were puzzles, segmented into layers that spun and moved.

Marked with golden sigils rather than pale ore like the tombs, they were untarnished by time, the gilded runes vibrant against all that black.

This obelisk was twice Elyasin's height but only a handspan thick, slim like a needle. She set her hand to its strangely warm surface, then startled to see Luc nearby. Leaning against a tomb in the near-dark, Luc had his arms crossed, a thoughtful scowl upon his face. His singing-stone cast a low light in a niche nearby, as if forgotten.

"Luc," Elyasin announced her presence. "What are you doing?"

"Fuck!" Luc visibly startled, then gave a wry laugh. "Don't sneak up on a man like that!"

"Be careful in the dark or you might lose yourself in it, Luc," Elyasin teased lightly.

"All too true." Luc sighed, his head falling back against the tomb. He was clearly not in a teasing mood, and Elyasin stepped over.

"Heavy thoughts?"

"You could say that." Luc rubbed his fingers as if they hurt. It was a distracted gesture, not unlike Elyasin's tic of rubbing her knuckles when she was anxious. Reaching up, he curried both hands through his golden mane with an exasperated sigh. Elyasin touched his hands and pulled them down. He blinked at her, then looked at her hand holding his, his smile awful.

"Care to share?" Elyasin prodded gently.

"Not really."

"Indulge me."

"Is that an order?" Luc eyeballed her.

"You're stewing, Luc." Elyasin stroked his hand. "Something's eating you up. You can tell me. Remember?"

Luc gave another hard sigh, then spoke, gripping her fingers. "Elyasin… the other day. When that wight appeared, I saw something manifest when you and Therel did battle. Like something was fighting the wight *through* you, directly from the Brother Kings. I can't get it out of my head and it's driving me crazy, thinking that the Brother Kings are just using you and Therel like puppets. That Morvein's pendants *meant* for it to happen to whatever poor sops inherited those damn things."

Elyasin was quiet. She'd been mulling over the exact same thing, in her own way. "It's like that and it's not, Luc. I can feel Hahled Ferrian inside me since that battle. Not like he takes me over, but that his *wyrria* flows through me. I felt *heated* when we were attacked, and I just knew how to move – how to gather this tremendous force inside myself and thrust it out at that thing."

"But Ghrenna's losing herself to Morvein's influence." Luc watched her with shrewd green eyes. "I can't – I can't sit around and watch that happen to Therel."

"And to me, you mean." Elyasin gave a sad smile. Luc couldn't hold her gaze and looked down. Elyasin's gaze dropped to their twined fingers, feeling Luc's care for her, though it was wrapped up in his torture about Ghrenna. Slowly, she disentangled her fingers and let him go.

His gaze was bleak as he found hers. "You know that I care for you. I never would have stayed at Lhen Fhekran if I didn't."

"I know." Elyasin reached out, touching a patch of luminous moss upon the tomb, as if it could ground this conflicted feeling inside her. "Luc. When we were young... I saw how you suffered at Roushenn, in your family. I never wanted to trap you into serving my line. You know I want the best for you, ever since we were children, but Therel's my true love. You only feel something for me because Ghrenna's pulling away, because she's changing. You need to let us all change, Luc. When I channeled Hahled's power against that wight, it was the most natural thing in the world. I've studied the sword for years, but I've never moved like that. It was mine as much as it was Hahled's."

"But what if his power breaks you, like Morvein is breaking Ghrenna?" Luc eyes were woeful.

"Morvein can't break Ghrenna," Elyasin felt a hard truth surface within her. "Because Ghrenna *is* Morvein, and you know it. They've never been different, Luc. Only a part of her was dormant before. A part that's stronger than the rest, and is waking now."

Luc went silent, staring into the distance toward the pinnacle of the cavern-mound. "A part that never loved me."

"A part that knows her duty above all else," Elyasin cupped Luc's face with her hand. "And so do I."

"But if it came to it," Luc's gaze pierced hers, "you'd choose Therel. I know it. You'd choose love over duty, your husband over your kingdom."

"My husband *is* my kingdom, Luc," Elyasin gave a soft smile. "He's a part of me. As are all of the people I need to protect. Including you."

"But you'll never love me, either," Luc gave a soft snort. "What a life I lead, falling for all the wrong women. I should never have left Fhouria."

"And yet, here you are." Elyasin let her voice go stern. It was time to teach Luc something about destiny, and Elyasin put a Queen's edge in her voice, something Olea had taught her long ago. "Take the path you've chosen, Luc. Do something with it. Your life is your own, and who you choose to help along the way is entirely up to you. If you call yourself a slave to monarchs or even to love, then you always will be. But though Hahled's power uses me, I am a slave to none, because my life is what I *choose* to make of it. So decide. Decide who you are, and quit this feeling of false responsibility you enslave yourself with. Use your gifts to help us or don't, your choice. Because you're not a slave, and you never were."

Luc stared at her – a level, weighing gaze as he pondered the full import of her words. He drew a deep breath in and let it out. "I guess I'm scared, Elyasin."

"Scared of being yourself?" Elyasin cocked her head, unsure where this was going now.

"Scared of my own power." Luc met her gaze squarely, raw honesty in his green eyes.

"Oh, Luc!" Elyasin reached out, cupping his face again. "You're more powerful than—"

"No. That's not what I mean." Gently, he pulled her hand down from his face, cupping it in his palms. "I've had this feeling for a while... what if something's happening to *wyrria* in the world?"

"What do you mean?"

"Like it's growing stronger, waking up?" Luc's gaze pierced her. "My healing has gotten stronger since Highsummer. So have Ghrenna's changes, and now, you and Therel channel the Brother Kings, and Elohl is some mythical savior of the world. Halsos, even Thad's manifesting memory-*wyrria* that puts any scholar I've ever heard of to shame! Fae-tales never hold so much magic, except when times are dire. Lhaurent, these wars… what if all this chaos and power rises because something worse than Lhaurent is coming?"

"The red-eyed demon of Elsthemi lore, you mean." A shiver rippled through Elyasin.

Luc nodded, his green eyes piercing the gloom. "And what if Morvein designed those pendants because she *knew* someone had to come back with power strong enough to match it? As many someones as she could make come back?"

Elyasin drew in a deep breath, a Kingsman breath, and used it to process all the things Luc was saying. They seemed too wild – yet, deep inside, her gut told her he spoke true. Heaviness settled in her heart. Stroking the moss upon the bier, she touched tiny fronds of a luminous fern but it failed to comfort her. The white and red inkings stood out upon the backs of her hands, running down her forearms like live fire, but for the first time it failed to make Elyasin feel warm in the blackness. A terrible chill stole into her heart and she shivered.

"Something rises in the world, Luc. Like a leviathan, provoking terrible crimes. I would pin the atrocities of the past decades upon Lhaurent, except that something within me says you're right. Facing that wight, I felt so alone. I've never felt so terribly alone, like a great darkness gathered all around me… What if Morvein felt this way?"

But just when she'd sunk into despair, Luc reached out and pulled Elyasin into an embrace. A warming sensation filled her; Luc's golden light pouring from his hands as he cradled her with one hand at the back of her heart. It filled Elyasin with purpose, with grace and strength. As the feel of a summer's day filled her, Elyasin shivered off despair, understanding the true blessing of what Luc was – light against the darkness.

They stood there, breathing together. At last, Luc pulled back to gaze at Elyasin with a stolid readiness. "Whatever you need from me, just say it. I used to think serving House den'Ildrian trapped me, but… I want to be by your side, Elyasin. I'm a better man, serving you, feeling you believe in me. Standing with you."

"Don't stand with me as my servant, Luc," Elyasin looked up into his eyes. "Stand with me as my friend. Be the man you were born to be. Independent and full of grace against the darkness."

Luc gave a chuckle. Reaching up, he stroked a lock of hair

from Elyasin's face. "Grace, huh? No one's ever said that about me before. Full of shit with cards up my sleeve, maybe. Weighted dice in my pocket, knives in my boots."

"Use whatever you have, Luc," Elyasin laughed back, feeling lighter. "Just do it for your own reasons."

He paused, watching her. Elyasin sobered, feeling a strange weight in the moment, but before she could say anything, Luc leaned down. Brushing his lips over hers – stealing a kiss in the gravitas. "Do not forget that there are people who will fight for you," Luc murmured. "Who love you."

"Not the least of which, are her King and husband." A strong baritone spoke from the darkness.

Luc startled, his hands dropping away as if struck by lightning. Elyasin glanced over, to see Therel approach from the dark, his white wolf-pelt and mussed blonde hair luminous in the shrouded gloom. Therel's pale blue gaze flicked over the scene, narrowed with regal fury. Luc turned, a flash of possessiveness in his eyes as he offered Elyasin a hand. She ignored it, stepping to Therel as her King arrived. Lifting up, Elyasin gave her husband a solid kiss, making him feel her heart. He gripped her with strong hands, pressing his kiss deep into her mouth as if claiming her like a wild animal. It was a moment before Therel let her go. When he did, he clasped her around the waist, turning her in his arms so she faced Luc, his hot breath giving Elyasin chills as he regarded Luc with a dangerous stare.

"I don't need to worry about my wife in her healer's arms, do I?"

"Therel—" Luc protested.

But Therel waved a hand, a glimmer of wrath in his eyes as he kept Elyasin close. "Peace. My Queen knows where her favored sword lies, and it's not between *your* legs, healer. But I heard what you said, and you're right. Love binds us stronger down here than *wyrria* ever could."

Threading his fingers through hers, Therel lifted up Elyasin's hand to kiss her knuckles. His tundra-pale eyes pierced her, and Elyasin felt herself shiver as Therel held her gaze with devouring lust and deep steadiness. Where once the wolf was wild in the night, he was now ready, a power running through him that made Elyasin tingle to the ends of her fingertips.

The power of the Brother Kings.

"We triumph where others fail," Therel spoke, "because like telmenberry, we are stronger together. Holding fast, clinging heart to heart and vine to vine. Making an impenetrable barrier that none can breach and protecting our sweetest fruits. The best parts of living."

Elyasin reeled, feeling Therel's power twist into hers, feeling her heat and Therel's smooth ardor twine together like the vines of telmen. The sensation flooded her, bound her, until Elyasin felt that she and Therel were two parts of the same twinned power – two sides of the same heart.

"Luc. Would you excuse my King and I?"

"As you wish." Luc's words were clipped. He moved away, sulking off into the mist, his lanky stride firm as if in challenge as he left Elyasin and her King alone. Reaching up, Therel stroked Elyasin's hair back from her face, cupping his hand beneath her nape.

"How long has it been since we made love?" He growled.

"Too long." Elyasin's breath quickened.

"How long?" Therel growled, moving in. His body pressed close, his soft lips beginning to kiss along her neck.

"Since the day before the invasion," Elyasin breathed, pulled in by Therel's warm hands at her neck and back. Yielding with a moan, warmth flooded her, tingling between her thighs.

"A mistake I aim to rectify." Holding her firm, Therel kissed deep into her neck below her jaw.

"The others will hear us."

"Let them," Therel growled into her throat. "My wife has needed her husband for weeks, and he has been a callous cur. Too caught up in my own bullshit until I saw you two together just now."

"So you only come to me out of jealousy?"

"No, jealousy was only the spark," Therel growled. "When we fought together against that wight – that's when I remembered. How it feels to move with you. To fight with you at my side or fuck with you in my bed. I am lost without you, and when I deny our love, I only make us weak. Love me, my Queen. Take me down, right now – don't say no."

Therel's hands were all over her. Cupping Elyasin's breasts, pulling the buckles of her jerkin. His lips were upon her neck, pressing her with lust and love. Therel was a madman of passion, but he was *her* madman, and she needed his love more than she needed breath. Elyasin pulled him down to the moss. They tore into each other like beasts, hands pulling at clothing, kissing as if they ate each other from the mouth down. Caught in their ardor, Elyasin hardly heard the shout that came from far up the hillside.

Until it came again – Thad's voice calling their names with urgency.

"What in Halsos?!" Therel growled, glancing up with one hand at the longknife in his boot-sheath. He gave an exasperated roar, frustration emanating from his entire body as he ground his hips down upon Elyasin. Thad continued to call them, and the area brightened as his voice neared. Elyasin lifted her chin to see Thad upside-down, waving at them vigorously with his glowing singing-stone through the mist.

"My Queen! My King! Oh!" Thad balked, his eyes widening as he registered the scene. His cheeks colored as he hastily swiped the spectacles from his face and turned his back. "Forgive me! But I've made a discovery, my lieges! Up at the central tomb. There's something you should see."

Therel growled again as the scribe scuttled back up the hillside. He pressed kisses down Elyasin's chest toward her breasts, but the moment was broken and they both knew it. Therel sighed, resting his forehead on her chest. "Karthor's sake. This better be good."

Elyasin shifted and Therel rolled off her so she could rise. As she fixed her clothing, Therel did the same, bucking his jerkin back up. Reaching down with a growl, he adjusted his member where it strained at the crotch of his breeches, then beckoned Elyasin on ahead of him. As she moved past, she paused to give his crotch a fondle. "We are coming back to this."

"As my Queen desires." Therel's smolder was deeply pleased as he took out his singing-stone and hummed it to life. Ascending the hill, Elyasin felt Therel's hand caress her rear as she walked. She turned and swatted him.

"What?" Therel grinned. "Can't a man enjoy his own wife's delicious ass?"

"We have to take command right now, Therel," Elyasin laughed back.

"I'd rather command you around the sack a little more." Therel growled, humor in his tone. He surged to trap Elyasin, his tundra-pale eyes shining, and Elyasin let herself be caught. Raising up, she brought her lips to his. A hot fire burned through her, matched by the slow pour of Therel's kiss down her throat. Deep like a river, the rush of his kiss was exhilarating. Elyasin wound her arms around his shoulders as he pulled her closer with a low growl, eating deeply at her lips.

It was a long moment before they separated, breathless. Something passed between them, like an understanding or a connection they'd never had before. A slow wash of light moved through Elyasin's red and white inkings where they stood out upon her arms and upper chest, echoed by the same upon Therel's skin in violet and white. Therel's gaze stalked Elyasin as she turned, making her skin heat as she headed up the incline again. When they reached the pinnacle, Thad's eyes were concerned as he took off his spectacles and lipped their ends watching a slow roll of light still passing through their twinned markings. Ghrenna stood by Thad with her long white hair bound over one shoulder, watching also, as Luc slouched like a handsome shadow against an obelisk, glowering.

Elyasin moved to where Thad stood beside a black obelisk – the nearest of seven that stood in a wide ring, their spire-sharp needles encircling a broad pool of black water. A gargantuan stone tomb rose from a bier at the center of that water, an isolated island in the middle of the small lake. Larger and more ornate than the others, this tomb was obsidian glass, but easily twice the size of the others and positively cluttered with white sigils. Every available space was inlaid; whorls of white, curls of silver, and script of pure gold writhed over the entire surface of the tomb and gabled lid. The only tomb set into the pool of water, the ring of black spires clutched the pool like some ancient creature's implacable grip – one additional spire rising from inside the pool at the foot of the sarcophagus.

"It's time we go where we were meant to." Ghrenna spoke as everyone arrived, her cerulean eyes almost fevered by the light of the singing-stones and the incandescence still sliding through Therel and Elyasin's new inkings. "Thad made a discovery this morning, and it has provoked memories long hidden inside Morvein's mind – the next step of our journey. But we cannot take that step unless we are aligned. We've lived dark days, but they will be worse if we cannot stand as one."

Elyasin did not miss the pointed gaze that Ghrenna shot Luc. Almost as if she were herself and not Morvein, that glance held both warning and affection for the surly thief. Luc flushed, though Elyasin could see his temper was not gone. Elyasin glanced to Therel, some part of her knowing that Morvein had spoken to her Brother Kings this way before they had traveled to the White Ring. She saw an answering knowledge in Therel's eyes, and worry as he reached out, claiming Elyasin's hand.

"Thaddeus," Ghrenna turned to the scribe, "would you explain your discovery?"

With a brisk nod, Thad traced a few sigils upon the near obelisk. They flared a wraithlike white-blue beneath his fingertips, like the sigils upon the tombs. To Elyasin's surprise, when Thad added humming to his endeavors the obelisk moved. Like a massive Praoughian clockwork, the thing shuffled through a few smooth clicks, pushing out pieces from its surface with a liquid fluidity, then re-placing them into the whole as entire sections twisted and rotated. What had been a six-sided obelisk now had eight faces with protrusions every handspan, the sigils on its face re-arranged into a different pattern.

"Amazing!" Elyasin stepped closer, reaching out to stroke the sigils. They flared under her fingertips, then went quiet.

"Indeed," Thad smiled brightly. "I discovered this a few days ago and have been recording the Giannyk sentences they form. Or incantations."

Elyasin chilled, not liking the sound of that, but Thaddeus merely plowed on in his scholarly excitement as he gestured to a group of sigils on the near surface. "I've recorded this pattern already. From my observation of the memory walls, I've come to assume that these sigils translate to *ice, travel, home, thought, bring*, and *wyrria*. It seems to mean something like, *by the power of wyrric thought, will you travel home to the ice*. Whenever the sigils rearrange, they always recombine in a pattern of six. On any obelisk in this room, each sentence has six elements. Noun-verb-noun, followed by another noun-verb-noun."

"What are you getting at, Thad?" Reaching out, Therel traced the sigil of *ice*, like seven stylized icicles or fangs in a row.

"Everything we've experienced down here makes music, or responds to it." Thad pulled off his spectacles and put them up on his head. "I believe Giannyk *wyrria* operated within that framework – sigils that are a living imprint, which respond to sound and vibration. When we interact with that – with the vibrations of our bodies through touch, speech, or singing – we get results."

Reaching out, Thad stroked the gold veins of the *travel* sigil, like an ornate cart-wheel. It brightened, then dimmed, but as he began to sing the sentence inscribed upon the surface, the brightening effect was multiplied. The pillar resonated, a low, thrumming vibration cascading off of its smooth surfaces, rumbling Elyasin to her core as waves of light rippled through the sigils Thad touched. Like thunder over mountains, the feel of it was carnal and Elyasin shivered at the thrilling sensation. Thad ceased singing and the hum of the obelisk faded, until his fingers merely traced pretty streaks of light upon its surface.

"Fascinating. How do you suppose it works?" Therel mused, riveted beside Elyasin.

"I believe that each obelisk is a puzzle," Thad spoke, "a tricky one. Just on this obelisk alone I've recorded thirty-six different positions, each with numerous faces, and each face having the recombinant six-sigil pattern. If you look at each obelisk, sigils will rise up from *inside* sections when it changes shape, revealing entirely new markings. Whoever created these didn't want them to be solved easily. Or perhaps at all. I also think—"

Thad cut off suddenly and Elyasin prodded him, "You think what?"

"That these puzzles protect something. Or perhaps incarcerate something." Thaddeus' gaze darted down, then back up as he cleared his throat. "I have the feeling these obelisks were put here to keep these tombs asleep. Every obelisk has one sigil that repeats. The symbol for *sleep*. In the tunnel pictures, the symbol for *death* was everywhere – a reclining figure on its side with coins over its eyes and arms crossed. But here, it's all *sleep*. A reclining figure on its side with one finger raised before its lips. What if – what if they're down here because Bhorlen put them to sleep *on purpose*? And created these obelisks with binding-magic in an unfathomable puzzle so that no one could ever wake them?"

Elyasin thought back to their battle with the Giannyk wight. How cold the thing had been, how inhuman. The wight had fled to this pinnacle when it flashed out. Elyasin shivered as her gaze met Therel's again. Therel took a deep breath, then turned to Thad.

"You're stalling, Thad." Therel admonished gently, his lupine gaze wry. "We know you've figured out more than you're saying."

Thad took a deep breath, and his next words ringing out among the obsidian obelisks like a death-knell. "I've learned enough of the Giannyk language that I'm able to read many of the glyphs inscribed upon this central tomb. Much of the text is historical, speaking of the entombed warrior's identity. This tomb identifies the occupant as King Trevius Stranik of the Heimhold Giannyk clan. Elected King of the North during the Giannyk-Albrenni Wars, when a vast evil swept the land. Wars, famines, plagues, purges, slaughters, natural disasters, you name it. An evil attributed to the *Utrus*, the Undoer, who is identified as a possessor-entity with red eyes."

"The Red-Eyed Demon," Elyasin murmured.

"Precisely." Thad's gaze held hers, troubled. "From the glyphs, I've pieced together that Trevius was actually possessed by this Undoer-entity. That he waged a horrible battle against his own kind, the Giannyk, and their neighbors the Albrenni, and nearly won. His own brother, named Archaeon Stranik in the glyphs, acquired a tremendous weapon, something called the Key of Fire, to halt Trevius and his warriors." Thad gestured to all the tombs. "And then this other fellow, Bhorlen Valdaris, created an unsolvable *wyrric* trap for Trevius and his warriors – to put them to sleep forever, away from the clutches of the Undoer."

"King Trevius' Sleep." The words breathed from Therel's lips with a terrible awe. "It's all real."

"So it is." Thad held his King's gaze. "There are dire warnings on the sarcophagi. To never solve *Karakhan nikh Obderheim*, the Riddle of the Obelisks. Lest it wake *Warrik schlafin k'Utrus* the Sleeping Warriors of the Undoer."

"Better stop fiddling with those plinths, kid," Luc murmured, only slightly acerbic.

"I have." Thad gave a cordial nod to Luc. "But I discovered that one had been tampered with long before we arrived." Gesturing to the second black spire in the ring, Thad stepped over to it, then began his routine of touching the sigils and humming, then singing again. But this one stood inert, not a single rune upon its surface flaring. Thad ceased his efforts, rejoining the group.

"So that one doesn't move," Elyasin observed, crossing her arms, intrigued.

"Its shape is final," Thad agreed with a nod, retrieving his spectacles and polishing them on one sleeve with a troubled look. "It has been *unlocked*, shall we say. It doesn't move anymore. No matter how many sigils I touch, or how I sing to it, it's done."

"So one of seven locks surrounding a sleeping Giannyk King possessed by the Red-Eyed Demon is open?" Therel spoke, his pale brows knitting in a frown. "I don't like the sound of that."

"I believe it's why we were attacked when we arrived." Thad put his spectacles back on his nose. "This lock was open prior to our arrival. Eight hundred years prior, to be exact. I spoke to Ghrenna about it, and her memories came flooding back."

"What do you mean?" Elyasin asked, turning to Ghrenna.

"Morvein unlocked that obelisk," Ghrenna cast her haunting gaze upon Elyasin. "The first time she came seeking the Giannyk to learn the Rennkavi's binding. She'd thought this was the place, when she arrived. She opened tombs, saw sleeping Giannyk warriors, and realized there were no doors leading out of this chamber, so she began fiddling with the obelisks, just as Thad did, learning the Giannyk language, figuring out their sigildry and incantations. She figured out two things while she was here. And a third that nearly killed her."

"What things?" Elyasin asked, crossing her arms over her chest, her fingertips touching her longknives and finding comfort in them.

"The first thing," Ghrenna gestured to the silent pool of water around the sarcophagus, "is that this pool is a portal, accessed by that obelisk at the foot of the sarcophagus. It leads to an underground citadel, to which Morvein traveled and found the White Ring of the Rennkavi's Ritual. And further, to the Giannyk Bhorlen who taught her how to bind the Rennkavi."

"Thank fucks we've got a way out of here!" Luc breathed.

"The second thing Morvein figured out," Ghrenna continued, "was how to unlock the obelisks. Her fascination with them outweighed her fascination with the tombs, and she was able to unlock one without having read the warnings. She freed something horrible. Just a bit of its wrath and power, but enough that she nearly lost her life battling it. She managed to get through the portal — barely, but Morvein didn't dare travel back this way until she had her Brother Kings."

"Morvein couldn't win against that wight we battled?" Therel and Elyasin shared a look.

"Not that creature." Ghrenna gave Elyasin and Therel a long look. "That was only one of Trevius' warriors. When Morvein unlocked that obelisk," Ghrenna nodded at the non-functional one, "she awakened Trevius himself, or at least a small part of his enormous *wyrria*, as well as the wights of many of his sleeping warriors. She nearly died, getting through the portal and out of here. When she was with her Brother Kings, they had more power to get through to the White Ring. Raising *wyrria* so close to Trevius' tomb will wake him again, but we must, in order to take the portal to our destination."

"Damned if we do—" Luc murmured.

"Damned if we don't." Therel glanced at the healer, then gave a battle-ready grin. "The only way out is through. Everybody take a half-hour to eat, water, and pack your things. We'll meet back here. Make ready to fight a demon."

No one spoke as they moved back down the hillside. Belongings and bedrolls were packed in a hurry; meals were quick. Canteens were filled at seepage-basins along the edge of the cavern, and then they were trekking back up to the mist-wreathed height. Packs were flung into the pool at Ghrenna's instruction. Everyone slid into the frigid water, cold enough to even give Elyasin a shiver, though it was only knee-deep. The fighters gathered around Ghrenna and Thad at the obelisk in the water, facing outward.

Ready for whatever might come when Ghrenna began opening the portal.

Tense silence breathed around them. Elyasin felt something hard rise in her, ready for battle. Heat flooded her, and as she gazed at Therel, she could almost see a cool flood of power surging inside him from the Brother Kings. Mist swirled over the waters of the black pool. Ghrenna's hands began to slide over runes upon the obelisk, igniting their blue-white incandescence. A vibration began in the chamber: a low, shuddering sound, like the growl of a mad animal. Ghrenna's hands were fast, her humming opening to singing in ancient Giannyk. The vibration increased, shuddering the hillside, making the black waters of the pool dance and the mist swirl up around them. Elyasin's neck lifted in hackles, the hairs on her arms standing straight as the entire chamber electrified.

Suddenly, a rippling concussion shot through the mist. Originating at the central sarcophagus, it hammered through the pool and down the hillside, lifting the mist in a macabre, shuddering dance. Upon its heels, light flared in a spreading wave down from the height. Bier after bier surged to life with a searing, terrible glow, the cavern flooding with a sinuous brilliance. Too bright, the light was obliterating, and Elyasin cried out as she shielded her face, longknives ready in her hands, but no matter where she looked it was the same. Like sun upon a snowfield, blazing sigils scorched her from every direction, the opalescent mist magnifying that brightness like diamonds.

Something came rushing out from the tomb in the center of the black pool. Terrible as a hurricane, it swirled the mist into a dazzling vortex. Elyasin had no time; it was upon them. Power hit her in a shuddering wave, and with a cacophonous howl, that power raised an army of wraiths in the mist all around them. The pressure of a thousand damned warriors slammed into Elyasin. It smote her to her knees in the water. A thousand gazes of terrible power – a vast, unimaginable *wyrria* that made the Brother Kings look like playthings.

A towering form rose from the central sarcophagus in a diamond light, cavernously dark in all that brightness. As if the light could not penetrate the ancient Giannyk King, Trevius Stranik's wight devoured all brilliance. Like a black hole, he ate all resonance – inhaled it, devoured it, as dead-bright blue eyes looked down upon them. Pain coursed through Elyasin's limbs like live lightning as his mind gripped her, forcing himself into her, demanding that she come to heel – and showing her his true essence.

Like a nightmare, red eyes stared out at Elyasin from a darkness so deep, it was the absence of all light. A world of endlessness and shadow, and the deep eternity of the Void. This was the force *behind* the wight-King. An enormous presence that wasn't in the universe, but *of* the universe. As its crimson, soul-staining eyes pierced Elyasin, devouring her mind and flesh, it ate up whatever was good and beautiful inside her. Leaving only terror and nightmares, and the worst parts of her nature, for her to examine at leisure. For an infinity of its pleasure. For an infinity of her Undoing – the annihilation of everything she had ever been, was now, or ever would be.

"No!"

The word scorched from Elyasin's lips like a firebrand from the forge. It went spearing into that darkness with all the power of Hahled Ferrian's *wyrria* behind it. She sent it right to those bloody eyes, spearing them, as her left hand shot from her body in a banishing movement, palm out – slamming that presence out of her soul in a wash of heat like a volcano's wrath.

She felt Therel do the exact same thing at her side. The red-eyed evil broke like a mirage, but it was not arrested, the wight-King surging in fast. Elyasin's hands flashed in a complicated warding on instinct, but the creature was faster. With one lance, the dark-wight seized her. The black mist wrenched her from the pool, lifting her high. Her limbs were freezing, her body devoured by pain and cold. Her ears heard Therel roar as Ghrenna's singing faltered. Flooding flows of power slammed the dark-wight from Therel, but it held Elyasin fast, tuning aside those *wyrric* attacks and sending them into his dazzling army – infuriating them.

As wights rushed in, attacking Therel from all around, King Trevius' eyes devoured Elyasin, a poisonous, terrible red. A face of massive stature and strong bones formed, made of the swirling black mist, staring down at her. A disembodied *wyrric* power, his body was still trapped in his bier, and on instinct, Elyasin seized the creature's swirling black *wyrric* hands that held her. Digging in claws of heat, she roared in its face, sending wrath out through her fingertips. Like lava flooding a mountainside, fire and molten gold seethed up its arms in crimson veins as she poured Hahled's defiance through the wight-King with a defiant roar, *wyrria* racing into her foe.

With a shriek of pain, it dropped her. The black mist flashed out as Elyasin splashed into the pool. Her bottom hit stone; her head plunged under. Golden sigils flared as she choked on icy water, thunder shuddering the pool from the dark-wight's wrath. He was coming. Black mist smote the pool, directly for her, but then, she was wrenched. Ripped away and threaded through nowhere, her insides twisted and eyeballs exploding as she traveled.

Thrust back into being with a splash onto hard stone – surrounded by a night full of stars.

CHAPTER 20 – JHERRICK

For three days after his death-rite, Jherrick sat in Flavian's oculus-room before the pool, feeling the Void surround him. Whispering energies of benign or curious intent touched at his hair, stroked his skin. Deep in trance as evening settled, Jherrick felt a malign touch seep into body, demanding energy. He shivered it off, blinking rapidly. Sweat stood out on his forehead from hours of rolling back such intrusions. His heart beat with a strange rhythm since his trials, and it did so now as he fought off the stealing touch from the Void, hammering his chest and making him cough.

Noldrones Flavian and Noldra Ethirae had been teaching him these past few days. Showing him how to immerse himself in the Void, yet remain above any energies that wanted to steal from him. After his encounter with the red-eyed demon, Jherrick was cautious, and it had taken the Albrenni a full day to convince him he could open himself up to the Void safely. Still, it was a struggle, venomous energies plucking at his body anytime he relaxed his vigilance.

Sensing a presence behind him, Jherrick released his trance as Noldra Ethirae ducked beneath the flowering vines that twined the stone doorway, carrying a silver tray of fruits. Her skin was the milky color of starlight in the violet evening, her hair a silver river that cascaded from beneath her hood. Her silk robe flowed over long limbs as she wove a table out of living vines that crept across the floor with an elegant gesture, then set the tray upon it. Her cheekbones cut across her immortal beauty, her eyes entirely black as she turned to evaluate Jherrick's aura in the Void. A midnight sky lived in those eyes, just like Flavian's – a miniature of the swirling cosmos Jherrick could now experience.

"Noldrones Jherrick," Noldra Ethirae addressed him with a slight bow and two fingers touching her brow. "Noldrones Flavian would speak with you after you sup. Are you well enough?"

Jherrick could feel her powerful presence in the Void, like a shudder through his bones. He had known little about her before his awakening, and now he almost knew too much. Ethirae was one of the oldest members of the Sanctuary, despite her youthful appearance. An orb of light glowed around her in the Void, an energy-sphere that now reached out to Jherrick with luminous tendrils, smoothing his jagged struggles. Every color light eased into his heart as she moved close, bolstering him. As if she was a strung harp singing through the dusk and he a coarse bronze bell, Jherrick tuned to her resonance, until all devious energies rolled back.

"How do you do that?" He sighed, bliss enveloping his Voidworld-vigilance at last.

"I make of myself a resonance beyond light and darkness," she murmured in her haunting alto as she came to sit upon the floor beside him. "And then creatures of lower vibration cannot touch my Essence in the Void."

Jherrick shuddered, feeling one of those touches try to invade again. Ethirae set her palm to his bare chest between the high open collar of his quilted silver-white robe. He panicked a moment, recalling the sensation of the imposter Olea reaching inside him during his encounter in the cave, but Ethirae's touch was warm and mild.

"Darkness haunts you since your Resurrection." Watching his eyes, Ethirae's silver-white brows knit. She cocked her head, pressing her palm deeper. Fingers of light eased through Jherrick, and then her presence slid up the back of his neck into his mind. Jherrick felt his thoughts sorted through, flipped fast like a deck of fate-cards. Until one memory rose: cold red eyes lancing straight to Jherrick's soul. Ice speared his veins and he cried out. Ethirae set her other palm to Jherrick's forehead, suffusing his mind with a wave of white light. The memory roiled back to a frozen nightmare and Ethirae lowered her palm from his forehead, though Jherrick could still feel a wave of light sighing into him from her.

"The Red-Eyed Demon has made claim upon you, Noldrones Jherrick," she breathed. "Only those of terrible power are so cursed by its choice."

"Why does it want me?" Jherrick shivered.

"The Demon seeks to walk the world again, in a body – yours." Ethirae sighed. "It possesses only the strongest of any Age. Only those who have the power to bring unfathomable ruin. Long ago, my people fought the Demon when it came to us."

Jherrick shivered as his heart gripped unnaturally. He knew that something dark lay inside of him, that understood death and annihilation. Ethirae's words sparked Jherrick's curiosity. "Your people, the Albrenni. They fought this thing?"

"Long ago." Ethirae let her other hand fall from his skin, as she watched him. "My people were Undone by the Demon. The Albrenni will never forget the taste of its destruction. There are but a handful of us left in the Manyworlds, most of whom are safe here in the Sanctuary, like myself and Noldrones Flavian. A few still steward the world you come from, hoping for a better Age. They hide themselves well, lest they attract the Demon's gaze."

"What exactly are Albrenni?" Jherrick reached out, touching her high cheekbones, running his fingers over her starlight skin.

"I am not forbidden to show any member of the Noldarum. Now that you are initiated, would you like to see my true form?" She smiled.

"Yes," Jherrick spoke before he could stop it, eager to see the truth of this creature before him.

With a soft smile, Ethirae turned her head and kissed the tips of his fingers. Still sitting upon the floor, she began to un-hook her silver-white robe from its high collar, revealing her smooth collarbones and chest. Slipping the quilted silk off her shoulders, she bared delicate breasts and slender, firm flesh untouched by time.

As the robe sighed down over her hips and puddled to the stone, Jherrick's breath caught. Not only was she beautiful, but her energy brightened the Void, swirling in a vortex of color. With an in-breath, she raised her palms over her head. And then with a swift cry, Ethirae brought her hands down, fingers gripping the Void with power. Light burst from her in a tremendous wave; like the explosion of a falling star, it smote Jherrick's senses. Enormous every-color wings burst from her spine in the world of the real, seven layers of them, surging to the far corners of the oculus-room. Her cry was that of a raptor as energy surged from her, slamming Jherrick back – a maelstrom vortex that thrust into the depths of the Void and made its ascendency known.

Fallen back to his elbows upon the agate-stone floor, Jherrick stared in awe. As the light dimmed, he saw before him a bird-woman with sleek down of milk-silver, angelic features and wings, her endless eyes boring into his soul. With a subtle shake, she riffled the wings, though they were not exactly feathers. Like filaments of woven light, they ran with rippling currents, like water pouring over cliffs, though they held the form of a bird.

"Aeon!" Jherrick breathed.

"See me, Child of Man," Ethirae spoke, her voice riven with an eagle's cry. "See an Albrennus Fellasti of the First Darkening. When humankind was in its infancy, we were ascendant. We held the darkness at bay with the Giannyk of Krethwathsten, of Heimhold, and of Hakkim Beldir; with the great tundra Kings of Rikiyasti, of Fithri Ile, and the desert-builders of Aj Naab. We were there to battle back the Demon's First Rise, though we lost everything. And we are here still."

Wafting out, one filament of those massive wings eased over Jherrick's forehead, pressing the center of his brow in a surge of light. Like a river's wash, Jherrick felt ancient memories flow into him. Five thousand years ago. Entire valleys running crimson from battles. Mountains exploding from terrible feats of *wyrria*. Herds annihilated in moments from a blast-wave through a grassland, killing everything it touched. Cities of men and women and children, walking mesmerized, coming to kill him. A tundra battle-plain, blue ice stained crimson with gore unto every horizon. The dead, rising to battle, their eyes blind red horror.

Jherrick fell back, gasping, his hands clutching his heart – trying to stop it, but Ethirae's memories flooded in, unable to be stopped. It was too much, the horror, the suffering. Jherrick's mind fled. His consciousness flashed out as he retreated to the furthest reaches of the Void to escape, but horror followed him into the Void, Jherrick's own screaming terror its doorway. Red eyes rushed up from the darkness, obliterating. Swallowing his vision, the red eyes eliminated stars, annihilated galaxies. The entirety of the cosmos was swallowed by cold, burning red, as despair screamed inside Jherrick.

Suddenly, an enormous wave of light and color sluiced around him. Pushing back the red, devouring it until nothing was left around Jherrick but a warming blue-white glow. Some part of him felt hands lifting him, raising him to a soft bed of woven vines. Gradually, his mind risked returning and found that three Albrenni held a circle around him, arms wide, miraculous wings spread to their fullest through the dusk-dark chamber.

Jherrick recognized Noldrones Flavian and Noldra Ethirae holding that circle, but the third was a stranger. A man that looked like he'd been ancient when time began, his face was gouged with lines and criss-crossed with scarring. One eye was blind and as he blinked at Jherrick, that eyelid did not close, leaking tears. His face was the visage of hawks in battle, his shoulders wide and straight. The feel of power wreathed his roped muscles and massive chest. A good deal taller and more rugged than his kin, he wore the silver robe of the Noldarum. Spread wide, his hands had black talons upon their gnarled fingertips as he gripped power into the Void, his forearms corded sinew and wreathed with arcane tattooing in a devouring black ink. That dead eye fixed upon Jherrick, and in it, Jherrick saw vast and terrible knowledge.

"Lay still boy." The ancient Albrennus commanded, his voice graveled like a battle-lord.

Ethirae held her spread-winged pose, reaching out a tendril of energy to press Jherrick back to the bed of vines. "Forgive me. Unveiling my true nature was too much. I had no idea how deep you could go into my memories."

But Jherrick was done being ignorant, struggling up to sitting. "No. I need to know what's going on. What is this Demon, and why is it after me?"

"At last." Flavian lifted an eyebrow with a subtle quirk of lips, a rare expression of amusement.

"Boy has some piss in him. Good. He'll need it." The ancient Albrennus spoke again.

"Need it for what?"

"To face the Undoer." The old Albrennus gave him a blind eyeball and Jherrick shivered under that uncompromising gaze. Red eyes rose in his mind, but distant, pushed back through a swath of everycolor light from the circle's power. With a hard in-breath, the ancient Albrennus broke the circle at last, catching himself upon a gnarled fist to the vines as his wings snapped down with a wrenching, haphazard motion. Crushing white flowers upon the bier with his fist as his mangled wings eliminated more around the room, the ancient Albrennus' gaze pierced Jherrick. "We banished it. But only for a time."

"What is it?"

"Such innocence," the old Albrennus snorted, his ancient eye flashing with temper. "To have lived in a world so safe for so many eons, all because we made it so."

"Come." Flavian was polite, gesturing for Jherrick to rise. "Your training among us will need to include far more than we ever thought, Noldrones Jherrick. Please. Walk with us."

Jherrick found his limbs stable as he pushed up off the bed of flowering vines and fell into step next to Flavian. The Herald's filamentous wings siphoned out to the Void as he walked, as if they had never been, while Ethirae folded hers neatly along her spine like a luminous cloak. The old Albrennus' broken wings merely dragged behind him, the group silent as they proceeded out beneath a flowering archway and into a vaulted corridor high above the minarets of the citadel.

But rather than take the winding stair that led toward the citadel's center, Flavian chose a lofty bridge toward the outer vistas of the city. Jherrick beheld the vastness of the cosmos as they moved down one corkscrewing staircase to a succession of vaulted platforms. At last, they came out upon a massive cloverleaf plaza, at the far edge of which stood seven white archways. Everycolor mist rippled through those archways like billowing silk, and Jherrick had the sensation of a thousand whispers in the Void. The hairs on the back of his neck pricked, his animal senses instantly alert.

Suddenly, a memory hit him. Of twisting upon that platform, spat out through one of those archways in pain and screaming, from the crystal blood Plinth near Khehem. Walking forward, Jherrick came to the center of the expanse of agate. Haunting strains of music with a thousand impossible chords moved through those archways, as if they accessed not just other worlds, but other universes through a vast and intelligent nowhere that sang as it danced. Mesmerized, Jherrick thought he saw sigils in the mist, strange and mutable, before they moved on.

"Haunting, isn't it? Seeing how the World Shaper moves?" Flavian stood at his side, gazing at the arches.

"The World Shaper?"

"That which creates." Flavian moved his hand in an expansive gesture, indicating the endless galaxies beyond the platform, that dropped off to an infinity of stars all around. "And the ability within us all, for us to create in turn."

"Is the World Shaper a god, or goddess?"

"Nothing so limited," Flavian's lips quirked. "The name was passed to us Albrenni eons ago by ones far more ancient than us, who fought for our maturation as a species. Like your humankind, we were once coarse, reckless, short-lived and short-sighted. We fought wars, decimated our brethren over land and ore, learned magic for power and bred *wyrric* bloodlines to dominate. But those who were old when we were young showed us the majesty of the World Shaper's benevolence, and warned us against the terror of her counterpart."

"Her counterpart?" Jherrick turned to Flavian, but it was the gruff old general who answered.

"The Undoer, boy. I do believe you've met." He gave an amused snort. Reaching up, he rubbed away leakage from beneath his ruined eye. "As I did, long ago."

"Who are you?" Jherrick's gaze sharpened upon the old warrior.

That ancient gaze fixed on Jherrick. "My name is Archaeon Stranik, of the Heimhold Giannyk and the Sephali clan of the Albrennus Fellasti. But you might know me by my shortened name. *Aeon*, I do believe your people curse to me."

Jherrick couldn't speak. He would have thought it a joke except that the old warrior held his gaze with such penetrating force that his guts liquefied. "Aeon? But Aeon is just a... symbol."

"Is he?" The ancient warrior chuckled, wrinkles of amusement pulling his scar-torn lips up. "Well, then I can just lay down in my grave and be *symbolically* dead, I suppose."

"You're serious?" Jherrick was a fool to ask, but the claim was so outlandish that he still couldn't wrap his mind around it.

Flavian actually chuckled beside Jherrick, a smile of amusement upon his features. "Deeds of heroes become legend. Legends die into myths when a culture falls and only stories live on, passed by mouth. Myths become gods eventually, worshipped as supreme, but supremely misunderstood. So did your people who once lived upon the tundras recount the deeds of Archaeon Stranik, King Trevius Stranik's High General, who sacrificed himself when all forms of battle failed against the Red-Eyed Demon. A warrior born of two ancient races with vast *wyrria*, who was strong enough to hold the World Shaper's Key, and brave enough to transform the world by allowing the Demon to take him instead of his half-brother Trevius. Archaeon became the Light of Creation, to save the world. He is the only one, as far as we know, who has ever lived to tell the tale."

"If you can call it living." The ancient war-general flexed his wings in a haphazard shuffle and Jherrick noticed that they moved in a cumbersome, jerking motion. Peering closer beneath the endless night, he saw the ancient man's filamentous wings were torn, broken, forming odd angles as if they had been shattered but never set right. Black scars rippled through them like waves of fire burned through and gone. As Jherrick peered at the man's skin, he saw Archaeon's flesh was the same, flowing with ancient burn scars, in addition to terrible slash-marks.

As a pained expression took Archaeon's face from trying to settle his wings straight, Ethirae moved to his back. Pressing her slender body to his spine, she wrapped her arms around his massive chest and set her lips to the center of his back, as high as her diminutive form could reach. Spreading her wings wide behind his broken ones, Jherrick felt her inhale the power of the stars. He saw her breath in the Void, gathering runnels of light. And then she pressed her lips deep upon Archaeon's spine, and breathed every bit of that light into him.

He arched in her arms, wings lifting, vibrating. He drew in a massive breath and for a moment, Jherrick saw the man's form brighten in the Void, whirling with color like the archways. And then he darkened, as if that light siphoned right back out through a thousand rents, flowing back to the universe. Archaeon relaxed in Ethirae's arms. Set a hand to her wrists where they encircled his massive but emaciated frame.

"Thank you, my dear," he rumbled gently. "That wasn't necessary, but thank you."

"I won't stand by and watch you suffer." She moved away, but

Jherrick could see how much that action had taken from her. Her aura guttered low in the Void, grey and slow in its ethereal spin. He thought she would have simply gathered energy to heal, but it seemed even her abilities had limits, as she did a rapid panting breath to increase her brightness by painfully tiny increments.

"Archaeon's wounds cannot be healed," Flavian spoke, watching where Jherrick was looking. "They are wounds of the etheric body, and no *wyrria* we've ever found, among any peoples or world, has been able to heal his tremendous sacrifice. Accepting the runic markings to become the World Shaper's Key, her instrument to battle the Demon, is not a thing to be taken lightly. It never was."

Jherrick's gaze roved over those burned-out inkings that swirled over Archaeon's skin as the man reached up to wipe his leaking eye. Like the emptiness in a house when the fire has left it in ruins, it was as if Jherrick could see the destruction within Archaeon. Black tendrils wove through his etheric body. Thousands of rents and ripped places where he leaked energy back to the Void. Those rents tore through his physical body also, a warrened darkness that ate him alive and left him a ruined husk.

"The magic, this – Key." Jherrick spoke, understanding. "It burned through you, left you unable to regenerate. You would be like them," he nodded to Flavian and Ethirae, "able to stay ever-young, had you not carried it."

"Great power comes with great sacrifice." Archaeon turned his formidable gaze upon Jherrick, piercing like an eagle's talons. "How does one transform ultimate destruction? Only by carrying the greatest creationary power any world has ever seen. A power that transforms the Demon when he tries to rise, and allows a Golden Age to finally come to fruition. Except for the Albrenni and the Giannyk and our human allies, our Golden Age fell with the Demon's Rise. We misunderstood *wyrria*, and we paid for it. Unto the last of our sons and daughters."

"What do you mean?" Jherrick asked.

"Power attracts power," Flavian interrupted, solemn. "The more one masters *wyrria*, the more that person becomes desirable for the Demon to inhabit. Our people were accomplished in *wyrria*. Though you are young and your power unlearned, the Demon feels what you might one day become, Noldrones Jherrick. Something

277

truly powerful. A power that can tear down worlds and cause the endless destruction the Demon covets – which was why the Giannyk and Albrenni were also desirable to the Demon, in our time."

"My half-brother, Trevius," Archaeon spoke again, "had the same *wyrria* that breathes in you, boy. The Path of the Dead, the Giannyk called it, where I was raised in the stronghold-citadel of Heimhold, which is far north in the lands now called Elsthemen. My father, Ulfgrad Stranik, bore four sons. Two with Giannyk women, great battle-Queens of the north. Another born of a human tundra-witch with uncanny ability, who saved my father's life in the wild. And the last born of the Honoress of the Albrenni, the Eagle-People's High Priestess, who gave her body to him as part of a truce our people formed then. I was the child of that union."

"Half Giannyk and half Albrenni?" Jherrick murmured.

"Yes." Archaeon nodded. "My Giannyk half-brothers, Bhorlen Valdaris, named for his mother's royal line, Trevius Stranik, and Vrennen Stranik Tundra-Born, were all great men. Bhorlen was a powerful Portalsmith and Sigil-Wright, Vrennen a masterful Portalsmith, and I held prowess as a Battle-Dremor, and a General in the field. But Trevius…Trevius had power. Fighting prowess, cunning, magnetism. Worst of all, he understood the Path of the Dead, which the Albrenni call *louve wyrdi*, and humans nicknamed Dusk *wyrria*. Trevius knew how to wield it. How to keep someone alive even after they were cut to ribbons upon the battlefield. How to banish life from a healthy warrior. And how to restore life to the dead."

A shiver passed through Jherrick. Archaeon's words held warning of something terrible. Something that ran in Jherrick's own veins, yet to be unleashed.

"Trevius began to raise armies of un-dead." It was Ethirac who spoke, taking up the tale as she stared out across the universe. "He found that arisen warriors fought harder – without pain, without a mind of their own. They could be controlled to his will, and his will at the time was battling the hordes of nightmares the Demon unleashed upon us through every gateway that connected to our world. You have heard of the Valley of Doors? Or perhaps the Aphellian Way?"

"I've heard of them." Jherrick's throat was dry.

Ethirae's gaze was level. "There are places in every world that must be *watched*, Noldrones Jherrick. Ways *through* the Great Void. Gateways like these we stand before here, to other worlds. Some worlds are not so forgiving as where you come from. Do you understand?"

"The Demon opened the gateways," Jherrick murmured. "Blasted them open, and unmentionable things attacked from these other worlds. Decimated your people."

"Indeed. Causing us many trials and vicious battles, before he possessed my brother Trevius, after Trevius rose as King of the Giannyk at the end of the Demon's Wars." Archaeon's voice was a hard growl in the luminous dark. "Twisted by the Demon's Rise inside of him, Trevius raised armies of the un-dead against his own kin, and against what was left of the Albrenni, the Tundra-Men, and our Ajnabi allies. Dead Giannyk rose upon the battlefields. Dead behemoths, dead creatures of nightmare, things we had already vanquished at terrible cost in the worst battles our world had ever seen. All of them rose – to fight us anew, and when one of our own was slain, he too would rise, turning on his companions and slaying on. The carnage was unimaginable. And unstoppable, except by fire. We learned to burn our dead in those days. Anything that died. The tradition of the pyre lives on among the Elsthemi, our Tundra-mated descendants."

"And the fire that burned through you?" Jherrick nodded to Archaean's wounds.

"Was sacred. Holy fire." Archaeon's tone was low, and in it, Jherrick heard strain. "I sought it out, a rumor of a rumor from the oldest Albrenni legends. Of a people called the Fyrrini, born of salt and ash, who could confer upon me the only thing that could stop the Undoer. The Key of Fire – the Key of the World Shaper. Needless to say, I found the Fyrrini, and they gave me what I sought. To my eternal damnation."

Ethirae set a hand to Archaeon's broad but emaciated shoulder. He did not shake it off, but slumped under her touch as if exhausted. "Forgive me. I will need to continue this conversation at a later time. Rising from my rest… has made me weary."

"Come." Ethirae moved under his arm, and Jherrick saw how old and worn the ancient battle-lord truly was. He leaned heavily upon her as he nodded his goodnights to Jherrick and then set two fingers to his forehead in respect for Flavian.

Jherrick and Flavian watched them go. When they ascended the first turn of stairs and were lost to view, Jherrick turned. "Will he be alright?"

"No." Flavian's visage was thoughtful, sad. "He will never live well again. I still hold out hope that we can find some cure for his malady, but," Flavian shrugged, an elegant gesture, "it is a dimming hope."

They turned back to the archways, staring at unseen winds that stirred the gossamer veils until at last, Flavian sighed. "Noldrones Jherrick. Ages turn, and the rise and fall of the World Shaper's spindle causes patterns to repeat. Societies rise and flourish, emerging into a Golden Age. When they begin to understand and weave currents of the universe, of *wyrria*, the Demon's mind is attracted from the nothingness where it resides. It begins to seek those who can wield the worst destruction – those of broken heart but of great magic. Those who are *susceptible* to the devouring darkness of its red eyes. Do you understand what I'm saying?"

Jherrick rubbed his chest. He could still feel it, the raw ache of Olea's passage from his life, and Aldris. The countless innocents destroyed by Lhaurent; and his Khehemni parents, dead by fire. Death followed Jherrick, and with it came this horrible darkness of his own broken-hearted sorrow.

"My grief. It lets the Demon in."

"Your *sundered heart* lets the Demon in." Flavian's dark eyes were compassionate. "The summation of your woes that you cannot move through. To find the light, Noldrones Jherrick, we have to embrace our darkness. See that which we hate about our lives, about our faults and wrongdoing. To conquer your grief and not be a lodestone for the Demon, you have to *face what you are.* You walk the Path of the Dead, *louve wyrdi* – Dusk *wyrria*. It is your nature, your power, and your bane. And it will be your Undoing if you cannot learn to face its dire magic."

"Dusk *wyrria*," Jherrick glanced at Flavian, "what is it, exactly?"

Flavian heaved a great sigh, turning his visage up to the endless stars. "How can I explain the vibration of the dusk? For such a thing is so subtle and powerful as to exceed all expectations and boundaries. In basic principles – the universe, the Great Void, breathes with currents that are all part of the World Shaper's creationary music. Vibrations that when harnessed, can create or destroy the areas they affect. Your people call the entirety of this vibrational system *wyrria*."

"*Wyrria* is magic, though, isn't it?" Jherrick frowned.

Flavian glanced at him, clasping his hands behind his back. "*Wyrria* is the vibration from which all things come. It is the summation of the World Shaper's music. Learn to hear different strains, learn to master the seven different vibrations of it, and you shall learn how to use it as the World Shaper herself does."

"To create or destroy."

Noldrones Flavian nodded. "For the Shaper herself made her Undoer. The Undoer is a natural process. It is something her Great Void *does*, as galaxies are born and die, as stars explode into being and snuff out. But when the Undoer possesses manifest flesh, it becomes unbalanced. Death exceeds life. Do you understand?"

"I begin to," Jherrick murmured. "But if the Undoer is a natural process, is it the same as the Red-Eyed Demon?"

A slight smile lifted Flavian's lips, his starlight eyes glittering with humor. "Astute, Noldrones Jherrick. Very astute. Indeed, we do not know. The Red-Eyed Demon is so vastly ancient and powerful that we are unable to tell any difference between it and the Original Undoing. If it is not Her Original Undoer, it is so corrupted by that vast discordance that even the ancient ones who taught us Albrenni could not say precisely what it was. Only that it has decimated worlds – entire galaxies – because it was allowed to come into being."

Jherrick shivered, a chill racing through him. "Is it only Dusk *wyrria* that the Demon corrupts?"

"No. Of the seven major strains of *wyrria* in the universe, the Demon can corrupt them all, except for the Shaper's original vibration." Turning towards Jherrick, Flavian watched him. Stepping close, he set his fingers to Jherrick's chin, raising it so he could look in Jherrick's eyes. "I see," Flavian spoke in a hushed whisper, his gaze moving from one of Jherrick's eyes to the other.

"What?"

"*Khehe wyrdi*," Flavian chuckled. "Conflict *wyrria*. I believe your ancient kin called it the Wolf and Dragon? It runs in your veins also. Though strangely enough, you do not carry it as your primary vibration."

Startled, a shiver raced through Jherrick. Heat shot through his veins, thinking about Khehem and the horror he had experienced in that dead place.

"Yes, *Khehe wyrdi* is there," Flavian breathed, watching him intently. "Conflict pours through your veins, just behind death. No wonder the Demon seeks you." Flavian's touch slipped away, and Jherrick shuddered to lose its cool calm. His gaze straying to the cosmos, Flavian's aura flowed out amongst the endless stars as he breathed in stillness for a long moment. He gave a long blink, and when he returned, he was still not back all the way, his gaze resting upon the seven archways before focusing on Jherrick once more.

"You have a hard road ahead of you, Noldrones Jherrick. Dusk and Conflict simmer in your blood. You will have teachers, but not here. We have no one here at the Sanctuary with enough strength in the *khehe wyrdi* to train you."

Jherrick went chill to the tips of his fingers. He shivered, watching the veils of muted light ripple and breathe in the archways. A dead boy's glassy eyes rose in his mind, then Olea's opal orbs dying to a flat grey.

And then Aldris, laying cold in kingly attire in the Memoriarium.

"I can feel your thoughts, Noldrones Jherrick." Flavian spoke abruptly, his endless eyes boring into Jherrick, stern and devouring. "I can feel you obsessing about resurrecting your dead friend. Trying to call his spirit back into his body. And I feel I must warn you: King Trevius Stranik was the same – vibrating with Dusk and Conflict *wyrria* both. The Demon rose inside him because of the terrible conflict that death brought him. And his equally burning desire – to end that death."

"Resurrection," Jherrick breathed, horrified. "But if I never train in my *wyrria*, then the Demon can never be able to use me."

"Ask Trevius Stranik how well that turned out for him." Flavian's words were soft in the darkness, ominous. "When he was young, he avoided developing his *wyrria* because he was afraid of its vast power, but every person's natural *wyrria* will out, in any way that it can, Noldrones Jherrick. Embrace yours. Or be felled by it when the Demon is stronger at wielding it than you are – from inside your very own body. Just like happened to King Trevius."

Turning, Noldrones Flavian gazed up at the seven archways, his hands clasped behind his back. Jherrick turned also, feeling the World Shaper's impenetrable music pour through him. Though it soothed Jherrick to watch that mutable flow, something dark roiled inside him.

Reaching out with hands of blackened starlight toward the Great Void – and the souls it wished to gather back.

CHAPTER 21 – THEROUN

After his meal, Theroun was led to a small chamber within the cloisters of the cathedral. A monk's cell, it had a simple wooden bed that Theroun collapsed into the moment he arrived. He'd awoken in the dregs of night having sweated through his shirt and trousers and stripped them away, drinking down a pitcher of water and collapsing to sleep once more.

It was deep night when he woke again, his muscles and sinews stiff. A single candle lit his chambers, flickering in an autumn breeze that fingered in through gaps in the stone wall. Theroun didn't remember lighting a candle. He sat up, rubbing his chest – his fevers had abated and his skin felt cool. The rioting of his *wyrria* slumbered, only causing a stitch in Theroun's old wound. Stretching, he realized a man sat upon a chair in one dark corner of his room.

Theroun knew that solid frame, that subtle regard. Khorel Jornath had him at a disadvantage. Theroun hadn't even heard the man enter the chamber through his obliviate slumber. He debated action, but against the mind-manipulator and without weapons, any action seemed moot. He settled for swinging his legs over the side and facing the man in his underdrawers as he stretched his side.

"Haven't you ever heard of knocking?" Theroun growled.

"I did knock." A rolling chuckle came from the shadows. "So many times and so loudly that I thought you might be dead."

"But you knew I wasn't." Theroun tested the man. "From your silver net in my body."

"Indeed."

"So why are you here?" Theroun growled, twisting the other way.

"To see how you fare." Jornath leaned forward into the candlelight with his elbows on his knees and big hands clasped, regarding Theroun frankly. "As High Priest at this encampment, it is my responsibility to shepherd my Brethren, and Initiates. Your welfare is of high priority to us."

"To join your ranks and serve Lhaurent?" Theroun snorted. "I'd rather die."

"You very likely will." Jornath was frank. "And our service to Lhaurent den'Alrahel stands only as long as there is not one to supplant him."

The answer startled Theroun, but he did not let it show. He ceased stretching and set his palms on his knees. "You would serve someone else against Lhaurent?"

"The Kreth-Hakir serve only the strongest." Jornath's smile was subtle in the wan light. "Only the most dominant power in any age may wield the might of the Scorpions. Lhaurent wears *wyrric* marks foretold by ancient prophecy, giving him a power so strong that it could unite the world in the most chaotic time ever seen. Unlike most who have heard the prophecy told from the tongues of lesser men, the Hakir remember the direct words of our god Leith Alodwine himself. We saw his fear of this future chaos, so we keep his faith and its primary tenet."

Theroun scowled, but the story was too intriguing to abandon. "Your god was afraid?"

Lacing his big fingers, Jornath's dark grey gaze evaluated Theroun. "Have you ever seen the eyes of a man who is so powerful in *wyrria* that he seems godlike, quail with fear?"

"What could such a man have to fear?" Theroun's brows furrowed.

"Destruction." Jornath's murmur eased through the room. "Ultimate destruction, of all places, all peoples."

"Don't your people destroy wherever they go?"

"We follow Leith's central tenet, and under it, atrocities can occur."

"Which is?"

"That we serve the one with the most power in any age. And watch him. For the ultimate corruption that Leith feared."

"You're spying on Lhaurent?" Theroun leaned forward.

"We serve Lhaurent." Jornath corrected, his gaze hard. "We serve him to the death of every last one of us. Our word to him is our bond, and our bond is everything. We shall continue to serve him until someone with a greater power bests him, but we also watch, Theroun. We watch Lhaurent den'Alrahel for a fate worse than death. For something Leith Alodwine, last King of Khehem, feared greater than war, greater than losing his family, his beloved city, even his life. We watch, for the Rise of the Red-Eyed Demon."

Theroun sat forward, mimicking Jornath's posture unconsciously. "You think Lhaurent's abilities and his power will turn him into some kind of monster?"

"Not a monster," Jornath shook his head. "*The* monster. Ancient lore mentions it only as the Destroyer of Worlds. The Red-Eyed Demon chooses only the most powerful in any age to seduce and enter. The most powerful, who are also the most alone."

"So this Demon, he's some kind of spirit?" Theroun knit his brows, trying to understand his enemy.

"He is a possessor," Jornath corrected. "A god who can slip into the mind. Take it in dreams, in nightmares, and eventually in one's waking life. Take a person to madness, and wield in them the ultimate chaos."

"And this possessor," Theroun continued, mulling it over, "could he enter a Kreth-Hakir?"

"No. In our training, the Kreth-Hakir do much to practice against such occurrence," Jornath commented. "Our god Leith commanded it of us."

"Was your god Leith possessed by this demon?"

"He never would say." Jornath's eyes darkened. "And despite our best mind-breakers, we could not wrest the truth of it from him. So we were formed to guard against the creature, to bind ourselves to the highest power in any land, to become close and learn their mind. To see if their eyes flashed red with the madness of the Demon."

"And if one comes who can best Lhaurent?"

"If Lhaurent den'Alrahel is cast down, though he is of our god's bloodline, we would marshal for him no more." Jornath's eyes were knowing by the candle's flicker. "You hate Lhaurent. I can feel it seething inside you. A lifetime of loathing. You believe his gains are all false and his motivations dishonorable. Such things are not of concern to me, Theroun, nor to the Brethren."

"So you serve a tyrant blindly."

"Not blindly," Jornath warned, his gaze dire. "In my span of years, I have seen the honorable and dishonorable rise and fall like the wheat and the scythe. Tyrants cause ruin; heroes cause gain. Lhaurent has been blessed by a new power, and this power will be watched and served like we have served others before him – until he either falls or becomes tainted in his soul. The greater mind of the Kreth-Hakir thinks in millennia, Black Viper, not decades. If you join us, if you decide to receive our training to wrestle the *wyrria* inside you, you'll understand."

"Join your hive mind?" Theroun growled. "Become a mindless cur to those more dominant?"

"Dominance is a training tool, nothing more," Jornath spoke quietly. "It is suffered until a Brother becomes strong enough to break a more dominant member's hold over his mind. I have three Brethren in this company struggling to break my hold over them right this very moment. Two full Brethren, and one Initiate who has powers far greater than he knows." Khorel Jornath's glance spoke volumes.

"Your Brethren are cruel in their ways."

"Have we been cruel?" Jornath eyed Theroun with a dark look. "When we took lives upon the battlefield, did we make them suffer? Or did we take their lives cleanly, making them slit their own throats with perfect skill? Did we not honor the best of the fallen, braiding their hair into adornments for our scorpions? Have we not caused a minimum of death as we rode through the countryside, sparing every hamlet and only making war upon the capitol? Have you seen a single Brother under the grip of my mind rape any woman or beat to death any man?"

"Adelaine Visek." Her name dropped from Theroun's lips before he could stop himself.

Jornath eyed him. "Would you have done any less, Black Viper, with a battle-maid who withholds information vital to the progress of your campaign?"

Theroun returned Khorel Jornath's steady gaze. Though he detested the man, he couldn't refute Jornath's words and Theroun hadn't seen any rape of the Elsthemi, nor beatings. They had been fed and watered as they worked, and only been mind-controlled enough to do their work without trying to escape.

It had been civil, really, for a conquering army.

"What do you want of me?" Theroun grated.

"I only ask that you hear my words," Jornath returned, his grey eyes frank. "That you consider a life among the Brethren. We have honor in what we do."

"But you suffer no resistance."

Jornath stood at last. Gazing down at Theroun with a complex look in his eyes, he spoke. "No. We do not. Those who oppose us are cut down. Any who cannot feel our mind-bending are of especial danger to the greater good. They cannot be controlled when the Red-Eyed Demon comes. Even with all our strength, my Brethren cannot pull the minds of the *wyrric*-blind away from the seduction of the Demon, and it would cause unimaginable chaos. We cannot have chaos, Theroun. Chaos is the enemy of order – of a strong foundation from which we can all flourish. Our god Leith understood how strong that foundation had to be against the Demon's Rise – he sacrificed everything for it. The question is: would you? Would you sacrifice everything you have to become something greater? To protect the world from an evil far worse than the rise and fall of nations or tyrants? Would you serve an Order that sometimes must make dire bargains, to prevent the destruction of all peoples? Think on it, for this world is far larger than Lhaurent, or you, or even Alrou-Mendera. Without a strong foundation when the Demon rises – we will all fall."

Theroun laced his hands, thinking. "What if Lhaurent is evil? What if he is this Demon you speak of, already possessed by this spirit of ultimate destruction?"

"I hate him as you do, Theroun." Jornath's smile was hard, his grey eyes dead as slate. "I hate Lhaurent den'Alrahel with all my heart. Many of my Brethren do. He has no honor, but we feel in him much strength, and though you do not wish to hear it, he possesses none of the red-eyed madness we have trained all our lives to know. You may not believe it, but my Order is ancient. We remember a time when the Red-Eyed Demon rose in ages past. And those who survived that madness founded my Order, many thousands of years ago."

"I thought you were the progeny of your god, Leith?" Theroun interrupted.

"No. The Kreth-Hakir Brethren are ancient, but we had fallen into disrepair when Leith came to us," Jornath corrected mildly. "We had forgotten our lineage when he revived in us the oldest memories of the Giannyk and the Albrenni, with whom the Kreth-Hakir were once aligned. Leith revived our power and solidarity; our long-forgotten practice of Knowing the Beast. For only those who truly know their darkest *wyrria* will be safe when the Demon comes."

"How does facing one's darkest *wyrria* keep them safe from the Demon?"

Jornath's words were very soft. "One cannot be a vehicle for the Demon when one knows and confronts the entirety of one's inner torment. When one embraces the very worst of who one is, and accepts it more deeply than any lover. Kreth-Hakir face our inner darkness. We face it and embrace it, Theroun, with open eyes. Once we understand and accept our Beast, we can calm it. And when a man embraces the deepest darkness of his nature, then *no man nor god* can control him with it. So will you accept your Beast, Theroun – to become part of something greater? Or will you let it take you down like a dog?"

With that, Khorel Jornath dipped his chin in goodnight and swept from the room. The wooden door clicked shut. Theroun was left with only a roiling and snapping of silver threads inside his body as he pondered everything the High Priest had said. Knowing he'd get no more sleep, Theroun moved to the floor.

Sitting in meditation, images came and went through his mind – of betrayal and death. The more he tried to banish them, the more they came, borne of darkness and annihilation. An energy built in him as he sat, a vast and terrible thing that soon trembled every limb. Some part of him that knew darkness, and was not afraid of being the terror in the night.

Dawn found Theroun moving through his fighting stances, flowing through sword-forms. He'd given up on meditation, the violence in his limbs far too much to contain. As the first rays of the sun seeped in through the cracks of his shuttered window, he dropped yet again into pushups upon the cold stone floor. Heaving through lunges to squats, flipping himself upside-down at the wall and doing pushups inverted.

Energy surged through his muscles like burning peat. It simmered within him, something he'd not felt for ages: a tremendous energy, filled with a lust for ruin. With every heave, Theroun tried to banish it. With every twist of his torso, he tried to wring it from his body. With every lunge and pivot he tried to spear it, to kill it with an invisible blade.

Memories dredged up. Theroun as a boy on his father's estate, watching his father's hired soldiers. Watching how they moved, the power in them as they fought on the practice grounds. Taking up the sword simply because he wanted to be among that hunt and bloodshed. To pummel, to strike and wrestle, even if it meant getting damaged. To have the power they had, the strength.

The killing strike.

Theroun pressed, lunged, flipped his bare feet back up the cold wall, holding his extension with strong arms. His face flooded with blood, wisps of steam curling from his body in the dawn. Thoughts swirled through him, each darker than the last. What if he was nothing but the hunt? Nothing but a killer? What if he had no loyalty, no honor? What if he stepped upon the battlefield only because he was actually darkness, and his will was only death?

The Black Viper.

Theroun's elbows buckled. He came crashing down, barely catching himself upon the balls of his feet before his knees drove into the stone. Theroun's fingers spasmed in his sweat-slick hair. Like a beast, all his anguish came roaring out of his mouth. He balled his hands into fists, smashing them into the stone floor. He gripped his head; pressed his forehead to the stone. His body shook as silver threads snapped and snapped again. The net around the black leviathan inside him was shredding, and with it came all the horrors Theroun had banished from his mind in order to survive the long drone of years.

He saw that day again; the day his life changed. The camp at the Aphellian Way. His Captain Aerundahl den'Bhern approaching, to ask if his General was alright. Red rage surging inside Theroun, a beast with nothing but the desire to kill. More than kill. To destroy the world, to bring it all crashing down in godlessness without a code of ethics in sight.

Theroun sat up, shivering in his sweat-drenched shirt and trousers. A tirade of silver threads snapped in his mind, and with it came a surge of agony. As if on cue, the door-latch clicked. The chamber door opened to admit the young Valenghian Brother with his short shock of silver mane. His violet eyes widened to see the state Theroun was in.

Banishing memories, Theroun hauled himself to his feet. He was a General. He served his Queen. The past was dead.

"Well?" He barked at the lad.

"Brother Jornath would see you." The young man gestured to the door, shrinking back slightly.

With a hard growl, Theroun gathered his ruined Elsthemi jerkin and slung it on. He strode through the hall and up the stairs to the chapel. Taking the steps two at a time, a fire lit his body as he pushed through the white-pine doors, slamming them back so hard they ricocheted off the stone walls with a boom. Standing at the war-table, Khorel Jornath turned from a scroll he'd been perusing.

"What do you want?" Theroun snapped, marching forward.

"My weave within you is breaking this morning, Theroun." The Kreth-Hakir's fingers slipped from the scroll as he straightened and faced Theroun. "You have far less time than I'd hoped."

"I'll give you none of my allegiance, Khorel," Theroun snarled. "I serve only my Queen. Your bastard tricks cowed me before Lhaurent, but I'll not succumb again."

"You must face the vastness inside you," Jornath spoke, watching Theroun carefully. "Or it will kill you, soon. We can help."

"I'll face it in my own way."

"Do that." Jornath's sneer was derisive.

"Did you call me here just to beleaguer me?"

"No. I called you here because I wish you to witness how one's deepest darkness can be used against them."

Jornath moved away from the table. As he did, eight Kreth-Hakir Brethren stepped from the shadowed gables, forming a circle in the open space of the cathedral. Suddenly, Adelaine was hauled in by two strong Brethren, dragged in on her knees like a dead cat. Stripped naked, her head hung with her tousled white mane tumbling around her bruised flesh.

Theroun surged forward with a roar. Khorel Jornath stopped him with a firm hand to his arm, and a vise-grip of silver around his flesh. "Try to free her and I will cut you down. With mind and blade I will flay you, no matter how valuable you may be. The others in my Order cannot penetrate your rising *wyrria*, but I can. The Dremorande will fall today and you are here as witness, nothing more. You will watch as I gain access to her secrets, because of what she fears. What she fears, and what she longs for with the darkest part of her being."

"And what is that?"

"Watch and see."

Khorel Jornath turned from Theroun. Four Hakir lowered Adelaine to the stone floor, legs straight together, hands by her sides. As twelve Kreth-Hakir Brethren ringed the fallen woman with their gazes fixed upon her, the High Priest stepped into the center. Adelaine seemed unconscious, her mouth open and head fallen to one side as shallow breaths rattled her throat. Her skinny ribs billowed like sails as she shivered, every muscle rigid. Her eyes rolled up, showing whites as her eyelashes fluttered. Though they stood in a sanctuary, Theroun knew this was was to be no holy right. This would be a breaking by demons, straight to Halsos's Burnwater, and there was nothing Theroun could do to stop it.

But he would be damned if he'd let her die this way. With a will, Theroun strained against Jornath's silver that held him. It gave with a sad sigh, and Theroun marched into the circle. As he crossed the boundary, the full weight of the Kreth-Hakir's combined mind-weave hit him like a furious silver ocean, something terrible already at work. Setting his jaw against the inundation, Theroun waded in to the fallen woman. The black oilslick nature of his own *wyrria* surged, fighting those silver waves and its own prison. It was because of its enormous strength of will that Theroun gained Adelaine's side, falling to his knees and taking up her hand.

"High Dremorande of Elsthemen," Theroun growled gently. "You're not alone. Even if you die, soldier, know that you do not go to that dark oblivion alone."

One ear turned his way, as if Adelaine listened even in her fugue.

"Say whatever you wish to comfort her," Khorel Jornath's baritone came at Theroun's side as he knelt. "But know that she will not suffer, not by my hand."

Jornath stroked Adelaine's face. A keening sound left her. She pressed her cheek into his touch as if it was the last comforting thing in the world. Theroun's bile rose at the High Priest's vile seduction. If he'd had a weapon, he would have buried it in Jornath's eye, but Theroun was also stunned to see that Jornath gazed at Adelaine with surprising tenderness, his visage a mixture of calm sadness and dominant benevolence.

"You fight so hard," Jornath stroked Adelaine's cheek. "Don't fight so hard. It doesn't have to be this way."

As Theroun watched, Jornath settled to a seat beside the fallen Dremorande. The rest of the twelve Kreth-Hakir prowled the circle, fixated upon their prey, pummeling into Adelaine's mind, but Jornath was the purveyor of mercy. With gentle hands, he stroked Adelaine's face, her neck, smoothing her tangled white hair away from her cheeks.

She keened harder, eyelids fluttering rapidly.

"Shh…" One of Jornath's big hands slipped behind her neck, cupping her nape. And suddenly, Adelaine was like a puppet with strings broken. One moment she spasmed, and the next she sagged. Jornath caught her with his big hands. Slipping his other hand beneath her back, he pulled her up into his lap. Wrapping her thin frame in those enormous arms, he cradled Adelaine like a child. Rocking her, he smoothed her hair, kissed her cheek.

"Easy. You're safe now," Khorel Jornath crooned. "I won't let them hurt you, ever again."

Suddenly, Theroun felt Khorel's mind surge in a wave of obliterating power. With the force of a maelstrom, he smashed back the twelve men who ringed them. The Brethren fell, stumbling to their knees, some crying out. Theroun saw one man's nose fountain blood as he fell back in a dead faint.

It was no ruse. It was real. Jornath had played the part of Adelaine's hero, commanding her foes to abandon their torment. Deep in Jornath's eyes was the last thing Theroun thought he would ever see in such a vile man – love. Not a sham, but real love, as if Adelaine was his most precious beloved. As if Jornath believed it to his fundament that he was her savior, her protector. Giving her the thing she desired most, and the only thing she feared. Her deepest darkness, the horrific shadow behind her *wyrric* power.

True love, and its protection from her nightmares.

"You're safe," Jornath murmured in Adelaine's ear. "They can't hurt you now. Let me see, my love. Let me smooth your pain... let me in..."

Theroun watched Adelaine unfurl for Jornath like a flower. She turned her face up, burying it in Jornath's neck above the high collar of his studded leather jerkin. She inhaled his scent, then rested her forehead against his neck. Her limbs relaxed. Her breath was shallow, laying at ease in his arms. Jornath lifted her with impossible gentleness, maneuvering her back onto the stone floor. With ultimate care, he laid her out, hands folded atop her breastbone, legs together in a position of repose.

Theroun could not take his eyes away. He could not bring himself to stop it, some fascination holding him to watch this terrible ritual and understand the true power of will-*wyrria*. Jornath smoothed Adelaine's hair to one side, then slid one big hand beneath her naked hips and the other beneath her neck, cradling her by her entire spine though she remained resting upon the floor. Lifting his face, Jornath closed his eyes in an expression of benevolent rapture.

Theroun felt a thickness to the room, a rippling heat issuing from the High Priest of the Kreth-Hakir. As if the very air simmered with quicksilver fire, it lipped over Theroun's skin with unseen fingers, compelling. The dark *wyrria* inside Theroun stretched, resonating with whatever was happening – but it could not break free, nor stop the ritual. Adelaine gave a deep sigh, feeling the energy build. She began to breathe faster, little sips of air. With subtle undulations, she began to writhe upon the floor, but Jornath made no move to consummate with her or touch her in any other way.

Undulating, Adelaine sighed hard, her legs pressed together with tension. She began to arch and heave, crying out not from pain, but pure, blissful pleasure. Her hands flew from her chest, slapping the stone near her hips. One of her hands contacted Jornath's wrist; gripped him. Theroun saw Jornath's lips twitch. He was rocking now, affected by the energy he wove, the interaction he willed. Adelaine arched, crying out in a wail of passion. Khorel Jornath echoed it with a gasp and a shudder, eyelids flickering.

Theroun's pulse raced, feeling it, the incredible *wyrria* they wove. He was a part of it as much as they, their weave rolling over his skin, raising his cock and driving deep into places untouched for years. The men in the ring had recovered and now faced the center with eyes closed. Hands palm-open, they directed their terrible focus into the circle, reflecting Jornath's weave of passion back upon those within – commanding it to heighten.

Adelaine surged. Khorel Jornath shuddered. Theroun gasped. The Dremorande writhed upon the stones, affecting them all as ecstasy flooded her. Fed back by the men at the perimeter and by the one touching her, it was an infinite loop of not just lust or pleasure, but pure, infinite lovemaking.

"Feel me…" Jornath whispered through the press of *wyrria*. "Know me. Open for your own beloved, come for you at last."

Adelaine climaxed in an explosion of bliss. Arching upon the stone, she screamed out in passion and love. Jornath cried out, bowing from the tension as the magic roared. The force of it hammered the men at the perimeter, who were driven to their knees, spasming. Theroun was slapped back, suffused with waves of gripping ecstasy.

Then, as if two bodies became one, Khorel Jornath's silver will-weave flowed through Adelaine completely, until she glowed beneath the colored glass windows of the cathedral like a Madonna of quicksilver starlight. Jornath took a tremendous breath. A satisfied smile lifted his lips, and though it was dominant, it was also tender. Moving his hands from beneath Adelaine, Jornath reached out, stroking her face with his fingertips.

"Thank you, my beloved."

Leaning over, he moved his lips over Adelaine's. She arched and shuddered, lifting her chin. Lips parted, the Kreth-Hakir High Priest gave her the softest kiss. Then inhaled, massive and slow, as if pulling the life of the world into the bellows of his lungs.

Adelaine arched beneath him. And then fell back, strings cut.

Her head fell to the side, pale eyes glazed like frosted glass. Khorel Jornath touched fingertips to her eyelids and drew them closed. Gazing down, Jornath paused a long moment, then pushed to his feet, his face set with careful blankness. The men around him were recovering to standing. Jornath continued to gaze down at Adelaine's corpse, an unidentifiable emotion in the hard depths of his eyes.

"She was a dedicated adversary," he murmured at last. "For

such a warrior of tremendous will, we show our highest respect. Brother Kiiar. Have a pyre made to burn her body in the Elsthemi way. I will give her the Rites of Kotar, the traditional right of passage for dead Elsthemi warriors, and chant over her until the sun dawns tomorrow. Then we will move as Lhaurent den'Alrahel wishes us to."

"Yes, Brother." White-haired Brother Kiiar signaled three others, the most recovered of the twelve, who came forward to lift Adelaine's body from the stones. They left the cathedral, followed by the rest of the Brethren with hoods pulled up, as if in respect for the dead.

The doors closed with a soft boom. Khorel Jornath's gaze swung to Theroun, empty as a barren winter night. "She gave me everything, Theroun. Everything I wished to know. Everything she spied upon, everything she held in her mind. Everything she feared and hated. Everything she tried to deny, so she could be hard and survive her bitter life. Pretending her conscious will was stronger than her darkest desire – to love and be loved. But none of us are stronger than our darkness. We all embrace our shadow-will in the end, one way or another."

Still affected by the emotions of the ritual, Theroun had no words. At last, he managed to growl, "In the throes of it – did you love her?"

Jornath's gaze was so empty that it shocked Theroun, unassailable. "Yes. Because of what I worked today, because of *how* Scorpion-*wyrria* works, some part of me does love her now. The gift we wield is a poison, Theroun, though we practice against poisoning ourselves. Invading someone's mind by the power of your will… you cannot entirely prevent yourself from feeling what they feel. When you open enough to truly possess someone, to take their mind and body that last final bit… some part of you is at the mercy of that union as much as they. You ask why our Brethren are a holy order? Because sharing such a thing is holy. Even when we kill with it. You must excuse me now, I have a warrior to consecrate. You were right, she was a formidable adversary, but she was also weak – because she never had our teachings to show her how to conquer her deepest darkness."

With that, Khorel Jornath turned, drawing up his hood and

leaving the hall the way Adelaine's corpse had gone.

CHAPTER 22 – DHERRAN

The day of the Commoner's Audience with the Vhinesse dawned early. As the first light began to simmer in the sky, Grump rose and dressed, taking off by himself on some final errand. A brisk breeze chilled the air, though the autumn day would be hot later, in classic Valenghian style. Dherran dressed in his new outfit, tan trousers and a white shirt with a fitted hunter-green leather jerkin that made the most of his brawn. Khenria wore similar attire – though hers came with a cinnabar brushed-wool corset and well-heeled russet boots. With leather bracers at their wrists, they both looked like Cennetian fighters, which was what Grump had intended today, and wore blades at their hips and in their boots.

Shouldering out of their inn after a quick breakfast, Dherran and Khenria took to the streets. The Obelisk Quarter near Delennia's manor teemed with hawkers, the streets already filled with an early throng. The oldest part of Velkennish, the Quarter was well-built, quarried from ancient alabaster stone. Moving into the thickest part of the crowd, Dherran and Khenria threaded their way into the commons at the center of the Quarter. A massive white obelisk rose up in the middle of this sprawling plaza, the plaza divided into tight alleys with thousands of merchant stalls. Four- to five-story buildings ringed Velkennish's trade-center, ornately carven out of alabaster blocks, lending the city an aura of grandeur beneath the autumnal sun.

Silk banners in vibrant colors caught the crisp breeze as the cacophony of early trade slit the air. The plaza surged with people, a festival atmosphere. Merchants shouted their wares as Dherran and Khenria threaded down a tight alley of garish tents and stout booths selling everything from fresh river-trout to ornate lapis jewelry to dark sweet figs. Dherran and Khenria's attire was fine enough that sellers accosted them, thinking they had money to spend. Dherran shouldered through the throng, waving hawkers away as Khenria stepped quickly behind.

Men and women of five nations moved through the crowd, from copper-haired Cennetians to swarthy Ghreccani with their dark ringlets and heavy-lidded eyes. A troupe of spry Cennetian jugglers in garish motley did fire-tricks in a cleared area. A whole section of alabaster cobbles had been roped off for a horse-auction, sleek steeds from Praough, attended by merchants in fine velvet. The air smelled of roasted meats, fruit chutneys, and caramel-nuts, the bounty of Valenghia famed. As Dherran pushed his way through, he couldn't help but marvel at the trade-hub of the continent. A wealthy land of grape and grain, Valenghia seemed somehow untouched by the endless war upon its western border.

Up ahead, Dherran fixed his gaze upon the natural pillar of alabaster surrounded by the sprawling fountain that marked the center of the Quarter. Pristine, the Obelisk of the Vine – also known as the Stone of Milk and Honey – was taller than anything else in the city. Levels of humped white crystal flowed down from the pinnacle, cascading with rivulets of cloudy water that emanated from natural fissures in the crystal, flowing down into the fountain's ornately-carven basin. The Obelisk was the reason Velkennish had been chosen as the seat of power in Valenghia, and as Dherran stepped to the fountain's rim, he felt the hairs lift at the back of his neck. Ancient *wyrria* seemed to breathe from the pillar. Tendrils of power seeping through the air that Dherran could almost see – misty flows that reminded Dherran of Delennia's ability. The hairs on his arms stood up as he stopped at Grump's meeting-point, staring at the mineral-rich water that flowed down into the fountain's basin.

"Impressive, isn't it?"

Dherran turned toward the commanding voice that had spoken from his left. In a new disguise even finer than his previous attire for the fight-rings, Grump was barely recognizable. A trim, rapier-brisk lord stood at Dherran's elbow in a deep plum Cennetian-style doublet, its buckles rich with plated silver. His shirt was fine silk, his trousers a soft black leather that spoke of money. Grump's hair had been cut in a short militaristic brush – a style favored in Cennetia – his beard impeccably trimmed to a sharp point. A silver hoop graced one ear, and the silver chain of a jeweled amulet dove behind his rakishly-unbound shirt collar.

"Who *are* you?" Dherran breathed. Realizing his mouth was hanging open, he shut it.

Grump lifted an eyebrow, imperious and far too like Arlen den'Selthir for Dherran's comfort, his persona as Grump entirely gone. Looking every bit the lord of mercenaries, and every bit like Grunnach den'Lhis, the Greyhawk, he strode up to the fountain. Dipping his fingers in, he brought them to his face, wiping mineral-rich water over his brow and cheeks. A ritual for good luck, to take the water and anoint the face, it was an action that people of all nations performed around the fountain's basin. Flicking water from his fingertips, Grump's gaze was flinty as he combed water through his newly-trimmed beard, then gestured north.

"Today, I am Lord Cebo Discanni of Scovira Province in Northern Cennetia," the Greyhawk spoke in flinty tones. His voice was low and resonant, without any trace of Grump's reedy warble – a lord's cultured accent running through his words. "And you are my indentured fighters, seeking their freedom. Which I am not inclined to grant you, even though your contracts have been successfully fulfilled. Time to go. Our audience begins in less than a bell, and if we miss it, there isn't another for two weeks. Plus, a lot more bribing that I'll have to do. This way, step lively."

Dodging through the crowd, Grunnach angled toward the north side of the plaza. Dherran noticed that his pace had a studied ruthlessness to it – as if the forest mouse had been eaten alive by this sword-honed Cennetian lord. Grunnach kept a hand on the ornate rapier at his side. Any jostle was met with a formidable scowl until the populace began to shrink back from him and his retainers. Reaching the edge of the plaza, they arrived at a thoroughfare free of booths – an elegant avenue that led directly to the White Palace, lined with gargantuan estates.

"Avenue of the Vine – the Valenghian royal houses," Grump murmured as they broke free of the crowd onto the ancient tree-shrouded thoroughfare. "Step lively now, and don't meet any eyes."

Dherran saw the wisdom in this, as crimson-liveried guards stood sentinel down the wide avenue, with one hand on a spear and the other upon a sword at their hip: Red Valor, the most elite fighters in Valenghia. Steely eyes watched their progress. Not Grump with his Cennetian lord's attire, but Dherran and Khenria. As they walked the avenue, Dherran found his interest in Grunnach's manner piquing. Bold, confident, he wasn't acting but *personifying* a Cennetian lord – as if he had always been one. This cleaned-up lord got alluring looks from noblewomen in horse-drawn carriages, and cordial nods from high-silver Valenghian lords out for a stroll. He was no less cordial, nodding in a brusque militaristic manner as he moved on.

With Dherran and Khenria pacing slightly behind to keep up the illusion of a lord and his retainers, they moved on toward the massive wrought-iron gate of the White Palace, set in a high alabaster retaining-wall at the end of the avenue. Grunnach moved toward the gate and the twenty Red Valor who guarded it, exuding an aura of a vicious fighter who was every bit the lord he'd dressed as today. Gone were his flitting mannerisms as he presented papers admitting them to the Commoner's Audience. This hard, ready warrior waited with regal attitude as the guard perused their papers and glanced at each of them – then finally waved them on.

They moved through, seeing enormous siege-doors drawn back behind the ornate iron grille. The fanciful gate of twining vines and blooming flowers was as lovely as the White Palace beyond, with its soaring turrets, domes, and minarets. The siege-gate was fully functional, though, and as Dherran glanced up at the portcullis it dwarfed his mind.

They were in. Grump led them east toward a topiary garden full of grape arbors and quince trees. Here, they found commoners and lords biding their time upon alabaster benches, waiting with fans in the sun or shrugging shawls in the shade for their audience with the Vhinesse. Grump gestured to an empty stone bench, far from any shrubbery or prying ears. He sat on the end of the semi-circular bench, Khenria next to him with Dherran at the other end.

Khenria crossed her knees in her well-heeled boots, eying Grump warily. "Are you ever going to tell us who you really are?"

Grunnach held Khenria's gaze a long moment. At last, he sighed, something of his old persona showing through at last as he smoothed his grey mustachios. "Don't look at me like that, little hawk. I did what I had to, to keep you safe. Becoming Grump for the time you knew me kept us both out of notice. The Khehemni who hunted me at the Vhinesse's command knew Grunnach, a warrior and a high lord of Valenghia from an almost-forgotten House. I've lived many lives in many guises over the long years, and this most recent persona was done for your safety."

"By *lying* to me?" Khenria hissed, her eyes flashing.

"By *obscuring* the truth," Grunnach was steady, though he did glance around to make sure no one was nearby. "Grump is the man I always wanted to be. Kind. Nurturing. Simple and without complication, but now that I am returned to Valenghia, the time has come for me to cease that persona. For what it's worth… I have loved every moment I've had with the both of you, as Grump. A life I thought I could have longer, until the Khehemni Lothren came hunting me again. Who are the least of my enemies, as I've said before."

Dherran crossed his arms. "Arlen recognized you in Vennet."

"He did." Grunnach's lips quirked, a shadow of the humor he'd had as Grump. He stretched his fine boots out upon the gravel. "But even so, when Arlen saw me at the tavern, he barely recognized me. I have changed from twenty years of living in the woods. A man gets old, and the muscles fail, but the heart remembers."

"Remembers what?" Dherran's voice was icy in the bright autumn day.

"Remembers being the Greyhawk, not a forest-mouse." Grunnach's grey eyes were flat. Dangerous. Yellow linden leaves fluttered down around them as a breeze whisked through. "And now that we are back in Valenghia, I must be the hawk once more. I cannot tell you both everything of my past, no matter how you push. Accept it or do not – but know that once again, I do what I do for your safety. In my current guise, the Vhinesse will think she is seeing a double of my old self – a different man who echoes one she used to employ. It will rattle her, which is what we want."

"Why?" Dherran murmured.

"Because Aelennia makes mistakes when she is rattled, Dherran," Grunnach's gaze was piercing. A leaf fluttered to the shoulder of his jerkin and he flicked it away. "Trying to control too many men with her *wyrria*. You are the one who will feel what she tries to do, and whether you can break free of it."

Dherran breathed slowly, trying to still his unrest. It was a risky plan. "What if she recognizes you for who you really are and sends her guards in?"

"There is always that possibility," Grunnach murmured with a nod. "Though if Arlen hardly knew me from twenty years of living rough, Aelennia will know me less."

Dherran glowered, crossing his arms tighter. "Talk, Grump. How do you know all these high-level players in Valenghia?"

"I was raised Khehemni, that much you know," Grunnach sighed, "born right here in this valley. In Valenghia, the Khehemni are sworn to the Vhinesse, like the Alrashemni in Alrou-Mendera. They are the Red Valor, and answer to Valenghia's Lothren, the pinnacle of which is the Vhinesse herself. In any case, the Valor have a Captain-General."

"You. You were their Captain-General once," Dherran murmured.

"Leave intrigue to your betters, Dherran." Grunnach gave him a pitying, Arlen-esque look. "No. I would never hold such a position. My talent is quiet-work."

"Spying. Shifting who you are to sneak around in the shadows." Khenria growled it at him, her pretty brows in a line.

"Yes." Grunnach nodded, acceding to it. "And during my time as a spy, it was my duty to report to two parties – the Captain-General of the Red Valor, and to the Vhinesse herself."

"Who is Captain-General of the Valor?" Khenria's arms were crossed like Dherran, though her head was cocked as she listened.

"That's where we're in luck," Grunnach's eyes twinkled, almost like Grump. "Once, the Captain-General was a man I vehemently opposed, but now it is High General Merkhenos del'Ilio. He's an old associate of mine from wet-work in Cennetia, and he's been ordered to serve the Vhinesse by his Cennetian Lothren, but he abhors it. So he's willing to help us, which is how we received our opportunity today."

"You were the Lothren's *assassin*?" Dherran's voice was cold, and he didn't try to warm it. Leaves fluttered down, as if stirred by Dherran's rage.

"Spy and assassin, yes," Grunnach gave a nod. "I went where they sent me. Cennetia. Praough. Ghrec. Alrou-Mendera. Which is how I met Arlen. He was the first person to ever capture me."

"You were sent to spy on the war-front by the Valenghian

Lothren," Khenria murmured.

"I was sent to *cause* the war, my dear." Grunnach's gaze was dire.

"*What?*" Dherran blinked.

"Thirty years ago," Grunnach continued, stretching his boots out upon the gravel and crossing his arms, staring off toward the palace, "the Vhinesse secured the allegiance of Cennetia and Praough via a hammering series of border invasions. Disorganized city-states historically without central rule except for a few brief periods, Cennetia was unable to gather a united front, so it collapsed. Praough wasn't long behind, though they fought bravely until their King had a one-on-one meeting with Aelennia. They fell under the Vhinesse's leash – and then she turned her greedy eyes to Alrou-Mendera, working with the Menderian Lothren. The Lothren's aim has always been to kill off Alrashemni in every country, and when the Vhinesse proposed to start a war between Valenghia and Alrou-Mendera, to let the Alrashemni kill themselves off during the fighting, the Lothren went for it. A rather ingenious, if diabolical idea. So, the Vhinesse sent my quiet-faction in to start skirmishes, in Quelsis and the neighboring regions, to fan flames that would eventually lead to war. Our targets were Menderian noble houses along the border. Which is when Arlen caught me, in one of those initial raids."

"You were murdering border nobles to start the war?" Khenria's words were bitter.

"And it was successful." Grunnach's gaze was level. "Next came retaliation from King Uhlas den'Ildrian, only recently stepped to the throne and still green in his Kingship. With the help of the Kingsmen, his generals coordinated with Arlen den'Selthir and quelled our attacks. But the Khehemni Lothren pushed back, raiding hard, slaughtering in the night."

"But how did the coup against the Vhinesse come about eighteen years ago?" Khenria asked, her brows knit.

"Ah." Grunnach sat up. "It was Arlen who convinced me to join him. I was a talented spy and assassin with underground contacts in Valenghia. There were factions on both sides that wished the Vhinesse deposed, and I was unrestful in my position, tired of being a blade in the night. Arlen wanted to protect his people at

Vennet. Purloch, a Vicoute from Quelsis, wanted his borderlands to stop getting pounded constantly. And Delennia wanted her sister stripped of the throne."

"So you joined forces," Dherran murmured.

"We did. Quietly." Grunnach spoke. "I turned coat, spying for Arlen, Delennia, and Purloch. Helping them organize through the Heathren Bog. Forming the drive that lanced to Velkennish and right through these very gates. Blasting open the throne hall doors and surrounding the Vhinesse. Which, as you know, failed. Colossally. But our drive earned a nickname – both for what it was, and for how it failed."

"The Bitterlance." Khenria sat up with interest.

"Arlen and Delennia fell in love during the planning of our coup," Grunnach spoke. "They were strong together, a cutting drive of purpose and passion. After the coup failed, the forces of the Bitterlance died and so did their love. Arlen abandoned us after his shame and subsequent humiliation as a Falcon of the Vhinesse. She allowed him to live, strangely enough, to take what was left of his Kingsmen back home. Purloch fled to the Heathren Bog, his lands near Quelsis razed to ashes. Delennia was stripped of her armies and confined to house arrest before Khenria was born, and I spirited her away at Delennia's request. In the years that followed, I lived in the Heathren Bog with Purloch. But then the Kingsmen Summons happened and I had to go – to find Khenria or die trying."

"That's when the war really began, didn't it?" Dherran murmured.

"Uhlas became wise to the Vhinesse's strategy," Grunnach nodded. "After the Kingsmen Summons, he sent commanders with more salt to the border. I daresay you remember General Theroun den'Vekir. He built his reputation in those days, though he later went mad, killing Valenghian Alrashemni as well as Kingsmen in his own ranks all along the Aphellian Way."

"But how did Mad General Theroun find so many Alrashemni in Valenghia?" Khenria asked. "Aren't they rare there?"

Gazing up at the swaying linden trees, Grunnach gave a grim sigh. "They are. But there was a . . . *fashion* begun along the Aphellian Way, some hundred years back. The Alrashemni Blackmark placed upon a youngster during times of border unrest could save a child from harm. Kingsmen would adopt Blackmarked Valenghian children, rather than kill them when skirmishes happened. So along the Aphellian Way, many Valenghians grew up with the Blackmark."

"Farmers. Tradesmen." Khenria had gone green. "Men who didn't know how to fight, who weren't Alrashemni. Those were the *Kingsmen* that General Theroun crucified!"

Still gazing up at the linden trees, Grunnach nodded, his flint-grey eyes grim. "Mad General Theroun didn't know about the Inking fashion. When he went on his fever-ridden rampage, he caught the easy ones – villagers who weren't actually Alrashemni. And he caught a lot of them. The atrocious death toll was the bloody banner the Vhinesse needed to convince her nation to go to all-out war. And they did. All because of one man's actions: mine."

Khenria's eyes widened, and Dherran's gut twisted. He reached down, gripping the stone bench. "But… how were you involved in General Theroun's madness?"

"After Khenria went missing ten years ago," Grunnach's gaze came to rest upon Dherran, "I opened up every contact I had, trying to find her. I re-infiltrated my Lothren, pretending to beg their forgiveness while secretly milking them for information. The price I paid was returning to the Lothren's service. I was sent with a secret faction to undermine General Theroun's campaign. Myself, a Khehemnas assassin falsely Inked with the Alrashemni Blackmark, and a Kreth-Hakir High Priest by the name of Khorel Jornath. Theroun was a strong commander, passionate. And though he had few weaknesses in battle, he loved his wife and children – desperately. His family were visiting the front that week. Someone had to give him a push, to make all that incredible passion break. To make it turn mad and recoil in the wrong direction."

"Someone quiet as a forest-mouse." Dherran's gut clenched, sick, as he wiped a hand over his mouth. "Working with the fucking Kreth-Hakir and the Lothren, headed by the Vhinesse…"

"The Kreth-Hakir have a longstanding alliance with the Khehemni Lothren, Dherran," Grunnach was impeccably still. "I worked with them upon numerous occasions. The blood of General Theroun's family is on my hands, but it was the falsely Blackmarked Khehemni agent who knifed Theroun. Theroun needed to think that *Alrashemni* killed his family. And with a push from the Kreth-

Hakir High Priest, Theroun's temper did what the Vhinesse intended – far better than she had ever hoped. He was the perfect desert-funnel, unstoppable in his fury and fever. It gave the Vhinesse everything she needed to retaliate. Severely."

"And you?" Dherran's gut turned over, miasmic. "You ran away, didn't you? Just like a rat."

"I did." Grunnach's eyes were sorrowful. He turned back to the trees, watching them sway. "Seeing what I had caused along the Aphellian Way was far too much, so I disappeared. For years, I had been tired of war, and this… it broke me. And so I became Grump – hiding in the forests, searching for Khenria."

"So you've been on the run ever since?" Khenria murmured, sorrow in her gaze.

Grunnach nodded, and the softness of his voice was Grump's. "Khehemni assassins were sent for me. I escaped through the Heathren Bog, to Purloch. I stayed there a while until my conscience drove me out, searching for you once more. I'd shaken the Khehemni assassins from my trail that winter and finally found you near Dhemman, wandering in the snowy woods and nearly starved. It broke my heart, that our war had turned you into a half-mad animal, so I took it upon myself to care for you, rather than take you to Arlen. Until you were strong enough to face this terror of a legacy you've inherited."

Khenria shivered in the cool breeze, her hands gripping each other in her lap. Her gaze traced the courtyard, lingering on the crimson-liveried Red Valor. "And now? Does my father even have a chance? Do any of us? Or will we all be ground down like the Bitterlance?"

"Perhaps." Grunnach shrugged, tracing Khenria's gaze. "But would you rather live your life having done nothing? When I saw Arlen again these past weeks… I realized how wrong I was to simply take you into the wilds. But men are flawed, Khenria. I did what I thought best at the time."

Suddenly, there was movement from the palace ingress. Two massive ashwood doors boomed inward, and a set of crimson-liveried guards beckoned. Petitioners began to rise from their benches, stepping along the gravel paths to the open doors. Grunnach pushed up from the bench. Brushing down his elegant attire, he spoke with command.

"Come. Gather yourselves for our audience. And remember –
there can be no mistakes this day, and *no* acts of bravado. Be civil. Be
irate at your lord, but that is all. And both of you – watch the
Vhinesse. If anything strange happens in that throne hall, note it.
For it is surely her diabolical magic, and nothing else. Let's go."

Moving off, Grunnach den'Lhis strode toward the open ingress,
without looking back.

CHAPTER 23 – ELOHL

Elohl's bare feet ached from standing upon hard marble. His knees creaked when he shifted, his low back throbbed. He almost didn't care that he was displayed upon his palladian chain, as he and Fenton had been standing at attention for hours. This morning's audiences in the Vhinesse's throne hall had begun at dawn. For the first few hours, Elohl had paid attention – listening to petitioners, memorizing the Vhinesse's responses, but as the rays of light streaming in the clear glass windows slowly changed angle through the high vaults of carven trees and vines, the series of open audiences for various sections of the populous became tiresome. Elohl heard nothing of the war, nothing about the Khehemni Lothren. Through it all, he stood, staring straight ahead beside the Vhinesse's alabaster throne without so much as a glance at Fenton upon the other side.

When suddenly, someone entering the far back of the hall caught his eye.

As the petitioners for the Commoner's Audience entered, a solid fighter strode in at the back of the long hall. Well-dressed but not ostentatious, he had sandy blonde hair and wore a Cennetian jerkin of hunter-green leather and a white shirt – but it was his stature that caught Elohl's attention. Muscled like a boar, the fellow spoke to a small older lord who was far more richly dressed. A thin young woman stood by them, watching the room with hawkish eyes, her coloring strikingly Alrashemni.

As the brawny man gazed toward the front of the hall, Elohl's breath caught. A tremor thrummed his body. He knew that square, bullish jaw. He knew those high, arrogant cheekbones. He knew those scowling blonde brows and piercing green eyes – eyes so hot with passion that they smoldered like emeralds in forge-coals.

"Dherran." Elohl's breath slipped from his mouth. He froze, wondering if the Vhinesse had heard, but she had begun to orate a judgement about a grape-blight, the first commoner's petition, and did not falter in her elegant speech. Though the Vhinesse had not heard him, it was as if Dherran had. Dherran's mouth dropped open in astonishment where he stood at the rear of the hall as his hot green eyes widened.

Elohl? He mouthed from the back of the room.

Elohl gave the tiniest nod. Dherran saw it. Elohl suddenly felt Dherran's energy hit him like a spiked mace. Dherran had always held a strangeness about him, something Elohl had never been able to define, but which could be felt. In Alrashesh, the elders had never been able to say whether or not Dherran had *wyrria*. But the fact was, his temper was palpable to those around him – a force generated by the pureness of his heart.

Dherran's eyes narrowed with that stunning temper now as they flicked to the Vhinesse – Elohl saw righteous wrath in those green eyes. Dherran's presence surged in the vaulted hall, that roaring sensation Elohl had known even when they'd been kids together. People felt it, shrinking back from Dherran with uncertain glances. So long sundered, having not known Dherran was alive until this very moment, Elohl found that surge of passion over his skin the same as it had ever been – but hotter, stronger. As if becoming a man had made Dherran a roaring volcano rather than the forge-fire he'd been when they were young.

Elohl watched Dherran's face turn scarlet. He turned to his lordly companion, growled a few words. The man's eyes went wide, blinking up to the dais in astonishment. He said a few words back, the girl now also watching Elohl with her pretty mouth fallen open.

His face a thundercloud, Dherran was gesturing emphatically at the lord. Elohl could almost hear Dherran's growl as he seized his older friend by the collar and tried to hustle him out of the chamber. The man stood his ground, but Dherran had a full head on him and a hundred pounds. The girl had her hands on Dherran's arm, trying to pull him off, but the commotion disturbed the hall.

The ruckus caught the eye of the Red Valor. They moved over the alabaster and marble floor, motioning commoners back as the Vhinesse continued her ruling. Elohl saw Merkhenos del'Ilio note the disturbance from where he waited in an alcove with his elite Red Valor for a war-meeting. Merkhenos had a hand on his sword, craning his neck to see what was going on. His seven Valormen, one a handsome Valenghian woman with a long silver braid, were drawing weapons, but Merkhenos motioned them to stand down when he saw that other guards had arrived and were now separating Dherran and his companions.

Hauling them to the front of the room.

"What is going on?" The Vhinesse ceased her ruling. Standing from her gilded alabaster throne, she motioned petitioners away so the space before her dais was clear. People shrank back like frightened sheep. Elohl could feel the Vhinesse's milky tendrils licking through the room. That sweet mist tried to ease into his thoughts, but he held onto the vision of Ghrenna's eyes and the sensations cleared.

"Bring that man to me. Just him. Not the others." The Vhinesse gestured imperiously at Dherran. Her Red Valor guards hustled him forward, leaving his two companions behind in the middle of the hall. Elohl saw a look he knew well upon the Vhinesse – a lecherous benevolence. The Vhinesse had seen Dherran's promise, a warrior of the highest caliber. Someone strong, handsome, vicious – someone she wanted to possess.

Dherran was marched to the front, his companions pushing through the crowd behind. He was more massive than Elohl remembered, his well-cut shirt and jerkin straining over fit muscles. He shivered with fury, though Elohl could see he was trying to contain himself. The clarity within Elohl sharpened as Dherran neared, as if someone thrust hot knives through the Vhinesse's weaves, her poison sighed away from Elohl like cobwebs, full of holes in the presence of Dherran's wrath. Elohl stilled his body, but a thrill of anticipation went surging through his limbs.

A humming sensation began to rise in the throne room. The closer Dherran was hustled toward the dais, the more it vibrated across Elohl's skin like a swarm of bees. As Dherran's gaze connected to Elohl's, Elohl felt a fiery lance rush through him. Like molten ore poured through his veins, his Goldenmarks buzzed through his body, though they had yet to light.

Memories knifed Elohl, then – of home and family, of friendship and childhood. His life came rushing back with Dherran's passion seething through his Goldenmarks. How he'd laughed, once, with Olea. How he and Dherran would climb the cendaries by the river and watch the girls bathe on late summer afternoons – Elohl cut by Ghrenna's pale loveliness; Dherran transfixed by the dark beauty of Suchinne. How they'd gambled at cards, stealing each others' arrows and laughing late into the night after the adults went to bed. The quietness of those hours, laying on their backs in the dusty fighting-rotunda, the five of them listening to the wolves howl as the moon rose in a clear midnight sky.

Dherran's gaze held Elohl's as he was shoved to his knees at the foot of the dais. Amazement conquered his arrogant face, and Elohl knew Dherran could feel it also – a synergy was happening between them. As if Elohl's Goldenmarks reacted to the passion of Dherran's intensely loyal nature, and Dherran's passion was heightened in the presence of the Goldenmarks. As the Vhinesse stepped down the dais toward Dherran, Elohl suddenly felt Fenton's electric presence shivering all around him like lightning barely constrained, pulled into whatever was happening.

Then, Elohl's mind was drowned by cerulean blue, like his resonance with Dherran and Fenton had called Ghrenna, and she was there. Her tundra-clean scent in Elohl's nose, her dark eyes in his mind; the feel of her body all around him. Elohl's pulse raced as his heart hammered with sensation. Her face clear in his mind, Elohl knew she was there with him – even though she wasn't.

Elohl's blood rushed in his ears as his Goldenmarks lit in a searing wash. A molten sensation filled him, like he'd caught fire – and that fire was fed by the wind of Ghrenna's etheric presence, the passion of Dherran's physical one, and the searing conflict of Fenton's *wyrric* one. As if alchemy existed between them all, Elohl's marks blistered like a desert sun, causing people to cry out all through the hall. The Vhinesse had been about to touch Dherran, to slide her fingers over his blonde mane and conquer him, when she halted, staring at Elohl. Fenton was suddenly beside Elohl, moved so quickly that Elohl hadn't seen it – lighting crackling to life in Fenton's palms as Elohl's *wyrria* surged to the screaming point.

As the Vhinesse paused, Dherran's woman dove in, lunging toward Dherran with a sword for him. The Vhinesse's cruel white eyes shifted, an inundation of white mist snaring the young woman. The girl spasmed to her knees with a cry before the monarch, the sword spinning from her grasp along the floor. The Vhinesse's hand snaked out – seizing the girl's sword and driving it home through her chest. Fingers clutching the blade, the girl's Alrashemni-grey eyes widened in surprise as crimson darkened her fighting-corset.

Dherran roared, a sound like a raging boar, as his woman came crashing down.

Elohl felt something expand out from Dherran. Hitting the room in a rush, Elohl saw a vicious mirage explode out from Dherran's body – a whirling maelstrom of sand and wind – as if a raging desert-funnel had swept into the throne hall from some far southern clime. As the mirage blistered away, history began again. The Vhinesse's lunge. The blade's plunge. This time, the hot whirlwind blew through the hall – arresting the Vhinesse's hand and plunging the sword through the outer part of the girl's shoulder rather than anything vital.

It was a light wound. The girl was up fast, whipping out a longknife at the Vhinesse in an arc of golden fire, causing the monarch to stagger back with wide eyes and drop Dherran's sword, but Dherran already there, his eyes fierce and boorish as he swept up his sword in a roll. Then lunged out of that roll – thrusting his blade right through the Vhinesse's pretty white chest.

Chaos erupted in the hall. Roars resounded as Red Valor raced to the Vhinesse. Fenton was in action, blasting the Vhinesse's men back from Dherran and his woman with strikes of lightning that exploded chunks of marble from the floor. Dherran's woman fought one-handed, rips of gold-red fire surging up her blade as Dherran roared up into the battle like a desert on fire, the small lord cutting down Valenghians like a grey hawk of death at their side.

Striking with a sword and longknife he didn't recall seizing, Elohl cut alongside Fenton's wrath, dancing the steps he'd known since birth with effortless tingles of his innate *wyrria*. Hewing down the Vhinesse's guard as they ran up the dais, he watched Merkhenos' group surge in to finish the Vhinesse. A vicious melee ensued as civilians fled, trampling each other to the doors. More Red Valor stormed the hall, surrounding Merkhenos and the silver-haired woman. Carvings were blown asunder, fountains blasted and rivers of water surging into the air as Fenton let loose. Golden fire devoured his eyes as he hammered back wave after wave of guards like children's dolls.

Protected by a knot of Valormen, the Vhinesse struggled for breath on her knees, one pale hand bracing the floor while the other clutched her crimson-stained chest. Staring through the melee, she watched not Dherran, nor Dherran's woman, nor even Fenton or Elohl, but the handsome Red Valor woman with the long silver braid. Fighting with a sword and spear with Merkhenos and his retainers, Elohl could see the woman's grim steadiness through blasts of lightning and flying chunks of rubble. Slicing down opponents with a look, then her bitter blades, some *wyrria* similar to the Vhinesse's arrested her foes, hewing them down around her.

"To me!" The silver-haired fighter's rousing alto split the chaos.

Elohl's Goldenmarks seared like the sun to her clarion voice, even as hundreds more Valormen poured into the hall, surrounding their paltry force and pressing in upon Elohl's senses. Elohl was motion as the chaos in the hall reached its peak, he was response, his blades like liquid light. Still alive, the Vhinesse's white sighs flooded the room, bolstering her men, causing them to drive in where Fenton's lightning wasn't. Fighting close to Fenton, Elohl could feel a cord of blistering resonance uniting them. A twisting bond that devoured energy from Elohl's Goldenmarks and funneled that power into Fenton – renewing him, making the lightning in his palms surge as he fought on.

As if the Goldenmarks had been made for this – to funnel power into the Kings of Khehem.

Yet Elohl knew it wasn't the Scion of Khehem that was their lynchpin today, but Dherran. If Dherran fell, their coup was lost. Elohl could feel the heart of all their passion blossoming out from Dherran's boorish frame, from his chest, from the screaming feel of a desert-funnel sweeping the room as he fought. Dherran had changed the outcome of events today – and continued to change them, simply by the power of his passionate rage.

The Vhinesse had enough life in her gasping body to deal them one final horror, and she did. As the allies began to stagger under sheer numbers, Elohl felt the Vhinesse's power roar. Felt her weaves of milk-mist cast wide like the silk of some enormous spider. Her poison erupted through the room, seizing her Valormen, wrapping them in a command that they give their all for her. Red Valor surged with renewed will, and Elohl saw weaves of white blossom in their eyes as he cut them down. As if the Vhinesse's control were a physical thing that tainted flesh, he saw why she'd ruled over three nations for more than twenty years.

Because she could summon her power to fill armies – to fight with no more mind than corpses.

As her horrors fell upon the allies, Elohl felt no fear inside them. They were dead men but for her will. Elohl gasped as a foe raked a blade across his hip. Even his sensate *wyrria* was slipping under the poison that coated the hall like a forest full of spiderwebs. He heard Fenton cry out, staggering as a Valorman slipped his guard, a dagger buried to the hilt in his left thigh. Dherran roared, falling to his knees clutching his sword-hand as his wrist spurted blood from beneath his cut leather bracer, the tendons severed, that hand useless. A foe barreled in, raising his sword to plunge down through Dherran's ribcage and into his heart.

No!

All at once, a command rose in the hall upon a surge of midnight wind. Like a glacial night, Ghrenna was there, her presence roaring all around Elohl. On instinct he drove toward her, as if she was the last thing in the world. Suddenly, he could see her, sitting alone under the mountains to the vigil of a small luminous stone; Ghrenna's cerulean eyes widened, seeing him, and Elohl knew that he was there with her, as much as she was here with him. Though his body hewed down foes, Elohl's consciousness wrapped around his beloved. Pouring through her like molten light, opening her. Lighting her up as bliss flowed from his heart through hers and back again. Their touch was fire. Their lips were breath. Their passion rose, cascading up into a tower of light, and Elohl felt their bodies merge across the long leagues – him becoming her; her becoming him.

Elohl was bliss in battle, his body pure movement and righteousness, and he was bliss in her arms, his soul pure devotion. As she poured her love through every part of him, Elohl's Goldenmarks blazed, alive. In that moment he felt the Marks expand. Roaring into the lancing conflict of Fenton. Twisting into the burning passion of Dherran. Devouring the drowning dusk of Ghrenna.

Drinking Elohl's own sorrowful dawn and exploding through the room.

With a striking thunderclap, the Goldenmarks concussed. Elohl was struck to his knees by the force as Fenton went down with a cry beside him. The shockwave spilled men to their knees all through the blasted-out hall, swords and spears spinning away from dazed hands. Halting the fight, men gaping as if their minds, hearts, and souls had been sundered.

The Goldenmarks shone like runnels of lighting in the sea, the war-riven throne room deathly quiet except for a chunk of marble falling from a shattered pillar. Elohl shivered in that immense space, to feel such power breathing through him. An uneasy silence devoured the hall, even the groans of the dying becalmed as the Goldenmarks blazed. Hard breaths echoed into the domes as warriors were stopped. Elohl saw their faces, and knew he could possess them. Dherran, green eyes wide, blood-splatter marring his blonde mane as he clutched his useless sword hand. Merkhenos, a searing readiness in his copper eyes, his garb crimson with other men's death. Fenton, standing tall with lightning snapping between his fingertips. Elohl knew he could thrust this bright *wyrria* through each and every one of them, not producing just this shock, but binding them. Taking their freedom and making his Rennkavi's marks do what they had been created to do – unite them under his yoke, forever.

Elohl took a deep breath and let it out, slow. Eagerness to finish the binding tingled in his every sinew, making his skin itch and his muscles surge: he wanted to use this magic. Some part of him wanted these men – all men – to understand everything he had endured since the Kingsman Summons. A military post he'd not wanted. A command he'd hated. A life that had taken him away from everything and everyone he'd ever loved.

Some part of him wanted to bind them, so that they would feel the desperation he had endured.

Not like this. Ghrenna's whisper filled him, and Elohl startled. The fresh-wind scent of her hair devoured him, the touch of her fingertips arrested him. The drowning beauty of her dark blue eyes pushed back the Goldenmarks. *Not like this, Elohl. The Marks have a will of their own, but they obey your choice. Would you unite us? Or ruin us?*

Elohl came to stillness, feeling the beat of his heart, seeing the steadiness of Ghrenna's eyes. Gradually, the Marks quieted within his skin and the moment passed. As his urge to bind sighed away, the Marks died until they were only golden inkings once more. People began to shift and blink, gazing around at the wreckage; some moaned, taking stock of wounds. Elohl caught Fenton's glance, then Dherran's. Then his gaze fell upon the fallen Vhinesse, clutching her chest and gazing up at him from the foot of the dais. An expression of fury twisted her features, even as blood soaked her white lace gown and pooled around her.

Elohl would not enslave men this day, but something had to be done about her.

Stepping down the dais, his bare feet touched the blasted marble of the main floor, warm with blood. Kneeling before the fallen monarch, he gazed into the Vhinesse's pale eyes with their ring of blue. Her face contorted, ugly. Elohl felt her energy expand in desperation, surrounding him with poisonous tendrils as she slid her palm, slick with her own blood, over Elohl's bare chest.

"You're mine," she spoke, her melodious voice ringing with bells as she pressed her sapping weaves deep into Elohl's heart upon the mark of her crimson blood. But her *wyrria* was hollow to Elohl now. Hollow like the sound of sleigh bells upon a winter wind.

"No." Elohl reached out, cupping her face in his hands. "You're *mine*."

Leaning in, he brought his lips to hers. As they touched, he poured himself into her. His calm. His peace. His desire to cease fighting. As Ghrenna's eyes lit his soul, Elohl's Goldenmarks flared, bright like the dawn.

When he drew away, the Vhinesse's face had fallen into a terrible peace – the peace of drowning under a highmountain lake, where all was darkness and silence. She wasn't his servant and she wasn't his slave. It was worse. She was *his*, united to the Goldenmarks in a way that could never be broken. But it was something Elohl had to do, to win this day, to save far more people from the oppression she would bring.

Slipping his fingers down her face from brow to chin, coated in the blood of the fallen, he whispered three words.

"Be at peace."

With a sigh, her pale eyes rolled up in her head. The Vhinesse of Valenghia collapsed to the white marble in a puddle of crimson. Dead, to the Rennkavi's command.

CHAPTER 24 – DHERRAN

Dherran stared at the scene, his maimed sword-hand forgotten even as he pressed down upon his wrist and ruined leather bracer to slow the bleeding. His eyes were wide in the sundered throne hall, bearing witness to the stuff of legends. Elohl, blazing with righteous light, had walked down the broken steps of the marble dais like some elder god. With a kiss, he'd sundered the seething power of the Vhinesse, cut it as neatly as a blade slices a thorny rose – and she had collapsed, dead at his feet.

Dherran knew that he'd been a part of that light. He could feel it still blazing through his body, commanding his passion. As if Elohl's golden inkings called to the ancient power in Dherran's veins, and knew what to do with it; Dherran shivered. Coated with blood, shaking with battle-fatigue, it wasn't his regular let-down after combat. It was this sundering command breathing all around him – *through* him. Spearing his heart like a thousand suns, making Dherran's passion flare and spin like a sand-funnel. Gripping deep into his heart, it left Dherran afraid, in a way he had never been afraid before.

Afraid of how it might use him.

"Who is he?" Khenria's words were soft as she bound a length of cloth around Dherran's slashed wrist, putting pressure on the wound that left his fingers useless.

"A friend. From my youth." Dherran pulled Khenria close and she gave a peep of protest. She was as blood-stained as he, and looking down, he saw the deep sword-gash on her outer shoulder that she'd already ripped her shirtsleeve off to bandage, the other sleeve sacrificed for Dherran's wound.

"Khen…" Dherran marveled down at her, his gaze lingering on her shoulder. "Aeon! I thought you were dead. I thought I saw – I thought the Vhinesse's lunge pierced your heart, for a moment there."

"I'm ok. She just got my shoulder. It's nothing." Khenria shuddered, looking back to Elohl, her brows in a tight line. "I feel him, Dherran. Your friend. Like he could make me do things—"

"I feel it, too." Dherran pressed his lips to her brow, tasting iron upon her skin, grateful that she was alive. He could have sworn he'd seen her die, seen her pierced through the chest, but he was just as glad she wasn't, that it had been some fever-mirage of battle and not the truth.

"What is it? *Wyrria?*" Khenria murmured against the thick hush. Valormen were moving now, tending wounds, helping the dying. Though the Vhinesse's poison had cleared, the throne room was red with massacre: bodies lay everywhere, crimson uniforms seeping with a deeper red, pools of filth slicking the floor. Dherran wondered if anyone would ever get all that gore scrubbed off the alabaster and marble, or if it would sink in, staining forever.

But Dherran had no more time to ponder, for Elohl was moving to him, leaving the body of the fallen Vhinesse behind. The man was captivating: intricate golden inkings still simmered over his blood-slicked frame, breathing with power. Not just the power Elohl had shown today, but a commanding presence he'd always held. As he approached, Dherran felt the weight of not just years between them, but *wyrria*. Of two lives, each desperate and wreathed with magic in their own way. He could feel command in Elohl's stone-hard gaze, in those lines at the corners of his mouth and eyes. Eyes of sorrow. Of battles won and lost, not the least of which were etched in the countless blade-scars that decorated Elohl's skin along with his rippling golden sigils and script.

He'd led a hard life, since that day they failed at Roushenn.

But a life that had honed whatever Elohl truly was.

"Elohl." Dherran breathed it, awed. His old friend was close enough in the stretched silence of the throne hall to hear now, and Elohl's lips quirked. His humor was still there, even if it was only a shadow of what it had once been. Dherran found himself smiling back as Elohl extended a hand – Dherran clasped Elohl's wrist with his good hand, feeling blood slick between them.

"Dherran den'Lhust." Elohl's opal-grey eyes sparkled. "Your passion for battle was welcome today, my friend."

"How were you—? I mean, what—?" Dherran had no words.

It was beyond description, everything that had just happened. They had won the day with magic: with *wyrria* — a resonance between them that wasn't even spoken of in Alrashemni lore.

"Later, my friend. But it's damn good to see you." Elohl clapped a hand to Dherran's shoulder and gave him a shake with surprising strength in his lean frame. This man was battle-hardened steel: a commander in every way, like Arlen den'Selthir. The mostly naked fellow who stepped down the dais to Elohl's side was no less so. And though his gold-brown eyes were calm, a smile of ready humor gracing his plain-yet-handsome face, Dherran was not fooled.

That man, whoever he was, had shot lightning from his bare hands.

The fellow stepped close, clapping a hand to Elohl's shoulder. "Fuck, it feels good to be free of that bitch!"

"You seem *quite* free, really." Khenria chirruped beside Dherran. It struck Dherran that she was staring at two gloriously naked men covered only by the triumph of battle, strange jewelry, and blood-soaked loincloths. Khenria grinned, her gaze taking in Elohl and his wiry companion.

"Hey!" Dherran gave her a little shake.

"What?" She retorted. "I can ogle. Your friends are handsome, Dherran. Deal with it."

"Handsome." The wiry fellow cocked his head, his gold-brown eyes flashing. "Now that's a word a man likes to hear. Fenton den'Kharel, milady, First-Lieutenant of the Roushenn Palace Guard. And you are?"

"Khenria den—" She hesitated. Then smiled. "Oblitenne. Khenria Oblitenne."

"*Oblitenne?*" Fenton whipped back the hand he was extending. His face held a battle-fierce darkness, his former placidity vanished.

"Stand down, *wyrric!*" A woman's voice suddenly boomed through the hall. Dherran glanced over to see Delennia Oblitenne in her bloodstained Red Valor gear rising from her dead sister's side. Moving toward them with a scowl on her fierce face, she whipped her blood-streaked silver braid back over her shoulder.

"And who are you?" Fenton hesitated, uncertainty moving in his eyes.

"She's the new Vhinesse." A wiry Cennetian approached,

dressed in Red Valor battle-leathers. His copper waves were streaked with grey, his eyes piercing. Grump had pointed the man out earlier as High General Merkhenos del'Ilio, their ally in the Vhinesse's court. Fenton moved into a guarded stance before Elohl as Delennia approached and Dherran felt the air shiver, like a gathering thunderstorm.

Delennia cocked a regal eyebrow at Fenton, her lips set in a hard smile. "Impressive. If I'd had a *wyrric* like you in my cadre eighteen years ago, our coup in this very same room might not have failed. I am in your debt." She gave a regal nod to Fenton, who straightened from his ready stance, then gave a nod to Elohl. "And am I in your debt as well. Whatever a Vhinesse may do for her new allies, she will. So do I promise."

"You're the Vhinesse's sister?" Elohl evaluated Delennia, no fear in his eyes.

"Twin." Delennia gave a small, ruthless smile. "By minutes. We never shared the bond twins usually enjoy. She was a bitch, by all accounts, and my nation has been at war for decades because of her, fed by stolen foot soldiers from foreign lands. I aim to correct that."

Dherran saw Elohl flinch at the word *twins*. The light of victory died in his eyes as they went flat, hollow. Agony twisted inside Dherran, seeing that look, and he knew that Olea was dead. The only one of them that Dherran had thought would actually survive all the tumult after the Kingsmen Summons. Dherran took a slow breath. Khenria must have felt it, for she snugged close, glancing up. He shook his head; they would talk later. Right now, there were more problems to sort out.

"This was not supposed to happen today." The Cennetian approached, motioning his exhausted retainers back so he could come to the impromptu knot of rulership. Grunnach moved into the parlay also, wiping down the longknives he'd been fighting with rather than his rapier.

"And yet happen it did," Delennia glanced to the Cennetian. "A stroke of luck."

"A stroke of destiny." Merkhenos' sharp copper gaze took them all in, finally settling upon Fenton and Elohl. "In Cennetia, we say *luck holds no coin, but destiny holds them all.* But when destinies collect," he glanced around them all again, with a thoughtful frown, "one must hold wariness in the heart."

"The tide of destiny is a fickle thing," Grunnach chimed in, sliding his knives away in twin sheaths on his boots.

"Indeed, Grunnach," the Cennetian grinned. "Indeed. It's been a long time. I hardly believed my eyes when Delennia pointed you out in the hall."

"Time is crueler than destiny, my friend. All of my joints can attest to that right now. Good to see you again." Grunnach reached out to clasp the Cennetian's wrist and they shared a moment. It held much; far too much for Dherran to even begin to puzzle out. Grunnach den'Lhis was not just one secret – he was a bundle of secrets, wrapped in a shroud of more, sunken in an ocean of them.

"Come." Merkhenos made an expansive gesture. "Destines turn, and we must decide what to do with a nation at war. We are in luck – the Generals and Captains who might have opposed us have been barricaded in the war-hall by my men as soon as I saw what was happening. We must devise a united front, before too many tongues can wag."

"Agreed." Delennia flicked her fingers at Merkhenos' men. One fellow with a band of silver at his collar moved up. "Seal the doors after us, Ghirano. None enter or leave. Let the corpses be, for now. Gather any others of you loyal to Merkhenos and round up all the healers from the palace infirmary. Bring them back here to attend the wounded. Ensure all these men are given food, water, and bandaged – but none are to leave this hall until you hear further instructions from me. Am I clear?"

"Perfectly, my Vhinesse." Ghirano snapped his heels together with a quick, though tired, bow.

"I'm not your Vhinesse yet," she murmured back. "But see that it's done."

"Yes, milady." Ghirano moved off at a brisk clip, summoning others of Merkhenos' guard as he began to organize the hall.

"Come. This way." Merkhenos led and the rest followed. No one spoke as he took them quickly down side-corridors and pushed through secret stone panels into servant's ways. As they maneuvered back-halls of alabaster stone, Dherran was amazed to find they came into contact with not a single servant. Clearly, the Cennetian didn't want anyone to know about the coup.

At last, they arrived at an out-door and Merkhenos hustled them across a broad hall filled with carvings of lustful creatures. The Cennetian's quarters were no less lewd, Dherran noted, as he and Khenria were shown to an opulent washroom, the others led elsewhere. A hot bath awaited in a large ceramic tub, with folded clothing in fine fabrics upon a gilded side-table. Avoiding his slashed wrist, Dherran stripped off his blood-soiled clothes, a stiff fatigue already settling into his muscles. Khenria was quick to the tub, stepping into the same white-slurried water from the Obelisk Quarter fountain, though she hissed as it sluiced over her torn shoulder. A lemony scent and the hint of basil wafted up from the steam.

"Shove over." Naked, Dherran stepped over the tub's rim. He eased into the water, carefully unwrapping Khenria's bandage and pulling the laces on his ruined leather bracer to inspect his wrist. The cut was clean, a fast slice that had cut partway through the main flexor tendons but not much else, not even down to the arteries. He was lucky he'd been wearing bracers, but the injury left that hand useless, unable to make a fist or flex toward his body. The white slurry ate the blood, dissipating crimson into nothingness as the oils in the bath soothed his throbbing wrist. Ducking under and using his hale hand to scrub out his hair, Dherran surfaced and lay back against the angled rest, letting the salts ease his muscles.

"Aeon, I could eat a house right now!" Khenria glanced at her shoulder – also a clean wound, the Vhinesse's sword gone right through muscle but nothing else – then laid back against Dherran with a sigh.

"That's battle for you." Dherran smoothed her curls away from her neck; kissed it. He was rising despite his fatigue and pain, and Khenria snuggled back against it.

"How many battles have you been in, Dherran?"

"Enough. Back before I left the Stone Valley Guard." He kissed her neck again, his maimed body not protesting as much as it should at his arousal.

"Is it always that… exhilarating?" She asked, as his good hand settled around her ribs.

His palm smoothed up, cupping her perfect little breasts. "Not for everyone. Only for those who don't fear death." He was lost in the touch of her flesh now; in the scent of her skin as he breathed against her neck, kissed under her earlobe.

"You don't fear death?" She breathed as the steam lifted up around them. His fingertips teased her nipples and she arched with a small gasp.

"No. I only fear letting someone control me." He kissed her neck deeper, biting. She cried out, grinding her rear back against his pelvis – against his member, now eager to do battle all its own.

"My fear's... being abandoned." She breathed as he bit her skin, deeper. "Don't ever leave me, Dherran. If you do, I'll hunt you down. I'll take your balls—"

"Shh..." Dherran turned her in his arms. She straddled him in the tub, her hands around his neck. She cried out as his cock brushed her, so thick and ready. Crushing her close with his arm, Dherran set his good hand to the bottom of the tub. Using it as leverage, he thrust his hips up, sinking into her. She arched back with a cry, but Dherran held her firm. She was not getting away from this. Not ever.

"You're mine, Khenria," he rasped as he fucked her, deep and slow, her ankles locked around his ass. "Until the last breath leaves my body. Until the light dies in my eyes. Even after death – I swear I'll haunt you..."

Dherran's breath failed. His words failed, lost in her. In the surge of her body and the flow of water and the tide of their breath as they moved. His breath came ragged and hers quickened. He thrust deeper, every ounce of his hard-won control used to prolong the moment. To feel her. To smell her – the hint of battle that still lay on her skin. To watch as she arched back against his grip, pulling upon his heart until he was buried with no escape.

Her long fingers slipped over his jaw, her grey eyes shining with a passion no woman had ever matched, not even Suchinne. Dherran quickened, lost to her touch. His lust and love surged to her beloved fingertips, called to the passion inside of him. He cried out, feeling them come together. In that moment, Khenria gasped, spasming forward so hard their foreheads touched.

A perfect moment filled Dherran, the twin of the one he'd felt in the throne room – a shockwave of pure glory. But this wasn't someone else's glory: this was his and Khenria's. A homecoming in her arms – again and again as their shuddering lasted a small eternity. As if the ecstasy couldn't stop, wouldn't. As if Elohl's *wyrria* had opened up something both their hearts had long hammered shut. Dherran's breath was hard upon the steam as he spilled into her, and Khenria gave it back until she collapsed and Dherran had to haul them both to the edge of the tub so they wouldn't drown.

Laying on his chest, she gave a breathless laugh. Dherran returned it, ecstasy still flowing through him as the chalky water moved in little currents around them both. "Gods in every heaven!"

"You said it." Dherran cupped her ass, drawing her close again. He was still half-hard and she shuddered from head to heels, crying out as she bit his neck with a laugh.

"No more! Aeon, I can't take it!"

"Whatever milady wishes." Dherran kissed her forehead. They lay there in the water, breathing softly in the steam as the glow slowly faded, though it wasn't gone. As if the alchemy between them would never let go. Dherran reached up, smoothing away her wet curls, unable to cease touching her.

He suddenly realized he was using his damaged hand. Pausing, he turned his wrist over. Where there had been rent tendons and sliced flesh, there was now nothing – only a thin white scar to show that Dherran's wound had ever been there. Marveling at it, he flexed his hand, making a perfect fist without pain. Then he glanced at Khenria's stabbed shoulder and saw that she was the same, idling with her eyes closed and her arms up around his neck like she'd never been hurt.

"Aeon and all the gods!" Dherran breathed.

"Hmm?" Khenria opened sleepy eyes, glancing up at him. He nodded to her shoulder. She looked over, her grey eyes widening, then snapping to his wrist. Shifting up in the water, she seized his arm, inspecting it, then looking at him.

"It's not even scarred!"

As Dherran looked again, he saw the white scar was also gone – as if brushed from his skin like a tide through ocean sand. They both sat there, staring at it, Khenria also glancing over to poke at the healed flesh on her shoulder.

"Dherran…" She looked up again. "Was that you, or me?"

"I don't even know," he breathed, astounded, smoothing

fingers over her healed shoulder. "After everything I felt in that throne hall today, Khen – I just don't know."

"Maybe both of us." Khenria shivered, her gaze going long. "My *wyrria* unbound today, Dherran. It's been useless, just a trapped rage inside me all these years, ever since I escaped my torturers when I was young. But today – today it came alive, when the golden marks upon your friend's skin called. They fed me, flamed me. Fired me…"

With a deep inhalation, Dherran sat up, winding her close in his arms. She shuddered, and even in his ecstasy and amazement at everything that had happened, a slow fear gripped Dherran's gut. If Elohl's power could give this gift of connection, of awakening latent *wyrria* in people, of strange healing despite fighting and war – could he take it away? Dherran kissed Khenria's forehead, wrapping her closer in his arms.

"We should get dressed," she breathed against his neck. "My birth-mother just asserted herself the new Vhinesse. I should probably be at a conference where I might be considered—" Khenria's voice quit with a deep inhalation.

"A crown princess of Valenghia?" Dherran murmured. "Fuck them. Let it wait. All I care about is right here, right now. And I will let no man take that from me. Ever."

Dherran smoothed a hand over Khenria's back and she cuddled closer. Wrapping her arms around him in the slick water, she rested her cheek on his collarbones. "I'll never leave you, Dherran. I hope you know that. Ever since we met, the only man I've wanted is you. Even—"

"I know." He found her lips with his. "You don't have to say it."

"You know?"

"I knew," he kissed her, "from the moment we met at the river. I saw it there in your eyes. Just as I've seen it every day since. Because it's the same thing I feel. Always."

"Always." Khenria breathed to him, fervent.

Passion poured through Dherran as he kissed her long and deep, in an endless moment that defied thrones and death and time.

CHAPTER 25 – JHERRICK

Jherrick sat before the seven archways in his quilted silk robe, listening to them breathe. Absorbed in the World Shaper's song as the dawn rose, he could feel the vibrations of music like currents through a vast ocean – liquid, unfathomable. Jherrick had been instructed by Flavian to sit here and listen, day and night, for the past week. And now, the sensation swamped Jherrick, filling him until nothing existed but awe. Swirling in through his crown and every pore of his skin, music of impossible harmony devoured him, illuminating places that seemed dark and endless. Crushing, it towed him under, made him feel like air was thicker than tar, until it would ease away, allowing his lungs to take a breath.

But there was darkness, too, that crept in when he lost focus. A jangle of disharmony that suddenly pulled him. A dead boy's glassy eyes rose before Jherrick, red as blood as he watched mist reflect off the seven archways in the luminous dawn. Shaking himself out of his reverie, Jherrick pushed back the cacophony and those eyes that tore him away from the beauty of the universe. With a sigh, he claimed a pitcher of water from the stones before him and drank.

Rubbing water over his face, he flicked it from his short blonde beard, his focus gone. Exhausted from his vigil, Jherrick's mind turned. Rising, he stood from his meditative seat and moved toward the egress from the cloverleaf plaza. His mind was lost as he ascended a succession of stairs and crossed bridges arching high over the morning-golden citadel. Descending, he found himself stepping into the Memorarium with its lofty columns, rectangular pool, and agate-stone bier.

Jherrick's gaze roved over Aldris' corpse as he approached, golden and red leaves shivering down as a morning breeze swept through the archways and colonnades. An urge seared within him and Jherrick's fingers twitched; wanting to use his *wyrria*, compelling his hands. He could almost taste Aldris' energy lingering among the colonnades and twisting maples, like iron upon his tongue. What Noldra Ethirae had told him was true. Aldris wasn't entirely dead, the sensation of tigers and hot-tempered smelting wafting through the open space. But as much as Jherrick could sense Aldris, it was maddening to feel so little of him. Like it was only an echo of what Aldris had been.

A step came behind Jherrick, a slither of silk over stone. Jherrick turned to see Noldrones Flavian approaching. Worry smote Jherrick, that he had been caught at Aldris' tomb, which had been forbidden until he had better control over his awakening *wyrria*. But Flavian seemed to be in a joyful mood, a smile upon his face rather than reproach. One hand was lifted, and Jherrick could see a tiny red finch perched upon the Herald's finger. It sang a trilling song as they approached, the sound lifting Jherrick's heart as the Albrennus stepped up beside Jherrick.

"What is this?" Jherrick asked, his mood lifting at the presence of the tiny red finch, stripes of cheery yellow under its neck and belly. As he raised a hand to touch it, the bird fluttered over to Jherrick's knuckles. It dug tiny talons in, ruffled its feathers and began to trill again, its throat vibrating with rapid pulses that echoed through the agate-stone dome. Jherrick gave a startled laugh, feeling brighter than he had in ages as a warming wind passed through the space. The finch cocked its head, eyeing him, then gave a laughing trill back like a mynah.

Flavian let out a rolling chuckle. He extended a finger and the finch let itself be petted under the throat like a tabby cat. "They're called *aurus excelsianni*, the soul-excelsior. It is said their song can call a man into joy so powerful that lifelong enemies become friends. I keep some in the citadel. They do wonders for lifting the heart."

"Indeed." Jherrick laughed as the tiny bird scratched its neck with one foot. "Is this for me?"

"It is." Flavian smiled, benevolent and mysterious. "He is very tame – treat him well and he will follow you everywhere. Every *louve wyrdani*, every Dusk Warrior, needs an instrument to train in feeling the soul-spark of a living creature. The soul-excelsior is the perfect instrument to practice on. Their vibrations coalesce around their being, and their souls are very present. Today, we will learn how to sense a soul in the Void – starting with your new friend here."

Jherrick laughed as the tiny finch hopped across his knuckles. It went to a more manageable perch upon his index finger, then fluffed up, its tiny stick legs disappearing beneath all that cherry-red down. As Jherrick watched, it shat, a tiny splat of white hitting the stones, then resumed its vociferous chirruping.

"Let us begin," Flavian intoned in a mystic baritone. "Close your eyes, Noldrones Jherrick. Feel the bird upon your finger. Feel the weight of it, the texture of talon and feather and the vibration of its heart. Feel what it is that makes this creature buoyant, that makes your ears happy to hear it, your heart happy to be near it. And when you understand these elements, open up and feel them in the Void."

Jherrick did as he was instructed, feeling the sweet presence of the finch. And when he had that happy nature solidly in his heart, he opened up, sensing the Void. Seeing it around him, vivid even through his closed eyelids. He saw the swirl of the finch's energy at once – a compact, cozy, yellow-white vortex upon his finger. Joy from that little swirl eased through his own body, Jherrick realized. As the finch continued its trilling laughter, its buttercup presence seeped into Jherrick's energy in the Void. He suddenly became aware of his own nature in the Void – tortuous, black and red with a violet halo, thick with tendrils of darkness that writhed through his being.

Jherrick gasped, as his eyes blinked open. "I see myself! My energy – it's dark."

"Indeed." Flavian extended his hand and the finch cocked his head, but did not leave Jherrick's finger. Flavian's endless eyes were reassuring as he smiled at Jherrick. "And yet, the soul-excelsior has chosen to be your companion. They do not choose those they dislike. Nor does the essence of joy befriend the truly dark."

Jherrick gazed down at the little bird. It looked up at him, trilled, then hunkered, closing its eyes as if drifting off to sleep. "Why me?"

"Because there is much good in you," Flavian murmured. "Despite the *wyrria* you carry."

Letting his concentration in the Void drift, Jherrick saw again the enormous presence standing firm just behind him in the starlit darkness. It was always there, he'd found – a part of him, limned in light, but something he didn't know yet how to truly access. "But I've let good people get killed. Because I followed a dark path."

"One always has a choice," Flavian murmured, "to be a better man."

"Olea told me something like that once." Jherrick laughed sadly.

"So can you be," Flavian intoned. "I feel your soul aching for such goodness to fill you, Noldrones Jherrick. It needs only a path."

"But my *wyrria* is evil, just like Trevius Stranik's was," Jherrick breathed, fear wisping through him. "It can raise the dead. And kill."

"Understanding death is not darkness," Flavian returned, his face peaceful. "Death is often a mercy, Jherrick. Rest your mind upon Archaeon, upon his ruination and damning immortality. Would he choose death if he could, do you think?"

"Yes." Jherrick's answer came without hesitation. "The wounds he was dealt from this Key of Fire – they consume him. It's a wonder he hasn't gone mad."

"He may yet." Flavian's tone was subdued. "He spends most of his eons in stasis, like we have done for your friend Aldris here. The damage to his physical vessel is so great that he is only able to remain within it for a few hours at a time. It is only with great difficulty that I can contact him when his mind strays through the Void during periods of stasis. But practice your *wyrria*, and you will also be able to find someone across that great expanse."

Jherrick glanced at Aldris' corpse. "I could actually contact Aldris or Olea, out there?"

A mysterious smile lifted Flavian's lips. "How did you find the soul-excelsior's energy in the Void just now, Noldrones Jherrick?"

"I focused on the feel of it, the emotions it raised in me," Jherrick answered. "And then opened to the Void to feel for the same pattern there."

"Precisely. It is through our *imprinting* with another soul," Flavian intoned, "that we are able to find them once they are dead. From their personality still memorialized within you – which you can follow to where the dead linger and call them back. *If* they are willing to return."

"The finch," Jherrick mused. "I saw yellow light easing into me from its essence in the Void."

"Yes," Flavian nodded. "The soul-excelsior is very bright and giving, which is why it tries to become one with you. Such creatures give naturally; they do not understand any other way. Find that sensation – of how it felt to be given that joy, that trilling song, the clutch of tiny talons upon your finger. And then you will find the soul in the Void."

Fast as thought, Flavian's hand snaked out. Seizing the little bird in a loose fist, he pinched its beak and tiny nostrils shut. The bird panicked, fluttering in Flavian's fist, struggling to breathe. Jherrick cried out, his hand shooting to Flavian's to get the Albrennus to release the bird. But Flavian gave a sudden explosion of power from his body, and a whip of manifested wings bowled Jherrick to his back upon the agate-stone. Before Jherrick could recover, the finch had ceased to struggle in Flavian's hand.

And when the Albrennus opened his fist, the bird lay upon his palm, dead.

"What have you done?!" Jherrick cried out, rounding upon Noldrones Flavian in rage.

"Calm your emotions." Flavian's tone was commanding and suffered no argument. Jherrick breathed himself to restraint, but his heart thundered and his breath was tight, wretched. Flavian made a settling motion, and as the Herald came to his knees upon the agate-stone floor, Jherrick did the same. Placing the dead bird down upon the floor, Flavian gestured to Jherrick.

"Close your eyes. Open your senses to the Great Void, and find the soul-excelsior, Noldrones Jherrick. Bring it back. Now."

Jherrick blinked. His first feeling was rage, but the thought upon its heels was, *can I?* A vast desire pulled deep within his body, like a hound upon the scent, ready to be unleashed and only needing its master's permission. But Jherrick was master and hound both, and when he closed his eyes and opened his senses to the Void, it was as if the leash upon the cur snapped.

Something in him burst outward, devouring the Void. Filtering, sifting, following a luminous yellow thread from the finch's memory that unwound from Jherrick's own heart. Feeling how the little bird had made him smile. Feeling the sensation of feathers, the racing of a tiny heart. Like Jherrick had been drowned for years and could finally breathe, his *wyrria* raced out, flashing faster than thought along that yellow-white filament and finding a sphere of swirling energy coalesced only a few handspan above the newly-dead bird.

Jherrick's *wyrria* roared. He felt something expand within him, triumphant. This was what he was – what he had been born to do. A dead boy's glassy eyes fell from his inner vision as he beheld the luminous soul of the dead finch swirling in the middle of the vaulted room.

He could bring it back. He would bring it back.

Without thought, Jherrick's hands lifted, expanding his energy in the Void. Surging to the bird's soul, wrapping that buttercup brightness in silver-dark light with violet and crimson edges. Guiding his *wyrria* in an intricate dance, Jherrick found the process innate. As his hands traced patterns in the air, caressing the soul, he found his *wyrria* understood death, how it felt, what it was – and how to capture it. His energy swirled around the finch's, curling it into a luminous sphere, engulfing the dead soul. He felt a sealing sensation once he had it, like a doorway slamming shut in the Void.

But it wasn't enough to simply find a dead soul, nor to contain it from dispersing. Pushing his energy into the bird's, Jherrick became one with its trilling death. As Jherrick's consciousness connected with the bird's, he found it wanted to return. It was sad it was dead, that it had been killed by someone it trusted. He felt it missing such a bright and happy body, and how it could sing. It had years left and it wanted to live them – to experience more of life.

Moving like mist, Jherrick's hands twined into that desire. He used it as an anchor to pull the bird's energy downwards. Easing his hands down, he rested one upon the tiny corpse. And then he directed two fingers down into the bird's heart as his other palm spread out, guiding the bird's soul back toward its inert body. When the soul finally came close enough, it funneled through in a rush, straight down through Jherrick's fingers and into the creature's dead heart.

The puddle of down and feathers seized beneath Jherrick's fingertips. It shrieked, a terrible sound, over and over. Hurrying in panic, almost losing connection to his *wyrria*, Jherrick picked up the little being, cradled it in his cupped hands. And suddenly, he could hear music. All around him, he could feel it, rushing like a vast ocean, singing in a thousand harmonies like a galaxy full of harps. The music filled him, thrummed through his foundation, and he became it – weaving it through his dark-light nature and pouring that vibration into the tiny creature's body.

The music of the World Shaper consumed him. Eons of harmonies. Lifetimes of melodies. His mind strayed far into the Void, and it was not until he felt Flavian's hands upon his shoulders that Jherrick at last began to return.

"Look in your palms," Flavian breathed by his ear.

Still delirious, Jherrick opened his cupped palms. And there was his friend, staring up at him with head cocked, curiosity in its gaze. As he watched the soul-excelsior, it trilled a haunting strain, a wisp of the World Shaper's melody that Jherrick had been consumed by only moments before. As if it could hear that otherworldly music along with him, and was filled by it also.

"You came back." Jherrick's breath was a bare whisper. His limbs were filled with a terrible languor, yet his entire being thrilled with the elation of his success. Like a drug, the desire to do more consumed him. Red eyes rose in his vision. Shock filled Jherrick, a hard slap of reality casting back that red gaze. He gave a shiver as an unnameable dread spiked into his veins.

"We will practice again," Flavian murmured, giving Jherrick's shoulder a small squeeze.

"I can't!" Jherrick choked out, terrified. "If I do this again – he'll find me. The Demon."

"You *can*," Flavian reassured. "And you will." Reaching out, he rested a hand upon Jherrick's shoulder, pouring warm light into Jherrick like Ethirae had done and pushing back his fear. "This is your nature, Noldrones Jherrick. Rarely have I seen a *wyrria* so effortless and ready to be used. You needed only initiation from us, not direction. Your body already knows the World Shaper's movements, your *wyrria* knows her vast song. This was a trial today, to see how much you could do upon instinct alone. And we have found that you already know the entire process, innately. You are far more than a natural at Dusk *wyrria*, Noldrones Jherrick. You are a savant. You are ready to proceed, whenever you feel you can master your fear."

Gazing down at the finch, Jherrick found himself terrified of what his ability could accomplish, especially in the wrong hands. But even as he despaired, the finch fluttered to his finger. With a steady trill, it poured the World Shaper's music from its throat, giving Jherrick hope that his curse could also be a gift.

Looking up, Jherrick's gaze fixed upon Aldris. He could see the cocoon of light now, that the Albrenni had encased the Guardsman in to feed his flesh vitality from the universe. Jherrick's *wyrria* breathed into the Void, following a sensation of tigers and iron and golden grass, the feel of Aldris' memory in Jherrick's heart. As if expressing his thoughts, the soul-excelsior finch took flight around the upper gallery of the dome. Mirroring it, Jherrick began to pace the perimeter of the pool. His gaze locked to Aldris as his *wyrria* flew through the Void like the finch flew through the air, searching. Immense, Jherrick's *wyrria* was like the entirety of the sky – untrained, but with all the potential of the universe behind it.

A light step came behind him. Turning, though still immersed in trance, Jherrick saw the ancient war-general Archaeon with his burned-out damage and broken wings. Lingering by an arch with arms crossed over his chest, Archaeon regarded Jherrick with his ruined white eye.

"Archaeon, welcome," Flavian bowed his head, lifting two fingers to his brow in respect. "Our Dusk Warrior is investigating his possibilities this morning."

The ancient Albrennus nodded to the Herald, but his galactic gaze was all for Jherrick, stern. "I can feel your restlessness in my dreams, boy, coveting actions far more impactful than you know. Beware your *wyrria's* eagerness to resurrect the dead. For that which you raise from death becomes your responsibility. A man's actions when he rises, what he chooses to do with his resurrected life, become yours – writ upon your very soul."

Jherrick ran a hand through his blonde mane, his *wyrria* still hunting far away. Fear and eagerness mingled within him. And upon its black tide, nightmares rushed in, red eyes swimming up from the depths. "I hear your warning, I can feel the truth of it. But this feeling – it compels me."

"Regrets drive your ambition," Archaeon stared Jherrick down. "And where there is regret, there lies the Demon's opening inside us. Master your regret, and master the Demon's voice within you."

Jherrick's eyelashes flickered. Archaeon had read him; the feelings that plagued him. But beneath the regret was rage.

Something rose inside Jherrick, bestial. Desire long suppressed flickered through him – to rip Lhaurent den'Karthus' entrails out. To keep him in a cocoon of *wyrria*, alive and suffering, and drain him over and over. To resurrect his corpse and do it all again.

"There." Archaeon's basso rumbled like an elder god, a knowing smile upon his lips. "There is the Wolf and Dragon I also feel inside you. Feel your conflict, your rage and violence. Open up and see it in the Void, the shadow of your tumult."

Jherrick's heart gripped, feeling the burning ruthlessness of his desires. Not able to meet Archaeon's gaze, he lifted his eyes to the oculus as he brought his *wyrria* back in the Void. Jherrick could see it: violet-black and swirling with crimson; roaring around him in a miasma tinged with hurricane-dark rage, sorrow, and loss. His conflict was so thick, he almost couldn't make out Archaeon's fading-star form as his tumult gathered bloody light from the Void, feeding the rage and destructiveness.

As it did, the shadow of a shadow surrounded Jherrick. A hulking shape with no dimension, just *immensity*. Not his protective aura that stood behind him, this thing surrounded him in the Void, and Jherrick trembled like he'd drowned in the darkest sea. Shivering uncontrollably, he felt darkness swirling in, choking him. Washing into his eyes, roaring in his ears.

A vast cold, that burned red.

He toppled. He didn't remember falling, but he was suddenly caught by Archaeon's enormous, ruined form, Noldrones Flavian upon his other side. Wings of light curled around Jherrick, tendrils of fierce benevolence. The filaments of mighty, broken feathers and hale ones brushed Jherrick's jaw, his neck, and temples. Where they touched, the poison of the Demon was lanced out of him, drained like pus from a wound. Talons dug into his shoulders, piercing through his robe, taking more of the darkness and letting it flow back to the Void. At last, the worst of it was gone. Jherrick came to silence in the Albrenni's grip. But he could still feel his conflict roiling within – a demon of suffering that would never quiet.

"Not until you embrace it," Archaeon's words were quiet by his ear. "Don't swallow your emotions, boy. Emotion is your power. Two ancient lines of *wyrria* move inside you. One hot with conflict, one cold as the shadows of the Void. The Wolf and Dragon battle inside the Dusk, and neither will ever go away. Embrace your conflict, for the vast conflict of what you still fear – being taken by the Demon – yields the bulk of your strength. *Feel* your conflict. Become the darkness… and then forgive yourself. We cannot divorce ourselves from our darkness, but we can embrace it, and turn it into light. Are you ready – to do what your power wishes to do?"

Inhaling a breath, Jherrick could feel the depth of his loss roiling deep inside. His miasma of rage and suffering more desperate than any lost wolf. It choked him, burning, as he gazed upon Aldris through the wings of the Albrenni, wanting to undo fate. Aldris' fate, Olea's, Vargen's – a dead boy who had died far too young.

A dead boy with Jherrick's own face – so alike they could have been brothers.

"I'm ready," Jherrick breathed.

Archaeon suddenly gripped Jherrick's shoulder, his talons puncturing deep as he reached up to touch two talons to the center of Jherrick's brow – just as Flavian gripped Jherrick's other shoulder and pressed two talons up to touch the base of his skull. Activation roared through Jherrick, a torrent of energy fed by the screaming conflict of his life. Emotions swept Jherrick as that energy raced in. He was a demon of wrath, of suffering. He was a beast of yearning and sorrow. He was the coldest depth of the universe and the brightest sun, swirling and churning and screaming with the power of his inner conflict. It swept him, chased all thought away. A primal roar ripped from Jherrick's throat, his body bowing backward as the daggers of the Albrenni's talons suddenly released his flesh like burning needles. Blood stained Jherrick's silver-white robe as he staggered forward through the pool, his hands slapping down upon the corpse on the bier.

Flooded with the vastness of his own *wyrria*, primal rage roared through Jherrick, in a bright, molten fury. Primal energy the likes of which he had never felt – never allowed himself to feel. Jherrick's hands moved on instinct; one over the Guardsman's heart, the other over his abdomen. He didn't know thought or rationality. He didn't know fear or joy or love. He only knew *existence*, and it was this understanding of living and death and eternity that roared through him.

Feeling the grip of his hands in the Void, Jherrick captured the thread of Aldris' soul-energy in his memory. The smell of iron, the taste of blood. The ferocity of emerald eyes flashing in the high desert sun. Gazing down, Jherrick saw the kingly nature of the man, dressed in finery for his death, layered upon his nobility in the Void. And like a lodestone for a shooting star, Jherrick's *wyrric* perception of Aldris' character brought the man home.

Jherrick felt his *wyrria* dig in to that tawny light as it returned. He felt Aldris' soul shiver as Jherrick's energy roared around it, binding it, his hands digging into the corpse's flesh and flowing over it quickly in uncanny patterns. Creating a funnel, a path down into the body through which Aldris' soul could find its way home. As Jherrick raised his right hand, leaving his left gripping Aldris' heart, the searing energy thundered down. The Albrenni cocoon was engulfed as the lion-tawny brightness of Aldris' soul came raging back from the Void – ripping into the cocoon, shredding it.

A sound like a brass war-gong rang in the darkness of the Void as Aldris' soul slammed back into his flesh. The Guardsman woke with a gasp, his green eyes flying open, clear and terrible like burning emeralds. Aldris' roar sundered the morning, thundering through the oculus-room, rippling the pool with whitecaps. The Guardsman thrashed in spasms as the soul-excelsior finch tore around the dome upon blood-red wings, its shrieks mimicking the man upon the bier.

Desperation filled Jherrick. Fear flooded him, slicing his power and sundering his connection to the Void. He couldn't find the World Shaper's song. He couldn't hear that endless tune that had restored the body of the finch. His energy was slipping; his control shredding upon the vast tide of his fear, watching his friend shriek and writhe upon his death-bier.

And he was losing the man.

"Help me!" Jherrick screamed at the Albrenni, desperate.

He was vaguely aware of three forms surrounding him now. Noldra Ethirae was there as the Albrenni encircled Jherrick and Aldris with luminous wings. Archaeon stood behind Jherrick, and drew a massive breath. Setting his hands to Jherrick's shoulders, his broken wings curled down, pinning the thrashing Guardsman with pinion-feathers strong as forged steel, the other Albrenni doing the same. As Jherrick watched, the universe cascaded through the Albrenni. The blood of stars, pouring down into Aldris' flesh – stabilizing the awakening Guardsman with the immense harmony of the World Shaper's music.

A concussion imploded the Memorarium, making Jherrick sprawl over Aldris as the three Albrenni staggered back, Archaeon falling hard with a splash into the shallow pool. His broken wings curled tight around his body, shuddering, as a horrible sound sliced Jherrick's ears. As the Albrenni rushed to Archaeon, Jherrick saw Aldris laying motionless upon the bier, eyes staring at nothing as his pulse beat in his neck. But the price for his return had been steep. Jherrick had failed to stabilize Aldris' body as the soul came home, and now, Archaeon suffered for it. The ancient warrior was in spasms in the water, curling and uncurling with flailing death-throes like some giant insect. Like the universe tore him apart from the inside, all the power they'd wielded now ripping flesh and soul and wing.

As Flavian and Ethirae pinned Archaeon with their wings, flooding the power of the universe into him, more movement rushed into the Memorarium. Six Albrenni Jherrick had never seen flew in, flooding vast flows of energy into Archaeon. His back against the bier, Jherrick was stuck in the Void, unable to return to sanity as he watched the chaos his *wyrria* had caused. Someone cursed – Flavian. Jherrick watched energy flush through Archaeon again and again, giving out to the universe through those terrible black burns. Flavian poured three times the energy through his own body as the others, searing like a falling star in the Void and proving why he was their Herald.

But it was not enough. Like a desert funnel, the emptiness inside Archaeon devoured that light, tore it away from the eight Albrenni and spat it back to the universe as if their efforts had never been. Suddenly, Ethirae shrieked like an eagle in battle. As one, all eight Albrenni hefted Archaeon, flying him up and out through the oculus.

Leaving Jherrick alone in the vast silence.

Jherrick's mind was still not inside his body from the shock of what had just happened. As if he watched from everywhere and nowhere, he slowly turned, staring at the man upon the bier. Aldris' eyes were wide, terror behind them. His breathing was fast, shallow. And as they stared at each other, Jherrick saw nothing: no fire of recognition, no spark of understanding in those burning emerald eyes.

With a sudden, primal move, the Guardsman was up. The magnificent crystal sword Aldris had clutched with his dead fingers flashed out faster than thought. But the resurrected man's precision was off – his slice ripping across Jherrick's shoulder rather than severing his head. Jherrick cried out in pain as blood washed down his arm. His mind returned as he jerked back from another sword-slice meant to disembowl him. Aldris snarled, his eyes flashing like emeralds on fire – but there was no one home behind those eyes.

Aldris struck again. Jherrick pivoted away, fast, splashing through the pool. His mind raced. His energy expanded, searching for answers in the Void. And suddenly, he found it. A thread of his own chaotic crimson-rage *wyrria* was still lodged in the Guardsman. Flowing out from Jherrick's lowest energy center, the origin of his fear and primal conflict, his Wolf and Dragon *wyrria* invaded Aldris, feeding Aldris with the power to kill and destroy.

With a cry, Jherrick tore that final thread of *wyrria* from Aldris. The Guardsman fell to his knees in the water with a short scream, his hands dropping the crystal sword. He slumped, breathing hard, head hanging. A paroxysm of coughing wracked him, and he took a deep, rattling inhalation. A long moment of silence echoed through the Memorarium, the soul-excelsior finch fluttering to land upon a trailing vine that hung down over the bier. Cocking its head, it watched the resurrected Guardsman gulp deep breaths of brisk morning air.

And then Jherrick heard the sound he longed for most – a short, wry laugh.

"Fuck me!" Aldris' head came up, someone home in those emerald eyes at last. "Don't you *ever* bring me back like that again, kid! Or I *will* cut your fucking head off next time, I swear to all of Halsos' Hells."

CHAPTER 26 – THEROUN

Theroun was in agony. Bedridden in his monk's cell and bare-chested in the chill autumn night, he burned with poison, fighting the *wyrria* that rose ever higher within him. For two whole days, his condition had deteriorated as his awakened *wyrria* snapped Khorel Jornath's silver net left and right. Acrid sweat stood out upon Theroun's body tonight, the reek that dead men suffering a blood-poison have at the end. Despite his concentration, despite everything he had tried, still it came for him – the massive darkness of his own vicious will weakening his body by the hour. Trying to kill him for reasons he didn't understand.

The midnight hour had come and gone, the depths of the cathedral silent. Propped up with pillows and doing his breathing to push back the pain, Theroun slid in and out of sanity. The young Valenghian with violet eyes and silver hair, Brother Antonius, sat by Theroun's bedside, as if in vigil. Leaning forward at intervals, the lad mopped Theroun's brow and neck with a cool sponge, letting water trickle down Theroun's poison-hot skin. About Thaddeus' age, Brother Antonius seemed to hold a sorrowful fascination for Theroun, and Theroun didn't refuse the lad's care, sometimes hallucinating in the height of his agony that the lad was actually Thaddeus.

The hour was deep when Theroun heard the door-latch click and the hinges creak. A chair was dragged up beside Theroun's bed and Brother Antonius was dismissed with a low exchange of words that Theroun couldn't make out. He felt someone lean in, then felt more than saw the massive quicksilver-woven paw of Khorel Jornath placed upon his brow. A deep ease poured from Khorel's palm, entering Theroun like a lifeline of silver light in his fever-fugue. But it was only enough to clear his mind a little, allowing him to see the room at last rather than the massive blackness that devoured him.

"You've not got much more time, Theroun," Jornath's voice

was soft, vague to Theroun's tortured ears. "Your choice is upon you."

Another wash of silver threads snapped inside Theroun as his *wyrria* roiled, striking at his insides. Theroun grit his teeth against it so he could speak, his voice rasping with pain. "I would rather die than fight for Lhaurent. I am bound to Queen Elyasin den'Ildrian Alramir's service. And to none other."

A great sigh issued out from the Kreth-Hakir High Priest. Jornath sat back in his chair, regarding Theroun like a stone watches time.

"I will save your Queen," Jornath spoke at last. "If you join our Order… I will save Queen Elyasin from harm."

Theroun blinked. He struggled to sit up, but only managed to produce a ripping pain that spasmed his back and lungs. When he could speak again, he fixed Jornath in his most formidable glower. "What are you saying?"

Leaning forward in his chair, Jornath rested his elbows on his knees and set the tips of his massive fingers together. "I know the secret of the tunnels out of Lhen Fhekran, Theroun. I gleaned from Adelaine's mind the working of it, how to place myself in the right kind of trance to make the music come alive as the woman Ghrenna did to open the passageway. I can have ten Kreth-Hakir Brethren in pursuit of your Queen within the hour. We have cleared the rose-crystal gateway beneath Fhekran Palace of the last debris from the palace's burning. All is in readiness for me to follow Lhaurent's command and chase my retinue in pursuit of your Queen and her King."

"What stops you?" Theroun growled.

"You." Jornath's grey eyes glowed like burnished opals in the flickering candlelight. "I sense within you a power too great to be ignored, Theroun. You have something that could change the game of ages, that could shape the world to come, if given the chance. My conscience cannot rest, knowing that you would so blindly take that to oblivion with your own selfish death. So I'm offering you a deal. The sweetest offer I could possibly fathom for you, based upon what you long for most, in your heart of hearts – your shadow-will."

"And what do you think I long for?" Theroun growled through his agony. "What is this darkness that breaks me to your command?"

"Absolution." Jornath's gaze was deep, penetrating. "You long for your Queen to set her hand to your brow. To tell you it will be alright. To tell you that you are forgiven for your atrocities against your King her father. To tell you that you are forgiven, for having this rabid Beast that lives deep within you."

Something gripped Theroun. It wasn't his rising *wyrria*, but his own heart, screaming in agony. It was his soul giving a horrible wail to know that Khorel Jornath was absolutely, terribly right. The man had read him like a hand of cards, and Theroun folded to that wretched understanding of his shadow-will. For a long moment, he could not even breathe, so keen was his suffering – because no one had ever forgiven him for the atrocities he had committed in his long and brutal life. No one had ever looked into his eyes and set their hand upon his head, and allowed him to kneel before them and pour out his guilt and regret for everything he'd done at the Aphellian Way.

And if Elyasin died, he would never have it.

"I'm listening," Theroun growled softly.

"Take our oaths." Jornath leaned in, his grey eyes intent. "Learn our ways. Choose our Order over your own death and I will spare your Queen from my hunt. I am the only one that knows the secret of the tunnels from the Dremorande. None of the other Brethren encamped here can penetrate my mind. If I say that Adelaine died with her secret firmly locked inside her, if I tell my Brethren and Lhaurent that I was unable to break that last piece of her, then so shall it be. The tunnels shall remain sealed. No Brethren will pursue your Queen. And we will move on to where Lhaurent wishes to send us, and engage ourselves elsewhere."

Theroun breathed softly, considering all that had been said. "Can you ensure Elyasin's safety against Lhaurent?"

"No," Khorel breathed. "But I can give her a fighting chance. If she comes forward directly against Lhaurent to take her throne back, I cannot protect her. But I can give her this escape. If we catch her in the tunnels, Theroun, she will die. But not before Lhaurent makes her suffer."

Theroun drew a breath against his pain, then let it out. "Lhaurent is a madman."

"Lhaurent is a tyrant," Jornath responded. "Nothing more,

nothing less. Will you take my bargain, Theroun? Will you save your Queen and yourself?"

"Will I have to serve Lhaurent?"

"Perhaps," Jornath murmured, his dark eyes ancient. "But I can promise you that as an Acolyte of our order, you will not be put to task for some time. You will be trained, tested, kept close to monitor your success in besting that which writhes within you. But we will not activate you in the field unless we have a dire need for your talents."

"So I become your peon."

"You become my Scion. Personally."

Something in Khorel's gaze was so penetrating, so ancient, that Theroun's curiosity rose. "Scion? What do you mean?"

Khorel breathed deep. "You are precious, Theroun, perhaps more than you know. The natural *wyrric* talents within you, which have been latent until now, are tremendous. Even without training, even without your *wyrria* awake and aware, you were able to best me, *thrice*. Do not think that has gone unnoticed. All my Brethren whisper of it. Contrary to what you might believe, I have not truly been bested in a god's age, and the last time I was…" Jornath's lips lifted in a haunted smile, "it was by the grandson of my god, a man named Fentleith Alodwine. I submit to Lhaurent because he carries the strongest power we've seen in over ten decades. But though I have let his power wash over me, thunder through me so all my Brethren could taste it and know Lhaurent for what he is, that power has not truly hammered me down in the way that you struck me. Thrice."

"So what is it that you want of me?" Theroun growled.

Khorel leaned forward in his chair, elbows on knees again. "I want to train you. I want you to take up my lineage. I want to give you the surname *den'Jornath*, so that all may know you are my Scion, my adept-in-training. The one who will replace me in my position of High Priest when I fall. There are only eight High Priests in our entire Order. Above me are only four Sages. And above them, only the High Master stands supreme. Who once was balanced by our High Mistress, Metrene den'Yesh – but that is a story for another day. You would come into our order twenty ranks above the regular Acolytes. It will cause a stir, but it is not without historical precedent for a man so highly accomplished and naturally talented."

"And what of the captured Elsthemi army?" Theroun spoke, processing this information.

Jornath sat back. "They will be used as Lhaurent sees fit. Conscripted. After I send pursuit after your Queen, I am ordered to take the entire host south, to fight at the Aphellian Way against Valenghia. Now that he controls Alrou-Mendera and has culled Elsthemen, Lhaurent sets his gaze upon the tilthlands of the Vine. And we will support him, until his aims are finished."

"What if his aims never cease?"

"Then we will continue to fight at his side," Jornath responded. "And watch behind his back. For as absolute power grows, so does the window to the Red-Eyed Demon. Lhaurent wishes to have control of the world. The Demon wishes for the world to fall. Some enemies are the ocean, Theroun, and some are but a drop of rain upon that ocean. I have learned to choose my battles over the millennia that I have been alive. And enduring the orders of tyrants has only made me know my deepest darkness, which makes me strong. Stronger, to face the Demon when he comes at last."

"You sacrifice the few to save the many," Theroun murmured.

"Just as you have upon every battlefield of every campaign you've ever fought."

"The soldiers I sacrificed knew what they were in for."

"Did they?" Jornath's grey eyes pierced in the candlelight. "Boys hardly grown into men. Green fodder for arrows and lances. Terrified and shitting themselves at the moment of death, their sword limp in their hands. Plenty of innocents die in battle, Theroun. And the ones who do not are forever changed. Stronger. Just as you will be to join the battle of the ages."

Theroun breathed softly in the dark night. A roiling pain gripped him and he grunted, resuming a brief spate of fast breaths. But upon its heels came another, and another. With a roar, the blackness inside him surged, slamming against the last threads of Jornath's silver net, ready to be free.

"Your time has come." Khorel Jornath sat up straight in his chair, his eyes narrowed upon Theroun. "In moments, your *wyrria* will be free and your sanity will be gone. Choose, Theroun. And choose quickly."

Theroun closed his eyes. Fighting back the raging *wyrria* within, he breathed steadily, processing his choice. If he took Khorel's bargain, it would make him a slave, entered into a contract he could never be free of. But that choice would save his Queen from a fate more horrible than death at the hands of his worst enemy. More than that, it would place Theroun in a position to learn a skill that might make him of tremendous use to his Queen.

Or perhaps learn enough to bring the entire Order of the Kreth-Hakir down from within.

Theroun took a deep breath and opened his eyes. "I accept your bargain."

Khorel said nothing. He watched Theroun for a long moment, something ancient in his grey gaze. "I see you, Black Viper," the High Priest murmured at last. "I see my death in your eyes."

"Take my acceptance or let me perish," Theroun growled, vicious. "For I cannot arrest what I am, not anymore. My *wyrria* longs to strike, Khorel Jornath. And if Uhlas learned anything during his kingship, it was this: that the viper cares not for friend or foe. It strikes the one who is closest to it – the hand who feeds it."

"And yet," Jornath returned, his dark eyes dire, "you have more loyalty to your dead liege than any man I've ever met."

"Because he was my greatest regret."

Theroun could say no more. The *wyrria* within him surged, ready for release. In a sudden burst, it roared free. Khorel Jornath's net exploded into silver mist. Theroun screamed, his body alight with pain. Poison ran his veins. Fire and ice, hot and cold, the fevers of the viper's venom, and there was no stopping it this time.

Some part of his breaking mind felt Khorel Jornath leap up from his chair, yanking back his herringbone-woven jerkin and exposing his chest as Theroun began to thrash upon the bed. A knife made of nothing but woven quicksilver threads flashed across the High Priest's chest over his heart. Blood blossomed crimson at Khorel Jornath's heart as he pinned Theroun down fast as a striking scorpion, seizing Theroun by the nape of his neck and drawing his thrashing lips to the blood.

Drink, viper. Khorel Jornath's command thundered through Theroun with the weight of eons. *Sink your fangs in and drink of our blood. Drink of our lineage, drink of our pain. Drink of our heart and our body.*

Let the essence of the Kreth-Hakir Brotherhood live within you. Take of our will, and be taken by ours in return. Theroun den'Vekir of Alrou-Mendera is dead. Let Theroun den'Jornath of the Scorpions be born.

Theroun's *wyrria* raged. It was ruin, it was death, and it wanted nothing more than to strike Khorel Jornath and drink him dry. With a roar, Theroun did, sinking his teeth into the High Priest's chest. Khorel Jornath cried out, and Theroun began to suck at the wound. Blood flowed into his mouth, sweet and metallic with the taste of life and death and ruin. A tremendous energy rushed through him and his hand flashed up, seizing behind Jornath's neck and holding him fast. Theroun's seizures abated as he drank and drank; all the pain, all the wretchedness. And what had begun with Adelaine ended with Khorel, as the waking of the Beast subsided within Theroun, and he felt the enormous darkness of his *wyrria* settle at last – awake, aware, and ready to be used.

"Enough." The words rasped from Khorel's throat. "Theroun, enough."

Theroun made a vicious hiss in his throat. It wasn't enough. It would never be enough. The blood was too sweet, the satisfaction of draining his enemy too pure.

"Enough, Scion!"

The command thundered through Theroun and slammed him backward beneath a pummeling wave of quicksilver. His lips broke from Khorel's chest and he drew a gasping breath. The High Priest shuddered above him, breathing hard, blood gushing from the mangled bite and blade wound.

Gazing down, Khorel stared into Theroun's eyes. Breath heaving and eyes misted, his voice was shaky when he finally spoke. "Scion of my Blood. I see you now for what you are. Others have called you a black viper, but there are many vipers of dark and destructive will in this world. You are something else. You are the *suna hebi*, he of black coils who rises up from the desert sands to attack without warning. With this consecration tonight, I commit you to what you are. Just as I also commit myself, to my own death in the *hebi's* black coils."

Lowering his head, Khorel Jornath brought his lips to Theroun's. The coiling *wyrric* darkness rose inside Theroun, enjoying the blood shared between their mouths. A promise between them, sealed in blood, of everything that had been and everything that would come to be. When Khorel drew away, his breath was shaky. For a moment he trembled with the power of what they had shared. And then his eyes hardened, until he stared down at Theroun with twin opals of utter dominance.

"This is the first and last time I will ever be at your mercy, *suna hebi*," Khorel spoke. "Come and kill me now, if you can."

With a fast whip-strike, Theroun's *wyrria* rose. He lunged at Khorel Jornath not only with his body but also with his mind, a wrath of oilslick black tendrils rather than quicksilver, shooting from his essence in a tremendous weave. A complexity he didn't understand but knew would kill. Jornath jerked backwards, eyes wide. And slammed Theroun's dark, venomous weaves back with a wall of solid silver, smashing him down through the bowels of the earth.

Theroun den'Jornath fell back to the bed, annihilated, as his vision flickered out to darkness.

* * *

No one came to wake Theroun. His door stood open, unlocked, as morning sunlight flooded in through his meager window. Kreth-Hakir and Menderian soldiers bustled about the cathedral's corridor, carrying sacks of grain over their shoulders, kegs of ale, and crates of telmen-wine. Theroun stretched, feeling better than he had in weeks. The *wyrria* inside him was quiescent, and even his regular aches and pains did not bother him. The old wound in his side was merely a twinge this morning, and Theroun marveled at the good that sleep had done him.

Or perhaps Khorel Jornath's blood.

The *wyrric* force within him stirred at the thought of blood. Of shedding it, of causing it, of drinking it, of watching it flow from his enemies. Theroun shrugged on his shirt, then the Elsthemi garb and furs he'd been captured in. He was most of the way through dressing when he spied something upon the bedside table. Frowning, he stepped over to it. It wasn't like him to miss a detail about his surroundings.

Standing at the table, Theroun stopped cold. His fingers

reached out, touching the garment that lay there. So neatly folded, with military precision. The weave of the leather and the setting of the silver studs were impeccable, the stitching detailed. His fingers slid over the jerkin, lifted it. The leather was supple in his hands, feather-light with a thin quilted silk under-jerkin.

All of it, black as death.

The herringbone garb made the reality of his decision hit him. Theroun was theirs. No longer Elyasin's, or Uhlas'. No longer a General of Alrou-Mendera, or a leader of armies. After whatever had passed last night, he wasn't entirely certain he was even a man any longer. But that was the question he needed answers to – where the Black Viper stopped, and the man began.

He left the garb upon the table. Pushing out the open door, he took the hallway at a military clip. Jogging up the stairs to the chapel two at a time, he pushed through the doors to find the cathedral's main hall in disarray, full of crates and barrels, sacks and provisions. Kreth-Hakir came and went through the open main doors into the high autumn sunshine, transporting goods. They nodded their notice of Theroun, but that was all, rushing silently about their tasks.

Reaching out, Theroun snagged a Kreth-Hakir Brother he didn't recognize by the arm, a sword-honed Cennetian man with short-shorn copper hair and beard, alchemical sigils tattooed up the sides of his neck. "What is all this? Where is Jornath?"

He felt a tendril of silver reach out to his mind. The oilslick-black venom of Theroun's *wyrria* slapped it back and the Brother winced, then spoke aloud. "Scion. The High Priest has gone to the Alranstone under the palace."

"He's gone into the tunnels?!" Theroun bristled, raging at having been so deceived.

"No, Scion," the Hakir Brother corrected mildly. "The white witch died with the information Brother Jornath needed locked inside her mind. He's been trying for three days to open the tunnels, without effect. He sent word to Rennkavi Lhaurent den'Alrahel this morning that pursuit of the King and Queen is futile. So Lhaurent has opened the Alranstone beneath Fhekran Palace. He bids us move the army with all haste to the Port of Ligenia to make ready for an assault upon the Aphellian Way against Valenghia. Excuse me, Scion. We all have much to do. If you seek Brother Jornath, you may find him near the Alranstone, orchestrating transport."

Theroun blinked. So Khorel had kept his word. And with Theroun's *wyrria* slamming back the other Brethren from his mind, the secret of their deal would remain. "I've been asleep three days?"

The Brother gave a frown, his green eyes penetrating. "Most sleep a full week when their Beast is finally tamed. Did Brother Jornath not instruct you in this?"

"Brother Jornath has not instructed me in much," Theroun snapped back.

"Did you not find the raiment we left?" The man inspected Theroun's filthy Elsthemi gear with a critical and somewhat disdainful eye.

"Oh, I found them."

Theroun shouldered past the Cennetian Kreth-Hakir Brother and out the doors. Jogging down the white stone steps to the avenue, his gaze took in the ruined city of Lhen Fhekran under the high autumn sunshine. Everything was on the move. Menderian soldiers and Elsthemi captives alike were busy transporting goods in wains, carts, and over their shoulders. Every beast that had survived the fires was being herded toward the ruins of the palace, a steady stream of livestock and horses rounding the palisade and moving toward the towering heap of black rubble that had once been Fhekran Palace.

Theroun picked up his feet, ignoring stares from both the Menderian army and the Elsthemi. He didn't have time to explain himself, and wasn't about to try. With a ground-eating stride, he marched toward the palisade, darting around men and horses upon a broad path that had been cleared in the debris. It angled down, deep into what had once been the hot-pools of the palace.

Theroun rounded a wall of blackened char and was greeted by the sight of a massive Alranstone of pure crystal standing tall and undamaged near a recessed alcove set with a rose-crystal door. Positively covered in runes and script of precious ores, both the crystal door and the Alranstone were pristine, untouched by the fire's ruination though all the stone walls bordering the once-underground space were cracked and blackened from the immense heat of the palace's burning. The pools that surrounded the Alranstone were filthy with ash slurry, though Theroun could see a few had already flushed themselves clean from the natural springs that welled up beneath the palace. Flowing away to the northwest in a meandering stream, the drainage found its way out of the palace's ruin by a newly-formed channel to the Fhekran River beyond.

Nature would take its course once they had gone, and this place would become a curiosity like so many other places sundered in war, Theroun mused. But right now, it was a staging-area for a massive operation of men and animals, barrels and crates. Khorel Jornath stood next to the Alranstone, directing traffic with his hands and smooth silver floes from his mind. As Theroun watched, Jornath beckoned for a group of ten Elsthemi to lead thirty blindfolded horses up to the Stone. The men joined hands and shared a look, but the man on the end gazed up at the Stone as if superstitious as his hand hovered over its smooth crystal surface. Theroun practically heard the silver command Jornath whipped at the man's mind to get him over his fear and proceed. The Elsthemi warrior set his palm to the Stone and a thunderclap filled the ruin, accompanied by a sucking of wind that made Theroun's ears pop – and then both men and horse were gone.

Theroun scowled. King Therel had said this Alranstone hadn't ever been active, not in living memory. Theroun wondered again how in blazes Lhaurent was able to wake and command Alranstones, surmising that this was how the eel traveled so quickly and in such secrecy from place to place. A hundred paces away, Khorel Jornath glanced to Theroun as if he'd heard Theroun's thoughts. Even from a distance, Theroun felt the man's gaze hit him like a quicksilver wall. Theroun staggered with a grunt and Jornath smiled, as Jornath's words broke through his mind, bright as the fucking morning.

That was a reprimand, Scion, for insubordinate willfulness. You were given a gift of our garb and were intended to take it. To wear the raiment of the Kreth-Hakir Order on this, your first day among us. You have insulted me, and your Brethren, by not joining us in this.

I'll not wear your colors. Ever. Theroun knifed it back, almost seeing an iridescent black tendril shoot out from his mind and cross the distance in a flash, striking at Jornath. But the vehemence of his will-sending hit a silver river, flowing away into nothing. Jornath smiled, and it was not kind. *I know a thousand ways to dissipate a mind-*

attack, Scion. You do not. You are bound to my blood now, and with that bond comes certain privileges, for both of us. I will not be so easy for you to block anymore, nor to attack. Would you like me to force you to make obeisance? Or will you obey my requests?

Theroun ground his jaw. Bristling, he opened his mouth to speak, but Jornath's silver line slipped into his mind, wrapping deep into his old injury. *I can make you writhe, Theroun. Or we can be civil until it is time for your proper lessons. The choice is yours.*

Theroun pulled his rage back. He could feel the promise of Jornath's words, already starting a hot lance of pain in his side. After days of suffering, it was the last thing he currently wanted.

I suppose I can maintain civility. Theroun thought back, though he still said it with a growl.

Master. Jornath's gaze was penetrating, even from a hundred paces.

Excuse me? Theroun bit back, hackles rising.

Master. Jornath's smile was exquisitely subtle and thrice as dominant. *You will call me Master, and I will call you Scion. And that is how it will be between us. Do you understand?*

A growl bubbled out from Theroun's mouth. Livid anger seethed through him, trembling his body. But before he could do anything, silver threads struck out from Khorel Jornath's mind again, wrapping into Theroun. Wrapping into his knees, his feet, his ankles. Suddenly, Theroun's body weighed two hundred stone. He sank to his knees in the sludge and char, fighting and losing. The weight of his head tripled, his neck bending in penitence. Simmering with rage, Theroun and the *wyrria* inside him both roared. But even his vocal cords weighed ten times what they should, and would not permit any sound. From the outside, Theroun simply looked like a man who had fallen to his knees for a moment of prayer. But from the inside, he felt his blood boil, fighting his captor's will with everything he had.

Khorel Jornath's rolling baritone laughed inside his mind. Theroun was allowed to lift his head, and as he gazed across the bustle, he saw the man was actually laughing where he stood near the Alranstone. Waving another group forward, Elsthemi soldiers carrying crates of chickens, Jornath directed them to assemble.

I could leave you there all day, Jornath chuckled.

Do that, and royally piss me off, Theroun bit back.

Jornath's gaze sobered. A small smile lifted the corners of his mouth, and it was not kind. *Stay, Scion. Remember today who I am to you, and you to me. Remember that your blood is no longer your own, nor your body, and certainly not your mind. We are one now, and even though you can fight the other Brethren off with your viperous will, you are one with them as well. Remain in a posture of humility today, and I shall summon you at sundown for your lessons.*

Khorel Jornath turned away.

And left Theroun in the slurry on his knees, stepped around by a group of soldiers leading goats.

CHAPTER 27 – ELESHEN

Two days after the keshari forces arrived, Eleshen stood at the
pockmarked ironwood table in the Upper Gallery of the fortress at
Gerrov-Tel, thinking. Arms crossed, her long fingers fiddled with the
end of her black braid where it cascaded over her shoulder, a frown
knitting her brows. Discussion had gone on for hours, and the grey
day had eased into a subtle twilight. Bullfrogs chorused outside as
the last of the light deepened, darkness now eating through the
arrow-slits of the round gallery on the third floor of the fortress. Oil-
lanterns had been lit and sat in niches in the walls, where ancient
rubble of broken statues had been cleared the day before. Eleshen
stood at the table, gazing at Lhaurent's maps of the southeastern
Menderian countryside, Ihbram, Khouren, Sebasos, General Merra
and her Captains Rhone and Rhennon Uhlki ringing the table.

General Merra spun a fly-blade upon the table as her ice-blue
gaze flicked cunningly over the maps, then reached up to flick a few
braids of her red-blonde mane out of her sightline. Eleshen
regarded the fierce, battle-ready General in her battered Elsthemi
leathers and shaggy grey wolf pelt. Her Captains, stout trees of
brothers with shaved mohawks of bright blonde braids, stood at
casual attention also, arms crossed as they examined the map.

The brothers Rhone and Rhennon Uhlki weren't identical, but
had fashioned themselves that way. Elsthemi dragon tattoos curled
down from the shaved sides of their scalps, their tattoos mirror
images of each other as they arced down behind their pierced ears
and disappeared under their shaggy brown-bear pelts. Cunning sky-
blue eyes connected to Eleshen's, as if they felt her watching. Each
brother gave a smile; Rhone's lecherous, Rhennon's just reassuring.
At her side, Eleshen felt the massive bulk of Brother Sebasos shift.
Crossing his burly arms, Sebasos gave the brothers a look of
hardened stoicism from beneath his heavy black brows. Their gazes
shifted back to the map, though Rhone's went with an even bigger

grin for Eleshen and a wink.

"All told," Merra continued in the discussion, "we've got five hundred keshari riders and cats, just over three hundred defected Menderians from Theroun's forces, and with your four hundred or so Kingsmen and Roushenn Guard, that brings us up to twelve hundred fighters. A goodly amount to bring to Arlen den'Selthir's aid."

"Who stays behind to defend Gerrov-Tel?" Eleshen spoke up, cognizant of the promise she made Temlin: to protect both the Kingsmen and the Jenners. "If we mobilize all the fighting men and women to aid Arlen den'Selthir, we leave Gerrov-Tel unprotected. Temlin charged me with keeping the Kingsmen and the Jenners safe – I won't have them all killed because of a single campaign."

"Sending our warriors down to Vennet may seem a foolhardy engagement, Eleshen," turning to her, the rogue Ihbram den'Sennia spoke in his lilting baritone, his green gaze fierce, "but trust me when I say that Arlen den'Selthir is no weakling. He could have been King Uhlas' top general, back in the day, but he chose not to be. It was more important to him to keep his position as leader of the Shemout Alrashemni, and that meant staying close to Vennet to ensure his *contingency plan* remained upheld. His emergency location has been cultivated in utter secrecy for over fifteen years, ever since war began to rumble on the Valenghian border. Arlen's played the lord in Vennet all these years because he is, but trust me when I say the man has contingencies for his contingencies. Some of us may die in this engagement, but I'm certain Arlen's planning will make certain those losses are minimal."

Eleshen fiddled with her braid, then turned to Sebasos. The massive brewer's muscled arms were folded at his barrel chest. Clad in his Alrashemni garb, his grey-streaked black waves were curried back from his forehead, his Blackmark visible upon his chest just above his shirt-lacings. His black brows made a scowl, his normal thinking face.

"What do you think, Sebasos?" Eleshen cocked her head.

Sebasos shifted his stance. "Temlin and I did not know each other in the Shemout, though he and I were both commanders of our cells, and thus independently had contact with Arlen over the years. What normal people would call an *emergency* plan to Arlen is simply good prudence. I believe Ihbram. Arlen would be prepared to defend this contingency location of his through Halsos' Burnwater and out the other side."

Eleshen was about to speak, when Ihbram suddenly chimed in again. With a twinkle of humor in his green eyes, he added, "If we make it to Arlen, he'll keep us safe. His emergency location has natural fortifications. It's a stronghold, a few hour's march northwest of Vennet, in the Great Forest – a place called the Vault."

"The Vault?" Eleshen spoke. "Aren't those the haunted ruins inside that old river-crevasse near Vennet? Fae-yarns speak of fortune-hunters that go there and disappear, and moaning spirits that drive men mad. Are you saying *that's* Arlen's stronghold?"

"What better a place to fight from than haunted ruins?" Ihbram's smile was eloquent. "Besides, Arlen's Kingsmen know how to deal with such things. And the stone walls are damn hard to climb up, but there are enough ledges for cats to leap." Ihbram nodded at General Merra, slipping into a sexy slouch with one hip against the table. Merra lifted her lips in a smile that was almost a snarl, ignoring his flirtation.

"So say we ride to Arlen," Eleshen took up the conversation again. "Who do we leave here?"

Sebasos stroked his grey-streaked black beard with one hand, then sighed. "As much as I'd love to join the battle, my knees aren't what they once were. I volunteer to remain behind with my Shemout cell to guard Gerrov-Tel – forty good fighters. This valley will be abominable with snow in a month or so. We just have to secure the fortress until winter. Lhaurent might risk sending a battalion up here in the snows, but he'd lose far too many men. And with the industriousness of the Jenners, we'll have it well fortified by then."

"The snows up here are harsh," Eleshen agreed. "You'd be safe until spring. The highway becomes impassable past Dhemman after Darkwinter."

"What about Elsthemen? In your absence?" Khouren spoke now, his melodious voice subdued as his gaze penetrated the High General. Something in his pale grey eyes was stronger than when Eleshen had first made his acquaintance. More human, somehow.

"Elsthemen is held in my absence." Merra spoke solidly, a fierce glimmer in her clear blue eyes. "Mikka Khuriye rounds up the

Bhorlen Rangers on my orders. She's rallied the mountain and tundra clans, in the Dhelvendale and Blackthorn ruins. They'll hold everything north and west of the Themi Sea. Elsthemen will hold on, by tooth and claw. But we need the Kingsmen ta truly rout Lhaurent's forces and regain our nation."

"Temlin left you in charge of this fortress," Sebasos turned to Eleshen. "It's your decision that matters in this. But what we cannot do is continue to deliberate. Every day we waste is another day Lhaurent can use his armies to crush what is left of the Kingsmen and the Elsthemi."

"Sometimes to protect life, you have to go out and fight for it," Ihbram agreed in a soft voice. He and Sebasos shared a long look, Sebasos giving the man a nod.

Arms crossed, Eleshen fingered the hilt of one longknife. Temlin had left her in charge of not only preserving Alrashemni treasures, but preserving the Alrashemni people. If she remained here, using the Kingsmen to protect scrolls and monks, she did Temlin a disservice. Eventually, Lhaurent would send an army – and if Arlen's Kingsmen fell, there would be no one left to help Gerrov-Tel.

Something clicked inside Eleshen. The attitude Elohl had once held, of doing what he had to, suddenly made sense. She was the tip of the spear now. She was the shield to save the Alrashemni Kingsmen from annihilation. And that meant taking them out to fight for what was theirs.

Their nation, their freedom – and their very right to exist.

Eleshen straightened. Her arms uncrossed as she set both hands to the hilts of her longknives. "Then we go. We live or fall together. The Alrashemni Shemout and Kingsmen failed to band together in the past, and they paid for it. Unity will be our strength. As Temlin den'Ildrian came out of the shadows to proclaim his strength as a leader for our nation, so will we come forward also – to be the heart of that nation. To fight, with passion and power, and bring all under the true light of the dawn at last."

"Stronger words than you know," Khouren gazed at Eleshen, his eyes sorrowful, but also simmering with fervency.

"And a stronger woman than *you* know, Khouren," Ihbram cocked his head, peering at Eleshen curiously. "Who *are* you?"

"I am still heir to the Dhepanship of Quelsis, as I was born." Eleshen gave a wry smile. "But now I know a larger truth. I'm the one who has faith in the Alrashemni Kingsmen. I will still have faith in them, even to the last Kingsman standing."

"Or woman." General Merra's blue eyes shone with a hardy fierceness. "Ah'v a cat who's recently lost a rider. Moonshadow needs a new lass. Do ye want a smooth fucker of a mount to go with that battle-sass, Wolf's Child?"

A ready smile lifted Eleshen's lips. Something passed between her and General Merra, and it was fierce in a way that only women can be. "I love cats."

"Ha!" Merra's laugh was throaty. Ambling around the table, she came to grip Eleshen's shoulder. "We'd love ta have ye. Yer a bitch like me, an' that's a compliment. Then I can ride back ta my contingent? Tell them of battle and get them on the road?" This last was addressed directly to Eleshen, rather than any of the men present.

"Indeed," Eleshen answered before any of the men could speak. "We'll make our forces ready to travel. Sebasos, will your fighters need anything to prepare the fortress before we set out?"

Sebasos shifted his stance, his black brows knit. "The main level of the fortress is solid enough, now that most of the timbers and doors have been repaired. We've got enough food for the winter if we supplement with hunting. The old armory beneath the Southwest tower has been unearthed finally. I've gone down there, and there are a number of useful items. Lances, swords, polearms, warbows. We ought to get it all lashed to available cats, take most of it to Arlen except for enough to outfit my fighters here."

"General Merra, can you bring cats up in three days to transport weapons?" Eleshen asked.

"I can do ye one better," General Merra answered. "I can have my entire host here by dawn. Tell yer rangers not ta panic and shoot at us – we'll circle up around the amphitheater. Then help load up those weapons ye mentioned and be ready ta set out by the second morrow."

"That will do." Eleshen looked around, evaluating each of them. Khouren with his fervent eyes and quiet calm, with more useful Aeon-given talents than she could shake a stick at. Ihbram with his cheeky grin, ready with mind-blocking abilities against the Kreth-Hakir. General Merra with her battle-hardy fierceness, a seasoned war-commander of dangerous regiments. The brothers Rhone and Rhennon, clearly fierce in their abilities and eager to jump into battle once more. Sebasos with his implacable demeanor, a stalwart protector who would do them well and hold the fortress.

And Eleshen – stronger under the moon than she had ever been under the sun.

"So be it," Eleshen set her fingertips to the tabletop, her demeanor hardening. "Let the Kingsmen make their last stand, or die in the attempt."

* * *

Deep in the armory catacombs beneath Gerrov-Tel's Southwest tower, Khouren Alodwine retracted his hand from the sword they'd both reached out to collect from a dusty wooden rack. Eleshen retracted hers also, startled by the electric energy that had rushed between them. Looking up, she was arrested by the intensity of the Ghost's gaze in the flicker of the oil-lamps, though he said nothing.

Eleshen and Khouren had been working side by side all day, packing up weapons and armor. Though he'd hardly said ten words, they'd passed the hours in an uncanny understanding. Through all the bustle of making ready to travel, he'd never left her side, haunting Eleshen's steps like a quiet, helpful shroud. A perfect gentleman since their kiss – almost too much so.

"Are you alright?" Khouren's dark brows knit and he cocked his head, his handsome jawline limned in the lamplight.

Eleshen blinked away her trance, tearing her gaze from his and back to the crate of longknives and blow-darts upon the table. "We should finish this load. Then get some supper. It's late."

"Of course." Lifting the crate to his shoulder, Khouren stabilized it with one hand. The vault was silent. Everyone else who'd helped move weapons and sundry to the prep area was long asleep after a busy day, and now only Khouren helped Eleshen burn the midnight oil.

Mounting the winding stairs, Eleshen navigated around

cracked boulders that still partially blocked the underground access from the toppled tower above. She could barely hear Khouren's step behind her, just a whisper of his leather boots. Gaining the upper landing, she moved out into an auxiliary courtyard of the main fortress, stepping around tumbled stones in a lofty midnight silence. The rain had broken at last, to a true autumnal chill with stars shining bright as diamonds above. The moon was a slim sickle in the clear sky, white and austere. Eleshen shivered as a cold breeze snuck in through her Kingsman garb and lipped across her collarbones. Blowing out the lamp, she set it in a niche, moving forward by the light of the midnight sky above.

"Perhaps this should be the last of it tonight." Khouren paced at her side with his crate, through the chill darkness along the edge of the collapsed tower.

Pulling the hood of her Alrashemni garb up over her hair to keep warm, Eleshen covered her surprise at his sudden engagement. "We'll secure this last crate near the Alranstone, then be done. We can do the rest at dawn before we march."

Khouren was silent a while more, until they crossed under a vault in the retaining-wall and into the rebuilt main courtyard, passing alert guards at the fortress doors. The main doors of fresh-scented cendarie were shut against the cold, though torches burned in iron brackets. With a nod to the guards, Eleshen stepped to the cluttered path that led through the main courtyard. Her glance was arrested for a moment by the three-story pile of rubble that gleamed in the moonlight nearby. Mature trees rose up out of that broken darkness, like much of Gerrov-Tel. Lights flared in the arrow-slits of the main fortress, bright like fireflies, but the fortress was still barely defensible. Worry devoured Eleshen for a moment, contemplating the formidable task Sebasos would have making everything ready for winter or a siege.

"Do you need to find Sebasos?" Khouren spoke, tracing her glance up to the ruined turrets, his voice soft in the night. "Leave him extra instructions?"

"I just—" Eleshen paused. "Temlin left me in charge. I hate to leave before I've hardly even done anything."

Khouren's smile twisted, but he gave a genteel nod as they continued on through the clutter. "A commander must make difficult decisions in times of war. Sebasos understands. So would Temlin."

Silence eased between them, punctuated by rustling cendarie trees and bullfrogs singing their last as autumn sighed in. Eleshen angled through the courtyard and down into the amphitheater where loads for the cats were being gathered for their departure tomorrow. Pale moonlight flooded the amphitheater as they moved through. Crowded with crates of supplies, weapons, and sundries, everything was nearly ready to be loaded at first light. Cats prowled in the darkness at the amphitheater's rim like muscled shadow, the entirety of General Merra's forces encamped just out of sight in the trees. Mirror-eyes flashed in the black, watching Eleshen and Khouren.

Striding on, Eleshen moved down the amphitheater's crumbling steps toward the bluestone Plinth. She didn't wait for Khouren, merely stepped down the incline, hands upon her longknife hilts as her eyes scanned the keshari presence at the tree line. It was a habit that had come with her new body, something she did as naturally as breathing now. Finding a likely spot, she paused as Khouren set his crate down atop a stack of others, a long silence drifting between them.

"I'll walk you back to the fortress," Khouren spoke at last.

"I can find my way." Eleshen waved a hand.

"I'd like to escort you."

Eleshen cocked her head at Khouren's quiet insistence. She thought to say something snippy, when she caught a glimpse of his pale eyes in the moonlight, steady and fervent. "As you like."

She turned on her heel and was about to stride back when she paused, arrested by the moon glinting off the Alranstone. Lit in stark shadows, something about it triggered her tonight: the angle of the moon; the presence of the Stone. It took her back to the first time she had been here, when Elohl had climbed that Stone and been given his Goldenmarks by the ancient king inside it.

"Elohl was changed after that," she whispered to the night.

"Elohl den'Alrahel?" Khouren's voice was low at her side. Eleshen felt him look at her. "You knew him, didn't you?"

"Not so well."

"What's wrong?" Setting a hand to her shoulder, Khouren turned her so he could see her eyes in the moonlight. His frown was dark, a possessiveness in it.

"It's nothing." Eleshen set her hands to her hips and found the hilts of her longknives beneath her fingertips.

Looking to the Alranstone, something dangerous glinted in Khouren's eyes before he glanced back to Eleshen. "Did Elohl hurt you?"

"Hurt?" Eleshen snorted. "Not really. But he didn't really care for me, either. He dumped me to go protect his Queen at her coronation. I never saw him again."

"He fought like a dervish that day," Khouren murmured, a thoughtful tone in his voice. "He was pursued on all sides by Palace Guard. He followed his only choice; leaving Lintesh with the Queen and the Elsthemi Highlanders."

Eleshen heaved a sigh. She'd thought it might have been something like that, though a part of her wanted to hate Elohl. "You were there in the palace that day?"

"I was. Watching from the walls."

"You do that a lot, don't you?" Eleshen quipped. "Watch. You were watching me when I was under Lhem's knife."

Khouren turned to gaze at her more fully, and the intensity of his presence under the moonlight made Eleshen shiver. "I would have intervened sooner. But Lhem was aligned with the man I served at the time. My obedience arrested my conscience. Forgive me."

Eleshen took a deep breath, realizing that they were talking at last. Truly talking. Sharing something about who they actually were, rather than this dance of intense attraction and silence they'd had so far. "You saved my life."

"I almost cost you your life."

"No. You saved me." Eleshen was firm. "Whatever you did with your magic, even though it gave me a new body – I don't regret it. You saved me. Made me stronger. I have a new life now, with purpose in service to the Kingsmen, all because of you."

"It wasn't I." Khouren's words were soft in the night. "My half-sister saved your life – Abbess Lenuria Alodwine. She had a great *wyrria* and used it to heal you because I asked it. But the price of that healing was high. My sister's magic resonates a new form for someone when it heals them, unless they carry Alodwine blood. Lenuria's healing made this body you now wear, Eleshen."

"The *Jenner Abbess* did this?" Eleshen blinked, astounded. "Made my new body?"

"Her *wyrria* chooses the form that serves someone best," Khouren's tone was melodious in the night, haunted. "A form that resonates with their innermost desires. Your new abilities resemble hers, you know. You fight like Lenuria once did. A master of blades, even with all her old moves. Her body knew survival. She was a demon in battle."

Eleshen took a long breath. Khouren's words made an uncanny sense to her. And yet, her new body knew other things than just impeccable fighting skills. She'd not felt anything the night Elohl had climbed the Alranstone and been Goldenmarked, but now she could feel energy breathing out of the nearby Alranstone like forge-fire. She could feel it, lifting the hairs all over her body. She could taste it like smelted metal on her tongue; an energy she hadn't known before that now livened this new body to the depths of her soul.

"And this energy I feel," she breathed, "this... strangeness I can feel flooding through me, and through the Alranstone?"

Khouren cocked his head, staring at her intently. Taking up her hand, his dark brows knit. And then lifted. "*Wyrria!* I can feel it... slipping through your veins. Did you know you were a *wyrric*?"

Eleshen blinked, comprehending but not understanding fully. She could feel it, sense this otherness within her, and had ever since her awakening in her new flesh. But it still seemed shrouded, dormant, as if it were yet to be truly unleashed.

"How can I have *wyrria* if I'm not Alrashemni?" She asked, her gaze perusing all the arcane sigildry on the Alranstone and its tower of closed eyes.

A strange light reflected in Khouren's eyes as he gazed at the Stone also. "You don't have to be Alrashemni to carry *wyrria*. Once upon a time, *wyrria* rose its cursed head throughout the continent, and still does, to a small degree. Stronger now, since Elohl was Goldenmarked by the King inside this Alranstone."

"So you're saying that *wyrria* strengthens in the world again," she spoke. "Because Elohl was marked with a destiny that links us all."

"For better or for worse," Khouren agreed.

"Do you really believe such things are a curse?"

"For my family." Khouren let out a soft sigh. "For others, perhaps not. But for the Scions of Alodwine, when the Wolf and Dragon *wyrria* rises in us, it always leads to terrible conflict."

"The Wolf and Dragon. Battling inside the flames." Eleshen blinked, recalling the colored glass window in the Abbey Annex, and the Goldenmark that had been writ all across Elohl's broad back after his encounter with this Alranstone. "It's an emblem of your bloodline?"

"Of conflict, yes. Unceasing conflict and a bitter darkness, that lives in our *wyrria*."

"Is that all you believe life is? Conflict and darkness?"

"Is there anything else?"

The way Khouren said it was so bereft that Eleshen reached out and took his hand. Feeling some strange kinship, she gazed down at their twined fingers as Khouren gently clasped hers. "We may stand in darkness, but I believe there is hope. Dawn never fails to rise even when snows choke the night. If there's one thing I learned living in the mountains for years, it's that."

"You sprang back from the grips of death. So strong. Like crocus of the mountains…"

Looking at her strangely, Khouren's pale grey eyes were vivid in the moonlight, his handsome visage riveted. Reaching out, he placed his fingertips to her cheek, his thumb caressing her lower lip. Eleshen shivered beneath his touch, but found the intimacy not unwanted as something heated deep inside her. He heaved a shaky breath and let his hand slip from her face – though slowly, as if he didn't want to relinquish the touch.

Eleshen was struck mute by whatever was rising between them. It was uncanny, a quiet darkness that gripped her yet gave her a light so bright she could barely comprehend it. She turned, shivering off the sensation, only to find a different sensation arrest her – the Alranstone calling in the moonlight. Entranced, she stepped down the ruined tiers to the monolith. But when she placed her hands upon the Stone, she suddenly felt inclined to do something she'd never done before. Setting her fingers to niches and the toes of her boots to rough grooves, she was suddenly climbing – her precision innate, her body coordinated.

It was a thrill, climbing. Feeling the danger of the height, knowing only her reflexes and strength could prevent a fall to certain death. Eleshen suddenly understood Elohl's urge to climb the monolith that fated night, and some anger towards him cleared from her. In a short minute, she gained the pinnacle and clambered to standing upon the Stone's top, taking in the arresting vantage of snow-shrouded peaks. Khouren was soon at her side. Breathing softly in the night, they gazed around in wonder, the moon blessing the glaciers with silver radiance as it held court over the world.

"I never thought the world could be so beautiful," Khouren murmured.

"Neither did I," Eleshen echoed, gazing around at so much beauty. "I used to think myself bright, but really, I have so much darkness in me from what Lhem did. But it goes back long before that, to the Raid of Quelsis. And the Kingsman Summons."

With a gentle touch, Khouren turned her to face him. "Your darkness is beautiful, Eleshen. Don't run from it. Lenuria's *wyrria* chose this form for you, because it knew you are stronger this way. More able to be what you wish to be, fueling your life with not just your light but also your darkness. Do you know what you want, from your life now?"

"I want to *be* Alrashemni, Khouren." The answer hit Eleshen like a forge-hammer, a truth that filled her core. "I want to be a Kingsman, to work through my Seals. It's all I've ever wanted."

"Then take Lenuria's gift." Reaching out, Khouren stroked a hand down her long sable braid. "Take it, and become what you were meant to be. Your *wyrria* was kindled in darkness and bitter conflict, but maybe that was for a reason. Because you're stronger with moonlight pouring through your veins than the light of the sun."

Something fierce rose inside Eleshen, triggered by Khouren's words. They saved her in a way she couldn't explain, much like his sudden action had saved her that fateful night from Lhem's torture. She stepped close, touching his silken garb. Opening his jerkin's collar so she could run her fingers over the bare skin of his chest. So she could lean in and smell him – his curious scent of cinnamon, musk, and bones.

Khouren let out a shaky sigh as shivers wracked him. One of his hands wound about her waist, drawing her close. The other went to her neck, gripping her nape and pulling her gently away. He breathed hard in the moonlight as he lifted those amazing pale grey eyes to hers, something in their depths burning gold.

"I don't want to take advantage of you, Eleshen. I—"

Eleshen didn't allow him a single breath more. Lifting up, she pressed her lips to his. Inhaling his strange cinnamon death-musk; feeling the tension of his body ripple all around her.

His tension broke. In a flowing rush, Khouren lifted her with his incredible strength. Holding Eleshen up as her legs wrapped around him like a midnight vine. Crushing her close into a kiss that had no end, only beginnings beneath the brightness of the moon.

CHAPTER 28 – ELOHL

An impromptu war-council had been convened in Merkhenos del'Ilio's chambers inside the White Palace. All were bathed and dressed, Elohl and Fenton in rich jerkins of dark crimson with silver detail that fit them like a second skin, their ornate jewelry discarded like so much trash. Elohl felt more himself, dressed at last and clean of both the gore that had coated his body in the throne hall and also of the Vhinesse's seeping taint.

His Red Valor attire fit well, a soft white silk shirt and black rough-silk trousers with black calfskin kneeboots with a high-collared dark crimson jerkin. The garb was not unlike the cobalt uniforms of the Roushenn Palace Guard, though Valenghia's elite uniforms buckled up the front with ornate silver vine-leaf buckles rather than have a crossover flap, dark crimson leather bracers tooled with vines gracing Elohl's wrists. Their gear from Elsthemen had been found in the Vhinesse's private quarters, and Elohl and Fenton had reclaimed their weapons harnesses and blades which had been gifts from King Therel and Queen Elyasin, along with Therel and Elyasin's signet rings. Elohl felt more himself with a satchel ready near the door, filled with his climbing gear just in case.

Trying to smother the worries that consumed him, Elohl moved forward to refill his wine goblet from a bottle of burgundy Valenghian Champelion that tasted of cherries and chocolate. It eased his mind and let his soul breathe to drink a bit; pushing back images of bodies spilling blood as he cut them down and the feel of his Goldenmarks pouring through disarmed men.

Leaning against the carven agate-stone wall by one massive fireplace, he watched the roaring blaze as the light beyond the gabled windows darkened toward evening. Dressed and picking through meats from a silver platter upon a side-table, Fenton looked up, then seized the platter and approached. Saluting with his wine goblet, he motioned with the platter.

"Have you eaten?"

"Just wine."

Fenton cocked an eyebrow, a small smile upon his lips. "You'll be worthless after all that fighting if you don't eat. Someone must have told you that up in the High Brigade."

"It was probably Ihbram." Elohl gave a slight smile back as his fingers took a chunk of roast beef from the proffered platter. He chewed slowly, though the flavors tasted like ashes right now.

Setting the platter down on a side-table nearby, Fenton leaned back against the wall, regarding Elohl with a level look. "How are you?"

"Drained." Elohl was honest. He didn't feel the need to hide anything from Fenton as he reached for more roast beef. "Whatever happened in there with the Marks, it took a lot out of me."

"No shit." Fenton's gaze was frank. "We need to talk, Elohl. I felt myself pulling power from you, from the Goldenmarks. You must know, that wasn't my intent—"

"I know." Elohl's words were soft as he settled against the wall at Fenton's side. "You don't have to apologize. The Marks... I believe they did what they were engineered to do. This goes deeper than us, Fenton. The Marks didn't just feed power into you, they used the power of everyone in that room whom I held dear. Ate it. Combining all of it together to cause something greater..."

"You could have controlled us." Fenton's voice was hushed. "I felt it, in that moment before you relaxed. You could have shot the power of the Goldenmarks through us all like you did the Vhinesse, taking us, binding us. Why didn't you?"

Elohl paused. Rubbing his fingers together upon the piece of meat he held, he stared at it. "Because then men are no better than slaves, Fenton. No one should ever be a slave. Not to any king, not to any throne, and not to me."

Fenton let out a slow breath. Elohl glanced up. The Scion of Khehem wore a complex look, but something in it was pleased. "I was hoping you'd say something like that."

"Were you afraid I'd choose differently?" Elohl ate his meat, chewing slowly.

"Perhaps." Fenton went for some cheese and grapes, popping them into his mouth. "Not all men would allow power like that to slip by their control."

"Not all men have lived a life like I have."

The words dropped from Elohl's lips like stones. He hadn't meant for them to sound so cold, but there it was. He'd hated his life in the High Brigade, pressed into military service like a common thug. And yet, honor had made him try his best, despite everything it had cost him.

"Perhaps you're the perfect person to wear those marks," Fenton mused, watching him. "I keep wondering *why* you were marked by Brother King Hahled Ferrian. It goes deeper than having twinned Alrashemni and Khehemni blood, Elohl. Plenty of babies have been born over the past thousand years with twinned bloodlines. But not many of them understood sacrifice. What it means to have your liberty taken from you, how that feels. A cautionary tale that you hold in your heart at all times."

Elohl looked up from the tray and met Fenton's gaze. "No man should ever be a slave."

"Nor will they be," Fenton lifted his goblet in a small salute, "not with you carrying those marks. But we have bigger problems to discuss at this meeting than the succession of the Vhinesse and how to stop the Menderian-Valenghian war. I fear we may be up all night, with the things I have to speak about."

"Lhaurent den'Alrahel." Elohl took a sip of his wine, his eyes dark in the fire's light. His voice was a low growl as he set his goblet down upon the gilded table with subtle force. "I can't hardly imagine a man such as that holding the Goldenmarks."

"It's worse than that." Fenton simmered also, a subtle prickling around his persona. Fenton took a deep breath and crossed his arms over his chest as if trying to keep his cool. "Lhaurent was given the Goldenmarks, just as you were, over forty years ago. And he's built everything he's created, every diabolical piece of it, over the past decades because he *believes* in those Marks. In his right to rule because of them. He knows the Rennkavi's Prophecy, because someone from my bloodline told him. Told him he was the Unifier. Gave him talismans from Leith, *important* talismans, that never should have been turned over to someone so black of heart. Lhaurent has his tremendous influence now because one of *my* line betrayed me. And gave a tyrant what he needed to rule, both in arcane objects and in ideology."

Elohl stood, stunned. His mind poured through thoughts yet was blank with shock. Fenton took up his goblet and drank deep, his gaze shifted to the fire. "I'm sorry I didn't tell you sooner, but I had to see what you were capable of first. What you would choose with those Marks. Lhaurent has chosen to do terrible things. I was fearful you might do the same."

"How could you think I would ever choose the same as that *madman?*" Elohl bristled.

"When we first met, I felt darkness inside you." Fenton's words were soft but his gaze was hard. "Olea was as upright as anyone I'd ever met. But you were an enigma. I'd heard from Ihbram how you'd tried to kill yourself – numerous times – in the High Brigade. I know conflict in a soul. Like blood on the tongue, I can taste it when I meet someone. You have it, in spades. But you also have something that Lhaurent never did."

"And what's that?" Elohl was still bristling, offended at Fenton's judgement.

"Love." Fenton gave a wry smile. "Lhaurent's never loved an Aeon-damned thing in his life. I don't even know if he *can* love. That man is a cold, murderous motherfucker, with a mind more twisted than the coils of an eel in the darkest sea. But you're not. You're a good man, Elohl. I felt your love today in that throne hall. We all did. Believe me, it's a feeling I'll never forget. Not even if I live a thousand years more than I already have."

Elohl's affront left him. He thought of Ghrenna, and as if summoned, her cerulean eyes returned to him. "It wasn't just my love you felt."

"No. It wasn't." Reaching out, Fenton gripped his shoulder. "Your love, what you wrought in that moment… it pulled up love in all of us. In that moment, Elohl, I *felt* every love I'd ever had. I saw them all. From the face of my first wife Levennia del'Mira to the chubby little fingers of the last grandson I saw birthed—" Fenton trailed off, his eyes lost before he took a deep breath, then smiled. "That's what you woke in us today, Elohl. The only thing that can unite men. Pure love, and the deep inner peace that comes with it. You are the true Rennkavi. Lhaurent is false. I need to speak about that tonight, and I hope you'll stand with me."

"Do you have any doubt that I would stand with you? After everything we've been through?"

"I've kept a lot from you." Fenton shrugged, an amused smile playing about his lips. "Some men would be sore about that. You were, as I recall, not so very many days ago."

"I could continue to be angry at you," Elohl gave a wry smile back, "but where would that leave us? It solves nothing. Not for our nation, not for Queen Elyasin or King Therel. If there's anything I've learned lately, it's what my sister already knew: keep Fenton den'Kharel close, whomever he might truly be. I'll want to know your secrets, eventually. All of them. But I've realized in the past few days that I don't doubt you, Fenton. I don't doubt your heart, nor what I feel when the Goldenmarks bind us together."

"Maybe you should," Fenton's gaze was dark by the fire's twisting light. "I'm not what I seem, Elohl. Maybe you should have a little caution around me."

"Maybe I should make that decision for myself," Elohl countered, "and not take the self-flagellating words of a guilt-ridden old *wyrric* for my guidepost."

Fenton's face opened in shock. He gaped at Elohl, lips asunder, hands unwinding from his chest. He set one hand to his belt, but not like he was angry or going to draw a knife. At last, an enormous smile split his face. "You fucking runt. Guilt-ridden old *wyrric* my ass."

Elohl shrugged, but his small smile betrayed him. Reaching out, he clasped the Scion of Khehem by the shoulder, feeling something resonate between the both of them. "You're constantly trying to atone, Fenton. Don't think I don't see it. I might not know the half of everything you've done in your life that you feel guilty for, but I'm not ignorant. I—"

"Gather!"

Their conversation was cut short by a brisk double-clap from Delennia Oblitenne, the handsome silver-haired woman from the throne hall, regal as a battle-empress in her clean Red Valor attire. Fenton gave Elohl a shrug and pushed from the wall, taking up his goblet and tossing more cheese into his mouth. Elohl followed, joining him as everyone gathered around the immense fireplace in Merkhenos' quarters. Chaises and settees had been placed in a circle, with the hearth left as a speaking-place. Fenton took a seat on a gilded chaise and Elohl claimed the space beside him. Dherran and his woman Khenria took a couch to Elohl's left with the aging lord Grunnach den'Lhis, Dherran giving Elohl a nod as he settled.

Elohl smiled back. It felt good to see Dherran again. As if something deep inside Elohl needed that passionate, driven spark Dherran held. As their gazes connected, Elohl felt a strange heat flow between them again, an echo of what had happened in the throne hall. Elohl suddenly thought of that mirage he'd seen surround Dherran when Khenria had been stabbed. Elohl's brows knit, noting that neither Dherran nor Khenria seemed to be injured any longer. But the council was starting, and he had no more time to think on it as Delennia Oblitenne stood before the hearth, hands upraised.

"Comrades," she began, her formidable pale blue gaze piercing each of them, "we are gathered tonight to determine the fate of a nation, and perhaps more than one. My sister, the Tyrant of Valenghia, has been deposed. By means and magic that none here in this room nor in any land could have foreseen. It will cause chaos and much suspicion among the populace, and we are here tonight to devise a strategy to minimize that chaos. I will not have any nation burn as a result of what has happened today. Not my own, and certainly not any of yours. So. I turn the discussion over to the High General of Valenghia, Merkhenos del'Ilio. Merkhenos, if you would."

With a graceful motion, Delennia gestured to the High General. He rose with a brisk clip, taking the center of the hearth. Staring at each of them in turn, he barked a single word, *"Battle."*

Some of the company shifted. Others sat easy, sipping their wine, most notably Fenton and Delennia. The wiry lord Grunnach den'Lhis sat erect and attentive, Dherran and Khenria the same beside him.

"That is what will surely happen," Merkhenos continued in his rolling accent, "if we do not organize. Lhaurent den'Alrahel has weaknesses, but information is not one of them. Even as we speak, he may be receiving word that a coup has happened here. How, you ask? Because it is the observance of those I employ in my intelligence, that Lhaurent den'Alrahel has a peculiar ability to make

Alranstones do his bidding. As such, he controls many inside and outside of Alrou-Mendera. There is one such Stone deep in the bowels of this palace. Which I have personally seen the late Vhinesse moving through – having had council at length with Lhaurent inside Roushenn Palace."

"How did you come by such information?" Fenton spoke, as easy interrupting a High General as he was sipping his Champelion.

"Please speak frankly, Merkhenos," Delennia added, a knowing look in her pale gaze as she set her wine goblet to a gilded side-table. "My sister's reign was tyranny. I intend to value openness and cooperation. But we cannot have that trust among this budding alliance of nations if we are all second-guessing each other. Please, state your alliances and how you know such detailed information about Aelennia's movements."

Merkhenos eyeballed Fenton, his copper gaze steady, before he gave a nod to Delennia. "My Living Vine. I was once upon Aelennia's palladian chain. And if our late Vine had a weakness, it was trusting that her kept men were completely brainwashed. As a Son of Illium, I have my ways against such mind-games. Cennetia, as you all know, is a nation of constantly shifting allegiances. But one faction, the Khehemni Lothren, has maintained an underlying stability there for centuries. After Aelennia hammered our nation and threatened to raze it to ashes a few decades ago, my Cennetian Lothren offered me up to be a *Generalisso* in Aelennia's army, as part of a peace pact. She soon became enamored of my talents, and through her poisonous persona, insisted to my Lothren that I become her *falcon*, just a few years ago. During that time, I learned a great deal about Aelennia's private meetings with Lhaurent, including the balancing act they engineered upon the Aphellian Way and the borderlands to keep the Menderian-Valenghian War stymied these past ten years – plans Aelennia thought she could one day usurp. Because of their hidden agreements, it is likely that Lhaurent has spies throughout this palace, and that they've already traveled through the Alranstone, giving Lhaurent news of today's events. I sent a cadre of men down to guard the Stone as soon as the battle ended, but I fear it may have been too late."

"How does that change the war?" Dherran spoke up, a thoughtful frown pinching his brows.

"Lhaurent will make a push, and soon," Merkhenos continued. "I have it on good authority that he already gathers a supplemental force of fighters at the Port of Ligenia, to augment his main forces at the Aphellian Way. He was already planning to break his agreement with the Vhinesse and drive hard into Valenghia's interior. Hearing of her disposal, he will move, and quickly. Before he thinks we can form a united force."

"Lhaurent has split his border-regiments," the wiry lord Grunnach spoke now, his fingers perusing his chin thoughtfully. "He sends forces through from Quelsis to overtake an uprising in the interior – the Alrashemni-aligned Vicoute Arlen den'Selthir in Vennet. They marched some three weeks past, likely having sieged Vennet already. A contingent of Bog-men under the direction of Vicoute Purloch den'Crassis have gone to their aid. "

Delennia shifted as she turned to Grunnach, her face flushed and scowling as she drank from her wine. Elohl was acutely uncomfortable, feeling the woman's *wyrric* power stalking around his body. "How many soldiers did Lhaurent send to deal with Vennet from the northern border?"

"Some five thousand, though they have likely sent in reinforcements from the Stone Valley Guard by now," Grunnach answered promptly. "I'd say they have eight thousand, probably. Plus at least three Kreth-Hakir, most likely more."

"I can gather half that in Red Valor Longriders stationed in Velkennish and the northern borderlands. We could be at Vennet in a week's time, if we push hard through the Stone Valley near Quelsis." Delennia spoke confidently, but her hands were tense where they gripped her wine goblet. In her strained visage, Elohl read all he needed to know – she cared for this Vicoute Arlen den'Selthir, deeply. Even if she was too proud to admit it, it showed in every line of her worried frown.

"Don't count on having an advantage," Fenton spoke quietly. "Lhaurent has the Kreth-Hakir Brethren on his side. One High Priest can control a hundred fighters. Add five Brethren together, and they can influence an entire battalion."

"When Kreth-Hakir join together," the wiry lord Grunnach chimed in with a glance at Fenton, "they create a synergy that ensnares minds by the hundreds or more. Most men are powerless against it, unless they've studied techniques to shield themselves."

"And Lhaurent has their alliance because someone else would not step in to lead them when he had the chance." Merkhenos' gaze was piercing upon Fenton.

Fenton sighed as he ran a hand through his thick gold-brown hair and riffled it. "I admit, it is my fault. Had I taken command of them eight hundred years ago, they would have gone where I bid. Now they run amok, choosing to serve tyrants who cause atrocity."

Everyone stared at Fenton in shock, except Merkhenos and Elohl. Fenton took his revelation in stride, gazing around the room with his posture easy as he lounged upon the couch. With a careful movement, he set his goblet aside upon a table, then rose to face the assembly. Though he did not change his demeanor or betray any emotion, power suddenly breathed out from him like the roll and bite of fire ants surging across Elohl's skin. All sat at attention, even though those present had already seen Fenton in action. Holding all gazes, red-gold fire began to writhe in Fenton's eyes, complementing the flames from the hearth.

"Gathered friends and allies. What you are about to hear does not leave this room."

Briefly, Fenton began his tale: of being Fentleith Alodwine the grandson of Leith Alodwine, Last King of Khehem. Of how that related to the Kreth-Hakir Brethren, the Leithren – now Lothren – and the Red-Eyed Demon. And of Leith's terrible restriction of the fountainheads of *wyrria* all over the globe, and the creation of the Rennkavi.

"I believe, as did my mother the Prophetess," Fenton murmured to the silent room, "that my grandfather was mad, using the tale of the Demon as an excuse to rule the known world. But the one blessing we have is that his legacy, the Rennkavi, lives." Gesturing to Elohl, he continued. "Once designed as a tool for Leith's use, it is now a free power. Because of the Goldenmarks, Elohl has the ability to unite all our nations and bring our continent to peace. Each one of you felt it in the throne hall today. Imagine *that* in battle, my friends – and know hope."

The room was silent as Elohl felt a press of eyes upon him. His gaze found Dherran, and Dherran gave a reassuring smile, though something about it was sad. "That's a fuck of a lot to carry, Elohl."

"You want some?" Elohl found himself smiling in return, just a bit.

"If I could shoulder some of it for you, I would. You know I would." Dherran's gaze was intense, honest. And gazing at his friend, even though they'd been so long estranged, Elohl knew it was true. Dherran would have taken this burden from him. Olea would have also, or Suchinne.

We'll all share the burden, when the time comes. Cerulean eyes pierced Elohl's vision, a thought from Ghrenna whispering through his mind. *When your power reaches its peak and we must Consummate the Goldenmarks, I'll be there. Trust in that. Come to me when the time is right.*

"Consummate my Goldenmarks?" Elohl breathed in the silence.

"What did you say?" Fenton turned, a puzzled expression upon his face.

Elohl realized he'd spoken aloud without meaning to. But Ghrenna's silver line of thought had already slipped away, and he said nothing more.

Merkhenos, sensing the closing of their agenda, rose and stepped into the center of the collection of couches beside Fenton. "My friends. We have heard much tonight, but perhaps the news we must hear most is that Elohl is not the only one who carries these Goldenmarks. Lhaurent den'Alrahel has them also, for many more years than Elohl, and is far more practiced in using them and their dire influence in addition to his own peculiar *wyrric* talents. My spies in Lintesh confirm a public unveiling of Lhaurent's Goldenmarked powers after a series of recent riots. They cowed the populace, made the people unite behind him, though he allowed terrible destruction to raze the city. Even with Elohl's masterful use of the Marks today, I fear that Lhaurent knows better how to wield his power. My deepest fear for our upcoming engagement is that, should any army face both Lhaurent and the Kreth-Hakir in battle, that we would be struck down. Decisively."

"I hate *wyrria*." Delennia Oblitenne heaved a sigh, then drank a large gulp of her wine.

"There's still a chance we might prevail," Fenton countered quietly. "Lhaurent doesn't know yet that Elohl exists – as another Goldenmarked, at least. He hasn't known to hunt Elohl, or even me.

376

But as of now, he is likely learning much."

"It is for that reason," Merkhenos continued, "that I petition this council to allow me to ride out from Velkennish with both milord Alodwine and the Rennkavi tonight, before we can be waylaid. Get them to the Aphellian Way posthaste, where they can remain hidden in plain sight among the Valenghian army. My Vhinesse, I have no worry that you can hold this throne. But if we lose these two *wyrrics* before we can bring them to battle, we are lost. And the Tyrant of Alrou-Mendera will have his way with all of us."

The room fell silent. Dherran glanced to Elohl from his couch, and though his arm was wrapped around his woman, his visage was bleak. Something inside Elohl echoed it. His heart gripped, to have found Dherran so suddenly yet have to leave so soon. To move on yet again – just a soldier in an endless war, forever without a home or peace.

"Merkhenos speaks wisely." Delennia caught Elohl's gaze, her white-blue eyes kind but stern. "He can protect you upon the war-front. I cannot protect you here, not if I am to convince a nation of my right to rule and also aid Arlen in Vennet. Make your goodbyes and ride tonight. Ride, Rennkavi, so that we all may survive the coming storm."

The Vhinesse's speech was like a death-knell in Elohl's heart. Taking a deep breath and letting it out slowly, he allowed himself a single moment to grieve. And then his gaze connected with Fenton's, and the stalwart support he found there gave him steadiness. Slowly, Elohl rose. Downing the last of his wine, he set his goblet aside. And then set a palm to his heart, his other hand dropping to the longknife at his hip. Sinking to one knee, he bowed his head in submission to duty once more.

"As you order it, Vhinesse, so shall I do."

"For the good of us all." Delennia gave him a sad smile.

"For the good of us all." Elohl echoed, though he couldn't feel it.

CHAPTER 29 – ELYASIN

Elyasin stood in the center of a vast eternity, surrounded by stars. Translucent, the smoky quartzite stone all around her held specks of diamond scattered through the black, glittering with a haunting brilliance. From every pillar, from every vaulted arch and portico, she was surrounded by darkness, yet there was light. As she gazed up from the smooth gloss of the plaza to the cavern's lost heights glimmering far above like a midnight winter sky, Elyasin had the euphoric feeling that she walked upon the universe.

Taking a deep breath of cool air, she watched that sky. A brisk chill sighed through the cavern, but she was not cold. Far above, a million stars studded the lost heights, the underground citadel meandering through a maze of diamond-black colonnades, luminous archways, and vast rotundas. Stars swallowed the sky. The buildings and colonnades were lost to stars also, leaving the impression of being swallowed by the cosmos. It was a retreat, Elyasin thought, as she set a hand upon a shattered column of milky white quartz crystal that she stood next to, larger than her and different than the rest of the stone in this hallowed place.

Standing in the center of a gargantuan plaza, the citadel surrounded Elyasin with columns and archways. Unique in the underground city, this plaza contained a circle of pure gold laid into the diamond-stone floor, and at the very center, a raised golden dais bright as the sun. Surrounded by the remains of seven shattered milk-crystal Alranstones, the White Ring was a ruin. Enormous crystal shards had been blasted across the plaza. In every direction, the diamond-black pillars of the surrounding archways had been gouged or tumbled entirely from the force of the calamity that had happened here.

Therel had stared at it like a man transfixed when they'd first arrived five days ago. This was the place where Morvein and her Brother Kings had failed to Goldenmark the Rennkavi over eight hundred years ago – the place of Therel's seeing-dreams. And though it was in ruins, the place held power, a *wyrria* so vast that Elyasin could feel it thrumming through her bones at all hours. Calling her to become one with that vast vibration. Calling her to work miracles and horrors here. Calling her to join with the ancient *wyrria* of Hahled Ferrian that now sung through her veins.

"My Queen! Supper is nearly ready!"

Elyasin glanced over toward Thaddeus' bright call. At the edge of the decimated plaza, Thad had his nightly cook-fire going beneath one massive, intact starlight arch. Therel sat beside him on a hunk of shattered milk-crystal, perusing an ancient codex by the fire's light, something they had found wandering the citadel on their first day. Elyasin moved toward them, stepping around enormous shards of shattered quartz. Even decimated, the jagged stumps of the once-powerful Alranstones with their flowing gilded runes made her body beat with power as she moved toward the campfire and the catch of iridescent fish roasting on grill.

At the boundary of the plaza, Elyasin crossed the gold circle set into the diamond-studded stone. Gliding over its pristine surface, she felt like she walked upon dreams as it caught the light of the fire, glowing with ethereal energy. Coming to the fire in its gilded brazier, she sat at Therel's side upon the long shard of shattered crystal. Thick as a downed cendarie-tree, the shard was warm where it caught the fire's brilliance through those milk-white depths. Therel snugged Elyasin about her waist and nuzzled his nose into her hair. Thad sat near the fire, poking at their grate of cooking fish with a long golden poker found in the abandoned citadel.

With all the trappings of a working city, they'd found the buildings held kitchens and larders, sleep-rooms and bathing-pools, libraries and gardens, as if the citadel had once held a few thousand folk. Elyasin imagined their lives had been spent in contemplation, as they had found countless niches for meditation, rooms of ancient libraries, and grottoes of flowing streams where one could sit amidst the moss and become mesmerized by the translucent fishes flashing through the water.

Gazing at the cook-fire, Elyasin enjoyed its welcome brightness, burning without smoke or fuel in the shallow bowl of the golden brazier. Kindled from pale stones they'd discovered, which burst into flame when sung to, the fire provided a welcome accent to the glimmering dark. It felt primal, uncivilized, as if Elyasin were one of the first people to walk the land, discovering fire against the vast night. Their first hour here, they'd walked past a brazier, humming to brighten their singing-stones, and been surprised when the brazier burst to life with flames. Braziers dotted all the pathways of the citadel, as if the long-ago occupants had preferred fire under their starry vistas, rather than luminescence, and Elyasin quite agreed.

"Where's Luc, and Ghrenna?" Elyasin asked, seeing that they were short a few people.

"Ghrenna's in her bower, in trance again," Thad supplied helpfully as he turned the fish.

"Luc's moping over her," Therel chuckled with a wry grin, unhelpfully.

Luc had haunted Ghrenna these past days they'd wandered the citadel, as they tried to figure out how to repair the White Ring. Ghrenna had gone into deep trance for the past many days, trying to find answers in Morvein's memories as to how such a thing might be done – still to no avail.

"I suppose I should go get Luc." With a sigh, Elyasin rose, stepping from the fire. Moving beneath the arch, she took a short avenue toward a small dome set with tall colonnades. Ghrenna's chosen meditation space was a modest rotunda, with nothing inside but a low stone bier right in the center, an oculus providing a view to the vastness of the cavern above. Elyasin moved into the dome toward the luminescence of Luc's singing-stone resting in a shallow golden bowl near the bier. As she moved into the chamber, her head whirled, feeling lost among the stars. Made of darkness and flecked with light, veins of violet and red flowed through the walls and ceiling of the dome, swirling in patterns like star-dust and galaxies.

Ghrenna's low stone bier sat in the middle of all those stars, a fountain of water burbling out of the wall and running through the floor in a meandering stream. Elyasin stepped over the stream and the iridescent fish that swam its starlit depths, approaching the bier. Ghrenna lay upon the stone in her bedroll, quiet as death. Her face was flushed. Her chest rose and fell with the shallow tide of her breath, her fingers clasped over her abdomen. Luc sat at her bedside upon a gilded chair, the fingers of one hand stroking Ghrenna's cheek.

He heard Elyasin's step and turned, regarding her with distant green eyes.

"How is she?" Elyasin spoke, arriving at Ghrenna's bedside.

"The same." Luc murmured, his musical voice grating. "Out there, wherever the fuck that is. She says things now and then, but she's gone into a trance so deep I can't wake her. And now... I feel her slipping away, Elyasin."

Luc choked to silence. Elyasin reached out and clasped Ghrenna's fingers. They were warm, hale and hearty, though something about it was distant. Like her body was here, but her spirit was elsewhere, traveling far out over the world – something Elyasin understood from Hahled Ferrian's *wyrria* moving within her.

"Ghrenna can send her spirit and mind elsewhere," she murmured to Luc. "She's... *traveling* right now, Luc. She's not here. We're getting supper prepared outside. You should come eat."

"I can't leave her," Luc rasped, petting Ghrenna's white waves. "It's like she's dead."

"Come get supper. Ghrenna will be fine. Her body is hale, only her spirit is elsewhere. We need to discuss the White Ring tonight."

"You don't need me for that. Besides, we haven't made any progress."

"Yes, we do need you. You're part of this. Come on."

Clasping Luc's hand, Elyasin hauled on him until he begrudgingly stood. Tearing his gaze from Ghrenna, he looked down at Elyasin from his tall height, their hands still clasped. Something complicated moved in his eyes, dark. "Why doesn't anyone love me?"

"Ghrenna loves you," Elyasin protested, giving his fingers a reassuring squeeze.

"No. She doesn't." Luc's green eyes burned, haunted. "She's with *him*. Elohl. She keeps breathing his name, like they're... you know."

Elyasin didn't know what to say to that. Luc's bitterness rained down all around her, and it was awful. Reaching up, she set a palm to his cheek and smoothed his golden beard. "We'll get through this. And when we do, Luc, there will be a thousand women who will see you for the man you are. For the bright heart and the beautiful loyalty you have inside you. Some woman will be very lucky to love you someday."

"Lucky like you and Therel?" Luc turned his lips into her palm, kissing it.

"Luc," Elyasin protested. She tried to draw her hand away, but he lifted one hand to hers, pressing her palm to his lips.

"Don't turn me away," he kissed her inner wrist now, making Elyasin's breathing heat.

"Luc, this isn't—"

"Isn't what?" Releasing her hand and pulling her in, he wound his arms securely around her waist. Gazing down, his green eyes were obliterated by need. "Isn't what you want?"

Luc's lips descended. Elyasin breathed hard, drowning in his need. Feeling the heat of his hands smoldering through her clothes and upon her skin. Something rose in her, some passion that had wanted many lovers, long ago. That had never been satisfied with just one. That had wanted a harem of women, a palace full of them, and had only been broken of that need when he'd seen Morvein for the first time.

Elyasin snapped back, just in time to turn her face from Luc's, breathing hard. Placing a palm to his chest, she pushed him steadily away. "I can't do this."

His hands held her, something fierce lancing through his eyes. She shifted, breathing faster, pushing but not with all her strength, not yet. She didn't want to have to drop Luc to the stones or hit him with a pulse of Hahled's *wyrria*, but she would if necessary.

With a horrible smile that didn't touch his eyes, Luc's hands dropped away. Elyasin stepped back, breathing hard, knowing her cheeks flushed from the burn of *wyrria* thrumming through her. She swallowed, one hand settling to the hilt of her longknife, the feel of cool leather and steel calming. Luc's eyes dropped to it, then roved up her body before meeting her gaze again.

"You're not breathing hard from fear," he spoke softly.

"No. I'm not."

"Then why push me away?"

"Because the lust of my body has nothing to do with anything, Luc," Elyasin was blunt. "I have the *wyrria* of a thousand-year-old King flowing in me. And eight *hundred* of those years, he's been trapped inside an Aeon-damned Alranstone. Don't try to kiss me again. I will cut you, I swear it."

He stepped back, raising his hands in surrender. But there was something obliterated in his eyes. Elyasin watched him stalk gracefully out the vaulted doorway. Smoothing her hair, she let a shudder pass through her. Straightening her jerkin, Elyasin gripped the handle of her longknife, but something inside her still beat hard at Luc's need.

Elyasin glanced at Ghrenna's pale beauty upon the starlit stone. She'd not moved, rosy and beatific in her trance. Elyasin stepped out of the building and into the open, moving back toward the fire at the plaza's rim. As she arrived, her gaze connected with Luc, who sat by himself upon a hunk of crystal across from hers and Therel's. His green eyes met hers, blistering, before he knelt to help Thad turn the fish over and roast some tubers they'd found. Luc began adding spices from a stash of crystal jars, as Elyasin moved to her husband and resumed her seat.

"It's a beautiful night," Therel snugged Elyasin close. He'd shed his down jacket and furs, his black jerkin unbuttoned and shirtlaces loosened. Elyasin watched the firelight flicker over his blonde chest hairs as Therel leaned close. Heat rose in her as Therel's hand cupped her jaw while he pressed soft lips to her neck.

But Elyasin's gaze found Luc staring at them from across the fire, wrath in the strung tension of his body. Something inside Elyasin shifted. One moment, she was angry at Luc, and the next, she wanted him to hurt. Wanted to turn her chin to Therel and meet her husband's kiss. Give it to him good and show Luc exactly whom she wanted in her bed. Some part of her wanted to be mean – Hahled's energy. As she stared at Luc across the fire, Therel's kisses broke from her neck.

"Seen everything you wanted to, healer?" Therel growled.

"I've seen enough." Luc stared back with wrathful heat in his green eyes.

"Just because you're not getting any doesn't mean we can't." Therel's short statement echoed the bluntness of the Brother Kings. Thad coughed nervously nearby, but none of them turned to look. He'd started to haul the fish out of the flames and place them on a gilded platter, but glanced at Therel, then Luc, uncertain.

But Luc was in a bad mood, and rifled his golden mane with exasperation. "Everyone can hear you two fucking at all hours! It's enough to drive a man insane."

"So use your palm, healer." Therel's smooth sass held the distinctive flavor of Delman Ferrian. "Healing hands like yours could do wonders on your cock."

"Is that right?" Luc crossed his arms where he sat upon the crystal pillar, putting his fingertips dangerously near the grips of his longknives.

Therel turned Elyasin, pulled her back against his body. His hands moved up Elyasin's waist, palming her breast through her jerkin. Possessing her as Luc's eyes followed, bitter. "I see how you look at my wife, healer, when you think I'm not watching. You've had an eye for her since Highsummer when you were at her bedside, realizing she was no longer the girl you remembered. And since Ghrenna eschewed your bed, its been triply so."

"Therel—" Elyasin protested as he kissed her neck. She had wanted Luc to know who had her heart, but Therel was being cruel. Luc had gone pale, and very still. His green eyes darkened in the light of the flames.

"Care to tell me just what specifically I'm accused of, Therel?" Luc fingered the hilt of one of his longknives. "Healing your wife when you couldn't do shit to help her after she almost died?"

Therel surged forward, but Elyasin braced her body and held him back, making him keep his seat. "What has gotten into you both?!"

"Ask your husband!" Luc gestured angrily at Therel.

"I've seen you, healer, touching my wife," Therel snarled, rigid, his pale gaze ice-cold with all the fury of a meltwater flood. "I can feel you coveting her, undressing her with your eyes. I can taste the blood rushing through your veins when you have a moment alone with her, wanting to take her down to the moss and fuck her in my place. I can hear the dark thoughts that rush through your mind, how many positions you would take her in, how fast or slow, and where."

Elyasin's lips dropped open. All thoughts fled as she gaped at Therel, horrified. But Therel was full of a deep, powerful wrath – a wrath that was his own but also wasn't. As Elyasin watched, his purple and white inkings from Delman Ferrian began to light across his chest, simmering to life all down his arms and onto the backs of his hands.

"I should gut you, cur—"

"*Delman Ferrian!*" Elyasin commanded. "That is enough!"

With her command, a blaze of light went rippling through her red and white inkings like the passage of a blistering fire. A fast wave of heat rolled off her body, and Therel blinked as if he'd been slapped. Something cleared from his eyes, and he breathed hard. His gaze blinked to Elyasin's as he shook his head. "Elyasin, what—?"

"He's going batshit," Luc snarled, "from that goddamn *wyrria* eating through his veins."

"Shut up, Luc." Elyasin smoothed her husband's hair to calm him while she pinned Luc with her gaze. Luc riffled a hand through his golden mane. His eyes went from bleak to furious to bleak again. And suddenly, Elyasin realized he was to shattering. As Therel calmed from his *wyrric* rage, Elyasin rose. Stepping around the brazier, she sank to her haunches in front of Luc. He wouldn't meet her gaze, looking down and massaging his knuckles. Reaching out, Elyasin raised his face so their eyes met. A tear slipped from Luc's red-rimmed eyes, then another as he met her gaze at last. Hitching a hard breath, he opened his mouth but nothing came out.

"How many hours a day are you watching Ghrenna?" Elyasin spoke, gently.

"All of them," Luc gasped, tears leaking from his eyes now. "This trance… I'm terrified she'll die if I'm not there."

"Aeon and all the gods!" Elyasin breathed.

Therel had risen now, coming around the brazier to stand by Elyasin. And to Elyasin's vast surprise, her King put his cruelty and jealousy away. Staring down, he settled to his haunches beside Luc. Reaching out, he gripped Luc behind his neck, pressing their foreheads together, then spoke in a soft tone Elyasin rarely heard from him. "None of us are getting out of here without you, Luc. We need you to rest. When are you sleeping?"

Luc hitched a hard breath, but he let his King hold their foreheads together. "I don't know."

"We need you to rest," Therel repeated. "I'll watch Ghrenna tonight. If anything changes, I'll come find you. Can I trust you around my wife?"

Luc looked up, pulled back enough that their eyes met. "Yes, my King. I swear. I'm so sorry... please forgive me."

Therel nodded. Immense compassion was in his gaze. Elyasin had seen it before and wondered how many times he'd watched men break on the battlefield. A vision poured through her. Of Delman Ferrian, kneeling before a soldier surrounded by a pile of bodies slain by the man's own blade. The blood-shocked look in the man's eyes. The way he'd breathed too fast, unstable. Of how Delman had cradled the man's neck, just like this. Pressing their foreheads together, giving the man the steadiness of his King. Even as much as Delman had been a dark bastard sometimes, he had also been capable of immense compassion. A compassion that Elyasin could feel now, resonating out from Therel's every sinew.

Hahled Ferrian's presence burst up within Elyasin like lava breaking stone suddenly, and she gasped. One moment, Elyasin was gazing at Therel, and the next, she saw Delman. Dysphoria flooded Elyasin, seeing two men upon Therel's face. One handsome and lupine, his blue eyes bright. One pale and alluring, with strong cheeks and grey eyes, long hair white as starlight. A reeling sensation pulsed through her, seeing her brother Delman comforting his liege-man. Not her husband – her brother.

"Elyasin?" Therel reached out, confusion in his gaze. "Are you all right?"

Elyasin flinched from Therel's touch and stumbled backwards, nearly tripping over the brazier. One hand out, she fell against the shard of milk-crystal on the other side of the fire. And suddenly, all that roaring energy within her needed to go somewhere. Without thought, only the feel of burning devouring her, Elyasin took all her surprise, her presence of Hahled Ferrian, and poured it into the Alranstone shard. Beneath her hand, the enormous spar of crystal groaned. All along its vast length, sigils of gold surged to life, sinuous like the blue-white of Elohl's *wyrric* marks. And before she could remove her hand, the entire spar of crystal shuddered, groaned, and lifted from the diamond-flecked plaza, hovering a foot in the air and making the gilded ring ripple with light where it crossed that hallowed perimeter.

Elyasin gaped at what she had just done. Everyone gaped. A

resonant vibration from the crystal roared through her upon the power of Hahled's screaming crimson *wyrria*. The fingers of her free hand clasped the gilded keshar-claw upon her breastbone, and it was scalding to her touch. Heat poured from her like a forge-fire and Elyasin growled, a sound she didn't associate with herself at all. She panted, trying to breathe off that simmering heat but the more she did, the hotter it raged, until sweat poured down her back as she shuddered from holding the immense weight of the crystal bound to her hand.

As if summoned from the grave, Ghrenna emerged from the dome nearby, stepping out into the plaza like a rare bloom swaying through a midwinter night. Luc stood quickly from his seat as she arrived, but Ghrenna stepped to Elyasin. Taking up Elyasin's free hand from her keshar-pendant, she held it, and those drowning cerulean eyes swallowed Elyasin's world. Elyasin stood there, riveted, shivering like a blown horse as she gazed into those infinite eyes. Ghrenna exhaled, and that breath eased into Elyasin's body like a cooling wind off tundra ice. One moment, she was raging with Hahled's *wyrric* fire, and the next, her heat sighed up on that vast wind, melding into it – strong.

"Move the stone into the ring," Ghrenna breathed, her voice like a nightwind curling through the etheric darkness. Elyasin felt that command sigh through every part of her. One moment she was trembling from strain, and the next, she was steady, moving her palm in a graceful dance and pouring Hahled's fire out through it – guiding the elevated shard of crystal fully inside the boundary of the golden ring. At the sweetest breeze from Ghrenna, urging her to let go – *gently* – Elyasin smoothed her palm toward the ground, settling the massive hunk of milk-quartz back to the plaza's surface.

The energy released her in a rolling wave. Elyasin rocked, ecstasy filling her, and a song like the bowels of the earth itself. And as she stood there, flooded with life and *wyrric* power, Ghrenna's wind swept through her again, calming that fire. Storing it back inside Elyasin's essence, saved for another time.

"What did you just do?" Elyasin breathed, astounded.

Ghrenna's lips quirked with a sad smile. "So it was for my lover Hahled, that it now is for you. Long ago, Hahled's ire and heat would rise in a flush of fury. And I—" Ghrenna twisted her neck.

"*Morvein* could direct that heat. Move it, wield it. Or smooth it out with a touch. Just as she could soothe Delman's cold wrath, also."

"You directed me to move that stone." Elyasin pressed Ghrenna's hand between hers. "I felt you inside my mind."

"Yes." Ghrenna's smile was complex. "I'm becoming more like Morvein everyday. Just like you and Therel are becoming more like the Brother Kings." Ghrenna reached out, brushing a lock of sweaty hair back from Elyasin's face. Ghrenna looked unreal, crystalline like a blossom in the snow. Her cerulean eyes were fever-bright. Her cheeks burned with a flush, her skin so luminous it seemed like snow upon shrouds. Her beauty was too fierce, those burning blue eyes staring out from dark sockets like a tundra-wight. She was beautiful, but it was a belladonna beauty – as if the *wyrria* surfacing within her devoured her from the inside.

As if Morvein devoured everything that was Ghrenna.

Ghrenna's eyes broke from Elyasin's, and she stepped back. With a deep breath, she turned to face them all, her gaze pinning Luc. "Though Morvein planned much, she did not plan for all occurrences. Her presence, her memories – they fill me now. And where once they tore my body apart, we have now come to accord. I know my true purpose – to bring the Rennkavi in our time and to wield the power of the Brother Kings to make that happen. But many things are unknown. Most of all, if I will survive this ritual we shall create, and the power I must hold to bring it to fruition."

"Ghrenna..." Luc reached out, woe in his eyes.

Ghrenna held up a palm, and Elyasin's heart broke to see the fierce love in her blue eyes. "You have always been in my heart, Luc. Though Elohl and I are mystically bound, I *chose* you, for years. And I will do my best for you – all of you – while I can."

"Don't talk like that." Moving forward, Luc gathered Ghrenna into his arms.

"I have to," Ghrenna breathed as she gazed up at him. Whatever Luc saw in her gaze, he didn't protest again. With a wretched sigh, he set his hand to her neck and drew her in for a long, slow kiss. Elyasin's heart broke to see it, and she turned away.

To see Therel, a deep worry in his eyes. A worry that Elyasin knew was echoed in her own. A worry that they would all go mad down here, living in the darkness like rats. But worst of all, she worried what would happen if she and Therel continued to channel the Brother Kings.

And if they channeled *wyrria* for the Rennkavi's Ritual, would they ever be the same.

CHAPTER 30 – THEROUN

Elsthemen had been left behind, and the last vestiges of Theroun's military career with it.

Salt spray was in the air this evening, though the weather was cool and fine. Seagulls wheeled over the cliff-camp above the bluffs of Ligenia Bay with its scrub grasses and coastal dwarf pine. Salal thickets divided the camp between the pines, but provided extra autumn rations with their furry blue berries. Theroun marched the cliff-height, watching soldiers haul crab-pots up a hundred feet from the surge. Supper on the Ligenian coast was fresh swordfish and crustacean, mussel and tiger-shell, with seaweed of twenty varieties and seagull eggs from the cliffs.

The Port of Ligenia marked the start of the arid lowland plains that stretched to the famed Aphellian Way – a region Theroun knew all too well. Only a league outside the city, the Menderian auxiliary camp was organized upon Ligenia's eastern bluffs. Their first days after traveling through Fhekran Palace's Alranstone had been spent organizing supplies and getting men re-formed into mixed regiments of Menderian, Elsthemi, and even more conscripted foreigners than before. The rebels that had survived, including Vitreal den'Bhorus, Jhonen Rebaldi, Lhesher Khoum, and the tall Jadounian warrior Duthukan, had been mixed back into the lowest ranks of foot soldiers.

There was nothing Theroun could do about that. He'd ensured those particular four had been placed in a company together, but with his low position among the Kreth-Hakir, there was little more action Theroun could take toward their survival. Marching through the camp now clad as one of the Hakir and finished supervising the camp's organization for the day, Theroun found himself grateful that his tall boots were soft as doeskin. Kreth-Hakir garb was lightweight but strangely resilient, and as Theroun strode past a cadre of soldiers emptying and sorting the evening catch, he ignored the scowls that tracked his herringbone-woven leather jerkin and silver-studded breeches. Red braids hauled back from her face and silt smirching her face, the tall Jhonen Rebaldi gave Theroun a dark look as he passed. Reaching out, she slapped the burly Lhesher Khoum on his filthy jerkin, and Lhesher gave Theroun a steady, chill gaze also.

Only Vitreal den'Bhorus watched with curiosity in his sharp green eyes as Theroun passed, his foxlike face absent of sneer where he stood next to the tall Jadounian Duthukan and his brothers. They'd not spoken these past days, but the Fleetrunner Captain and Duthukan were the only men who watched Theroun with interest, wondering what he was up to. No one else gave Theroun anything less than hostile glares. If these soldiers thought Theroun was a traitor before, they were convinced of it now. There was no more leadership from any council, no more puppet Generals on this campaign. Lhaurent gave orders directly to his most trusted, and those men wore the herringbone black.

And Theroun was now one of them.

Taking ancient steps cut into the rock and giving a nod to Vitreal before they broke eye contact, Theroun continued up the high bluff toward a pavilion of red and silver silk. The pennant of the Kreth-Hakir Brethren, a silver scorpion on a red field, snapped in the high ocean breeze. Above it upon the pole was another pennant, a white field with a golden starburst and curls of white-gold flame. Theroun scowled at that showy banner. The bastard Lhaurent wanted all to know he was god-touched – ordained to lead by some fucking arcane tattooing and a questionable ancient birthright.

Patience, Scion. Khorel Jornath's mind eased into Theroun's upon a silver thread, with a small smile of humor. *The Rennkavi will have his day. And we will have ours. Hasten. Our command meeting awaits.*

Theroun knew he was late for the evening Kreth-Hakir command meeting – he didn't need to be reminded. Jogging up and down the cliffs all day supervising various aspects of camp was exhausting. But Theroun found his body felt more hale each day since Khorel Jornath's blood-oath. Mounting the last stairs, he gained the promontory's rocky overlook. With a nod to four Menderian soldiers that flanked the entrance of the pavilion – so woven through with quicksilver that Theroun wasn't even certain they had their own thoughts anymore – he entered the tent.

Theroun allowed his eyes a moment to adjust to the dim light, his gaze flicking to every corner of the wide rectangle before marching forward. It was habit, searching a room for assassins. Amused faces showed on the twelve Brethren around the stout madrona map table as he joined them, a breeze wafting in from two panels open to the coastal view in the rear of the pavilion. Setting his fists to the red wood, Theroun looked around. The Kreth-Hakir watched him, a few of the younger ones like Brother Antonius with twisted smiles, as if trying to hide amusement.

"What?!" Theroun snapped.

"Do not mind the teasing of your Brethren," Khorel Jornath's voice came from a shadowed alcove, where he splashed water over his face from a silver basin and wiped it with a length of red silk. Moving forward from the shadows, his own amusement lit his dark-opal eyes. "They're not used to one of such power having so little idea of what to do with it."

"What do you mean?" Theroun snapped, irate. He crossed his arms over his chest with his usual scowl.

"Searching the corners of the room with your eyes," Jornath chuckled. "Expanding our minds to sense our surroundings is training every Kreth-Hakir receives within our first year as Acolyte."

Jornath stepped to the table next to Theroun. The man regularly stood next to Theroun in public, as if marking his territory. Theroun set his jaw. He belonged to no one, no matter some dire blood-oath, and eventually Jornath would learn that. A subtle smirk lifted Khorel's lips, sensing Theroun's thoughts, before the man spread his hands for the meeting to commence.

"My Brethren, let us begin. We have news this evening. Lhaurent den'Alrahel has informed me that the status of Valenghia has changed recently. The old Vhinesse has fallen in an unexpected coup, and her sister has risen to her place. Lhaurent wishes us to take advantage of this instability and march out posthaste, to join the main army upon the Aphellian Way. We will maintain a garrison here to provide support and monitor the coastline for naval interference. Two shipments of recruits are scheduled to arrive from Jadoun in the next week. I would like three volunteers to remain and master them, then follow the main host in a week's time. Who would enjoy this duty?"

Hands went up around the table. Theroun knew the Brethren only raised hands or spoke out loud for his sake. Normally, these proceedings would happen mentally, unless there was a very untrained Acolyte in attendance, like Theroun.

But he found himself impressed with the inner workings of the Kreth-Hakir. They were organized, prompt, educated and articulate, even those who had originally come from a marauder culture. They had systems for any occurrence, and functioned more like a council of peers than what he had previously thought was a pack-like hierarchy. It was true, they had ranks, and one had to mind-best a Brother of an upper rank to advance. And the most senior Brother on any campaign was allowed to seize control of everyone's minds, as Jornath did for coordinated attacks in battle.

But otherwise, it seemed damned egalitarian.

Jornath nodded to three less accomplished Brethren with upraised hands, including the young silver-haired Valenghian lad, Brother Antonius Ossenheim. "Thank you for your service. I will give you an especial briefing at dawn before the main host departs. Please remove yourselves to meditation, and prepare to bend highly defiant minds in the next few days."

The three Brothers nodded and turned from the table, departing through the tent flaps. Theroun now knew the Kreth-Hakir spent hours in trance daily, honing their focus. Khorel Jornath eyed the remaining Brethren, mostly comprised of senior Order members.

Calm and highly-educated, Brother Arlo del'Vonio had grey streaks in his military-short Cennetian-copper beard and hair. He made eye contact with Theroun, exuding a brusque but pleasant nature and smiled, his eyes green as the sea and tattooing of Cennetian alchemical sigildry rising up both sides of his neck. Arlo supported Theroun's position as Scion, Jornath's chosen replacement, and was Jornath's top commander on this campaign. His position was Priest of Letters, which meant that Arlo was both historian and historical tactician for the group, as well as their resident authority on the arcane.

Brother Kiiar dhim'Erle stood at the end of the map-table, given a slight space of honor around his person by the Brethren.

Small, with a frizz of white hair haloing his head, his birdlike face was pensive as he regarded the map of the Aphellian Way spread up the table and weighted down with longknives. He glanced over as if feeling Theroun's regard and gave a comforting smile with his bushy white brows and sparkling black eyes in his half-burned visage.

Brother Kiiar came from an ancient race of desert people upon the far southeastern peninsula, beyond Ghrec and the Twelve Tribes. It was a lawless place, known as the Wasteland, though its proper name was Aj Naab. Brother Kiiar had told Theroun briefly of his home, a place where all were warriors or mystics out in the unforgiving sands and obliviate crevasses, no oases to save them like the Twelve Tribes. A place where men battled upon massive lizard-like mounts called kuori for the scant remains of an ancient technological civilization that had once dominated the southern peninsula.

Brother Kiiar's position among the Brethren was High Priest of the Watch. Technically, he was Khorel Jornath's superior, though his position here was more as mystic guidance for the campaign rather than as a tactical strategist, and he spent four-fifths of each day and night in deep meditation inside his tent.

Then there was the surly Lefkani pirate, swarthy Brother Caldrian hek'Khim, Jornath's third-in-command. Gazing at the map upon the table, Caldrian scowled, his long black mohawk braided back from his crown and cascading down his spine full of feather fetishes, gold trinkets, and bone beads. He reached up, scratching at the hole where his right ear had been next to his scarred temple. His left ear was full of pierced gold hoops in the Thurumani privateer way, in addition to his left eyebrow.

Caldrian's position was Priest of Wrath. Theroun had seen enough of the man's temper to know Caldrian could spread his rage through an entire battalion and make men fight past death and out the other side. But in meetings he was civil, his rage well-controlled for the most part. Glancing up at Khorel, Caldrian's near-black eyes flashed as he spoke in his burly baritone. "I don't like leaving such a paltry force to guard the coastline, Brother Khorel." He gestured at Theroun. "Even your Scion would agree, I'm sure."

Theroun was allowed to speak at these meetings, and he did so now. "I do agree with Brother Caldrian. Menderian ships are currently being blasted by the cannons of the Tourmaline fleet, on as many shales as King Arthe den'Tourmalin can hound them. We're only a Tourmaline spy-vessel away from word reaching Arthe that Lhaurent masses a force here intended to drive into Valenghia. Arthe is no friend to Valenghia, but he is even less of a friend to Lhaurent. He would seize the opportunity to attack Ligenia Bay and cut off our provisions from the sea."

Jornath regarded Theroun, then Caldrian. "Lhaurent assures me a Menderian fleet will maintain position in Ligenia's harbor to guard our rear for the duration of the campaign."

"How many ships?" Brother Caldrian crossed his arms, scowling in a very Theroun-esque manner. Theroun found himself smiling internally. This man, he understood.

"Some twenty strong." Jornath's eyes narrowed on Brother Caldrian. "Don't veil your thoughts, Calo. You know I can punch through them if I have to. Tell me plainly what you suppose."

Interesting, Theroun thought. He filed that information away for later, that Brother Caldrian was defiant and willfully secretive.

The Lefkani pirate's pierced nostrils flared, but he made a gesture of respect to Jornath with two fingers to the center of his brow. "Forgive me, High Priest. In my old life sailing with my people, I had the opportunity to fight Tourmaline fleets regularly. They are vicious, and their ships slice the water faster than hawks fly. A fleet of twenty is not enough to keep Ligenia Bay secure, should they put their minds to interfering. Not to mention that there are no fewer than fifteen other accessible inlets along this strip of coast."

Brother Jornath's gaze flicked to Theroun. "I respect the opinion of my Priest of Wrath, and his significant naval history. Brother Theroun, do you have an opinion on this matter?"

"I do." Theroun was blunt. "This section of coast has many access-points, as Brother Caldrian has noted." He nodded at the former pirate; the man nodded back with a pleased glint to his black eyes. "And King Arthe den'Tourmalin has detested Lhaurent and the Khehemni Lothren for many a year. The Lothren are destroyed in Alrou-Mendera due to Lhaurent, but they still exist elsewhere, and Arthe remains a vigilant man. His spy-ships run the oceans. He will come for our tail. And since he has declared a cessation of his treaty with Alrou-Mendera, it is only a matter of time before he decides Lhaurent's dealings upon every coast are to be utterly halted."

"Is King Arthe's fleet strong enough to stop all the Rennkavi's coastal activities?" Khorel Jornath crossed his arms, a position Theroun now knew meant the man was thinking deeply.

"His isn't," Theroun growled. "But it's a hop, skip, and a jump for him to notify Valenghia. They control the fleets of Cennetia, Praough, and have a historical alignment with the Independent Island of Crasos and the Lhemvian Isles. Five fleets against Lhaurent's one. I enjoy bad fucking odds, gentlemen, but not that bad. Lhaurent plays a game he is a novice at, and it shows. He should have stayed with primping, perfuming, and back-stabbing in the shadows."

Brother Kiiar gave a snort. All eyes instantly looked to him as he chuckled, waving one gnarled old hand. "I appreciate your candidness, Brother Theroun. It's been a long while since we've had a new member with such fire and blatancy."

"The Scion doesn't mince words, that's for certain," Brother Arlo spoke with a laughing smile. "Piss and vinegar and little else."

Theroun despised being treated like a new recruit, and was about to open his mouth when Jornath scowled, tapping one finger against his leather-clad arm. "Focus please, gentlemen. Lhaurent knows his game of spies, but this game of nations is foreign to him. Brother Theroun's insights are valuable, as close as he has been to Lhaurent's person these past many years at Roushenn. As such, even if Lhaurent sends more ships, he risks a sea-battle in Ligenia, corrupting our supply-lines to the Aphellian Way." Jornath gave a measured out-breath. Not a sigh, but not far from it. He scowled deeper, reaching up to rub his smooth lips.

Brother Kiiar perked, his sharp black-on-black eyes piercing Jornath. "Our Kreth-Hakir fleet is tied up in Ghrec and the Twelve Tribes, Brother Jornath. It will be weeks before they can aid us, even if you do have me send word."

"You have a fleet?" Theroun raised an eyebrow at the news, as he filed the information away that Brother Kiiar could read Khorel's mind fairly easily. "What is it doing at the southeastern peninsula rather than running support for this campaign?"

"*We* have a fleet, Scion," Jornath corrected, his gaze pinning

Theroun. "And it runs the coast of the peninsula because our Order have business in the Twelve Tribes. Part of our arrangement with Lhaurent was his assistance in an Order-arranged takeover there, which is in progress. The ancient Oasis of Ghellen has fallen and so have the coastal Oases. But the *berounhim* rangers of the desert have waged a war of unprecedented skill against us. And so our Order is split right now, our fleet and many of our Order members occupied."

Theroun blinked. That was insanity. Why split the ranks of the Order and of Lhaurent's armies at such a critical juncture? What could it possibly gain them, battling in the desert of that obscure and mostly wild land?

"The Order has many interests, Scion," Jornath's eyes turned steely, reading Theroun's thoughts. "Not all of them are your burden to understand. Focus on our situation here."

Theroun bristled. Crossing his arms, he adopted his best glower.

"I was once like you, Brother Theroun," Brother Arlo spoke up with a smile. "Full of piss and hot water. A martial commander with decades of accolades dripping from my belt, not to mention excellent alchemical training. I served under King Iccio del'Carrini of Legate, and I lived to unify the Cennetian city-states under his banner. Being green as the lowest footsoldier chafes for men such as us. Use that to propel you upward in our Order, Theroun. Let it fire you on the inside, while you give respect to your superiors on the outside. Your energy is wasted in direct defiance of your Master."

Theroun was irked at the speech, but something about Arlo's words tripped his mind. Theroun shuffled back through his history lessons. "King Iccio del'Carrini united the city-states of Cennetia over four hundred years ago. How——?"

Arlo smiled, patience resting in his sea-green eyes though they were also stern. "I am four hundred and seventy-six, Theroun. You stand in a room of men who are all no less than three hundred years aged. Every man here has spent the entirety of their lives commanding armies. Brother Jornath is our superior for this campaign, but even with his ten centuries of life, he is but a junior to some of the men and women in our Order. Think about the vast honor you have been given to stand at this table. Particularly, at

Brother Jornath's side."

Theroun had no words. His lips had fallen open and he shut them, but he still found he could not scowl. His gaze tracked around the command tent, noting each face. They all stared back at him frankly, no lie in their eyes.

Theroun stood in a room of ancients. He *was* the greenhorn. Theroun swallowed, and he knew it looked weak, but the film in his mouth had to go somewhere. His mind reeled, trying to take it in, when Jornath's hand settled to his shoulder. A comforting energy flowed into Theroun and he took a breath, steadying himself.

"We will risk Lhaurent's gambit." Jornath did not address him, but spoke to the group. "I see no other options. Brother Kiiar, please find a meditative seat tonight and send word to High Master Yesh that we require the fleet's support, and a full battle-cadre for this operation, as many as can be spared, as I am loathe to risk so many of our Brethren on ill-devised plans. Lhaurent may be a weak tactician on the field, but I will not underestimate him. He wears the Goldenmarks, and all of us here know the harbinger of that anointment."

Heads nodded around the table. Sober scowls filled the room. "The Age of Chaos comes," Brother Kiiar spoke softly. "The Demon's Rise is upon us."

"*Agate brithii discenzio.*" Brother Caldrian growled. Screwing up his face, he spit upon the rug. "I don't believe Lhaurent is the Uniter of the Tribes. He is a fool."

"You felt his power, the same as I." Jornath's eyes were icy. "And though we have received word from Lintesh, before we felt our Brethren perish there, that Lhaurent's birth line was possibly not Khehemni as we supposed, he still wears Leith's ruby ring and is able to wield it. You will serve our Order in supporting him, Brother Caldrian. So did Leith order us, to watch closely anyone who demonstrates astounding *wyrric* ability, and to serve the Rennkavi. If you have dispute with that, I invite you to take it up with High Master Yesh personally."

Theroun watched the pirate blanch. His black eyes flickered down and stayed down. Whoever this High Master Yesh was, he was enough to intimidate even the most violent mercenaries.

"I like Lhaurent no better than you do, Calo," Jornath's words were soft. "Do not make me remind you what it means to serve our Order. Especially not with the Rise of the Demon at stake. You are a formidable warrior and we would have you among us. We need every possible man, when that time comes."

Jornath's eyes flicked to Theroun. All eyes flicked to Theroun. Theroun could feel slips of silver wafting between them as the Kreth-Hakir shared thoughts – thoughts he wasn't party to because of the ferociousness of his inner *wyrria*.

"The rest of you," Jornath's gaze traversed the tent, interrupting the silvered conversation to conclude the meeting, "please engage yourselves making the camp ready to march to the Aphellian Way in three days' time. Dismissed."

* * *

The meeting adjourned, leaving Theroun alone with Khorel Jornath in the command tent. It was where they both slept and took meals, as Theroun was expected to remain close to his Master during his early training. Drinking deep from a chalice of wine, Theroun refilled it and sipped. His mind spun through all the snippets of information that had been so casually dropped at the meeting. It was plain that the Kreth-Hakir were far more powerful than he knew, though their reasons for tethering their formidable power to other men baffled him.

After kindling some oil in a bronze brazier against the night, Jornath sank into a stretched-hide chair. Leaning back with his boots up on a footstool, he sipped a wine also. His searching gaze fixed upon Theroun before he spoke. "You are wondering why we don't just crush tyrants like Lhaurent."

"Among any number of things I've been wondering, that does top the list." Theroun had grown used to this kind of interaction with Khorel – him not speaking but Khorel reading his thoughts anyway. It was irksome, but there was little Theroun could do about it. Claiming a plate of cherries from the table, Theroun sat in the chair next to Jornath's. Picking through the plate, he found the cherries tangy and refreshing after a long day in the hot Ligenian sun.

"Could you break Lhaurent's hold over Alrou-Mendera, do

you think? With the full power of your order?" Theroun wondered aloud, sipping his wine.

Khorel Jornath swirled his goblet, his grey eyes faraway. At last, they focused upon Theroun. "We could. Though I cannot best Lhaurent personally, I believe under High Master Yesh's coordination, we could flay Lhaurent's mind and be done with his idiocy."

"I think you and I share some things in common, Khorel," Theroun chuckled.

"Far more than you know." Jornath regarded Theroun with a candid gaze. "I have judged Lhaurent to be a petty tyrant. So have you. But he has something that turns petty tyrants into dominators of their time."

"*Wyrria?*" Theroun sipped his wine.

"Belief." Jornath heaved a sigh. "He *believes* in what he is, Theroun. He believes he is the Uniter of the Tribes. And he will do it in the only way that makes sense to him, with domination and cruelty. I have seen deeply into his mind. It is a thing of oily depths and slipping shadows. Your nickname for him, *eel*, is far more appropriate than you know."

Jornath lifted his goblet with a nod. Theroun raised his goblet in response, but another question needed answers. "If you don't trust him, why serve him so blindly?"

"Kreth-Hakir never serve blindly." Jornath leaned forward, cradling his goblet. "We serve tyrants because we must make them trust us. So they will let us in, let us see if the Demon has turned their eyes and mind red. Before this strange accident I felt in Lintesh recently, I had men close to Lhaurent in Lintesh. Watching him, feeling his mind, even as they did his bidding. It is a dire loss that we no longer have anyone in the capitol monitoring him, but I can still feel Lhaurent from afar, and I meet with him almost daily through the Alranstones. Lhaurent has to trust *us*, Theroun. We don't have to trust him."

"Would you ever leave his service?"

"If he dies," Jornath nodded. "Many a nation has lost our support because their heir was not worthy of our watching. Empires fall fast without us."

"I can imagine. Have you ever taught anyone the secrets to

your longevity? So that they could rule longer than their normal span?"

"We do not share our Order's secrets," Khorel continued. "Such mysteries are too powerful in the wrong hands, without the Mind of the Brethren to moderate for the Demon's Rise."

"Moderate," Theroun cocked his head. "The mind-connections of the Brethren provide security against any of you becoming possessed by this Red-Eyed Demon creature."

"Indeed." Khorel nodded with a slight smile. "As a hive, like the shared minds of the diamanne scorpions of the southern deserts, we are able to force out any mind that might possess any one of us. Even if the Demon were to enter our pinnacle member, High Master Yesh, the rest of us have a ritual where we could join as one to cast the Demon out. It is a thing of dire magic, passed down from ancient times, but recorded as effective."

"Dire magic? What does that mean?"

"It means that none of us would survive the ritual," Jornath gave a bitter smile, "but neither would the one possessed. A win, but at great cost."

Theroun rubbed the old wound in his side, though it was only a slight annoyance tonight. "All of you are committed to going down with the ship if this Demon rises. Using your lives to drive the Demon out of anyone powerful enough to garner its attention."

"We would use far more than our lives to cast out the Demon, Theroun. We'd use our *will*." Jornath leaned forward, setting his wine goblet aside. "For as you are learning, bending minds has everything to do with willpower. The man with the strongest will shall prevail even when his mind has fled. Hone that, and one can control madness even as it rages."

"Like a warrior in the grips of the red rage upon the battlefield," Theroun mused, "who practices fighting so that when battle sweeps him, his movements will be innate."

"Indeed. At its foundation, Scorpion-*wyrria* is will-*wyrria*." Jornath nodded. "How do you live in the world? How strong is your force of person?"

"What do you mean? How strong is my will in battle?"

"Perhaps. Or consider this." Jornath countered with a knowing glance. "Is the force of your will the means by which you understand your world? There are seven major types of *wyrria*, Theroun. People who show aptitude for *wyrria* are not limited to the type in their bloodline, not in as specific a way as most men think. It's your way of *understanding the world* that determines which type of *wyrria* you favor. Most children acquire the same aptitude for the *wyrria* of their ancestors's bloodline because they have a shared milieu – an enculturated way of understanding the world from their people, which begins even as the baby listens to life through their mother's womb before birth."

"And my way of understanding my world is via my force of will." Theroun mulled that over, feeling how it made sense.

"Indeed. Many commanders of battle who show *wyrria* have will-aptitude. You have accepted your *wyrria*, Theroun. But now you have to understand how to wield that power. So that when your time comes, you have the full strike of the *suna hebi* behind the lance of your will. Tell me. What does your inner Black Viper long to do? What does it lust for? What is the thing for which you would seek Queen Elyasin's absolution?"

Theroun took a deep breath. The tone of the conversation had changed, and they'd entered his training now, just as they'd done each evening. "My *wyrria* longs to desecrate. To kill for sheer pleasure, without restriction."

"And how is your viper's killing restricted?" Jornath's eyes were knowing, dark.

"I am limited to killing only adversaries," Theroun responded promptly. "And only upon the battlefield where such things are normal."

"What did you experience when you drank my blood, Theroun?"

Theroun shivered as his *wyrria* stirred, eager. "Pleasure. The satisfaction of feeling your lifeblood slip away. I wanted to see the light leave your eyes, to know that I had conquered you. To experience the sheer pleasure of dealing your death."

"If we were not adversaries, what you lust for would be called murder." Khorel's eyes bored into Theroun. "Tell me. Would you kill someone in the height of passion, would you murder someone – if it were allowed?"

"No." Theroun's answer was prompt.

"Would your viper?" Jornath's smile was knowing.

Theroun hesitated. He could feel his *wyrria* rise with a spread of unfathomable blackness as he pictured a scene he'd so often tried not to – a dark fantasy. Something forbidden, something he never let himself imagine, though he'd hedged upon it many times. What came to him was terrible, but it fed the vile power within.

"Yes," he rasped.

Jornath slid to the edge of his chair, his gaze penetrating. "Stay with that scene you are thinking of, Theroun. Picture it. I want you to *feel* it. Feel what happens. Place yourself in that passion and that desire for death. Let the fantasy run riot and see where it goes…"

The scene rose, fast as a viper's strike in Theroun's mind, and he could not deny it now. It was his dead wife he saw in his fantasy, so beautiful in her heyday. Lissendra del'Mira had been a Cennetian goddess, and had let Theroun fuck her as hard as he wanted. In his fantasy, her copper-gold locks were fanned out upon the pillows in his command-tent upon the Aphellian Way. Theroun gazed down into her jade eyes, screwed up in aching pleasure. He kissed her full, red mouth in the dusty heat, sweat slicking them both. In their passion and the stifling afternoon heat, he turned her over, gripping her by all that hair, forcing her up on all fours in a tight arch.

"Take her, Theroun." Jornath's command roiled through Theroun, as he watched the scene like a silver nimbus within Theroun's mind. Theroun's *wyrria* rose, feeling the scene, living it. He felt oilslick-dark coils unwind, surging through him with a heat more vicious than the pounding of his blood. Theroun took his wife harder in his fantasy, pushed them both to terrible limits. Lissendra cried out for him, blissful as he rammed into her, over and over. And Theroun knew what he wanted, what his *wyrria* wanted. A searing sensation surged through Theroun's body, washing through him with shivers of hot and cold poison.

A painful sensation, but pleasant. So fucking, terribly good.

Do it! Jornath's silver command slammed Theroun, breaking his last restraint. Theroun's *wyrria* flashed in a venomous strike as he slashed his wife's throat in his fantasy with a black knife, just as she came screaming his name. Shuddering with orgasm, pumping blood out upon the bed, she gave Theroun her everything. And he came for her hard, giving her his all – claiming her sex, her blood, and her beautiful death.

Something tremendous exploded from Theroun and he screamed as his viperous *wyrria* roared out. He felt that oilslick-black energy hammer Kreth-Hakir to their knees all around the camp, as cries of pain echoed in Theroun's mind. When he opened his eyes, Khorel Jornath was on the rug, knocked out of his chair to his knees. One fist upon the carpet, he breathed hard, his gaze still locked to Theroun.

"*That* is the power of your darkness," Jornath grated softly.

Theroun's throat closed. His mind rang like a war-gong. Even as his *wyrria* surged with glory, Theroun's humanity wailed. How could he fantasize about his wife's death? How could that be what his *wyrria* craved? Theroun collapsed to the floor, gasping. Eyes tight, he could not stop the horror. The scene replayed, over and over. Her corpse upon the bed. Her corpse in his command-tent upon the Aphellian Way in the sweltering afternoon. Her throat slit by his hand, and by another hand, but her beloved eyes dead all the same.

"I killed her!" Theroun gasped. "I brought her to camp… it was my fault she died! Aeon forgive me—!"

Theroun broke, roaring upon his elbows and knees. Mind-blind, wild, a black vastness roared through him and all around. He felt the power of that scream lance out in a second strike, piercing the ears of every Hakir within a five-league radius, making them shudder. A heavy hand settled to Theroun's shoulder and quicksilver serenity poured through him, Theroun drinking it as gratefully as he'd devoured Khorel's blood the night of his binding. Gradually, the scene faded. Theroun's *wyrria* slipped back into a quiescent state, the immensity of the blackness at the edges of his thoughts coiling away for another time.

"How can *this* be a part of me?" Theroun rasped as he clutched his chest.

"*Keep your friends close, and your enemies closer,*" Jornath spoke softly. "There is only one thing that is a man's natural enemy, Theroun. The shadow-side of his own true *wyrria*. But knowing your enemy is power. And knowing what gives your enemy power is even moreso."

"I have to become this thing inside me?"

"You have to not be *afraid* of it." Khorel gave his shoulder a small squeeze. "Having dark desires and acting them out are two separate things. But if you face your desires, your Beast will become your friend. More than that, it will allow you to harness its power, and fight *for* you rather than against you. Do you understand?"

With his forehead pressed to the carpet, Theroun nodded. Swallowing back bile, he was at last able to sit up. "I begin to."

"Good." Jornath's smile was pleased. "Your training will now include far more than the calming meditations I have shown you. Now that you know how to raise your *wyrria*, we begin the Harnessing Sigils. I will show you how to bend your *wyrria* to your will. We can't have you blasting every Brother in a five-league radius with your inner torment, now can we?"

Jornath laughed, amused but with pride ringing through his deep voice. Seizing Theroun's shoulders, he helped Theroun to his feet. He stared Theroun down, but not without compassion. "The road you shall walk is long and difficult, Scion. But I promise you, it will not be without assistance, nor without rewards. Mastering your shadow-will is the greatest pleasure a man can know."

"And why is that?"

"Because nothing is forbidden." Jornath's mouth quirked. He opened his lips as if to say more, then shut them again with a rueful smile. "Take some time. Walk along the bluff or down the cliffs. Clear your mind. A man's first time opening to his shadow-will is not an easy thing. Ask forgiveness of your dead wife, for the things you desire."

"You saw all of that, just now?"

"We are linked, Scion." Jornath's face was impassive. "Learn to use your power to shield your mind from mine, and I will see no more. Every man here has personal things he keeps to himself. The nature of one's shadow-will is the most personal of all. Go. Take a walk. A meal and a hot bath will be prepared for you to enjoy later. At midnight tonight, you and I have a personal mission to attend, but you may rest until then."

"And this mission is?"

Jornath's eyes darkened and Theroun could read distaste in them. "I'm going to send to Lhaurent in meditation tonight and ask for more ships. As my Scion, it is your rightful place now to attend all my meetings, so you will attend tonight, and try to penetrate my mind as I converse."

"Lhaurent won't enjoy that, being gainsaid. Or feeling me with you, given any sort of position in this army other than shit-keeper."

"No." Jornath's hands slipped from Theroun's shoulders. "And it will make him suspicious, but he depends on my Brethren and will not cut us loose."

Theroun cocked his head. "Do you fear Lhaurent? His retaliation upon you if he's displeased?"

Khorel Jornath gave Theroun cold eyes. "Yes. I am not a fool. But learn one thing, and one thing well, Scion of my Blood. I did not last a thousand years in the Kreth-Hakir Brethren, breaking my challengers and those I challenged as I ascended the ranks, for being an idiot. I will not risk my Brethren on an ill-conceived battle, not for any king or tyrant. Like your wife was to you, they are family to me, though of a different sort, and I will protect them from those who threaten them, even if it means breaking a few to save the many. You are now family to me. And Lhaurent, though he carries Kreth-Hakir blood in his vicious veins, is no family of mine."

With those fierce yet strange words, Jornath turned, striding out into the settling evening. Leaving Theroun alone with the last remnants of his *wyrric* power and the dark shadow within him.

CHAPTER 31 – ELESHEN

The ride south out of the mountains and into the deep forests of central Alrou-Mendera had taken less time than Eleshen anticipated. Keshar-cats moved fast through the lowland pines and alder, and they'd traveled hundreds of leagues in only four days of hard riding. A day's ride north of Vennet now, the morning brooded with autumnal storms and a drizzling rain as their company slid through the shadowed forest.

Eleshen's dappled grey keshar, Moonshadow, was smooth as silk beneath her saddle. Though they'd traveled hard, the massive cat had muscles in places where muscles ought not be, and Eleshen relished riding her. Keshari fighters in wet furs and motley leathers moved around Eleshen like stalking shadows under the heavy canopy, many riding double with Kingsmen in their Greys with hoods up against the rain or stalwart Palace Guardsmen in military oilcloaks. Towering fir and darkoak trees crowded close in the rolling hills, interspersed by white-ash and populus whose leaves stood out golden in the somber light, fluttering in a chill breeze.

Eleshen's cat paused, lifting her great head and opening her mouth to snuffle the increasing drizzle. A low yowl mourned from her throat. Other cats heard it, halted, lifted their heads to the scent and yowled. Merra's massive white cat Snowscythe stopped beside Eleshen's with a growl.

"The cats ahv scented blood on the storm – battle." Merra reined up, setting her long polearm in her stirrup's pocket and palming back her wet braids. She flicked her fingers to her top commanders, Rhone and Rhennon, who ambled their cats to her flanks. "Stalk the ridge ahead. Kill any Menderian sentries."

Rhone and Rhennon gave quick hand-signals to their elite keshari teams, then stole away upon their mounts through the dense alder and wet loam like muscled shadows.

"Advance! Silent!" Merra hissed from her mount. The entire

company was soon moving, though all talk was absent now. Slinking through the trees and the wet, Merra led them up the ridge rather than down into a deepening gorge, making sure her forces stayed to the shadows. Soon, they had a high overlook of the river cutting two hundred feet down to their right in a narrow gorge. The gorge opened out into a broad river-valley, and Eleshen's breath caught as the view expanded at a rocky promontory.

The seeping drizzle marred the view, but nothing could obscure the arresting citadel that rose up before them. The river broke around a massive upthrusting of red stone cliffs that rose up in a high-walled city, glowing crimson as the sun dipped under the clouds to the west. Rainbows shimmered as minarets towered up into the bruised sky, Eleshen craning her neck to fully take the city in. The lower vaults were entirely cliffs; sheer walls of cinnamon stone – a natural upthrust in the middle of the river. Fifty feet high, the cliffs rose to arched ingresses set in midair. There was no bridge to those doorways, no way to assail the cliffs. Each arch was flanked by towering carvings of winged men and women thrusting spears to the sky. Doorways to nowhere dotted the city's spiraling reaches. Bridges spanned the heights, vaulting from tower to tower – a city wreathed in clouds yet anchored in the riverbed.

Eleshen's breath caught as she gazed upon the camp in the river-valley just south of the citadel. Menderian soldiers filled the valley, a sea of tents and picket-lines and avenues. Smoke raised in thin streams from braziers and cook-fires as Menderians in battle-leathers moved upon the plain like ants, hedged in by enormous cliffs to the east and west.

A skirmish was in progress at the river between the camp and the fortress. As Eleshen watched, a volley of flaming arrows went shooting up from a battalion of men upon the river's bank, hitting the vaulted archways of the fortress with a splatter of fire, setting the wooden bulwarks in the fortress' archways aflame. Enormous trebuchets had been erected upon the top of the fortress' archways, but were not in use, archers below in the vaults returning fire down across the river.

Sneaking out of the shadows from the ledge, Rhennon and his group returned, Rhennon sidling up to Merra with a low report. Looking through a copse of alders to the left, Eleshen could see a catapult upon the rocky promontory. The rocks there were smeared with fresh blood, the mauled bodies of ten Menderian soldiers still as stones. Khouren's tawny cat slid up next to Eleshen's, ruffling its bedraggled fur with irritation, Ihbram's big roan male sliding up next to Merra and Rhennon. Eleshen shivered in the drizzle, something in her veins thrumming for battle and blood.

"Scouts are encamped on all the ridges surrounding the valley, in groups of ten or fifteen," Rhennon reported, low. "The Menderians have catapults here and on the western ridge. We assume they've got an evening report-signal, but we've not seen anything. Rhone's gone on with his team to take them all out, quietly."

"Well done," Merra spoke back softly. "Let me know when Rhone returns and confirms kills."

"General." Rhennon nodded soberly.

"That's Arlen fortress, the Vault." Ihbram spoke beside Merra on his big cat. "Parts of it were ruined when I last saw it, but looks like Arlen's done repairs over the past decades. And those trebuchets atop the archways are definitely his. We're in for a fuckstone of a fight if we go down there, though. I estimate eight thousand Menderians, give or take."

"Berlunid's fury!" General Merra gave a hard sigh. "We need ta get into that fortress, but it's suicide ta barge in on a force that large in a tight valley like this, especially when they're already at arms."

"It's worse than that. See that splatter on the wood and how the rain can't put those fires out?" Ihbram gestured at the fortress, where men were now dumping cauldrons of water down from the upper archways to try and douse flames in their bulwarks, as the steady rain couldn't sate that twisting green-gold fire. As they watched, one bulwark crumbled, then another. Far below, using oxen and men protected by a turtle of shields, the Menderian army was rolling six siege-towers to the edge of the quick but shallow river. Another volley of arrows sailed up to splatter the fortress with a greenish-yellow fire.

"That's Pythian resin, lit aflame," Ihbram growled, his face hard and drawn. "Splatters far, sticks to anything like a sonofawhore. Burns like phosphorus while it eats a hole right through anything except stone."

"Pythian resin." General Merra watched the battle, her face tight. "That bastard Lhaurent. If we go down there, they're going to start shooting all that at us. We'll lose everyone."

Merra lifted her chin, watching as the defenders sent the flaming bulwarks down into the river now with battering rams from the inside, blocking the river where the siege-towers were supposed to be rolled with green fire. The towers had been nearly ready to enter the water, but the oxen began to panic at the flames. They watched as oxen snapped their traces, shying from the burning river and trampling men. They couldn't hear screaming from their high vantage, but they watched as men scattered like ants and left the towers standing still.

"Clever fucker, Arlen," Ihbram grinned as the flaming bulwarks in the river began to catch aflame two of the siege towers that were too close. They went up like chimneys, as men strained at thick cables to haul the other three back to a more secure location on the stony shore. A few burning bodies went floating downstream, searing yellow-green in the vicious twilight.

"There. Look at the southeast tower." Ihbram gestured to the nearest wall of the fortress, set with narrow ledges leading up to a few massive ingress-arches fifty feet up. "Those ledges are big enough for cats to jump up, make it to those near archways. That's our way in."

"Those ledges're narrow, an' they face the battle," Merra fixed her gaze on the route they scouted. "Five hundred cats ascending a few at a time would be easy pickings fer Pythian arrows, an' the Menderians would see us fer sure, if we climb while they're active."

"Dammit," Ihbram murmured, throwing down his hood to bare his red braids, palming them back in a rare show of frustration.

The setting sun began to die over the western cliffs. Within seconds, that thin strip of golden light between hills and sky had been snuffed out, the valley plunged into a suffering twilight beneath roiling thunderheads that intensified the rain as a wind picked up. All their allied commanders were pulling up hoods now, huddling in their oilcloaks and furs – watching the battle below with futility in their eyes.

The two flaming siege towers crumbled, falling into the shallow river and burning on. Still, the Menderian army sent volley after volley of flaming arrows up to the fortress' arches, picking off archers who sent flights of arrows down. It was a stalemate, Eleshen could feel it. Even after weeks, neither force had vanquished the other. The fortress was nearly impenetrable, but it left the defenders with no real way to retaliate against their foes, either.

"The Menderian army isn't going to be stopped long," Ihbram observed. "As soon as those bulwarks in the river burn up, they'll begin rolling siege-towers back in. We've got a night before that happens, tops. They were going to take the fortress today, but now they have to wait. Arlen bought himself one night with his little trick, but not a lot more. I don't know why he's not using those trebuchets of his, but maybe they've been sabotaged. It's hard to tell from here if they're operable."

"There could be another way in, away from the fight." Khouren's eyes narrowed upon where the northern split of the river rounded the city's cliffs and was lost to view. "But I don't see any ledges up into the fortress anywhere else."

"Brenner knows how the people who built that fortress got into it," Merra snorted sourly. "I don't see any ramps or bridges or anything."

Eleshen gazed through the rain that sheeted in curtains upon the wind now, seeing that Merra was right. The fortress had no ingress, only a broken ramp in the river that had probably been Arlen's way in. The archways began fifty feet up and there were no bridges to the surrounding cliffs. Eleshen's gaze lingered upon the statues of winged people that flanked every enormous arch. Some were headless, some had spears or half-broken upraised arms. But seeing them, gazing up at the towering minarets and doorways that went nowhere, Eleshen finally understood.

"They flew."

"What?" Khouren glanced over, watching her intently.

"The people who built this citadel. They had wings," Eleshen spoke again. "They didn't need a ground-level ingress or bridges to their fortress." Khouren and Eleshen returned to watching the battle. The Menderian's remaining siege towers were out of the river and safe, their soldiers once again in protected phalanxes with shields. Khouren sidled his cat closer to Eleshen so their legs touched as they stared out over the battle below. He smoothed his hand over Eleshen's thigh and she shifted into his touch, welcoming it.

"Lhaurent's forces will be up inside that city at first light," Merra growled from atop her snowy mount. "And then it's sword on sword. How many fighters does Arlen have in there?"

"Arlen doesn't have eight thousand fighters," Ihbram spoke soberly. "Maybe he's got fifteen hundred. Maybe. The rest would be just villagers."

"He's going to get clobbered, even with the skill of his Alrashemni," Merra growled, her blue eyes furious in the darkening twilight. "We need to move. Tonight. But I won't send our forces in ta die in droves."

Suddenly, Eleshen had a thought. "Khouren, you can walk through walls. Could you get inside and alert Arlen that we're here? Have him make a distraction for the Menderian army while the keshari sneak down in the dark tonight and jump up those ledges into the fortress?"

"The fortress' walls are natural stone down below," Khouren lifted his chin, his blue-black braids haloed by the wet. "I can't breach natural stone. I'd have to climb up."

"I could climb lead, you could follow," Ihbram glanced over, a sparkle of intrigue in his green eyes. "Get us high enough so you could pull us inside. We could find Arlen and get him to make a diversion tonight as Eleshen said. Arlen knows me. He'll trust my information."

Merra had ceased pacing her mount and drawn close, a thoughtful expression upon her face. "If Arlen can make a big enough distraction at the fort, we can slip up and in with minimal losses. Cats are stealthy in the dark, an' this rain will cover any noise an' make it hard ta see us from across that river." She glanced at Ihbram. "If ye can find Arlen tonight, we can do the rest."

"Done." Ihbram nodded briskly, his grin vicious. "Khouren?"

"Shouldn't be too hard to get us inside. Up the northeastern face, where the army can't see us." Khouren glanced at Eleshen, something worried and protective in his gaze. She knew what he was thinking; that she would be left with Merra's riders, away from his protection.

Suddenly, a flaming shot went up from the western ridge,

where they could just see another catapult through the curtaining rain. Merra flicked her fingers and Rhennon jogged his cat to a brazier under a guard-hut. Dipping an arrow into the flames, he shot an answering flare from his enormous Elsthemi warbow. Another shot came from the northeastern cliffs, and Merra cussed. Rhennon returned and Merra growled at him, "Take twenty down to the river and up the northeastern cliff. Eliminate the watch there. We can't have them spying on us tonight. Join us down by the river after dark."

Rhennon gave a quick nod, then signaled his elite group to peel away. Twenty cats slipped out of the trees and over the shadowed northern edge of the cliff – gone down the side. Eleshen blinked, that the keshari could just jump down cliffs like that. But she had no time to ponder, as Merra signaled them to retreat back into the dripping forest. They soon returned to the main host, who idled, taking a rest in the dripping gloom.

"Finish yer food and empty yer loins!" Merra hissed to her company as she moved her cat into their midst and briefly summarized their plans. "Check yer weapons! Tonight's silent running, hear? Kingsmen, watch yer keshari Lieutenants fer hand-signals. Once we go down into the gorge, if I hear so much as a growl from cat or rider ye'll be shot full of arrows!"

A brisk nod came from the keshari riders, with a two-finger affirmation. The Kingsmen saluted with a palm to their hearts and the Roushenn Guard with fingers to the brow, though many shifted in their saddles. Riders dismounted, bumping heads with their cats. Saddles and cat-bridles were left on and the keshar-cats didn't wander, knowing that it wasn't yet time to rest. Fighters hauled out jerked meats and nut-and-berry waybread baked just before they'd left Gerrov-Tel. All supplemented their meal with boar-lard, dipping fingers in the grease and licking them off. Eleshen had seen how the keshari riders took lard and salt during the day, eating little else on the road.

"Fat's the best meal before a fight," General Merra sidled up, offering Eleshen an oiled pouch of lard. "Light on the stomach and ample fuel. Have a good dip, lass. We'll be hard in it tonight. May not be a chance ta eat again fer a while. Doan' want yer muscles ta fail if we see battle."

413

Eleshen dipped her fingers in and licked them, finding the fat gamey and thick. But it cleared her tired mind and smoothed her parched mouth, though she turned away Merra's second offer. Khouren sidled up as Merra left to give fat to her snowy cat.

"How are you?" Khouren's smooth voice slid down Eleshen's body like something alive as he stepped close.

"My ass hurts, wouldn't you know?" Eleshen quipped.

Khouren missed her humor, his opal eyes narrowing with tension. "You may see battle soon, if things go wrong. Are you ready?"

Eleshen eyeballed him. She couldn't deny that she was developing feelings for Khouren, but his hovering had begun to grate. Whenever they stopped, he lingered like a specter. When they bedded down, he slipped to her like a shadow with a hand on his blades, watching the night until she invited him to lay beside her in his bedroll. She lifted her eyebrow. "Are *you* ready? What if you run into a problem in the fortress?"

"I know how to solve problems." Khouren's eyes were dark, a look Eleshen was beginning to know well. He moved in, catching her around her waist, his grey gaze fervent. "Stay close to Merra if there's any fighting. I couldn't bear it if—"

"I'll go where I please, thank you *very* much." Feeling irate with all this jangled energy flowing through her for an upcoming battle, Eleshen picked his hands off her waist and squared her shoulders. "I don't need any man telling me what to do."

"I just meant—"

"I know what you meant," Eleshen flicked her sable braid back over her shoulder. "And I'll not be patronized. I appreciate you trying to protect me, but—"

"But you don't want me." Something in Khouren's eyes died, going from worried to utterly bleak in an instant.

"No, I just meant—"

"I know what you meant," Khouren set his jaw. "But it's my right to care about you. I—"

"Your *right?*" Eleshen had been about to apologize, when his possessive tone caught her all wrong. Her heart boiled; her limbs trembled. She didn't know where this fury came from – as if her body wanted any battle it could get. Stepping back into the fur of

her dappled grey cat, she gave Khouren a nasty look, as
Moonshadow turned her great head and gave Khouren an
additional nasty look. "Saving me from death at the hands of a
madman doesn't give you any ownership over me."

A stricken look seized Khouren's face. He reached out, but then
his hand fell to his side. Eleshen watched a bleak woe take his opal-
dark eyes before they went carefully blank. "As you wish." Turning
away, Khouren stalked to a copse of sycamore trees to the north and
slid through them, lost to sight.

"Oh, Halsos!" With a frustrated sigh, Eleshen turned into her
cat and buried her face in her cat's silvery fur, her heart hammering
with twin emotions of fury and heartache. With a growl, Eleshen
pulled one of her longknives. Setting the blade back along her
forearm, she focused on the deep rhythm of the cat's breath. She'd
once dreamed of finding a man like Khouren: someone strong and
passionate who idolized her every move. But now, she'd been so
eager for battle that she'd provoked a battle with Khouren.

"Don't take what he says to heart." Ihbram's smooth voice
came from her left, with a hint of sad amusement. "Khouren really
has no idea what to do with women."

"He is infuriating!" Eleshen snapped, pushing up from her cat's
fur. She rounded on Ihbram, her longknife still to hand as she set
fists to her hips. "He's so – old-fashioned! If I needed a man to step
all over me, I'd lay down like a daisy in a cow pasture!"

"Easy, keshar!" Ihbram's green eyes flashed humor.

"Well? He pissed me off." Eleshen slid her blade back into its
sheath with a huff, wiping rain off her forehead with the back of her
hand.

"Khouren has that effect on people."

"So do you. You're a rogue."

"Always." Ihbram gave a grin, but it didn't touch his eyes.
"That said, I do know a bit about women. Give Khouren a little
patience. He doesn't know how to court."

"I don't need to be *courted*."

"That's where you're wrong," Ihbram's emerald gaze pierced
Eleshen. "You do need to be courted. You think you don't, but
you're a Dhepan's daughter. You're well-bred, Eleshen. You have
high standards for your men, and only court the most noble.

Khouren's a challenge to your sense of nobility. But you see something in him, something that has only begun to know its own honor. Love him for what he is, milady. And pardon my nephew for what he's not yet become."

"You're silver-tongued," Eleshen blinked, her fury cooling somewhat.

"Unlike Khouren, I've spent hundreds of years navigating royal courts." Ihbram's renegade smile didn't touch his eyes. "I know love and loss. And I tell you this: don't push Khouren away. He may be rough, but his heart is more passionate than any man I've ever met. Excepting one."

"Yours?" Eleshen snorted.

"No, not me. Someone you met... a while back."

Unbidden, his face rose in her mind, and Eleshen knew exactly of whom Ihbram spoke. Sea-grey eyes full of loss and woe. High cheekbones and black curls brush-cut for a soldier's life. Brooding brows, with a lean and regal strength to match any king.

"Elohl." Eleshen's heart gripped her, and she fought back a sudden sting of tears. "How did you know?"

"Back when we first met, I... read your thoughts, just a little." Ihbram's gaze was apologetic. "I didn't mean to pry, I was just curious who you were. And Elohl's image—"

Eleshen stared out through the settling darkness, fingering her longknives. "He still haunts me, sometimes. When he—"

"Left you. Alone. I know." Ihbram moved closer, taking up one of her hands. "I cannot apologize enough for Elohl. He's got trouble down deep in his soul. I was his friend for many long years and it never got any better. His love is deep, but it's a frightening thing. That kind of love only goes two ways – bliss, or destruction."

Eleshen sighed, staring down at Ihbram's hand. He was a rogue, but something in him was also kind. "I know. If I die tonight, I'll go knowing it was better for Elohl and I to part ways. His love for Ghrenna – how could any woman match that? I felt lost when he left me for her. But I won't go to my death tonight pining."

"Don't go to your death tonight at all," Ihbram squeezed her hand. "Khouren offered you good advice. Stay close to Merra tonight, or Rhennon. Don't remain alone if it comes to a fight, Eleshen, just because you're pissed off at Khouren. Let your friends have your back."

Eleshen breathed deep as she considered his words. She watched rain gather upon a golden alder-leaf and splatter to a dark hummock of moss in the waning light. "So. I suppose you and I are friends now?"

"I'll be your friend if you'll be mine. Comrades-in-arms." Ihbram gave her a hot glower, subtly shifting his posture so it simmered with sex. "Unless you'll come to me at night and be comrades-in-bed."

"Rogue!" Eleshen pushed him with a laugh. And suddenly, her spirits brightened. The gloomy nightfall looked more luminous, the rain less chill. The autumn leaves were a warmer shade in the heavy twilight, and the forest loam smelled rich and earthy. Reveling in it, Eleshen gave a smile at last, her heart easing for the first time in days.

"Ready for battle?" Ihbram eyed her, not the look of a rogue but the frank gaze of a comrade.

"Yes." Eleshen lifted her chin, and with that word, something in her was set free. As if she could feel her soul winging away already into any possible fray. Feeling the jolt of a sword-strike shivering up her arm, hearing her own battle-roar calling for blood. Eleshen set a hand to her heart, feeling it. She'd never been in battle, but this body understood it.

And was eager for it.

"Ihbram, mount up!" Merra's low bark came in their direction suddenly. "Rhennon's cats ahv decimated the watch at the northeast ridge an' returned. Ye've got a clear path to the fortress. Find yer kinsman and take yer mounts down. When ye've got Arlen's assistance, light a signal fire east where the Menderians canna see. We'll be waiting in the gorge. Swift riding."

Ihbram gave a quick nod and mounted his cat. With a last look at Eleshen, he gripped the reins and moved off into the trees where Khouren had headed earlier. As Eleshen watched him go, Merra signaled the group, her voice ringing out softly from where she sat ready upon her snowy mount.

"Time ta ride! We pause in the cliff-shadows until dead midnight. When we see a signal fire, it's chase-me-fast! Tonight, it's stealth an' glory — let no man take ye down!"

Merra made a hand signal at her heart, her fingers clawed, then thrust her polearm to the charcoal sky. The signal was repeated all around as riders set foot to stirrups and vaulted up. As Merra thrust her polearm again into the wet dusk, the Elsthemi riders repeated it, wheeling their mounts into a long column that spanned the northern drop-off and sidling through the last of the brush. Eleshen twitched her cat's reins so it fell into line at the ridge past the last clump of alders. Rhennon, returned from his mission atop his blood-smirched cat, gave Eleshen a wink as they came shoulder-to-shoulder at the edge of the steep cliff down into the gorge.

"What does this mean?" Eleshen hissed, making the cat-claw signal at her chest, as all the cats lined up at the drop-off, shivering with eagerness.

"*Victory!*" Rhennon growled back, a battle-ready grin upon his lips.

A third time, General Merra turned in her saddle and made the signal, death and purpose in her ice-blue eyes. As one, the entire battalion repeated it, and then the riders found their stride, flowing forward and down over the jagged northern cliff.

CHAPTER 32 – KHOUREN

The grey night was nearly full dark by the time Khouren and Ihbram ran their cats to the fortress' northeast wall. Though Khouren's cat was old, it was still fleet, out-pacing Ihbram's on the rocky flats as they slid through the shallow river and dismounted by the upthrust crimson rock. Ihbram glanced behind and Khouren's gaze followed. No flaming arrows had been shot from the rim of the canyon nor from the edge of the Menderian camp, now obscured from sight at their position behind the fortress' stone.

"Thank fuck for small favors," Ihbram breathed in the darkness. "You're up, *ghendii*."

Khouren set his cat free, no love lost between them, and approached the sheer wall. He slid his hands over the rock, closing his eyes. Feeling subtle vibrations in the stone, he tried to match it and slide his way in, but at last shook his head. "We'll have to climb, just as I thought. The stone is solid down here, for at least ten lengths. I can feel a cavern on the other side, but it's too far."

"Damn." Ihbram's voice was hardly a breath as he gazed upward. Following his uncle's sightline, Khouren saw that this entire wall of the fortress was smooth, no ledges to rest upon. The first archways began higher than on the southern side, one hundred feet up rather than fifty. His uncle's visage was shadow-on-shadow in the shrouded night as he slung a rope from his shoulder. "Time to climb."

They worked quietly and quickly, in a coordinated rhythm both knew well from long ago. Khouren readying knots and clips that made makeshift harnesses in the line, Ihbram setting them in with metal clips and then thrusting a bolt-setter to the rock. Ihbram covered it with his *shouf* to mask the noise, but the sprung hammer inside the bolt-setter made a hard *ka-chunk* as it hammered the bolt in – rippling every nerve in Khouren's spine.

"The army's going to hear that."

"Not if we move fast." Ihbram checked the short rope-knife at his hip, making sure it was secure, then set his fingers and the toes of his flexible boots to the wall, finding small holds. Then he was up, another *ka-chunk* coming ten feet above Khouren's head. The line took up slack and Khouren set his fingertips to the wall, gazing up to watch his uncle's route as the last of the light failed.

Thrusting with his thighs, Khouren heaved upward, struggling to keep his diagonal motions as fluid as his uncle's. The rock face was sheer, chilly beneath his fingertips, and the holds were small. But Ihbram was an expert, and set a true route with the best holds available as they worked steadily upward. Climbing wasn't Khouren's best activity, and he was all-over sweat when suddenly, fifty feet up, he felt the vibration of the stone change beneath his fingertips. All at once, the stone felt like a viscous liquid, and even as he thought it, one hand slipped right through. Khouren lost his balance and his footing – falling straight through the wall.

He heard a shout from Ihbram as he fell through into a black void. Panic took Khouren, free-falling. But he was yanked to a halt by his harness, sending the breath out of him as it jerked up into his balls. His eyes watered, but living was worth it. Gazing down, he couldn't see anything. There was no above, no below. No here nor there – just a suffering blackness permeated by a chill draft. Though Khouren's vision was impeccable, this was unlike anything he'd ever experienced – as if the void ate all light.

With steady hands, he hauled himself back up the rope. He came to the place where he'd fallen, feeling where the rope went through the stone to the outside. Sliding one hand through solid stone, he reached out. With a meaty slap, Ihbram's hand gripped his, skin to skin. Slowly, Khouren relaxed his focus on his hand, without losing focus on his body. It wouldn't do to pass through his harness and send both himself and his uncle plummeting to their deaths in this black abyss. Like jelly pulled through a strainer, Ihbram was moved through the wall by Khouren's *wyrria*. All the way in, Ihbram set a fast bolt into the wall with a *ka-chunk* that reverberated through the darkness, anchoring them.

That sound rolled through the void like thunder through a bottomless night. And then, Khouren heard an answering sound. Like someone hummed through a glass vial, a singing came back to him from below and far above. As he stared into the nothingness, light seeped into his eyes. Hundreds of feet below, far lower than the river-bed they had climbed from, he saw crystal towers. Thrusting up in a razor-keen maw, they whispered with a subtle blue light that went surging through their surfaces, playing through the deadly tableau below like a moonlit tide.

"That would have been a bad end," Ihbram chuckled, but Khouren heard the tension in it.

"The worst kind of stop," Khouren agreed, swallowing hard. He'd never tried passing through crystal pillars before. He didn't know if it could be done, or if they would simply skewer him. The echoes of their voices amplified the resonance, the light below brightening until Khouren could see Ihbram's face in the soft glow.

Ihbram glanced up to the ceiling of the chasm, his face angelically lit. "Up there."

Khouren followed his uncle's gaze. The ceiling of the vast cavern was a mirror of the floor – a jagged maze of enormous spires, spiking down like jaws clamping upon them, a subtle blue light writhing through it all.

"Chilling," Khouren murmured.

"Not so friendly," Ihbram agreed. He pointed right, and Khouren glanced over. A crimson stone bridge protruded from the wall they were anchored in. Spanning the chasm, the bridge ended at a set of grand stairs that regressed beneath a massive arch carven into the cavern's wall. That wall was a maze, set not only with that one enormous archway, but riddled with vaulted doors and recessed alcoves of every size and variety, pockmarked into the stone. All those impossibly delicate archways led to stairs that regressed, tunnels burrowing up or downward into a dark unknown.

"Must be five hundred of them," Ihbram's voice was soft, stunned. "Whoever built this place didn't want to make it easy for anyone to get in."

Khouren nodded. Without a word, they began to move along the wall. Ihbram set anchors and Khouren removed rope as he arrived. Looking up, he saw there were actually crystal bridges far above, that appeared transparent until the eye glanced upon them. It was the same below – bridges and platforms among the crystal teeth that seemed to appear and disappear as they moved. Gradually, they moved the hundred feet sideways and down, until they both stood upon a half-moon dais that led to the stone bridge.

Ihbram un-clipped the rope, his critical eye assessing the bridge. "Why the fuck did someone build a bridge to this solid wall?"

With a frown, Khouren had a thought. Placing his hands upon the wall to the outside, he changed his body's harmonics, vibrating his hands upon the stone. It caused a humming sound, and as it did, the wall began to light in fantastical whorls and sigils made of the same blue ether that slipped through the crystals below and above. Khouren could see veins of crushed crystal inlaid into the red stone, camouflaged until it caught that blue-white fire.

"Beautiful!" Ihbram ran his hands over cascading sigils as Khouren stepped back. Looking up, Khouren could see the symbols created a haunting scene of winged men and women clad with bright helms and armor taking flight off a ledge into thin air, brandishing spears for battle beneath a blazing sun. The tableau was bounded by two columns and a high arch, as if a doorway.

"The right kind of *wyrria* must create a door to the outside," Khouren murmured.

"Think yours could do it?"

"Perhaps," Khouren shrugged. "But there are no ledges leading to this spot, if you're thinking about getting Merra's cats in here."

"You're right." Ihbram sighed. "We need to find Arlen. If this bridge leads to the center of the fortress, we'll be in luck. But all those doorways make my balls cling, Khouren. I've never been inside this place, but the stories I've heard are terrifying. Keep your wits close."

"Agreed."

Turning from the door, they clipped the rope to their harnesses, but remained attached to each other. Ihbram went first along the narrow bridge, shoulders tense and hands ready. But nothing accosted them and they were soon safely over the chasm. Khouren paused, eyeballing the wall now before them with its countless ingresses, as trepidation washed through him. "If the people who made this place flew, they wouldn't have needed a bridge. So why build one? Trap?"

"Probably," Ihbram grinned. "But since when do Alodwine

men run from a conflict? Just be ready to drag me through a wall, yeah?"

Khouren lifted an eyebrow as he rolled his sleeves up to his elbows, and Ihbram did the same. It was familiar, their battle-routine of long ago – readying for skin contact to phase Ihbram through something along with Khouren in a pinch. Banishing distractions, Khouren regarded the massive archway. Far up in a shadowy alcove near the turn of the stairs was a cluster of crystals. He hummed, and Ihbram joined in. As if called to awaken, the crystals at the turn in the stairs brightened to a flowing blue-white, like milk and phosphorescent algae stirred in a glass.

"Up we go," Ihbram murmured.

Khouren took the lead now – his reflexes faster in the dark when climbing wasn't involved. One hand hovered near his longknife as he ascended, the other ready to clasp Ihbram's wrist. But nothing accosted them as they wound up to the next turn. Another set of crystals in an alcove appeared, dark and slumbering. Khouren hummed to light them. They began to glow softly, when suddenly, something shot from the cluster. Fast as a strike of pale lightning, it lanced Khouren in the chest and he gasped, pain like a flood of bees spearing through him.

"Khouren!" Ihbram rushed forward. The crystal shot another blast of vaporous lightning, but he ducked fast, seizing Khouren and dragging him back down the turn.

"I'm alright!" Khouren coughed, rubbing his chest. Unbuckling his charcoal silk jerkin, he hauled open the laces of his grey shirt, gazing at his chest. A bloom of pale wraith-vapor moved beneath his skin. "What in Undoer—?"

Ihbram moved a hand over the *wyrric* marks, tracing their movement. "Damned if I know. You sure you're not hurt?"

"I'm fine." Khouren blew out a steadying breath. "Though it stung like that hornet's nest in Althumma we got into that one time."

"Not a fun time, that little outing. We learned better than to crawl through mesquite bushes on the Lhemvian Isles to scale that fucking fortress of Jhorenni al'Ban's." Ihbram offered a hand and Khouren clasped it as his uncle hauled him to his feet. "Different door?"

"Different door."

Moving back down to the egress, they clipped in to the wall. Ihbram took them up a few levels to a different ingress, jumping down onto a balcony and brushing off his hands. The balcony entrance had columns carven like lilypads, with dragonflies and frogs hiding in the greenery. Traces of green paint adorned the ancient arch, with a rich violet color to the lilies and insects.

"Looks nice," Khouren murmured.

"I thought so. Pleasant." Ihbram flashed a ready grin.

They moved into the gloom, finding a tunnel rather than a staircase, broad enough to walk side-by-side. Hairs prickled on Khouren's neck, but it was only the air. Alcoves held crystals, but Ihbram and Khouren kept their silence as they passed and they didn't brighten. At last, a glimmer of light ahead caught Khouren's attention and he nudged Ihbram. They put their backs to the wall and inched toward the exit, hands ready at weapons.

The tunnel opened into a vaulted space. Muggy, the air in the broad chamber had a sulfurous stink, and as Khouren glanced around, he saw crystals of every color glowing softly in niches in the walls. The chamber had flowing water, the burble of sound creating the source of the crystal's light. Ripples of reflected light poured over the walls of the cavern from ten steaming pools edged in a white sulfuric brine. As they inched closer, Khouren saw the pools were lit from within, water moving over more crystals within the pools themselves.

"Dangerous?" Khouren murmured.

"I wouldn't dip my balls in it."

Moving to another pool, Khouren gasped. "Shaper!"

"What?" Ihbram stepped to his side, then blinked. "Oh. Shit. Is it dead?"

The first pool had been empty, but this one contained a creature. As Khouren peered closer, he couldn't precisely call it human. It was long-limbed and pale, with webbed fingers and toes, ripples of flowing fins emerging from its shoulder-blades and long thighs. It had fins for ears, and its eyes were closed as if in repose. Silver scales with an opal sheen shimmered over its bare body, in long lines down its decidedly feminine nakedness.

In all his long life, Khouren had seen nothing like this. And from the way his uncle gaped at the thing, he suspected it was the same for Ihbram. Reaching toward the pool, Khouren felt compelled to dip his fingers in – to touch that long, flowing body, and stir the water around its fins.

Ihbram's hand slapped to Khouren's forearm, arresting him. "I wouldn't."

Khouren startled. Blinking, he looked around as if seeing the cavern for the first time. Glancing into the pool, he was startled to find not a winsome woman in the water, but a shriveled thing, mummified with grey-silver skin stretched tight over rotting bones and fins.

"What in Aeon—?"

"Something's fucking with us." Ihbram's gaze swept the shadows. "There's mind-*wyrria*—"

Suddenly, the thing in the pool opened rotten eyelids, baring two pale, cloudy globes. A hand shot out from the water, gripping Khouren's neck with furious strength. Only part of him heard Ihbram's battle-roar as rotten things surged from the pools, launching through the water and hurling themselves at the intruders.

Five of them were on Khouren, two more on Ihbram, seizing them with slick, webbed hands and talons like raptors. Khouren couldn't phase through their grip. *Wyrria* pummeled him, surging from the mer-creatures. Fangs thrust from the creatures' mouths as they shrieked, lancing cries that made the cavern blaze. Moving fast, Khouren gutted one in the belly, skewered a second in the neck. But a third sank talons big as knives into his leg and dug in.

Wyrria flooded Khouren through those talons, the cold, dead feel of the darkest ocean floor. Overwhelming pain shocked him and he screamed, as others impaled him from the rear and sides, pinning him. He lost control – an unconscious fury – slashing wildly for throats, bellies, anything he could get. The odious horrors shrieked as he cut, slashing him back even as pieces stinking of high tide fell from them like rotten shrouds. Enormous fangs bit into his shoulder. That hand went limp as he roared, one longknife dropping to the cavern floor with a ringing clatter.

Khouren could see Ihbram battling nearby, but his uncle couldn't help, two of the mer-things still assaulting him. Khouren jabbed for eyes with his remaining knife, got one. The water-being shrieked, but claws ripped into Khouren's back, digging into his spine and deep into his lungs. The horrors shook him like terriers with a rat, the last two of them that remained on him trying to tear him apart. With a desperate surge, Khouren plunged his longknife into the neck-muscles of fish-woman in front of him and cut her spine. She went limp, falling on Khouren and he managed a roll, flinging her body at the creature behind him, blood and acidic fluids cascading as he crushed the one behind, then skewered it.

But fangs and talons were still buried in Khouren to the hilt, broken off from the mer-beings like a lizard's tail and left inside his body. He could barely breathe, the pain unimaginable. The appendages of the water-creatures had been poisonous and his flesh burned with ice even as it healed, his body trying to repair as he coughed blood. He tried to sit up, but the talons in his back and shoulder went deep.

He yelled for Ihbram. Through his agony, he heard fast footsteps. Ihbram's face had been raked, his jerkin and shirt torn at the shoulder and chest, but he was mostly intact as he sank to Khouren's side with a stream of curses. His green eyes darted to the damage even as he slit the throats of the limp creatures near Khouren to make sure they were dead.

"I'm healing around the talons and fangs!" Khouren managed. "They're poison!"

"Fuck!" Ihbram cursed. All of Leith's line had fast healing, but Khouren's was uncanny. Quickly, Ihbram readied one longknife as Khouren gasped, his insides full of caustic ice. With a roar, Ihbram thrust his knife into Khouren's shoulder. Flicking his blade, he popped the fangs out with his knife-point, to a gush of blood as Khouren screamed in agony. Some artery had torn and his vision swam, his eyelids flickering.

"Stay with me!" Ihbram growled, slapping Khouren's face with his free hand.

Fighting unconsciousness, Khouren gasped as Ihbram set his knife to Khouren's back, slicing faster than a surgeon on a battlefield. He ripped the claws out of Khouren's healing flesh, and Khouren coughed blood, vomited. With the impalements gone, he fought for air. But things were wrecked deep inside, poisoned, gushing bile and blood. His lungs wouldn't obey and a whistling came from his punctured chest as he spasmed.

His vision flared white and the world fuzzed out.

"Khouren, *stay with me!!*"

Stay with me.

His uncle's *wyrric* command blossomed through Khouren like an emerald ocean, tingeing Khouren's fading world green like gazing through a peridot crystal at dawn. Part of Khouren wanted to die, thought he should die, for all the terrible things he'd caused in this life. But his uncle's command seized him, filling Khouren to the brim until he could feel nothing but the fire of Leith's line burning in his veins.

Suddenly, another face swam into Khouren's vision – a heart-shaped face with sleek black hair, eyes like violets in the rain. Khouren roared, the sound of beasts in torment as the Wolf and Dragon fought within him. His body spasmed upon the cavern floor and Khouren screamed as fire filled him. Raging to die, raging to live. Raging to love and be loved. And with it came healing; uncanny, racing through his body. Muscles knit as Khouren spasmed. Poison was neutralized, sinews rejoined, arteries surged closed. His lungs popped back with a deep wrenching that made Khouren cry out.

And then it was done. The fire left him; everything left him, and Khouren's mind evaporated upon the emptiness in its wake. Above him, his uncle was crying. Tears slipped down Ihbram's face, his eyes red-rimmed in the fey light as he helped Khouren up to sitting.

"You ass!" Grasping Khouren's head, Ihbram set their foreheads together, half-laughing. "Gods of the sands, don't you *ever* scare me like that again! There are few enough of us left as is. We can't afford to lose you! Not now, not after everything…!"

"Maybe it would be better if I was dead." Tears stung Khouren's eyes. "I cause ruin."

"Don't be daft!" Ihbram gave him a little shake. "We love you. Even your grandfather. And Eleshen – Don't throw all that away, Khouren! She loves you, you fucking idiot!"

Khouren swallowed hard as tears slipped down his face. "How can I ever make it right? All the people Lhaurent's killed because I gave him power? What if he kills her?"

"We'll find a way, *ghendii*. We'll find it together."

Ihbram pulled Khouren into his arms, hugging his nephew fiercely amidst the stench of reeking fish. Khouren seized his uncle, feeling the comfort of family before he pulled back and Ihbram let him go. Gazing down, Khouren found he was a mess. Blood and limpid scales desecrated everything, his shirt and charcoal jerkin ripped to pieces. And though everything still ached, he pushed to standing and discovered that his body obeyed.

"Damn if that wasn't thrice-fine *wyrria*, Khouren," Ihbram's eyes were impressed as his gaze roved Khouren's mangled gear. "You had five of those things on you, fuck if each one wasn't strong enough for seven men."

"Conflict has its uses."

"I've never seen you heal that fast before. Not even at Lintesh." Ihbram opened Khouren's rent shirt, gazing at the flow of etheric light that still trickled through his skin from where the crystal had seared him earlier. Khouren's skin was immaculate, not a scratch left behind.

"That's because I never have. Not like that." Khouren spoke softly, also amazed.

"Your grandfather would be proud."

"Grandfather never wants to see me again." Khouren wiped his knives on the dead creatures before sliding them home in their sheaths. The cavern was quiet now, but for the rippling of water.

"Fentleith loves you. No matter how angry he is that you got tricked by Lhaurent," Ihbram murmured. "As does Eleshen. Don't think I don't know what's going on there."

"What if she finds out I'm no good?" Khouren murmured as he sank to a seat upon the rim of the nearest pool, staring at the dead mer-creatures seeping a viscous white blood onto the cavern's stone. Ihbram sank to a seat next to him and Khouren glanced over to see his uncle's green eyes were wistful in the moving light, a wry smile of heartache on his lips.

"Did I ever tell you about Helene del'Ilio, the first woman I ever loved?"

Khouren stilled, watching the eerie cavern light play over the pools. He and Ihbram had been close before Khouren had retreated to Roushenn. Once, Khouren had loved his uncle's stories of wine, women, and song – before he found out Ihbram was a two-faced hypocrite when it came to love. And though he'd heard his uncle talk of women again and again, he'd never heard of Ihbram's first obsession.

"How did you meet?" Khouren asked.

"It was in Cennetia," Ihbram smiled softly. "In Duomini, the City of Waterways, built upon pontoons in the Ciari River-delta."

"There's no city at the mouth of the Ciari," Khouren cocked his head, intrigued.

"Not anymore," Ihbram chuckled. "That area of the delta has sunken now; it was underwater before you were born. But it used to be a glorious citadel. It would flood when the rains came. The pontoons would go up and down, lifting the buildings. The walkways were built on floats, trussed to arching stone bridges anchored deep in the silt. This was back when I was still young, less than a hundred years. I was a callous fucker then – I had five women at that time who knew nothing of each other. They were stunning beauties, but Helene put them all to shame."

"Was she a noble?"

"She was an assassin," Ihbram chuckled, lacing his fingers to pop his knuckles one at a time. "Hired by my noble lover, Ruitia del'Mar. Ruitia had a sense of honor, and when she found out she was getting royally fucked, literally, she retaliated. Most Cennetians like their poison, but Ruitia wanted me gutted like a flounder, my corpse tossed into the canals for the alligators and ripfish. So she hired the Sons of Illium to come after me. And when her assassin accosted me one misty night, I gave the woman what-for."

"Did you hurt her?"

"Badly," Ihbram chuckled. "Got a shoulder in her gut, slammed her face into the stones of a bridge. Knocked her out. When I hauled off her face-shroud – Shaper's tits! I scooped her into my arms and took her to our Alodwine safe-house in the city, to Minareth. You never met your aunt Mina, but she had healing *wyrria* similar to Lenuria's. She saved the girl a broken nose and cheekbone. By the time Mina left, the girl was unmarred. And more beautiful than anything you've ever seen."

"I doubt it." Olea's face surfaced in Khouren's mind, followed by another beauty – Eleshen.

"Well, there she was, starting to stir," Ihbram continued. "Hair that amazing Cennetian blonde-copper. Dark eyelashes. Tattoos of real gold ore curling around her cheekbones, in the style of Old Illium. She was Illianti. When she opened her eyes, fuck me Khouren, if they weren't the purest lavender I've ever seen."

"Like Elemnia's. And Eleshen's."

"Just like it." Ihbram gave a sad smile. "Elemnia was one of the most beautiful women in the world, Khouren, also from the Illianti line, did you know? Lavender eyes only surface in Illianti blood. Well Helene had those eyes, and dammit, if I didn't fall in love right that very moment. I leaned over her. I set my lips to hers for a kiss. And felt a damn knife snicked to my groin."

"Serves you right." But Khouren twisted inside, knowing that he'd never done Olea any better. And now he was doing no better with Eleshen, suffocating her.

"Well, she had me," Ihbram chuckled. "She held me at knifepoint all night, riding my brains out. To say we fucked is saying too little. I gave myself to her – heart, body, and soul." Ihbram sighed in the dim grotto. "What I'm trying to say, is that when I met Elemnia – a part of me fell in love with her, too. She was dangerous, alluring, ruthless in battle, fierce. She was everything Helene had been and everything Eleshen is now."

"You *punished* me for loving Elemnia."

"I can't say it was right, or fair." Ihbram drew a long breath. He let it out slow, his gaze a thousand leagues away. "But you have to understand. I watched my own lavender-eyed lover succumb to time, Khouren. When it began to devour her, when we had children, and time began to change her, and me… I ran. I blocked my mind hard and never looked back. Because I knew if I didn't, I would stay. I would stay and be a father and a husband. Raise my children and forget being Alodwine – sending so many weaves through my own mind, that I would become no better than a common farmer. Losing myself."

"Was her love so terrible?" Khouren murmured, tired.

"No." Ihbram's gaze met his, devastated. "It was everything I'd ever wanted. I was there with Helene, at the end. Our children had all been killed before her – assassination, accidents, sickness, and one other had disappeared without a trace. She was alone upon her deathbed. The day the light left her eyes, when she was white-haired

430

and frail, I was the only one there to watch her die."

"You didn't stay and watch the rest of your lovers die," Khouren murmured.

"I couldn't." Ihbram's words haunted the cavern. "But I found them every few years, saw my children from afar. Watched the years turn in their faces, life dimming from their eyes. I watched all my lovers expire, Khouren. Watched my Khehemni children die, too, not enough of Leith's *wyrria* in their veins to sustain them. After a while, it started to seem futile. Loving. And when I saw you and Elemnia fall in love—"

"You were jealous." Khouren spoke, so much about their history coming clear at last.

"I was jealous." Ihbram's eyes lifted, their emerald depths piercing. "I know what I am, Khouren. I've seen my shortcomings in the face of every child I've sired and left unclaimed. But maybe Lenuria gave you a gift before she died. Maybe she saved Eleshen – so you could be saved, too."

Khouren took a deep breath and let it out slowly. "I love Eleshen, Ihbram. It's in the way she moves; the way she argues. It's in the flash of those eyes when she's pissed or thinking. Eleshen echoes Elemnia and Olea – yet, she's so different."

"Eleshen's a noble, Khouren," Ihbram's mouth quirked. "Elemnia and Olea were only fighters. Eleshen needs a man who's more than just a good sword. A man who can stand in the fire, and love her no matter how heated it gets. She needs someone who's a zealot for her love. Like you."

"What if I'm not what she wants?" Khouren's hands trembled and he laced them together.

"Become the man she wants. Become the man you want to be, *ghendii*." Ihbram jostled him, then clapped him on the shoulder and pushed to standing.

"What about you?" Khouren asked, sadness moving in him for Ihbram's predicament as he rose to standing also.

"What about me?"

"Who do you have to love you?"

Ihbram's face closed like stone. His green eyes glittered in the low light, pained. "We should get a move on. Merra's forces aren't going to wait." Glancing down at the corpses, he nudged one with his boot. But they were motionless, desiccated flesh hanging off their bones as pearly blood spilled over the floor. "These fuckers were strong. Could be we're on the right path."

Khouren glanced at his uncle, and they watched each other a long moment. At last, Ihbram's mouth gave a sad quirk, as he palmed his red braids back into a half-bound bun and glanced off around the grotto. Khouren's gaze followed, seeing a few low tiers and a flight of stairs that led up at the far end. It was the only exit, as if whoever had built this place had wanted intruders to be tested by the mer-creatures. In the cold light that simmered off the crystal alcoves, that dark ascending staircase looked almost preferable.

"That looks as good a way as any," Ihbram spoke, gesturing Khouren onward.

Moving to the ascending stairs, Khouren headed up with Ihbram on his heels. They didn't talk again, though the tension of all that had been said still flowed between them in the darkness. But they'd not ascended hardly a minute, when the staircase suddenly ended in a blind wall. Khouren set his hands to it, feeling the vibrations of the stone.

"It's thick, but there's a large space beyond it. Maybe another grotto, or a room."

"Then let's go," Ihbram nodded.

Weapons ready, Khouren seized his uncle's wrist, then stepped them through the wall. To find themselves emerged in a massive armory, lit bright to the vaulted caves with torches and lanterns. The armory bustled with men and women in war-gear, the vaults filled with stands of armor, sword and bow-racks, wall-stands of pikes, and baskets of arrows. All of the warriors within looked up at once. Pikes were suddenly leveled, swords whipped from scabbards and aimed at the intruders.

"Whoa!" Ihbram held his hands up, a roguish grin upon his face. "Peace! We've come to find the Vicoute Arlen den'Selthir. Any who can point our way to him is going to win this war single-handedly."

"That's a pretty promise. One that half-Elsthemi curs shouldn't make, if they value the length of their dirty red braids."

A gravel-hard voice turned Khouren's head. A man stood nearby at a rack of swords that shone with impeccable care. Wearing older grey Kingsmen battle-armor, the aging lord had a tough yet elegant demeanor. His thick sandy hair was combed back from his forehead and shot with streaks of iron. A neatly-trimmed beard graced his jaw, unforgiving blue eyes staring out from a stern face. But moving forward, his austere face broke into a welcoming smile as he clasped arms with Ihbram.

"Ihbram Alodwine den'Sennia," the lord chuckled, his eyes glittering. "How long has it been? Thirty years?"

"Never underestimate my ability to survive a fight, Arlen," Ihbram chuckled back. "Or your own meticulous planning to survive even worse."

"I never do." Arlen clapped Ihbram on both shoulders like the man was his own son. "And here you walk straight through a wall into my stronghold, looking as young as ever! Your *wyrric* wonders never cease."

"Not mine, actually," Ihbram gave a small nod to Khouren. "Arlen, meet my nephew, Khouren Alodwine."

"How are you both here?" Arlen gave Khouren a gaze that missed nothing, suspicious suddenly as his gaze roved Khouren's mangled gear.

"From Temlin den'Ildrian. He hadn't received word from you in some time and feared the worst." Ihbram's face fell suddenly. "You should know, Arlen – Temlin has fallen. And the First Abbey with him."

Arlen's face fell, suddenly grim as stone. With a deep inhalation, he nodded. "Temlin will be honored, as fits his station. But now is not the time. Did anyone survive from the Abbey?"

"Most everyone survived, actually," Ihbram continued with a ready grin. "And Temlin ordered us to come to your aid, before he died. We've arrived with some twelve hundred keshari riders, Kingsmen, and Roushenn Guard – all waiting outside your walls atop cats in the northeastern canyon. We need a distraction to get them inside the fortress. Tonight."

Arlen's face opened in shock, but his surprise was quickly mastered. Khouren saw the quick mind of an old fighter churning as Arlen squared his shoulders, turning from a lord into a war-general in the blink of an eye.

"Come, gentlemen," the Vicoute Arlen den'Selthir barked,

making an efficient gesture for them to follow as he threaded briskly back through the armory. "I know just the distraction we need."

CHAPTER 33 – ELESHEN

From her place hiding in the shadows of the canyon-ridge, Eleshen saw a small flame kindled at the fortress' eastern archways. Just the flicker of a single torch illuminated in a night black as tar, but she felt a breath of relief ripple through General Merra's forces around her, hoods of fur and leather up in the driving rain. Rhennon gave a soft curse from atop his big cat next to Eleshen, as the same came from his brother Rhone, having re-joined them, puncturing the rain-washed silence of the past four hours.

Suddenly, Eleshen saw fires rise from the line of enormous trebuchets atop the fortress archways, their slings loaded with immense boulders burning with pitch. As alarms rang in the Menderian camp, the peal of hammers on massive bronze war-bells, Eleshen saw additional movement at the grand archways of the fortress. Brazier-fires suddenly blazed in every arch, lighting the red fortress like a bloody wall of eyes. In half a breath, lines of archers in the fortress had lit arrows – each archer sporting tremendous silver-white warbows taller then they – and now the darkness spawned fireflies. Before Eleshen could gasp, the enormous boulders of fire and all those fireflies launched into the night, beautiful arcs that came hurtling down into the northern edge of the Menderian camp – thudding into wains, bowling over barrels, and lighting up siege-towers not rolled back far enough from the river's edge.

It was a masterful attack. Clearly, Arlen den'Selthir had been waiting to use this powerful ploy, and the Menderian forces scrambled in the deep of the night, waking to fire lighting up their northern camp. They'd thought Arlen's trebuchets inoperative, just like Ihbram had, a line of pretty toys unused for weeks, and Eleshen guessed they'd not seen these silvered warbows yet. Bronze alarms pealed throughout the camp as men rushed out of burning tents and others rushed into the fray, trying to capture horses and pull wagons back from the rapidly-spreading line of fire.

Which had blocked the Menderian's access to the river. It was time. Hand signals fluttered through the keshari riders and in a massive surge of muscle and power, General Merra's forces leaped forward like a single organism. Eleshen was one with her cat as they bounded forward, Rhennon on his big beast beside her. Hunkering low over Moonshadow's shoulders, she felt the rain slice her cheeks like wasps as they ran with silent elegance over the rocky flats at an impossible speed toward the river. No horse could move like this. Exhilaration filled Eleshen; a roaring sensation in her body. She was lightning, she was wind.

She was the night, and the night had claws and fangs.

They hit the river in a rush of darkness. Water hardly splashed at all around them, as Eleshen's great cat heaved into the stony watercourse, swimming with ready strokes. The driving rain was still heavy, and though Eleshen could see the perimeter of surging fire blocking off the Menderian camp, she couldn't make out much else. Merra's forces gained the shallow ledges, and cats began to leap up the fortress' walls. Above, Arlen's archers were cunning, directing their fire deep into the central and western camp to turn all eyes away from the eastern wall of the fortress the allies ascended.

Eleshen's cat came to the wall, and as Moonshadow began to heave upward next to Rhennon's big male, Eleshen watched the Menderian camp blaze. Soldiers ran, scrambling in the driving wet and churning muck. Siege towers too close to the carnage caught alight in a whirlwind from the burning pitch coating the boulders, funnels of red fire twisting into the darkness despite the driving rain. Fire held a line at the bank of the river now, as the trebuchets were re-loaded again and again, hurling flaming boulders into the closest Menderian's resources. Merra's forces leaped fast up the narrow ledges to the fortress' great archways, silent as ghosts as the distraction raged. Keshari surged before and behind Eleshen with not a single yowl – a flowing sea of silent fang and sinew thrusting in great leaps up from the river and into the fortress.

The shore was devastated – bodies burning, siege towers collapsed, mess-tents and command-tents, and every last thing that could burn alive with fire. Eleshen hunkered low over her dappled cat, feeling the muscles of the beast coil and explode, leaping them up one ledge to the next. When she at last slid from its back high

436

upon the smooth flagstones beneath one vaulted archway, Khouren and Ihbram were there, rushing to her side as she moved out of the way to let more cats and riders flow past.

The sweet song of victory ran in Eleshen's veins as she and Khouren embraced, his arms crushing her breathlessly to his strong, lean chest. She hardly even registered his torn and mangled garb as the whomps of more launching trebuchets thundered through her ears like music. The rhythm of the archers' volleys beat in her heart as they loosed again, and again. And as Eleshen turned her eyes to the night, watching the Menderian camp burn, she felt no sadness. Staring down at the carnage, Eleshen burned with triumph. As Khouren stepped close, watching the devastation with her, Ihbram marveling next to them, a song of wrath in Eleshen's heart surged.

"We have waged death this night," she spoke. "Behold its glory."

Khouren turned to look at her, his opal eyes carnal as his blue-black curls reflected the fire below. Reaching up, he touched Eleshen's chin, his gaze fervent in the light. Eleshen watched him, feeling her own fierceness in the light of the flames. Khouren hitched a hard breath, then drew her in. His lips found hers and they kissed in the burning night as cats ascended the wall, flowing in through the archways all around – a living sea of fang and claw beneath the storm.

At last, Eleshen pulled back. "I'm sorry. For provoking a fight with you earlier. I didn't mean to."

Khouren's grey eyes shone with relief and fervency. "It's alright. I know how it feels, the battle-rage. It's part of the *wyrria* that's been awakened in you Eleshen, and I—"

Khouren was suddenly cut short as General Merra pushed through the throng upon her massive white cat. Vaulting from her saddle with a wide grin and a laugh, she faced their trio. "Ronins! Well done! Savin' the day was the least of yer accomplishments tonight! I am in your debt."

Merra gave a deep nod to Ihbram and Khouren. It wasn't quite a bow, but it was significant. Khouren and Ihbram blinked, but then both set palms to their hearts, gripping their blades like Alrashemni.

"Well!" Merra clapped their shoulders. "Time ta find this

bastard of a Shemout Kingsman ye've told me about, this Vicoute Arlen den'Selthir."

"Search no more." A smooth, iron-hard voice cut the din and Eleshen turned to see a tall, lean lord approach behind them, clad in the Alrashemni Greys. He moved forward through the mass of cats and riders with a retinue of dangerous charcoal-clad Kingsmen, plus archers clad in woven garb of green moss carrying those tall silvered warbows. All six Kingsmen including the lord himself had nicked their chests at their unbuckled jerkins, showing stylized blood-red Inkings of the Mountain and Stars between their shirt-laces.

With swift grace, the lord made a deep bow, one palm to his heart over his blooded Inkings, one to the sword at his hip. "High General Merra Alramir of Elsthemen. I am the Vicoute Arlen den'Selthir of Vennet, commander of this fortress and Rakhan of the Shemout Alrashemni. My Kingsmen and I are in your debt for arriving with reinforcements this night."

"Thank me not, fer it is I who am in yer debt, ye ballsy fucker." General Merra strode forward, her great white cat upon her heels, extending a hand. Without batting an eyelash, the Vicoute clasped her arm hard. A moment passed between them, like a meeting of kindred souls as a grin split Merra's lips and Arlen echoed it with a soft chuckle. Merra's grin grew wide and she laughed, hale and hearty. Moving in, she slapped Arlen upon the shoulder.

"And indeed," General Merra laughed, gesturing at Ihbram and Khouren, "it's these three ronins ye have ta thank. Had it not been fer them an' their ideas, we'd all be nae but torches in the night out there."

"Indeed. Fighters with many uses." Arlen gave a cordial smile to Ihbram and Eleshen, then a tighter one to Khouren.

"Arlen," Ihbram gave a courtier's nod to Merra, "it is truly High General Alramir you have to thank for your reinforcements today. Had we not met her keshari contingent up near the Elsee a week ago, we'd not have had the ability or the numbers to come to Vennet's aid, even as much as we might have wanted to."

"High General," Arlen gave Merra another deep bow, one hand upon his heart and the other upon his sword, his stern face split into a fascinated smile. He rose with consummate grace, far more the lord than fighter now. "Anything an old war-maker of

Alrou-Mendera can do for you, he will."

"Elsthemen will be takin' ye up on that." Merra's smile was strained.

"Indeed." Arlen's eyes hardened, glittering with a fire of battle.

"Arlen, may I also present the Lady Eleshen den'Fenrir, a close personal friend of Temlin's." Ihbram gestured to Eleshen, who stepped forward and gave a Kingsman bow to Arlen.

Arlen's hard blue eyes flicked to Eleshen as his brows rose. "Den'Fenrir? Do you hail from the eastern borderlands?"

A smile lifted Eleshen's lips as her cheeks flushed under the lord's intense scrutiny. "I was raised in Quelsis, actually. My father was Dhepan Eiric den'Fenrir. I'm his eldest."

Arlen's iron gaze flicked over her as his lord's manners dropped, his persona suddenly chilly. "I met Eiric's eldest daughter once, before their family fled to the mountains after the Kingsman Summons. She was a sun-haired beauty with green eyes. You'll find that lying to me is rather *unhealthful*, young woman. So I ask again – who are you?"

Eleshen's lips fell open as she flushed, stammered, panicked. It was Khouren who stepped to her side, and slightly in front of her in a protective stance, one hand resting upon his blade. "Milady Eleshen is who she says she is. She's been through far more than you ever might. She was King-Protectorate Temlin den'Ildrian's true friend, given command of the Kingsmen at the Fortress of Gerrov-Tel, and is a blessing to those who know her. Be careful how you treat her."

Arlen's eyebrow rose, his hard eyes wrathful as if Khouren had personally taken a shit on his boots. Stony with fury, he turned to Ihbram. "Ihbram? Can you vouch for any of this?"

Ihbram coughed, not a little bit of chuckle in it. "Please forgive my nephew. He's a bit – enamored. And his manners are thin. But trust me, Arlen, milady Eleshen is everything she says she is. She has a strange history, one touched by *wyrria*."

Arlen narrowed his eyes, and their intense searching returned to Eleshen. Those piercing blue eyes bored into her for a very long moment, and it was all she could do to not back down from them. But as they held their strange duel, Eleshen felt something flare within her. Some heat and attitude that she'd always had, and she opened her feisty mouth, giving him what-for.

"If you'd like to question me about all the little or notable things about my family and my lineage, then go right ahead," Eleshen sassed the Vicoute, setting her hands to her hips in challenge. "But if you *really* knew either me or my father, then you'd know that neither of us had any tolerance for shit. So *if* you're quite done, I believe we have larger problems, such as what to do about that massive force down there that we've only managed to burn back a fraction of tonight. And if you're a *lord* as you say you are, you'll show your reinforcements some hospitality, in the way one should for the Heir to the Dhepanship of Quelsis and the High General of Elsthemen."

Eleshen's tirade was the lordly equivalent of a smack in the face with a fry-pan. The aging lord blinked, his blue eyes wide, before he laughed, then bent in a deep bow to Eleshen. "Forgive me, milady. I was callous. I can see now that you are who you claim to be. I do recall a very young version of yourself giving me a similar speech when you were only six years old, about how I should protect my neighbors better against Valenghian invaders. Please accept the apologies of one who has lived too long interrogating every shadow."

And suddenly, the memory returned to Eleshen also. Her, just a little thing with a fiery temper and an even more vicious tongue, lashing some tall, handsome lord with bright blue eyes about the situation of their surrounding countryside. "*You* were the lord I berated when I was six?" Eleshen blinked. "Aeon! Forgive me! I—"

"It is nothing," Arlen's lips lifted in a kind smile as he lifted a hand to stop her apology. "You were a spitfire of a girl, and your father and I laughed late into the night about your vicious tongue, a welcome thing in a desperate time, and the true spirit the heir of any Dhepanship should show. Please know that I was sorry to hear of your father's passing in exile. Forgive me for not sending men to your aid, I shall forever regret that. War devoured the eastern reaches, and I was much preoccupied. Your father and I held the border together many a time during the Raids, along with Rakhan Urloel den'Alrahel of Alrashesh, and Vicoute Purloch den'Crassis, back in the day."

Eleshen had nothing to say, finding her self strangely tongue-tied as too many emotions rose, too quickly. Arlen's gaze pierced her, though a deep sadness lingered in his warrior's countenance.

"Come," Arlen smiled, and with a genteel bow, extended his arm to Eleshen. "A tour of the Vault, I believe, is in order. War devours us, but we have had a victory tonight, my friends. The force that Lhaurent den'Alrahel sent to rout the Kingsmen out of Vennet wasn't enough, but you've walked in on their reinforcements, a full eight thousand now. I fear you are here to stay, as further war will be our pastime come dawn. But let us rest tonight and plan for the battles ahead."

The Vicoute Arlen den'Selthir stepped forward, offering Eleshen his arm as if she was already of the station she should have inherited. She accepted it, but her gaze found Khouren. He held a dark look, his jaw set, his eyes piercing the aging lord.

The mood might have remained somber but for High General Merra Alramir. With a hearty laugh, she strode forward, her massive white cat looming over her shoulder. "Piss on bones! Have we not got the most talented warriors the continent has ever seen right here in this very fortress? Let the ghosts of the dead see how we come, in battle and glory before we fall. Come on! Ale fer parched throats!"

Merra moved forward, slapping Khouren on the back as if sensing his unrest. Giving Eleshen a wink as she passed, Merra stepped away to her riders, her great white cat ambling at her heel. With a nod and a courtier's smile, the Vicoute Arlen den'Selthir followed, leading the way into the fortress with Eleshen's fingers clasped lightly upon his arm.

CHAPTER 34 – KHOUREN

The following morning dawned cold and clear, the brisk scent of autumn in the air. Khouren sat upon the edge of the bed in the filigreed bower of stone inside Arlen's main keep, watching Eleshen. How calm she was, her breathing deep and even in sleep, oblivious to his watching. He'd not made love with her after the allies' war-conference the preceding night, only held her with their clothed bodies twined close until her breathing had evened out.

Then stayed awake as the night drowned on – watching her haunting loveliness in the flickering shadows cast by the torches.

Eleshen had accused him with her violet eyes last night, about not telling her the dangers he'd faced inside the citadel, as Ihbram had recounted the tale to Arlen and the rest. He'd not been able to meet her steady look, unused to telling anyone about his activities. Massaging his bitten shoulder in his new charcoal Kingsmen garb rather than his ruined sneak-thief attire, he watched Eleshen's sleeping loveliness. Though his body had healed from the mer-people attack, he was still stiff. Rolling his shoulder out, he glanced out the carven window of their filigreed bower, to see the sky lightening in the east.

Slipping out of bed away from Eleshen's intriguing warmth, Khouren slid from the bower like a wraith. Stepping into the hall of filigreed stone, he watched torches flicker in niches, lighting the lofty dome all around him as water burbled from clever fountains set throughout the massive space. Staircases wound up to vistas through the outer wall, creating a warped feel that twisted Khouren's mind. Filigree was carven into the stone at every turn – fine as lace with curling scripts and tendrils. Ringing the cavernous hall were statues of winged men and women in elegant poses, all carven from towers of rose quartz. Scenes of people at rest – laughing, playing musical instruments, eating a peach. Like an artist's gallery, the domed space soared around Khouren, though it could not uplift his tumultuous heart.

As he passed one statue, Khouren felt the quartz's pleasant heat in the chill dawn. The hall was heated not by fireplaces but by the luminous effigies, curled into private alcoves by filigreed stone dividers that towered up inside the dome. Orbs swirled above, much like the ones that haunted the blue halls of Roushenn, though these were pale pink and rose-gold, swirling with an easy grace down from the latticed vaults.

Khouren moved on, out of the dome that was Arlen's primary command-area, taking a high-arching bridge over to the fortress proper. Turning, he looked upon where he'd egressed from. The dome, an enormous hall of twisted crimson pinnacles, rose beyond the vaulted walkway from a high cloverleaf plaza reached by three arching bridges. Hovering upon that graceful curve as if suspended in the lightening morning, a filigreed wall of stone surrounded the dome like a hedge of vines, set with arched doorways into the air all the way up the curving sides.

Turning, Khouren moved deeper into the massive citadel, thinking again of Eleshen's supposition, that this place had been built by winged people. It was a warren, a labyrinthine beehive. Pinnacle-towers spiraled up all around, sharp as needles in the heavy dawn sky. Staircases wound to lofty balconies and suddenly ended. Vaulted archways opened into thin air. To Khouren, the Albrenni bird-people were a legend, tales passed down through his family line from stories his great-grandfather Leith Alodwine once told. But what if the stories were true – of the winged Albrenni and the massive Giannyk who had fought the Red-Eyed Demon in the greatest and most sundering battle the world had ever known. The Albrenni were said to have been fearsome and accomplished *wyrrics*. Seeing this place, these lofty pinnacles and arcane doorways, Khouren almost believed it.

As he walked on toward the southern wall, Khouren found his mind twisting trying to memorize the layout. It would have been easier to move through the walls rather than navigate all these twists and turns, except that the Vicoute didn't seem to know just exactly who or what Ihbram and Khouren really were – though he seemed to know that Ihbram was long-lived and both the Alodwines had *wyrria*.

In his brooding, Khouren's gaze strayed to a brazier-lit plaza. Keshari riders cared for their cats as Khouren gained the courtyard with the rising dawn – brushing them down, feeding them lard, butting heads. The mood was joyous, keshari fighters cracking lewd jokes of battle and bravado as they went about their early duties. Not a few of the Elsthemi were still embracing with abandon right there in the courtyard on piles of shed furs, filled with the heady triumph of the night before. Others lay in trysts with grinning fortress defenders or Vennet-folk, some of whom staggered under their fierce mounts at the nearest wall.

It was practically a bordello, half-clad couples fucking in every archway Khouren passed. Sounds of ecstasy accompanied the crackle of brazier-flames and the yowls of cats. A colonnaded causeway led to another courtyard with more of the same, but despite the lewd scenery, Khouren found himself at ease as he walked on. Taking a winding staircase up, Khouren sought the highest vantage to clear his churning thoughts. He finally found himself atop the southern wall of the citadel, gazing down upon the river-plain below.

Glancing up at the lightening sky, Khouren shivered in his new charcoal Kingsmen garb, his hood up. From his vantage atop the ramparts, up by the now-silent trebuchets, he took in the valley. It was still filled to the brim, despite how many had perished last night. There was barely any room for the river with all the men, tents, livestock, and sundry moving below, though the Menderians had cleared out of the burned area that Arlen's trebuchets and longbow archers had decimated near the river's bank.

Khouren's head ached, from dire thoughts and the endless battle-conference last night. Maneuvers and feints fluttered through his mind like moths. He didn't have a mind for battle-plans. He was a knife in the night, and would kill whom he had to when the moment came. Until then, planning only made his mind swim like wayward minnows.

"I should warn you to not go about the Vault without one of my Kingsmen as a guide. This fortress has many unexplored dangers still lurking within."

A smooth voice with iron tones cut through Khouren's reverie. He turned, finding the Vicoute Arlen den'Selthir's blue gaze piercing

444

him like the talons of an eagle as the sword-honed lord emerged from the shadows of an arch. He moved toward Khouren as the sun finally crested the eastern ridge and dawn began in truth, tendrils of gold and rose flaring through the clouds high above.

"This fortress is no more dangerous than some places I've haunted," Khouren spoke, wondering if the man had followed him or had simply been here already, watching his trebuchets in the rising dawn.

"Indeed." Arlen stepped forward, approaching the retaining wall and leaning a hip against it, his arms crossed. "Long ago, this place had some sort of *wyrric* charm upon it. Hunters and trappers passed stories of Devil's Mountain from father to son. Until forty years ago, none could even cross between the river's cut. Misfortune occurred to any who dared approach the cliffs. But forty years ago, a party of my Kingsmen hunting nearby were able to not only cross the river, but climb the walls. I rode out to assess the situation immediately, and though we suffered casualties over the years breaking into the Vault, and we've only got a tenth of it functional for our purposes, it's proven its use these past weeks."

"Casualties?" Khouren glanced at Arlen, rubbing at his shoulder.

"*Wyrric* traps and trials," Arlen chuckled darkly, "much like you and your uncle endured yesterday. I lost a lot of good men in those early days. You're rubbing your shoulder like you were damaged far more than Ihbram described in your encounter with the beings in the pools. Perhaps men with strange talents fall into those traps as readily as normal ones do."

"Something like that." Khouren didn't feel like explaining their encounter with the water-wraiths, and ceased rubbing at his stiff injury. Arlen eyed him but didn't press, though Khouren had a feeling the man would, later. Not about the mer-things, but about what and who exactly Khouren was and why he had come here.

"You don't have sentries posted on the northern walls," Khouren settled a hip against the berm, unconsciously mimicking the Vicoute. "Aren't you worried Lhaurent's forces will cross the river and climb up behind you?"

"No." Arlen's visage was stony as his impassive gaze devoured Khouren, trying to figure him out. "They've already tried, and found the same trials. They've given up all avenues other than the south face. I only defend the portion of the Vault we've commandeered, because the rest defends itself." He glanced at Khouren pointedly. "Other than your ingress."

Khouren returned the gaze, not feeling like apologizing for what he was. "You trust my uncle."

"Are uncle and nephew alike?" Arlen watched Khouren carefully.

"No." Khouren said it plainly, letting the Vicoute make his own judgements.

A slow smile crept over Arlen's face, but it was a cold thing. "*Wyrria* doesn't make a man powerful, you know."

"I don't want power."

"I see how you watch her, shadow, how you covet her," Arlen's eyes narrowed in a shrewd warning look. "The lady Eleshen den'Fenrir is not yours. She is Heir to the Dhepanship of Quelsis, a lofty title and a great responsibility. I would counsel you to caution in that arena, whoever you are. She may rise to a great station if this war ever ends, or perhaps because of it. Her father was an excellent Dhepan, and was beloved in his city. Eleshen has the makings of the same."

"She doesn't need your protection." Khouren held the Vicoute's chill gaze, matching him.

"Neither does she need yours."

A ripple of shock went through Khouren's body, and Arlen's chin raised. His keen eyes missed nothing, and Khouren had a feeling the man possessed a *wyrria* he didn't speak of, a way of evaluating the characters of men. He had already judged Khouren's soul and found it lacking. Khouren felt certain the only thing that stopped Arlen's blade from piercing his heart was a long association with Ihbram.

Sunlight blazed over the red minarets, but the sight didn't fill Khouren with bliss. Gazing down at the activity below, all he could feel was a sinking sensation. Another soft step upon the stone made him turn. Ihbram stood there, his mane of russet braids vivid in the golden light. He said not a word as he stepped to Khouren's side, giving a nod to Arlen as he moved forward to stare out over the valley.

"They look so small, don't they?" Ihbram spoke, his tone somber.

"Except there's eight thousand of them." Arlen crossed his arms, gazing down at the sea of soldiers. "At least they've not started re-building their siege towers yet."

"They're doing something else." Khouren nodded at a sprawling tent in the western camp, his keen eyesight evaluating the movement. "Rolling barrels out from that tent there. Putting them on carts and moving them to the river near that catapult, just out of the burned area." He nodded at a small catapult just behind the line of char that didn't look like it could throw anything a hundred feet, much less up and over the fortress' walls.

"Interesting." Arlen scowled. He turned to Ihbram, tapping the fingers of one hand on the wall. Khouren rubbed his shoulder and Ihbram eyed him also, though he said nothing in Arlen's presence.

"Watch their movement," Arlen spoke at last, his gaze pinning Khouren, then Ihbram. "Report to me at the dome the moment anything changes. I've counsel with General Alramir and Vicoute Purloch this morning, otherwise I would stay and watch. But I am afraid I'm needed elsewhere. Gentlemen."

"Vicoute." Ihbram gave a genteel nod as the battle-hardened Kingsman moved off. Once Arlen had jogged down a far flight of stairs, Ihbram turned to Khouren with an appraising eye. "You're still hurt. From our encounter with the water-wraiths."

"It's nothing." Khouren ceased massaging his shoulder, again.

"What did Arlen say to you?" Ihbram's russet brows knit.

"He spoke to me of power, and Eleshen. Warning that *wyrria* doesn't make a man powerful. And warning me to stay away from her."

"That's where he's wrong," Ihbram spoke. "Leith's line is dangerous, but I don't think Arlen understands the truth of it. I haven't told him of our real origins, and he knows nothing of Fentleith. He's never experienced true Khehemni *wyrria*, not like our bloodline. If any one of us starts to break from being exposed to Leith's original power, or what's waking inside Roushenn—" Ihbram's eyes went distant as he hitched a hard sigh.

Khouren caught his uncle's gaze. They still hadn't had a good moment to speak about Temlin's revelation concerning Lhaurent, but it seemed the time had come.

"Do you think it's true, what Temlin found out?" Khouren murmured, watching his uncle. "That Lhaurent isn't actually a Scion of Khehem? That he's not really twinned blood of Alrahel and Khehem?"

Ihbram blinked as if focusing his thoughts before speaking. "I can't rightly say, Khouren. I've never been able to penetrate Lhaurent's mind, and Fentleith told me it was the same for him. I feel Lhaurent's substance, a treacherous thing like eels in black water. And though he has rage within him, it just doesn't feel..."

"Doesn't feel what?" Khouren pressed.

"Conflicted," Ihbram continued. "With every child Fentleith's spawned, or me, even if they only had a hint of the Wolf and Dragon *wyrria*, they've always had a conflicted righteousness about them. Hotheaded? Sure. Warlords? Sometimes. Zealots? Many. But no true Scion of Alodwine ever had such cold calculation as Lhaurent. He's not *conflicted*, Khouren, about anything he does. His mind has the darker feel of Scorpion-*wyrria* to it, like the Kreth-Hakir."

"I defied him," Khouren murmured. "When I carried Lenuria's body away from where he'd tortured her – he ordered me to stop. I didn't. And I didn't burn."

"Why did you not tell me that?" Ihbram gazed at him, his brows lifted.

"I didn't know what it meant at the time." Khouren avoided the topic of the Kreth-Hakir High Priest's silver weaves in his mind, which had guided the entire episode and leant him strength. Both then and later, when he'd watched Lhaurent from atop the ramparts at the public unveiling of his Goldenmarks.

"I wondered how you managed to escape Lhaurent's service without burning into ashes," Ihbram mused, scratching his short russet beard. "But I took grandfather's oath too, Khouren. There was a lot more to it than just swearing ourselves to the twinned bloodline of the true Rennkavi. Did you ever see it in Lhaurent, the red eyes?"

"Sign of the Demon, or sign of the Wolf and Dragon?"

"Both. Either." Ihbram's gaze was intent.

Khouren heaved a sigh. "No. As much as Lhaurent tortured for pleasure, as much as he ruined men and women for the sheer atrociousness of it – no. I never saw his eyes flash red. Either with the Demon's Rise, or with ours."

"Have you ever had the dreams?" Ihbram gazed at Khouren, with the desolation that always lurked beneath his blithe exterior. "Of the Red-Eyed Demon Fentleith described from his nightmares?"

"Never." Khouren shook his head. "But Lenuria had them. She managed to keep the Demon out. She told me that when she began to meditate at the Abbey and examine her own deepest darkness, that the Demon's nightmares began to go away. It didn't want her to know herself. It wanted to use her darkness to break her. But she never let it."

Ihbram leaned against the berm, staring out over the valley. "Would you kill Lhaurent? If it came to it?"

Khouren stared up at the towering red minarets, rising like twisting spires of blood in the dawn. "I would now. Would you kill Fentleith?"

"In a heartbeat." Ihbram's answer was prompt. "I know what he's capable of, Khouren. If he went wrong, if the Demon ever rose inside him… he could tear our continent apart. Especially if *wyrria* ever manages to wake completely in the world."

"Even though Fentleith's our blood?" Khouren murmured, his heart twisting.

"Even so." Ihbram's face was stone. He was silent a long moment, then turned to Khouren. "What about Eleshen? Do you think Eleshen has our *wyrria* now, since her healing?"

"I can't say," Khouren murmured, returning to a thought he'd often had since Eleshen's salvation. "Eleshen can feel *wyrria* now that she's changed, and I can sense something moving inside her, yet to be unleashed. But I haven't seen her do anything uncanny, other than fight like a well-trained swordswoman." Glancing to Ihbram, he picked up their previous thread of conversation. "What about Fentleith? I put his palm on Leith's talisman, Ihbram, it drank his blood. If he has any of Leith's ability running though him now——"

"Lenuria was the strongest at taming Fentleith," Ihbram eyeballed Khouren with a sigh. "She used to give him calming treatments, did you know? Fentleith called her his *blessed daughter*, because of us all, she was the only one who could get through to him during his rages. It was because of her that he became so calm in later years and learned to control that diabolical battle-*wyrria* of his."

"And if he begins to rage again?" Khouren glanced over.

"I don't know." Ihbram answered with a tired rubbing of his hands over his face. "I don't have any answers, Khouren. If Fentleith begins to rage again, he's at risk for raising the Demon's nightmares that plagued him in the past. If I were the Red-Eyed Demon, I would go straight to him – and pummel him until he broke."

"Unless it chooses one of us to haunt this time," Khouren's words were black, a despair taking him that their future would be anything but bloody. The Scions of Alodwine both settled at the wall, silent now, watching the army below. Suddenly, Khouren perked. The barrels he'd been watching were being opened near the line of archers, slouchy bags loaded into the cup of the rickety catapult. The bags were sloppy, shifting around like wheat-flour. But the material they were made of was too fine for a flour-sack, thin and friable.

"What the—?" Ihbram asked, watching it, too.

"Devil's Breath!" Khouren straightened at the wall as live lightning shot through his limbs.

"Fuckstones!" Ihbram glanced to a set of Arlen's banners flying on a pole near one trebuchet. "Wind's coming up steady from the south. They're going to poison us out!"

"Hold on!" Khouren gripped his uncle's wrist, skin to skin. Faster than thought, they were falling through the floor to the level below. Roaring for archers to retreat from the vaulted ingresses, Khouren and Ihbram hurled their face-wraps into the nearest water bucket and swaddled them around their heads, protecting their noses and mouths. Yelling for everyone else to do the same, *now*, they hurtled along the wide causeway that led toward the courtyards and the dome.

Just as they did, they heard the sharp sound of the catapult released. A *whump* hit the side of the arch, white powder exploding through the air. Puffs of deadly powder swirled on the morning wind, rushing down the causeway and blooming up like fungal spores.

Thundering orders through their facecloths to get noses and

mouths wrapped, Khouren and Ihbram streaked past the first courtyard. The Bog-archers in the hall had been spared, swaddled before the first bag hit, but here, it was too late. A number of keshari riders made it to water-buckets and had facecloths in place, but few made it to their mounts in time. Cats began to go down; yowling, gasping, tongues lolling as they strangled. Eyes bulging, they panicked – shredding anything nearby, contorting into impossible shapes. The courtyard roiled with shrieking, rasping death. Even as Khouren stared around in horror, another *whump* hit the fortress wall behind him. Even one sachet of Devil's Breath was enough to kill a keshar-cat – and he'd seen dozens of barrels unloaded this morning.

His heart thundering in terror, Khouren ran on, Ihbram at his side, roaring for wetted facecloths. The surviving keshari riders and Bog-archers raced in every direction, roaring for the same, all of them trying to outpace the deadly bloom of powder upon the crisp morning air. Twin streaks of purpose, Khouren and Ihbram made it to the second courtyard of keshar-cats before the drift of deadly white, shouting for everyone to get to a water-barrel and wet whatever they had. Keshari riders launched into mad action. Faces of man, woman, and beast were wrapped fast, the cats' heads entirely swaddled so they couldn't shake off the wet wrappings.

The second courtyard of cats had been saved, but only just. Khouren's mind was madness as he left Ihbram, streaking through wall after wall in a direct route back to the dome. All he could think of was how porous the walls of the dome were, how many spaces there were between the delicate stone filigree – how exposed Eleshen would be.

His lungs burned as he gained the bridge arching up to the grand dome. His mind was a single point of focus as he raced inside, roaring for people to soak clothing in the fountains and guard their breath. Racing through to the main fountain, he roared at the morning war-council. General Merra, Purloch, Arlen, and the rest jumped quickly to the water, wetting garments and slapping them over noses and mouths.

But Eleshen wasn't there. In a surge of desperation, Khouren raced past. Through the next hall, to the semicircle of filigreed bowers beyond the main vault. He raced to the bower he and Eleshen had taken the evening before, but the bed was empty, the covers thrown back, a half-eaten breakfast upon the stone bedstand.

"Eleshen!" Khouren roared. "*Eleshen!!*"

His mind spun. He couldn't think. His lungs burned from running. His eyes watered as powder blew through the dome, caustic dust making him shed tears. With a hard inhalation, Khouren did the only thing he could think of. Closing his eyes, he focused on Eleshen's smile. On her beauty. On her nature, dark and light, tempestuous and loving. On how she laughed, so suddenly and full. Her scent of violets and rain filled his nose, the feel of her soft skin beneath his fingertips devouring him. In desperation, Khouren opened himself wide, and from his heart a cord of golden flame went lancing away into the morning beyond the dome – east.

With a prayer, Khouren dashed through the filigreed eastern wall to find himself upon a broad balcony. Golden sunlight smote his eyes, the brilliance of the day rising over the forest. And there, to his left, a woman had collapsed to the stone, her sleek black hair puddled around her lean and lovely form. Khouren raced to her, his heart screaming. As he turned Eleshen over, he saw that her lips and eyelids were blue, her violet eyes shot through with red veins as she gasped from asphyxiation.

"*No!*" Khouren knelt over her, hauling Eleshen's spasming body up from the balcony. Tearing his wet face wrap down, he set his lips to hers, elevating her head at the neck and exhaling down her throat again and again. His eyes burned from poison in the wind, tears spilling from his lids as his throat began to close. Torment roared through Khouren, anguish like he hadn't known in a hundred years. As Eleshen spasmed in his lap, dying, Khouren screamed, and something exploded from his being. A concussion of power, it thrust into Eleshen's body. Roaring through her, carrying all of Khouren's love and *wyrria* with it.

He felt something grasp his power from deep within Eleshen's body. Something that felt like it ate Khouren's power alive – feeling all his abilities, sifting through them. It latched on to one, twisting into something that went deep into Khouren's bones. As he spasmed hard, feeling her *wyrria* dig into that energy deep inside him, Eleshen twitched. Gasped. Drew a horrible, rattling breath and began to cough, her eyelids and lips regaining color, fast.

Khouren didn't know what exactly had happened, but some

resonance between his *wyrria* and hers had saved Eleshen. Khouren held her fast, gasping with relief as he wound one end of his wet face wrap over her mouth and nose, the other over his own.

"Khouren?" Eleshen spoke through the wet cloth as she gazed up. Still cradled in his arms, she was so warm, so beautiful, and looked strangely hale, as if she had healed fast via Khouren's own innate ability. Reaching up, she touched his face, his hair, tears shedding from her lovely violet eyes. "You're alive! I thought... when you weren't there this morning, I thought——"

"I'm here." Khouren breathed through his cloth, setting his forehead to hers as grateful tears slipped from his eyelashes. "I'll never leave you again, I swear it."

"Don't swear to me. Just be with me," she murmured, her violet eyes haunting and beautiful.

"Always." Leaning down, Khouren moved their facecloth aside, pressing his kiss to her lips. It was deep, and it held everything his heart wanted to say. Pressing up, Eleshen kissed him back, as the vile white mist dissipated upon the morning breeze.

* * *

In the deep of the night, Khouren woke the moment rain struck the stone of the dome outside. A patter at first, then a deluge, he lay still listening to the steady drumming with Eleshen wrapped in his arms in the solitude of their bower. Pressed close to her naked skin, he breathed her in, smelling rain and violets, and an undertone of mountain spices. His bare body drank her warmth, exhausted and invigorated from their lovemaking earlier.

Nothing moved in the dregs of the night, and Khouren realized it was still an hour or so pre-dawn. The forces of their allies slept deep after such a horrible day. Almost two hundred cats had been lost to the Devil's Breath. Almost a thousand men and women, too – fighters and farmers alike succumbing to the Devil's luck. And though Khouren felt bliss, lying here with his arms wrapped around Eleshen's lean curves and his lips softly kissing her shoulder, his mind knew no rest.

Lhaurent's forces would strike again. And if they did, Khouren might lose her – for good this time.

Khouren hardly knew his own intentions as he shifted away from Eleshen's warmth and out from beneath the covers. A strange fervency gripped him as he slipped naked out of bed, silent as shrouds. He was a wraith in the night as he donned his charcoal Kingsmen gear and weapons harness, his mind moving in a haunted darkness as he raised a new *shouf* over his mouth and nose, and his hood up over his hair.

As if sensing his departure, Eleshen turned over in her sleep and made a peep. Khouren stared down at her for a moment, drinking in her beauty, feeling her again with his body. After their rush of heady lovemaking, they had lain together, all night. Khouren could still feel the softness of her curves in his hands. He could still feel how she arched for him, how she breathed to his rhythm as he moved his fingers over her lovely flesh, stroking her hips, her shoulders, her thigh. Taking her slowly with the softest kisses to her drinkable lips.

Leaning over, Khouren slipped a kiss over those beautiful lips again. They curled in a smile just for him, and Khouren's heart broke to see it. But it was well that she did not wake. Khouren was night itself as he moved through the walls and out of the dome, his mind churning with dark thoughts as he made a straight line toward the southern wall. Stepping through an alcove by the first courtyard, he saw piles of bodies of cat and men alike, waiting for the pyre. Sobbing eased through the night. Eerie and haunting, it spoke to Khouren of what he had to do.

He was a wraith in the shadows as he gained the southern wall. Materializing through the stone, he was about to pass under an open archway and let himself down the rock face, when he suddenly heard voices in the chill night. Slipping into the column of the massive arch, Khouren watched two men approach in the shadowed gloom, one bearing a minuscule lantern in his palm, turned down extremely low. He wasn't surprised to see Arlen, wondering if the Kingsman lord ever slept. But the other man was a stranger, an enormous, brawny fellow with a bald pate positively devoured by crimson tattooing, wearing the classic crimson jerkin of a Red Valor soldier.

Holding his breath and honing his hearing, Khouren paused, listening.

"And you say Delennia's longriders are just northeast of Vennet?" Arlen growled, piercing the big man with his fierce blue gaze in the wan flickering of the small lantern. "How many?"

"We bring four thousand Red Valor cavalry lancers," the tattooed bald man spoke, hushed. "She'll be here by dawn, Arlen. I must get back to the main host. I know our combined forces still do not even your odds, but what reply can I give my mistress?"

"You can very well reply that we'll blaze from this fortress the moment we see her crimson on the horizon, Emeris," Arlen spoke back, somber but fierce. "Delennia's arrival is the best odds we can muster, even if we are still a few thousand short. I will make use of her drive, to the last man or woman standing, you can be sure of that. I still can't imagine how she ever decided to come to my aid, though."

The enormous man chuckled, placing a hand on Arlen's shoulder. "She loves you more than you know, my Lance. She never stopped, even though she's hated you this whole while, also. Grunnach was quite convincing with the gifts he brought, though I hate to admit it."

"So I take it Dherran arrived in one piece?" Arlen's smile was pleased, yet sad.

"He was demon in that throne hall." The big man chuckled again. "You should have seen it. *Wyrria* like one never would have guessed. He reset time. You would have been proud."

"And his trigger?" Arlen's words were so soft, Khouren could hardly hear.

"Your daughter," the big man Emeris spoke solemnly. "She was stabbed by the Vhinesse, through the heart. He reset time, changed that event. Bringing Aelennia down instead."

"Indeed." Arlen's gaze was infinite, and something in it vastly sad. At last, he heaved a breath, his iron-eagle gaze fixing upon Emeris once more. "Return to Delennia. Tell her we'll be ready. And tell her... I'm sorry."

"Tell her that yourself, my Lance." With a secret smile and a nod of his chin so deep it was almost a bow, the big man cracked his knuckles and walked toward the wet ledge, slinging himself over the side by a set of grappling hooks and out of sight. Arlen watched the space where he'd gone, one hand upon his sword. But there was no commotion from the Menderian camp, no sound other than the driving of the rain. With a small smile, his gaze far to the south, Arlen extinguished his lantern, then turned in the darkness and made his way back through the deep halls.

Khouren found his heart beating hard inside his pillar, his mind whirling. They had reinforcements coming. He didn't know how or why, and most of the conversation had been Ghreccan to him, but it was an advantage he was not about to waste. Moving silently to the ledge, Khouren found rough handholds and eased himself down the narrow ledges, moving carefully on the slick stone. Before long, he was down at the river's rim, slipping into the water like ghosts through sepulchers as the rain pelted down around him.

With silent stealth, Khouren emerged upon the south side of the river. Making sure his hood and face wrap were in place, he was a specter in the steady rain. Just a shadow moving over the muddy ground in the darkness, not a squelch to his footfalls. His heart blew with cold readiness as he paced west, to the oiled canvas tent he'd noted earlier in the day. Sentries huddled around spitting braziers as he passed, miserable. They didn't see him. Khouren's own darkness was ever his friend, and no man wanted to see true dark on a night like this. Khouren couldn't blame them. These men were just doing what they were told.

Soldiers convinced to give their all for Lhaurent – just as Khouren had once done.

But he was finished with that now. As he slit the throat of a sentry with a fast headlock and a quick strike, his mind was already upon his objective. A second sentry was stabbed through his throat before he could shout, eyes bulging as Khouren eased him down to the splattered mud.

"Be thankful you died this way, rather than what's to come," Khouren blessed him as the man's soul left his eyes.

Ducking under the oiled canvas tent-flap, Khouren surveyed his mark. It was utterly dark inside, rain spattering hard upon the covering above. Shadows upon shadows devoured the interior, no one so idiotic as to light a torch or a lantern in this tent, if Khouren guessed rightly what it contained. Moving through the wooden shelving and racks, Khouren smiled beneath his wet facewrap, knowing his guess had been right. All those barrels with their pretty sachets of powder. All those hundreds of palm-sized porcelain pots, lined up in neat rows. Khouren was darkness itself as he stole back outside. He was a knife in the night as he slit the throat of a sentry moving by with a torch. He was the thief of all thieves as he stole back into the tent with the torch casting a guttering light – as he opened a row of flammable ceramic jars.

Moving his torch over them all, setting each and every one of them alight.

The green-gold fire of Pythian resin surged to life, roaring with an eagerness to destroy; to maim and ruin. Khouren watched it spring to life as a vicious light took his eyes. Taking up two of those flaming pots in his gloved hands, he went to the tent-flap – hurling them out into the night. Fire exploded in a group of tents nearby. Screams rose. Khouren went back and seized another two, hurling those after the first. Another burst came from where he'd thrown the second volley. Moving with strong strides, he seized more burning pots of Pythian resin and hurled them as far as he could. Horses screamed at the picket lines. Men were up now, dashing through the driving rain. Muddled in a melee as fire exploded to life all around for the second time in as many nights.

But far worse.

The peal of hammers striking bronze bells came, as the tent containing the poisons and resins caught fire from the burning splatter. Twisting emerald flames erupted all around Khouren, pots blazing in every direction. Still, Khouren seized burning ceramic urns and hurled them. His gloves had burned away. His hands caught fire, searing with pain. But Khouren's mind was lost to the specter of the flames, bright and terrible. As his skin seared and his clothing charred away, his weapons harness snapping off, his hair searing up to his scalp with the blistering scent of burning animal, he smiled a ghastly smile. He was death. He was glory. He was the wraith in the darkness, but now he was a burning torch as fire consumed him, a beacon of destruction in the night.

The tent disintegrated from exploding pots of resin. Khouren hurled pots in every direction, volley after volley. Into a smithy, racks of swords and armor consumed by spring-gold flame. Into a picket-line of horses, causing them to rear and scream, scattering as their tethers and withers were eaten away by caustic resin. Into groups of soldiers shielding their faces from the flames as Khouren roared out to the thunder of fire and rain. Roaring out all his pain, all his passion. All his rage, all his glory. All his love and all his hate.

All the power of his endlessly conflicted *wyrria*.

With a burst of energy, Khouren's *wyrria* overtook the fire. As fast as his skin charred, it was replaced. Burning resin ate through sinew and bone and Khouren's own *wyrria* replaced everything just as fast. Devil's Breath charred upon the blaze, but his lungs heaved like bellows, replenishing his tissues as they were poisoned. Sinew surged to life, muscle replenished. New skin flowed, spitting resin out of his body in spatters of flame that arced into the rain. Flowing down around his shoulders, his hair was restored even as it burned again.

The Menderian camp twisted with green fire. A volley of arrows was launched, but Khouren's *wyrria* was untouchable now within the flames of his majesty. As fire and sinew flowed, the arrows passed through him, thudding into burning canvas and timber behind.

Khouren's smile was darkness, his eyes opal annihilation as he walked out from the burning, men cowering back from him all around.

CHAPTER 35 – DHERRAN

A sickle moon shone high above the Vhinesse Delennia Oblitenne's forces, wan in the night. Its silver glow cast the fields outside Vennet in an odd hush, made even more strange by the humps of blackened char to either side of the road. A swath of destruction had been revealed by the pre-dawn moon for the last five leagues, as Delennia's forces marched from Quelsis to Vennet. Blackened farmsteads punctuated horrific scenes of eviscerated cows and sheep, livestock left to rot piled in the moonlit ditches.

Dherran shivered upon his roan gelding, the ten-abreast column of four thousand Red Valor cavalry lancers progressing at a brisk walk along the rocky highway. Many of Delennia's company had secured a cloth over their noses and mouths at the stench, and Dherran, Grump, Delennia, and Khenria had done the same at the lead of the army. Coming through this decimation at night, having pushed their march out of Velkennish this past week, Delennia had sent her man Emeris on ahead to find out if their path to Arlen's fortress was clear, or if they would face an army on the road. And though they had come across no one, the road smelled like an abattoir, char and bile and rotting things wafting to Dherran's tongue with every breath.

Dherran glanced over from his roan gelding. Delennia sat tall upon a stallion so white it shone silver beneath the high moon, matching her long silver braid and an ornate Valenghian war-saddle. The new Vhinesse's gaze was grim as she gazed over the silvered landscape. Dherran saw Khenria shiver in her buckled crimson leathers, Red Valor battle-gear that suited her well. They were all clad like Red Valor, except Delennia, who wore chevron-slashed crimson and black leathers with blackened steel fittings. An older style of Valenghian battle-gear, and one that bore the crest of her house burned into the leather chest-plate. Apparently, it was the gear Delennia had worn during her first coup against the Vhinesse her sister.

It made for an interesting statement.

Delennia's coronation as the new Vine of Valenghia had been performed with the appropriate pomp the previous week. Though the populace had been stunned at the sudden coup, there had been no riots. Apparently, changes in Valenghian rulership were often bloody, rivalries between the Royal Houses a vicious thing, and dignitaries and commoners alike had taken it in stride.

The Red Valor had bowed to Delennia as their new commander and head of the Valenghian Lothren, led by Merkhenos before he spirited Elohl and Fenton away to the war-front. Grump had disappeared for a number of nights, returning to the palace exhausted and filthy, his charcoal assassin-gear crispy with the dried blood of other men. Dherran and Khenria had asked no questions, and Grump had supplied no explanation, only insinuating that Delennia's naysayers had been permanently removed from the Valenghian Lothren. For her part, Delennia had made provisions for the security of her palace and nation, including trying to have the Alranstone in the bottom of the White Palace toppled to prevent Lhaurent's movements. When that had failed, she'd set a guard of a hundred Red Valor on that passage – with orders to kill anyone who came through on sight.

All in all, the coup had gone rather well. But now, traveling the long dark road from Quelsis to Vennet, it wasn't hard to see why Delennia was perturbed. Though Lhaurent's forces to subdue Arlen had been Menderian, they had been coerced into razing their homeland.

"Well, the Scorpions have been busy." As if reading Dherran's mind, Grump gave a harrumph to Dherran's left, where he rode upon a short grey gelding beneath the sickled moon.

"This is their doing?" Dherran glanced to him as they walked the horses past a pile of black flesh that might once have been a sheep.

"Indeed, Dherran," Grump waved a hand at a burnt-out farmstead huddling in a charred grove of matchsticks to the left of the road. "This is Kreth-Hakir work – encouraging Menderian soldiers to commit atrocity against their own people for Lhaurent! But what have we not seen that one would expect in such a cruel invasion?"

Dherran glanced around, noting downed sing-leaf and alder trees where a farmstead had torched the brush nearby. It was a wonder that the whole forest hadn't caught flame, dry as it was. But heavy black thunderheads sat firm above the trees to the west, the brisk smell of rain wafting upon the midnight air despite the stench. "It's pretty grisly, Grump. I think we've seen it all."

"No bodies." Khenria spoke up, riding upon Dherran's flank. "Lhaurent sends a message, that any who oppose him will lose their lands and livelihood with all this decimation. But we've not seen human bodies."

Delennia glanced over to Khenria, and Dherran thought he saw the hint of a smile lift her lips before they set in a hard line once more.

"Which means," Grump continued, waving a hand to indicate the charred farms on either side of the road, "that Arlen had a very good warning system. He knew exactly when Lhaurent's forces marched from Quelsis and how fast. Arlen got his people and his surrounding noble allies and their retainers out ahead of Lhaurent's army, to his contingency location."

Rounding a line of cyprus trees, they saw a blockade of dead cows stretching across the road. Delennia flicked her fingers to one of her captains and he moved his horse forward, summoning riders from the front of the column. The blockade was set upon, Valormen hitching ropes to rotting legs or horns, then to their saddles. Whipping their horses lightly, they began to drag the carcasses into the ditch, which the trained war-horses did with only minimal tossing of their heads.

"Why didn't Lhaurent's forces just take the livestock?" Khenria asked as they waited.

"Vicious statements spread fear." Delennia's answer was cold in the slanting moonlight, the roiling clouds at the edge of the forest beginning to swallow the night. "Lhaurent is no fool. He wanted the Vhinesse's army to see this if she pushed into the interior. An invading army will become skittish if they see that a king is willing to ruin his own lands to deal with insurgents. What more would he do to invaders? My sister would have thought twice about that. She might have turned around, fearing a trap."

"And you?" Dherran directed his question at the Vhinesse.

"I know it's a trap." Delennia returned his gaze squarely, her pale eyes shining under the disappearing moonlight. "We march a force of four thousand upon a force of at least eight thousand. My Valormen are elite, but it's still a numbers game, one that is *not* in our favor. Lhaurent knew my sister had committed the bulk of her strength at the Aphellian Way. And clearly, he has forces in reserve from their little *arrangement*, enough to siege Arlen into the ground if he so wishes."

The road was clearing, as Red Valor lancers in the column behind Dherran idled upon their horses, checking swords, reins, and sundry. Dherran saw how they passed the time just like Alrashemni Kingsmen – never a lost moment to prepare for an upcoming battle. Red Valor from the Stone Valley and Long Valley had been co-opted into this push, in addition to Valormen from Velkennish. The upcoming engagement would use Khehemni to liberate Alrashemni, the Red Valor predominantly Khehemni in their ranks. Most didn't know or care about Khehemni-Alrashemni feuding, raised in their cities to become elite fighters for the crown.

But those that did, had given Delennia fierce looks when she had addressed them at the Stone Valley five days ago. And yet, they had organized under her will. Whether it was simply for a chance to invade Alrou-Mendera, or because they were consummately loyal to their Living Vine, Dherran couldn't say. But he'd felt Delennia spread her powers during that speech, soothing unrest. She had Oblitenne *wyrria*, and she'd used it to get the Red Valor behind her.

"So we march, knowing Lhaurent has a good chance of besting us? Why would you take such a gamble?" Khenria bristled, staring at her birth mother. She'd been doing that a lot of late, sizing her mother up, challenging Delennia, her gaze hot and hawkish.

Delennia stared her daughter down. It wasn't a mean gaze, simply tough. Until at last Dherran saw Khenria wilt under her birth mother's stare. The woman was formidable, and Khenria fidgeted in her saddle.

"I march," Delennia spoke firmly, "because having a tyrant-king for a neighbor is not healthy. If he can do this," she gestured to the road, cobbles smeared with filth as rotting flesh was hauled away, "to his own people, then what will he do to mine? To *ours*, my daughter. And when a king is a tyrant, no matter how convincing his *wyrria*, eventually he will lose his people's support. And that is where we win – by picking them up when he lets them fall. By providing help until they rise up and rip out the throat of the master who whips them like a broken cur."

The road was finally clear. The captain and the rest of Delennia's soldiers returned to the moon-shadowed line, having cut the putrid ends of their ropes and left them to lie with the corpses now seething a bloated odor from either ditch. But Delennia held the line, not motioning them forward yet, staring her daughter down beneath the cold silver of the moon. Impressing upon her daughter, the Vhiniti and heir to the throne, a lesson.

"Tell me you understand," Delennia spoke quietly to her daughter.

"I understand," Khenria murmured upon the cool wind, though she bristled.

"I do not expect you to call me mother," Delennia spoke, low enough for only Khenria, "but like your father Arlen, I do expect you to absorb what we know. To prepare to someday lead in our stead, Khenria. If I die tonight, what does that mean for you? Think on it, and decide what it is you would do, should Lhaurent win this battle. If I should fall, or your father, and all the protectorates you hold dear."

Khenria was silent a long moment, absorbing her mother's words. The column shifted behind her, eager to get going, but waiting for their lead. At last, Khenria spoke again, her brows knit. "Do you think you will die tonight?"

"It matters not to me," Delennia's gaze pierced Khenria like a lioness' claws. "But it matters to you, because you have let others hold you up. The time for that is past. Now you hold *yourself* up. Enter your own becoming, before we continue a step further. Because if you know who you are, when everyone else falls down around you – you will stand tall. You will fight for what *you* believe in. And *that* is the only way to triumph."

The army was silent behind them. The road was silent ahead. Khenria was deeply silent. Her gaze lingered upon the ditch at the side of the road, now filled with bloated black shapes. Khenria squared her narrow shoulders, filling out her dark battle-leathers, sitting straight in the saddle. Reining her horse in, she seemed to look down on her mother the Vhinesse beneath the disappearing moon, as if she'd somehow grown tall.

"Ride on!"

Khenria's bark was piercing in the midnight chill, as she turned to command the column. As one, four thousand Red Valor heeled their horses, stepping forward upon the stony road. As the moon disappeared behind the clouds, Khenria clucked her horse into the lead next to the Vhinesse – a princess of Valenghia beside her Vine, leading an army to war.

The column was deathly silent as they progressed, the smell of dawn rising in the air as the sky at last began to change. All around, the road was subtly visible in the lifting light, a white stripe in the deep grey. But as they rounded a line of felled cyprus trees that had been piled in a barricade, that barricade subsequently dismantled for Lhaurent's army to pass through, Dherran saw the vast ruin of Vennet.

It was hardly recognizable. Everything had been razed. Every building loomed in the pre-dawn, stove-in, rooflines collapsed, foundations blackened. The scent of char was thick and heavy despite the slurried mud of recent rain the horses trod through. As a thin drizzle began to claim the air, then deepened into a steady downpour, the column moved forward through the decimated town. Here and there lay a body, and more livestock, charred. The trail toward Arlen's contingency location was not hard to find. Just past Vennet's blackened plaza, a swath of destruction headed off down a cart-track and deep into the forest to the west.

Delennia pointed and Khenria nodded. Without any chatter in the greying light, they led the column toward the broken swath of an army's passage. Lhaurent's forces had been as callous with the land here as they'd been with Vennet, all the underbrush hacked down and trampled in a swath a hundred feet wide. Bits of detritus had been left behind. A broken wagon-wheel; a set of busted leather straps for a baldric. Another dead cow, this one butchered for its meat, the bones and hooves left behind. A worn-out pair of boots.

Delennia's forces rode the trail in a tense silence. They'd only traveled into the forest an hour when a big black horse came galloping toward them out of the deep shadows, Emeris' strong mount returning with its master riding tall upon it in his Red Valor gear. To the north, Dherran could see a glow on the horizon, red like fire. The scent of char filled the wind despite the steady rain, and as Emeris hauled his stallion to a stop, his words confirmed everything Dherran already knew.

"Conflict ahead, my Vine!" Emeris gasped. "The Vicoute's forces are safe in the Vault, but someone's made a push from the fortress into the river-valley. It's chaos. Something's blasted up a good half of the Menderian camp, but there's still a hell of a lot of them left. Our approach is clear, though. I've alerted Arlen to our position and he promises his men will be ready to push when we arrive. With this chaos happening in the Menderian camp, we should be able to pin Lhaurent's forces between us and Arlen, drive hard with the cavalry."

The man spoke with utter confidence about the location of the battle, and Dherran raised his brows at that. Delennia was likewise unfazed, and Dherran surmised that they had been here before and knew the terrain.

"Thank you, Emeris," Delennia spoke, and her liege-man nodded. The slick night had lightened, the black-on-black succumbing to a grisly dawn of grey shadows with crimson fire illuminating the underbelly of the clouds directly north. Delennia was motionless upon her mount for a moment, deep in thought. At last, she gave a sharp whistle through her teeth. Her Red Valor captains moved their horses up into a huddle around her, Dherran, Khenria, Grump, and Emeris among them.

"This will be a straight drive," Delennia spoke succinctly. "Emeris, lead your lancers up the western flank and take out any trebuchets up on the ridge——"

"Forgive me, Vhinesse," Emeris interrupted, wiping rain from his crimson-tattooed pate. "But the catapults on the western and eastern ridges have already been taken out. Keshari-work."

Delennia's eyebrows rose and she glanced to Grump. "You didn't tell me Arlen had keshari."

"I didn't know he did." Grump looked nearly as astounded as Delennia before his brows pinched in a thoughtful frown. "But it's to our distinct advantage. Keshar-cats and Elsthemi riders will fight harder when inspired by our drive."

"Indeed." Delennia took in the group again. "Emeris, hem in the western flank, then. Captain Rhoric, take the right. My drive will go up the middle, with you three," her gaze pinned Dherran, Grump, and Khenria. "No one breaks the line. We push as a group and fill in any gaps from fallen cavalry. I will have this tight and coordinated, gentlemen. We are the anvil, and Arlen is the hammer. He'll know what to do once we arrive. Our goal is *surrender* for the Menderian forces. Captain Thorvel, have your archers target any Kreth-Hakir you see. They are to be taken out at all costs. Gentlemen. Prepare your companies for battle."

Delennia's captains heeled their horses with a salute of two fingers to their brow and trotted back to their companies, relaying orders. Emeris glowered at no one in particular as he checked his weapons. Dherran did the same, though it was going to be tricky fighting in the driving rain and bloody slurry that was sure have engulfed the camp already from whatever chaos was occurring.

They marched forward as a unit, companies organized to the right and left. The trees soon opened out into a broad river-valley seething with fire and uproar. No one was watching their rear. Dherran had been in battle numerous times, but had never seen anything like this. He sat tall upon his horse, seeing a tight valley surrounded by ridge-cliffs. Bounded by a river to the north stood the most incredible fortress he'd ever seen. Stark red in the grey morning, it looked like pinnacles of blood piercing the sky. Like massive talons ripped through the clouds, it was more than a fortress, this citadel of vaulted arches and impossible height.

And before it, hemmed-in upon river-plain to the west, was chaos. Swaths of land had been scorched black, tents and wains afire and blistered with holes. An acrid scent seared the morning wind, bitter with the tang of blood and death. As they approached, they saw a mass of keshar-cats lining up at the archways of the fortress, wooden ramps being winched down to splash into the flooding river below as lines of archers with enormous silver-white warbows lined up on the heights before a row of trebuchets.

As promised, Arlen's fighters were ready for them.

Delennia's cavalry were formed. Lines were ready, swords were out, her Red Valor eager in their stirrups as the dawn lifted in the stark grey morning. Khenria snarled with weapons bared, Grump the same. New alarms were rising in the Menderian camp, the harried clangs of bronze bells smiting the chaos as Dherran drew his sword from over his shoulder and blew out a steady breath, his ears ringing with rage and a shudder thrumming through his body.

"*Charge!*"

Delennia's roar was lost to the thunder of hoofbeats, even as a ringing blast came from an Elsthemi war-horn at the fortress. Dherran was at the front of the line, his sword already swiping down as the Red Valor cavalry galloped into the Menderian forces, hamming them hard. Horses reared and kicked as Red Valor stabbed with their silver lances, their precise Valenghian battle-maneuvers cracking skulls and spines while keshar-cats flowed down from the fortress into the river to pound the northern camp.

Somewhere through his red rage Dherran saw Grump and Khenria holding their own, fire surging up Khenria's blade, as Delennia fought like a blistering star in the bleak dawn at her daughter's side.

And a vicious smile lifted Dherran's lips, as soldiers cowered back before his raging sword.

CHAPTER 36 – ELESHEN

Eleshen woke just before dawn to find the Vault a beehive of activity.
She sat up in bed, blinking awake to noise and bustle. Glancing
through the filigree of her bower to the hall beyond, she clutched the
blanket to her bare chest. Through the partition, she could see hard-
eyed Bog-archers in moss garb readying baskets of arrows. Keshari
riders in fur and leather strode through, cinching on ancient armor
as they thrust swords home over their shoulders – many of them
now without cats, but not without ferocity.

Kingsmen in their Greys strode past, checking longknives.
Ihbram approached, his russet mane pulled back, his green eyes
shining with battle-fever as he ducked beneath the woven door-cover,
carrying a plate of food. Eleshen could tell by the low braziers and
chill air that it was barely dawn, rain drumming a steady
counterpoint upon the dome to accompany the bustle.

"What's going on?" Hauling on her silken undergarments and
battle-halter without caring about Ihbram's presence, Eleshen began
to eat hastily from the plate; roasted goat, fresh apples, and a cold
peach chutney with a sharp white cheese.

"We're staging an attack." Ihbram sat on the bed, stretching
out his legs and crossing his boots as he watched her eat. "Within the
half-hour. Arlen said to let those affected by Devil's Breath recover as
long as possible before we saddle up."

"Didn't most of the cats die?" Eleshen spoke through
mouthfuls, ravenous after her poisoning.

"Just a turn of phrase," Ihbram smiled ruefully. "Your cat
made it, actually. Someone got a rag over her nose and mouth in
time, and someone also saved mine. Khouren's cat perished, but he
can ride behind you." Ihbram frowned, glancing around the filigreed
bower. "Where is he, by the way? I've looked all over, but I thought
he was with you."

"I thought he was with you." Eleshen slurped down the peach

chutney. "He was with me last night. Anyway, why attack now? Aren't there seven thousand soldiers out there?"

"There's been some sort of accident in the Menderian camp," Ihbram's eyes shone with violent satisfaction. "They managed to catch their stores of Pythian Resin and Devil's Breath on fire somehow. It's still going on, and their camp is in chaos – everything's going up in flames."

"How many have been killed?" Eleshen set her meat down.

"Arlen estimates at least a sixth of their forces so far, mostly their support-tents and horse lines on the western flank. But he received word early this morning that we have Valenghian Longriders on the way to support us. Red Valor cavalry lancers, some four thousand of them. We'll never have a better opportunity to hit the Menderians, and General Merra and Arlen are mustering all hands. Hurry and get dressed."

Eleshen was already tumbling out of bed, hauling on her Kingsman Greys over her silken undergarments. Smooth as doeskin, the lightweight leather cinched close to her lean curves. Flipping her hair out of the way of the high collar, she plaited her sable locks into a long braid and pinned it up tight. Buckling on her weapons-harness, she hauled the sword out from over her shoulder and checked the edge with the back of her thumbnail. Thrusting the sword home, she checked her longknives. They were sharp – honed to perfection and ready for throats.

"Fast as Lenuria ever was." Ihbram murmured with a mystic smile upon his lips. "You've got a fair amount of her traits in you with this new body. Khouren and I have both noticed it."

Eleshen was about to reply, when her dream from the night came roaring back. In it, she had seen Khouren, burning with fire, his blue-black hair a wreath of flames. His body had been a living torch, regenerating beneath a searing resin as fast as it could eat him away. He'd been hallowed by fire – a beast of darkness and power. But that darkness had held screams. Soldiers running; burning tents. The horror of countless lives being taken rang in Eleshen's ears. And yet, it stirred her, something fierce inside her resonating with the destruction.

"Are you alright?" Ihbram cocked his head, watching her.

"It's nothing. Just fever-dreams from the Devil's Breath."

"Can you fight?" Ihbram moved closer, smoothing back a strand of her hair with his fingertips, his eyes concerned.

"I'm fine." Eleshen slapped his hand away, peeved. "Let's go."

"As milady wishes." Ihbram's smile was renegade, but also somber. With a crisp military bow and a clack of bootheels, Ihbram led the way. They strode fast through the commotion. Joining the bustle, they moved from the dome into the lifting grey dawn and over the vaulted bridge to the fortress. Torches burned in brackets, illuminating the fierce tension of riders preparing the surviving cats in the courtyards. Bog-archers jogged past with baskets of arrows and their hardy silver-white longbows.

Threading through the commotion and finding their cats already prepared, Eleshen and Ihbram took their reins and led their cats toward the main archways at the southern side of the fortress. Gazing down upon the valley, Eleshen saw that fires raged below, fully a third of the camp burning with green-gold flames twisting up into the dawn and devouring the western flank. Screams of men and horses could be heard everywhere. Whatever accident that had occurred had taken the destruction far. Splattering Pythian resin had devoured holes in men and beasts, tents and barrels, wains and winches. The western side of the Menderian camp looked less like an army and more like a burning tar-vat. A red eagerness for battle rose in Eleshen, as Ihbram moved to her side with his big roan cat.

"We survive today," Ihbram spoke as he mounted up. "Stay by me. I always did fight better with a woman of spit and vinegar nearby."

Eleshen butted heads briefly with her dappled grey Moonshadow, then slung up into the saddle. "*I'm* surviving. You have to make that decision for yourself. Will Khouren find us?"

Ihbram gave a laugh, his eyes alight in the burning grey dawn. "I think he'd find you at the end of the world, milady. He'll find us. Trust me."

Their interlude was interrupted by a pouring of moss-clad men and women out from the fortress and up to the vaulted egresses above. Purloch's archers lined up in their moss-green garb at every archway, ready with their enormous white warbows. Keshari forces swarmed the causeway behind Eleshen and Ihbram, many of the cats carrying double riders. Ramps were lowered from huge winches

470

rolled into the archways, settling into the river with a deep splash in the driving rain, lodged in the boulders of the rising water below. Wide enough for five keshar-cats to storm down, niches in the sides of the ramps accommodated the Kingsmen and other foot-soldiers – who now set hands to long ropes with grapples, setting the grapples and heaving the ropes over the edge.

Vicoute Arlen den'Selthir strode to the front near Eleshen's arch, clad in Kingsmen Greys without a scrap of heavy armor to weigh him down. With a glance at General Merra upon her snow-white cat, who had ambled up to the front of the keshari, he evaluated their press of hide extending down the long thoroughfare behind Eleshen and Ihbram. Across the way, Menderians rushed to the river – pikes at the front with archers and swordsmen behind, desperately trying to form up in time to meet the charge they could see coming from the citadel.

Looking out over the Menderian camp, Arlen's steel-blue eyes narrowed. Following his intensity, Eleshen looked to the far south of the valley, to the treeline. And there, she saw a line of cavalry push through the trees, a solid wall of horse and men in crimson, their drawing of cold steel shining in the morning's grey light. As they formed up, horses prancing eagerly as bronze bells pealed with frantic urgency in the Menderian camp, Arlen's lips twisted up into a cold, immensely pleased smile.

"*To war!!*" Arlen roared down over the citadel's edge.

A tremendous roar went up, as General Merra thundered out three sharp blasts from her battle-horn. Like liquid energy, the keshari forces went pouring down the ramps from the fortress. Led by a roar from Merra's great white cat, Eleshen's cat was in motion, Ihbram on her flank. Behind them, Kingsmen flooded down their ropes into the shallow river. Soon down with a splash into the water, Eleshen's cat waded fast across through the swift current.

Eleshen's sword was out as they gained the far side of the river, clashing into the melee. The keshar-cats were vicious, destroying pikemen and archers quickly. Eleshen and Ihbram dashed in, pressing hard to create space upon the river's bank for the swordsmen on foot behind. Under an arching volley of arrows, Arlen's and the Abbey's Kingsmen rushed to battle behind them, preceded by fang and muscle that barreled into the Menderian lines and sent them scattering like mice.

Eleshen slashed and pivoted on her cat, whirling and roaring as men came at her on foot and horse. The Menderian pikemen had broken to the keshari's charge, and now it was a melee, with no time to coordinate their attack, especially with the rear of the camp getting hammered by the Valenghian cavalry. A battle-grin slit Eleshen's face as blood spattered her. It was not she who was afraid as she sliced her sword with a roar and barreled into a forming line of Menderians. It was they whose eyes showed fear.

Blood and battle filled Eleshen. Her dappled grey cat was a menace in the burning grey morning, biting heads, raking horses, barreling into foot soldiers. Atop it, Eleshen moved like the breath of death, fast as darkwater's flow. Cutting, parrying, slipping, striking. Her blood boiled with death; her body screamed for it. Blood washed her as a throat opened to her blade, the hot metallic taste filling her mouth as she struck again, roaring into the faces of her enemies.

Menderian soldiers began to scramble back in droves, breaking their line at the river's edge, cats and keshari riders and knots of accomplished Kingsmen hammering them back. Eleshen took a shallow slash upon her shoulder, but spun her dappled cat in fast, slicing up under her adversary's armpit. Another took his place, and Eleshen stabbed him through the eye with her longknife, then kicked him in the face with her boot.

Eleshen's spirit soared, a vicious energy taking her as she fought. Blissful, her body flowed with her breath through cut after cut. Ihbram fought upon his big roan cat to her right. Like they had been born to battle together, they kept a tight formation that left room for each to pivot as bodies piled up around them. Eleshen and Ihbram pushed their cats to a more open area, taking on a cadre of Menderian cavalry lancers.

Suddenly, Eleshen saw Rhennon's cat go down from the strike of a Menderian lance, a volley of arrows turned upon General Merra beside him. Merra batted them away with her polearm, but two arrows struck deep into Snowscythe's hindquarters. The great cat gave a wicked roar, its hindleg buckling, spilling Merra down into the battle. Rhennon and General Merra were trapped as a burning catapult collapsed around them. Hemmed in by fire and enemies, they fought in a quick dance of brutality, while Merra's cat yowled and swiped, pacing to find a way through the fire.

Eleshen had a moment to see Rhennon and Merra move, deadly with Elsthemi grace, before she shouted at Ihbram and reared her cat in with a roar. In one massive pounce, her cat and Ihbram's leapt the burning debris, barreling into the soldiers that assailed Rhennon and General Merra. Smashing them, mauling them, seizing them and hurling them into the splattering flames. Merra's great cat saw the breach and leaped in also, striking, biting and mauling in a dance of pure hell despite its injury.

Eleshen fought with sword and longknife, standing in her stirrups, Ihbram causing havoc beside her. She saw her battle-madness reflected in General Merra's eyes as Merra vaulted up to the saddle of her cat, Rhennon fast up behind Ihbram. Eleshen's cat mauled one last man with a screaming hiss then turned, leaping them back across the flames, Ihbram's cat and the determined Snowscythe leaping behind them.

Heavy rain-clouds bruised the eastern sky, when an explosion suddenly rocked Eleshen. She realized with a jolt that the rescue of General Merra and Rhennon had put them too near the western ridge, and fire now surrounded them on three sides. A flare of gold-green flames shot up from an armory-tent, churning the grey morning as twisted lumps of shields and horseshoes hurtled past. Eleshen ducked, moving her cat into a tight spin to gut a foe behind her – when a figure walked out of the burning debris.

Like a mirage of Halsos' Hells, it came, writhing and shifting as it melted and formed and melted again. It was a man, but it was not – twisting with fire like some demonic beast. Screams of terror sounded nearby; the foes Eleshen fought retreated. Her dappled grey cat gave a vicious hiss, arching so hard that it shed Eleshen from the saddle, before it streaked off. Ihbram's cat did the same, fearing this blazing effigy far more than any battle the keshar-cats had ever faced. As Rhennon vaulted up to the back of the snarling Snowscythe with Merra, her cat also backing off quickly, the burning thing approached. Eleshen and Ihbram were left alone as the cats panicked – throwing up an arm against the scorching hell and readying weapons.

And yet. Peering through her fingers, Eleshen cut the searing light to see that the demon of gold-green fire was a man. Moving toward them, he heaved exploding pots of flame out into the camp with tremendous throws, splattering a yet-intact wain and a mess tent. And in his lean height and sinewed muscles, burning and melting, Eleshen saw a miraculous horror. Flesh knitting even as it sloughed away, muscles tightening even as they were eaten by the fire, hair growing into a river of blue-black curls even as it singed back to the scalp.

Opal grey eyes piercing from the flames, wraithlike, even as they boiled from the heat.

"Khouren!" Eleshen's whisper was nothing upon her lips, and yet, he heard. Ears melting and sloughing only to be replaced, the creature arrived before her. The demon of flame stared at her with longing in his scalding eyes, and rasped three words through his charred and blistered throat.

"I love you."

A Menderian soldier with more courage than most ran up with a roar, his blade swinging for Khouren's fiery head. Eleshen dispatched him, driving her blade through his throat and letting him fall in Khouren's flames, as Ihbram held off a party that rushed them nearby. But she couldn't take her eyes from this man before her, this creature who burned through his own hell and the driving rain as the morning lifted in grey fury. He was both horror and magnificence, and as much as it shocked Eleshen, it also spurred her. Here was a man who stayed in all adversity. Here was a man who would stand by her, through all of Halsos' Burnfire.

Here was a man who would become a demon, just to protect her – to be hers.

"I love you, too." The words choked from Eleshen's throat, the scorch of Khouren's flesh billowing into her lungs. And yet, as the words left her, Eleshen knew their truth.

A smile rose upon Khouren's blistering lips. As if fed by her words, his opal eyes burned gold in the grey light. With a mighty roar, Khouren rushed forward, charging the net of soldiers that tried to hem them in. He was fire in the morning. He was a beast of death to their enemies, and Eleshen glorified in it for one endless moment before spinning into the carnage. Shoulder-to-shoulder with Ihbram, Eleshen saw Khouren reborn as his flames finally put themselves out from the swiftness of his healing. As they spun and stabbed, cut and swiped in a trio of death, Eleshen saw that Khouren's hair was glossy, reaching down his back in a river of loose curls. His skin was young, clean of lines as if he'd been renewed by the flames and scorch.

His eyes were molten like gold as he fought for the people he loved – his soul redeemed.

Suddenly, something hammered Eleshen to her knees. She'd thought it was a horse that slammed into her, so badly did it throw her down, her sword jolted from her hand. But then black boots stepped in, separating her from Khouren and Ihbram as fighting raged all around. Eleshen was ready with her longknife, surging up – to find herself facing an enormous man in herringbone armor with an ornately shaven head.

Pain roared through her as their eyes connected. Eleshen spasmed, her back arching like a bow. Some part of her heard Ihbram and Khouren's shouts, saw them surrounded – by six more Kreth-Hakir Brethren. But Eleshen saw nothing else as pain ate her from inside out; seizing every sinew, mauling every limb. Unfathomable, it woke a memory in her body – of twisting beneath Abbot Lhem's knives. The Kreth-Hakir brother used that memory as he seized her by the collar, commanding her to obey and hurt as he hauled her head up so she'd be devoured by his dark eyes. Wave after wave of silver weaves ripped into Eleshen's mind, making her re-live Lhem's torture, enhancing it tenfold. She shrieked, feeling his cuts again, feeling her desperation – knowing she could never escape.

Knowing she was trapped, helpless in the dark.

Hauling upon Eleshen's hair, the Hakir brother with the ornately shaved head shoved her down at his knee, forcing her to watch the battle at his boot like a cur. Like an ocean of silver light, Eleshen could feel the Brethren's terrible influence engulf the battlefield. Arresting the allies' best fighters and whipping Menderian soldiers to frenzy, the Kreth-Hakir Brethren had rallied against the coordinated charges. Khouren trembled beneath the gaze of two, paused mid-strike. Ihbram was gripped in the stare of five, shivering like a beast on his knees in the char. Near the river, Arlen had been seized by one with a hand to the throat, Merra and

Rhennon down to two more, Snowscythe roaring and swiping as a group of twenty soldiers with pikes held it off.

Bolstered by the Kreth-Hakir's presence, Menderians hammered in, slaughtering cats and riders at the northern line; ringing Kingsmen and isolating them. Eleshen screamed in pain and frustration, watching their line fail. Using her hair, the brute hauled her face up to meet his as his mind smashed into hers, a horrid grin beneath his ornate head-shaving and brooding brows.

Lhaurent den'Alrahel sends his regards.

But as his silver weaves pummeled in to annihilate her mind, a roaring sensation filled Eleshen's head. Like the sound of surf pounding ocean cliffs, a terrible shuddering filled her. She couldn't remain still; couldn't control her limbs. Vibrating like a lute-string tuned too far, her body shuddered as something enormous built within her, and not from the Kreth-Hakir – with no outlet and no release. A terrible churning of conflict and horror built within her, and Eleshen screamed – consumed by something far worse than the allies' demise.

As silver weaves ate the dawn, a violet energy burst out from Eleshen in a flooding wave, roaring up the Hakir brother's arm and casting back his silver intentions – right into his own mind. The brother went down with a scream, writhing with his hands over his eyes. Eleshen's mind was suddenly clear, crystalline, her vision painfully acute. Whirling on her knees, she sliced his throat so deep it took his head off. As his hand spasmed, releasing her, she was up from the mud with a battle-roar unlike any her throat had ever issued.

Somewhere nearby, Eleshen could hear blasts of a trumpet sounding yet another Valenghian cavalry charge. The forces around her were splitting, shaken by what Eleshen had done to the Kreth-Hakir brother. She was pure motion as she used that opportunity, vaulting to Khouren. Fury raging inside her, she thrust its magnificence at the nearest Kreth-Hakir who pinned her beloved. She could see his silver weave, rolled back by her wave of violet like a tidal surge and cast into his own mind like lances. He went down, screaming, clutching at his eyes. But Eleshen didn't pause. Throwing that enormous violet energy at the other Hakir, she charged in and decapitated him as his mind was eaten alive by his own *wyrria*.

A shiver raced through the Kreth-Hakir as Khouren sprang up, longknives out, protecting Eleshen as she raced toward Ihbram. Hakir were breaking from Ihbram, turning toward Eleshen with alarm on their faces, casting a massive silver net all around her – only to have it thundered back, smiting them through the eyes and dropping them, shrieking as they twitched. With a roar, Ihbram was freed from their vile machinations. Thrusting out an enormous wave of crimson thought-energy, he enveloped Arlen, Merra, Rhennon, Khouren, and Eleshen in a burning net of protection as Eleshen cast her mind out, throwing back wave after silver wave.

Herringbone men went down all around, clutching at their eyes and screaming. Ihbram raked his way through the fallen, kicking one in the face as he gutted others. Khouren eviscerated the men who'd held him, and Merra had bitten the ear off one assailant before skewering him in the neck. Arlen was past his downed foe as well, roaring at his Kingsmen and the Elsthemi to regroup as the next flare of Valenghian trumpets slit the morning.

Back up on her blood-streaked white cat, General Merra gave an answering three-blast of her horn. Circling her polearm for her keshari to form up on the riverbank, they found the Menderian force now cowering back. United in their blood-soaked Greys, Arlen's and the Abbey's Kingsmen held steel in their eyes as they readied their blades for death.

With another deafening three-blast, Merra sounded the charge, echoed by Valenghian horns.

Pulling into a bristling circle in their burned camp, the Menderians defended their rear, but the combined Valenghian and allied charge was vicious. Ears ringing and muscles burning, Eleshen felt as if she'd only been fighting a minute, when she saw one last man in herringbone black rush her, silver weaves pummeling in to break her mind. Without thought, Eleshen let her fury flood her, and her violet wave rose one last time, sending all those cunning silver weaves back into his mind as she stabbed him through the eye with her longknife and kicked him to the ground.

Suddenly, a feeling of silver cobwebs lifted from all around her, as if blown through the air on the morning wind. Utter dominance was in their sensation – as if a tremendous mind had been controlling the Menderian forces and was now blown away to nothing. The Menderians suddenly broke, sharp whistle-blasts sounding a retreat as they blinked like they surfaced from a trance. Soldiers flooded back from the allied army, retracting into a tight position inside their camp – no longer touching the keshari and Kingsmen at the river. General Merra blasted a halt as she stood high in her stirrups, watching them.

Suddenly, Menderian soldiers began to throw down their weapons in droves. Falling to their knees, they succumbed all through the ravaged camp, some with surprised expressions, as if they had no idea what they were doing here. As quickly as their charge had begun, it was over. Ihbram and Khouren stepped to Eleshen's side, Ihbram wiping his blooded sword on his thigh before thrusting it away over his shoulder. Breathing hard from the fight, Khouren was naked as the day of his birth, coated in other men's blood, his eyes searing gold as he stepped close to Eleshen with lithe muscles rippling and longknives bared. Eleshen's heart hammered, her body still engaged for more battle, though even from the blood-churned ground she could tell it was over.

"Why are they surrendering?" Eleshen heaved, shaking out her sword-arm and catching her breath.

"I don't know." Ihbram was less winded, standing up high on his toes to see. "There!"

Eleshen followed his indication. One brawny man with sand-blonde hair and brooding eyes walked through the soldiers on their knees in the blood and scorch. Menderian General's pins upon his collar, he motioned for his men to stay down. Glancing at a tall silver-maned woman who rode a white charger from the Valenghian cavalry, then at Arlen den'Selthir, now standing with his sword-tip planted in the ground at the head of the Kingsmen, the Menderian General moved toward the river and the keshari. The Menderians made themselves comfortable in their camp's ruins, tending to injuries as the Valenghian woman on the white horse motioned for a few of her Red Valor captains, who broke from the cavalry, making for the parlay near the river. Eleshen, Khouren and Ihbram moved to join them, the factions meeting at the riverbank as the Menderian General tossed his sword to the stony ground.

"In the name of Alrou-Mendera, we surrender." The man spoke plainly. He glanced to Arlen, something like apology on his hard-lined face. "Arlen. I had no idea it was your people we were sent to rout out. When we received orders at the Aphellian Way to pass through an Alranstone to Quelsis and fight a group of insurrectionists who planned a coup out of Vennet, I never—" The man shook his head, one hand to his temple, flinching as if in pain.

"General den'Albehout." Arlen's voice was cold, his blue eyes penetrating. "You and your men were duped by the Kreth-Hakir Brethren among you, the fighters in herringbone black. Duped into attacking your own people at Lhaurent *den'Alrahel's* bidding."

"He speaks true." Ihbram stepped forward, his face hard like a roaring lion. "Your minds have been taken by mind-bending *wyrria*, for some time now. You'll have that headache for a few days, General, as will all your men."

"*Wyrria?*" A horrified expression consumed the Menderian General's face. "Are you saying that magic has been used to make my men and I fight our own people?"

"*Wyrria* takes many forms, General," Arlen spoke back. "And all of it will break the unsuspecting. If you wish to blame anyone, blame Lhaurent den'Alrahel, who wields the spear of that vile magic used upon you."

Turning his head, the Menderian General spit into the rocky mud with a nasty twist to his lips. "Fuck Lhaurent. Long live Queen Elyasin, Aeon hope she lives. Vicoute," the Menderian General sank down upon one knee, "do with us what you will. But spare the army, please. We had no idea we had been sent to wipe out our own people."

"I accept your surrender, and your army will be spared," Arlen spoke tersely. "If any of your men show signs of continued Kreth-Hakir influence, however, they will be put to death. I cannot allow any exceptions."

"I understand."

Arlen gave a heavy sigh. Reaching up, he rifled a hand through his iron-shot hair. His eyes raised to someone in the Red Valor cavalry, a broad boar of a fighter with sandy hair, and he gave a hint of a smile. Then his gaze found the handsome silver-haired woman in her crimson and black battle-garb upon her white charger. The smile fell from his face, replaced by the most honest look Eleshen had ever seen.

"Delennia," Arlen murmured with a nod.

"Arlen," the woman spoke back, not quite frosty but not far from it.

"*Vhinesse*, actually," an aging lord coughed from atop a grey gelding, discreetly for all to hear.

Arlen drew up tall, a cascade of emotions roaring through his blue eyes before they were banished. The Vicoute and the woman on the white charger stared at each other, cold yet somehow intimate. Eleshen could see instantly that these two were cut from the same cloth as the regal woman sat tall upon her mount, not about to give Arlen an inch of satisfaction at their win. From her austere expression, it was clear that she was going to give him hell — perhaps later, in private.

"Vhinesse?" It was General den'Albehout who broke the silence, staring up at the Valenghian woman, stunned. "*The* Vhinesse?"

"As of a short week ago." She gave him a hard smile. "My predecessor was unnaturally dispatched. My name is Vhinesse Delennia Oblitenne, General, and I want no war with Alrou-Mendera. But I will fight to protect my lands and allies against Lhaurent den'Alrahel's tyranny. He is a beast, and needs to be culled. The question is — are you with us, or do you need to be put down as well?"

A long silence devoured the morning. The rain had slackened, leaving only a thin mist in the autumnal air. As the Menderian General stared up at the Vhinesse, he bowed his head. Gazing down at the stony mud, he held it a beat before his gaze came back up, his pale green eyes vicious. "I am your servant. If Lhaurent den'Alrahel wields treachery to attack his own people, then he is no King of mine. Long live Valenghia, and long live Alrou-Mendera, and long live Elsthemen. But down with the King, until Queen Elyasin rises once more."

"If she lives." Arlen's voice was hard, his gaze even more so.

"If she lives," General den'Albehout nodded, sober.

At last, Arlen heaved a sigh. Placing his hands on his hips, he glanced up from the kneeling General to the Vhinesse, his gaze softer than it had been. She held it, imperious, proud, a glacier that would need tremendous thawing. But she was here, and for some reason she had come to aid him in his hour of need. As Eleshen watched, she saw something soften in the woman's white eyes at last, the tiniest smile quirking her lips.

"Come." Arlen beckoned the Menderian General up. "Let us return to the fortress, for we all have much to discuss this day."

But though his words were for the assembly, Arlen's gaze strayed back to the brawny fighter with the sandy hair with a soft smile, then to the Alrashemni-looking young woman beside him with something like pride. But the Vhinesse's near-white eyes avoided Arlen as she turned her horse toward the river-ramps and the fortress. Arlen issued a hard sigh. Moving to the Menderian General as he rose from his knees, he set a hand to the man's shoulder.

"Send a few of your captains back to deal with your men, Khaspar, then meet us inside. I'll send down healers to help the wounded and start moving the dead so the river and your camp don't become diseased. I'll not lose more countrymen in this vile war than we have to."

General den'Albehout stood. Clapping a hand to Arlen's shoulder, he set his jaw. "This war is madness, Arlen. Something's not right in Alrou-Mendera."

"Indeed." Arlen gave a tight smile and clapped the man's shoulder also. "Far more is wrong in our fair nation than you know."

With that, they turned, Arlen moving off after the Vhinesse. General Merra prowled after them on her enormous cat, while the young Alrashemni woman among the Red Valor barked orders for the Valenghian cavalry to begin setting up a camp on the eastern edge of the river-valley.

But Eleshen's eyes were all for Khouren as he clasped her hand in the cold morning, his gaze upon her fierce. Eleshen smiled up at him as he took her in his arms, cradling her to his gloriously naked body and forgetting the rest of the world as they breathed together in the chill morning. As the rest of their allies moved horses and cats toward the river, its brisk flow smelling of fresh rain and victory, Eleshen lifted up and kissed her man.

Tasting ash and fire upon his tongue and loving him all the same.

CHAPTER 37 – ELOHL

The Aphellian Way was a triumph of ancient civilization – and a bane.

Elohl stared up at the Monoliths of the Way in the late afternoon, feeling intense emotions war within him as stark shadows grew long over the cracked red earth. Even under the shade of the red silk awning that served as a command pavilion, the sun wrecked its wrath upon the spreading plain. Zephyrs careened in the shadows, swirling red silt up around the bases of the dual line of Monoliths that stretched all along the thirteen bone-dry leagues of the Way, raising a cloying smell of peat and scorched herbs. Sounds of war-camp and the smells of horse and piss mingled with the swirling dust, coating everything that had the foul luck to move under the lowering azure sky.

War was hell to Elohl, and even in such a fantastical place, it was no better than it had ever been. Sitting upon the steps of Merkhenos' command tent with one ear upon the discussion taking place inside, Elohl watched the Valenghian camp as he carved a piece of gnarled white yither-wood with his belt-knife, trying to soothe a battle taking place inside himself.

In the slanting shadows of the two-hundred-foot Monoliths, men toiled. With cloths wound about their heads, wetted against the parched air and red dust, soldiers heaved sacks of grain to mess tents. Under the vicious sun, men hauled on lead-lines of burdened oxen, who lay down in the shadows refusing to move; soldiers lingering in the relief of the Monoliths, resting for a smoke or dunking their heads in water-barrels.

The camp was a pressure-vat, cooked too long and ready to explode. Elohl could feel it, simmering through his every sinew as he carved. Blowing a shaving from his yither-wood, Elohl ground his jaw, furious that it still had no shape; no function. White as bleached bones and still formless even after days of crafting, the fragment of wood mocked him. Fragrant mesquite-citrus oils bled from its pale grain as Elohl carved, the bittersweet scent making his thoughts churn like the dry winds. Looming over the camp, some alabaster, some pure jade, others obsidian with runes of gold, the Monoliths around him were as varied as the clouds in the high, barren sky. Carven to resemble every fantastical being that had walked any earth, and even some that could barely be imagined, they seemed to watch Elohl's frustration with accusatory eyes.

Lined up all along a road that went nowhere, there were no temples upon either end of the Way. No destinations, no palaces. Nothing of significance, although trade-villages had sprung up here time and time again as an important crossroads. Dead cities were buried in the edges of the flanking bogs, but there were no roads to those places – as if whomever had built those ancient citadels hadn't dared encroach upon the Way. The broad, exquisitely level and un-marred highway of crimson stone simply passed through this dry and desolate plain, lined by effigies. And then returned to the earth at either end, giving up to arid grasslands to the west and cultivated fields of grain to the east.

Here Elohl sat, right in the middle of it all, torn once again from everything he loved and cast into the fires of Halsos for nations and kings. And yet, Elohl knew his purpose now, knew it to the depths of his being. He could feel the peace he desired – the deep peace that fed the Goldenmarks – there just out of reach. He'd felt it so strongly in the throne hall of the White Palace, as he'd been surrounded by Dherran's passion, Ghrenna's love, and Fenton's blistering conflict while he bared his own nature to the furies of fate. But now, it seemed so maddeningly out of reach – those intense emotions and connections distant like a fading mirage.

Mirages surrounded him, here. Mirages of heat, war, and stark reality. The Aphellian Way was arid, and underneath the red silk awning of the command tent, the temperature was currently as blistering as Elohl's internal war. Valenghian High General Merkhenos del'Ilio had just told his Generals and Captains that the Vhinesse had been killed in a coup, and Merkhenos' best, a combination of soldiers from three nations, were in an uproar.

White or red scarves wound up over their heads and making them look like desert-striders, all of Merkhenos' commanders had been stationed here at the Way for far too long. Flaxen-haired Praoughians stared Merkhenos down with defined jaws, their cobalt eyes the only cool thing in the suffering day as they held their long-lances, butt-ends planted stiffly upon the boards of the pavilion's platform. Copper-haired Cennetians with dark brows and dangerous eyes watched Merkhenos with thoughtful scowls and arms crossed, fingertips perusing the daggers each wore in profusion upon their weapons harnesses.

The Valenghian commanders were no less adept in their austere fury, sun-chapped hands resting on tall silver spears or on sword pommels. Their long silver hair was braided back against the constant winds that dried their parched skin. These Valenghians were nobility, second or third sons and daughters of high houses conscripted into a decades-old war and left here to hone or die. As such, they wore finery to battle, even if only a pearl earring or an emerald pin in their jerkin's collar.

One man, a trim, tall Praoughian General by the name of Greghane des'Finnes with a short blonde beard, spat onto the platform, speaking in a thick-slurred Common speech as his cobalt eyes flashed anger. "A coup? Good. With all respect, High General, if the old Vhinesse is dead, then Praough no longer has any stock in this war. Aelennia Oblitenne held our King Eleps des'Levanne in dangerous thrall, and he regrets acquiescing to her all those years ago. We all know it was *wyrria*. But an alliance no man of honor could go back on once he gave his word."

"Truer words have never been spoken." Merkhenos set his fingertips to the map table – currently covered in vellum charts of the local region – his copper eyes pure in his hate for the old Vhinesse. Dressed in crimson with his silver General's pins of a trailing vine upon either side of his high collar, Merkhenos shifted, his tall black boots creaking at their knife-sheaths. "Cennetia, likewise, has no more stock in this endless border-battle."

"See?" General des'Finnes waved a hand to his comrades, "even the High General agrees."

"We all know whose vicious blades were instrumental in *offing* our Vhinesse," one tall Valenghian General with a long silver braid, Suxisse Osenneaux, snorted, as his lips curled in contempt for Merkhenos. "Her disgruntled fuck-boy. Or is that, fuck-*falcon*?"

Merkhenos straightened, going dangerously quiet even for a Cennetian, his copper eyes flashing murder. Leaning casually back against one pillar beside Elohl's place on the steps, Fenton shifted, sliding into a stance that was not quite ready for a fight, but not far from it. Merkhenos had warned them that the command-meeting would not be pretty today, but Elohl had not imagined it would be this ugly. Clearly, the factionalism was deep, the simmering tension Elohl felt flooding him here at the Way a problem that had mired this campaign for years.

The Vhinesse had united three nations under her reign, but as Merkhenos' copper eyes flashed, Elohl felt the temperature spike under the pavilion's silk like a fever. A hot wind blew through, adding to the sweat that poured down Elohl's back. And though the octagonal pavilion was set at the northern edge of the Way where the grey trees of the northern Bog rose up to command the sky, there was no relief here. The Cennetians and Praoughians were furious at having had to fight a war for decades that wasn't theirs.

And the Valenghians were furious that their Vhinesse had been killed.

"Your High General didn't kill your Living Vine. I did." Elohl spoke abruptly. Tucking his whittling into the inner breast pocket of his crimson Red Valor jerkin, he rose from the pavilion's steps to standing. Though he wore crimson vine-tooled bracers at each wrist, Elohl's white sleeves were rolled up in the heat, his jerkin unbuckled and his lacings open, the Goldenmarks clearly visible at his forearms and on his chest with his Blackmarks. And even though the Goldenmarks weren't currently lit, all eyes turned to him, especially the Valenghians, as Elohl stared them down. "And I would do it again."

Uproar swept the pavilion. Suxisse Osenneaux lunged at Elohl, but Fenton was there, holding the man back with a blade to his throat. "I wouldn't."

"Hold!" Merkhenos' whip-sharp command stilled the outburst. All eyes assessed Elohl, but not all of them were hostile, he found. The Cennetians were grinning, and one moved forward to slap Elohl heartily upon the back, while the Praoughians stared down their long noses at him, uncertain but appraising.

"And who, pray tell, are you to have killed such a powerful

personage, Kingsman?" General des'Finnes lifted a flaxen eyebrow, his cool eyes roving Elohl's borrowed garb and visible marks. "You're no Red Valor, or I'll eat my moustache. Neither you nor your companion." He nodded at Fenton, who was slowly easing his blade away from Suxisse Osenneaux's throat. Suxisse stepped back with upraised hands, though his pale eyes were bestial.

"My name is Elohl den'Alrahel, First-Lieutenant of the High Brigade and Kingsman-Protectorate of Queen Elyasin den'Ildrian. And this is Fenton den'Kharel, First-Lieutenant of the Roushenn Palace Guard, also Kingsman-Protectorate of Queen Elyasin." Elohl used Fenton's known name, as all had agreed it was a better idea to keep Fenton's true identity hidden upon the Aphellian Way, for the time being.

"Two Kingsmen." General des'Finnes wore a bemused smile. "And sworn to Elyasin? I thought she was dead."

"She's not." A hard smile flashed in Fenton's eyes and lifted one corner of his mouth. Elohl saw a twist of burning gold move through those eyes, and General des'Finnes startled.

"Your eyes!"

"These Kingsmen are being impressively modest, gentlemen," Merkhenos smiled languidly, patient like a stalking forest-cat despite the heat – perhaps the only patient personage in the pavilion today besides Fenton. "You'd do well not to cross either of them. They have more talents than they show."

"Talents?" General Osenneaux's haughty voice was cutting. "Such as?"

"*Wyrria.*" Merkhenos' indulgent smile turned upon the high-silver Valenghian noble. "You don't think we simply danced our way into the Vhinesse's throne room, do you Suxisse? Aelennia had no idea just what she'd put on her palladian chains this time. And it cost her."

Six of the male and two of the female commanders under the fluttering silk awning startled. Their eyes connected with Elohl as they nodded deeply in respect. Elohl didn't know the reasons, but felt intuitively that each had suffered at the Vhinesse's hands, or knew someone who had, perhaps as a Falcon. But each of them wore pain in their eyes as they gave Elohl their silent thanks, hearing what position he'd held in the Vhinesse's court and what he'd subsequently done about it.

All at once, some part of the conflict that simmered within him firmed. Elohl was glad he'd used his Goldenmarks to kill Aelennia Oblitenne. He'd debated over his decision as they'd traveled with a cadre of Red Valor Longriders from Velkennish to the war front, thinking perhaps there had been another way. But gazing at them now, those who had suffered under her leash, Elohl was glad he'd done it. Glad that he'd had the ability to roll her under his *wyrria* and use that moment of unity to send her back to the Void.

His Goldenmarks flared, as if recalling his decision and firmed by his sudden resolve. Commanders stepped back with a cry. The skin above Elohl's open crimson jerkin and upon his forearms showed the Goldenmarks writhing an etheric blue rather than their usual sunlight-underwater, something harder, more edged than his feelings of peace and love. As commanders reacted to the sight, Fenton suddenly had a crackle of lightning between his fingertips, stepping in front of Elohl. Merkhenos raised his voice, ordering everyone to settle.

But the flare of power was like tinder in the dry heat, and the simmering tension exploded in the command pavilion. Swords were pulled by Valenghians, knives in the hands of Cennetians. Praoughian long-lances were leveled, the tall elegance of those eastern people bristling. The first flames roared with Suxisse Osenneaux's quick strike toward Merkhenos, though the High General was already blocking the sword at his neck with a snarl. But in that moment, Elohl's Goldenmarks exploded. A concussion of power hammered the men around him, staggering everyone back from an impending bloodbath.

"*Enough!!*" Elohl bellowed with fury as his Goldenmarks roared through his veins. "*Be the fucking commanders you're supposed to be, or I will do it for you!*"

Commanders gaped. A few had been blasted to their seats and were scrabbling up, stunned by Elohl's *wyrric* outburst. It surprised Elohl nearly as much, as if all his pent-up conflict had suddenly exploded into a steaming pit-vapor.

He let it take him – a scalding passion re-awoken by Dherran in Velkennish. Letting those emotions roil through the pavilion, Elohl flared with power so scorching that men flinched back with hisses of pain as if they had been stung. Many shielded their eyes as Elohl's Goldenmarks dazzled the late afternoon, Elohl staring around, surging with wrath. He knew that he could take every man here. That he could master them. Force the Unity upon them, as he had done with the Vhinesse, until they'd no longer bicker and rake one another over the coals. Until they would fight as a united force against Lhaurent.

Brainwashed – no better than the Vhinesse.

The thought brought Elohl up short. His Goldenmarks pulled back to a simmer as his eyes connected to those who'd suffered the Vhinesse's wrath. Those men and women had not joined the near-melee. Off to one side, they hovered with hands upon their weapons. Mostly Valenghians, but also one petite Cennetian woman and one tall Praoughian man, their eyes watched Elohl as they stood far back from Suxisse and his bristling guard.

"Would you?" Merkhenos' smooth speech interrupted the stunned silence. "Would you use your power, Rennkavi, to force us to become one?"

"*Rennkavi!*" Suxisse's white eyes widened. "Merkhenos—! What?!"

"Your Rennkavi has come, Suxisse," Merkhenos gestured at Elohl with a deferential elegance. "You might wish to bow."

The Valenghian's eyes were enormous, as he trembled from head to heels. And just like that, he was down upon one knee, ducking his head with a fist to his heart. "Rennkavi! Forgive me!"

Three of the Valenghians and five of the Cennetians were now upon one knee before Elohl, as his Goldenmark continued to surge with light, though it was diminished. None of the Praoughians bowed, though they gaped at Elohl's *wyrric* display. But Elohl understood that these nine who bowed were high up in the Khehemni Lothren of their nations, and knew what the Rennkavi was. It made Elohl uncomfortable suddenly. His Goldenmarks flared and Elohl resisted the urge to touch fingers to his weapons. He was about to say something, when Merkhenos spoke once more.

"You will all bow, gentlemen," Merkhenos's musical tones held a hard edge as his copper gaze raked his commanders, "if Rennkavi *Lhaurent den'Alrahel* has his way upon you. *Elohl* den'Alrahel is a reasonable man, and the power he has flared just now is little more than a reminder for all of us to be civil. But Lhaurent is not. He'll *make* you bow if he gets ahold of you. He won't give you any options."

"Lhaurent den'Alrahel?" Suxisse Osenneaux's head came up, confusion in his haughty pale eyes. "What do you mean? The Menderian warlord is another Goldenmarked? Is this some kind of trick?"

"Far from it," Merkhenos spoke darkly, his copper gaze pinning his commanders. "Lhaurent is also Goldenmarked, and using them. Believe me, Suxisse. You do not want to be on the losing end of *that* battle. Which is why we must have patience and come to accord today. I have news that Lhaurent builds a strong army to push toward this encampment, even as we speak. A force intended to break our stronghold and invade *all* our nations, now that he believes Valenghia is weak. The Aphellian Way is our choke-point, gentlemen, against the tyranny that is coming. If this avenue falls, believe me when I say that we will all face a fate far worse than our dearly departed Vhinesse, or the power you feel flooding from our comrade Elohl right now."

Those who had knelt now rose, wary as they glanced from Elohl to Merkhenos. Elohl's Goldenmarks were settling now as the tension under the pavilion began to fade, though they didn't die out completely. Briefly, Merkhenos held court, explaining to his commanders the short version of what Elohl was and what Merkhenos' spies had also witnessed of Lhaurent. He gave a succinct explanation of Fenton, and the Scion of Alodwine lit a small golden flame in his palm, which drew shocked epithets. By the time Merkhenos was finished, all of his veteran commanders watched Elohl and Fenton with a level thoughtfulness.

Elohl knew that look; he'd worn it on countless occasions – the look of a commander judging his assets in war. All faces held it now, no matter their nationality. These men and women hadn't risen high in their military careers for being reckless. They were calculating what Elohl could do, and Fenton, and how that could be put to use in battle. Elohl stood firm under their scrutiny, pleased that they were thinking as a unit again, rather than a squabbling bunch of renegades about to defect in the army's hour of need.

Just then, a scout swaddled in a filthy red facewrap galloped a lathered horse up the dusty avenue. Vaulting from this mount and throwing the reins at a startled groom near the horse-pickets in the shade of a tall jade phoenix-Monolith, he ran up the pavilion steps two at a time, heaving to a halt in front of Merkhenos. The man was all-over sweat and red dirt, his dun-colored jerkin's buckles undone, soaked at the pits and chest. Hauling down his facewrap, he panted out news.

"High General! We have movement at Ligenia Bay! The Menderian host encamped there, some twenty thousand strong now, is preparing to march. Our spies estimate they will join Lhaurent den'Alrahel's main force at the Aphellian Way within three days, five at the most. The Menderian forces upon the western Way make ready for their arrival. This mustering will put Lhaurent's combined might upon the Aphellian Way at some seventy thousand strong, by our Watch estimates."

Merkhenos stood very still as his Captains and Generals shifted, a few cursing softly as they took in this dire news. If their situation had been bad, it was now exponentially worse. Elohl didn't know exactly how many fighters the Valenghians and their conquered nations had here on the eastern Way at their massive fortifications that spanned into both bogs, but it wasn't anywhere near the force Lhaurent was currently mustering. With a hard smile, Merkhenos set a hand to the man's heaving shoulder. "Get some water and a meal, Lieutenant des'Pannes. You've done well."

"Sir." The Lieutenant snapped a weary salute, practically falling back down the pavilion steps so tired was his jog. Merkhenos turned, watching the faces of his commanders. A brisk wind whipped through the air in the pavilion, cooling the tension as the sun finally touched the ramparts of the enormous Valenghian fortifications that spanned the entirety of the Way in the west. At last, Merkhenos spoke.

"Let this be a lesson to you all – a demonstration of Lhaurent's power. What you felt from Elohl today is but a fraction of what Lhaurent is using to amass this incredible force against us. All of you heard the words of our Watch-scout. Lhaurent uses his gifts to smash men's hearts, not just influence them – to take away their freedom so he can build this army that is double our forces here at the Way. His army is composed of slaves, gentlemen, stolen from many lands. We are all soldiers of our nations, my friends. And like any good soldier, what we long for is peace. But would you rather have that peace come amiably, or because someone forced it into you, breaking your will and taking your lands? For that is precisely what Lhaurent will do, if we do not rise up in a unified force against him. As much as I would like to return home, I cannot. For my duty is to oppose any who would take my freedom – especially since, like most of you, it has already been taken from me for so very long."

A breathing silence moved through the pavilion. It was flaxen-haired General des'Finnes who broke it at last. "And Lhaurent? Would his abilities out-match Elohl's in battle, do you think?"

"That, I believe, is up to Elohl."

Merkhenos' copper eyes rested upon Elohl, a deep thoughtfulness in them. Elohl understood the Cennetian's meaning: that it was Elohl's own strength of will which would face Lhaurent in battle, not the strength of the Marks themselves. Lhaurent was no stranger to his power, and he didn't hesitate. If Elohl shied from stepping into the power of his own Goldenmarks, Lhaurent would vanquish them – and enslave them all to his will.

Elohl saw the man again in his mind; Lhaurent's opal-grey eyes glorifying in the melee in Roushenn Palace. The Queen stabbed, the Elsthemi First Sword dead by Elohl's blade. Lhaurent had stared Elohl down with all the coolness of darkwater eels strangling sailors. And that was exactly what he'd do, if Elohl couldn't re-find the passion he'd felt in the White Palace, and use the fullness of his Goldenmarks.

A shiver moved through Elohl as the swirling air became brisk upon the arid plain, the pavilion cast in shadow now from the western fortifications. Looking out, he watched the fast-falling night, his heart simmering with trouble. Round and round his emotions went, like they fought inside him as the dry grasses rustled near the open-air octagon, picking up the evening wind. As if feeling his tension, a pheasant took wing fifty paces out from an open field near the edge of the northern bog.

As Elohl stared out into the settling evening, he found his heart filled with tumult, but lacking the steady passion he needed to best the man who was coming for him. He'd felt it in the throne hall of the White Palace, his heart bolstered by the raging heat of Dherran flowing through him and the connection of Ghrenna's incredible presence. But without those aspects now, Elohl felt strangely uncoupled from the vision of peace he'd had then – all of his heat and power churning in a circle and dis-coordinated.

Come to me tonight. Elohl blinked as Ghrenna's words breathed through his mind. Her cerulean eyes drowned his vision suddenly, as she rose like an evening mirage inside him. *We need to talk, Elohl. I need to tell you things I'm remembering from Morvein Vishke, the woman whose soul I share. It has to do with the battle you now face, both inside yourself and upon the Aphellian Way. Come to me, tonight...*

Her scent wisped away upon the dry evening and Elohl shuddered, feeling bereft. She was his passion; the only thing he had ever loved, the only thing he'd ever found worth fighting for. It staggered him to feel her touch slip away – leaving him feeling more churning conflict than ever. Elohl hardly noticed that Merkhenos had dismissed his commanders. They passed by Elohl on their way down the pavilion's steps, skirting him with awed and wary frowns.

"So the Unifier commands men at last." Merkhenos' rolling accent brought Elohl back from his reverie. The High General stood before Elohl beneath the red silk awning, something flinty and pleased in his copper eyes. "My commanders were quite impressed by your outburst. Indeed, I wasn't sure you had it in you anymore, so quiet have you been since we left Velkennish. But I see now that you simmer, deep with the challenges of the Wolf and Dragon, which springs forth when it reaches its own inner boil."

"I'm no stranger to commanding soldiers in desperate situations." With a deep breath, Elohl squared off to Merkhenos, shaking off the last of his strange fugue as he touched the cool steel of the longknife at his hip. "If they need someone to marshal them, to command them into cooperating with one another, I'll do it. My own inner demons and conflicts will not prevent me from doing my duty here, though I would regret to have to force them to come to accord. But if I must, I will."

"Your fortitude is well-timed," Merkhenos gave a beleaguered sigh, eyeballing him. Shifting his attention, the Cennetian gazed out over the western fortifications, then to the south, watching horses and soldiers move in the whipping evening dust along the Way. Fenton had settled back against his pillar once more, arms crossed, watching Elohl thoughtfully. Elohl returned his gaze, unafraid of his choices, though his heart still felt like it tumbled around inside him. Moving to the command-table, Merkhenos stared down at the maps of the Thalanout Plain unrolled upon it, weighted at the edges by knives. At last, he heaved a deep breath and looked up, his copper gaze roving from Fenton to Elohl.

"Gentlemen," Merkhenos spoke, "all has been said today that can be said. My commanders need some time now, to consider the things they have heard and make their own decisions about where they stand. In the meantime, although I am loathe to do it at such a critical juncture, I must take my leave tonight upon an errand. I will be gone two days; perhaps less. With Lhaurent's army soon upon us, my return will be a close thing. In the meantime, you shall have my personal guard."

Merkhenos nodded to Ghirano and four of his elite Cennetian Red Valor guards who lingered nearby at the foot of the pavilion, watching the discussion intently, before Merkhenos continued. "Now that the Rennkavi and his Wolf and Dragon protector have unveiled themselves here at camp, word will spread. I ask you both to learn the temperature of the camp in my absence – feel what the men are thinking about you. Walk among them and hear their thoughts, let them see you and something of your abilities. I worry not that we shall attract Lhaurent's attention now, but more that my men need something worth fighting for once they hear that we have a force twice our size barreling down upon us. I also ask that you be political, Rennkavi, in my absence – notoriety is upon you. If you are a commander of men in hard times, then be that – for all of us need it right now."

Elohl was stunned by the Cennetian's frank words. But he found the man's cultural directness refreshing, and instead of being offended, Elohl set a palm to his heart and bowed. "Merkhenos. I will do everything that I can."

"Are you certain you have to leave right now?" Fenton had crossed his arms at his pillar, staring Merkhenos down with an intent look. "This is a critical time for your men, General."

"So it is." The Cennetian nodded back, his battle-lined face frank. "But destiny waits for no man. Not either of yours, and not mine. This errand I do not with a willing heart, but because I must.

Believe me, I would rather be here, preparing my soldiers for what faces us. But this errand, I'm afraid cannot wait, and may be instrumental in sealing our fortunes in the battle ahead. If I do not return—"

A strange look came over Merkhenos' face suddenly. Reaching up, he unpinned his silver High General's vines from his collar, pressing one into Elohl's hand and one into Fenton's. And then turned with a brisk nod to each of them, motioning for his guards to remain behind as he strode down the pavilion's steps and through the horse-lines to the south.

Copper-haired Ghirano and the rest of Merkhenos' guards gaped at what their High General had just done, their eyes wide from their spot at the base of the pavilion. And though they shifted uncomfortably, they stayed near, keeping their silence and slowly closing their mouths as they glanced askance at each other and watched Merkhenos disappear around a mess tent.

"Did he just—?" Elohl watched the Valenghian High General go, astounded.

"I think so." Fenton watched Merkhenos go also, a troubled frown upon his features. Fenton's gaze tracked Merkhenos until they could no longer see him through the fluttering mess of dust-streaked silk tents and awnings. Fenton scowled, and a prickle began to lance the air around him.

"Do you you know where he's headed?" Elohl spoke, concern sifting through him as the bite of Fenton's magic slipped over his skin.

"Not a clue." Fenton heaved a breath and his prickling gradually subsided, as he glanced down at the pin in his palm. "But he really thinks he may not return from wherever he's going. I'm usually able to read people better than that, but his mind is closed to me, Elohl. Illianti poisons, I'm sure, strong ones. But turning over his command... *a silver dagger does not make a man an assassin.*"

"No." Elohl watched where the Cennetian had gone, deeply troubled. With conflict roiling in his heart, he tucked the pin into his jerkin's breast pocket without putting it on. "I need to go think a while. You alright here?"

"Are you?" Tilting his head, Fenton gave him a searching gaze.

"No. Not really."

To his credit, Fenton didn't pry. Stepping forward, he set a hand to Elohl's shoulder and gripped it. "Go have a breather. Come back when you're ready, and we'll talk about possibly leading a war without the one man all these soldiers really trust."

* * *

Elohl stole through the shadows of the dark pre-dawn, dodging tents, stepping over awning-lines pegged into the parched ground, and skirting animal paddocks. Copper braziers crackled in the night and Elohl skirted by them, dodging Red Valor sentries. A shadow in the crisp night air of the Way, his crimson hood was up, darkening his visage as he slipped through the hush, moving around horse-lines without even a whicker from the drowsing beasts.

His *wyrric* sensation breathing around him, he moved toward the one place in the shambling, dug-in city that was unoccupied. Beyond the mess-tents and empty command-pavilion, the clutter along the northern edge of the camp gave way to a grassy greensward. Untouched by boot of man or hoof of horse, the clearing the pheasant had risen from earlier gaped at the edge of the northern Bog like a wound. As Elohl crossed into the field, he felt a prickle race over his skin and up through his spine, making him feel suddenly heated. As if his inner tumult raised twenty-fold, his skin crawled, and he pulled the hood of his Red Valor jerkin forward more as he felt his Goldenmarks light in a simmering flow.

No one went near this clearing, because of the thing that stood at its center – and this sensation it produced. No horses could be walked through this field, much less cattle. The Valenghians said it was haunted, with a specter of furious doom that arose in man or beast as they passed that invisible boundary. Energy burned in Elohl's marrow as he crossed through the waist-high grasses toward a massive stone effigy in the center of the clearing. Conflict emanated from the ancient Monolith, carven like an enormous red dragon coiled into a ball with its snout beneath its tail. Unlike the rest of the Way, this Monolith stood alone and not in-line with the rest, as if its furious power might infect the other effigies of the highway. Gazing up, the sculpture blocked out the stars as Elohl neared. *Wyrria* poured from the thing as Elohl moved nearer. Heat roiled off its russet stone even at midnight, producing wavering currents that shivered the chill air.

Images of battle flashed through Elohl's mind. As he put a hand to the dragon-stone's warm shoulder, scenes of his own life tumbled through him. Elohl flushed, watching men slain. Seeing crimson blood wash over cold white snow and shed steam. Feeling his strikes as he slit throats, stabbed hearts, cut unprotected knees. As if the thing could read all his history of bloodshed. As if it ate that energy, drawing him in, emitting a slow pulse that matched Elohl's own heartbeat.

He shook himself out of trance and pulled away. But as he did, Ghrenna slid into his sensate sphere. Near all night yet distant, her presence suddenly coalesced around him. As if the dragon-stone also powered their connection, Elohl's sensation of Ghrenna became painfully clear. Even his feeling of embracing her in the Palace of the Vine hadn't been this prescient. As if she manifested in the starlit dark, he saw her luminous outline – felt her touch like flesh as she set warm fingertips to his chest and traced his Goldenmarks, making them flare with blue-white fire, a sound like music and wind in his ears.

Elohl's breath caught. He stared. Ghrenna's body pressed against his, warm, nearly real. Layered upon the real world, she was an etheric shadow. But in Elohl's mind-vision, she was there; and to his skin, she was there. And in his nose, she was there as he pressed his lips to her hair, feeling silken white strands move beneath his breath. Elohl's hands stole up, holding her, slipping over the soft skin between her shoulder-blades. Ghrenna was naked beneath the stars. Her skin was supple, strong with muscle. Elohl inhaled her tundra-musk scent, sweet like wintermint and pines rooted in an icy stream. Her hands lifted, her fingertips touching his face. Pulling back, he watched her, their bodies pressed close in the night.

"How is this possible?" Elohl breathed to the darkness.

Ghrenna beamed up at him, her cerulean eyes full of love. Her beautiful lips curled in a smile both haunting and blissful, and it filled Elohl's heart. For the first time since the White Palace, Elohl's Goldenmarks blazed beneath his jerkin, flooded with their togetherness and with the oceanic sensation of peace he recalled. He wound his arms closer, drinking her in, never wanting to give this sensation up.

Your power grows, Elohl, Ghrenna breathed. Her lips seemed to move, but her voice entered Elohl's mind with the night breeze that swirled around him. *Do not fear your current conflict. The Wolf and Dragon battle in your blood because of your tumult, and so do the Goldenmarks feed, biding their time for when they will finally be unleashed.*

"Conflict magic," Elohl set his forehead against hers. "I can feel it. Just like in the White Palace."

With each torment you face, Ghrenna breathed back, *your magic grows. I know you hate it. You long for a home, for peace—*

"For you." Elohl slid his lips over hers. "I've only ever longed for one thing in my entire life, Ghren, I—"

I know. Ghrenna lifted up, placing the softest kiss upon his lips. *I can feel it, just as I felt your call all those years. I knew we were destined, but I had no idea why or how until now. Ancient magic is wrought in your blood, Elohl, and mine. I am the rebirth of the only person who ever had the power to begin the Rennkavi's Ritual, the final ceremony to bring him into the fullness of his Unification. My magic exists only to bring yours to fruition, Elohl – so you can Unite all of us against what's coming.*

"Lhaurent." Elohl's heart gave a flash of rage, and he stilled beneath the stars.

Perhaps. Perhaps not. Ghrenna's cryptic answer made Elohl pull back until he could see her drowning blue eyes.

"Lhaurent has the marks, too, Ghren. He's coming. If I can't find it in me to bind men to me before he does—"

I know. Ghrenna's face was somber, her high cheekbones catching the starlight. *Lhaurent threatens all we hold dear. And if he wins at the Aphellian Way, nations will fall.*

"Have you Seen it?" Elohl cupped her face, searching her eyes.

Not precisely. Ghrenna held firm, taking the deep breath of her Kingsman training. *Morvein's memories recall a tyrant, King Alcinus den'Alrahel of Alrou-Mendera, who had much power back in her day, even though he wasn't Goldenmarked. Because of his immensely dominating* wyrria, *that man brought nations to ruin eight hundred years ago because he believed in his right to rule, similar to Lhaurent, and he had the Kreth-Hakir Brethren on his side. The Brother Kings fought him hard, but no power was enough to overcome him. It was utter chaos, Elohl. I fear—*

"That Lhaurent would bring such chaos upon us."

And worse. He will bind every living soul into his madness.

"How do I stop him?"

Find the reason the Marks chose you.

"What do you mean?" Elohl pulled Ghrenna closer, watching her face.

The Goldenmarks… Ghrenna's brows knit, as if recalling something. *Morvein received a vision through the sands of time, Elohl. Of a king with umber hair out in the desert at a ruined city. He sent a desperate jumble of thoughts* through *time, Elohl. Like a lifeline flung out with every power he had left. He sent it to find the one person strong enough to continue his work, to complete the Rennkavi's Ritual. That vision found Morvein, two hundred years after it was sent. She ventured under the mountains to find a Giannyk named Bhorlen, to learn how to create the Goldenmarks the way this desert king had shown her.*

"Leith Alodwine. Last King of Khehem…" Elohl's gaze lifted to the massive dragon-stone, and he felt it give a slow pulse, as if acknowledging his attention.

You know of Leith? Ghrenna blinked, startled.

"I met Bhorlen. And I'm traveling with Leith's grandson, Fentleith Alodwine," Elohl chuckled, finding some amusement in fate at last. "I'm blood-kin to Leith, apparently."

The Wolf and Dragon rise within you. Ghrenna's hand pressed his chest at his Blackmarked Inkings, but it was the Goldenmarks that thrummed to her touch. *Leith created the Marks you wear. When his plans were sundered by his untimely demise, he threw them through time to Morvein, who learned from the Giannyk how to fashion them. When her attempt to impart the Marks to the young Theos den'Alrahel failed, destroying the White Ring of power before she could even get to the true Rennkavi's Ritual, Morvein thrust her understanding of the Marks into her Brother Kings and trapped them in Alranstones, binding herself to her bones so her soul would rise again when she was needed once more. Hahled Ferrian marked you because the Marks resonated with you, Elohl. You are the Rennkavi. And your destiny with me is bound, leading us to the White Ring to complete this eons-old magic.*

"But what of Lhaurent? Why did he receive the marks?" Elohl countered.

I don't know, Ghrenna breathed to the night. *I only know that Hahled felt compelled to Mark Lhaurent, because the Marks understood Lhaurent also. Perhaps it was a mistake, perhaps there is a reason for it. Leith didn't pass his whys along to Morvein in his last desperate feat of communication, Elohl. He only passed on what had to be done to prevent the rise of an ancient evil. Without the Rennkavi brought into the fullness of his power by the Rennkavi's Ritual, to unite the world against the Red-Eyed Demon, we are all destined to fall.*

"The Red-Eyed Demon. It sounds like a nightmare," Elohl mused, a shudder sweeping him in the starlit night.

It's more than a nightmare, Ghrenna cuddled close against him, burying her nose in his chest, her warm cheek to his skin. *It's ultimate, fathomless destruction. Long ago, two wyrric peoples united to fight against it, the Giannyk and the Albrenni. They banished it, but against such an evil even winning was a loss...*

Elohl brushed back strands of Ghrenna's luminous hair back from her face. She glanced up beneath the starlight, her drowning blue eyes filled with ancient pain. Ghrenna had always been in pain, abandoned, alone, and Elohl wanted to banish that pain. He wanted to take it and shred it with teeth and claws; to coil around her and crush her close until she understood that she was never alone, – and that nothing could separate the powerful love they held between them.

Pulling her close, Elohl let that feeling flood him. His Goldenmarks blazed beneath his jerkin, scalding his skin like they breathed fire. Ghrenna inhaled, her eyelashes fluttering, and Elohl knew she could feel it, everything he was feeling. All his raw emotions and his love with it. The roar of his Goldenmarks filled the night, shuddering the tall grass. Sliding over the dragon-stone and making it heat with a mirage upon the midnight wind, like it writhed beneath the stars – talons stretching, coils sliding, jaws snarling.

"What do we have to do?" Elohl held Ghrenna firm in his hands and in his power, even though she was a thousand leagues away.

Find me, Ghrenna breathed. *I am under the Kingsmountains, at the place where I must work the Rennkavi's Ritual – the White Ring. The Rennkavi can't hold the Unification without this final piece, Elohl. And this is what we have that Lhaurent doesn't – me. I am your Gerunthane, the one who can begin the ceremony, channeling it for you, that you will complete. A ceremony that will open all the ways of wyrria for you to bind and use. Lhaurent's efforts at Unification will be incomplete without this. I can deliver this power to you, and you alone. Watch for me, Elohl. I will find you when the time comes.*

Holding her close, Elohl didn't want to let her go, no matter that dire fates were being planned this night. "Stay. Be with me tonight. Tomorrow we may go to war. But tonight—"

Tonight we love.

Ghrenna moved in. Pressing her body against his, her spirit molded to Elohl's flesh. The taste of evergreen and wintermint slid across his tongue as she set her lips to his. Her arms wound around his neck as he crushed her close. Her midnight breath sighed through the field, kissing him in a thousand ways as Elohl took her body down to the tall grass. His power blazed, heating the night as they moved in the darkness.

Consummating their love in bliss, even though their heart's other half cried out a thousand leagues away.

CHAPTER 38 – THEROUN

Come, Scion. It is time for our meeting with Lhaurent.

Khorel Jornath's grey eyes sliced Theroun like cold steel as Jornath stormed into the command tent in the depths of the midnight hush. His high-cheeked face a thundercloud, he flicked his fingers, an imperious gesture he hardly used with Theroun. Theroun had been packing extra armor in a trunk, preparing for their march out of Ligenia at dawn, and he straightened, massaging out a cramp in his side. Khorel was obviously in a terrible mood, and Theroun lifted his eyebrows at that, as the man rarely let his emotions be seen.

Theroun kept his cool far better than the High Priest tonight, moving toward the tent-flap in his Kreth-Hakir garb and ducking out into the luminous night after Jornath. Three days after their mind-meeting with Lhaurent, they still had no answer about the extra naval support Jornath had requested. And though Theroun had been predominantly unsuccessful at joining in that meeting, Lhaurent had felt his presence, and his displeasure had tainted the entire negotiation. Jornath had been visibly tense ever since.

Ships far down in the harbor gleamed beneath the sickle moon, deck-lanterns flickering like fireflies in the brisk night as Khorel strode quickly down the cliff-walk through the salt spray, zigzagging down the steps that led away from the harbor and towards Ligenia's Alranstone at the edge of the cliff-camp. The camp was quiet tonight, only a few soldiers striding about with final preparations to move the army out in the morning. Khorel threaded through it all with hooded eyes, acknowledging no-one, and Theroun followed. Through a copse of salal, they came to the small Alranstone clearing. A three-eye Stone, it wasn't a terribly impressive one, squat and tapered to an oblong point. Formed of a smoky Hellenthine quartzite that was native to the area, the Alranstone had only the top eye open to the moonlight, casting a hazy carmine glow through the night.

Menderian soldiers with lanterns ringed the Stone, hands ready at their weapons. They nodded to Jornath as he stepped up, and Theroun could see with his improving mind-sight that the smooth character of the quicksilver weaves threaded through these men were Jornath's impressively subtle bind. Since his blood-oath to Jornath, Theroun was seeing mind-weaves more and more, sometimes just a subtle flash of silver at the corners of his vision, sometimes strong and glowing so bright in his mind-sight that he was surprised they weren't visible in the real world.

Jornath's binds were such; bright, impeccably created, strong. The soldiers who guarded the Alranstone made no move to intercept Khorel and he did not address them. With a look from Jornath, the soldiers parted, permitting access. Striding forward, Khorel set a hand to the Stone, then turned to Theroun, his grey gaze piercing in the wan moonlight.

"Put your palm to the Stone," Khorel commanded. "When we arrive at Roushenn, you are to be *absolutely silent* unless instructed by me to respond. Am I clear?"

Theroun lifted an eyebrow. "Do you expect trouble?"

"From Lhaurent? Always." Khorel's thick lips lifted in a small smile, but it was quickly doused. "Don't be a problem tonight, Theroun. Remember that you and I are far more aligned in interest than he whom we serve. But we go because we must. Place your hand upon the Stone."

Theroun didn't like the sound of that, but he did as he was instructed. He promptly felt that horrible, vise-grip sensation of being sucked into the cavernous maw of the universe, ground up into powder, and spat back out the other side. He stumbled as he emerged from an Alranstone upon the other side and caught himself from falling.

They'd come out in an enormous, vaulted room. Flickers of images showed high above – vantages of the City of Lintesh, the Kingsmount, the Elhambrian plains. Theroun knew those vantages well. One was of the First Abbey grounds, but he hardly recognized it, as if some enormous earthquake had swallowed the Abbey whole. They stood upon a high dais in the center of a vast sea of Praoughian clockwork machinery that chugged on in a thundering drone.

"This way."

Khorel flicked his fingers, and they moved across the high dais and down along an avenue through the machinery, coming to the wall of the dome. Khorel pressed his hand to a section and a door opened in it, where only seamless bluestone had been before. The door swung outward and Khorel strode into a dim hall, lit by vapid blue globes that swirled in the high vaults.

"Where are we?" Theroun murmured.

"Have you never been back here, behind the walls of Roushenn?" Khorel turned a slightly surprised glance upon Theroun as they ducked into another hallway, vaulted like the last. Theroun gazed up and around, impressed even as he set his jaw, realizing how many secrets Lhaurent had kept from him, and from his Queen. Blue globes whirled overhead, some wisping down near his face as if curious.

"I've never been in a part of Roushenn that looks like this. Are these Lhaurent's secret spy passages?"

"Among other things. Here."

Khorel turned, pushing against another section of rough bluestone wall. It moved to his touch as if it had been primed; swinging inwards and admitting them to a vast octagonal room full of bookshelves. Crammed with arcane items, tomes, and scrolls, the room was elegantly appointed like a lord's reading-room. Lush Perthian carpets were strewn over the cold bluestone floor, velvet chaises grouped here and there. A fireplace blazed in one corner, though as Theroun approached, he saw it was not a real fire but a swirling collection of the same globes that haunted the hallway, except these were crimson and gave a deep heat like real fire.

Theroun's eyebrows climbed his face as he and Khorel approached the fireplace. And then promptly scowled, to see the man sitting in the ancient leather armchair there, sipping blood-red wine from a golden chalice as he perused a slender volume bound in cobalt leather resting in his lap. A second matching volume sat upon the table next to him; a rack of resplendent white armor made of a silvered metal Theroun didn't recognize stood near the fire also. Matching weapons with rubies in their hilts glimmered in the fire's sorcerous light, as if their jewels drank the blood of the flames. The ruby ring upon Lhaurent's index finger did the same as Lhaurent set aside the cobalt volume with practiced stillness, then gestured to a chaise near his chair. Khorel Jornath dipped his chin in respect before settling to the chaise. Theroun, wondering what this was all about, did the same.

Lhaurent den'Alrahel regarded them with cool dispassion, but did not rise. His grey-opal eyes shone in the false firelight, as if they drew energy from the swirling globes. Immaculately trimmed, slicked, and perfumed as ever, he nonetheless had a haggardness about him. Highlighted by the sorcerous fire, Theroun could see that Lhaurent's cheeks were gaunt, and a fever seemed to burn in the hollows of his eyes.

As Theroun's gaze fell to the man's royal white robe chased with golden thread, he couldn't hide his surprise. Lhaurent was missing an arm, right from his Aeon-damned shoulder. His left sleeve draped, empty, only his right hand protruding from his right sleeve and bringing his wine goblet to his sallow lips again before setting it aside.

"The prodigal General returns." Lhaurent gazed upon Theroun as if someone had taken a shit on his shoe, his lips twisted in distaste. His voice held his regular smooth tones, but raspy, as if the man had done much screaming of late. Theroun wondered again how Lhaurent's arm had been taken, and couldn't stop the small smile that crept in around his lips as he glorified in Lhaurent's maiming. He wanted to stride over there and grab that stump; dig his knife into that tender flesh. But Khorel Jornath's slicing quicksilver words inside Theroun's mind made him flinch.

Envision our Rennkavi again in such a manner and I will make you grovel, Scion.

Theroun took a steadying breath, then gave Jornath a nod. "Forgive me, Brother Jornath."

He watched Lhaurent's black eyebrows climb his forehead, an astounded watchfulness tensing his lean frame. "So. It is true. You have broken him to the Brethren."

"As I said before, Brother Theroun is an asset to our cause, Rennkavi." Khorel Jornath's words were placid, and he let no emotion show, not upon his person and not from his mind.

"He was supposed to die in Elsthemen, as an example. Not be

broken into your Order."

"Brother Theroun's mind is tethered to mine," Jornath was pleasant as he argued back, giving nothing away. "His stratagems, his battle plans, his knowledge of the Aphellian Way. When we are finished with our campaign, he will be dealt with. But for now, his asset is his living memory."

"Can you not simply drain his memories and stick a knife in his gut?" They were talking about Theroun as if he wasn't there. Theroun wondered if Khorel had told him to be silent because they needed to show Lhaurent he was essentially a prisoner. But he'd been allowed to wear the studded black of the Brethren to this meeting. Theroun puzzled on that as Khorel answered his Rennkavi.

"Our mind-abilities don't work that way, Rennkavi," Khorel gave Lhaurent a thin smile, but a deferential nod. "Memories degrade quickly when stolen from the host. I would have Theroun's memories a few days, little more. Not long enough to fight this war for you. Keeping Theroun alive and tethered to me allows his thoughts and memories and planning to be ever-available to my inquiry. Which is essential to our success upon the Aphellian Way."

Lhaurent's gaze narrowed upon Theroun. And then his smile grew cruel. "Show me. Show me the cur has been tamed."

Theroun had but a moment of Khorel's thought wisp through his mind, *this will hurt,* before he was suddenly twisted with so much pain that he spasmed off the chaise. Falling forward, he landed upon the rug before the hearth, seizing uncontrollably. Pain exploded through his body – ripping, twisting, devouring, exploding behind his eyeballs in lurid starbursts so badly he couldn't even scream. The vastness of his torture was unlike anything he'd ever felt, besides the roaring agony of his own *wyrria* rising.

Suddenly, his own power whipped back. Like a lash of black oil, it struck at Khorel Jornath. The man didn't shudder and his body didn't wince, but Jornath rolled back his power, something like a smile twisting into Theroun's dazed and ravaged mind.

Very good, Scion. Your abilities are growing. Now play along, or get us both killed.

Theroun gasped with his cheek upon the carpet. His breath was pure fire, his body worse, but at least he had his mind back. Tears of pain leaked from his eyes, and he barely heard Lhaurent's

505

smooth voice when the bastard said, "Now. Have him kiss my hem."

Do it. Jornath's voice was inside Theroun's mind, but without any pull against Theroun's will. It was simply one man urging another to not be stupid. Theroun struggled to his hands and knees, everything an aching fury. His mangled side hurt most of all, but he managed to struggle over to Lhaurent and press his lips to the hem of Lhaurent's robe down by his feet.

The man struck out like a whip, booting Theroun up under the chin. Theroun's jaw clacked hard, gouging his tongue with his teeth. He was kicked over, his palms barely finding the hearth before his head smacked the lintel of the fireplace. Blood filled his mouth, dripping down his chin. Theroun gasped, additional pain rioting through his head.

Lhaurent rose. Staring down with vast pleasure in his fevered eyes, he came to one knee. Before Theroun knew it, the bastard had gripped Theroun's hair in his fist. Gazing into Theroun's eyes, he let Theroun see his mind. Something awful moved there. Something dark and bright at the same time, that held nothing but evil. A shiver of shock lanced Theroun, horror fast upon its heels. Suddenly, the empty sleeve of Lhaurent's silk robe filled. Like an eel slithering out of dark waters, the fabric now had mass behind it. A writhing, terrible presence, as if the sleeve was occupied by a nest of snakes.

Shrugging down his robe without releasing Theroun, Lhaurent bared his left shoulder. Showing Theroun a new arm made of dark matter that twisted through with writhing golden sigils. As Lhaurent's arm filled out to a fully-functional hand, Theroun saw it was being emanated *from* the sigils that cascaded across his pale skin. As if the golden seal written inside Lhaurent's flesh caused this arm to be made from the vastness of the cosmos itself. That spectral arm moved with inky currents, swirling and spreading out from the Goldenmarks and being resorbed. As Theroun watched, a slow sunlight blaze seared through those marks, lighting them up like a night full of imploding stars.

"Behold," Lhaurent murmured, using the knuckles of his spectral hand to stroke Theroun's face, to touch the blood upon Theroun's lips. "Destiny runs through my veins, Theroun den'Vekir. Would you continue to fight such a destiny?"

Lhaurent gripped the back of Theroun's head with his right

hand, as his spectral one tasted Theroun's blood. Theroun found himself struck mute by that touch – horrified and riveted all at once. Waves of power flooded from Lhaurent, pummeling Theroun, unimaginable. Cold and warm, Lhaurent's spectral flesh pulled him like a siren song; commanding him not just to obey, but to love. To adore – and to worship Lhaurent like the god he was. Overwhelmed, Theroun found himself wanting to be closer. His hands had slipped to Lhaurent's neck, drawing the man in. As if Theroun *wanted* to become one, in the fullest sense of the word.

Stand firm, Scorpion.

Khorel's voice inside Theroun's mind was like a hand upon his shoulder, pulling him back from a terrible abyss. As if a quicksilver lifeline had been cast to Theroun in a maelstrom, he seized that thread as Lhaurent's power stormed him. And in that moment, Theroun found his Beast, and understood it. Lifting his hand, Theroun settled his grip behind Lhaurent's neck, sealing them together.

"So be it," he growled.

And then he thrust the power of his *wyrria* like a serpent's strike through that drop of blood Lhaurent touched – hard. Making the man feel it. Forcing it to shiver up inside that swirling hand of power and death; making Lhaurent understand the madness that was the Black Viper of the Aphellian Way. All of Theroun's rage; all his fury. All of his blackhearted existence inside this twisted body. All his lust for killing, his desire to murder unimpeded. Theroun let his venom flow through his blood, pouring out of his body like an oilslick darkness and into Lhaurent.

Lhaurent stared at him in wide-eyed surprise, then flowed to his feet quickly, shaky, releasing Theroun so fast he was almost shoved over backwards. Staring down upon Theroun, he breathed hard, uncertainty in his oceanic grey gaze. His brows knit, his spectral hand and the inky darkness around the golden sigils swirling in a chaotic maelstrom, as if whatever he had felt from Theroun had rattled him.

"Kill him," Lhaurent spoke at last, "when our war is won. As far as our campaign, you will march out at dawn. Your previous request for more naval support is denied – you have all the ships you need for this engagement. Report when you arrive at the Aphellian

Way. "

"Rennkavi. As you bid." Khorel rose from the chaise with steady grace. Stepping behind Theroun, Khorel touched his shoulder. "Come."

Theroun came to his feet, not unsteady anymore but immensely calm, flooded with the searing black poison of his *wyrria*. They turned and Lhaurent watched them go, and were soon out the bluestone door into the hall. The door sealed with a sigh. Once it was shut, Khorel gave a sigh of his own. Theroun followed as they made their way back through the vaulted byrunstone halls, and Khorel led them back to the dome-room with the chugging gears before he finally spoke.

"You did well," he murmured, quietly. "Come. We still have much to do tonight."

"What happened in there?" Theroun followed as Khorel descended into the pit along the bluestone walkway.

"You subsumed the Rennkavi's Unity. By the power of your own *wyrria*." Khorel glanced over at Theroun, his gaze frank.

"I thought the Rennkavi was infallible." Theroun growled, still feeling his dark *wyrria* moving inside him, unwilling to be completely put away yet.

"He should be." Khorel gave Theroun a level stare as they stepped up before the Alranstone.
"Something is wrong with him, with the Goldenmarks. When I first met Lhaurent our Rennkavi, I expected a man of such overwhelming will and heart that his power would shine brighter than a thousand suns, the twinned blood of the Dawn and the Wolf and Dragon surging through his veins. But when Lhaurent unveiled his Goldenmarks to me at Highsummer... I was able to turn them from my heart, just as you did now. He still does not know that he did not command me to his service completely. And through me, the rest of the Kreth-Hakir have not been entirely commanded to the Rennkavi's service, either."

"But you're telling me they should have been. So Lhaurent's power isn't all-consuming, as your Order expected?" Theroun growled as they mounted the wide dais, the towering Alranstone ahead.

"It's enough to be vastly dangerous." Khorel shot Theroun a

warning glance. "Even if he can't completely compel you or me, or the entirety of the Kreth-Hakir nor this Alranstone in the bowels of Roushenn, he can Unify armies of common folk, legions of them. And he still wields peculiar powers of his own, amplified a hundredfold by Leith's ring and other *wyrric* talismans that Lhaurent has learned to use. And *that* is something to gravely beware."

Theroun glanced at the Stone as it gave a pulse of light from an opal eye at the top of six closed ones. "Is that how Lhaurent attains passage through these things – he Unifies them to his will, just like he does with men?"

"Not all of them." Khorel stroked the Stone lovingly. "This one is still able to resist him, though she plays along with his schemes."

"She?" Theroun cocked his head. "Are you saying a person is inside every Alranstone?"

"Yes. Just as Lhaurent poisons the hearts of men into worshiping him, he can poison the hearts of Alranstones into doing his will. It's part of why his campaigns were able to spread so far and so quickly, in secret. But this one closest to him is not poisoned. Metrene only makes him think she's a slave, so she can watch where he goes. And report – to us."

"She's Kreth-Hakir." Theroun's eyebrows rose. He set a palm to the Stone and felt an enormous weave of opal strands smooth as pearls settle over his thoughts, soothing.

"Metrene den'Yesh, consort to our High Master, and the strongest Kreth-Hakir High Mistress who ever lived. She's been inside this Stone since Leith committed her here, a thousand years ago."

A smooth surge came from the Kingstone again, but there was no more time for talk as a blinding flare of light seared the cavern, and Theroun was once again threaded through annihilation and back out the other side. They emerged at the Stone in Ligenia, and Jornath wasted no time recovering. With long strides, he led Theroun down another set of cliff-steps, winding them far down into the harbor, to the slurry of floating piers that formed the oceanic trade of Ligenia Bay.

They continued along the quiet docks in a tense silence. Few people were about this time of night. A trio of old duffers smoking pipes gambled at cards across a barrel by the light of an unsteady lantern. A ship's dog barked, growling at Khorel as they passed. Khorel gave it a sharp glance and it yelped, cowering behind a stack of crab-pots and whining as if struck. A waifish whore in salt-starched rags showed Theroun a shoulder and an unenthusiastic smile as they moved by, blisters encrusting her lips. Theroun hadn't allowed sick whores in his army camps, and Jornath was no different – she was down here working the docks because she couldn't get coin on the cliffs above.

Theroun walked on, moving briskly to keep up with the powerful strides of Khorel Jornath. The man was brooding, though on everything that had happened with Lhaurent or on something else, Theroun couldn't say. Curious, Theroun brushed up against Khorel's mind, his control over his oilslick mind-weaves better in the vast quiet of the bay. Only to find Khorel's thoughts vacant as graves. The man was hiding his mind from Theroun, very carefully, though his emotions were all too plain upon his body.

Theroun didn't know where they were going next, as they wound their way through the docks to the far western edge of the squalid city. Squat stone buildings populated the wharf, fisheries and salting operations, trade-houses and gambling inns. Cracked wooden placards creaked in the autumnal wind, paint flaking and crusty from sea-spray. A circle of unsavory characters occupied the dock ahead. Though they numbered eight swarthy men, they took one look at Khorel and Theroun coming down the dock and broke apart, stepping back, wariness shining in their eyes. Not the looks of men whose minds had been cowed, but of wolves who naturally feared a predator in the dark stronger than they.

Khorel and Theroun strode by without a second glance. At last, they reached a sea-cave on the western side of the bay. It was high and dry, the tide washed out to its lowest point. Khorel rounded into the darkness and Theroun followed, letting his eyes adjust to the deep interior. Gazing around, Theroun saw that a short Alranstone occupied the vaulted sea-cave. High up in a cluster of volcanic rock, it thrust up from a vein of smoky Hellenthine crystal. Streaked with yellow quartz that gleamed gold in the lantern light like a tiger's eyes, the striped crystal Alranstone stood only a handspan taller than Theroun.

Up on the volcanic bedrock, three Kreth-Hakir Brethren gave

cordial nods to Khorel, standing from where they had been sitting in silent meditation next to the lantern. Brother Kiiar was there with his flyaway white hair and enthusiastic smile through his half-melted face. Brother Caldrian gave Theroun a welcoming scowl with an amused quirk of lips, and Theroun gave one back. Rising with impeccable fluidity, Brother Aldo curried back his copper waves and gave Khorel a nod, saluting with two fingers to his inner eye.

"Brother Jornath. All is in readiness for the Heraldation."

"Thank you, Brother Aldo. Brother Caldrian, my Scion's accoutrement."

Stepping forward, Brother Caldrian held out a bundled harness of black leather, complete with longknives and a longsword. "You might need these tonight."

Raising his eyebrows, but seizing the weapons-harness anyway, Theroun buckled on twin longknives at his hips, settling the sword over his shoulder, also noting that a number of fly-blades were sheathed up the harness on his chest. There were also two longknives for his boots, and as Theroun slid them home, it felt right, returning to his battle-self. Though he didn't question why he'd suddenly been gifted weapons – Jornath's tense attitude tonight said enough. As Theroun prepared, Khorel leaped up the steps in the bedrock, waiting up by the Alranstone with hooded eyes. Theroun ascended the flights quickly with the other Brethren, soon standing before the tiger-striped Stone in the damp cave.

Jornath gave Theroun a warning look. "If Lhaurent is deadly, our next meeting is doubly so. Keep your mouth shut and your ears open, Scion. Do not worry, I will guard anything within your mind that needs guarding, but I implore you to be as cautious as you have ever been, as the night moves forward. Are we clear?"

"Indeed." Theroun responded, wondering what was coming. But he had no more time as everyone set their palms to the Alranstone, and were flashed through – into the most enormous cavern Theroun had ever seen.

It didn't smell like ocean detritus anymore, but cool and old, like they were buried leagues beneath the earth. A hollow breeze sighed through a space so gargantuan that Theroun couldn't see its boundaries, licking Theroun's skin. Faraway, light from deep inside the monstrous cavern showed edged contours in the black, of upthrust glassy obsidian crags nearby. As Theroun followed Jornath and the rest of his Brethren down an obsidian staircase from the high vantage they'd come through, he glanced back to see they'd been spat out of a massive Alranstone of pure obsidian ten man-heights tall. It had no eyes and no markings, and neither did the tremendous flow of black glass they now traversed.

Rounding upthrust pillars of obsidian as they descended, the entirety of the cavern was suddenly exposed to Theroun's view, and it was far larger than Theroun had initially thought. Of a vastness that boggled the mind, Theroun found himself humbled by the power of nature. As if he gazed down upon the Lintesh from the slopes of the Kingsmount, he saw a vast chasm of darkness below, ringing a tremendous plaza of natural obsidian that had thrust up from an oblivion of nothingness all around it, floating in the cavernous black.

Like fireflies in the night, the plaza below sparkled with light, and activity. A host was gathering, perhaps some five hundred strong, in the center of thirteen enormous obsidian archways that formed a ring in the center of the natural glass. As Theroun watched, enormous copper braziers were lit between every obsidian arch, blazing a hearty light through the darkness in a vast ring. Men moved about inside that ring, most clad in black. The glassy black lava-floe was connected to the far reaches of the cavern by arching obsidian bridges that spanned the ring of nothingness at the plaza's rim.

Following Jornath down the winding stairs carven into the near wall, Theroun and the rest were silent as they finally arrived at one of those ancient glass bridges. Narrow and without rails over the nothingness below, the bridge had an arching slickness that made even a hardy warrior like Theroun get a thump of trepidation in his chest. He tried not to stare down into that nothing, but he found he couldn't tear his eyes away from it. Endless it was, down into the bowels of the earth. One wrongly-placed foot would send Theroun sliding across the obsidian and down into it, his screams forever lost.

He pushed it from his mind, taking a deep breath and fixing his gaze straight ahead to the plaza. They were soon across the bridge, and Theroun breathed internally in relief. Before him, he could see the gathering at the center of the thirteen arches. Most of those here were clad in the studded silver and black leather of the Kreth-Hakir, though some weren't. As they neared one gargantuan arch, Theroun picked out the crimson of a Red Valor uniform moving in that sea of black, though the man who wore it was a slender copper-haired Cennetian. Silver flashes of Lefkani privateer's garb caught his gaze, their coins of wealth smelted into their salt-wrecked sea-armor. A few swarthy Ghreccani moved in that casual melee, scimitars at their colorful sashes and tattooed geometric designs of their kills across their cheeks, foreheads, and down their necks. A smattering of Unaligned men of massive stature towered above the rest, clad in herringbone huntsman's fawn leathers.

But the thing that truly caught Theroun's attention was the dragon.

Astonishment hit him as he stared. This creature, if indeed it was what Theroun supposed it was, though he had thought such things only the stuff of fae-yarns, had been dead a very long time. Large as a hundred men and coiled in a fetal position in the center of the plaza, it was surrounded on all sides by massive upthrust jags of obsidian. It looked mummified; scaled skin thin as vellum stretched over jutting bones, its color perhaps once a brilliant red with golden stripes along its length, but which now looked like a lord's finery gone to ruin.

An opalescent dust coated the beast, making it appear bleached of its once-luminous color, though that dust shimmered in the darkness like powdered diamonds. Sinew could be seen all along the length of its rib-sunken body and vertebrae, where spines jutted out in a long double-row upon its back. Its enormous head was blocky, its thick jaws snarling with black fangs. The scaled skin had sunk over hollowed eye-sockets and filled with dust, giving the thing a haunting, pale stare. A mantle folded along its neck, furled in death but comprised of a vicious spread of spines. Its muscled forelegs had massive claws, but it had no hind-legs that Theroun could see, nor wings. Only a body and tail that coiled like a serpent, the spiked tip curling back around its forelegs and snout in death.

Staring at the dead beast, Theroun realized they had crossed under the obsidian arch. The gathering turned to watch their arrival, except for a few servers moving through the throng with refreshment upon silver trays, dressed in Kreth-Hakir garb with their cowls up. Upthrust areas of obsidian had been commandeered as high seats for whatever was about to occur, providing a view over the plaza. The area within the archways descended at a slope to the upthrust obsidian platform and the mummified dragon in the center, like a giant amphitheater.

Theroun could feel thunder moving around that bowl. As if the obsidian floes amplified all thought, mind-weaves hit Theroun like an ocean as he crossed under the arch behind Khorel Jornath. Theroun staggered, feeling like his head would explode from the sudden roar of it. And yet, the gargantuan chamber was silent, only the sounds those of breathing and the clink of drinks set aside as Theroun crossed into the assembly's midst – curious eyes staring and minds pressing from all around.

With a snarl, Theroun felt his oilslick-black *wyrria* rise, spearing minds back from his person with a renegade rabidity. A number of eyes went wide, and the thunder of minds hissed upon the perimeter as if Theroun had bitten them. A passing serving-lad collapsed in a faint, shattering the crystal chalices upon his tray and spilling blood-red wine over the plaza's black glass at Theroun's boots. Three others hustled to the lad, hauling him up and out of the circle toward far passages in the cavern, staring back at Theroun with wondering eyes.

Everything inside Theroun told him he'd just entered a den of thieves, as his *wyrria* bristled. These were men of the most vile and dubious sort. Cons, thieves, murderers; night-workers, wet-boys, pirates. Manipulators who wove in the shadows and turned kingdoms to their liking. His spine tingled with danger, and Theroun found his hands upon his knife-hilts.

But some of those nearest Theroun in Hakir black gave him thoughtful looks as they glanced to Khorel, then back to Theroun. One ancient man in a plain black robe rather than studded leathers gave a small smile, his black-on-black eyes piercing from beneath his cowl, and Theroun saw Brother Kiiar nod. A group of Lefkani pirates in their smelted silver coin armor and fetish-strung mohawks approached, and Brother Caldrian clasped arms with them. Like a cool wind, Theroun felt Khorel's mind move through his – calming him, pressing his unease back, assuring him there was no immediate danger, yet.

"Steady, Scion," Khorel murmured at his side. "Be still and stay silent until I introduce you before the Heraldation. Keep a civil tongue. And know that there are those here who can read your mind flawlessly – and compel you to do things just as flawlessly if you are found wanting as a new member among our Order."

"Define *things* and *wanting*," Theroun growled, hands on his longknives as his careful gaze scoured those who watched him.

Khorel turned dark eyes to Theroun, quicksilver warning pummeling from him. "Death, if you are found too dangerous to let live. Or worse."

"How much worse?" Theroun growled.

"Far worse. Come. And try to keep a leash on your darkness." With that, Jornath strode forward through the throng, Kreth-Hakir and others sighing back from his presence like wheat before the scythe.

CHAPTER 39 – JHERRICK

Aldris had spent a number of days recovering from his ordeals of resurrection. The Albrenni had been caring for him, and the Guardsman had regained his health well. Now, the Kingsman and the Khehemnas stood face-to-face upon the cloverleaf plaza with the seven crystal archways, listening to the portals whisper in the violet dusk, flowing with the deep breath of the Void. Standing before Jherrick, Aldris set his hands to his hips, far more sober than he'd once been. A dusk breeze stirred his bright mane above his careworn smile, his black crystal death-sword in a harness upon his back with two matching longknives at his belt. Clad in his royal green silk jerkin tooled with silver thread, Aldris looked regal, hardened, his short golden beard luminous in the settling dark.

"You look good, kid," Aldris spoke at last.

"You look better than I might have thought," Jherrick returned with a slight smile.

"I look better than I feel." Aldris gave a low chuckle, his smile wry. "Death, you know? Takes its toll."

"What do you remember?" Jherrick had not been permitted to see Aldris while the Guardsman recovered, and he and Aldris still had not spoken of what had happened during Aldris' resurrection. Commanded to sit and listen to the World Shaper's song for the past week once more, Jherrick hadn't been sure if the Albrenni were punishing him for his inability to finish Aldris' resurrection, or if they'd simply had their hands full healing Archaeon Stranik. But now, watching the Guardsman returned, hale and whole, Jherrick knew he'd made the right decision, to bring the man back. Staring at each other, something flowed between them, some understanding that there was more they both had yet to do in this world.

"I remember enough." Aldris' gaze slid past Jherrick's shoulder to the seven archways, and Jherrick watched tendrils of lion-tawny light ease toward that otherworldly flow in the Void. "I remember music, and… love. No woman in the world can love a man like that, kid, I tell you that much."

"Do you want to go back?"

Aldris drew a deep breath as his piercing green gaze flicked back to Jherrick. "No. I have a duty here. Just because we've come through to some mysterious realm ruled by ancient beings doesn't mean we're not needed back home. We took oaths to be in the Roushenn Palace Guard, kid. Oaths to Queen and country. I stand by them."

"I don't know if I do anymore." The evening breeze rippled Jherrick's hair and he combed it back out of his eyes, longer than it had once been.

"Maybe not." Aldris' smile was wry as he took in every inch of Jherrick's frame. "You've changed, kid. Queen and country don't seem to be your thing anymore. Maybe they never were. So. You can resurrect people, huh?"

Aldris' gaze was frank, searching. Jherrick knew the question in the Guardsman's mind and he shivered. "I almost lost control of it, Aldris, trying to bring you back. I don't know… if I can bring *her* back."

"But you might be able to." Aldris' gaze pierced Jherrick to the quick, intense as he moved a step closer in the falling dusk with a gesture at the cosmos brightening all around them now. "Lhaurent's out there, Jherrick. Back home. Reaping Aeon-knows what destruction in our absence. The Albrenni have seen war surrounding Alrou-Mendera. He needs to be stopped." Aldris scuffed a boot upon the stone. "Our world needs a hero, Jherrick. We need Olea."

"But what if I can't—?" Jherrick's heart clenched, fear gripping him.

Aldris moved forward. Reaching out, he gripped Jherrick's shoulder and Jherrick winced, the talon-punctures from Aldris' resurrection still resisting Noldra Ethirae's healing. "The Albrenni told me about the power you unleashed to bring me back. They told me they've only seen anything like it once before – in a time of *real* warriors, Jherrick, men and women with *wyrric* powers the likes of which we can only dream. Even if you lost control of it resurrecting me, you're a power to be reckoned with. I know it. Halsos, I *felt* it. I can still feel those talons of yours dragging me back from wherever I was. There was a part of me that didn't want to return. But you dragged my ass back, because I have a duty here, unfinished. And so do you."

Aldris' emerald gaze was sharp. Jherrick felt a dire energy flow between them, as if the bond he'd hauled Aldris back from the Void by had never truly severed. "You want me to go with you. To return to Alrou-Mendera."

"The Albrenni say we can leave by those anytime." Aldris nodded at the shimmering archways. "That they'll take us where we need to go."

"Need is a funny thing."

"Yeah, no shit." Aldris growled with a darker humor than Jherrick had ever heard from the man. Releasing Jherrick, he stepped up to the grand arches and scuffed one boot upon the stone, marveling up at their immense height. "Ever wonder if our need was what fucked us? Right from that damn Alranstone out of Lintesh?"

"The Albrenni say that the souls bound inside Alranstones hear the music of the World Shaper," Jherrick stared up at the shifting portalways also. "They go mad, unable to return to that vast music. They make choices based upon what they hear, a choice subtler than thought."

Aldris gave a harsh laugh, then curried a hand through his golden mane. "We're gonna end up three galaxies over, if we take one of these damn things again. That Flavian fellow said this realm was carved out eons before his people were even born – that this is a space *between* time. Fuck if I know what that means, but apparently, passing a span here means nothing – we can go back to when we left, if we need to. Unless a portal-keeper stops us, I guess."

"These portals don't have keepers, not like Alranstones," Jherrick mused, feeling etheric currents move through the Voidworld. "These arches are *open ways*, Aldris. They operate on resonance – our own soul chooses the destination."

"Then it should be easy-peasy," Aldris chuckled, his green eyes dark by the light of the shifting archways. "My soul wants to get the fuck home. And kick Lhaurent's ass. You with me?"

"You know it's not that easy."

"Yeah. I *really* fucking do." Aldris turned, giving Jherrick a hard stare like chips of burning flint. "You recovered from that

Bloodstone near Khehem. I was *dead*, Jherrick. I was out there a long time. And even though it was only a month, it felt like centuries. A part of me can't help but wonder… if I went through one of *those*," Aldris nodded at the archways, "whether I would come back at all."

"Do you want to return to the Void?" Jherrick's breath was soft. "Or would you rather return home?"

Aldris' gaze strayed far for a while, fixed upon the archways, then at last came back. He was silent for a moment more, then gave a wry chuckle. He was about to respond, when Jherrick suddenly felt a ripple pass through the Void. Like an exhalation, a tremendous wind sighed over him. The stars and galaxies stood out in high relief above, as if a dark moon had covered the night.

Turning, Jherrick watched the archways shift and shiver in the Void. Suddenly, the centermost arch flashed, swirling fierce and chaotic. An explosion of heat knocked Jherrick and Aldris backward as the pillars of that arch writhed with luminous fire. Gold and red twisted in a vicious dance, as the World Shaper's music screamed like a beast writhing in the grip of seven burning hells.

A man was spat out from the centermost arch, landing with a wretched crunch upon the plaza's stone – unmoving. Jherrick was already racing to his side, Aldris upon his heels. Decimated, the man's flesh was gouged with talon-rips, as if an eagle the size of a bear had tried to tear him apart. Blood was already soaking the agate-stone plaza, pulsing from a dozen rents in the man's abdomen, his neck, his thigh. His shredded charcoal silk garb was of the Twelve Tribes' *berounhim* caravanserai, but as his hood fell back, Jherrick saw russet-red hair like a man of Cennetia.

As Jherrick's hands touched the man to roll him to his back, his eyes flew open. Gold-red and twisting with wildfire, his eyes burned in his bloodshot whites. Unseeing, those eyes were dazed with pain and a terrible battle-fury. Searing like suns, the image of a red-gold dragon flamed up around the man in the Void. He roared with all the power of that massive beast behind it – and then his breath was gone.

"Fuck!" Aldris felt for a pulse at the man's ripped neck, more mincemeat than flesh, blood flowing out over his fingers. "Do something, Aeon-dammit! Use your gift!"

Jherrick's hands were already moving with the flow of his

wyrria; his mind was already in the Void. Jherrick felt the man's soul swirling around his body upon wings of gilded red flame, roaring for a way back in but not finding the means. This soul wanted to come back. It *needed* to. Surging around Jherrick in the Void, it blistered him with power and the agonizing need to have its body again. Moving on pure instinct, it was not a conscious decision Jherrick made, to bring the man back. It was as if Jherrick's *wyrria* was compelled, his left hand slapping to the man's heart, pressing to his rent chest as his right hand raised, his *wyrria* reaching out, up – everywhere.

And as Jherrick acted, the man's soul understood implicitly what was about to happen – roaring into Jherrick with the exultation of suns exploding.

Jherrick screamed at the immense power heaving through him. Muscled with scales and burning flesh, it was chaos, a churning miasma of conflict and power. Using his body as a lightning rod, all that bestial energy roared inside Jherrick. His insides burned as his mind sundered trying to contain the man's essence. It poured through him like lava as it slammed back into the man's body. The man beneath Jherrick's palm raged to life, roaring like his *wyrria*. With both hands, he seized Jherrick's face – and a desperate hurl of memories went flipping through Jherrick's mind.

Destruction and death. War, terror, horror. Vast fields of blood, creatures of nightmare pouring out of open portalways, decimating armies like phosphor matchsticks. Upheavals of the land. Explosions of *wyrria* from deep within the earth, blasting cities to ruin. Everything he had seen in Noldra Ethirae's memories of the Demon's First Rise – to the last image and detail. But this remembrance was of modern vistas flooded with carnage and nightmare. In the man's vision, Jherrick recognized the Aphellian Way, the Valley of Doors upon the Elsthemi border, the oases of Ghellen and Khehem – and the City of Lintesh.

And through it all, cold red eyes, glorifying in the destruction to come.

"*Utrus!*" The dying man croaked. "*Khehe ahlwe—!*"

Shock smote Jherrick, to hear the man's heavily-accented Old Khehemni. But his meaning was all too clear. *The Utrus. Battle it.* With his final pronouncement, the man's umber-gold eyes rolled up.

He seized, his broken body unable to contain his soul's return. Blood poured from his mouth, a gurgling bloody froth.

"*Hemna ahlmine!*" Jherrick shouted. "Stay with me, dammit!"

Jherrick couldn't let him die. This man was a power to be reckoned with – one who had seen the Demon's Rise, not in elder times but in the modern era. The man's golden-flame gaze tried to hold Jherrick's, an animal determination within him. Before his soul could flee again, Jherrick raised both hands to the cosmos. With a primal roar, he did the only thing that came to him. He made his body a channel, a through-way – a portal in and of itself, through which the vast energy of the World Shaper could flow.

And it came. Thundering through him with the sound of a thousand trumpets, roaring down through his hands and in the crown of his head with the power of a million drums. Ripping through every pore like the scrape of endless bow-strings, the vast creationary music of the cosmos came into Jherrick like a maelstrom wind through the harmonies of time. Unskilled, unlearned, Jherrick was drowning in the sound, tuned too far, being pulled down with it – all his body's vibrations rushing into the dying man upon the bloody agate-stone.

The man's body took that harmony without apology or remorse. Like a thousand beasts opened their maws and drank that enormous sound, it ravaged Jherrick, devouring him alive. Jherrick screamed, desperately trying to get out of the way. But the red dragon ate his resonance, merciless. All heat left him. Jherrick's blood slowed to a thick syrup, even as some part of him saw the man's ruined body snapping back together. Wounds roared shut; bones hammered into place. Sinews stretched, thrumming as they knit, and the dying man arched in a spasm.

But as his living gasp poured forth, shaking the tremolos of time, Jherrick's own breath sighed out. Jherrick collapsed to the bloody stones, his own life exchanged for the man's – even as some part of his dimming vision saw the man rise, hale and whole.

"No! You are not to perish!"

The man's baritone was urgent, his speech a heavily-accented Common tongue now, flavored with the rolling lilt of the Twelve Tribes. Burning gold eyes were visible above Jherrick as scalding hands held his face – and then, the man's lips were upon Jherrick's.

A tremendous beast of *wyrria* emanated from the man, power boiling through the Void. Like a storm in the darkness, it crackled with crimson fire and bursts of golden *wyrric* lightning. As the man exhaled, a raging fire of ether poured into Jherrick's mouth. Cascading down Jherrick's throat, it flamed his heart and lungs. Jherrick gasped, life flooding back as the man poured fire like liquid honey deep into his body, reviving that which had been ready to die. Jherrick gasped, watching the man's *wyrria* manifest – terrible and magnificent, an immense power channeled directly into his veins and blood. After the third breath, Jherrick shuddered back completely, stabilized by that enormous flow.

The man set their foreheads together, gripping Jherrick's nape like they were brothers as he gave a breathless laugh. "You return, my savior! Thank all the gods!"

Jherrick blinked up, seeing fire-gold eyes roiling with ancient power set in the man's strong, handsome face. As his *wyrria* settled in the Void, the man's eyes shifted from writhing fire into a pleasant gold-ochre color, reminding Jherrick quite suddenly of First-Lieutenant Fenton den'Kharel. His features were handsome, high-cheeked and chisel-jawed, with humor and kindness. He even looked like Fenton, as if they could have been brothers – one the essence of midday heat, the other evening's last gloaming, his body wiry and lean and of a similar stature, though slightly taller.

"Who *are* you?" Jherrick breathed, still feeling a nimbus of prickling energy all around him, as if the man couldn't quite control his vast *wyrria*. A thousand ants stung Jherrick's skin, marching along his pores, making him wince.

The man chuckled, and with a knowing look, he shook out his body, hale now and without a scratch on him, though his charcoal *berounhim*-style silken garb was ripped to shit and soaked with blood. Doing a deep series of breaths, the pricking energy around the man gradually subsided as Jherrick sat up on the plaza, staring at him. Aldris knelt at Jherrick's side, his eyes wide as their gazes connected, Aldris' hand ready upon one longknife as he looked back to the stranger.

"You ok, kid?" Aldris growled low, his vicious green gaze locked upon the russet-haired man.

"I'm fine." Jherrick reached out, settling his fingers to Aldris' wrist. "I'm fine."

The Guardsman didn't quite stand down as he helped Jherrick to his feet, his eyes never leaving the russet-haired man doing his breathing practice. At last, the man opened his eyes and with a fluid movement, rose, the prickling nimbus that had previously surrounded him smoothed out into an easy golden glow. Through his torn *berounhim* garb showed lithe, desert-honed muscles just like Lourden and his *Rishaaleth*. Lean as a sword, he looked no more than twenty-eight or thirty, hardly older than Jherrick – but held the command of a battle-lord as his eyes flashed crimson flame.

"Forgive me," he smiled wryly at Jherrick, with a nod to Aldris, "the dragons of our blood dance together, my friend. Thank you for restoring your liege, Khehemnas. Whatever the Scion of Khehem may do for you, he will."

"Scion of Khehem? Who are you? What the hell is this?" Aldris cut in, his eyes narrowed, his hand back on the knife at his hip.

The man set his hands on his hips with an exhilarated laugh. Bright like a lion yet smooth like a wolf stalking dark shadows, he lifted one hand in a gesture of peacemaking. "Forgiveness! Please. I have come straight out of a dire trial, and my wits and manners scatter. It is not a daily occurrence that a man finds himself nearly torn apart and then just as suddenly corralled back into life. Forgiveness, please. My name is Leith Alodwine, Scion of Khehem, son of King Orihout Alodwine, of the Thirteen Tribes. And you are?"

"Leith *Alodwine*? Last King of *Khehem*?" Aldris' hand pulled his longknife now, both of them, as he moved into a fighting stance in front of Jherrick. "Hold right there, fuckstone! I don't know who you are, but that isn't Aeon-fucking funny."

Jherrick was as shocked as Aldris, but menacing the man at blade-point had been a bad move. "Careful, fighter." The man's eyes flashed crimson fire, his smooth baritone devoid of all pleasantness now, that strange nimbus prickling with energy around him once more. "Those who pull blades on the Scions of Khehem live short lives. Especially upon Khehem's soon-to-be King."

"You really think you're Khehem's last King?" Aldris' snort was derisive, his blades still out. "That city's dead. No one's lived there for a thousand years. Good luck getting crowned by anything other than char and sand."

The man's russet-gold eyes narrowed, twisting with a maelstrom of heat and a dark temper. "Dare you to loose such an idiot tongue steeped in lies at me? Telling me such odious falsehoods —"

"Peace!" Jherrick moved in fast, extending a hand to forestall the bloodshed he could practically feel coming. "My comrade speaks the truth. Khehem has no King, and no one has lived there since it was destroyed in a terrible war a thousand years ago. It's a dead city, my friend. We've seen it, with our own eyes. We've been there."

"How can it be? The vision that beast gave me…" The man went pale, his russet eyes terrible. All fire dropped from his eyes as an annihilating fear roiled through his gaze. With a shudder, he wiped a palm over his face, his fingertips lingering at his smooth lips. His hand drifting away from his face, he stared at it, as if it was not quite there. Jherrick drew a deep breath as he and Aldris shared a look. Aldris lowered his crystal longknives, watching the man closely as Jherrick took a breath, his brows furrowed.

Jherrick was about to ask if the man really was who he said he was, and what he recalled of these trials he had just come from, when he felt a movement of air from above. Five Albrenni flew down through the dusk-lit sky like eagles diving, slamming to the plaza with ephemeral wings wide and rolling with power. It was not Noldrones Flavian, but Archaeon Stranik who stormed forward with all the wrath of a burning sun, a massive javelin of pure rose-crystal hefted in his right hand. His broken wings spread wide, they trembled as he devoured the essence of the stars, his gaze pinning Jherrick like firebrands.

"What have you done, Noldrones Jherrick?" Archaeon rumbled, his voice pummeling the air like thunder. "Have you not learned that those you return from death become your responsibility?"

"This man has had a vision of the Red-Eyed Demon, same as I have." Jherrick rose, standing his ground before the ancient Albrennus, not accepting criticism for something his *wyrria* had done on pure instinct, and something that had felt so right to do. "I saw my nation destroyed in his vision, Archaeon. I couldn't let him die."

The man who professed to be Leith Alodwine had stepped beside Jherrick. His fugue passed with the arrival of this new danger, his palms were spread at his sides in peacemaking. But his gaze was level, focused, wary: and in it Jherrick could see red fire begin to twist – as that tremendous energy bubbled up in the Void again, swirling around him.

"You have resurrected something you can't control, Noldrones Jherrick." Archaeon's voice was cold, his iron-hard gaze shifting to the newcomer as if he also watched that tremendous *wyrria* seething up through the Void. "Someone whose fate is now intertwined with yours."

Four Albrenni flanked Archaeon, including Ethirae and Flavian, their infinite eyes full of a vast and terrible sorrow. Ethirae opened her mouth as if to speak, but at a shake of Flavian's head, she closed her beautiful lips. There was to be no mercy here. Whatever Jherrick had done, resurrecting this man here and now who professed to be Khehem's Last King, it was something terribly proscribed. Jherrick could see the enormous wave of energy the Albrenni pulled from the stars, channeling all of it into Archaeon. Ruined though he was, he was still powerful, the immensity of his rising energy lighting the air with curls of white vapor, the same as rippled through the archways – limning his crystal javelin with white sigils and coursing *wyrric* flames.

"I am no threat to you, whoever you are," Leith's voice was low at Jherrick's side, but the air around him crackled with answering power, his eyes molten gold as his hands transitioned to readiness. "But I tell you here and now, if you threaten a brother of my city, one who has saved my life, you will face my wrath. I have battled a beast of legend today and survived – and I'm of a mind to battle more if necessary."

The entire breadth of the cloverleaf plaza suddenly began to crackle with power, both from Archaeon and the Albrenni and also from the newcomer. With a florid curse, Aldris seized Jherrick by his collar, hauling him to the side near the archways. Archaeon's gaze pinned Jherrick, austere and terrible, before it slid back to the newcomer. But it was Noldrones Flavian that spoke up, his gaze infinite with sorrow as he pressed one hand to his heart.

"We have come because we feel the call of the Undoer within

the both of you," Flavian breathed, his starlit eyes devouring Jherrick. "Buried deep in a place where it was not before. Innocence remained until the Void shuddered with a deep and powerful knell just now, the likes of which I have not felt in a god's age. For at the touch of each other's *wyrria*, Noldrones Jherrick, the saving of each other's lives, you have saved a vision of Undoing that would have died to the Voidwinds had your souls both fled tonight. I am sorry. Though you made it all unwitting, the choice has been made. Two fates have been twined as one – for as long as you both may live it. We can no longer harbor you here, Noldrones Jherrick, for your learning will take a harder path than we ever could have imagined."

"Punish me for this profane act within your starlit realm, not him, god of whatever people you come from," Leith Alodwine spoke up, his voice cold with power. Jherrick glanced over to see that Leith's gaze had gone flat as that enormous power rose up behind him in the Void. Devouring light, it spun in crimson and gold shadows like a vortex of endless motion. Flavored with the snarl of beasts in battle, a red wash of color filled the Void, fueled with conflict and rage.

"You will find no mercy here, Scion of conflict and deathmaking." Archaeon's answering growl was summer thunder upon a wind of ether. Drawing an enormous breath, he filled his emaciated chest like a powerful bellows, the crystal javelin in his ready hand flaring white-hot as he raised it.

And Jherrick knew that if battle began, only the Undoer would reap the harvest. Without stopping to think, he tore from Aldris' grip and stepped in front of the Scion of Khehem, raising his voice to Archaeon's etheric surge.

"Please, I beg you——!"

But Jherrick got no further. With a mighty throw, Archaeon hurled his crystal javelin, the lodestone for all the Albrenni's tremendous might – just as Leith Alodwine threw a concussion of power straight from the Void. Colliding, a tremendous sound rang through the Void and the Albrenni's realm, deafening Jherrick. A shockwave concussed the air from those two enormous powers, sundering the air with a blast as a torrent of sigils smote themselves into being and the crystal javelin exploded in a rush of *wyrric* flame and searing shards. Power ricocheted; crystal archways cracked.

Voidworld energy was released and Aldris was thrown backwards through the leftmost arch with a shout. Hammered by that enormous wave of force also, Leith's body hit Jherrick, the both of them tossed backwards through the crystal pillars of the central arch.

And as the vapors of the World Shaper's mist consumed him, Jherrick heard a cacophony of sounds in the Void, the most sundering, terrible thing he had ever heard in his life – before he was wrenched through the crystal pillars, his body exploding into nothingness before it was once again formed upon the other side.

CHAPTER 40 – THEROUN

Khorel Jornath took the lead with Theroun and his other Brethren at his heels, striding into the throng of thieves and Kreth-Hakir upon the obsidian plaza. A soaring silence devoured the bowl between the thirteen black glass archways. Theroun kept his hands on his knife-hilts as he moved through to the front, near the jagged obsidian upwelling and the preserved dragon covered in glittering white dust. A dais of obsidian thrust up in the creature's midst, encircled by the dragon's tail and neck, reached by a narrow bridge over the tail and a set of obsidian stairs.

Upon that dais stood a massive man, raised up above the dragon's body and visible to the entire amphitheater. He watched Khorel and Theroun approach, though he had no eyes from which to watch. Chin uplifted, the towering, muscled warrior had a white mane thick as a lion's, raked back from his forehead and braided into long twists. Upright and strong, with massive shoulders and powerful limbs, he wore the studded black herringbone leathers of the Kreth-Hakir, an enormous battle-axe riding his back rather than a broadsword.

The warrior's proud face was strong-boned, and Theroun realized his stature was truly massive as they ascended the stairs to the dais. The man stood a full head taller than Khorel Jornath, and Khorel was already a head taller than most. The old blind warrior made Theroun feel like a sewer-rat as he came to stand before the dais and adopted his best glower. Riven scars criss-crossed the warrior's stoic face, like a keshar had ripped up a mountain, deeper than any keshar-marks Theroun had ever seen. The broad scars continued down his neck, under the high collar of his studded jerkin. His bare hands were ripped up also and Theroun's brows rose, wondering if it was the same beneath all that leather.

"Indeed." The old warrior broke into a rumbling chuckle, gazing down at Theroun with an amused smile twisting his thick lips.

"My scars go all the way through my flesh and out the other side. Master your pain, and pain will no longer be your master. Welcome, Theroun den'Vekir den'Jornath, Black Viper of the Aphellian Way, newest member of our Order."

"And who are you?" Theroun growled, his hackles high as kestrels that this man had slipped into his mind so easily that Theroun felt not a single trace of it.

"Magnus Yesh. But you may call me High Master." The man's blind sockets stared down at Theroun, vastly cunning. Even though Theroun could not feel a single silver thread, he knew that massive, ancient presence was rolling through him, feeling out his every last thought and memory.

"Stay out of my head." Theroun growled, a lance of oilslick-dark energy spearing out of him on instinct. Master Yesh did nothing, his posture and subtle smile impeccable. But Theroun's own *wyrria* came hammering back at him, smiting him to his knees upon the obsidian glass. Theroun gasped, feeling like he'd taken a swipe from an ice-bear. His knees screamed, ground into the rock as the pressure pummeled him, his spine bowing and head pounding beneath that tremendous force.

"Khorel. Did you not suggest that your Scion be civil at these proceedings?" High Master Yesh spoke in an amused tone. Theroun couldn't look up. Incalculable weight pressed him – only his shaking hands kept him braced from being flattened upon the dais.

Chuckles stole through his mind from those filling the amphitheater's bowl. Not a few of the Kreth-Hakir were grinning, enjoying the show. But there were those who did not grin. The Cennetian in the Red Valor uniform, for one, far back up on a crag of obsidian stone. Through his pain, Theroun caught the man's gaze, saw his careful copper eyes as he lifted one hand surreptitiously to his longknife. The Lefkani pirates were no less uneasy, their eyes darting as they maneuvered into a tight group with the feel of a bristling sea-urchin. And the Ghreccani moved restlessly, swarthy faces scowling with hands on their scimitars.

Just as Theroun thought some of these non-Hakir would leave, High Master Yesh raised a hand to the assembly. "Brothers! Lothren! All those who remember Leith Alodwine, Master of the Dragon and Great Unifier of our time, gather! For tonight we hold the

Heraldation, as we have not had in many a long year. For those among the Lothren who know only of this gathering from their forefathers, know this: no harm shall be visited upon you, no matter how willfully you debate tonight. All may wear weapons in this hall, but none may draw, on pain of Annihilation. My Kreth-Hakir Brethren are included in this truce. Should any draw blades or mind-weapons, only Annihilation shall be the result. Those who are new to the Brethren," Master Yesh gave Theroun the full force of his scar-blind gaze, "would do well to remember consequence in this sacred place."

Theroun's body was suddenly released. The weight upon him evaporated and he was able to take a shaky breath, then push to his feet. Master Yesh's blind gaze lingered, before he turned back to the hall.

"Now!" He bellowed, his voice amplified through the natural bowl of obsidian and reflected back by the archways, "We have been called together tonight by High Priest Khorel Jornath, who asked for this assembly some months ago to discuss matters of import."

Master Yesh opened his hand to indicate Khorel – who gave a nod, then flicked his glance to Theroun. Theroun understood and stepped to Khorel's side, but Khorel slid a step forward, so Theroun stood just behind. Theroun set his jaw, chafing, until a soothing wash of energy sluiced over him. *Peace, Scion. Pay attention. You may find your insights needed here.*

That statement cooled Theroun. He settled into watchful silence, arms crossed and his scowl in place, his gaze raking the crowd from the high dais as Master Yesh began to speak again. "We live in dire times, my friends – for the Rennkavi has come!"

The hall erupted in furor, but only from those who did not wear the herringbone-black. Theroun glanced to Khorel, but the man stood firm, gazing straight ahead. Master Yesh raised his hands for the gathering to quiet, then motioned Khorel Jornath forward to speak.

"The Rennkavi has indeed come," Khorel spoke in his low, dominant tones. His voice blossomed through the hall, resonant with his rolling Unaligned accent. "I have seen his Goldenmarks and felt their power. The Kreth-Hakir have felt it also, when the Rennkavi sought to break me to his Uniter's bind near Highsummer."

Khorel glanced to Master Yesh, who nodded and gestured for him to elaborate.

"Lhaurent den'Alrahel of Alrou-Mendera bears the Goldenmarks," Khorel intoned, continuing. "Long have the Kreth-Hakir Brethren monitored both tyrant and benevolent for the coming of the Rennkavi or the Demon. One has arrived. And yet," Khorel rubbed his lips and gave a hard sigh, something Theroun rarely saw him do, "he is not the Unifier we might have hoped."

Master Yesh beckoned for him to continue, and Khorel Jornath launched into a summation of Lhaurent's atrocious character. He detailed vile deeds and horrid deals the likes of which Theroun had never even imagined. From hundreds tortured in Roushenn's bleak halls, to thousands murdered in foreign lands, to using the Kreth-Hakir to smite down opposition, it was a stomach-churning list.

"Lhaurent is a tyrant," Jornath finished. "But I have seen the fervor of purpose in him. He believes he is the Uniter. He has a singularity of will that lends him power, gentlemen. A power not to be underestimated."

"Not to be underestimated at all." Someone spoke up from the audience, a slight but tall man wearing the herringbone black with Lefkani piercings up both ears.

"The Heraldation recognizes Brother Coralim hek'Enni," Master Yesh looked to the man and nodded.

"From our watching of Lhaurent by my contingent in Lintesh," the man continued, "which is now decimated but for myself and Brother Arno del'Legate, who remains there, Lhaurent has caused much distress in the population. But I have felt his Goldenmarks, same as Brother Jornath. They bend my will and make me wish for nothing but to make Lhaurent's glorious vision come to life, regardless of personal cost. Lhaurent has the power to unite us – to truly unite nations and armies against the coming of the Demon. And yet."

"Yet, Brother Coralim?" Master Yesh prodded in a gentle but firm tone.

"Yet," Brother Coralim continued, his glance darting to Khorel Jornath, "just a few weeks ago, the King-Protectorate from the First Abbey, one Temlin den'Ildrian, asserted that he had learned of Lhaurent's familial origins – that Lhaurent is not born of Leith

Alodwine's line, as we initially supposed. I passed this information on to Brother Jornath as soon as I heard it, though it cannot be substantiated. The King-Protectorate's mind was being artistically blocked at the time, by a ronin mind-bender who continues to slip out of our clutches in the mountains near the Elsee."

"Thank you Brother Coralim," Master Yesh nodded levelly. "What other opinions do we have on this matter?"

Theroun blinked, realizing it was to be a debate. He opened his ears, listening with rapt attention.

"Lhaurent is a bad man." This came from an enormously tall fellow of dark black skin down near the bottom of the dais. Countless white Jadounian scarifications of battle prowess were etched across his hands and up the backs of his forearms, even across his high cheekbones and down the sides of his neck. The man didn't wear black, but saffron silk garb with a wrapped headscarf – dual scimitars and countless knives on his harness.

"The Heraldation recognizes Prince Bitko Melo of the Sunwarrior tribe, Second-Head of the Jadounian Lothren." Master Yesh nodded to the tall fellow.

"Long have I done the bidding of my Lothren," the fellow nodded back and continued. "I respect and honor my father Ketko and my mother Botana, dual heads of our Lothren. We are warriors and fierce, but our hearts break for the wreckage done among our people at Lhaurent's command. My tribe has become little more than slavers. We are not warriors. We are not fierce. We ply our own people into service with threats and tainted water. More than half our population in Jadoun is already lost to Lhaurent's designs. We seek a pardon from this council tonight. We no longer wish to serve the Rennkavi. He is a bad man, and our country is dying because of him."

"Do you not serve your Lothren with glorious purpose?" Another man spoke from the side of the gathering. He had the stocky build of a Ghreccani, with blue-black ringlets down to his shoulders and a geometric tattoo across his forehead. Colorful ochre silk desert-garb was cinched close to his muscled personage, though he wore no weapons. As he approached, Theroun was stunned to realize the man's irises weren't Ghreccani black but a stunning ochre color that matched his garb. Those eyes fixed upon Theroun a moment as he pushed forward, rage in them, and cunning.

"The Heraldation recognizes Passiros Eluvios of the South Desert Raiders in Ghrec, First-Head of the Ghreccani Lothren, and Raiding Priest of the Brethren of the Kreth-Hakir."

Raiding Priest was a new title to Theroun. His gaze sharpened upon the man, interested that this fellow was Brethren and Lothren both, yet did not wear the herringbone black. Boorishly handsome, something about the Raiding Priest was also unique. Theroun heard Khorel take an inhalation, his presence stiffening as the Raiding Priest came all the way to the front. Their eyes locked – Khorel and Eluvios. Plain hatred seethed between them.

"You do Leith Alodwine a vast disservice," Eluvios continued, staring at Khorel though his body faced the Jadounian. "Losing heart in his designs during our time of trial."

"We do not lose heart in Leith," the Jadounian protested. "But we lose faith in this Rennkavi of such cruel nature."

It was as if the Jadounian had spoken right from Khorel's mouth. Theroun's attention sharpened, watching this interaction. He could feel testing lances of energy slicking out from Eluvios toward Khorel Jornath, who had erected a firm wall around himself and Theroun.

Master Yesh's hard gaze fell upon the Ghreccan. "You will cease, Passiros. State your opinions but leave off baiting Brother Jornath."

"As you will, High Master." The Ghreccan gave a florid bow. His broad-cheeked but handsome face was smug. Theroun surmised that whatever the man had been doing wasn't technically illegal here, but it was invasive. Khorel Jornath's face was tight; his jaw set. He actually crossed his arms over his broad chest.

"Are we such gutless curs?" Passiros faced the hall. The man used none of his *wyrria* now, but his presence was strong and his voice artful, capturing attention with ease. "Will we fold when Leith asks us to stand firm? If the Rennkavi has been Goldenmarked, no matter his bloodlines, it means the Demon's Rise is imminent. The character of our glorious Rennkavi is not to be questioned. Many have plainly stated tonight that Lhaurent den'Alrahel is of powerful personality and *wyrria*. It is our duty to follow him – *support* him in his every design."

Passiros stepped back with a florid bow. A low murmur of voices and minds spread through the cavern. Master Yesh let the hubbub rise, watching with his scarred and sightless hollows. Even as Theroun watched, he could see the assembly becoming divided. Mind-weaves moved through the amphitheater – Theroun could almost see them like silver fishing-lines cast between members of the Brethren as they conversed. Some shook their heads, arguing. Others had the glow of true zealousness. While others had roguish grins and spoke with serpentine gestures that churned Theroun's stomach – privateers who wanted to use Lhaurent cruel Unification as an excuse to rape and plunder.

"There is another!" A voice pierced from the rear of the throng with a clipped Cennetian accent.

Master Yesh raised his palms, urging the space to quiet, his absent eyes training on the Cennetian in the Red Valor uniform. "The Heraldation recognizes—" He paused, his brows knitting, then lifting as a hard smile stole over his face. "Recognizes one of the Cennetian Illianti, if I'm not mistaken."

"Indeed." The Cennetian leaped down from his obsidian crag and shouldered his way to the front, one hand upon his blade. Theroun sensed a battle-hardy presence in that wire-honed frame. Gazing at him, Theroun realized he recognized the fellow. Theroun had accompanied Uhlas into Velkennish once to try and reason with the young Vhinesse during the border-raids she'd commenced upon her inauguration. She'd had a Cennetian High General at her side in the throne hall – the same man who now stood before the assembly, doing Theroun's hard gaze one better with his sharp copper eyes – Merkhenos del'Ilio.

"You do not trust us, Son of Illium, to poison your mind from intrusion," Master Yesh chuckled, though his face was a hard mask.

The Cennetian gave a vicious grin back, his copper eyes flashing. "Illianti grandmothers pass on their knowledge and recipes, High Master Yesh. All children of Illium learn their grandmother's tales well. Tales of mind-reading manipulators. And which draughts one can take that make such efforts null."

Theroun's ears perked, to learn that this Cennetian knew a poison that kept Kreth-Hakir out of one's mind. Clearly a well-guarded family secret, it was nonetheless extremely valuable information.

Master Yesh chuckled again, but his blind gaze was fierce. "You have something to say before the Heraldation, Son of Illium?"

"I do." Without invitation, the Cennetian stepped up the stairs to the bridge over the dragon's desiccated tail. He didn't take the dais, but wasn't far from it. "Comrades! I come from the Aphellian Way with news of dire importance to this assembly. That there are not one, but *two* Rennkavis! And that I have in my care the second one – a young man by the name of Elohl den'Alrahel, a man strong of heart and stronger in love. A man who puts the atrocities of Lhaurent in their place, who shines with the glory of the true Rennkavi, rather than one who is false."

"*Two* Rennkavis?" Master Yesh's face slacked, his dead sockets seeming to bug from his astonished face. Theroun knew a moment of satisfaction, that Master Yesh didn't know everything. This Cennetian war-general had trumped the Kreth-Hakir. Theroun's gaze found Merkhenos'. They shared a fierce glance, a touch of a smile upon both their faces, before the Cennetian looked back to Master Yesh.

"I speak true!" The man produced a small glass vile from an inside pocket of his crimson jerkin. Capped tightly, it contained a foul brown sludge. "One sip of this antidote and the front of my mind will clear to you, Master Yesh. Or any others powerful enough to find the truth in my mind through my poison's fog. Shall I? Would you like to know if you have options other than Lhaurent den'Alrahel as your Rennkavi?"

"Clever, Son of Illium." Master Yesh's smile was no longer welcoming. "You are a cagey man from a long line of wary curs."

"Cagey to the end." Merkhenos gave a wicked, rakish grin. "Bastards, every last one of us."

While Master Yesh lifted his chin at the Cennetian, Theroun noted that Khorel Jornath held a slight smile of amusement. And a touch of something else, as he looked upon the Cennetian. The two knew each other, Theroun realized. But as soon as he had that thought, he felt it quenched under a drowning weave of quicksilver. Khorel, insulating Theroun's thought from the assembly. But Khorel's quick action had confirmed everything Theroun suspected. Jornath and the Cennetian knew each other. Mutual spies of common purpose, friends – or more?

That thought was surrounded by waves of silver, too.

A smile lifted the corner of Theroun's mouth, to know one of Khorel's secrets at last. Merkhenos had taken a sip from the vial and re-capped it. Wiping his lips, he lifted his brows at Master Yesh, challenging. Yesh frowned, and lifting his chin, appeared to retreat within himself. It seemed personal secrets were rife among the Kreth-Hakir, if one was strong enough to keep them. And this Cennetian Lothren member had more secrets to hide than the Hakir did. At last, a sigh issued from Master Yesh. The ancient man's chin dropped, his dead eye sockets staring the Cennetian down. "He speaks true. A second Rennkavi has been Goldenmarked."

Silence smote the hall; mind-silence, vocal silence. The kind of silence that takes a man when they've been stunned dumb. When at last thoughts and whispers moved again, they were shocked. Feeling out with his new abilities, Theroun found them tinged with a strange darkness – and fear.

"If two Rennkavis walk among us, it can only mean the Demon's Rise is imminent, Magnus."

A slender woman dressed in herringbone leathers stepped through the throng, down to the edge of the dais. But where all the Brethren wore black, her leathers were bone-white, the color of bleached skulls in desert sands. Throwing back her deep hood, she bared her visage. Her hair was a fiery copper, braided into an ornate twist over one shoulder. Her skin was the bronzed loveliness of Cennetia, or perhaps even Lefkani, a bloodline Theroun couldn't pinpoint.

Lean as a whip, she had a delicacy about her that was belied by the power that seethed from her person. High cheekbones made her emerald eyes pierce Theroun as her gaze raked the dais. She was breathtaking and Theroun found himself staring, not because she'd put any weaves into his mind, but because of her sheer animal magnetism. Theroun watched Khorel Jornath sink to both knees, bowing his head in a Kreth-Hakir position of ultimate submission – a gesture Jornath hadn't even shown High Master Yesh. Theroun's eyebrows rose. And rose even further when High Master Yesh struggled to not do the same as the woman gained the top of the dais.

"Metrene!" High Master Yesh rasped, his breathing ragged as she neared. Reaching out, her fingers slid over his cheek, and Master Yesh came to a shuddering silence. He stared down at her, his scarred lips fallen open. One touch, Theroun saw. This woman had given the High Master of the Kreth-Hakir one touch and he had fallen into silence. Though whether it was from commanding him or the sheer astonishment of her presence in the hall, Theroun couldn't say.

The hall erupted in confused whispers, the name *Metrene den'Yesh* sighing across lips and minds as all eyes fixed upon the dais. Some of the oldest Hakir in the hall had taken a knee like Khorel. Among them was Brother Kiiar, a kind of rapture upon his half-melted face as he gazed at the regal woman in her bone-white leathers.

"Why have you come?" The low words were Master Yesh's, his gaze rapt upon the woman as she stroked a thumb over his lips, making him shudder. That shudder was echoed all through the hall as a sigh of rapture passed through every mind. It slid through Theroun like a pleasurable wind, making him gasp, even despite Khorel's strong mind-blockade.

"Am I not your High Mistress still?" Metrene den'Yesh's voice was low, a whisper in the sands of time. Her presence stalked like a panther as she stroked Master Yesh's neck, giving him a lift of one regal copper brow. Her gaze broke from him and swept the hall, and in that reprieve, Master Yesh took command of himself. Though he breathed hard, Theroun could feel the man re-mastering his impeccable will. She had surprised him with her presence here, but not for long. Impenetrable silver walls rose up around the High Master, and Theroun smirked, wondering who else had secrets. Metrene's eyes turned back to Magnus Yesh and they locked gazes – vibrant emerald to scarred and empty sockets.

"I feel the ages turn," she spoke in a dark tone that echoed through the space. "Though my mind can range far from the blessing of Leith's Alranstone to which I am bound, I am not content within its granite confines. Threads flow, fast and faster in the weaves of time, Magnus. They torment my mind. I could not in good conscience be absent from this assembly when dire fates manifest."

Proceeding to the Cennetian, Metrene den'Yesh reached out, brushing a hand over Merkhenos' cheek. Theroun heard her whisper, "Fear me not, Son of Illium, your secrets shall remain safe," before the Cennetian suddenly went down upon his knees with a short cry. She collapsed with him, sinking gracefully to her knees and maintaining her touch as he cried out again in a sound of ecstatic release, clutching his heart. By the time the woman stood, the Cennetian was upon hands and knees, gasping. Theroun felt Khorel Jornath shudder, tension rippling in his shoulders – wanting to go to the Cennetian.

Again, that thought was sluiced away by Khorel's quicksilver wave.

"Two Rennkavis... fascinating," Metrene spoke softly, a curl of a smile upon her lips as her words echoed in Theroun's mind, singing like summer reeds. Sighs echoed around the room. Men sank to their knees, feeling the sensation of wind and silk blowing over their skin. A thrill washed through Theroun at this woman's tremendous power, his cock stiffening. Metrene looked back to Merkhenos, who had come up to his knees and took deep breaths.

But Master Yesh's immense frame filled out, challenging the woman, her body wan compared to his enormous stature. "What is your business here, woman? You are no longer part of our Order."

"Am I not, my beloved?" Her cunning lips smiled sadly, just a little, her panther-smooth gaze roving over Magnus' proud frame. "I feel your mind, Magnus, and whom you would support. But know that I have seen much of Lhaurent den'Alrahel. Enough to know that his will is powerful – and powerfully black. Lhaurent holds a natural ability to poison with his will, and whenever he walks through my Kingstone, I feel..."

Turning her head, she closed her eyes. As if gathering memories, Metrene took a long breath. When her eyes opened, they burned like green fire, furious. "*Lineage.*"

The effect of that one word upon Magnus Yesh was tremendous. His face fell into a stony darkness, his body hardening as his enormous hands gripped the pommels of the longknives. Her knowing gaze bored into him as a tense silence breathed through the vast cavern. All eyes were fixed upon Metrene den'Yesh, High Mistress of the Kreth-Hakir, facing off with the High Master.

I feel your power, Black Viper. Metrene's sinuous voice slid into Theroun's thoughts suddenly, though she did not turn to look at him. *Like barbed coils upon my tongue. You are like I was once, a wild thing. Khorel tries to help you master your gifts because you have volatility and power – a wrathful combination in the Demon's hands. Do not think him a hard master. Like I have, he has felt the Demon's touch. Felt it, and turned it aside by mastering his own darkness.*

The Demon has already tried to possess Khorel Jornath and failed? A stunned silence filled Theroun. But she said no more. Facing Magnus Yesh, she stared up at him from her slim ferocity. Gazing down upon her, the sightless man's face had taken on an ancient sadness. "Will you so willfully resist me again? Like it was with the Brother Kings?"

"You were wrong to side with King Alcinus den'Alrahel," she countered, "despite his many lands, powers, and influence. Just as you are wrong now, with the terrible sequence of events you have fathered here."

Magnus Yesh drew up tall, staring her down with his scarred sockets. "The Kreth-Hakir will follow where I lead."

"*Right to the Demon's Lair!*" Metrene hissed, her voice slicing through the cavern like a braided whip.

And though everyone in the amphitheater trembled from this vicious utterance, Magnus Yesh stood before her like a stone now, unmoved. "Go, woman. Take your vile white weaves and go, before I am of a mind to make you do so."

And to this, she laughed. Like flails raining down upon the entire assembly, it wasn't a force even Khorel Jornath could deflect. Pummeled beneath that scourging, cries came from the hall, Theroun grunting from the mercilessness that assaulted his flesh. But her caressing wind and silken voice trembled Theroun just after, a sluice of bedchamber sighs arresting him as she spoke, turning away from Magnus Yesh.

"I fear for you, my beloved. I fear for you all…"

Theroun was left with a hunting melody in his mind, a sound like mournful reeds as Metrene den'Yesh moved like a bone-white ghost across the platform and down the obsidian stairs. Halting, she gazed at the mummified dragon. Reaching one hand out, Metrene set it to the dragon's bony cheek-ridge above its grinning row of fangs. The fine diamond dust brushed off upon her fingertips like shimmering chalk. Closing her eyes, she pulled into her core until Theroun could no longer sense that she even existed at all. But Theroun realized he still felt her thoughts – connecting him in a faint spear of stunning opal light with Khorel Jornath and Merkhenos del'Ilio in a private conversation.

Khorel Jornath, Merkhenos del'Ilio, Theroun den'Vekir. Harken. Your clear wills arrest me. The three of you have other designs than the support of a madman. And so I need you to do a duty – and be my spear. She breathed it through the three of them. Finer than spider's silk, it siphoned into them like a single hair upon the morning breeze. *Be my bones. Be the righteous weapons you all were made to be, against the Demon's Rise. For time quickens now, and we have run out. Stand with me – as One.*

With that, Metrene *pushed* something through them all, like a breath of wind. And to that call, the dragon's bones woke. Theroun jolted; his hands went to his weapons, but the creature hadn't moved, not exactly. But it was as if that thread of life from Metrene had proven that the beast wasn't in fact dead – only in a fugue so deep it appeared so. As Theroun watched, shocked, the mummified lizard took a single inhalation with its emaciated ribs, then let it out through a flare of slitted nostrils.

A gust of heated air roiled over Theroun, the creature returning to stillness as shocked gasps filled the underground space. With a stroke to its scaled cheek, Metrene whispered in a thought that only her mind-linked could hear, *Farewell, Agni, fiercest of the Protectors. Slumber on. Dream good dreams of battle and vanquishing.*

Turning, she threw up her hood and stepped down the obsidian stairs, a pale specter against all that black. Retreating through the parting throng, she moved through one of the towering archways and vanished – as if she had never been.

* * *

The Heraldation ended at last, too many hours passed in the fathomless dark. Theroun's eyes felt like ground glass, and he'd taken countless cups of kaf-tesh the acolytes brought around. Though High Master Yesh had made up his mind about following Lhaurent den'Alrahel, debate had raged for hours. The Kreth-Hakir had a pseudo-democracy, and all would be heard before the assembly concluded. Analyzing the situation from every possible angle, calculating every outcome – especially in regards to Metrene's warnings and her effect upon the dragon, that everyone had presumed was as dead as Theroun had thought it was.

Khorel Jornath had held Theroun's thoughts in a vise-grip the entire time. Shards of obsidian crunched under Theroun's boots now as they retreated up the winding stairs toward the obsidian Alranstone, Brothers Kiiar, Caldrian, and Arlo behind them. Up ahead, Theroun saw Merkhenos walking alone up the stairs. Khorel picked up his pace, as if to gain on the man's egress. The Cennetian arrived at the obsidian pillar, glanced down to Khorel, then bent, adjusting his boots – stalling. Khorel hurried up the last four staircases, gripping Theroun's shoulder and placing a hand upon the Alranstone at the exact same time the Cennetian did. Brothers Kiiar, Caldrian, and Arlo had slapped hands to the Alranstone also – all six of them spat out together into the ocean-cave.

A grey pre-dawn glimmered off the ocean at Ligenia Bay, reflecting in the tiger-striped crystal of the Alranstone. As Theroun turned, he saw Merkhenos clasp arms with Khorel with a wide smile, then do the same with Brothers Kiiar, Caldrian, and Arlo. Turning to Theroun, he gave a chuckle. "General Theroun den'Vekir! Will wonders never cease. We meet again."

"High General del'Ilio." Theroun nodded at the man, though he didn't offer to clasp arms. "You're a long way from your battle-front."

"My army is in good hands." The High General of Valenghia's copper eyes glinted, before turning to Khorel Jornath. "So. Where do we stand?"

"We're with you, Merkhenos." It was Brother Kiiar who answered, his black-on-black eyes glittering in the rising gloom as he settled his hands inside the long sleeves of his black robe. "Metrene den'Yesh herself supports our endeavors to follow this Elohl den'Alrahel as our Rennkavi rather than Lhaurent. I do believe your cunning plans are quite in luck. Quite."

Khorel Jornath inhaled, turning his eyes to the old man, and Brother Kiiar chuckled. "Don't think I can't see where a person's *wyrric* imprint goes, Khorel. Metrene is cagey, and frankly insane sometimes I think, but she's not infallible. She had private conversation with you and the High General and your Scion. Don't deny it."

"Did you know she could manifest outside her Kingstone?" Jornath asked Brother Kiiar.

"Metrene is ancient, who knows just what exactly she can do?" Brother Kiiar chuckled. "And that was no mere manifestation we saw tonight. She was there, in the flesh – created anew to journey out from her Alranstone. Her power is like wind on my tongue, ever-shifting, ever-present, ever a surprise."

"Is Metrene strong enough to oppose High Master Yesh?" Brother Caldrian was scowling, arms crossed at his chest.

"Perhaps." A frown took Khorel's features. "Master Yesh has been our head for some three thousand years, but Metrene is his rival. Once she was wild, a chaotic thing. She was stripped of her official standing among us at the time of Leith, due to the untamable nature of her *wyrria*."

"It's why she wears white instead of black," Brother Kiiar interrupted. "But those who knew her back then, as Khorel and I did, know her power is stronger than all of us, perhaps even stronger than Magnus, though no one knows for certain. Only two creatures were ever able to break her. Leith Alodwine and Agni."

"The dragon?" Theroun startled.

Khorel turned his way. "The dragon is far more than he seems, Theroun. I have never seen him breathe before, though something inside me always knew the creature was not quite dead. And now, as *wyrria* wakens in the world again with these Rennkavis—"

"Fentleith Alodwine will rise." Merkhenos del'Ilio interrupted, his copper eyes flashing, ferocity in their depths. "The long-lost Scion of Khehem is alive, gentlemen, something I did not tell the assembly tonight. I have found him, recently, in Valenghia, acting as protector to Elohl den'Alrahel. His magnificence causes all words to fail."

"So Fentleith Alodwine is alive," Khorel Jornath breathed, a dark look of relief and pain crossing his features. "The Scion of the Wolf and Dragon. I didn't think it was possible. He's been dark in my mind for eight hundred years... damn Magnus Yesh and his lust for glory!" Khorel growled, his features twisting up with dominant contempt. "I will never forgive him for yoking us all against the Scion of Khehem."

"It was a bad move," Brother Kiiar commented soberly, his hands tucked deep in his sleeves, "I can only imagine how much better the world might be now if we had been able to follow Fentleith at our lead all those years ago. But his *wyrria* was a maelstrom then, gentlemen, and if he has shut it down all this time, I wonder – how much stronger may it have grown where he cannot see it? And has he taken a long look at his shadow-will, my Brothers, in all these centuries?"

The gathering stood silent a moment in the sounds of the ocean echoing off the walls of the sea-cave. Theroun was beginning to understand how much emphasis the Brethren placed upon understanding one's shadow-will, and it seemed they feared what this Fentleith Alodwine might do if he didn't understand his deepest darkness.

At last, Khorel turned his gaze to pierce Theroun. "Join us, General Theroun. Though your powers are wild still, you've got enough instinct to be of use to us."

Theroun blinked to be addressed by his old title. He shifted, crossing his arms at his chest, scowling. "What exactly are you asking?"

"I want you to defect from the Kreth-Hakir, with me and my Brethren here. When the time is ripe." Khorel's gaze was level, no subterfuge anywhere in his mind or dark grey eyes.

"I thought that treason against the Brethren was a death sentence," Theroun countered, interested but wary, his mind clicking through the potential outcomes. "Isn't that your historical precedent?"

"It is." Khorel's look was level, his voice stone cold. "But history concerns me not. Our High Mistress has given us a charge that splits the Kreth-Hakir Brethren. Decide now if you wish to be a part of it. If you do, you'll be hunted for the rest of your days for defection from the Order. But I have seen deeply into Lhaurent, and eels move through his depths, slithering in to choke everything in their path. He will kill this world, you know it as well as I. I am strong, but combining minds of the Kreth-Hakir are stronger. Together, with Metrene, we are finally strong enough not to follow

Magnus Yesh's blind orders – allowing us to aid the true Rennkavi, Elohl den'Alrahel. What is your will, Theroun? The choice is yours."

Theroun's gaze flicked to Merkhenos. The man wore no expression in his cinnabar eyes, his hands resting lightly upon his weapons. Theroun's mind clicked through possibilities, considering his options. A long moment passed. At last, Theroun drew a breath, then nodded. Jornath's smile grew pleased, his gaze penetrating as it swept every man before the tiger-eye Alranstone.

"Hold firm. We will turn on our Brethren when the time is right, but Lhaurent and High Master Yesh *must* believe we give our all until that moment. And when it is over, we will stand side-by-side, Shaper-willing. In a better world."

With that, their coup was sealed. Wrists were clasped, slivers of mind-promise shared. High General Merkhenos del'Ilio stepped to the Alranstone, disappearing in a clap of thunder that reverberated through the vaulted cave. In silence, the five Brethren stepped down the volcanic bedrock to the cavern's sandy floor, squelching through the brine of a high tide come and gone.

They had an army to march out today, and each man would play his part – for now.

A low growl stopped Theroun in his tracks suddenly. A growl that curled his hackles high – of a beast on the hunt, ready to eviscerate the thing it had stalked. A growl Theroun knew well. He turned, glancing up to a ridge of bedrock just above his position. A pair of cursed yellow eyes met his from the vaults of the cavern, vivid and daring, a hulking shadow behind those devil-orbs coiled to pounce.

"You again," Theroun snarled, his lips curling into a smile to see his nemesis had tracked him all the way to the sea-shore by some ungodly instinct. "Give in to me or eat me, but either way, quit being a bastard."

A wicked snarl lifted the Black Bastard's jowls. With liquid grace, the ronin keshar-cat leaped down from the ledge, its enormous jaws closing over Theroun's head. That sandpaper tongue raked Theroun's face, marking him, as astounded chuckles moved through the cavern from his Brethren. By the time the Black Bastard released him, Theroun was all-over spittle. But his grin was viperous as he mounted up, riding his wicked cat high as the sun rose over the southern sea.

CHAPTER 41 – ELYASIN

Elyasin's body was all-over sweat as she extended her hands in a bracing grip, feeling for the energy of the massive, broken shard of milky quartz before her. Concentrating on the crystal, longer than she was tall and ten times as thick, Elyasin wiped sweat from her eyes with her inner arm. Clad in only her silken undergarments with her boots on for protection and rags wrapping her knees, she radiated heat like a forge-fire from where she stood in the White Ring, the diamond-black citadel lifting to its ever-night all around. Thaddeus approached cautiously, eyeing her in the light of the three lit braziers nearby as he ran his fingertips across the golden runes upon the crystal boulder Elyasin was about to move, igniting them with white-blue wisps to check their phrasing.

"This one belongs halfway up number four." He nodded to the position of the Fourth Plinth nearby, at the edge of the White Ring. Judging the distance to the plinth's jagged origin, thrust up from the diamond plaza like a broken stump, Thad narrowed his blonde brows, then took off his spectacles to polish them. "That's a twenty-foot move, my Queen. Would you like me to call King Therel to assist?"

"No. Therel's done for the day. I can do it."

Elyasin wiped her brow again with her arm, sweat pouring down her body in runnels, soaking her garments. She'd never sweat this much in her life. Thad offered a goblet of water thickened with salts, but Elyasin shook her head. She was already in the flow of Hahled's *wyrric* power. Brimstone coursed through her muscles; lava ran her veins. She was burning up inside, but somehow her body contained it all, guiding the energy along the focus of her mind and down the *wyrric* red inkings that coursed along her flesh.

Gathering Hahled's *wyrria* from every corner of her sinews and pushing it down through her arms to her fingertips, her crimson inkings lighting with blue-white ripples, Elyasin tensed her hands.

Hands partly aimed at the jagged mass of crystal, partly aimed at each other to concentrate the *wyrric* flow, she took a deep breath, then began a series of deep pants to flare her fire hotter – wilder. Pumping her breath like a bellows, she fed the fire inside her with everything she had, making her dizzy as heat rippled from her skin in a mirage.

Thaddeus stepped back, warding his face with one hand. Like a bonfire, Elyasin's body shed heat in waves, and she gathered it with flowing movements, down her body and into her hands, tensing her fingertips in a keshar-grip at the massive piece of crystal as her inkings rippled and flowed. The broken shard shuddered, then scooted along the ground with a screaming shriek – enough that Elyasin could feel the crystal's innate *wyrria* caught in her grip. Like a lion with a bull in its claws, Elyasin sank her claws in, feeling the stone's resonance. Wrapping its signature around her fingertips, thrusting in until she came to the core of its essence.

With a resounding shudder, the fragment of crystal rang like a struck bell. A sweet chime filled the air, like a finger run around the rim of a wine goblet. With one last out-breath, Elyasin thrust her hands up over her head and stepped in. Like a live bird in her fingertips, the gargantuan shard heaved up, six feet above the ground.

The massive weight of it pressed down upon Elyasin. Tremendous, it felt as if it would break her spine; as if she heaved a millstone up over her head, thrusting down on her bones and making them grind. With fast pants, Elyasin flamed Hahled's *wyrria* higher. She'd practiced this numerous times now, first with shards no bigger than her arm, then with fragments the size of her body. Through trial and error, and muscle-memories she'd never had before, she'd begun to learn Hahled's vast *wyrria*.

Even so, this fragment was a challenge. A third larger than any she'd attempted to move these past six days, its humming filled her bones and shivered shockwaves down her arms. Though she didn't touch the shard's mass, she touched everything that mattered. Its resonance was the vessel through which its *wyrria* flowed, and it was this that Elyasin interacted with.

Sliding her feet forward, Elyasin chose each step with careful grace. Without Therel to help stabilize this massive hunk of quartz, one mis-placed step could send it crashing to the plaza and shatter, or careening off. She and Therel had already made that mistake four days ago, and one piece of crystal that had been large as a bull-ox was now in fifty pieces no larger than a housecat.

Thaddeus was their rune-cataloguer. He watched Elyasin's movements, staying well out of her way, not making a sound and letting her concentrate. From her peripheral vision, Elyasin could see Thad's astute gaze sliding over the shard, noting each and every sigil upon it, especially on the underside where they had been hidden from view before.

"How much further?" Elyasin gasped through gritted teeth. Her arms were shaking, her chest collapsing beneath the weight. Her knees began to buckle, and her thighs trembled like she heaved a dead keshar in her hands.

"Five more steps," Thad breathed. "Three...two...one. Gently. Gently, my Queen..."

With a smooth out-breath, Elyasin eased her hands down. Backing up, she brought her hands down in front of her core, shifting their lotus-position into a carrying position as the enormous weight came down near her pelvis. At the end of her breath, Elyasin's silk-wrapped knees buckled, slamming into the plaza. The spar of crystal came down hard, crashing down on the diamond-black stone. Elyasin knew a moment of terror; but the crystal held fast, not so much as a single crack lancing its core or marring its surface.

"Well done!" Thad clapped his hands.

Elyasin collapsed. Splaying out upon the cool diamond-stone plaza, her chest heaved. Sweat dripped into her eyes, but she had no strength to wipe it away. Every muscle trembled as if she'd sprinted five leagues. Her heart hammered and heat swirled around her, making wavering images in the chill air.

"I think that's it for today." Thad's face appeared above her.

Elyasin nodded. She didn't even have words yet. Swallowing hard, she rasped, "water."

"Coming!" Thad darted off, soon returning with a golden pitcher. He didn't ask, just doused Elyasin with it, sluicing her face and chest as he'd done numerous times before. It was bliss. She tilted her chin up, reveling in the ice-cold stream, then opened her mouth and swallowed over and over. Somewhere during the second pitcher, Elyasin was able to push up to sitting and scrub sweat from her face as Thad doused her with the rest. A third jug was proffered, and she took it with a grateful nod, heaving it to her lips and drinking thoroughly.

At last, her vision cleared; her head ceased pounding and her bones quieted. Her muscles still shivered, but she'd been at this for over four hours today – a full thirty minutes longer than yesterday, and an hour longer than Therel. Elyasin gazed upon the massive spar of crystal she'd moved, a smile blossoming over her face. Thad heaved to a seat next to her upon the wet stone and gave a chuckle.

"Well done, my Queen! You've put your King to shame today."

"Therel has no shame, but I'll take it." Elyasin's smile brightened. These past few days, learning how to heave these shards around to get them organized so they could re-build the Alranstones at the White Ring, had been some of her best days in a long while. She felt cleansed, sweating and heaving, as if her body had been made for this. To fight – to wrestle with impossible odds and come out the victor. A deep pleasure filled her, and she turned her smile to Thaddeus.

"Where is my lazy husband?"

"I just saw him, relaxing in the heat pools, before we started with this last shard." Thaddeus gave her an even bigger grin. "He's addicted to them."

Massaging her bare arms, where Hahled's crimson and white inkings curled down over them to her wrists, Elyasin gave a laugh. "I don't blame him. I don't know which *wyrria* is worse – one that burns a person up like a forge, or one that cools right through the core. I'll go see him in a moment. Is this placed where you need it, Thad?"

"Oh yes." The scribe smiled brightly. "I got a good look at the sigils underneath, and it's right in the position it needs to be to assemble the pieces of Alranstone Four. When Ghrenna does the binding-runes tomorrow, they'll go up in a counter-clockwise spiral, starting from the broken base to the pinnacle, just as we planned."

"So that's all of them?" Elyasin asked.

"That's all of them, my Queen," Thad chuckled. "Thanks to your impressive feat today. Quite the capstone on our endeavors of the past week."

Elyasin glanced around the wide plaza of smoky black stone with its circle of bright gold and gleaming golden dais. Each of the seven broken quartz pillars now had all their gargantuan shards arranged in a spiral around their base. Most of the largest pieces were near their bases, but some of the crystal pillars had shattered all the way down. Alranstone Seven was a mess, its spiral more like a field of crushed stone than anything that could possibly become a Plinth again.

"Have you finished arranging that one, Thad?" Elyasin nodded at Alranstone Seven.

He glanced over at it and shrugged. "As best I can. All seven eyes of the Plinth are in order. The runes too, as best I can figure out. I tried to group the smallest shards near the pattern-whorls I think they came from, but some of them are so small, they've got no markings of any kind. It'll be up to Ghrenna to get everything back in place. I've made it as simple as I can for her, but—"

"She's still going to have to do a hell of a lot." Elyasin palmed her sweat-streaked gold locks from her face and flicked water from her chin. "How is she?"

"Still traveling in trance." Thad shrugged, his visage thoughtful and green eyes appraising. "I don't think she's found all the answers she wants yet, about how to put all this back together. Tomorrow will be as much experiment as anything, I think."

"And Luc?"

"Luc is getting some much-needed rest," Thad grinned, taking his spectacles down from his head and polishing them on his breeches. "He's still out as we speak. Ever since breakfast."

"Did you check his breathing?" Elyasin chuckled. It was partly a joke, but partly not. Luc had been horridly sleep deprived from watching over Ghrenna by the time Elyasin recognized what was happening six days ago. Tempers had calmed since then, and they'd had no more flares of wrath – the air cleared now that Luc's frustrations had been exposed and both Elyasin and Therel were exercising the hot and cold twinned tempers of the Brother Kings out of their bodies daily.

"He's breathing," Thad's lips curled in a small smile. "Just recovering."

"Thank Aeon," Elyasin chuckled. "I thought he and Therel

were going to tear each other apart a week ago."

"Thank Aeon indeed." Thad nodded, sober. He gestured at the organized shards of crystal all through the black-diamond plaza. "Do you think we'll really be able to put all this back together? It's like the children's rhyme of Dildrum the Egg-Man who got crushed beneath the ox-cart."

Elyasin smiled; she hadn't thought about that nursery rhyme in ages. "We'll have to, Thad. We came here to perform the Rennkavi's Ritual. We can't do that with broken Alranstones. They won't vibrate properly to amplify the *wyrria* of the ceremony. And from Ghrenna's reports of her mind-travels, Elohl doesn't have much time. None of us do. Battle is imminent upon the Aphellian Way, and if that happens——"

"Our nation falls."

"Or rises with a tyrant behind it that none can ever stop."

Thad was very quiet. Picking up a small shard of milky-white crystal beside them, he twiddled it through his fingers. "Are you really going to go through with it? The Rennkavi's Ritual? You'll have to – you know – in front of all of us."

Elyasin glanced over and Thad's green eyes shied away before they came back, seeking truth, his ash-blonde brows knit in a troubled frown. Elyasin took a deep breath, then sighed. "Ghrenna explained the steps of the Rennkavi's Ritual to us all, Thad. The binding we need to open the portal to the White Tower involves passion. Carnal passion. Originally, that would have been between Morvein and her Brother Kings, so they could get through to the White Tower and channel *wyrria* for the Rennkavi. Now, it's Therel's and my responsibility. What I'll be doing is no less or more than any man or woman on the battlefield – I'll be fighting to protect something I love. My nation; Therel's nation. All the people of the world who are being torn apart by Lhaurent's atrocities. I keep that firmly in mind when squeamishness tries to make me shy from my duty. Besides," her lips quirked, "it's nothing Therel and I haven't done before. And Therel saw it, over and over, in his seeing-dreams long ago. We're ready for it."

Thad flushed to the roots of his hair as his gaze tracked to the broken stumps of the Alranstones. "I've never… I've never done… *that.*"

"You've never been with anyone?" Elyasin's eyebrows rose, a small smile upon her face.

He shook his head and took a deep breath. "I mean, I think about it. I've kissed a few girls. Palace maids, mostly – you know, quick down in the larders. But Theroun kept me so busy at Roushenn, and I was shy before I came into his employ. When I wasn't taking notes for him I was in the palace annals, researching until all hours of the night. I don't drink, and I never learned how to approach women. They terrify me – especially the lovely ones."

His glance shifted to Elyasin, then away.

"Thad!" Elyasin linked her arm in his, giving him a playful jostle. "I'm flattered!"

"You should be," he murmured, turning ferociously red. "You're beautiful."

"Well." Elyasin jostled his shoulder again. "When we get out of here, I promise I will teach you how to approach women. What they like, what makes them interested. What they enjoy in the bedroom."

"My Queen!" Thaddeus turned to her, his eyes scandalized. "Won't your husband—"

"Relax, Thaddeus!" She laughed, enjoying his befuddlement. "I'm not going to *show* you what women like. But I'll find you someone who can."

His flush deepened. "But… you will be showing me. Tomorrow, if all goes according to Ghrenna's plan."

"I suppose you will get an eyeful tomorrow." Elyasin blinked and her arm slid out of Thad's. It was Elyasin's turn to look at the shattered fragments of crystal, hi-lighted by the braziers that blazed with sorcerous fires around the plaza to cast light upon their re-assembling work.

Thad ran his shard of crystal between his fingers. "I won't watch. I swear it."

"You have to," Elyasin spoke frankly. "You're a part of this, Thad. And I'd rather have you watching out for my safety during the ritual than turning your back. Therel and I will need you and Luc to stand ready. To – pull us out – if something goes wrong."

"Like when the Alranstones shattered the first time Morvein tried this?" Thad spoke softly.

"She didn't even get this far, Thad," Elyasin reminded him.

"The Rennkavi candidate they had wasn't even Goldenmarked yet. All this destruction was because the lad they chose wasn't strong enough to hold the Marks. But the Rennkavi's Ritual is a hundred times the magic used to imprint the Goldenmarks. If just the marking went wrong last time, and caused all this…" Elyasin waved a hand at the destruction, feeling tired finally.

"Then who knows what could happen during the full ceremony," Thad finished, bleak.

"That's why I need you." Elyasin glanced back to him. "Therel and I will be flooded with *wyrria*, channeling the power of the Brother Kings. I don't know what's going to happen. Ghrenna doesn't even know, because Morvein never got that far. She has a vague image of what may happen, based upon the vision Morvein was sent through the ages, to Consummate the Rennkavi. But what's actually going to happen?" Elyasin shrugged.

Thad's breath was steady, and he said nothing for a long moment. "I won't falter, Elyasin. I'll stand firm during the Rennkavi's Ritual, and watch out for your protection. I swear it."

Elyasin nodded. Reaching out, she clasped his fingers. Thad's long thin fingers wrapped around hers, and they shared a comfortable silence. But with a strange bleakness in her heart, Elyasin at last sighed and rose. Her euphoria was wearing off, and now her body just hurt. It ached in places she didn't even know she had, from days of prolonged exertion. Rubbing her neck, she glanced down. "I'm going to find Therel at the hot pools. Would you like to come?"

Pushing to standing, he shook his head and adjusted his spectacles. "I need to get supper ready. Luc is grumpy when he wakes and there's no hot food."

"Isn't he just." Elyasin smiled.

Thad met her gaze at last, utter earnesty in them. "You know I… care for you, don't you? The other men may bicker and fight over you, but… when you need me, I'm here. My Queen."

"I know." Elyasin smiled gently. Reaching out, she placed her hand upon Thad's thin shoulder, gripping it in camaraderie. "Love for your Queen is a beautiful thing, Thad. It makes you righteous and bold. It makes you push yourself to your limits and beyond, to make the right decisions. And you have. At every turn, you have been there – moving us forward. Helping where we didn't even know we needed it. Theroun was right about you; you are an asset, Thad. But you're so much more than that. You are a *good man*. Someday, some other lucky woman will see it, too."

"Someday." Thad's soft smile was haunted, his cheeks flushing behind his wire-rimmed frames. "If we ever make it out of here, I suppose."

"We've all been pushed to the breaking point," Elyasin cupped Thad's cheek. "But if love is the result of that stress, like the diamond compressed from coal, then it's a good thing. Let your heart be love, Thad. Let it hold love. For me, Luc, Therel, and Ghrenna. And for yourself. It's what keeps us going, when all things fail."

Thad pressed Elyasin's hand to his cheek, his green eyes shining with devotion. "You are a beautiful woman, Elyasin. But more than that, you are a wise and stalwart Queen. I will see you sit your throne again someday. Even if I have to move mountains to do it."

"Start by helping us thread broken Alranstones back together," Elyasin spoke gently. "And then we'll repair my nation."

With a nod, Thad released her hand. Sinking down upon one knee and lowering his head, he set a palm to his heart and one to a knife on the belt at his hip. Without a word, he rose and retreated, off to the underground river where they'd had luck catching their supper. Elyasin watched him go. There was something that shone in Thaddeus' soul, as if darkness could not touch him. And she wondered if he had his own particular *wyrria*, other than his impressive memory.

The magic of an unquenchable heart – that could move mountains when it had to.

* * *

The next morning, everyone assembled at the center of the White Ring. Time could not be told in the infinite diamond darkness of the underground citadel, but Elyasin felt refreshed by her long sleep and the gentle, exhausted lovemaking she and Therel had shared before curling up in their little nest in their own private dome near the plaza. She'd slept hard, the first dreamless night she'd had since arriving here. And now she stood, holding Therel's hand and gazing at Ghrenna, who stood in the center of the burnished golden dais in the middle of the plaza.

Ghrenna looked astounding. A riot of health was in her cheeks, her eyes bright in their cerulean depths. Dressed in her Elsthemi buckled leathers and snowhare pelt, her long white waves were plaited in a loose bun at the nape of her neck. She wore longknives in her boots and upon her hips, and her body surged with vitality – a fighter to her very essence, ready for battle. Ghrenna gazed at them each in turn – Luc, then Thad, then Therel and Elyasin. Her glance dropped to the monarch's clasped hands and her full lips eased into a smile. Her gaze flicked up and she spoke, her haunting alto filling the plaza and weaving currents upon the chill air.

"Is everyone ready?"

"We are." Elyasin spoke, strong, echoed by the others.

"Everyone is to do their part." Ghrenna's strong gaze pinned them all by turns. "Luc. You will heal anyone who begins to tire. Move freely, judge who needs you most, balance your efforts. *No one* is to be given especial preference, or we will fail. Is that clear?"

Holding her gaze with steady ferocity, Luc gave a sharp nod. He appeared far better today, also. More robust, standing taller, his lion-gold mane bright like his refreshed emerald eyes. Something had steadied in him since his near-break seven days ago, and his tall, lean frame was easy and relaxed in his buckled tan leathers.

"Thaddeus," Ghrenna continued, continuing on to the lean scribe, "you will be my voice. I will yoke your mind to mine as you sing the sigils inscribed upon each of the Plinths, when you and I arrive at them, from root to crown. You have the sequences locked in your memory?"

"I do," Thad spoke softly but with confidence. His gaze never wavered, and Ghrenna gave a small nod. None of them doubted Thad's meticulousness, or his excellence.

"Elyasin and Therel," Ghrenna turned to them last, command in her iron-willed gaze. "You will be my hands. As Thad's song vibrates the Plinth back into harmony, you will engage the flow of the Brother Kings, lifting every last piece of each Plinth back into place and holding them steady until Thad's song and my binding-runes can put them back into their original unity. Are you prepared?"

"We are." Elyasin and Therel spoke in unison, their combined voices bright and hard – ready to do any kind of battle they had to.

"I will orchestrate the proceedings," Ghrenna lifted her chin. "When you feel my mind slip inside yours, do not fight me. Our body needs a mind to sing the voice, to work the hands, and to heal the flesh. I will be that mind, your Gerunthane, and we will all be one body in this. Your own *wyrric* abilities will be pouring through you, and mine will direct your flow. Fight me and we fail. Allow me to breathe through you like the Nightwind, and we will succeed. Are you ready?"

Heads nodded; shoulders squared. Elyasin took one last glance around, seeing the impenetrable steadiness of their cadre. Everyone here would do or die – and dying today was not an option.

Without another word, Ghrenna turned. She led their steps, moving the party to the base of the first sundered Alranstone at the far edge of the diamond-black plaza. This one was in the best shape, over half of the natural milky quartz crystal still upthrust from its base in a jagged spar and swirling with golden runes, only fourteen shards of moderate size to piece back together. It was the easiest one: Ghrenna had numbered the Plinths in order, starting with the most intact, because this one would be practice for all the rest.

Practice, so they could get it right – or keep trying until they failed.

Ghrenna lifted her hands, and an etheric wind began to move through the underground space. Or perhaps it was inside Elyasin's mind, but she felt the power of the group rise suddenly. Heat flared inside her as that etheric wind rushed in through her nostrils, first the left, then the right – and the heat inside Elyasin scorched to a furnace. The wind moved through her, diving in through her ears and parted lips, pouring in through her eyes like a splash of water upon her face. Licking up her legs and diving in lower places, a beautifully erotic sensation that made her gasp.

Elyasin's body burned to Ghrenna's Nightwind touch. She was the mountain, she was the volcano. She was the roar of a lioness under the scorching grassland sun. She was molten gold, pouring through her veins, blistering the air and sending vapors steaming off her body as Hahled's crimson inkings simmered blue-white upon her skin.

As she glanced to Therel, she could see his *wyrria* had risen, but in inverse. He stood strong and cool, his white-blonde hair shining like moonlight on snowfields. A haunting darkness was in his ice-blue eyes and a chill wind eased off his skin, moving the ripples of mirage around Elyasin as his purple inkings from Delman rippled like ocean water capturing the light beneath icebergs. As his gaze met hers, an electric sensation filled Elyasin, raising every hair on her body. And feeling his magic taste hers, lick around her with its cool moonlight to her scorching heat, Elyasin understood.

They were twin *wyrrias*, balanced. Twin hearts, matched in ability but opposite in temperament. And strangely enough, Elyasin felt an additional balance inside her own skin, easing the torrent of the Brother Kings. As if Elyasin's own calm balanced King Hahled within her; and as if Therel's innate temper livened the cold darkness of King Delman.

The contentious Brother Kings had never been so well balanced before. As Thaddeus' lilting tenor was raised before the first shattered Alranstone, beginning to confidently sing out the combinations of Giannyk runes from base to pinnacle, Elyasin twined her fingers in Therel's. They simmered together, ice upon flame, scorch upon water; a livid sensation that made Elyasin's awareness of her own vibrating skin and her cavernous surroundings blossom. Her consciousness expanded upon that burgeoning wave, and she felt Therel's go with it. Her etheric body, her *wyrric* power twinned and twisted into Therel's as they sighed out – filling the massive plaza.

Within Elyasin's inner vision, a rune writ itself in golden fire suddenly. Blazing to life within her, it was so vivid she could see it in her waking vision, the sigil of her essence forming from all this incredible power and harmony she experienced. She felt the Nightwind catch that rune in talons made of flowing wind. Ghrenna's command – that Elyasin surrender to the mind that would direct her. That Elyasin become one with it, and allow it to use her. With a deep breath, Elyasin bowed before that power like stepping off a ledge into the rushing wind – allowing the golden rune in her mind to be swept away, replaced by one that shimmered white like ether inside her.

And then the Nightwind filled her, raising her arms and guiding her into the dance.

There was no other word for it. Thad's voice strengthened, similarly yoked into the body Ghrenna had formed, an eerie melody that provided their rhythm and flow. Elyasin felt Therel's cool nature yoked into that body as well, then the sweet golden ease of Luc being bound. As their cadre came into balance, the body prepared by the flowing command of the Nightwind, sigils of white etheric flame began to write themselves in the air.

And then they were all dancing to that haunting music, together.

Moving side-by-side, flowing with smooth steps, Therel and Elyasin made complex gestures that rose on instinct from Ghrenna's yoking – dancing their combined power into the shattered crystal shards as Thad sang and Luc's golden healing monitored them all. And not one shard, but all of them for the first Alranstone began to lift at once. Those lowest in the spiral began to wind up first from the base of the Plinth, organizing in midair, sliding into their long-lost place. Moving in a powerful flow, Elyasin's skin simmered as she watched etheric sigils writing in the air around those crystal fragments. Slipping into cracks, the sigils unfurled like vines of language, forming a spider-thin net that licked out, binding through the fragments. Tendrils of blue-white fire curled deep into the shards, the sigils pulling the fragments together – unifying the base of the Plinth and cascading all the way to the top.

As they united the base, the golden runes inscripted upon the Plinth seared from a mellow white to a blistering luminousness. As the enormous edifice came together with a blinding blaze in every fissure, all seven eyes upon the Alranstone flashed open. They blazed white, dazzling the cavern, before cooling into their sequence of colors – a dark onyx and crimson at the bottom, to a luminous violet-white at the pinnacle.

With a sigh of release, Elyasin felt Ghrenna's grip inside her body ease. Elyasin's hands fell to her sides; she breathed hard from exertion, even though she hadn't even known she'd been exerting herself. She hadn't even known her muscles had worked so hard until she felt the staggering ache hit her – so great had her euphoria been, seized in grip of the Nightwind. Fear rushed through her in a jagged wave, that she'd not been aware of her own body's limits as they'd danced. Elyasin shuddered as she felt her body again at last, realizing that she ached all over like she'd been beaten. Her shoulder twinged, as if she'd carried something far too heavy but not known she was hurt until this moment. She heard Therel swear at her side, rubbing his wrist.

As if the Nightwind had sent him, Luc was there. Placing his hands upon Elyasin's shoulder, pouring his healing gifts through her in a wave of warm golden light. The Nightwind still moved through them in unseen currents; Ghrenna hadn't released them yet, only allowed a reprieve. Moving to Therel next, Luc cupped Therel's damaged wrist until the Elsthemi King breathed in relief. Luc stepped back, finished, though he twisted his neck and massaged his knuckles with a scowl as if experiencing his own pain. Ghrenna gazed at him, her cerulean eyes unreadable, then turned and walked to the second Alranstone.

And on we go, Elyasin thought.

Alranstone by Alranstone, they called their combined magic. Thad's music became a song Elyasin danced to with her beloved by her side. Their flow became a dream, Elyasin's mind broadening to view the proceedings from outside herself and above the plaza. Watching their body work; watching Ghrenna orchestrate their combined *wyrric* powers. At every Stone, it was the same. Their dance, Thad's song, the sigils Ghrenna commanded with her power, to bind the shards of quartz back into one, and then a round of Luc's healing to rejuvenate them all.

But this time, Ghrenna did not allow them to feel their discomforts, only sent Luc where she judged he was needed, not releasing the flow of the dance. Euphoria filled Elyasin as they continued on, making her lose herself upon a tide of opiate-smooth bliss, over and over. Her body quivered after the fourth Plinth; she fell to her knees as it nearly gave out. The song jangled, a sensation like screeching animals ripping through Elyasin – but Luc rushed in, his seeping golden light sluicing through her flesh, removing all her concern.

Removing all her reason – to resist the call of the Nightwind.

On and on they worked. Elyasin's body was a forge, her hands were smelted fire. Her dance was lava's flow down the mountainside, meeting with the cool rush of the river that was Therel. The music filled her in haunting strains like wind though the darkness of time. Therel failed in the middle of the fifth Stone. With a cry, he collapsed to his knees just as Elyasin had earlier. The music jangled; the dance spasmed with a vicious chorea. Massive shards of crystal jittered in midair, lifted halfway into place but not yet set. Thad's voice cracked as if he'd felt Therel's pain, and a hard thrust of icewater ripped Elyasin's veins – sharp as a dagger.

She cried out, her limbs freezing from the cracking of Delman's *wyrria*.

But Luc was there fast, his hands upon Therel, pouring his gifts through his King as the rest of them held the dance steady from its near-collapse. But with her euphoria interrupted, Elyasin could see suddenly. How pale Luc was, sweat beading out upon his forehead from healing them all, over and over. How Therel's muscles jerked and spasmed as he was healed, his breath a hard rasp in his throat, his skin dusky with cold, ice beading out around the edges of his searing blue eyes. Elyasin's body poured sweat, soaked and searing with heat-blisters as a horrible thirst filled her, her tongue bloated and a headache screaming in her temples.

"Luc! Quickly!" Ghrenna's true voice was surprising in all that cacophony. Elyasin felt a push of ether whisk past her and slam into Luc – a command from the Nightwind. She could almost see sigils of white fire blaze in Luc's wrists, seeping into his hands, forcing him to heal Therel faster. And then Therel was up, steady, breathing out a hard plume of chill mist and re-joining the dance.

The harmony fused. The crystals lifted and ceased jittering – and they continued.

But Elyasin knew the truth. Even as her euphoria resumed, a dark fear filled her as they turned to the sixth Alranstone. As Morvein's Nightwind consumed her again, that dark pleasure coaxing Elyasin back into the dance, she knew it would devour them. This power consumed all that it commanded. It opened them wide, ate them up, taking their vitality – coercing a person to give their all for the Nightwind. And like a threllis or fennewith high, the user who'd been yoked into this bliss didn't even know they were being devoured.

Until it was too late.

On the seventh and final Plinth, Elyasin felt her body give up at last. Unable to supply any more energy, her *wyrric* furnace ripped apart and a vast explosion rocked through her. One last surge of heat flared through the cavern, as the crimson inkings all over Elyasin's body blazed. Ghrenna's white sigil in her mind seized that power and focused it, sending it like a comet to the thousands of fragments in the final Plinth.

Zooming upward, the crystal shards thrust into place upon that hard wave – not a gentle, controlled rise but a shocking burst of organization. A similar blast of power shot from Therel as he failed upon the backlash of Elyasin's collapse, his own purple inkings flaring vivid, lighting up the Alranstones all around. He went down to his knees with a cry as the last of his blistering ice hammered the fragments with such power that it slammed them into their final places. Sigils blazed into being as Elyasin fell, hitting the gold of the dais on her side – burned-out.

Used up.

As the seventh Plinth blazed into becoming, every Alranstone in the White Ring searing with blue-white light, complete at last, Elyasin gasped her final breaths upon the cool gold of the plaza. Her vision flickered; darkened, her hearing buzzing out to a thin whine. Someone's fingertips found hers – twined in hers. Elyasin rolled her eyes to look as her breath fled, seeing Therel collapsed on his side next to her.

His wolf-blue gaze flashed for her one last time, in love, before dimming out to frigid winter snows.

CHAPTER 42 – ELOHL

The Valenghian camp upon the Aphellian Way was in a ruckus as night settled over the arid plain. The final preparations for battle, which was coming for them like the hammer to the anvil, were well underway.

Desperation surged from all sides as the heavy grey twilight deepened into a brisk darkness. As torches and braziers were lit against the lowering night, Elohl watched the tension in the air. Irate Praoughian long-riders whipped horses that had no need to be whipped, who reared and whinnied in distress. A group of Valenghian heavy infantry in full silver battle-armor rushed past a Cennetian cook, slamming into the man and spilling his pot of potatoes. The Cennetian stepped into the torchlight, spewing epithets in a florid rush and shaking his fist while making devil-cursing gestures at the Valenghians. Two Cennetian soldiers dressed in night-shade gear and bristling with knives came to the man's aid, calling for the Valenghians to halt, then rushing after them with daggers half-drawn when the silver-haired men did not.

Tension had intensified in the ranks. Just today, Elohl had broken up no less than twelve fights between men of different nationalities, and a few women warriors, too. With the threat of battle looming, each and every soldier now aware that Lhaurent's forces outnumbered them two-to-one, the Vhinesse's former army was cracking. Breaking, as if without her *wyrric* tyranny, they had no glue to force them together any longer.

Sitting near the horse-pickets adjacent to the command-tent upon a rough wooden plank over two water-barrels, Elohl roiled with the tension simmering through the air and through himself. Since he and Fenton had been given the High General's pins, to take over command of this fracturing army in Merkhenos' absence, Elohl had led just as he'd done in the High Brigade, only on a larger scale. Issuing commands to Merkhenos' Generals and Captains, working with Fenton to secure a moderately competent plan against the arrival of Lhaurent's forces. They were dug-in, supply-lines were set, any last cracks and chinks in the towering fortress-wall that the Valenghians had built across the Way near the center league had been repaired. Sentries had been set to watch for the Menderian approach; signal-fires were ready, barrels of boiling oil atop the ramparts. Supplies of arrows and healing-resins, salves and bandages were fully stocked, and the countryside around the Way had been evacuated of farmers and villagers, excepting those who knew how to heal or fight.

They were ready – as much as they could be.

And now, Elohl was alone with his thoughts, whittling, the scent of spicy citrus coating his fingers with every curl he shaved from his creation. Elohl smoothed the hunk of yither-wood in his hands, lit in stark definition by the crackle of a nearby brazier. It was taking shape finally, inspired by the creatures of myth that writhed up every Monolith all along the Way. Elohl narrowed his eyes and blew a few shavings into the dust beyond his boots. He could almost hear the shavings screaming as the cracked earth sucked out what little moisture was left to them, even at night.

"Centime for your thoughts." Fenton clapped him upon the shoulder as he settled to the bench with a tired sigh, stretching his boots out before him in the shifting light of the brazier. Unwinding a silken red wrap from his mouth and nose, Fenton rubbed the palms of both hands over his face as if fatigued. He probably was; they hadn't gotten much sleep in the three days since Merkhenos had departed – and still, the Valenghian High General had not returned.

"Why are we here, Fenton?" Elohl spoke, watching his carving take shape beneath his knife, thinking about Ghrenna and everything they had discussed three nights ago. "In the middle of all this chaos, trying to unite men who just want to break apart?"

"Why do the night breezes blow?" Fenton was winsome tonight, as if their being hours from battle eased him. Leaning back onto his palms with a ready grin, he gave a soft chuckle. "Enjoy being alive tonight, Elohl. You might be dead tomorrow."

"Is that supposed to calm me?"

They'd be fighting in the dark tonight, unlucky and chaotic no matter how one did it. At least it wouldn't be the scorch of the day, but it would be Halsos' Burn of its own variety. Elohl had fought many a highmountain skirmish in the dark, and they never went well. Too many wounds, too many wild sword-swings even in the hands of allies. Lhaurent's forces had marched at dawn, but the two camps were at the opposite ends of the Way, and the field of approach was long between them. Fenton and Elohl had left explicit instructions to hold their position behind the Valenghian guard-wall – their army would not waste energy and resources crossing the leagues, and would let Lhaurent come to them.

But Lhaurent's army hadn't stopped their march as the sun eased past midday. He'd not paused them leagues out, to water and rest and prepare. He was coming – and he was coming tonight. No one would see any sleep from the spears of tension that surged now through the camp. Midnight would come and go in a wash of fitful dreams and watchfulness, and they'd clash sometime in the early hours before dawn. Elohl turned his whittling over, examining what was turning into a coiled serpent with strong forelimbs and claws – the dragon-stone in the field near the Heathren Bog.

"I don't think it's a matter of being calm," Fenton murmured, watching brazier-fires spring to life all over the camp like lightning bugs in the night. "Just knowing one's own mortality."

Chill stars had popped out through the velvet darkness. But even as Elohl glanced up, he saw the stars to the west blotting out to a suffering crimson above the fortress-wall. A wind blew, thick with heat and change. There would be a storm tonight, and it rolled in from the western Way as if pushed ahead of the annihilation that came for them.

"No, I mean," Elohl spoke again, watching the molten sky to the west, "what point is there to all this?"

"Saving the world?" Fenton chuckled, leaning back on his hands again.

Elohl gave him a look.

"Alright! Alright." Fenton held up his hands, then settled back with them laced behind his head. Gazing out over the nighttime bustle, his lips curled into a small smile as the brazier's flames cast his face in a red glow. "Do you see them, Elohl?"

"Who?" Elohl squinted out in the lowering dark. A mirage of changing temperatures moved across the dusk, obscuring the far row

564

of Monoliths beyond the enormous, sprawling encampment.

"These people," Fenton continued, nodding at the soldiers moving through the chilling night. "They know nothing of dire times and deep magic. They only know what is before them tonight. To fight; to kill or be killed. To love and hopefully get loved before you die. It's something I cherished about being among the Elsthemi. Merra, Therel, and the Highlanders didn't live for tomorrow or yesterday. There was only today. And today is what you make of it, for good or for ill."

"Wise words." Elohl brushed dust from the coil of the serpent's tail, examining its long line.

"Some might say so. Sometimes I think I'm foolish, Elohl, but there's one thing I've learned through all my thousand terrifying years."

Elohl glanced over. Fenton wore a strange expression in the brazier's light, deeper than pondering and more expressive than judgemental. It was more real than his usual face, this pensive wonder; and as Elohl watched, he gave a slightly etheric smile.

"I almost never thought I'd meet you," Fenton spoke at last. "The Rennkavi. Part of me disbelieved that any creation of my grandfather's could possibly be as wondrous as my mother's Prophecy described. But when I met you, when I saw those marks flare on your skin – I felt their honesty. *Your* honesty. You may hate being a slave to fate, Elohl, but you have a gift no one else could master, simply *because* you hate being a slave. And that gift gives us hope. All of us. It has the power to bring us together into one enormous, slightly less dysfunctional family. Maybe, anyway. How could you not wish to gamble on such a thing? It's a beautiful *wyrria*… no matter how it began."

"You really believe your grandfather was evil? That he created the Rennkavi to enslave the world?" Elohl couldn't meet Fenton's eyes as he smoothed his carving.

"I do." Fenton's voice was calm, and something about it made Elohl look up. Fenton's eyes curled with a slow fire, the gold in them bright in the evening's starkness. "But my grandfather died. Whatever ensnaring purpose those Marks were originally meant for, it can't happen now. You're free, to use the Marks how and when you will. You showed that in the Vhinesse's throne hall. You have a choice – to bind with those Marks and enslave or to elevate people's hearts, uniting them not as slaves to your will, but simply because love is powerful. Think about it. And then decide whether you want to continue stewing."

Fenton kicked Elohl's boot teasingly, then jostled Elohl's shoulder with a chuckle. Elohl drew a deep breath. He didn't share Fenton's lighthearted mood tonight. The simmering tension within him had been eating at him ever since they'd left Velkennish, since he had been torn away from Dherran, and it was only stronger now. But Elohl's ethereal meeting with Ghrenna at the dragon-stone had been astounding, and it bolstered him, thinking perhaps she was right. That he needed this surging tension inside him; that it was part of his power, through the Wolf and Dragon lineage. That every moment of friction, every hour he simmered in conflict, battling his emotions that would no longer be suppressed under any kind of glacial calm, was another moment his *wyrria* strengthened.

Another moment that *he* strengthened – becoming ready for when he would have to face his destiny at last.

Elohl's head lifted and he inhaled a steadying breath. Something hot swirled inside him as the air stirred, dry as the dust and with the iron tang of blood. Clanging drew his attention nearby. A Valenghian blacksmith one tent over plunged a hot-forged sword into a sizzling vat of cold water.

"Elohl?"

Roused from his trance, Elohl turned. "What if love isn't enough, Fenton? What if this force inside me only grows out of conflict, only grows because of these writhing emotions I feel? Like the sword being honed in the forge, what if strength rises in the world only because we battle, like the Wolf and Dragon – rather than through peacemaking?"

Fenton gave a subtle chuckle in the red night. He leaned back, stretching into his laced hands at his head. "I feel it, the tension in the air. It sears my limbs, Elohl, makes me feel like I'm on fire, through and through. When I have those sensations, when conflict and that simmering feeling roar through me like you're describing – I feel how it makes me strong. But conflict isn't the reason we fight. Too much conflict causes ruin: in the flesh, in the bones, in the mind. In our people. A world based on conflict is only anarchy, from which nothing can grow. No, we fight because we *want* a better tomorrow. We ache for it, would kill for it, desire it. Love is the *reason* we battle, Elohl. Love is what's beneath the Wolf and Dragon. Because if you never cared about anything, what would you fight for? Nothing. Think about the people you love, Elohl – *that's* why we have conflict. So really, it's your love that gives you strength. You might ask Ghrenna what she feels beneath the roiling storm you hold inside you, when you and she meet at night." Fenton's smile was knowing.

Elohl set his whittling down. He gazed at Fenton, level. "How do you know about that?"

"Come on," Fenton's lips quirked. "You steal off at night when you think I'm asleep. I can't let you wander alone right now, Elohl, you're too important."

"You've followed me when I went to the dragon-stone?" Elohl paused, unsure if he should feel betrayed or thankful that Fenton hounded his sojourns these past few nights. Though he and Ghrenna had really only spoken the first night, Elohl had returned both nights since – reveling in her, feeling her body and his entwine in the deepest darkness, coiled in the protection of the dragon-stone as they shivered and gasped in lovemaking.

"Everyone here shuns that spot," Fenton spoke, his gold-brown eyes knowing, "except those who feel its pull. Conflict *wyrria* is a hard curse, Elohl; the line of Khehem's Kings is no easy blood to share in. Someone, eons ago, bound so much conflict *wyrria* into that damn dragon-stone that sometimes I think that's why this Way attracts wars. These thirteen leagues are some of the most bloody on our entire continent. And yet. This place is also one of the most powerful on our continent. Whatever my grandfather Leith did to snuff out *wyrria* a thousand years ago, he couldn't quite do it here. Power lives here. Fuck, it *breathes*. And that dragon-stone breathes more than most – allowing other powers to strengthen around it."

"So you've heard me speaking to Ghrenna."

"*Speaking* isn't the word for it, but yeah." Fenton held a slight smile, though it was kind.

Elohl flushed, but Fenton spoke again before he could. "Elohl. You have a powerful connection to Ghrenna. It's only grown since that coup in the White Palace. Use it. The love you bear each other is only more powerful for the distance that separates you and the conflict that creates. I've seen how the Goldenmarks light when you two are in contact at midnight. Your love feeds them. Instead of running from that, try using it. Indulge in your love, Elohl – and see how strong it can make you."

Fenton's speech came to an end. Elohl sat, digesting all that had been said. As if summoned, Ghrenna's cerulean eyes came, rising up like the dust that blew across his boots in the whispering night. She was there, breathing all around him. Moving in his heart and skin, slipping into his body, waking every part of him. Without pain or any kind of searing sensation, only a beautiful wash of warmth this time, the Goldenmarks began to glow softly on Elohl's chest and down to his forearms and hands. Like curls of ocean sunlight, they flickered and moved under his skin – tender and calm, but strong.

As if they needed his love to truly come alive.

Without a word, Elohl unbuckled his crimson Red Valor jerkin and shed it to the bench. His shirt went next, pulled off over his head and cast to the pitted wood, then his leather bracers. Taking long, slow breaths, he focused on that feeling. Of Ghrenna and their connection. As he did, the Marks flared brighter. Not to bind, and not because he was in dire straights trying to unite bitter enemies or stop a conflict, but because Ghrenna's love moved around him and through him like the curls of the nightwind – raising his own powerful love in return.

Elohl felt her respond, sitting in meditation thousands of leagues away under the mountains. Ghrenna turned, came to his arms, molded to his body. As they breathed together in a space that had no distance and no time, feeling each other's hearts and the bliss of their togetherness, the Goldenmarks surged, bright.

People stopped their activities all along the nearby Way. Through half-lidded eyes, Elohl saw them staring at him through the fire-studded darkness, not just seeing his Goldenmarks light, but *feeling* them brighten with a powerful, timeless love. A Valenghian soldier dropped a saddle from his shoulder and sank to his knees, his astounded face bathed in that pure etheric light. A Cennetian cook-girl gripped her filthy apron, tears blinking from her startled copper eyes to be cast in that radiant glow. A Praoughian tinker dropped his basket of wares to the dust, his round face made even rounder by the *o* of his mouth as he watched curls of bright love flow through the darkness.

Elohl saw them, felt them, as his peaceful love and gentle bliss with Ghrenna reached out in every direction; sighing through every mind, easing into every heart. As a crowd gathered in that strong white-blue luminescence, Elohl realized that he felt love for them – all of them. Not because they were infatuated or impressed by him, but simply because he was touching their hearts. Something about the power of the Goldenmarks opened men up; allowed their hearts to be seen and felt. Allowed Elohl's own heart to touch theirs and commune in this powerful, peaceful feeling. It was gentle, beautiful, blissful – warm and wild in the panicked night.

Elohl's lips fell open. He took steady breaths, feeling this vast love that moved like an oceanic sea in every direction as the Goldenmarks surged, casting the entire camp nearby in a godly, incredible light. Far away, he felt Ghrenna smile, her sigh lovely as a midnight wind.

Elohl. It happens tonight. We are ready to bring you into your full power as Rennkavi. And now I know that you are ready, too. Come to me, when you feel the power rise to its peak. Come to me – and become who you were meant to be.

Her blessed vision faded from Elohl's mind and she slipped away. But the sensation of love that had triggered Elohl's Goldenmarks was not gone. The Marks breathed through Elohl's skin, sending waves of heat and chill through his body as they gave a blissful light to the thickening crowd. Men and women watched him, hushed and reverent, in a ready way that Elohl could feel. As if he could reach inside them, he knew their hearts as well as his own, and could feel the loves and longings of each and every person bathed in that *wyrric* oneness.

As if he had become their hearts, and they his.

Taking out the Valenghian High General's pin that Merkhenos had given him, Elohl ran his thumb over its silver vine, gleaming by the strong light of his Goldenmarks. It was smooth and dotted with tiny flowers under his roughened skin. Glancing at his hands with their luminous ink, twisting and curling like true sunlight now without any underwater constraint, Elohl turned them over. Staring at his old self-inflicted scars upon his inner wrists, he allowed himself to feel all these men and women. How tired they were; how bone-weary. How much they just wanted to go home to their families, their children and loved ones.

How much they longed for all the same things Elohl did – as much as the first day he'd come to the High Brigade, and through to this very moment.

"Ever led a war before?" Elohl spoke to Fenton at last.

"In my time," Fenton's demeanor was calm, a kind of awe upon his features as a liquid golden fire burned in his eyes. "Eight hundred years ago, it was all war, Elohl. I led men and they died. I led them again, and still they died – all because we didn't have a Rennkavi. Don't let that be our fate. Be our hero, our leader. The man you were born to be. The man that King Hahled Ferrian marked you for all those months ago."

"Lhaurent is Goldenmarked also." Elohl slid his thumb over the silver pin again, feeling as if he touched eels in all that smoothness. "He has the same power I do."

"No, he doesn't." Fenton's smile was kind in the night. "He doesn't have a quarter of the strength you possess, Elohl. Because he doesn't have *this.*" Reaching out, Fenton set his palm to Elohl's heart and the Goldenmarks flared beneath it. Elohl felt a bolstering strength surge through him, as if Fenton had actually pressed some of his own mighty *wyrria* right through Elohl's heart. Taking a deep breath, Elohl shivered, feeling something inside him rise, strong with coils and scales and talons in the night.

"Unite these men around us," Fenton breathed softly, "before Lhaurent has a chance to take them away. Peace comes at a price, Elohl; all men pay that price in war. But the only way to find true peace is to allow yourself to become what you need to be. To marshal this army and lead them – as you were born to."

With a last deep breath, Elohl rose. Fenton's palm slipped away, and Elohl turned, taking up his crimson jerkin from the bench. He slung it on sans shirt, leaving the Goldenmarks open for all to see. Setting the Valenghian High General's silver pin to his collar upon the left, he squared his shoulders. Eyes were upon him, watchful in the night. Not just Merkhenos' captains and personal guard, but this entire region of the camp. The Way was choked with tired faces illuminated by Elohl's Marks and in the burgeoning crimson of the oncoming storm – faces of men who had seen too much war.

But they had strength, and so did he. They would stand and

face Lhaurent's army with courage this night, no matter what they could or couldn't do. As Elohl stepped forward into their midst, he felt something rise in his heart, an expansion of understanding. And as he reached out to clasp the arm of the stunned Ghirano before him, Elohl felt a smile lift his face.

A true smile. A smile that knew suffering and hardship. A smile that knew peace and plenty. A smile that knew love and rage, hate and mercy, as he clasped Ghirano's arm. And Elohl's deepest love flared his Goldenmarks through the night, expanding them tenfold like the coils of some ancient creature unfurling to embrace the world.

Because he knew, that all their hearts held the same love.

"*Gottio!*" Ghirano breathed, his eyes enormous, bathed in that light.

"I'm no god," Elohl murmured, "just a man. Spread the word, Ghirano. For how you feel tonight is how we all can feel if we unite and finish this. I'm tired of war. Aren't you? Isn't it time this was over?"

Copper eyes shining, Ghirano nodded. He let Elohl's wrist go then sank to one knee, setting a fist to his heart in a strong Cennetian salute. All through the nearby Way, men and women sighed to their knees in the luminous darkness. But it wasn't what Elohl wanted. Resolutely, he knelt, helping Ghirano back to this feet, clasping the man by the shoulders and giving him a shake of camaraderie.

"Don't worship me – fight with me. Help us unify tonight, so we can end this with minimal bloodshed. Put any differences you have with the other nationalities aside, and we can win a lasting peace for all our lands. Are you with me?"

"Rennkavi," Ghirano breathed. He swallowed, then gave a curt nod. "*Rennkavi!*" He shouted, to be heard over the midnight wind and blowing silt.

In that moment, Elohl lifted up his voice also, his strong baritone rebounding off the Monoliths as his blazing *wyrria* lit the night.

"Tonight, we become one!" Elohl thundered. "Though we shall see battle, do not see the man across the field as your enemy. See how your enemy may become your brother! For are we not all brothers and sisters of the same heart? I feel the same loves and losses in you that you feel in me. These Marks I bear do nothing but make plain that which is right in front of us – that men are made to live and love in peace and companionship. Join me! For I fight this night against a tyrant, because sometimes killing a rabid beast is a mercy. Just as we feel mercy when we stare into our lover's eyes, so we will *be* mercy when we stare into the eyes of our enemy. We will drive straight to his heart, and bring his slaves over to our love. *That* is what we are – we are *all* Rennkavi! And none may sunder us with their hate!"

A rousing roar went up through the red night. Hundreds of men, thousands. A rhythmic clapping came nearby, as Ghirano and his Cennetian guardsman started a song, beating a complex rhythm upon a water barrel. Something in it called to Elohl, moving his veins and spearing his mind. He felt Fenton rise to it, too, the man's lightning suddenly prickling around them in flashes that slit the gathering night. It was an old song, an ancient song. A song that had been created to move power when that power had been young. It wasn't in Cennetian, or any language Elohl knew. That song seemed *wyrric*, full of bright chirps and sliding syllables – like birds of hope soared to the midnight sky, and Elohl's hope surged with it.

Borne upward upon the tide of a thousand soldiers and more feeling the pulse of that song, Elohl's Goldenmarks spread wide, flaring out through the burgeoning night. Each curl of script unfurled like massive coils though the air, their etheric light touching every person there. Each sigil upon his skin dug in like enormous talons, piercing into every heart. Even the oxen lowed in the sylvan darkness, the horses whickering, moving toward him with a peaceful, steady gait.

In that moment, Elohl felt the Dragon within him unfurl. He was no longer the Wolf, alone and lost in the darkness. He was both Wolf and Dragon; and as he set his coils around the world and his talons into every heart, he knew the true power of the Goldenmarks.

He could unite them all, without enslaving them.

And he would – with love.

CHAPTER 43 – KHOUREN

Khouren was pacing. Their allied army had halted for the evening meal, in a swath of rolling hills a few days south of Vennet. The evening was on fire with golden light as Khouren's boots crunched in the sandy soil, hills of grass waving around him. He moved like a stalking specter, kicking at a spiral seashell in the dirt. The Thalanout Plain had been an inland sea long ago. Carven out by glaciers, swallowed by saltwater, then raised up with treacherous bogs upon either side, it retained a prehistoric feel – as if behemoths still roamed its waving grasslands.

A mound raised nearby, made from thousands of ancient corpses piled high under the withering sun. Thigh-bones taller than a man, claws as long as Khouren's femur; gargantuan skulls with tusks and spikes in ridges along their spines. Skeletons of animals so old their bones had petrified. Beasts damned to destruction, then piled by some long-lost people to rot upon the plains until their bones were bleached into stone.

The Hills of the Damned were avoided by caravans and armies, superstition rife about it. Only the bravest snuck into this dead zone to plunder ivory and sell it for atrocious sums, or powder it into costly aphrodisiacs. Gazing upon an enormous mound ten man-heights tall, Khouren's spirits fell, feeling like they were cursed. Ihbram had ridden his keshar-cat back early this morning, giving a scouting report that had darkened every heart. The slave army with the captured Elsthemi that they sought out of Ligenia had already rendezvoused with the main Menderian host.

Ihbram estimated Lhaurent's army at nearly seventy thousand now, from his spying upon a hilltop. It was a force the allies could never hope to breach, even though they had gained Delennia's Red Valor cavalry and a significant portion of the Menderian host from the Battle of the Vault and General den'Albehout's decision to join Arlen. The allies numbers were nearly ten thousand fighters now, but it could not compare to the annihilating presence of Lhaurent's mustering. Even worse – Lhaurent's forces were already marching to war. Ihbram had raced his cat back so hard it had frothed at the mouth and collapsed when he arrived to tell them that battle was imminent upon the Aphellian Way.

The allies had halted their column today after Ihbram's report, two days' ride from the Menderian encampment. An afternoon of wretched discussion passed, full of bad options and worse. All non-fighting personnel had been left behind at the Vault – including injured Menderian soldiers, or those who had lost all heart for battle. But Khouren knew they'd been the smart ones, to relinquish their place in the coming mess.

"Khouren?" Eleshen's step was light and Khouren startled. With more gravitas than she'd had before, she stood tall as she approached – the bearing of a true warrior, which was what she was now. Khouren reached out and wound her into his arms. Breathing softly, he buried his nose in her long sable braid.

"Are you all right?"

"This place is cursed." Khouren's mood was dark under the lowering sun. A specter rode him, telling him that marching against Lhaurent's army was death. "If we ride out to free the Elsthemi slaves, we'll be crushed."

"I know." Eleshen murmured, pulling back slightly. "Everyone's still discussing it, but —"

"What's there to discuss?" Khouren spoke, certainty filling him like sand siphoning into a bottle. "Even a midnight raid upon a force like that would annihilate us. Aeon, everything's all wrong—!"

"Shh," Eleshen set a hand to his chest. "What's gotten into you?"

"Death. Can't you feel it?" Khouren gazed around, shivering in the brisk wind.

"It's just the bones," Eleshen soothed. "Everyone knows this place is haunted."

Khouren breathed out slowly, trying to ignore the creeping fear that prickled over his skin and failing. At last, his gaze returned to Eleshen. "What are the commanders discussing? Are we to attack?"

Eleshen fiddled with her long sable braid, turning to gaze back from where she'd come, facing into the brisk evening wind. "Merra is hot to advance. Arlen is advising caution, Delennia and den'Albehout with him – to watch and gather intelligence. Ihbram's vastly worried over the Kreth-Hakir he saw. He counted more than thirty of them among the tents of the main host."

"We'll be annihilated." Khouren closed his eyes as certainty filled him.

"Delennia's advising we circle through the northern Bog and give support to the main Valenghian force, rather than charge or raid Lhaurent's army. She's counseling Merra to abandon the enslaved Elsthemi. Ihbram thinks he can get us to Valenghia faster, through these barrows here in the Hills of the Damned. Apparently, some of them acted as portal-ways long ago, into some dead city just inside the Heathren Bog near the Valenghian fortifications."

But Khouren knew those passages through the barrows. Even though Ihbram counseled it as a wise move, he didn't agree. Things lived inside those humped mounds of bones; things that were just as voracious today as they had been when Khouren and Ihbram had traveled this way over three hundred years back. It was part of why he trembled, standing upon the low hill, watching the piles of bones in the settling evening.

This place was for the dead, far more than the bowels of Roushenn had ever been.

Suddenly, Khouren heard a roar that sounded like the Elsthemi High General. Like live lightning, Merra came storming up over a hill from the commander's parlay. With a snarl, she drove the long blade of her polearm into the sandy soil. Her breath heaving, she sank to her knees. And then down to her butt, ripping up the tall grass in fistfuls.

Eleshen moved forward as if to console Merra, but Khouren gripped her arm with a shake of his head. A mournful yowl wafted on the wind, and Merra's great white cat ambled up over the hill, bumping her blocky head into Merra's back. With a hard sigh, Merra stroked the cat's tufted ears. The big creature sank to its belly and curled around Merra like the world's laziest couch, its tail-tip flicking with the gusting of the wind as it reached around to lick at the place where arrows had been removed from its haunch at the Vault.

Ihbram came over the rise next. He glanced at Merra, then

headed in Khouren and Eleshen's direction. Stopping, he curried his fingers through his trimmed russet beard, then itched it. "Well, we're no closer to solving this fuckwad than we were hours ago. Any way you slice this meat it's rotten."

"You want to take us through the barrows?" Khouren glanced at Ihbram.

Ihbram caught his glance, sober, then shrugged his shoulders. "Delennia has a solid force upon the Way, though they're outnumbered a good two-to-one by Lhaurent's army. Elohl's there, and Fentleith. Far more power than we have now. If we can't get through a wight-barrow to the northern Bog... I'd have to say we're minced meat if we attack the Menderians directly."

"What's Arlen going to do?" Eleshen glanced at General Merra again, who now leaned back against her cat with her arms crossed and eyes closed.

"Not much he can do," Ihbram sighed. "He promised to aid General Alramir, but not at the cost of all of us. I think the barrow-passage is the most strategic plan. The Alrashemni are for it. So are Delennia, Purloch, and the rest. Arlen is trying to be magnanimous, but you can see it all over his face that he agrees with us. But he fears that if we leave, Merra will—" Ihbram rubbed a hand over his red braids, flicking away a light sweat from his brow.

"Arlen fears General Merra will go after her people. On her own." Eleshen finished, horror filling her violet eyes.

"And that she'll take her keshari riders with her," Ihbram nodded. "Severely diminishing the strength of our forces."

"But it's suicide!" Eleshen retorted hotly.

"Don't we all know it." Ihbram glanced to the Elsthemi High General. Khouren watched the woman with her great cat. Its ears flicked their way, its whiskers riffled. It opened one big golden eye and stared Khouren down. With a deep breath, Merra opened her eyes. As she did, her cat snuffled the wind, mouth open. Suddenly, Merra slung up into the saddle and wrenched her polearm from the ground, her cat on its feet. They moved off, up and over the hill.

"Shit!" Surging forward, Ihbram was fast on their heels over the low rise toward the impromptu cat-cradle. Foreboding in his gut, Khouren jogged in pursuit, Eleshen on his heels. As they crested the rise, he saw General Merra reign her cat close to her Captains, the hulking brothers Rhone and Rhennon Uhlki, issuing low commands. Ihbram dashed down the hill, barreling toward the cats. Hauling out his sword, Ihbram thundered, "*Halt!*" – raising every head and making the cats yowl.

"Draw no steel unless ye plan ta use it!" General Merra barked at Ihbram. Khouren held his ground with a hand on his weapons, watching the scene. Eleshen was no less cautious, sliding her longknives out with slow stealth as she and Khouren stood on the flank of the hill. Tension simmered through the air, as Arlen, Delennia, and their contingent crested the rise, stopping to watch what was happening below.

"I won't let you leave." Ihbram's stern words to General Merra wafted upon the wind. He shifted his warrior's stance, stepping in front of Merra's great white cat. "You'll die if you go. And you'll take the strongest part of our forces with you."

"They're my Elsthemi! Enslaved!" General Merra's blue eyes blazed.

"They're still *alive*." Ihbram's gaze was somber, his voice calm. "Your Elsthemi have been biding their time. It's not pretty, but if you go now, you'll all die. Then where will Elsthemen be?"

"My people need me ta rescue them!" Merra's gaze was fierce, her visage a thundercloud.

"Your people need you to stay alive." Ihbram had dropped his voice, but Khouren had sharp ears. "The Menderian forces will *annihilate* you. If you had twenty thousand *maybe* you'd have a chance. But against what Lhaurent's got? Even I can think of no plan to rescue slaves against that."

Merra gazed down at Ihbram. Khouren could see the brightness of tears in her fierce blue eyes. As he watched, Ihbram slid away his sword, stepping close to the big cat, lifting a hand to smooth its rippling fur. *Wyrria* prickled through the air, a pressure Khouren could feel up on the grassy knoll. In his mind-sight, he watched soothing flows of crimson ease out from Ihbram into the Elsthemi High General.

"Don't throw your life away," Ihbram murmured. "There is a time for motion and a time for stillness. And a time to regroup with your allies – who are here. And who need you."

Merra choked. She gazed down into Ihbram's solemn face and

Khouren saw tears fall. "Where do I have allies anymore? Where will Elsthemen go if our warriors die?"

"To Valenghia." Delennia Oblitenne strode down the grassy hillside, Arlen in her wake. The new Vhinesse was impressive in her crimson and black chevron battle-armor, broad-shouldered and strong in her ground-eating stride as she came to pause a short distance away. "Where we will fight with strength and get all our lands and peoples back from this abominable tyrant."

"We need you, High General." Stepping up next to Merra, Ihbram laid a hand upon Merra's boot. Khouren saw clever threads of crimson mind-*wyrria* easing up her calf, seeping into her thigh. Merra bristled like a mongoose facing off with a snake, then kicked out at Ihbram's hand as if she could sense what was happening.

"Take yer mitts off me."

Khouren's ears perked at that, and he heard Eleshen catch her breath.

"We need you, High General," Ihbram echoed again, his strength of persona easing into Merra again on ruby tendrils. Ihbram's flows were potent, but Merra broke her palm from her saddle-horn with a brisk movement, slapping *wyrric* threads out of the way as if she had felt them. Ihbram's eyes flashed in the lowering sunlight; Merra gave a low, simmering growl. Khouren's gut twisted at that sound, watching their standoff of wills.

"Why won't she see reason?" He breathed softly.

"Warriors have passionate hearts," Eleshen spoke, her gaze rapt upon the scene.

"We need you, Merra. Please. Don't throw your life away." Ihbram repeated it a third time, tension simmering through the air upon his crimson threads.

And suddenly, the Elsthemi High General broke. With a crushing sob, she threw her polearm down to the grass and fell forward over the neck of her great cat, burying her face in its fur. Even from a distance, Khouren could feel the thrumming of the keshar-cat's rolling purr as it turned its blocky head, licking Merra's red-blonde braids; comforting her. Their bond was tender, and something about it hitched Khouren's chest. His heart swelled and he reached out to collect Eleshen close. She wound her arms about his waist as they both watched.

Down below, Ihbram had claimed the reins of Merra's cat, petting it soothingly. Khouren watched Delennia and Arlen move in, Delennia speaking low to both Ihbram and Merra. Merra rose, palming away tears as she nodded to Delennia's words, then glanced at Arlen, who nodded also.

And Khouren knew that Ihbram had convinced them. They were headed to Valenghia, and it would be through the barrows as Ihbram willed. As Merra roared for her keshari to mount up, the sharp five-blast of her horn echoed through the grasslands. Within a quarter-hour, Khouren was mounted up behind Eleshen upon her big dappled cat, their allied army being led by Ihbram as they wound through the rolling hills of barrow-mounds. Eleshen guided her cat around sharp rocks as their army swarmed the low hills. At the top of one sandy rise, Khouren saw they moved toward a particularly large mass of ancient bones piled atop a cairn.

Built of shale-rocks and obsidian flint, the enormous barrow Ihbram led them toward was roughly constructed. Forming a ring of doorways below, the barrow dug into a hill of sod topped by a massive pile of petrified bones. But every doorway in the lower part of the structure led nowhere. Bricked up with sharp pieces of flat shale, each doorway was capped with a long spike of obsidian – entrances closed up long ago. The sun lowered, expanding over the golden hills, lighting the cairn with a fiery luminescence. Khouren watched obsidian glint like vicious, knowing eye-slits, as if those spikes belonged to some ancient reptile. A chill swept him as Eleshen's cat stepped over a boundary of scattered obsidian that might once have been a wall. He felt some massive darkness stalk him, aware of his presence.

Others felt it, too. A number of Valormen made a superstitious warding with two fingers drawn in a line over their brow. Horses reared and snorted, keshar-cats snarled and hissed, backs arched and ears flat to their skulls. It took a lot of shouts and slapping of reins to get the cats to continue forward. The column halted, leaving only the commanders and Ihbram riding forward to investigate the cairn. Khouren watched as Ihbram stalked his cat past a few doors, listening at each one as if waiting to hear something.

"Is Ihbram sure about this?" Eleshen shivered before Khouren, as if sensing the danger Khouren felt in this place.

"This is where Ihbram and I came through long ago," Khouren spoke tersely, the feeling of being watched eating at him. "From a lost city in the northern Bog near the Valenghian fortifications on the Way. Ihbram believes we can get through again, without trekking for days. Make it in time to help the Valenghian forces, before Lhaurent's army arrives."

"Do you think we can get through?" Eleshen asked, snuggling back into Khouren's arms.

"I don't even think we should be here," Khouren breathed, fear rippling through his sinews. Ihbram had stopped his cat before one shale doorway. The cat gave a low yowl, twitching its whiskers at the door. Ihbram gestured and Merra gave a sharp whistle for the other commanders in the lowering darkness. Then, Ihbram ambled his cat toward the bricked-up doorway – and disappeared.

Khouren blinked. One moment, his uncle and his cat had been there, while the next, they had shivered like a mirage upon a scorching plain, gone from sight. But presently they returned, slipping back through the solid doorway, Ihbram beckoning. Arlen and Delennia moved their steeds forward, and Eleshen clicked her tongue to move her dappled cat also. Khouren watched as Ihbram returned to the door, slipping through like smoke again, followed by General Merra and her big white beast. Khouren's brows knit, as he and Eleshen gained the spot where Merra and Ihbram had disappeared.

In the shivering light of evening, Khouren suddenly saw a great truth. Though all the other doors into the barrow had been blocked-up, this one was a cleverly-disguised mirage of *wyrria*. From a distance, the doorway looked solid, but now that Khouren was close, he saw the image of solidity was created by a crystal set into the obsidian spike, catching the last of the sun's rays and creating an illusion that confounded the mind. Even as Khouren stared at it, his mind still couldn't tell it wasn't a solid wall, except that he could actually perceive the dark shadows inside the barrow. As he stuck a hand into the arch, it met nothing; no stone, no obsidian. Just a mild sensation of chill – as he watched his own hand shimmer and disappear.

"Get your asses in here!" Ihbram's voice called out from inside the barrow. Khouren could just make him out in the gloom beyond the mirage. Moving their cat forward beneath the arch, Eleshen guided them through a blowing sensation of cold into the dim interior.

Circular, the space had a packed dirt floor, shadows devouring the inside. All along the curved walls, Khouren saw human skulls staring back at him. Thousands of them, carefully stacked and interspersed with arrangements of femurs and longbones. The entire cairn seemed to watch him, with a haunting stillness that made every hair on his body stand up. Not to mention the black pool that waited in the middle of the floor. Dismounting, Khouren walked up to where Arlen and Delennia crouched, hovering their fingertips over the pool next to Ihbram and Merra. Eleshen was quick to his side as Khouren gained the rim of the pool, crouching.

This was the same place, just as he remembered it from hundreds of years ago. He stared down into black, far down as if through another universe. Ancient, an abandoned city grew up thick and rancid from a devouring bog on the other side of the black gateway. A city of tumbled ruins covered by vines and overgrowth with a sloping amphitheater in a mud-choked hollow. Khouren stared, as Eleshen breathed softly by his side. He could almost feel the slow evening in that other place, filtering down from a high canopy of trailing vines and spreading foliage.

"Where is that?" Eleshen spoke, her voice hushed in the dim cairn.

"It's known as Wayfarer," Khouren breathed. "A city of ancient peoples long gone. It's just north of the Aphellian Way, on the Valenghian side."

"This is the portal Khouren and I came through before," Ihbram spoke solidly, glancing up at the others, though his gaze fixed upon Khouren.

"How do you know it still works?" General Merra breathed, stretching out her fingertips but not quite daring to touch that viscous black surface.

"I don't," Ihbram's smile was wry, "but it's worth a shot. Everyone step back. This might take some convincing."

Stepping forward in the dim space as everyone else took a few steps back, Khouren knew his duty. With a deep breath, he focused on the pool as he gained Ihbram's side. Though Khouren quailed, a glint in Ihbram's sharp emerald eyes said he was ready to do battle.

And battle it would be – Khouren knew all too well.

With the lightest touch, Ihbram stretched his fingertips down from his crouch, slowly, until they met the inky surface. Instantly, something seized him. Ihbram went rigid, his eyes rolling up in his head. He began to shiver in a palsy, his eyelids fluttering, his eyes rolled so far back they were only whites. As Ihbram shuddered, breathing hard, Khouren could see what was siphoning out of his uncle. Tendrils of crimson were being sucked out of Ihbram and into the pool – hundreds of them, the thing trapped within the portal drinking the man's *wyrric* lifeblood alive.

Ihbram spasmed and cried out, and Khouren responded. Seizing his uncle's shoulder with one hand, he thrust his other hand into the inky blackness. Pain gripped him. A sensation like the pool was alive, though it had no mind. And within that sensation, he felt a thousand gaping maws suddenly open, eager.

One meal of *wyrria* wasn't enough – it would have more before it allowed passage.

Khouren screamed as he felt crimson and gold floes of Wolf and Dragon *wyrria* sucked out of his very bones. Every eye of those skulls watched him from the walls, laughing with madness. And he knew, that each and every one of them had been devoured by this thing over the eons. All of their *wyrria* drained – to death.

Khouren screamed again, pulled so hard that his supportive hand fell from Ihbram's shoulder, splashing into the blackness. Ihbram was dragged forward, stumbling into the viscous black liquid as the pool's pull increased a hundredfold. Eating, devouring, draining them. Sucking the life from their flesh and the magic from their veins. It hadn't had a good meal in ages, and it was far more ravenous. Khouren felt himself desiccating, aging fast, becoming brittle – becoming death as it ate. The toll had to be paid for them to pass, but in this terrible devouring – so much worse than it had been before – Khouren knew they had made a vast mistake.

Eleshen's scream was faraway. He barely registered her, vaulting from her cat and striding into the black pool. With a scream like a harpy, she thrust both hands deep into the pool. It roared in exultation, eager to devour whatever additional *wyrria* she held.

But suddenly, Khouren felt something compress through the

pool. Like Eleshen had slapped it, he felt the tides turn. As she roared at it like a warrior gone amok, Eleshen raised one black hand to the bones surrounding the cairn. Fixing them in her violet eyes as Khouren shuddered with the last of his life, she roared.

He felt her take control. It was then that Khouren understood her strange *wyrria* as she shuddered hard, draining the creature right back. She hadn't battled the creature, her *wyrria* simply echoed its own – taking on its qualities, its motions and desires. She was suddenly the ravenous devouring of a starlit ocean inside Khouren's mind. Violet consumed his vision as Eleshen drained *wyrria* back from the creature's talismans – from the bones that supported its vast magic. Filling her to the brim, pouring it back into Khouren and Ihbram.

Khouren gasped as his *wyrria* returned. Seething through his sinews and flesh like hot lightning, it burned him as it returned, but its flood was welcome. With Eleshen growling like a demon, Khouren and Ihbram were able to stand, wading into the center of the pool. Standing with her, seizing hands, they combined their might.

Eleshen's *wyrria* gained their qualities – Ihbram's adept convincing and Khouren's smoky inability to be grasped. With a roar, she slipped all three of them away from the creature's hunger by Khouren's magic. She trapped it inside her mind, by Ihbram's ability. The thing howled, a terrible cacophony of a thousand beasts being tortured, struggling. *I don't think so.* Eleshen's mind breathed through all of them, surging with violet light. *You will allow us passage. And exact no more toll, from any that pass through this place.*

Like a beaten thing, its power flashed away. All those seeping, draining maws were just gone, to the bright wrath of Eleshen's nature. Khouren heaved a breath and shuddered to stillness, returning from his far trance as the pool cleared. From an inky darkness it surged out in a bright wave, the surface rippling to a crystalline white. The city in the bog looked like a paradise now upon the other side, and Khouren could practically hear the calling of birds as they fluttered through the verdant trees. Glancing at Ihbram, he saw his uncle's eyes were open. His russet braids were streaked with white, two prominent streaks in his red beard, his skin creased with lines. The man had aged years in moments, and

Khouren gaped, astounded.

But even as he stared, Eleshen turned, setting a palm to Ihbram's heart. Her eyes glowed with violet light as she poured the last of his *wyrria* back into him, brightening his hair back to a fiery russet and smoothing lines until he looked barely forty once more.

"Eleshen—!" Ihbram gasped. With a shiver, Eleshen seemed to dispel the trance that consumed her, and the power in her eyes flashed out – back to a normal, though lovely, color. Blinking around, her gaze fixed upon the skulls for a moment, then upon Khouren.

"We can take the army through now," she spoke shakily. "It'll give everyone passage." Stepping up to support the still-unsteady Ihbram, she got under his arm and helped Khouren move them all out of the crystalline pool. Delennia, Arlen, and the rest of the commanders gaped from the boundary, eyes darting as if unsure what had just happened. Arlen stepped up, setting a hand to Ihbram's shoulder, his iron-hard gaze vastly concerned.

"Are you all right, my friend?"

"I'll be fine." Ihbram's lips quirked, though Khouren could tell he was faking it. Khouren's uncle was still in pain, even if he played strong. Eleshen had reversed the *wyrria* used on them by the thing that lived in the pool, but it wasn't the kind of sacrifice a man recovered from. Even though flesh could heal and *wyrria* be returned, that feeling of being helpless never went away.

Arlen said nothing, only nodded. Glancing at the pool, he narrowed his eyes. And without further hesitation, strode in.

CHAPTER 44 – DHERRAN

Dherran gaped as Arlen disappeared in an instant, into the crystalline pool within the dim barrow. There was nothing for a long moment, only ripples in the viscous water, until suddenly he was back, striding out of the pool with only his boots wet.

"It works," Arlen growled at Delennia. "Muster the army."

The Vhinesse's eyes were wary, but she didn't gainsay him. Moving out with General Merra at her side, Dherran soon heard Delennia's formidable shout ordering the columns into ranks to come through the barrow. The three *wyrrics* who had done battle with whatever had been in that pool stood to one side, visibly shaken. The woman with the violet eyes was staring at the water, and as Dherran looked at her, she turned her gaze to him. He shivered, unnerved, suddenly aware of all the skulls lining the cairn staring at him with dead eyes. Dherran could almost see them in her violet gaze – thousands of dead, standing at the walls.

Waiting for the moment he would join them.

Setting his jaw, he firmed his resolve. That wouldn't be his fate today, nor any day soon. Khenria gripped his fingers and he looked down, seeing her beloved face. Those big grey eyes, her fierce cheekbones. She was ready for whatever was coming and so was he. Dherran squeezed her hand. At Arlen's beckon, they led their horses forward – into the crystal pool.

With a gut-wrenching, eyeball-popping contortion, they traveled through. Dherran staggered but managed to maintain his balance, holding on to his horse's lead with Khenria at his side. Dusk choked the evening and as he glanced around, he knew they were in the same city they had glimpsed from the pool. Bog-birds whirred and clicked overhead, flitting from tree to tree in a soaring canopy. A snarling yowl came through the dense forest. Midges whirred around Dherran's head, the ruined city topped by a shuffling canopy of living green, a rippling chorus of bullfrogs beginning far out in the dense grey-green.

They'd come out in a rectangular pool at the center of an overgrown, tumbled rotunda. A stone rim only a handspan high surrounded the pool, but as Dherran and Khenria walked their horses out, he saw the water of the pool was pristine, though everything else around them was completely overgrown with vines and rooting trees. Stepping out with only his boots and his horses' fetlocks wet, they moved to the side. The three *wyrrics* were soon through with their cats, then Grunnach and his steed.

In tens and twenties, their allied army began to come through the pool. It took over an hour to put nearly ten thousand warriors, horses, and supplies out into the overgrown city. Campfires were kindled as night fell, kills made by Purloch's archers now roasting upon spits to feed their host. A blithe mood had taken their forces, having braved the barrow and saved many days of impassable travel and precious time. Songs and Bog-flutes lifted around campfires as men took their rest, far from the creeping unease of the haunted hills.

Snugging Khenria close as they lounged with their backs against a tumbled stone wall, gazing into the fire as the flutes changed into a somber tune, Dherran suddenly felt a prickling along the back of his neck. It had been assaulting him, on and off, since they had come through. As if someone watched him, as if something called through the depths of the night. Squeezing Khenria's shoulders, he kissed her forehead, then her lips as she looked up with a question in her eyes.

"I need to get up for a while. Go walk a bit," Dherran murmured.

She nodded, lifting up to kiss him again. "Be careful. Take Yenlia or Bherg or one of Purloch's archers with you if you go out into the forest."

"Sure."

Sliding out from beside her, Dherran rose. With a fleeting smile, he turned toward an overgrown arch, ducking through a cascade of vines to leave the tumbled plaza the army was now encamped on. Sliding through the hushed grey-green of overgrown pyramids, colonnaded walkways with no roof, and past cisterns sporting fully-grown trees and ponds of duckweed and pink lotus,

Dherran followed the tingling sensation. He thought it would have led him back to the rectangular pool in the rotunda they'd come through earlier, but it led him off to the south.

His eyes adjusting to the solid night as he moved through the peeping darkness, night-birds whooping calls to each other in the canopy above, Dherran walked through the tumbled ruins. Pushing through tall ferns and cascading vines, he moved through the dead city like a specter. As he gained the rim of the citadel, where the stony plazas suddenly gave out to the forest proper, he saw a shadow sitting upon a low wall in the black-on-black. Dherran had thought this was the source of his tingling sensation, but noticed that his heart was pulling him past whoever lingered upon the wall – into the forest.

But this shadow had to be dealt with first. Putting a hand to his sword, Dherran crept forward, keeping behind arches as much as he could. But as he neared, a grating, lordly-smooth voice issued from the man upon the wall.

"Draw no steel, Dherran."

Dherran blinked, recognizing Arlen den'Selthir's voice. Straightening, his hand left his sword as he moved forward to the shadow. "Arlen? What are you doing out here?"

"Same as you." Dherran felt more than saw Arlen's shadow turn toward him. "I feel him. Calling us."

"Feel who?" Dherran sidled to the wall, his hackles rising high, unnerved.

Arlen gave a mysterious chuckle in the dark. "I've heard the tale of the coup in the Vhinesse's throne hall. Delennia told me how her *wyrria* was pulled by the Rennkavi, enhanced, engaged to do his bidding. Even without binding men, he has a sway, Dherran. The Goldenmarks call us all. I can feel it, same as you. He may not know it, but he's been calling us, ever since that moment. I feel it – to come and be one with his magic, tingling through my blood as we speak."

"*Wyrria.*" Dherran leaned a hip upon the wall, crossing his arms. "Grump said you have it."

"And I do." Arlen lifted his chin as if scenting the night. "It may not be manifest, precisely, but I feel it, hammering in my heart, enraging my fury as I fight. It's one of the reasons I train hard,

587

Dherran. Because battle never leaves me. So I make the most of it."

"You have a Khehemni ancestor."

"A few of them, if the stories in my family are true. The Alrashemni and Khehemni have a far more messy past than any of us would like to admit." Arlen glanced over, considering Dherran by the wan light of a sickle moon that crept now through the canopy far above. The clouds had shifted, and a fey silver edged the ruins. Dherran could see Arlen's austere profile, and the outline of shapes in the low wall. It shivered Dherran suddenly, to see that the wall was made entirely of skulls. He shifted his stance with an alert tingle, moving his hip off the wall.

Arlen gave a low chuckle in the limned darkness, as if he'd read Dherran's thoughts. "Ask me anything, Dherran. You've earned it."

Arms still crossed, Dherran pondered that. It felt like ages since they had last conversed this way, in the relative peacefulness of Arlen's manor in Vennet, training hard by day and learning as much as Dherran's mind could handle. But life had changed – moved on – in so many ways since that relatively peaceful time. As Dherran felt a tingle seize his neck again, he saw an answering shiver ripple through Arlen.

"Do you trust Ihbram, and his companions?" Dherran asked, starting with the obvious.

Arlen gave a hard sigh, his iron-blue eyes piercing in the moonlight. "Ihbram and I go back a long way, Dherran. Nothing he's done has ever given me reason to doubt him. I know he's far more than he seems – more than I could ever imagine. But I trust him, and so should you. He has a very good heart, and believes in peace."

"What about the Rennkavi?"

Arlen gave a soft chuckle. "He's your friend, not mine, Dherran. But I feel his call. And whether that's a good thing or bad, I can't rightly say. It could be a curse or a blessing in this upcoming battle. Only the death toll will tell."

"Do you think we have a chance?" Dherran murmured, sobered by Arlen's words.

He heaved a deep sigh. "I have to believe that we do. Otherwise, my courage would fail and then where would our armies be? But know when I tell you that Lhaurent has assembled a truly annihilating force. We are outnumbered, out-maneuvered, out-*wyrria*'d. If your friend the Rennkavi cannot work miracles…" His voice drifted off, into a midnight chorus of bullfrogs. But then, Arlen's gaze shifted to Dherran. Giving him a long, thoughtful gaze, a mysterious smile quirked his lips.

"What?" Dherran bristled slightly.

"Khenria's done well to choose you," Arlen's gaze pressed under the wan moon. "As her father, I can't say I'll ever be un-protective, especially with all the years I lost not knowing her. But you've risen to all challenges with a tenacity and heart that shows who and what you are. You stood firm in the White Palace, against an onslaught I once collapsed under. Your heart has its own *wyrria* and its righteousness surges in your eyes. I saw it the first day I watched you fight and I see it still. But it's matured now. Stronger, wiser."

Dherran found himself speechless at Arlen's praise. Praise from the Vicoute Arlen den'Selthir was a rare thing, he had learned. "Heart magic. You saw it in me."

With his mysterious smile, Arlen nodded. "*Jinne wyrdi* is an ancient conundrum. A magic that seldom flows in human veins, and is practically unknown in either Khehemni or Alrashemni bloodlines. It makes the bearer wild and willful with raging passions, but also able to change outcomes in an instant, because of their heart's truest desire. What will you do with it when your back's up against a wall? What you've always done, Dherran; win. And that's why, when we join the Valenghian army for this battle – I'd like you to lead the charge."

Dherran was stunned as the moon eased behind a cloud above, abandoning the dead city to a dusky shadow. Even as much as Dherran surged with satisfaction to hear Arlen's words, something else inside him bristled, uneasy. As if a massive presence watched him in the dead city, just as it had in the barrow – turning its head to stare at him with renewed intent. As if destiny had a feel – of darkness that swallowed all light. Taking a deep breath, Dherran felt a heavy weight settle upon his shoulders. Yet, with it came promise. To lead men in battle; to become a fighter worthy of a place at Khenria's side once all this was over.

Glancing at Arlen, a black-on-black shadow now, Dherran

nodded. "I'll lead the charge."

Dherran couldn't see it, but he could feel Arlen's gaze lingering upon him, before he nodded. "So be it. I must head back to our forces, to discuss our upcoming strategy. Are you headed onward tonight?" Arlen nodded his chin at the looming black that rose up before them at the southern edge of the citadel.

"I am," Dherran nodded. "If it's Elohl calling, this feeling we're having, then I need to go to him. Even if just for an hour."

"Do so." Arlen pushed off the wall of skulls, standing tall. "Have him alert Valenghia that we are here. I will arrive with our commanders to parlay in two hour's time."

Arlen extended his arm. Dherran clasped it, feeling a strange sensation pass between them – like a meeting of equals rather than teacher and pupil. And with that, Arlen turned, slipping off through the black night.

With Elohl's strange call prickling his shoulders and the enormous presence watching him in the darkness, Dherran turned to face the forest's boundary and stepped in. Pulled on through the black, he didn't have to navigate the midnight forest with his eyes. Threading past the humped ruin of an ancient pyramid in the trees, he moved on. Guided by something he couldn't understand or predict, Dherran only knew he had to follow, pushing through the forest by the instinct of his heart. It was only a short way. Before a half-hour passed, he found himself upon the edge of the bog, striding out from thinning trees onto a hard-packed plain with tough clumps of sedge-grasses – an abrupt change in the night.

There were no stars above now, no moon. A seething mass of clouds devoured the deep midnight, red suffusing their underbelly. Dherran realized he had exited the bog near the towers of the Valenghian palisade across the Aphellian Way, watch-fires casting a glow up into the storm-shrouded night. Adjacent to a row of towering Monoliths – some dusky, some luminous – Dherran could see a fluttering crimson command-pavilion limned by torches. Red Valor guards flanked the entrance, their steely eyes searching the dark.

But Elohl wasn't there. The tingling sensation called Dherran east, as he moved on in the hushed night, not announcing his presence just yet. The temperature of the camp was tense but ready as he threaded through mess tents steaming with stew and smelling of spice-jerked meat. Soldiers came and went with wooden bowls, or sat dicing upon barrels, not sleeping though the hour was deep. Lightning flickered in the clouds, blooming in rosettes before dying to the torchlight. War-horses whiskered as Dherran threaded through their lines. Reaching a broad field that whispered with tall grass, at the center of which loomed a massive edifice of pale stone, he arrived.

It was here that Elohl had been calling him this strange night. Moving through the waist-high grass, Dherran felt a sudden charge dig into his body. As if his fighter's passion had been amplified tenfold, he felt it screw into his nerves and deep into his chest, setting his teeth on edge and tensing his muscles. His entire body buzzed with the unpleasant, though enlivening, sensation. As if hornets raged through his veins, ready to unleash their fury upon the world.

Dherran shivered as he approached the gargantuan stone edifice. Carven in the shape of a curled-up dragon with a flared mantel of spiked thorns, long spines ran the length of the dragon's back, its blunt nose snarling with fangs beneath its armored tail. Something about the beast was powerful, eerie, and explosive like Ghreccan fire-cannons. Every hair on Dherran's body stood up as he neared, until finally he saw a shadowy figure sitting cupped in the dragon's front talons.

The figure rose. Clad in crimson, he seemed like a Valenghian soldier, but as Dherran stepped close, he saw no shirt beneath the man's leather jerkin. It was unbuckled at the collar and chest, baring a rippling, incandescent light to the darkness. The simmering beauty of those marks caught Dherran's breath, mesmerizing.

"Dherran." Elohl's low voice aroused Dherran from his reverie.

"Elohl." Moving forward, Dherran suddenly felt at a loss. Unsure of how to greet his friend, who was so much more than he'd once been, Dherran paused, then extended a hand. Elohl glanced at it as a wistful smile quirked his lips. Reaching out, he clasped Dherran's proffered wrist.

"Do we know each other so little now?"

"Seemed odd to take you up in a bear-hug," Dherran spoke, "being what you are now."

"Rennkavi."

"I suppose." Dherran shifted, restless, the prickling sensation still sluicing over him. "We've got a backup force inside the northern Bog, Elohl. Kingsmen, Bog-folk, Elsthemi, Red Valor, defected Menderians – some ten thousand strong. When it's time to do battle, we're here for you. The commanders are coming to parlay in another hour or so."

"I know." Elohl's smile was haunted.

"You know?" Dherran startled.

"Ghrenna told me."

"Ghrenna—" Dherran swallowed, an urge to run pouring through his veins suddenly. It was primal, the feeling predators get when they realize something stronger than they has flown overhead. "She told you of our movements? Of our allied army?"

"Ghrenna sees far these days," Elohl's Goldenmarks gave a stunning ripple in the night.

Dherran chuckled, trying to be easy but his hackles rising high, spooked. "You two against the world, huh? Just like you always were… with more *wyrria* now, I guess."

"I guess."

A haunted silence stretched between them. Dherran shifted again, unease pouring through him. But seeing his friend standing there, still so much the Elohl he had known, even though he wasn't anymore, Dherran's heart surged. No matter how much power he had, no matter how much *wyrria*, Elohl was like a brother to Dherran, and the ease of family and love suddenly warmed Dherran. His prickling sighed away beneath that glow, and he took a deep breath, speaking from his heart.

"Elohl. When this is all over, I'd like to catch up. I know it seems trite, everything we've been through these past ten years, but… I'd like to have an ale. To put down all these dire things we've become and just talk. I know I was never one for expressing myself, except with my fists, but… you mean a lot to me. You were my best friend. Maybe I didn't value your friendship back then, not like I understand friendship now. But I'd like to have a chance to know the man you've become. Beneath all—" he waved his hand at the flowing marks, "those."

"I'd like that." Elohl's baritone was hushed upon the storm-wind that rippled the dry grass. But Dherran saw the small smile that lifted Elohl's lips at the corners, a rare thing that truly expressed what he felt. "When this is all over, we'll have an ale, just the two of us. Before Ghrenna and I set out to find a little farm in the mountains."

"Going for the farm-dream?" A true smile lifted Dherran's face at last, bolstered by the glow in his heart. "I guess some things don't change. Think you'd be happy milking cows and herding goats the rest of your days?"

"I know I would be." Elohl's level gaze gave Dherran a chill. As if specters danced across his grave, laughing at the life a fighter could never have.

"Think we'll live long enough to get peace, Elohl? Milk cows and curly-haired little brats?"

Elohl's lips quirked more, a wry humor in his dark eyes, though Dherran could feel the wave of deep ease that flowed out from Elohl upon a surge of his luminous inkings. "Cut the shit. You'd never be happy in a quiet life. You'll be a fighter to the end of your days, Dherran. You always were."

Elohl's words hit Dherran like a punch in the gut. Perhaps he hadn't meant it to be sobering, but the smile slipped from Dherran's face as a heavy sensation settled upon his shoulders. As if Elohl had pronounced Dherran's death, Dherran found himself recalling Elyria's dire words as a flare of heat-lightning flickered in the black morass above, a brisk storm-wind rippling the grass.

"And you always were a lover," Dherran murmured, feeling something bleak eating through his heart. "But only the poets will sing our fate. For lovers and fighters both bleed when the horn of war calls."

"Tonight's not the night we die, Dherran." Elohl's voice was firm against the darkness. Reaching out, he clasped Dherran's shoulder, his Marks giving a steady flare. "We're in this battle together, until all of Halsos' Hells open and swallow us. I felt what happened between us in that throne hall in the White Palace, and I know you felt it, too. Don't let your heart fail us now. Your passion is the fuel for my fire, Dherran. Your stalwart heart gives me strength; it always has. And if there's one thing I know about your passion, it's that it will never die. Stand by my side; be strong for us all tonight. Because lovers need love to make them stronger, so we can all prevail against what's coming."

"And fighters have strong hearts to give." Dherran hitched a breath in the red darkness. Reaching up, he set his hand to Elohl's shoulder so their embrace formed a ring. Something fierce went surging through Dherran, then. Something born of wind and heat and scorching desert sands. As if his passion had an origin, borne of hurricanes through searing canyons. Inhaling a breath, a funnel of red sand appeared in Dherran's vision, blinding him for a moment. Setting him trembling from head to heels – for a fight.

"And so we die," Dherran murmured. "Together."

"And so we live, asshole," Elohl crushed Dherran's shoulder in his grip, shaking him. "Whatever we are now, remember that we are Alrashemni. Lead with me, Dherran. Help me lead tonight. These men who will soon battle are afraid of their annihilation and they look to you, and to me – Blackmarked and Goldenmarked – to command in this battle. So do it. With me. Please, my friend. My strength as the Rennkavi is nothing without you at my side, giving me hell."

Dherran was silent a long moment, his brows knit. At last, with an enormous inhalation, he straightened, feeling all hesitation flee from his heart under the impeccable steadiness and strength he felt emanating from Elohl. Gazing at his old friend, Dherran saw purpose set Elohl's jaw, and every line of his sword-honed sinew. The Goldenmarks flared – a clear, vibrant blue that dazzled the night as Dherran felt their hearts resonate. Their eyes locked, and it was as if Dherran could see the entire universe in Elohl's steady opal gaze.

"There's nothing I'd love to do more," Dherran spoke, his heart firm once more with purpose. "Use my strength and finish this. Face this blight Lhaurent den'Alrahel has unleashed upon us and tear it down. Take his army away from him; take our people back. Menderian, Kingsmen, Valenghian, and all the rest. We're ready to win our lives back from this storm, Rennkavi. And when we're done, we'll have that ale."

"Done." Gripping Dherran's nape, Elohl drew their foreheads together. With a soft laugh, he said, "I love you, you know that? I know I've always been one somber, hell-eyed motherfucker, just as you've always been a torrent of passion. But I'm learning how to love with my whole heart, not just bury my emotions anymore. Learn with me."

"Learn?" Dherran laughed, feeling lighter than he had in ages. "I'm already a roaring beast for the people I love, Elohl! But one thing I'm learning from all this is to not accept failure. Not even if I have to go to Halsos and back to make it happen."

With their foreheads pressed together, Elohl gave a soft chuckle. "Never would have pegged you for a deep thinker, Dherran."

"Yeah, but I always knew you were an asshole." Dherran let Elohl go with one last shake, then grinned, feeling like they had come to accord at last. "I should get back to the Heathren Bog. I'll return with Arlen, Delennia, and the rest when they get here, so we can discuss the battle."

Elohl gave a nod and Dherran turned away. But before he could stride off, he felt Elohl's iron grip upon his arm. He turned. Elohl stood tall before him, filling out his sinewed height with strength and quiet surety – just like his father, Urloel, but far more. Elohl's eyes were steady as he and Dherran faced each other, his Goldenmarks flaring strong in the night. Ready, for whatever happened next. Dherran found it spoke to something deep inside himself that understood life and death. Standing there in the heavy dark, Dherran smiled, his heart surging. For the first time, Elohl looked like a Rakhan – a leader for the Kingsmen.

And a leader for everyone else this black-hearted night.

Reaching out, Elohl clasped Dherran's shoulder. "Come on. Let's get this battle planned, as much as a fucking enormous melee can be."

CHAPTER 45 – ELYASIN

Elyasin returned to consciousness staring up at a starry night. Her vision swam, stars whirling. Time had no meaning and for a moment she felt the universe breathe. All around her, an endless susurration flowed without limitation. Deep and sensual, it caught her breath and made her pause. For a moment, there was nothing but stars, forever – and the feeling of a presence behind those stars.

Her body shivered and the moment broke. As that shudder passed through her, she was hit with pain. An enormous, suffering pain, as if every muscle had been beaten with sledgehammers. A cry issued from her lips – the only sound she could make.

"She's awake." A soft voice sounded nearby – Thad's voice, gentle and melodious.

"Thank all the gods." Therel's voice caused relief to flood Elyasin. She remembered his eyes dimming; she remembered seeing his face go slack. But as she craned her neck to see him, she felt Therel's hands, warm and gentle, slide under her. Sitting at her bedside, he lifted her, his wolf-blue eyes alive and filled with relief as he cradled her to his chest. Every bone and muscle in Elyasin's body screamed, and yet, feeling Therel's smooth rise and fall of breath, their hearts beating as one with their chests pressed close was more soothing than any balm. With careful movements, Elyasin managed to lift her arms and wind them around Therel's neck, pressing her lips into his skin.

"I love you," she sighed.

"My sweetgrape—!" Therel choked, cradling her neck so he could pull away slightly and lay their foreheads together. "Don't ever scare me like that again…!"

"As long as you don't, either," Elyasin spoke as they kissed, tired and gentle through her pain. "I couldn't bear to watch you die again, Therel."

"Someday we'll have to," he rasped. Tears slipped down his

cheeks, and Elyasin kissed them away.

"Not here. Not now." Setting their lips together, she gave him a real kiss. Deep and slow, inhaling his lupine musk and river-water scent. Therel wound his arms around her, and they kissed deeply, feeling each other's presence, soft and slow. It ended gently, and Elyasin sighed as they rested foreheads together once more.

"What happened?" She asked at last. "Did we finish it?"

"The White Ring is complete, my Queen." Thaddeus appeared in her field of vision and sat on the edge of her bed. A soft smile lifted Thad's lips, but there was something haunted about it, and Elyasin knew that look from her scribe. Glancing around the room, she saw they were in the same small rotunda that she and Therel shared, their furs and bedrolls beneath her. Elyasin was still dressed in her shirt and silk undergarments, though her breeches and boots had been removed and her legs were bare under the furs she was snuggled in. A brazier was lit in a cheery fire nearby, but other than Thad and Therel, the chamber was empty.

"Where are the others?" Elyasin asked, struggling to sit without Therel's help. Therel eased his grip and allowed her to try her strength, even though every sinew in Elyasin's body screamed.

"Ghrenna's outside," Thad spoke softly. "At the Ring. This past day."

"I've been out a whole day?" Elyasin eyed Thaddeus. He wasn't telling her the whole truth, and she knew it. His gaze dropped from her question, shied away.

Therel reached out, smoothing a lock of her honey-gold hair back from her face. "I've been out most of that time as well. Thad's been watching over us. I just woke an hour ago."

Elyasin noted Therel's bedroll rucked-up next to hers. "Where is Luc? Is he outside with Ghrenna?"

Thad swallowed and his gaze flicked to Therel. Elyasin's gaze followed, and her King and husband met it squarely, sorrow in his eyes. "Luc didn't make it, Elyasin. I'm so sorry."

Elyasin's head swam. The stars in the walls multiplied, too many, as her eyes burned. Therel reached out to soothe her but Elyasin pushed him away. And then swung her legs over the bier and heaved to standing, though the rush of a river filled her ears and her body ripped with agony.

"Show me to him."

Therel stood with a slow movement, as if his body hurt as much as hers. Taking her hand and placing it on his arm, he escorted her. Elyasin forced her limbs to move, stepping with slow footfalls to the vaulted doorway. Moving outside, a bright light smote Elyasin – and despite her woe, her eyes opened in awe.

In the plaza, where once all had been tumbled and broken shards, there now stood seven enormous monoliths of milky white quartz, thick as cendarie-trees and towering over the other structures in the underground citadel. They glowed with a swirling light, like honey flowed in their vast depths. Though their eyes were closed, a dazzling brightness poured through the golden sigils upon their faces. Flowing like sunlight underwater, the sigils blazed and then receded, in spreading patterns like the ripples of an ocean wave. A sighing hum moved through the cavern, as if the ring of white Alranstones breathed with the universe itself. Low and melodious, it was composed of countless tones, yet all had perfect harmony as their subtle flow rose and fell. It was haunting, achingly raw. Elyasin felt her heart pulled to a kind of ecstasy despite her grief, and elevation filled her even as she was gripped in despair.

She moved forward upon Therel's arm. That raw and beautiful sound with the waves of rippling light pulled tears from her lids. As they crossed beneath the diamond-black archways and over the golden ring, then stepped past the white Alranstones, Elyasin felt a smooth ripple shiver through her. The Stones were aware, easing into Elyasin's gripping heart with etheric fingers, as she moved toward the light that flowed over the central golden dais.

Ghrenna sat in the center of the dais. Cross-legged with her palms resting on her knees, her chin was lifted, her eyes closed as she sat, perfect and luminous as a pearl in all that haunting light. A body lay before her. Tall and lean with a mane of golden hair, his chiseled, handsome profile was even more pronounced in death, his thick tawny lashes closed. The gold of his short beard gleamed in the lilting light as he lay in his fawn-brown Elsthemi leathers. As Elyasin mounted the dais, she saw a smile haunted his lips, though his roguish face was waxy and pale.

"Luc!" His name sighed from Elyasin's lips as she sank to her knees. Reaching out, she laid her hand atop his. Someone had placed his sword between his hands, and Elyasin gripped his cold, dead fingers, pressing them into the leather grip.

"He gave his all for you." Ghrenna's low voice made Elyasin look up. Tears spilled from Elyasin's lids and down her cheeks as she met Ghrenna's ancient blue gaze.

"Thrice he saved me from death. One time too many."

"Luc feared being a slave." Reaching out, Ghrenna brushed her fingers tenderly over Luc's bright waves. As she gazed at him, a sad smile touched her lips. "He told me that, long ago in Fhouria, when he finally came clean about who he was. He feared going back to Roushenn; to face his destiny and become the plaything of Kings. But you treated him with honor, Elyasin. You treated him as an equal. And so he gave everything for you – to save not his Queen, but his friend. You should have seen the look on his face as your first breath surged in and his last sighed out. I've never seen Luc look so fulfilled. Never in all the years I knew him."

Tears poured down Elyasin's cheeks and she let them fall. A hard sob choked her throat. Leaning over, she pressed a kiss to Luc's cold, dead lips. "I should have let you go. I should have set you free."

"He was as free as he wanted to be," Ghrenna spoke from across Luc's corpse. "He couldn't leave you, just like he couldn't leave me. But some loves make a man's heart sing, and others make it grip in chaos. His heart sung for you, Queen of Alrou-Mendera and Elsthemen, even though his heart gripped for me."

Elyasin looked up, watching a tear slip from Ghrenna's dark blue eyes. "I never loved him like I should have," Ghrenna murmured, "like he deserved."

Elyasin watched Ghrenna for a long moment. Luc's hand was stiff and cold beneath her touch. But it was not the dead that needed her sympathy right now. Rising as fluidly as she could manage, Elyasin stepped around the corpse and sank to her knees beside Ghrenna. Wrapping the woman in her arms, Elyasin held her in that soft, moving light. Ghrenna was still a long moment, as if her being had evaporated into the chill air – but then, with a shudder and a gasp, she began to sob.

And where that misery had been unleashed, there was no end. Elyasin petted a hand down Ghrenna's pale locks as the woman shuddered in her arms, breaking. Carrying such a heavy burden, that even Elyasin, as Queen of a nation being devoured by chaos, couldn't truly understand. Ghrenna's hands spasmed, gripping Elyasin's jerkin as she sobbed harder. Her shoulders shook and she gasped between sobs.

Elyasin heard a soft footfall and looked up to see Therel. Thad stood somewhat further off, past the edge of the golden dais, as if he were afraid to tread upon it. But Therel mounted the short steps up to the gold disc, his wolf-blue eyes full of sadness and quietude. Sinking down next to Elyasin in his buckled Elsthemi leathers, he set a hand on her shoulder, massaging it while Ghrenna continued to break in Elyasin's arms.

"I can't!" Ghrenna choked. "I can't do this—!"

"Yes, you can," Elyasin shushed, petting Ghrenna's white waves with soothing strokes. A memory of Olea holding her this exact same way just months ago struck Elyasin and she straightened, letting her body fill with strength for the woman breaking in her arms. "And you will. Where Morvein failed, you will succeed. You will bring this world to unity, Ghrenna. You will work the Rennkavi's Ritual and we will have the great peace we all hope for. Luc gave his life for that. He stayed with us, because some part of him believed in what we're doing. This world we'll build is not just for you and I. It's for everyone who has suffered injustice, to bring them out of the darkness and into the light. I know you're tired, and I know your heart breaks and so does mine – but do other hearts break any less when they lose a husband, or a father, or a son in battle?"

Ghrenna quieted in Elyasin's arms. She gave a shudder, then a deep sigh. Slowly, she pulled away, her gaze bright and bleak. "I killed him. It was my *wyrria* that killed Luc. It nearly killed all of you. What if... what if it kills Elohl?"

Reaching out, Elyasin cupped Ghrenna's lovely face, wiping a tear away with her thumb. "We all must risk what we love in times of war."

"How can you be so strong?" Ghrenna's shoulders shivered as a tremor took her.

Elyasin took a deep breath and let it out – the trick of Kingsmen patience that Olea had taught her long ago. "Because I had a good teacher. And because I have to be. For my nation, for the world – and for you."

With another shiver, Ghrenna nodded. Her blue gaze fell to Luc's corpse and lingered. "We have to engage the ritual soon. These Alranstones have amplified my ability to send myself through the ether to Elohl. A great battle is soon to break upon the Aphellian Way. Lhaurent has a force twice the size of the new Valenghian Vhinesse and our allies. And Elohl hasn't the magic to bind the Vhinesse's entire army yet against Lhaurent. He needs the Rennkavi's Ritual. The time is nigh."

"How nigh?" Therel's voice was low in the murmur of the Stones. His hand stroked Elyasin's back with calm, steady movements.

"Hours," Ghrenna's blue gaze pierced Elyasin to her core.

"*Hours*," Elyasin whispered. Something rolled through her, like the giant presence of Hahled Ferrian's magic turning over, excited for battle – even as the rest of her shivered in fear. Therel's hand gripped her shoulder, steadying.

"I've tried to delay as long as I could," Ghrenna continued. "You and Therel needed to wake, and I needed to regain my own strength after our reparation of the Alranstones. But Lhaurent's forces are mustering. The Vhinesse's army is readying to meet them. The Way will run with blood by dawn, and Elohl needs our help to stop it."

"Can the magic of the Rennkavi stop such a thing?" Therel spoke darkly at Elyasin's shoulder.

"Yes." Ghrenna's gaze flicked to Therel, certainty returning in her. Sitting up, she let herself draw back out of the comfort of Elyasin's touch, shivering off her uncertainty and moment of weakness. As Elyasin watched, Ghrenna became harder, stronger, as if the persona of Morvein penetrated to her core as her unfailing certainty returned. Watching them all, Ghrenna spoke with a lower voice, a deep, strong alto, her tears drying upon her cheeks.

"If the vision Morvein received about the Rennkavi's power is correct, then he can stop any conflict. Once he is fully in command of the *wyrria* he needs."

"Then we mustn't delay." With a deep in-breath, feeling Ghrenna's certainty fill her, Elyasin sat tall – ready for battle. "Let us begin the Rennkavi's Ritual."

* * *

Elyasin stood in the center of the golden dais, ready in her white silk shift. Therel stood facing her, clad in a silken shirt and trousers. Standing to their right, Ghrenna was clad in similar fashion, and to their left was Thaddeus, dressed like Therel. They'd found the soft garments in a stone chest in the citadel, and Ghrenna had insisted upon their use. Heavy clothing impeded the vibrations of what they were about to achieve, and ornamentation was the same.

Luc's corpse had been removed from the burnished dais of gold, taken to the rotunda Ghrenna slept in and laid out carefully upon the diamond-stone bier. They'd all taken a moment to say goodbye, Elyasin sitting quietly at his side and holding his beloved hands, thinking about all the ways Luc had been her protector, her friend, and a good man. With a last kiss to his cold lips, Elyasin had risen and returned to her and Therel's rotunda to shed her Elsthemi gear and dress in her white silk shift for the ceremony.

Elyasin and Therel had shed all their jewelry and other clothing, except for their keshar-claw pendants, in preparation for the ritual. They'd taken time to bathe each other in the shallow river that ran behind their rotunda, a slow thing of kisses and gentle touch as they stood in the calf-deep water, feeling their sorrow; sharing it. Cleansed now and dressed, Elyasin felt more herself, her aches from the reparation of the White Ring gone as the fire of Hahled's *wyrria* resurfaced. Her body felt hale once more, a heat and gentle fire simmering through her crimson Inkings, though her heart still hurt.

Now, she and Therel shared a quiet solace as they faced each other, ready, Therel clasping Elyasin's hands with a solemn smile. Thad stood to Elyasin's left, wearing his spectacles with his silk shirt and trousers. His participation wasn't needed in this ritual, but he was part of it – to observe the proceedings and stand strong if any of them should fall. Gazing up at Therel's beloved wolf-blue eyes, Elyasin heard Ghrenna began to sing a haunting melody from their right, with the guttural, lilting syllables of the Giannyk.

Elyasin shivered as an etheric wind swept her, her senses heightening as fire kindled in her veins – the same as when the Nightwind had touched her before. As Ghrenna's alto voice wreathed the Alranstones, they began to brighten, their humming rising to a musical cadence. Elyasin's skin shivered as she felt all seven Alranstones entrain to Ghrenna's voice, tuning with each other and thundering through Elyasin's bones in a weaving, sinuous, penetrating harmony. As that music intensified, braziers of fire-rocks began to flare to life all around the perimeter of the plaza – bursting into flame in a ring between the Alranstones.

Elyasin heard Therel's sharp intake of breath. His hands clenched hers. Gazing up into his eyes, she saw the shock writ in them; that the braziers had flamed, repeating his seeing-dream of fire ringing them in the darkness. Humming filled Elyasin's bones; music filled her body. A languid bliss began to surge through her with her burgeoning heat as Hahled's inkings brightened on her skin, pouring through with a weaving, sinuous fire. That same golden-bright rune appeared in her mind again, when suddenly, it was carried away by a series of white sigils blazing within her. Like a rippling wind, that binding language sighed through Elyasin's consciousness as Ghrenna sang; as Ghrenna called their meaning with her *wyrria*.

Sigils began to flare in the air also, upon ripples of etheric vapor, true manifestations that Elyasin could see with her waking vision. Like the coil of a vast serpent, they surrounded Elyasin and Therel. Pulling them closer; binding them into one heart, one mind, and one body. Elyasin flushed and she stepped in to Therel's body, compelled by the sigils that wreathed them, as Therel moved forward into hers. Cool vapor sighed off him, catching her breath, gripping her belly, tightening her thighs in an erotic pleasure like ice smoothed over her skin.

Elyasin's breath caught, captured in Therel's flow, feeling the currents of a highmountain river surge all around her. Her heat flared, a surge in her crimson inkings like lava moving through a channel, seeking the cool of the river to capture it – to bind it into impenetrable strength and stone. A shimmering mirage lifted up around them as Elyasin's fierce heat met Therel's smooth cold, twisting with vapors as their purple and red markings simmered and lit. Etheric fire surged through her and Elyasin cried out, caught in the power – and the passion, as Therel gripped her around the waist, tight, and drew her in.

His eyes burned like icebergs and tundra-wights as he twined her fingers in his, lifting them to his lips. Kissing her fingers softly, his blue gaze devoured her, just like the first time they'd met. Elyasin heard a wolf howl in the rising music that shivered all around her, Ghrenna's voice droning on in lilting patterns that caught the power of the crystal Alranstones and shuddered it back through Elyasin's most intimate places.

Therel stared down at her, devouring her with his need and the feel of a desperate winter's night. All Elyasin wanted was to heat, to sear in the depths of that flow, her power brightening tenfold as she shuddered to that carnal pull in her husband's being. Devotion shone from his eyes. Passion and lust surged from his flesh where he pressed her, hard, commanding her body to be close to him with his hand strong upon her back. In the darkness, strong as mountains and howling wild in the night, Elyasin could feel the triumph and fall of the Elsthemi people and their King, holding her so strong and ready – ready to give his all just as she gave hers to this last hope they shared.

From his body, from his eyes, from their lips as hers reached up and his descended, she felt his fury and howl – that he would stand with her, loving her, until the end.

Elyasin's heart opened as their lips met. Pouring up through her, rushing up from her heart and through her lips into his, Elyasin's *wyrric* heat exploded. Devouring her husband as his eternal darkness came flooding down her throat with cold clarity and unimaginable power. Elyasin felt them take each other, eternally. Power flowed through them; her into him, him into her, forming a double-matched ring within their bodies – and then, in a towering wave of heat and cold flame, exploding through them both. Erupting Hahled and Delman's twinned *wyrria* and flaring the braziers to columns of fire all around.

Therel cried out, seizing Elyasin around the waist, crushing her to his body with lupine madness and passion. Releasing their twined fingers, he hauled her up with both hands under her thighs and Elyasin seized him with her legs around his waist. A powerful strength shuddered through them both, upon a surging rip-tide of need.

Sigils poured through Elyasin's mind as she was taken down to the golden dais by her husband. White fire rippled around them, flaring inscriptions upon the air as their silken clothing was torn away by their own hands. Therel was a wild beast as he attacked her, kissing her neck, kneading her bare breasts with his hands, gripping her waist. And Elyasin surged for him, growling, her own passion flaring high as she bit his neck and cried out her own need into his beloved flesh.

Positioning himself at her opening, Therel gripped her hard by the neck, holding her still, feeling her writhe beneath him, taking her with his burning blue eyes and the searing chill of his body before he took her with the rest. Elyasin burned, a towering inferno of passion, her inkings searing through her flesh, on fire with light. She needed him – it couldn't wait. With a cry of rage and passion and devouring lust, she thrust her hips up onto him, hard – slamming him into her and spilling an obliterated cry from her lips as he roared out in agony and triumph, his body spasming and his fingers seizing her throat.

And then it began.

There was no time as Therel fucked her. There was no space as she clutched him, wrapping her legs around his hips, pulling him on and on. There was no mind left in Elyasin as she devoured her husband like an animal, like rutting beasts, furious and wild upon the passion and power now pouring through the ring of Alranstones. The braziers roared, flooding the plaza with fire. The Alranstones flared, sigils igniting upon their surfaces in coiling spirals as they resonated the heady power of the raw union inside their ring. The diamond-black darkness flooded with light as Therel heaved and gasped, gripping her throat while Elyasin seized his nape and held on, digging her fingernails in like claws until he roared with pain and fury.

She was fire on the mountains. She was molten ore moving inside the earth. She was the power of that flow, just as Therel's wildness was the thrust of rivers in flood and oceans smashing cliffs into ruin, breaking icebergs to its raw glory. As they sundered each other, through each other, an impenetrable ring of fire and ice and might flooding the plaza, all the eyes upon the Alranstones began to open. Starting from the base, sigils flared with rippling white ether as the onyx eyes eased open first, then the crimson. One by one, all eyes opened, rising up through the pinnacle of pale violet, until all were wide, upon every Alranstone, all around them.

Seven eyes upon seven Alranstones – all flared to the carnal *wyrria* being wrought in their midst.

As they fucked within that all-seeing ring, Elyasin felt power flood from her skin, devoured by those eyes. As if the world watched her carnal glee; as if the entirety of the cosmos could see their bliss and devoured their heady abandon. An explosion thundered through the circle, blasting out from the Alranstones – a shockwave rushing into the center, hitting Elyasin and Therel with a hammer of power and ecstasy that made them both cry out in their final moment. And as Elyasin came, in completion and glory from Therel's last wild thrust, pouring her fire up and out through her husband, he came with an obliterating roar that poured a cool river through Elyasin's core – and Elyasin felt them twist into one.

One heart. One body. One mind and one strength. One swirling vortex of *wyrria*, flowing upon each other's tides – the perfect balance within the perfect union. As the power twisted into an inseparable coil, pulling them through each other as they collapsed, an immense blossom of white etheric fire exploded around them. Sigils flared through the shivering air – and a portal opened in their midst, swallowing the golden dais.

Reeling in glory, her heart thundering as Therel crushed her beneath his exhausted weight, Elyasin lost herself to that *wyrric* flow. Some part of her saw that they were elsewhere, no longer in the diamond caverns. That she and her beloved were somewhere in the sky, a lightening dark which held burgeoning clouds above and all around. Therel's heart hammered upon her chest and his deep breaths heaved, his exhausted lips at her neck. Wind licked Elyasin's bare back, and she gazed over her shoulder, seeing nothing but clouds and a golden dawn beginning to seep through the endless sky.

Floating upon her bliss, she realized she and Therel were suspended in midair, wreathed by etheric sigils that flared up from the air itself, rippling with white-gold curls of *wyrria*. Looking down, she saw Ghrenna, laying upon a white stone altar ten lengths beneath them, sundering to a ring of etheric sigils just the same. Surrounded by three massive archways, each rippling with pale fire in a *wyrric* barrier that surrounded the central space, Elyasin saw

Ghrenna writhe upon the altar. With sinuous movements, she surged, as if aroused by the touch of the dawn wind that curled past Elyasin and licked the altar below.

The entirety of the white tower and its cloverleaf platform began to swirl with that wind. In her exhausted, blissful fugue, Elyasin saw Thaddeus, on his knees upon one of the clover's petals, his wide-eyed gaze devouring the scene from where he watched from outside the *wyrric* barrier. As the wind swirled and the tower began to hum, and Ghrenna surged upon her altar below, clasping her breast, gasping and arching as she touched between her legs, Elyasin felt a devouring wind of ether pour through her.

A sundering, opiate ecstasy, the powerful sweep of the wind made Elyasin's mind flee and her muscles lax. She felt Therel shudder atop her, their magic still twined deep in a blissful coil as the Nightwind poured through them both. Ghrenna heaved in sinuous glory below, the wind surging through her, pouring from her, opening within her. Elyasin felt that mighty call resonate in the stone of the White Tower and explode outward – devouring the land. Calling everything; everyone. Calling the *wyrria* of the earth itself to hearken to the last Wind of Night before the Rise of the Dawn.

And they came. Like the a sundering ocean, they came, flooding Elyasin's bliss-emptied body. Focusing in her empty vessel and twisting into one stream of energy, with a second stream of wild power coursing through Therel. Twin channels for the vastness of the world's *wyrria* and every living heart upon it, Elyasin and her King combined that rushing, annihilating flow – pouring it down into Ghrenna upon the white altar.

Elyasin cried out; Therel did the same, sundering to that rush of *wyrria* pouring in from the world and through her body. Their inkings flared with blue-white light as Elyasin came again upon the tide of that terrible, wild power, shuddering as Therel hardened inside her and erupted also, roaring in exhausted bliss. But the *wyrria* flooding in now from the entirety of the world and all its people didn't release them, only used their twisting glory as fuel – pouring through them faster, snaring them harder into the river's rush and cascading all of that power like a waterfall down into Ghrenna, writhing with ecstasy upon the white altar.

Caught in the passion and fury, Elyasin couldn't even cry out as the next climax hit her, and the next, and the next. Her consciousness expanded in annihilation, Therel surging atop her as they twisted together, their bodies lost to the river of *wyrria* as dawn's light lifted in the rose-gold sky, brightening the thunderous underbellies of the clouds.

At last, the tower rung like a struck bell from all the raw power resonating through it, and Ghrenna screamed in a terrible bliss below upon the altar. That peal of power rang out in the heavy morning, shivering the air and calling to the world. Its sundering knell shook the snowcapped highmountains as it banished clouds from the sky in a wide ring around the tower.

Calling the Rennkavi – as dawn's first light flooded over the mountains at last.

CHAPTER 46 – ELOHL

Beyond the Valenghian guard-wall, Elohl held the line in the depths of the night. Cavalry stretched to either side of him and behind, filling the Aphellian Way, foot soldiers and pikemen behind, ready for the forces that were coming. Shadows moved far out along the western Way, dotted with thousands of points of fire. Thunder pummeled the dry air as a lance of lightning slit the heavy crimson clouds. Elohl glanced up but felt no stir of rain as he watched heat-lightning flicker again, tingeing the roiling cloudmass red.

"Yours?" He glanced to Fenton, sitting tall upon a black warhorse beside him.

"My tension's got to go somewhere, Elohl," Fenton nodded tersely. "I can't spark my hands right now. It scares horses."

A low rumble of thunder rolled over the plain as blossoms of light flickered above. Tension filled Elohl, too, as he watched the dark mass creep closer. Lanterns of green-yellow fire twisted at intervals among the Menderian army, shedding an eerie light on the black sea of men and horses approaching. Watchtowers in the Valenghian fortifications blazed behind Elohl, enormous signal-fires lit to give those who battled at least a slanting light in the heavy dark. Dawn was near, but the night was still dark as a sharp ozone scent slit Elohl's nostrils, dry dust swirling in the wind. Fenton was containing himself, all in all. A hard readiness set Elohl's jaw, anticipating what Fenton could do when he finally unleashed that energy in battle.

Elohl's Goldenmarks cast a flickering glow, muted in his simmering tension. The light shivered over the recently returned Merkhenos del'Ilio to his left. Merkhenos said not a word, but watched the Menderian host approach with narrowed eyes. With the rumble and chunk of tens of thousands of soldiers and horses stopping all at once, the Menderian force halted at last.

Thunder rippled the air. Branch lightning lanced the heavy

clouds, illuminating the battlefield in a flickering light. Watchtower fires and Menderian lanterns cast an upward luminosity on that roiling black mass, haloing the night like fresh blood and bruised flesh. Elohl inhaled, knowing the stones of the Way would run far more crimson than the sky tonight. In the punctured darkness, he saw a group of riders form at the front of the Menderian army.

"Parlay," Merkhenos spoke curtly, flicking his fingers to Elohl and Fenton and summoning them as he stepped his horse forward. Five of Merkhenos' top Generals plus Ghirano moved forward with the group, silence swaddling their hoof-falls as thunder rippled above.

Tension filled Elohl's neck and shoulders. A battle-ready, fierce tension he knew all too well. Breathing deeply, he fed that sensation through his body, allowing it to spread into his limbs. For the first time, that hackle-high readiness had somewhere to go, rushing through his veins and into his Goldenmarks – the conflict of impending battle flaming them luminous in the crimson night.

Suddenly, Fenton stiffened at his side, then swore. Reaching out, he gripped Elohl's reins. "I feel Kreth-Hakir. Merkhenos! Stop your Generals. They can't come into the parlay. I can hold off a cadre of mind-benders from you and Elohl, but I can't do it for your entire leadership."

Merkhenos halted his warhorse. But to Elohl's surprise, the battle-readiness upon the man's face hadn't changed, as if he expected this. "Take them back, Ghirano." Ghirano opened his mouth to protest, but Merkhenos waved a hand at him and he went, wheeling his horse and making the other Generals retreat with a sharp whistle.

"No need to block the Kreth-Hakir for me, Scion of Khehem," Merkhenos spoke again. "I have my own protection against mind-benders. Save your strength for battle."

Fenton paused in the saddle, narrowing his eyes upon Merkhenos as the darkness flickered, before a wry smile lifted his lips. "Illianti bastard. More tricks up your sleeve than a whore of Tellurium. You'll have to share that mind-blocking recipe of yours with me someday."

"The Illianti have many surprises against many foes. But we never share them." Merkhenos gave a renegade smile, but his hard copper eyes never left the men that had halted a hundred paces distant. He nodded to Elohl. "Shall we?"

Elohl moved his horse onward, taking the lead. Though Merkhenos was the High General of this army, it was Elohl's power that would turn the tides tonight. Lightning rippled above as the trio closed the distance, Elohl's Goldenmarks searing with a slightly stronger blue-white light as he moved into the familiar rhythms of impending battle.

A lantern slung from the pommel of a horse ahead, lighting their destination and the four men who waited. But a dark space gaped in the middle of the line, as if the night had swallowed the center of the group who had come to parlay. Then, the air wavered before Elohl's eyes. Like a leviathan rising, a massive scorpion appeared, its diamond-black chitinous plates glittering in the lantern's light as sheet-lighting raced through the clouds above. Its arched tail rose high, a searing barb longer than a man's arm shining with venom in the red night. Enormous claws cluttered and clacked as it gave a restless sidestep – as if it couldn't wait to slice horses apart.

On its back, a man sat tall. As Elohl's group halted at fifteen paces, he could see the strong set of the man's shoulders, an enormous broadsword upon the man's back. His silver-studded herringbone leathers glittered in the night as much as his horrific mount, and Elohl's chest gripped as his Goldenmarks flared. The man's deep hood was raised, his face shrouded, but Elohl felt that penetrating grey gaze. Those thick, dominant lips curling up in greeting, sending the darkest moment of Elohl's past smashing into his present.

The night Elohl had failed at Roushenn Palace, and the black scorpion rider who had nearly severed his arm in the Kingswood, then captured them at Alrashesh. The memory came rushing into Elohl's thoughts like black water. His body was suddenly vibrating, thrumming like a harp string played too violently, and his Goldenmarks blazed as he set his jaw in fury. Elohl could feel Fenton feeding off it, drawing from the Marks as Elohl shivered in wrath. A crackle of lightning spread above, illuminating the sky and hammering their ears with thunder.

The man gave a brief nod from the depths of his hood,

acknowledging everything that had passed between them.

But as the lightning in the sky cleared, the line of Lhaurent's captains parted, the hooded black rider even shuffling his massive scorpion to one side. A white horse stepped up, a man dressed in the regalia of kings riding tall upon it. Clad in armor that shone a silvered white in the darkness, the rider's white jerkin was chased with gold, giving the man a ghostly look in the flames' stark light. Matching sickled longknives glimmered at his hips with a longsword across his back, a massive ruby in the pommel devouring the crimson sky like it drank blood. Starbursts of gold inset with rubies were pinned to his collar, the chest-pieces of armor and the man's shirt left open to bare his pale skin to the night.

Skin that glimmered with the Goldenmarks.

Lhaurent den'Alrahel's smirking grey eyes found Elohl's by the lantern-light, and another rush of Fenton's lighting slit the heavy sky. That arrogant visage with high cheekbones and smooth lips repulsed Elohl. Carefully slicked back from his high forehead, two streaks of silver in his hair and short beard were the only things to betray Lhaurent's age as he opened his chest-plates – baring a ripple of light in his Goldenmarked skin. Lifting his left hand, he also displayed an arm made of dark ether twisted through with golden sigils and flowing light. The spectral arm swirled with inky currents, issuing out from the Goldenmarks. An arm made not of flesh, but from the Marks themselves – like a night sky full of imploding suns.

As Lhaurent's gaze roved Elohl, he smiled – a thing of odious and terrible delight. "Elohl den'Alrahel. At last, I meet the man with the twinning of my Marks."

That statement punched Elohl in the gut, shocked to think that this could be the answer to the Rennkavi's twinned blood – that there were supposed to be two of them. Elohl heard Fenton take an inhalation as well. And then let out a slow, measured breath, as if trying to control himself from simply blasting a lightning bolt at Lhaurent and burning that smug smile from his lips.

"Perhaps you weren't fit to wear them, eel," Fenton's voice was hard as another branch of lightning flickered through the sky, "and the Goldenmarks chose another."

"One more valiant than I, I suppose." Lhaurent's odious smile remained. "It took me a while to figure out who you were, Fenton den'Kharel. Or should I say, *Fentleith Alodwine*. You've allowed your grandfather's toys to languish unattended. One does not need valiance in this game of nations, Scion of Khehem, but prudence; patience. Forging ties of cooperation even between those with different theories about how the world works than you. I have forged such bonds. And you have failed to do so. So what do you have? One weak Rennkavi who does not know his power, and a scant half of the forces your enemy possesses, when you could have had it all. The Khehemni; the Kreth-Hakir. Armies of many nations behind you and true belief in every heart – binding them together as one. Such as I have now."

With the barest motion of his spectral hand, Lhaurent signaled his men. The hooded rider upon the scorpion changed his posture, just a fraction. Suddenly, behind the parlay group, a line of glittering chitin appeared in the red dark, unveiled from nothingness. A full line of massive black scorpions – over a hundred of them. Each one straddled by a man in herringbone black, hooded upon their glittering monstrosity like a line of diamond stars in the maw of death.

"Shaper of the Fields—!" Fenton breathed.

"Stand strong." Merkhenos' rough growl cut the night. "Do you know me, Lhaurent den'Alrahel?"

Lhaurent's lip curled with distaste, and Merkhenos' lack of the honorarium *Rennkavi* was not lost upon Elohl. "I do, Son of Illium. Long did Vhinesse Aelennia Oblitenne have a watch set upon you and your ilk. As did I. You'll remember my agent, High Priest Khorel Jornath?"

With that, the scorpion-rider next to Lhaurent lifted his silver-studded hood and shook it down. Elohl's heart burned with fury, seeing that dominant visage. He was the same – as if the man had not aged at all. Smooth black hair braided back with a streak of silver at each temple. Cutting cheekbones on a strong-boned face, his dark grey eyes piercing with humor and belligerence, his stature enormous as he sat upon his scorpion with his greaved hands resting upon its plated back.

A hard smile lifted his thick lips, his dark eyes even harder as they penetrated Elohl. And then his gaze flicked to Merkhenos, and he gave a nod.

"Khorel." Merkhenos' voice was flat. "I suppose it's good to see you again."

"Merkhenos." The man said no more, but a simmering tension stretched between the Valenghian High General and the Kreth-Hakir High Priest. Khorel Jornath's lips turned up in a deeper smile as his gaze flicked to Fenton. "The Kreth-Hakir have been searching for you, Scion of Khehem. Eight hundred years, I believe the count is now. When you would not take us up in our offer to support Leith's original aims, we had to look elsewhere for inspiration. You'll have to forgive us, of course. As Leith Alodwine's most direct blood-kin, your leadership would have been our first choice. But now our Rennkavi has arrived. I'll give you one last chance to join us, Fentleith. Abandon your false Rennkavi. Be who you were meant to be, and unleash *that*," he glanced up at the flickering sky then back to Fenton, "in the way you were meant to. Help us unite the world, in strength and purpose. Just like your grandfather once tried to do."

"*Never.*" Fenton's voice was such a low, murderous growl that Elohl almost didn't recognize it. Lightning erupted across the sky and thunder made all talk impossible for a moment. When it finally died down, the Kreth-Hakir High Priest was smiling wide, as if tremendously pleased.

But all he did was give his elegant, brutal shrug again, and say, "As you wish."

"I suppose we're done here." Merkhenos' voice was a curt snap, his Cennetian accent clipped.

"I suppose we are." Lhaurent was gracious, giving a small nod. "Good luck to you and yours, as I shall weep when the ruby blood begins to spill from your throats. Oh, and speaking of blood and throats," his gaze flicked to Elohl. Something terrible was written in those shining grey eyes; some knowledge that Lhaurent was simply aching to reveal. As Elohl watched, the man's smooth lips lifted in the most satisfied smirk Elohl had ever seen.

"Speaking of blood and throats," he repeated, "Olea's white throat was most lovely when I slit it with my knife. You should have watched her gurgle her last. I'm sure she would have cried out for both of you, Elohl, Fenton. If she could have."

Elohl's mind roared; his lips fell open. He stared into that odious face and something that had been good and tempered inside him fled. His righteousness gave way, replaced by a snarl. Or perhaps it was a battle-roar, as Fenton hurled a lighting-strike straight at Lhaurent. Lifting that arm of dark smoke and *wyrric* sigils, Lhaurent cast Fenton's strike away, sending it careening into a Monolith. The pillar of obsidian exploded, hurling shards of black glass out upon the battlefield as cavalry-horses reared and men cried out.

And just like that, the battle began.

Merkhenos sounded a horn and the Valenghian forces charged. Khorel Jornath surged forward, his scorpion-riders with him. Elohl's body moved on instinct as the melee crashed around him, feeling where foes came from, hewing them down, wheeling his impeccably-trained war-mount to rear and kick.

Snarling filled him; the sound of a roaring, rushing river, like a dam had broken and a highmountain lake now cascaded through Elohl's limbs with abominable power. Elohl's sensate sphere seared as he put down foes all around, his Goldenmarks blazing white-hot from the power of his wrath. Battle-fugue took him, red and monstrous. Like a beast that coiled in and in upon itself, his conflict was a devouring rush with no end. Fenton's lightning was everywhere, blazing with the enormity of the wrath that filled Elohl, spilling out from his Goldenmarks. Elohl heard the man's roars with concussions of thunder as the Scion of Khehem fought like a dervish, while Elohl's body fought upon washes of instinct, taking down enemies left and right.

Expanding out, Elohl's Goldenmarks were a flooding wave, *wyrria* seizing allies around him and making them surge into the fight, roaring for death and vengeance. But even as they did, Lhaurent cast his black-smoke hand at the Valenghian army, his own Goldenmarks blazing with darklight – making them shift and attack their own. The line of scorpion-riders darted in, causing Valenghian cavalry to turn, rounding upon their allies, cannibalizing the ranks behind. Elohl's horse was gutted and tossed him, but Elohl rolled up from its throw, lithe on his feet. Soldiers came at him and he cut them down. Horses reared and he spun in, gutting them. Blood coated him as he slashed a quick strike across a Menderian soldier's unprotected throat.

Fenton's horse went down nearby, but Fenton rolled up on his feet, gaining Elohl's side as he hurled lightning toward the scorpion-riders from his bare hands, skittering their black mounts away. A chorus of Elsthemi war-horns and Menderian trumpets blasted from the tree-line of the northern Bog, and the allied forces came pouring from the trees. Elohl caught sight of Dherran in the front of that spear as they crashed into the flank of Lhaurent's forces. With a thundering concussion, the armies met. Snarls of keshar-cats joined the melee, war-horses whinnying in terror as cats swiped their way in.

Whinnies crunching out as horses' faces were bitten off.

Leading the charge, Dherran roared like a boar in the brightening grey light as he gutted and slashed with a massive broadsword. Wheeling his charger, power poured from Dherran, like he was born for war – fighting with a soaring bliss in the fray and the slash, the gore and the glory. Dherran's searing *wyrria* flooded his allies like a blazing sun, redoubling their passion, making the allies fight like mad banshees. Elohl's heart roared with it, his Goldenmarks flaring and sending waves of light pounding out as he watched his best friend command the way he was meant to – as a beast of passion and battle.

That flank was rallying, despite the Kreth-Hakir Brethren who raced in to betray it. Dherran's mad roar was echoed by horns and sharp blasts from bog-whistles keeping the charge together. With Fenton's thunder and Dherran's rage surging through his Marks, Elohl seized a horse and flung himself up. Dherran saw him and gave Elohl a vicious smile. A tremendous burst of energy shot through Elohl, like a leviathan freeing itself, the Goldenmarks seething from his skin and writing sigils of blinding ether in the blood-spattered air. Those sigils curled into men around him, the allies surging with vigor as sigils wrote themselves like the body of some massive beast through the battle.

But something else shivered the air, then. Like a massive gong struck by a war-hammer, a pummeling energy of silver weaves thrust through the battle. Elohl had only a moment to see a semicircle of twenty Kreth-Hakir scorpions unveil near Dherran's charge. In a fast, coordinated strike, the Kreth-Hakir Brethren surrounded Dherran in a tight circle, their chittering black horrors cutting him off.

With a cry, Elohl turned his horse. But the solid wall of flesh left no space; he couldn't get close. Roaring, Elohl used his Goldenmarks to hammer etheric fire into the men nearest Dherran, making them attack those scorpions. Battling five Kreth-Hakir, Fenton felt Elohl's desperation, turning to blast his way through and reach Dherran's side. But the glittering black beasts held their ring as Dherran roared in frustration and turned his horse in a tight circle inside, isolated.

Dherran's woman Khenria and an older lord assaulted the edge of the ring, Khenria with fire searing up her sword, but they were battered back into the melee by the whip of barbed scorpion tails. The ring of black riders upon their clacking mounts raised their arms, as if gathering energy from the lancing sky. And then, thrust their tremendous net of silver weaves to their pinnacle member – an enormous man with silver-white braids, who cast back his hood and raised scarred and sightless eyes to the bloody sky.

Elohl screamed, knowing what was coming. When suddenly, three scorpions in the group broke rank, barreling into the others. The silver net faltered. Elohl thrust etheric sigils into the men nearest those renegade riders, aiding the confusion, and saw one rider note him. Khorel Jornath's dark grey eyes held his and surprise filled Elohl. But before he could respond, Jornath and his renegades hammered the other Kreth-Hakir with mind-weaves, shredding theirs. A rippling black oilslick energy joined the renegades, from a lean lord with a battle-hardened visage riding a great black keshar-cat. Joining Khorel Jornath with other renegade riders, that rippling oilslick energy struck into the heart of the silver being woven against Dherran.

Scorpions went down; the circle broke. Dherran drove his horse toward the gap, almost free. When all that silver power was suddenly *pulled* from the Brethren by their leader. Ignoring the renegades, the blind-eyed leader reached up over his shoulder, seizing a double-terminated silver lance from a sheath, snapping it out to full length to form a seamless javelin in his strong hands. Like quicksilver threaded through the eye of a needle, all the power of his Brethren poured through his hands into the lance, blazing with pure silver light. Raising it, the blind-eyed leader hurled it with a mighty throw – piercing Dherran's heart.

Elohl screamed, pain erupting through him as if the lance had gone through his own heart. Dherran gasped, clutching his chest where a silver burn marred his jerkin around the embedded lance. Lifting his gaze to Elohl, their resonance snapped out as the blind-eyed rider surged in – seizing the lance and ripping out Dherran's bloody heart from his chest in a burst of silver light.

Before he could so much as topple, Dherran's body began to unmake itself, sluicing away in an unholy zephyr of searing blue light. Shimmering sand cast him apart, pouring down over his saddle as a funnel-wind siphoned up, blue light blazing. A sound like screaming banshees filled the air, like the roar of a storm though canyons, staggering the blind-eyed rider back as wind whipped the battle. Curling white sand up into a towering desert-funnel that surged with blue light, the wind sluiced up every last grain of sand, taking it high into the lifting sky – and was gone.

Elohl's heart guttered, stunned. His Goldenmarks flashed out, white sigils dissipating from the air in the lifting grey light. All around him, men shifted in confusion as the passion and unity abandoned them and the Menderian forces swept in. Screams returned to Elohl's ears, scents of blood and shit hitting his nostrils as he was caught in the backlash, flooded with death, icy fingers buried in his heart. Riding on a blood-slicked white charger, Lhaurent suddenly charged through the broken pennants of the five allied nations, glowing like a comet of annihilation, his grey gaze fixed upon Elohl. Turning aside foes with a wave of his *wyrric* fingertips, darklight seared through him, bright and terrible, making Elohl's horse strangle as it whinnied and fell suddenly beneath him.

Elohl rolled, hitting his shoulder hard upon the bloody stones of the Way, turning to face his enemy as Lhaurent charged in with that sorcerous hand splayed. As he came, something inside Elohl surged, roaring. Fighting for Olea's memory; for Dherran's passion. Rushing to the surface, the beast of Elohl's *wyrria* surged and Elohl rolled in as he charged – seizing Lhaurent's leg with white *wyrric* fire and hauling him from his horse down to the stones of the Way.

Elohl's beast rose. The creature inside him expanded as his Goldenmarks raced into the world, writing sigils of etheric fire through the air like a thousand coils in the rising dawn. Lhaurent scrambled, throwing his *wyrric* arm up against Elohl's onslaught as

618

Elohl hurled more coils of white fire, binding Lhaurent to the ground. Blistering ether wrapped Lhaurent's black arm, ensnaring it. Elohl stormed forward, his skin searing with *wyrria* as he seized Lhaurent's hand of darkness in his grip and thrust it to the red stones of the Way, golden sigils on his hand burning with power.

With a roar, Lhaurent whipped out a sickled white-silver longknife, stabbing for Elohl's flank, but Elohl's blade was there with the speed of instinct, catching him in a clinch and holding him off. As they struggled in the clinch, Elohl's blazing hand pinning Lhaurent's darklight one, a shuddering resonance passed through them both.

Digging into Elohl's wrist at Elohl's old self-inflicted cut-marks, Lhaurent lifted his lips in a snarl, his swirling black fingers suddenly writing onyx sigils through the passage of Elohl's Goldenmarks. The cascade of black sigils burned like poison and Elohl screamed in a bestial roar, furious. He pushed harder, struggling in the clinch, and sigils of golden-white flame began to surge from Elohl's fingertips, inscripting through Lhaurent's dark black waters.

The eel screamed, but as he did, tentacles of surging darkness shot out from him, racing up Elohl's arm like a leviathan. Acidic obliteration speared through Elohl's body and he screamed, their knives shuddering against each other in the clinch. And as dawn crested over the battlefield, the sun's first rays slanting beneath the heavy clouds, Elohl and Lhaurent's gold and onyx sigils raced to consume each other – sending a pulse out into the world.

A call, generated by their twinned *wyrria*.

Ghrenna's cerulean gaze hit Elohl like an ocean wave. Sucked into their blue depths, he was drowning in her. He heard Fenton's shout, as a barrier of *wyrric* vapor blossomed to life all around. As Fenton raced near, Elohl was wrenched sideways through space and time; ripped from the battlefield and dumped onto a white platform ringed with three towering archways.

Elohl's *wyrria* flashed out as he hit the stones of the white tower with a hard grunt. Lhaurent's *wyrria* did the same, and he rolled onto his back, coughing from the impact. He heard Fenton cry out, heaved to a far cloverleaf. Black sigils cleared from Elohl's skin as he pushed up fast, knowing where he was. The White Tower rushed with *wyrria*, obliterating, and the center of all that might was

Ghrenna. Ghrenna, her pale beauty pristine as she writhed with ecstasy upon a low stone altar in the middle of the tower. Ghrenna, her beautiful waves tumbling free as she heaved and gasped in a surging wind of ether, as if she made love to the entire world.

Power poured down into her, in a torrent of white *wyrric* fire that arched in from the golden dawn and flooded the highmountains. A barrier of *wyrric* fire surrounded the center of the platform between the archways, Fenton trapped upon the other side. But Elohl had no mind for the Scion of Khehem as he moved, rushing to Ghrenna's side, his hand clasping hers upon the altar. As her eyes opened, burning with cerulean fire, Elohl felt all that *wyrric* power from the dawn go roaring through her body – straight into his. With a cry, she arched up as he lowered, power swirling out from her heart and up through her throat, exhaling into him as their lips touched and kissed. Bliss filled Elohl, as the entire *wyrria* of the world filled him, cascading to the dawn in ripples as endless as the rising sky.

Suddenly, a sharp pain hit him like an avalanche. Stabbed into Elohl's back; ripped into his kidneys like daggers of fire, again and again. He screamed, torn backward by a hand of black ether and flung to the tower's stones. He heard Fenton's roar, saw blasts of lightning hitting the barrier in a wretched fury. But Elohl couldn't breathe; couldn't move. He didn't know how many times he'd been stabbed, but blood pooled beneath him upon the pristine stones, vivid red upon the white, Lhaurent's sickled silver-white knife laying beside it. Rolling his eyes, Elohl saw Lhaurent seized by the flooding power as he took Elohl's place over Ghrenna, caught in the unification rather than Elohl. As Lhaurent caressed Ghrenna's cheek with his writhing black hand, he gasped, flooded with power – and then thrust that hand of darkness deep into her chest.

Ghrenna screamed, arching like she was on fire. Fenton screamed, hammering the barrier with lightning as Lhaurent leaned in, his *wyrric* hand gripping inside Ghrenna, pulling all the power of the world through her heart and into his swirling darkness as the first rays of dawn smote the tower. Black sigils of ether began to write through the air as Ghrenna's body fell slack, her fingers trailing over the edge of the altar and into Elohl's blood. His heart wailing, his world collapsing and Fenton screaming as that black fire curled out,

Elohl willed the last of his fleeting strength into the tips of his fingers. They twitched, moved – and with a final tingle of his sensate sphere, his fingertips found Ghrenna's.

Elohl gripped her fingers; she gripped him back. And Elohl felt Ghrenna divert that massive wealth of power, all the world's *wyrria*, away from her violated heart and through her fingertips – straight into him. For one endless moment, all the *wyrria* of the world flooded Elohl as he and Ghrenna kissed through their touch.

And then Lhaurent's boot stomped down, crushing Elohl's fingers to the bloody stones and breaking their hands apart.

Their connection snapped out; the power faded. And Elohl faded with it, lost to the Void.

CHAPTER 47 – JHERRICK

Pain raged through Jherrick. Crimson light seared his vision. He couldn't move, couldn't think. There was only pain, and red, and the sensation of laying upon hard ripples of sand. Jherrick knew he was still alive, his body twitching like a spider in death throes, while his mind roamed the Void, fleeing to the safety of space. The wrenching of coming through the crystal arch from the Sanctuary of the Noldarum had been agonizing, and Jherrick saw others who truly were dead move by upon the Void's etheric currents.

Phantasms brushed him as they sped away to their ultimate homecoming, and Jherrick's *wyrria* began to turn – seeing the dead, feeling them. The stalwart honor of a warrior, the scheming precision of a money-lender, the slippery consciousness of a thief. The true dead passed by, luminous in their satisfaction with their life and eager to move on. They took no note of Jherrick; just another untethered soul. Some lingered, however, hovering around dying bodies. While some yearned for bodies already gone, burning upon a pyre in the cold northlands or being sealed into a tomb underground.

Hungry spirits of tundra-wights, barrow-vampires, and other unfinished dead turned in the Void to gaze upon Jherrick. Curious, wondering if he could be a way for them to re-enter the world. Tendrils seeped into Jherrick's shuddering flesh, trying to wrest his body from him. Like spiderwebs, Jherrick's *wyrria* burned them from his etheric body – their dark, writhing energies taking up a vigil at their death-haunts once more.

But there were others in the Void, also. Ancient energies deep in stasis, minds that twisted and roiled, caught between this world and the next. Locked in place, subjugated and shackled, they were trapped by *wyrria* that held them like ghastly chains. Visions flashed in Jherrick's mind – rose quartz columns, smoky crystal pillars, Byrunstone Plinths, obsidian tombs. Alranstones. Shock filled

Jherrick as he saw complicated glyphs in the Void, locks that shifted and re-formed. The work of an adept jailor who had created ferocious sigildry to bind these souls for all time – the minds within these prisons gone to a place even Jherrick could not touch. They were not dead, but un-released – and that torment had forced them into places so dark and mad, that Jherrick could not feel anything human left in their terrible silence.

Shuddering away from the bound ones, Jherrick reached out, feeling for people who had come and gone in his life. Currents of ether moved his violet-crimson aura through the Void, as he searched for constellations of memories that had been a friend, a foe, or a comrade. The tortured souls Lhaurent had killed came back first. As if summoned by Jherrick's guilt-ridden consciousness, they slipped out of the Void, surrounding him with faces of torment. Blame seared from their eyes. Hate surged from them, attacking Jherrick's Void-body. With nasty fingers, the wrathful dead bit at his energy, crowing with glee to damage a man they blamed for their end. Jherrick issued a cry in the Void, unable to halt their fury with his untutored *wyrria* – drowning in a sea of vengeance.

Suddenly, a strong pulse shocked them back. A blessed light swirled in, pushing back the menacing dead. Olea's face rose in Jherrick's mind, smiting the darkness with hot longknives of light. A furious battle-cry echoed in Jherrick's ears. As if he'd called her soul, Jherrick felt Olea's energy flood into his with luminous tendrils. Olea's honey-leather scent was in his nose. The way her eyes flashed when she was disrespected; the way she laughed in the Guardhouse. The feel of her, calm and tired after a long day of training as she sat in a chair with her boots up on her desk, rifling through lists. Her sudden smile when he bumbled his spectacles, just so she would pick them up and offer them back.

Olea's glow surrounded Jherrick, slipping into his mind and heart with sweet fingers. Her grey eyes shone like fire-opals, commanding as she slit knives of fury through the wraiths, dissipating them. She was a dervish of purpose as she annihilated Jherrick's foes and seized his wrist in a grip so hot it burned.

Come with me, Olea's strong alto commanded, pummeling Jherrick's ears in the Void. *You must save him. Quickly.*

Save who? Jherrick's voice was a disembodied nothing as he was hauled by Olea over leagues of desert and mountains, rivers and oceans, taken far from his body upon the hard sand. Dawn broke below, over a long expanse of blistering land between two thick grey bogs. Searing down like a falling star to a thinner space, Jherrick was drawn to chaos and confusion. The press of expired souls hit him like a tidal wave – a battlefield choked with the new dead. He staggered in the Void; his barely-living body convulsed upon the sand. War-torn souls screamed around him, disoriented. Confused, betrayed by battle, trying to shake their sword-maimed corpses awake. A sea of carnage – tens of thousands of dead howling, the winds of the Void churning in a vast and terrible whirlpool.

And still, the battle raged in the world of the living. Jherrick could not make out the factions, the ripped pennants of at least five armies trampled among the dead. A churning mess of men fought each other, dying. Jherrick fixed upon Olea's energy, willing her to move on through the madness.

Fast as thought, Jherrick was whisked away, high over the bloody plain and up into the highmountains. His etheric body was sucked close to a white tower of alabaster agate, that rose from the depths of a cerulean lake ringed in glacial peaks. A glorious citadel with spires and arches and high doorways led into thin air – their pinnacle tower piercing high into the luminous sky, dawn already broken over the eastern horizon.

Jherrick could feel the vibration of the White Tower swirling in the Void. It was a lodestone; a place to harness power, to gather it from the universe and transmit it back in works of glory. As Jherrick's etheric form rose to the topmost spire, he felt the soaring energy within the tower's ancient agate-stone. It vibrated and swirled with the same opalescent light that moved within the archways of the Noldarum's realm, writhing glyphs in an endless dance through the Void.

Bound power; pure *wyrria* of the cosmos. A citadel built upon an ancient upwelling, a structure that captured the earth's own incredible flow. Jherrick felt its vast music, waiting to be harnessed – to be *tuned* – just like he felt other *wyrric* geysers bound with tight caps waiting to erupt all through the world.

But only one of these *wyrric* founts had been harnessed into a lodestone, ready for some magnificent event. Jherrick shivered, feeling the enormity of the tower's vibration in the Void, fearing what it could do. A vast power, he felt innately that it could destroy or create, depending upon its use. Depending upon the nature of the soul that set that power free, that harnessed it into concordance. One mighty *tuning*, that caused it to strike like a bell over the entire world. And Jherrick knew, that this power could Undo all the caps on the *wyrric* founts; could release all the mad souls trapped inside their prisons. This power could wake it all – magnificently, terribly. As Jherrick's etheric body flew to the tower's highest pinnacle, up through the ring of clouds, his heart seized in his chest to feel someone at the very top.

Someones. Already commanding that terrible flow.

Energy raced toward the pinnacle from all over the earth. Jherrick could see it, a vast umbrella of opalescent light in the Void being sucked toward the peak of the spire by whatever *wyrria* was being worked high above. As he gained the tower's height, he saw that vast energy coalescing like a fevered star in the center of three tremendous archways. Ten feet up, Jherrick saw two bodies trapped in the ether, intertwined in glory. A man and a woman converging and channeling all the power of the world into a spiraling stream that flooded down to the center of the tower's white dais.

But down below, in the center of the archways, was horror.

At the convergence of the three-petaled white platform lay a woman, her soul blazing in the Void like a tundra-wight. She screamed, rapturous and in pain – channeling all that immense power into a man writ through with blazing golden marks, his black *wyrric* hand thrust right through her chest and gripping her heart. She was coming unraveled, sundering with Undoing. Black fire was writing though the air upon terrible *wyrric* currents as Jherrick could feel her soul shredding from the immensity of what she channeled, and the pain being gripped by the man's black hand. Caught in the flow, being devoured by the man who held her, she was lost – unable to halt his taking.

Jherrick quailed in the Void – to see that the man was no other than Lhaurent den'Karthus.

Lhaurent was the sun. He was horror. He was the convergence of the world, of all *wyrria* and every soul. He was ultimate darkness, taking every last thread of that energy into himself and binding it into his Goldenmarks. Binding the heart and essence of the woman beneath him and her channeling into a vast and terrible unity that shook the Void with a thundering howl.

In his eyes burned crimson – the crimson of a thousand exploding suns; the crimson of a world of blood. The crimson of upheavals devouring the earth, killing every living thing upon it, and Jherrick suddenly knew him for what he was. A manifestation of the Undoer. A soul taken so long ago he may never have known it, taken during his birth by the Utrus with red eyes. A soul who had so long ago succumbed to the Undoer inside himself that it had lain hidden, unknown by any who had ever touched that dark energy, though all had felt it.

Here, was the demon of time.

Here, taking what it wanted – so it could Undo whatever it liked.

Revulsion surged through Jherrick. Rage devoured him. Something rose inside his body with a roar of flame, furious at Lhaurent's terrible works by the Undoer's hands. Like Jherrick had suddenly grown a thousandfold in the Void, energy surged into him, filling him, expanding him, making his aura of violet and crimson sear like a night on fire.

As his gaze strayed to the side of the altar, he spied a disembodied soul who watched it all from his knees in a pool of blood. Though Jherrick had only met Elohl den'Alrahel once, the day he'd come to the Guardhouse to receive his pension, he'd seen how much Olea's twin had been just like her. Tall, sword-honed, commanding but sober in a way that had made the Alrahel twins seem like two sides of an inseparable unity – two sides of the same incredible light.

Ravaged, Elohl's soul watched with a tortured heart, kneeling inside the ring of arches. His fallen body had poured out the last of its life in a pool of fresh crimson, though Elohl's knees left no imprint in the blood-pool as he watched in horror while Lhaurent sundered the woman upon the bier. First-Lieutenant Fenton den'Kharel stood upon one cloverleaf of the tower, a slender young man beside him that Jherrick recognized as a scribe from Roushenn. A wrath of motion, Fenton lanced lightning at the dais, at Lhaurent. But none of Fenton's fury could touch the Castellan, protected by a *wyrric* barrier that flowed between the archways, wrought with white and gold sigils.

Only Elohl was inside the barrier, watching helplessly as Lhaurent drained his beloved with his ghastly black hand – draining away all the power of the world that had collected in the depths of her heart.

To the Undoer's delight.

Help him!!

Olea's scream was wretched in Jherrick's ears. Jherrick was pure instinct as he flung his etheric body to the fallen soul of Elohl. He was the talons of the Void as he seized Elohl den'Alrahel in his grip. Jherrick was pure motion, his *wyrria* flaring, ravenous as he connected to Elohl's mind. Before his energy concussed in the Void with a tremendous thunderclap, slamming Elohl den'Alrahel's soul back into his body. It was not a nice reunion. It was not a gentle homecoming, this thing Jherrick had done upon wrath and instinct. His *wyrria* was the fury of a fell demon as it thrust Elohl's soul back into his cooling body. Elohl's flesh jerked upon the stone, shuddering the blood-pool – re-ensouled, but not yet alive.

Gripping his talons into the Void, Jherrick seized anything nearby. Any power, any life. Any mystery, any light, any vibration, any music. Anything he could find to restore Elohl, to return him to life so he could punish Lhaurent den'Karthus and halt the Undoer's rise. Stars dimmed. Galaxies shuddered. Jherrick heard souls scream from the battle far away. A cacophony of voices cried out as Jherrick seized any available vibration and poured it into Elohl's body.

But the largest source was the flooding power that raged into Lhaurent from the dying woman, and Jherrick seized that, too – diverting the entirety of its thundering flow and thrusting it all into Elohl den'Alrahel.

Vicious, grotesque, the flood of that tremendous power awakened Elohl's body with a sudden fury. Elohl's flesh rode that power, lancing and rolling through the Goldenmarks like lightning. Sinews knit in a rush. Bones popped back with a wrenching grind. Elohl's blood surged back from the blood-pool until it filled his veins. And then Elohl came up from the stones with a devouring gasp and a scream like a dragon as his heart hammered its first beat – his Goldenmarks on fire with the light of the dawn.

The white tower rang like a bell, exploding the Rennkavi's power out into the world. Jherrick felt it, concussing open places in the earth that had been capped for centuries. Places that had once run raw with the carnal essence that hammered through his veins, places where the world had been bound into slumber. Those places exploded open to the shock of the Rennkavi's awakening. Alranstones sundered, all eyes upon them cracked, souls flooding out, released. Fountain-heads of *wyrria* that had been subsumed burst open in torrential rivers, flooding the land. Where magic had only simmered before, arrested for a reason Jherrick couldn't fathom, it was now unbound – its fury and bliss magnificent.

Jherrick stood in rapture, feeling the world come alive. Feeling it wake. Feeling the Rise of the Dawn, where unity yoked the world as one and every heart awoke to that magic. Feeling every head turn. Feeling every battle and devastation cease as all turned to the White Tower and beheld with cries upon their lips – the return of *wyrria* to the world.

For a moment, all hearts beat as one. For a moment, all breaths came and went in the same tide. For a moment, a vast bliss spread out from Elohl den'Alrahel, his Goldenmarks blazing like a fallen star in the dawn – devouring Jherrick and all the world as it sang Elohl's bliss in one united moment.

And then his rage, as he glanced upon Lhaurent.

Jherrick felt it – like a scream through all that bliss. Suddenly, all that light and rage transformed Elohl's *wyrria*. From a man speared by bliss, his *wyrria* became a beast in the Void, expanding, twisting with a sudden rise. In the Void, Jherrick saw an enormous energy expand out from Elohl's shoulders and spine, spreading out muscled white coils through the black. Engulfing the dawn, swallowing all that power being funneled from the world, the creature that arose behind Elohl den'Alrahel was magnificent, and terrible. Like the power of red and gold Jherrick had seen behind Leith Alodwine in the Albrenni realm, he saw the truth of Elohl's essence now – a white dragon made of pure *wyrric* fire, dwarfing the arches, the tower, and the brightening sky.

As that creature expanded from Elohl's essence, harnessing the Rennkavi's power and concussing it back a hundredfold in the dawn, Jherrick saw its opalescent scales, talons, and ridge-muscled coils.

Though it had shape and strength in the Void, it had only a shivering menace in the world of the real, a vast potential roaring to be released. It was a demon – magnificent and supreme. With a scream of fury, the entirety of that enormous form suddenly poured into Elohl and out of him at the same time, as he roared – the sound of a thousand beasts of death, ready for blood.

The expansion of Elohl's enraged *wyrria* slammed Jherrick, hurtling him back through the Void. Thrusting him back into his own suffering body, where he woke with a wrenching cough upon a rippling expanse of white sand. But not before he had seen what Elohl den'Alrahel had become – a beast of light in the Void, a dragon of pure *wyrria* flowing through the man – ready to devour the dawn with his fury.

Jherrick gasped to wakefulness, back in his rent and devastated body, and thought he heard a laugh roll through the Void. A blissful laugh, a heady exultation, tinged with the autumn tones of Olea's voice. As Jherrick lay there, gasping, embroiled in a terrible agony from what he had just endured, he thought he saw Olea's eyes in the Void.

Thank you, her voice sighed all around Jherrick, *for all that you have brought to fruition. I will see you again soon, Jherrick. Expect me.*

Gazing down upon him, Olea's eyes gleamed red. Before a beautiful laugh spilled from her smiling lips and she flashed out – gone.

CHAPTER 48 – ELOHL

Power blossomed out into the Void from Elohl den'Alrahel.

Ancient, volatile power. Bloodlust stole Elohl's vision; fury devoured his mind. A tremendous wave of energy shuddered through him – the coalescence of the White Tower, taken from Lhaurent den'Alrahel and thrust back into Elohl, magnified a hundredfold. He was nothing, he was everything. The scream of a million souls filled his body. Every heart of the world beat in his chest. Every flood of battle raced through his veins. Every glory, every madness. He was the pinnacle of the magic, and it devoured him and spat him out – as something new.

Transformation devoured Elohl's *wyrria*. A transformation unlike anything he knew. And though his body shook, weak still from the vast wrenching of being resurrected from oblivion, his energy was consumed by the sundering power of all the world's *wyrria* flowing through him. Something enormous roared to the dawn inside him. Something powerful not of body, but of *wyrria* – that lashed out with a luminous tail shot with golden sigils and searing white fire. That tail was barbed and thick, long with flexible muscle, accurate to an infinite degree. And as Elohl felt it whip, his body was suddenly in motion.

Devoured by white flames, his vision seared with the rising dawn at it fixed upon Lhaurent. Surging forward, Elohl found his body lithe, magnificent. Muscled in places it had never been, he felt talons beneath his fingertips, scales on his fists, his energy of a stature that could have swallowed the tower had it been allowed to take shape inside his sinews.

A roar resounded in his ears, but it wasn't Elohl's. It was Fenton, surging with wrath out beyond the barrier, a desert funnel of lighting and fury as he blasted the *wyrric* energy that isolated the center of the dais. Unhinged, Fenton raged with renewed power – liquefying the pale stone of the dais and archways and turning them to white glass as he fought to get in and battle their enemy.

Because he could now. Because all the founts of *wyrria* in the world had been released, opening that power to the Wolf and Dragon *wyrria*.

Because all that power now surged – in Elohl's veins.

The opalescent stone around the barrier was melting to Fenton's fury, but this battle was Elohl's. Elohl's gaze of white fire pinned Lhaurent as he came – the man who had ruined something beautiful. Who had Undone something holy; something Elohl had longed for with all his soul – and now would repay in spades. There would be no mercy; mercy was not a thing his mind understood anymore.

He was pure light; he was wrath as he came for the once-Castellan, power singing through his veins. Lhaurent saw him coming. His face twisting with a vile sneer, he threw up that black arm, still surging with the power of his Rennkavi's Marks like blackwater eels in the deep. Fingers splayed with unholiness, Lhaurent clenched his black hand, a focus and tremendous hatred surging through him and making that black grip swirl like a mad cosmic dance. He gripped the air and Elohl felt something clench around his heart – a touch of fathomless leagues and strangling black depths.

But Elohl was the dragon now. With a single inhalation, he flexed his massive, world-devouring *wyrria*, and burst that black grip upon his heart in a wave of fury. A terrible reverberation slammed through the White Tower, and Elohl felt the world around him crack. The barrier around the dais sundered with a concussion so vast that an enormous crevasse split the tower like a death-knell. Fenton surged through as the barrier broke, two of the archways melted to liquid glass, their portals flashed out and the wall of *wyrria* between them vanished. A lanky young man dashed in, claiming two unconscious, naked forms that were Queen Elyasin and King Therel and hauling them out of the way as Fenton stormed in.

But Elohl hardly saw it. As the barrier broke, it concussed Lhaurent, hurling him off his feet, smacking him up against Ghrenna's altar, dazed. Ghrenna lay motionless upon the altar, but Elohl could see her breath and knew she lived. *Wyrria* and vengeance roared in Elohl's veins, as he reached the stunned Castellan, striking down with his left hand gripping Lhaurent's shoulder from where that terrible black arm emerged.

With a ripple of sinew and flesh, opalescent scales with golden sigils went surging down Elohl's arm from elbow to fingertips. Manifesting from flesh, from *wyrria*, and transforming Elohl's body, Elohl felt the strength of his true nature seethe down that arm with his matching fury. White talons tore from his fingertips, puncturing deep into Lhaurent's shoulder. The Castellan screamed as Elohl's talons punctured flesh, deep into Lhaurent's Goldenmarks.

As Elohl sank his talons in, he gathered the full force of his *wyrria* – and *pulled*.

A terrible cry ripped from Lhaurent's throat as his Goldenmarks flared white-hot through his entire body. In one breath, Elohl inhaled, and Lhaurent's Goldenmarks surged towards Elohl's talons, drawn out of Lhaurent's flesh like poison to the blade. Elohl's gaze burned as he took back what was his. In a searing wave, white light scorched through Lhaurent's Marks, leaving black lines of impotent char in their wake. Gathering in Elohl's talons, the Rennkavi's power went screaming up out of Lhaurent into Elohl in a burst of *wyrric* fire as the last of Lhaurent's Marks burned out.

Lhaurent screamed, his black hand evaporating in a sizzle of vapor. He flailed backwards, stumbling from the altar. Elohl roared as his open hands hit Lhaurent, pure *wyrria* hammering his foe in a tremendous strike. The Castellan was hammered hard, hitting the white dais with a crunch. Sliding into the pool of Elohl's blood, he shuddered, heaving rasping breaths.

Elohl rushed in fast, quick with a beast's instinct. Digging his talons in, Elohl hauled Lhaurent up. His soul blazed as power surged through his free arm, tingling his fingertips, ready to transform and finish the job. Lhaurent screamed and struggled, but he couldn't counter the power coursing through Elohl. Blood surged from Lhaurent's mangled shoulder, darkening his white robes crimson and devouring Elohl's vision. Crimson was his only perception; annihilation his only thought. As red drops of Lhaurent's life fell, a presence burned through Elohl's mind – seizing Elohl's body in a sundering cold as clear as the cosmos.

Thrust your enemy down, the being with red eyes whispered through Elohl. *Unmake that which has sundered your blissful unity.*

"What are you waiting for?" Fenton's voice was barely recognizable at Elohl's side, the growl of a thousand beasts as lighting shivered around him in a nimbus. Fenton's words echoed the whispers in Elohl's mind, and every sinew in Elohl's body trembled, raging to do as the being with red eyes whispered.

To Undo his enemy.

"Elohl—!"

Ghrenna's weak call turned his head; sharpened his eyes. She lay still as death upon the altar, a blackened burn spreading like poison from the center of her chest. Her sweet flesh, once so pure, was now marred with lines of char that obliterated her Blackmarks, snaking out over her collarbones and beautiful breasts. The sight of her ruin drowned his fury, just for a moment. As her cerulean eyes arrested him, the crimson cleared from Elohl's vision and the sound of whispers was pushed away.

Lhaurent seized that moment, wrenching free of Elohl's talons and lurching toward the only remaining archway. With a livid curse, Fenton seared lighting after him, but Lhaurent threw up his remaining hand – casting aside Fenton's fury by the flash of a ruby ring upon his index finger. Lhaurent turned, racing again for the portal, and with a roar, Fenton pursued. Elohl's sinews trembled to chase after them and finish it – when he saw Ghrenna spasm upon the stone altar. A terrible rigor, it bowed her spine, a wail issuing from her throat.

In that moment, Elohl chose. It wasn't a choice of mercy or vengeance. It wasn't a choice of thought or reason. It was a choice of his heart – to be with her, until the end of the world, until the end of all things.

His love was never a choice – it was always her.

Rushing to Ghrenna's side, Elohl let Lhaurent go. Fenton flashed out through the portal, fast upon Lhaurent's heels. Dawn rippled off the opalescent scales of Elohl's transformed arm as he gained the altar, the beast of his *wyrria* curling around Ghrenna. His heart seared with pain as her fingertips reached up weakly to stroke his jaw; but her touch was all he needed. With a gasp, Elohl felt his rage break. He felt it burn down into ash as her Nightwind caressed the massive beast of his nature and soothed it.

Bones snapped, sinews re-made. Talons condensed and scales

flowed back – Elohl's arm regaining the shape of a man, his
fingertips and hand crimson with blood. Hauling Ghrenna up, Elohl
cradled her close. Her heart beat like a poisoned bird against his
chest, her breath coming in shallow sips. Spirals of black charred
through her skin, her white shift burned away where Lhaurent had
desecrated her. A white keshar-claw pendant lay sundered upon her
breast. A sob rose in Elohl's throat, seeing how she had been abused
at the height of her ecstasy – an ecstasy that was supposed to have
been his, and hers, united.

His body shivered with *wyrria* again, ready to transform. Ready
to annihilate the world for what Lhaurent had done. But Ghrenna's
hand came up, touching his face. Arresting him with her luminous
cerulean eyes.

Don't hate him, my beloved, she breathed out with her mind.
Forgiveness is the only path. Please… the Undoer—

But she couldn't finish the thought. Her mind snapped out to a
gasp. Her eyes rolled up as a chorea took her limbs, so terrible that
Elohl couldn't even hold her. She jerked out of his arms, spasming
upon the white altar – and then lay still.

Elohl seized her cheeks. He pressed fingers to her throat,
searching for her heartbeat. Bringing his lips to hers, he kissed her
desperately, hoping he would feel the sweet bliss of her breath. With
a wail, Elohl cradled her to his chest, roaring out to the cold new
dawn like an animal. His scream continued in the Void, endless, the
White Tower echoing it in a ringing swath. He could feel the battle
at the Aphellian Way, finished with their clash of swords and magic
– sundered to the power of the Unification. And though all hearts
surged with connection and togetherness in the new dawn, for Elohl,
everything he had ever hoped for was as ashes now.

But on the heels of his cry, he suddenly heard an indrawn
breath. Looking down, he saw Ghrenna's eyelashes flutter. Her
cerulean eyes opened; devouring him, bright and full of life. Elohl
flooded with joy. His heart expanded to the cosmos, to see her
returned from the brink of death. Leaning in with ecstatic release
and a sudden laugh, he bent to kiss her. But Ghrenna startled. And
where Elohl thought she might have surged to kiss him back, he saw
her recoil.

"Unhand me, *haldakir!*" Power flooded from Ghrenna's voice

like driving winter snow. A voice Elohl didn't know; a voice of pure fury. Elohl flinched back, shocked, as Ghrenna pushed away, clutching her burned silk gown to her blackened chest.

"Steal kisses from Morvein Vishke and face a Dremor's wrath!" She seethed at him, her white gaze flashing cold. "Know that I will eviscerate your mind with all the fury of the Nightwind if you even so much as *try* that again."

Blackness stole Elohl's heart, and his joy died in his throat.

CHAPTER 49 – KHOUREN

The Rennkavis had disappeared from the battlefield, leaving hell in their wake.

Khouren fought like a dervish, whirling and slicing, ripping open throats and cutting tendons. Eleshen fought at his side, a demon just as much as he was, and Ihbram roared like a lion in the dawn, his bright Elsthemi braids spattered with other men's blood.

Their keshar-cats were already down, rent with too many wounds, and so Ihbram, Eleshen, and Khouren had compacted into a tight knot, fighting in their own little hell. Chaos reigned upon the Aphellian Way, but Ihbram had a plan, guiding their vicious knot toward scorpion-riders. Fighting through Menderians, through mind-controlled Valenghians, Ihbram was their guidepost as their trio smashed through the ranks. Surrounding Kreth-Hakir Brethren; darting in, eviscerating their scorpions. Leaping to the diamond-backs of the ruthless mounts, Ihbram protected their group while Eleshen turned the Hakir's weaves back on them, severing them from the hive.

Before Khouren sliced their guts out.

An unholy fire filled Khouren, his *wyrria* surging through his veins. Eleshen roared at his side, lopping off a swiping scorpion-talon with her sword and rushing in to stab out its eyes. It flailed, striking blind, but Ihbram was already up on its flashing back, cutting off the tail as Khouren ran under the beast and took out its legs. It hit the bloody battlefield with a clatter. The rider tried to arrest Eleshen with his mind, and she turned it back on him, making the man scream and claw at his eyes. Khouren hurled his longknife with all the force of his *wyrria* – straight into the man's neck.

He went down gurgling. And they were off again.

Khouren had little sense of the battle raging around him. Men roared and cried out, horses reared and shrieked. Armor clattered to the stones of the Aphellian Way, bodies torn by blades slicking everything a hellish crimson. Khouren saw the fallen in flashes and moments. A roaring keshar-cat with a rider struck down by a scorpion's tail. A Kingsman in Greys lopping off the head of a Menderian soldier with one powerful strike of his longsword, sending the head rolling. The horn of General Merra sounding a regroup, battle-cats darting through the chaos to rejoin her. An entire swath of crimson-clad Valenghians turning as twenty Kreth-Hakir rode into their midst, falling upon the keshari riders like a red rain.

Suddenly, a massive black scorpion roared up before Khouren. He towered upon his black beast, an enormous warrior of the Unaligned Lands wielding a huge broadsword one-handed as his creature darted and killed. A thick silver mane was braided back from his face, old talon-scars raking his flesh. He had no eyes, and yet, Khouren felt the man's mind pin him like a lance. Ripping through Eleshen's violet tide to do so – slamming her back so hard she stumbled to her knees and held her face, blood spurting from her nose.

Jornath's pet. The man's voice was like summer thunder as it hammered down all Ihbram and Khouren's mind-shields in an instant. *You have caused far more chaos than you know, cur.*

The blind fighter leveled his sword at Khouren, and his scorpion rushed in. Twice the size of any other creature upon the battlefield, the beast raked with enormous claws as Khouren darted beneath its strikes. But the man's mind smashed into his again, and with a cry, Khouren's steps faltered. The scorpion swiped, gripping Khouren in its enormous claw, pinning his arms to his sides, squeezing. Khouren screamed, razor-edged chitin sawing his flesh.

"Khouren!" Ihbram roared. Khouren felt his uncle and Eleshen dash in, Ihbram hacking to distract the scorpion while Eleshen darted in to sever its claw at the joint.

I don't think so. The man's mind flooded Khouren and he screamed. It was echoed by Eleshen and Ihbram, their trio's *wyrria* split. The scorpion swiped at Eleshen and she ducked and rolled. It made a brisk turn, hammering Ihbram, but he darted, trying to get the claw that cracked down upon Khouren's ribs and spine. Khouren roared, his body in agony, trapped and unable to heal. A mind-shift flowed from the blind-eyed rider into the beast. The blind man watched Ihbram's movements with his terrible *wyrria* – and sent the scorpion's barbed tail down, right into Ihbram's chest.

Ihbram staggered, eyes wide. His hand clamped on the stinger and his sword was fast, slicing it from the creature's tail before it could release. It screamed, shuddering, dropping Khouren. As it convulsed, Khouren rolled away, his breath heaving through countless broken ribs, his legs paralyzed. Near Ihbram, Khouren reached out, hauling the stinger out of Ihbram's chest as Eleshen ran in, striking at the scorpion. It whirled, but she stood her ground, a clever strike sending its left claw to the ground in a swath of black gore.

Khouren could feel his spine knitting. Already, sensation in his toes began to return. His body flared like fire as he watched Eleshen fight. She'd redoubled her violet floes, and the blind-eyed rider dodged as some of his energy came back at him. But he countered in a tremendous mind-strike, paralyzing her to fall rigid before his beast. Helpless, Khouren could only hold a hand over Ihbram's wound as his uncle gasped from poison and Eleshen's fight failed. Desperation surged in Khouren. He couldn't heal Ihbram, couldn't stop the blind-eyed rider, and there was no talisman of Leith's to save any of them now.

Suddenly, another scorpion appeared before them. Skittering up fast, the beast was ridden by a man Khouren knew all too well. That strong-boned, haughty face. That cool confidence and smooth, thick lips. That arrogant demeanor pinned Khouren, and Khorel Jornath's voice pummeled through his mind.

If you value your life and those of your friends, stay down.

Khouren blinked, astounded, as Khorel Jornath and his scorpion faced off with the blind rider. Eleshen was freed from her bind, rolling away as the two massive scorpions began to engage, stabbing at each other, slicing. She panted as she came to Khouren's side, black blood from the scorpion coating her. Longknives ready, she placed two fingers to Ihbram's throat, checking his pulse. "He's alive. Just."

"Give him this, quickly!"

A glass vial went flying through the air. Eleshen's reflexes were fast, catching it in the chaos. Khouren had only a moment to see the Valenghian High General, Merkhenos del'Ilio, rein in his black charger with a glance at the battle between Khorel Jornath and the blind-eyed priest, before wheeling his horse off to the remains of the allies. Eleshen poured the vial down Ihbram's throat, and he coughed. But his breathing stabilized and his eyes snapped open, even as he clutched his pierced chest and tried to rise.

"Lie still!" Eleshen commanded, pushing him back down.

Khouren could twitch his feet now. He rolled to his side, watching masterful mind-weaves being thrown between the two Kreth-Hakir Priests. Silver waves of incredible power that Khouren could actually see with his true eyes rushed in the space between the scorpions, but neither seemed to be winning. A cadre of three more Kreth-Hakir surged in as the stalemate ensued, but a mean black ronin-cat leaped into their midst, swiping them back, the stern commander upon it none other than the steel-eyed Theroun den'Vekir. Throwing black oilslick weaves at the Kreth-Hakir Brethren, devastating as a viper's strike, Theroun fought with his mind, sundering the Kreth-Hakir's unity. A grisly smile rode Theroun's face as he struck – and with his mean black cat barreling in to finish them, the cadre was bleeding out upon the stones.

But it wasn't enough. Even though so many Brethren were dead, there were still more. A sea of Menderians surrounded the allied forces. Like an ocean, they were closing, cutting off the allies from their battlements. Sharp horn-blasts came from General Theroun, General Merra, and the Vhinesse. Cats snarled backward in retreat, horses whirled about, and foot soldiers turned, hightailing it toward the battlements.

But like a great beast of tooth and fang, Lhaurent's forces hemmed in the resistance. Sealing them off from safety – into the doom of the melee. Kneeling by Ihbram and Eleshen, certainty flooded Khouren's gut. They had lost. Even though Khorel Jornath and General Theroun battled back Kreth-Hakir and the blind priest, there were others still turning wave after wave of allies. Thirty men here. Fifty there. Soldiers fighting shoulder-to-shoulder turning on the ones in front, eviscerating them. Breaking any phalanx the beleaguered allies tried to make.

A group of grey-clad Kingsmen turned upon each other, fighting with bitter, terrible skills. A trio of Cennetians captains in the crimson of the Valor clashed with snarls. Riding upon warhorses, Arlen den'Selthir and the Vhinesse Delennia Oblitenne suddenly wheeled their mounts and came to arms, roaring with a hatred the likes of which Khouren had never seen. Khouren trembled beside his uncle and Eleshen, despair taking him. Ihbram gripped his hand, gasping for air. Khouren gripped Eleshen's fingers, ready for the end.

Suddenly, a massive sound rang through the air, like a tremendous war-bell. A shockwave ripped the battle, hammering men and horses to the ground. It hit Khouren with force, slamming him to his knees on the blood-slick stones of the Way. As it did, an incomparable euphoria blossomed through Khouren's body, opening his heart. Gazing up at the sky, he saw white etheric fire ripple out in an enormous arc like the wave of a volcano's eruption. Sundering into every man and woman, it blasted through them all. Lighting their eyes with luminous *wyrric* power. Opening them up, baring their hearts to the sky and their blood to each other. Raising their vibrations with the sound of the struck bell – tuning them all into one incalculable harmony.

The most beautiful sound Khouren had ever heard was the silence of a hundred thousand men in battle suddenly stopping at once. The most beautiful tympani ever concussed upon his ears was the clatter of weapons hitting stone as knives and daggers, swords and polearms were dropped from astonished fingers. The most beautiful sight he had ever seen was a hundred thousand fighters staring up at the sky, then staring at their kin with open lips, tears bright in their eyes. And the most beautiful thought Khouren ever had was how luminous they all were, stunned into this moment of peace and bliss. A moment where every heart opened as one, and all hearts knew each other – loves and sorrows, losses and joys, annihilations and becomings.

"Khouren—what?" Eleshen managed to gasp next to Khouren.

"The Rennkavi has risen!" Khouren rasped, joy flooding him. Taking up her fingers, Khouren kissed them, staring into her beautiful violet eyes. "The Unity has come!"

"He did it!" Ihbram gasped next to them. "Elohl, that fucking bastard! He fucking did it!"

Battle ceased. Men waited, staring at the sky and at each other, though the vast inundation of euphoria was now fading. As Khouren watched, they began to stagger to their feet, helping each other with clasped wrists, leaving weapons where they had fallen in the carnage. Gazing around with shocked eyes, a great hush settled over the Aphellian Way, except for the groans of the dying.

Khouren helped Eleshen up. He had a moment where they found each other's eyes, before she seized his nape and kissed him, hard. Khouren kissed her back, pouring everything he was into her. Every dream he'd ever had, every love he'd ever lost, every yearning to be complete. His arms wrapped tight around her lovely frame, before she pulled away with a gasp, her violet eyes shining.

Ihbram had struggled to his feet beside them. Khouren extended a hand, though he did not let go of Eleshen's waist. Ihbram coughed, spitting bloody phlegm, but even as he pulled back his jerkin to touch where the scorpion had impaled him, Khouren saw the flesh was mostly healed. His brows rose. Ihbram had never healed so fast before, but something had happened when Elohl sent that shockwave of Unification through the world. Something unprecedented, that Khouren could feel suddenly – Ihbram's wide emerald eyes telling Khouren that he could feel the same thing breathing through the dawn.

"Can you feel it, Khouren?" Ihbram laughed as he gripped Khouren's forearm. "Shaper of Life! Can you feel it?!"

Closing his eyes, Khouren felt out along the morning wind with his *wyrria*. Through the blowing dust and carnage, he sensed something immense vibrating the world. All around him; humming in his ears, whispering in his thoughts. A tuning of his bones into a flooding harmony that eased his sinews, a vibration that poured through the earth beneath his boots. Khouren adjusted his stance, feeling that strange flow rush up from the ground into his body. Carrying him, sweeping him up – from the bones of the earth itself.

"*Wyrria!*" Khouren breathed. "Shaper – it's everywhere!"

"Fuck me." Ihbram clapped a hand upon Khouren's shoulder, then gave a lively laugh. "The Rennkavi brings peace with the dawn!" He yelled at the top of his lungs.

As if Ihbram's pronouncement broke the spell that lay upon the battlefield, a great roar went up through the army. Unified, men and women all around Khouren broke into laughter. Arms were clasped, enemies pulled into embraces. Foes became friend as nations forgot their swords and stripped off helms and vambraces.

But as Khouren watched the celebrations, he saw a group that were not jubilant. The Kreth-Hakir Brethren had gathered in a tight knot on the south side of the Way, some still upon scorpions, others on foot. The blind-eyed priest sat tall upon his chittering black mount, though it shuddered, seeping a tarry blood from numerous wounds. Across from the forty or so remaining Kreth-Hakir, facing them in a tense standoff, Khorel Jornath sat tall upon his smaller scorpion, Merkhenos del'Ilio upon his left and General Theroun den'Vekir upon his mean black ronin-cat to Jornath's right, with a few others at Jornath's back.

There were no words among the Kreth-Hakir, not that Khouren could feel or see. But it was as if a chasm had opened between the rebels and the hornet's nest they faced. Khouren felt silver weaves rise. There was a fight coming like a thunderstorm, that even the Rennkavi's moment of vast unification had not been able to quell.

Suddenly, a woman strode out of a massive alabaster Monolith upon the southern edge of the Way. Wearing white leathers the color of bleached bones with her hood up, her long fiery hair was done in a complex braid, cascading over one shoulder. Moving with graceful, unhurried steps, she parted the army like a sighing sea. Stepping through death so lightly her feet barely made an imprint in the filth, she moved right into the midst of all that building silver power, positioning herself between the hive-mind and Jornath's renegades.

Staring straight at the blind priest, her emerald eyes sliced through all that impending annihilation with a thought. But even as she did, the blind-eyed priest reached for something lashed to his scorpion's neck – raising up the bare and bloody heart that had come from Dherran den'Lhust's chest. The woman in white took a quick inhalation, her gaze fixing upon that bloody organ gripped in the man's fist. He stared down at her, seething with menace and utter dominance.

As that silver wave rose again, the entire remaining hive of Kreth-Hakir surging with yoked purpose under the blind rider's command, the woman in white whirled, flicking the fingers of her left hand at Khorel and his renegades. In a flash of light, they were suddenly gone, her with them. And just like that, whatever fight was to be among the Kreth-Hakir was over. The silver wave subsided, though the blind priest's lips twisted down in a vicious scowl. Turning his chittering black monstrosity away to the south, he abandoned the battlefield, and as one, the remaining Kreth-Hakir melted away with him, lost in the trees of the Visken Bog.

A great ease swept the battlefield. As if the last of the tension for a fight had gone with the mind-benders, men began to speak again, to jostle each other in camaraderie. Khouren's heart lightened with them, turning to kiss Eleshen, when suddenly, a dire call hammered his mind. It hit him so hard he staggered, and he felt Ihbram cry out next to him. The imprint in Khouren's mind wasn't Hakir silver, but red-gold fire – Fentleith's burning signature twisting in from a thousand leagues away.

Sending a thought – an image – right to Khouren's brain.

Roushenn Palace, blocks of blue byrunstone exploding to vicious strikes of lightning from his grandfather's hands. The palace's halls churning like a maelstrom as Lhaurent moved through it, wielding Leith's ruby ring and turning the palace into a morass to avoid Fentleith's wrath.

"Grandfather!" Khouren gasped. "He's after Lhaurent!"

"We have to go, Khouren!" Ihbram gripped his wrist, his eyes screwed up in pain from the force of the sending.

"You're weak." Khouren gripped his hand, pulling it away. "I can make it through those churning halls, I can't have you slowing me down."

"Khouren!" Eleshen stepped to his side, weapons ready. "I'm coming with you."

"No!" Khouren reached out, touching her face. "I lost Lenuria to that man, I'll not lose you, too. Guard Ihbram. I'll be back soon."

"Khouren!!" Eleshen gripped his arms, but he was like smoke on the wind, shifting through her touch. Stepping back, he admired her – all of her vicious, haunting beauty.

"I'll return to you. I swear it. Stay with Ihbram."

Her pretty lips fell open and rain shone in her violet eyes. But Khouren couldn't stay to watch those lovely raindrops fall, nor even kiss her lips one final time. Fentleith roared in his mind again and Khouren turned, sprinting toward the Monolith the woman in white leather had emerged from. If he was right, the Rennkavi had unlocked all the doorways of this world. If he was right, this Plinth was open now, ready to accept Khouren and fling him where he needed to go.

As Khouren crossed the Monolith's boundary, a tingle like fire-ants raced over his skin. Obsidian sigils came alight in a rippling wave, ready. And the only need in Khouren's heart as he slapped his palm to the alabaster stone was not for honor or glory or even for retribution.

It was for redemption.

In a rush of wind and a hurtling of ether, he was sucked through the Stone, and traveled.

* * *

Khouren emerged from the Kingstone inside Roushenn, to a palace gone mad.

The clockwork mass at the center of the palace heaved and shuddered, gold and bronze gears grinding in cacophony, entire swaths of gears not working at all. A hole the size of a ship had been blasted in the side of the massive dome, the byrunstone liquefied to molten glass. The dome-room buzzed like a hive of hornets, *wyrria* so thick upon Khouren's tongue that he could practically lick it from the air. The Kingstone burned hot with white sigils and curling ether, and Khouren stumbled away from it, shielding his eyes.

Wyrria sluiced him from all around. Thick, he waded through its substance like a fly through molasses, swaths of etheric flame blossoming in the air like a forest fire blown by an invisible wind. The Rennkavi's Ritual had sundered whatever devices had been holding back *wyrria* from upwelling through the earth in geysers of terrible glory. And struggling to breathe in the heavy density, Khouren now felt the true power of the earth's *wyrria* – the enormity of it – unleashed.

Hauling in deep breaths, Khouren tried to get his head above water and stop this drowning that suffocated him. He struggled to move, to make his body turn to a path where he could breathe. From somewhere far within the palace, he heard blasts. The foundations of the Kingsmount shuddered. Gears groaned as walls jammed, then ground to a halt with a series of ear-slicing shrieks. Something exploded and metal shrapnel whizzed above Khouren's head.

Stumbling into the pit of gears along one submerged walkway, Khouren felt a pulse near the center of the clockworks. A place where *wyrria* flowed in an easy harmony, rather than the thick syrup up near the Kingstone. As Khouren phased through clanking metal and screaming gears, he knew where he'd been called to – emerging by the small pillar of stone buried deep in the pit. He knew what had to be done. Slicing his thumb on his blade, Khouren set his hand to Leith's filagreed pyramid – his blood seeping into the filigree, dripping onto the river-stone at its heart.

Power flooded Khouren in a wave of crimson gold. He rocked but it did not fell him, his hand clamped to the talisman. Suddenly, the air was easier to breathe. The *wyrria* flooding the chamber was like wind blowing his steps toward his goal now – and Khouren's steps were fleet as he ran through the blast-hole in the dome, enormous blocks of bluestone thundering down around him as the palace shuddered again. Feeling his grandfather like a burning beacon in his mind, Khouren raced through wall after broken wall, gear after blasted gear, fey blue halls lit bright with molten rock.

Bodies littered the carnage. Khouren focused on his feet, to not trip on charred and mangled flesh or the exposed gears of wrecked walls. His gut twisted to see the bodies Lhaurent and Fentleith's fight had left behind. The destruction of Wolf and Dragon *wyrria* had never been so keen as Khouren surged through a blockade of thirty dead Palace Guardsmen, their cobalt jerkins charred and smoking from their silver buckles.

The palace shuddered around him. Khouren ran through the destruction, higher and higher through the Tiers, following the fury of his grandfather's ruin. Through a blasted-out wall, through a vaulted atrium burned into black glass and scorched plants, through palace dressing-rooms with chamber-maids crisped into blackened flesh. Through a kitchen on fire from exploded ovens, pie jam and pastry scorch filling Khouren's nostrils along with billowing black smoke.

Until he came to the battle at last.

Roushenn's Throne Hall was blasted to pieces. As Khouren watched, a section of marbled floor went sliding out from the far end, racing toward where his grandfather Fentleith held his ground near the high dais. Fentleith leapt it with a roar, trying to get to where Lhaurent stood before his white-wrought throne – and though Lhaurent bled out from a mangled wound on his left shoulder, soaking his white battle-armor, he was far from finished.

Lhaurent's Marks were entirely black now, and Khouren no longer felt any power emanating from them. But his cleverness in taming Leith Alodwine's sacred artifact, the ruby ring of dusky white star-metal, knew no bounds. As Khouren watched, Fentleith cast a swath of lightning, and Lhaurent threw up his remaining hand, Leith's ruby ring flashing with light as it battered that hot blast away – sending the lighting hammering into the pillars nearby. Byrunstone exploded with a deafening concussion. Spears of glass, melted by the heat, hurtled past Khouren and he phased, letting it shatter against the rear wall. At a gesture from Lhaurent, a whole section of the eastern wall opened up. Guardsmen, maids, porters, and servants flooded in through the breach, rushing Fentleith with their eyes taken over by crimson fire.

Fentleith roared in anguish from the power of Leith Alodwine released upon the masses of Roushenn. But he could not stop it, and with a terrible cry, sent a sheet of blue-white lightning to scythe down Lhaurent's pawns. They fell, tumbling like paper dolls aflame, and Khouren's gut twisted so hard he doubled over, vomiting on his boots.

Lhaurent's grey gaze pinned Khouren, noting him. Khouren felt it like a blow from the rear of the hall – demanding his submission not to the Rennkavi now, but to the command of Leith Alodwine, ancient master of Khouren's line, his talisman in use upon Lhaurent's hand. Khouren dropped to his knees gasping, as his ancestor's command, wielded by Lhaurent's willful *wyrria*, demanded Khouren to fight against his grandfather Fentleith. To turn on his own flesh and blood and kill the man who had given him life, and love.

Khouren felt Fentleith turn, noting Khouren's presence with widened eyes.

And Khouren felt Lhaurent's command, wielded by all the power of the Wolf and Dragon, and Lhaurent's own oceanic madness – to end Fentleith.

"Khouren!" He heard Fentleith shout through the grinding walls and the simmering thunder. "He's not our master! He's not Wolf and Dragon! Break free, Khouren! Break free with me!"

Something shivered deep inside Khouren. Some beast came awake in him, roaring up inside his flesh. Suddenly, he felt all the hate he'd harbored against Lhaurent. All his hope, dashed upon the black tide of Lhaurent's ruthlessness. All the disappointment, that his Rennkavi had been a madman, a thing which never should have seen the light of the Goldenmarks. And the fear that had once swamped Khouren, the conflict that had raged inside him for centuries, of wanting a strong leader to follow, suddenly focused. All Khouren's loves and losses sharpened – his battle of the Wolf and Dragon coming to perfect balance inside him.

He felt the air shiver around him. A nimbus blossomed from his core, and it was not the lightning that surrounded Fentleith, but the devouring darkness of Khouren's own *wyrria*. Striding forward like a dancer, Khouren was lifted into the air by his dark nimbus, the marble of the floor phasing out beneath his steps. Lhaurent cast his hand out, commanding bluestone columns to shift and the floor to open, but all of it disappeared in a devouring arc to Khouren's *wyrria*, sections of ceiling crashing down as he walked on. Falling gold and marble phased out as it hit his sphere. Lhaurent's grey eyes widened. Fentleith leaped back, to not be touched by that dark halo as his grandson drew abreast of him.

"Shaper's mercy, Khouren!" Fentleith breathed, his eyes burning gold in astonishment.

"Not for Lhaurent, grandfather," Khouren breathed back, ready to finish it.

Raising his voice, Fentleith Alodwine, Last Scion of Khehem, addressed Lhaurent as blasted chunks of marble crashed down though the ruined hall. "You have shown no mercy to the world, Lhaurent, and so from the Scions of the Wolf and Dragon, you shall have none! Prepare yourself for the Void, spawn of the Undoer!"

"The Order of Alrahel will never surrender to Khehem's Kings!" Lhaurent's grey gaze was cold, imperious. His chin rose, eyes glittering with righteousness. "We are the Thorn that pierces the Dragon. We are the Last Night that silences the Wolf. We are the Rose that will come again with the Dawn, uniting all under our glorious light. We are the Linea Alrahel – the true Line of Kings – *the Order of the Dawn!* Even if you kill me, the violence of Leith Alodwine will never prevail over this world. She who Shapes us all, will never allow it."

"You really believe that?" Fentleith's voice was astounded. "You really believe that you are a vehicle of the World Shaper?"

"I do. Because I am." Lhaurent's voice rang with belief, echoing through the hall. "I am the Light of the Dawn!"

"You are *nothing.*" Khouren's growl was low like an animal. "Elohl den'Alrahel is the Rennkavi, and has brought our glorious Dawn, not you."

Khouren knew a zealot when he saw one, and Lhaurent's power simmered with a crimson annihilation that could never have been the World Shaper. Furious, Lhaurent's eyes burned red as he suddenly flung up Leith's ruby ring, gripping into that dark nimbus of Khouren's, trying to command it. But Khouren was done being the servant. He was done being someone else's cur.

He was done believing in others – before he believed in himself.

Like a demon, Khouren dashed in. His will was a spear, his devouring ruin sharpened into a lance. Lhaurent deflected, using Leith's ring to throw up the marble of the floor between himself and Khouren, but Khouren's spear ate through it all. A howl ripped from Khouren's throat as he felt his grandfather attack also with a shattering lance of lightning that surged upon Lhaurent as Khouren's black nimbus speared toward Lhaurent also. A cold fury drove Khouren as he lunged toward Lhaurent, implacable as the fall of night.

But before his spear could reach Lhaurent, the once-Rennkavi flung his right hand out. Leith's ruby ring flared, bright like an exploding volcano. His grandfather's careening bolt of lightning turned, flashing back – and smiting Khouren right through his chest.

Pain exploded through Khouren. He barely heard his grandfather's scream as he felt his heart burst; his body spasming as he fell with a crash, his black nimbus gone. Falling to the marble dais, Khouren felt Lhaurent's hand flash down, pressing that burning ruby to Khouren's sundered heart and turning it to stone so he could not heal. Khouren saw his death arrive through the Void. But as Khouren's life sighed away, he slipped out one dying fingertip

– and touched Lhaurent's soft boot.

Lhaurent immediately shifted through the floor of the dais, pinned in solid bluestone to his shoulders. Sweeping forward with a blitz, Fentleith Alodwine, Last Scion of Khehem, seized Lhaurent's startled face in his grip. And thrust all of that *wyrric* lightning, all that power of the living Wolf and Dragon, right through Lhaurent's skull with a sundering roar.

Lhaurent screamed, searing in lightning-swaths through his skin. His eyes charred out to scorched sockets, and still Fentleith's lightning roared through him, Khouren's grandfather's wrath twisting through his molten eyes. Lhaurent's head fell back, black smoke exhaled upon his last breath. And then his body burst into ashes, piling upon the stones of Roushenn as the clink of a falling ring came from far below.

Fentleith rushed in, cradling Khouren in his lap, his vivid golden eyes lost in tears. But Khouren's soul had already fled, watching from the Void. Roushenn Palace was wreckage, his grandfather screaming in wretchedness as the new day shone beyond the ruined domes. From behind Roushenn's throne, the tableau of the Wolf and Dragon in their ever-battle lifted Khouren's eyes, still intact. Their gazes penetrating him, the beasts seemed to judge Khouren.

Then smiled – deeming him worthy of their lineage at last.

Turning away, Khouren lifted his eyes to the Void. And saw it brighten for him, lit by a million stars.

CHAPTER 50 – ELESHEN

Eleshen rode tall through the streets of Lintesh, upon her dappled keshar cat Moonshadow. At the front of the Elsthemi royal retinue, just behind King Therel Alramir and High General Merra Alramir, Eleshen had been given a place of honor as they paraded at an easy pace through the crowded streets of the Queen's City. A brisk wind skirled the sunny morning, snow glimmering off every bluestone gable. Riding at Ihbram Alodwine's side, Eleshen's white shrug of snowrabbit fur ruffled in the crisp breeze, her long sable braid spilling in a complicated weave over it. General Merra herself had woven Eleshen's braid this morning, once Eleshen had finally awakened from her khemri-venom dreams.

Merra had insisted that Eleshen be sexy as hell today, resplendent in the vicious finery of the Highlands. Eleshen rode tall in her charcoal corseted leather jerkin with its plunging neckline, her buckled leather trousers and boots with their knife-sheaths, and her pelt buckled on around her shoulders. All of which left the most important feature of Eleshen's attire visible – the stark black ink of her new Kingsmount and Stars – finished just yesterday and still red-limned from fever dreams.

Darkwinter Fest had never looked so bright, as their retinue of five hundred Highlanders continued through the streets. Elsthemi war-horns blasted their arrival. The populace thronging the streets cheered, pushed back by cobalt-clad Roushenn Guard to make way for the massive cats and their wild northern riders. Eleshen could see that Lintesh was being rebuilt as they entered Roushenn's main plaza, to a fanfare of Menderian trumpets from the Fourth Tier. The city had been scrubbed of soot and grime from the midsummer burning, and the blue-grey byrunstone shone with flecks of quartz under the bright snow. Taverns and shops had been restored all around the broad circular plaza, strong new cendaric timbers and blue roof tiles hale beneath the winter drifts, cheery smoke issuing from chimneys.

The shanty-cities in the outer Tiers had been disassembled, although some places in the city were still ruined. Though the winter day was bright, the First Abbey of the Jenners haunted Eleshen. As they'd come through the city, she'd seen it was still a jumbled mess of broken stones. The two months since the Rennkavi's Unity had not been enough of a span to rebuild it, and Eleshen wondered if it would ever be done. But as they rode through the main plaza, packed with a carnival atmosphere, food booths, acrobats and sundry, Eleshen's heart lifted – as eager as the rest of the city for the Pact of the Coalition that would be signed today between seven nations previously at war.

Threading their column around the main fountain, its frozen spume carven into an enormous sculpture of roaring lions and keshar-cats encircling the Kingsmount, they eased through the cheering throng to the massive portcullis of Roushenn. Just after they'd crossed under the bluestone wall, carven and far more ornate than Eleshen recalled, Ihbram gestured at a section of collapsed wall near the gate and chuckled.

"Well, well, well," Ihbram spoke smoothly. "Fucker's showing off. I swear, that man is too much these days, now that *wyrria's* returned."

Glancing over, Eleshen saw a crowd gathered near the breach in the wall. As she watched, a massive tumble of byrunstone blocks near the breach lifted into the air upon invisible hands, shedding snow as they rose. Moving in a slow spiral, the sundered blocks began to arrange in mid-air, wintry blue-white sigils curling in the thin cold, pulling them together. Suddenly, all the broken bits and boulders were pulled tight, then fitted seamlessly back into the thirty-foot high breach. With a flash of blue-white light, the blocks flared with sigils all across their surface, then died out – leaving an intact section of wall.

Applause broke out among those watching, and cheering roared from the plaza beyond, which had seen the event from the far side.

"Fentleith Alodwine, ladies and gents," Ihbram chuckled. "As I live and breathe."

At last, Eleshen saw the man who stood before the wall, a man she'd once known as Fenton den'Kharel. Wearing a crimson jerkin tooled with the Wolf and Dragon, he wore no jacket nor furs in the cold air. Steam wafted up around him, shimmering in a mirage as if he'd expended a great heat in his exertions. His white shirtsleeves rolled up, his arms rested upon his head as he heaved a sigh with a pleased smile. The column of Elsthemi halted in Roushenn's broad inner courtyard, watching. A woman in a long white ermine cloak stood next to Fenton, and with a strangely simultaneous movement, they turned toward the Elsthemi's arrival. Eleshen was shocked to recognize Ghrenna den'Tanuk as the woman in that snowy cloak, as she and Fenton turned. But Ghrenna was as distant as Fenton was elated to see them, parting his throng of admirers immediately to stride across the snowy courtyard.

Fenton's stride increased to a jog, his grin elated as he neared. With a roar and a laugh, King Therel slung down from his keshar-cat to greet him, but General Merra beat her brother to the punch. Vaulting from her saddle, she landed neatly in Fenton's arms as he rushed up, her legs twined around him as she devoured his face in the most immodest kiss Eleshen had ever seen. Holding her up effortlessly with his hands gripping her leather-clad ass, Fenton broke from her lips with a hearty laugh, gold and red fire twisting through his eyes, then dove in more. Everyone cheered and hollered as the King of Elsthemen waited on their pleasure beside his cat, grinning from ear to ear. When Merra at last released Fenton, Therel hauled him in for a hearty embrace.

"Why do I never get homecoming welcomes like that?" Ihbram chuckled near Eleshen, his elbows resting on the pommel of his cat-saddle.

Turning to him next, Fenton gave a pleased grin. "Because you've never settled long enough to require a home, miscreant. Come here."

Ihbram slung down from his saddle with a laugh and stepped in to embrace his father. It was long, and both heaved a great sigh before setting their foreheads together – the homecoming of family. It made Eleshen's heart grip suddenly. She gazed up at the palace, feeling it loom above her. Much of it was repaired, and like the city, it had been scrubbed of brimstone from where it had burned from Fenton and Khouren's battle against Lhaurent – but still. Entire

652

wings were yet crumbled, collapsed in upon themselves or spewing enormous stones into the courtyard like a giant's playthings. As Eleshen viewed the destruction, her chest clenched, her breath shallow in the crisp air. Seeing the palace, even largely restored as it was, reminded her of only one thing.

That Khouren was gone, and had sacrificed himself to bring down their enemy.

Eleshen had not been to Lintesh in all these months. When she'd received the news from Fenton that his grandson, her lover, was dead, Eleshen had stood by, numb with shock. Ihbram and Fenton had wept out their pain that horrible day. But when they'd traveled through an open Alranstone to Lintesh from the Aphellian Way and seen the swath of destruction, Eleshen had stared, mute and hollow inside.

Khouren had gone in there ready to die for what he believed in, zealous to the last.

Eleshen's gaze strayed. She found herself looking down at her russet leather boot in its stirrup. Suddenly, a hand appeared, resting on her boot, then rising to give her calf a kind squeeze. Swallowing a shine of tears, she looked up – to find herself gazing into the stalwart kindness of Fenton's lovely eyes.

"Eleshen," he murmured.

"Fentleith," she spoke back.

A hard knowing rested in his gaze. His eyes were peaceful but sad, with only flickers of gold as he gazed up at her, then gave her leg a squeeze again. "Your Inking looks well on you."

"Thank you." She shivered, dispelling her fugue and sitting tall upon her dappled grey cat. "I'll be formally recognized tonight at the festivities."

"The Kingsmen have gained a valuable asset. And ascending to become Dhepan of Quelsis also," Fenton's smile was kind, though wistful around the edges. "Khouren would be proud of you, and so am I."

"Thank you," Eleshen murmured again, subdued.

"Come." Fenton gave her boot a light slap, breaking the mood. "Queen Elyasin makes ready for everyone inside. The Council begins in a half-hour. I was just finishing up here with Morvein."

Eleshen's brows knit, and she glanced from Fenton to Ghrenna.

Ghrenna had not approached the Elsthemi party and stood aloof in her white ermine cloak. No one approached her, as if she was too intimidating or perhaps too frightening to be near. Her beauty was pale as tundra-snows as she returned Eleshen's gaze with calm cerulean eyes. A breeze stirred and Eleshen shivered, unnerved at Ghrenna's unearthly presence.

She'd only heard the basics of Ghrenna's story from Ihbram as they had helped rebuild Lhen Fhekran these past months, and Eleshen had progressed through her formal Alrashemni training under General Merra. Of Ghrenna's damage from Lhaurent upon the White Tower, of how Elohl had died and suddenly been returned to life by unknown means, only to have Ghrenna nearly die in his arms. Of how she had awoken, changed – now someone else entirely, because of everything that had happened.

A fanfare of horns sounded, breaking Eleshen's thoughts. A retinue of liveried guards, dignitaries, and servants began pouring from the palace ingress as the doors boomed open. Stepping down the wide bluestone steps, they fanned out in a welcome-arc in the humped snow, with proper decorum but delighted smiles. No one's smile was more delighted than Queen Elyasin den'Ildrian Alramir, who swept down the stairs in a stunning outfit of dove-grey battle-leathers to embrace her King and husband almost as passionately as Merra had Fenton, though Elyasin's feet remained on the ground.

Cheers exploded around the square, whoops roaring from the Highlanders as their King and Queen kissed. It was passion, and it was steadiness, and it was bliss. Watching the fierce, true love that had united two nations and was about to unite many more, Eleshen finally smiled, her heart swelling with an infectious joy.

Queen Elyasin broke from her husband's kiss. She beamed one last smile at him, then turned to face the Elsthemi. Raising her hands, she roared, "Highlanders! Tonight we shall dine and drink, tell tales and dance! For no man nor creature will keep us from our celebrations – for your homecoming, to a nation that is as much yours now as it is mine. Elsthemen, be welcome! Be welcome in Alrou-Mendera, and let us celebrate a new era of Unity at last!"

Her words were devoured by roars and cheers. The plaza behind them erupted, trumpets gave fanfare, and Elsthemi war-horns blared. With their arms around each other, Queen Elyasin

and King Therel bounded up the stairs of the palace and
disappeared inside.

Eleshen slung down from her keshar-cat with a smile. Grooms
came around, collecting her cat's reins and leading the beasts away
toward the stables. Eleshen was left standing among the milling
Elsthemi as Fenton and Merra embraced again with throaty laughs.
But Merra pulled away, bounding up the palace steps to attend to
the duties of her rank. Ihbram and Fenton began to talk, and
Eleshen joined them as Elsthemi moved into the palace to the
welcome of maids and butlers – others picking up handfuls of snow
and beginning an impromptu snow-fight in the courtyard.

Eleshen ducked a wayward snowball and stepped to the palace
ingress. Joy surged all around. But there were some who were not so
joyous. Eleshen's gaze connected with Ghrenna, who still stood aloof
by the guard-wall. Her hands were folded into the voluminous
sleeves of her white cloak, the hood of fur framing her pale locks like
a wintry pane of glass. With a shiver, Eleshen suddenly realized that
Elohl was not there. And as she glanced around the milling
courtyard, she saw no sign of him.

Only Ghrenna, standing alone by the wall, watching Eleshen
with those drowning blue eyes.

Eventually, the party moved inside, into the high-gabled entry
hall of Roushenn. It had been charred and blasted, littered with
dead bodies when Eleshen had seen it after Fenton and Lhaurent's
battle. But now it was pristine, every block refitted, not a pock to mar
its soaring elegance.

And it was elegant. More so than Eleshen had ever seen it. She
stared around, her lips fallen open in wonder as she took it all in.
The hall was bright, not just from the winter sun pouring in through
massive windows of pearled glass that had never been there before,
but also from globes of swirling white light that danced like drunken
fireflies upon the air, leaving wisps of ether in their wake. As the fey
globes wove up into soaring gables, Eleshen saw that Roushenn was
entirely carven now. Trees arced up columns, wreathed in flowering
vines. Tableaux of harvesting wheat and tending animals, of raising
children and singing harpers were carven everywhere she looked.
Like the Jenner Abbey, these were scenes of prosperity, of love and
peace. And as Eleshen glanced to the far wall beyond the checkered

white and blue marble floor, she saw an enormous carving of Queen Elyasin with six other monarchs, the likenesses of King Therel Alramir and Vhinesse Delennia Oblitenne familiar.

A smile lifted Eleshen's lips as she took everything in. She hardly noticed when Fenton stepped to her side, following her gaze around the enormous hall to every pearled-glass window and portico. "Do you like it?"

"It's beautiful!" Eleshen breathed. "I came to Roushenn a few times when I was young, but it never looked like this!"

"I made a few improvements. With the help of the Jenners and Morvein, of course," Fenton chuckled.

"You did all this?" Eleshen turned and found Fenton grinning, a subtle recklessness in his brown-gold gaze.

He shrugged, and there was modesty in it, but the pleasure of pride shone through. "The Jenner architects and Valenghian stone-wrights did the re-design. I merely worked with Morvein to carry out their schematics. It's far from finished, but we've got most of the central halls repaired. Elyasin wanted a palace of light and community to replace the old Roushenn. A place where all could feel inspired rather than a stark fortress. She's opened up the hidden passageways of the Hinterhaft and made them new public halls for everyone to enjoy. If Roushenn could house tens of thousands before, it could now house thrice that. No more secrets. Just Unity."

"Incredible!" Eleshen still couldn't adjust to how much power Fenton hid inside that unassuming frame of his. Even as she watched, he slouched genially against a column, crossing his arms and marveling up to the vaulted gables. Swirling globes wisped down from bluestone arches and veins of pearl inlay, as if attracted to Fenton's attention. He looked back to Eleshen, and the white globes wafted away.

"Is Elohl here?" She couldn't help but ask, noticing Ghrenna standing alone by the entryway.

"Supposedly." Fenton followed her gaze and his demeanor darkened. "Elyasin said he arrived last night. But I've not seen him yet."

"He's avoiding you? And her?" Eleshen blinked, glancing to Ghrenna.

"Apparently."

Fenton looked as if he would say more, but just then, a fanfare sounded in the hall from a trio of trumpets. Eleshen saw Queen Elyasin and King Therel move off toward a vaulted gable at the far left and up a grand staircase. Fenton pushed from the wall, gesturing to Eleshen and snapping his fingers at Ihbram, who chatted with General Merra. Merra barked orders to her keshari to gather, then glanced at Fenton with a sexy smile. Fenton stepped to her, falling into an easy stride at Merra's side as she moved away after the King and Queen with her elite retinue.

Eleshen went with Ihbram, winding up the grand staircase to the upper galleries. A cobalt carpet woven with gold and silver lions was set up the stairs with golden runners. The hall above was luminous with chandeliers, enormous pearled-glass windows at either end of the causeway. Eleshen blinked stupidly at all the light, each chandelier blazing with hundreds of fey-globes that twisted around them in sorcerous swirls. She didn't recall chandeliers inside Roushenn. And this hallway hadn't had windows – especially not colored glass.

Hearths crackled with fires along the hall, as Eleshen followed the royal retinue to a set of open doors at the south end of the corridor. They entered a vaulted hall decorated with gilded furniture and lit high with chandeliers, fae globes, and pearled windows. Fires roared in every hearth. A wealth of potted plants were arranged by each column, giving the hall a comfortable feel. Tables were arranged in a broad circle around an open space with a podium, and Eleshen saw representatives of the seven allied nations mingling with wine, starting to take their seats.

Eleshen moved toward the table where King Therel now sat with General Merra and their Highlanders. But she hesitated, noting the table where the Menderian host gathered with Queen Elyasin, her new Castellan Thaddeus den'Lhor, and her High General Arlen den'Selthir – who was also High Rakhan of the Alrashemni Kingsmen now. Another table was appointed for the Kingsmen, who had gathered with Brother Sebasos and a few of Arlen's best. That table had Jenners also – quite a few with quill and paper, ready to scribe the morning's proceedings.

Three factions – and suddenly, Eleshen felt torn between them.

"Eleshen. Over here."

She glanced over to Fenton's smooth voice and saw him and Ihbram settling at a table to the right of the Menderian contingent. Ghrenna was seated there, sipping a chalice of wine as she gazed around the room with wintry poise, her white hood lowered. Eleshen moved to their table, accepting a cup of wine from a serving-lad.

"Which table is this?"

"*Wyrrics* table," Ihbram chuckled, leaning his chair back on two legs with a roguish grin. "Misfits table? Whatever you want to call it."

"It's an honor for our kind to be included here, Ihbram. For any magic-users at all, especially Khehemni ones." Rising from his seat, Fenton pulled out a chair beside him for Eleshen and raised his eyebrows. She moved forward and sat.

"Why is there a *wyrrics* table?" Eleshen glanced at Fenton as she sipped her wine.

"There was a time when *wyrric*-users of all kinds were hunted, hated." Fenton's gaze flicked to Ghrenna before he nodded to the Kingsmen table. "Only the Alrashemni fostered *wyrric* abilities among their children this past thousand years. But since the Rennkavi caused *wyrria* to flow through all lands and peoples again, *wyrrics* have a much larger presence in the world. Already, spontaneous openings of *wyrria* are starting to happen in the general populace, something that hasn't happened since the time of Leith. Khehem's knowledge is needed here, even though the Lothren caused trouble for centuries. As Scion of Khehem and head of the Alodwine clan, I take personal responsibility for that, and aim to repair it. But Khehem receives a chance to unite with the world now – to undo Leith's fractiousness. As powerful *wyrrics* of an ancient lineage, Queen Elyasin and the Coalition need our perspective on how to deal with magic rising in the world again."

Eleshen sipped her wine, considering Fenton's words. Gazing around, she took in the settling Coalition groups. Each of the ten tables held a retinue, for the seven nations present, plus one for the Kingsmen and another for the *wyrrics*. A last table held representatives from a number of miscellaneous nations – tall dark-skinned Jadounians, swarthy Ghreccani with their geometric facial tattoos. Plus a few tall spearmen wearing crested red helms and thin desert silks with reed-woven red breastplates.

"Sweet Aeon!"

Fenton suddenly rose from his seat. He stepped briskly toward the table with the southern ambassadors. A man dressed in Roushenn Palace cobalt with a golden lion's mane and smiling green eyes chatted with a strikingly handsome spearman with blue-black curls cut in a short brush. The tall foreigner had a long blade-scar on one cheek, still red from recent healing, and cradled a red-crested silver helm under his arm. The green-eyed Guardsman laughed at something the spear-captain said, then turned as Fenton swept in on him.

The Guardsman's eyebrows rose. And then he and Fenton collided in a crushing embrace, full of back-slapping and jubilant laughter. Fenton laughed a few words – returned by the Guardsman – but the hall was settling and Fenton moved away with a last shake of the man's shoulders, reclaiming his seat beside Eleshen.

"What was that all about?" She asked him.

"An old comrade from the Roushenn Guard. I hadn't thought I'd ever see him again." Fenton's eyes sparkled, but suddenly darkened. "He and I have a lot of catching up to do. But not right now."

At that moment, the only person Eleshen hadn't seen came slipping through the doors. All eyes turned to him – how could they not? Elohl den' Alrahel was magnetic, handsome, and the entire reason the Coalition was here today.

Eleshen's thoughts dropped away as he entered. Clad in a midnight-blue jerkin tooled with gold whorls that mimicked his Goldenmarks, his sea-grey eyes scanned the assembly – not flinching from all the scrutiny, but not embracing it, either. One might not have thought he was a hero, so silent the room became at his entry. And where his sleeves were rolled up at his forearms, Eleshen saw the Marks. They weren't gold anymore upon his left arm and hand, but a flowing, opalescent white, and she wondered at the change. She had heard from Fenton about the events upon the tower, but he'd not said anything about Elohl's Marks having changed, and Eleshen wondered at it.

Elohl's gaze met hers, briefly, without recognition. She supposed he'd not heard about her transformation yet, and he'd not seen her ride in with the Elsthemi – but still, it gave Eleshen a pang.

Elohl's gaze paused as he found Ghrenna. Eleshen watched them stare at each other, a moment that stretched in the room's soft hush. And then his eyes found Fenton and he moved forward, claiming a seat at the *wyrrics* table, though not next to Ghrenna. Fenton gripped Elohl's shoulder briefly, and Ihbram jostled him. Elohl nodded to them, though he sent a curious frown past Fenton to Eleshen.

But there was no more time for re-acquaintance, as Queen Elyasin rose and stepped into the central space and up to the podium erected in the middle of the tables. Raising her hands, she commanded the room to hush as servants continued to move in elegant patterns, settling refreshments and pitchers of water at every table.

"Friends, be welcome!" Elyasin began, her lovely voice resonating through the hall. "You have gathered here today, because we experience a new world in our time. *Wyrria* has arisen in all our lands these past two months and causes unprecedented chaos, but also unprecedented delight. Our wars are ceased for the first time in forty years, soldiers returning home to rebuild, to renew, and to decide what to do with their future. As must we. In an era of open travel through the Alranstones, now freely admitting passage to anyone, we have come to a turning-point in what it means to have national borders, standing armies, and trade. Today, we begin the discussion of these concerns. At the end of our time, we will sign the Pact of the Coalition that has been drafted these past two months with significant input from you all. We will add any last majority-vote clauses to the document. And we will understand that this is a living Pact, a breathing thing that will change and change again as we refine governing in this new time. Let us now begin. I invite King Therel Alramir to open with a discussion of the Elsthemi, the rebuilding of Lhen Fhekran, and magical tumult inside their borders. We will proceed 'round in order, ending with the opinion of the *wyrrics* on all that has been said, before we move on to the Pact proper. King Therel, if you would."

Elyasin made an elegant gesture to Therel, who rose from his seat and came to the center as she left. A brief touching of fingertips between them showed their love as Elyasin resumed her seat at the Menderian table, Therel's wolf-pale eyes following her all the way.

And the Council of the Coalition began.

CHAPTER 51 – THEROUN

Theroun den'Jornath leaned against a column with his arms crossed over his chest, listening to King Therel Alramir make his statement about the condition of the Elsthemi nation. It was a grim description, the mess Lhaurent had left in his wake, not the least of which had been perpetrated by the Kreth-Hakir.

Scowling around the room, Theroun took in the assembly. Hidden in plain sight in his herringbone-weave leathers, no one in the room even knew he was here – and he received no return gazes from those he watched. Taking in the Rennkavi Elohl den'Alrahel in his midnight-blue and gold finery, Theroun watched the impressive warrior listen to King Therel's speech. The man glanced over, and for a moment his storm-grey eyes narrowed. But Theroun suspended his breath and let his intention drift back into the oilslick haze of mind-weaves that coated his body like a living skin. Exhaling slowly, Theroun thickened his black weaves like a scorpion's armor – making his presence impossible to be seen.

Theroun's sight-dampening weave flowed around him, and Elohl's glance traveled past. The Rennkavi looked back to King Therel as Therel now described magical chaos erupting at the Valley of Doors – that three Doors there had opened and caused natural laws like gravity and daylight to bend in the area. Theroun continued his watch, absorbing the meeting. After the Aphellian Way, where he had been seen fighting at Khorel Jornath's side, Theroun could never show his face in an assembly such as this again. And though the Kreth-Hakir had been split from Jornath's rebellion, it didn't mean that Theroun was liberated of his bondage. Khorel Jornath and Metrene den'Yesh would take his full report later, and there would be no escaping it.

Under Khorel and Metrene's tutelage at the rebels' stronghold upon the Isle of Crasos these past months, Theroun was developing into a mind-master far quicker than even Khorel had anticipated.

Obfuscation of intent, creating weaves to cause the eye to travel past, had taken Theroun only a week to learn. With the explosion of *wyrria* in the world, his abilities had grown from a chaotic strike to something he could use at will now – allowing him to spy upon the assembly. It was a worthy skill, though Theroun despised deception. His thoughts drifted to another of such black arts – the Ghost of Roushenn. How that man had gotten the drop on Theroun inside his own chambers. And how he had seen that fellow again on the Aphellian Way, fighting like a dervish in the night for the allies.

Theroun hadn't seen the Black Ghost again. And though he abhorred these dark deceptions, his future depended on it – even if it took him to Halsos' Hells and back.

Gazing over the nations present, Theroun took in all the eager faces. Tall Arthe den'Tourmalin was cool as ever, but the aging Isleman King nodded as Therel thanked him for sending shipwrights to help re-build Lhen Fhekran. Vhinesse Delennia Oblitenne also gave a regal nod as she was thanked for sending Valenghian stonemasons. The Elsthemi were rabid with pride for their King – High General Merra Alramir, her Captains Jhonen Rebaldi, Lhesher Khoum, and the twins Rhone and Rhennon Uhlki. Theroun hadn't approached them after the battle at the Aphellian Way. He had disappeared under a mind-weave, rather than try to explain his complicated allegiances to the Kreth-Hakir and why. This assembly held only hate for the herringbone black, despite Khorel Jornath's and Theroun's betrayal of the Brethren upon the battlefield. No story Theroun could ever offer would hold water with his former allies after they had watched him fight at Khorel's side.

He was a traitor in truth, now – against all nations and peoples.

Theroun's gaze drifted to Merkhenos del'Ilio as he listened. The war-general had broken his ties with Valenghia and sat at the Cennetian table as temporary Regent of Cennetia now, though the proud and vicious city-states continued to squabble like always. Merkhenos gave Theroun a subtle smile and a cordial dip of his chin as their eyes connected. Theroun's lips quirked. Of all those present, Merkhenos was the only one who could see him, with his drowning Illianti poisons flowing through his veins. Though the man wouldn't divulge Theroun's presence here. Merkhenos was aligned with Khorel Jornath – for now – his lips as full of secrets as his veins were of deadly poison.

King Therel sat. Vhinesse Delennia Oblitenne was next, rising to orate the status of Valenghia's armies and the steps being taken to return Cennetia and Praough to full sovereignty, including the return of land-grabs and excess taxation. Valenghia would have lean times ahead, but Delennia held a stalwart belief that her nation would be better off working in cooperation with others rather than dominance.

It was a good speech, and received applause.

The meeting droned on. People began to eat delicacies and drink kaf-tesh as the sun's angle changed through the gabled windows. Theroun's glance came to Thaddeus, at Queen Elyasin's side. Pride warmed his heart, Theroun's only uplifting emotion today. His own children were long dead and buried, but Thad had been almost a son to him. And now, Thaddeus had risen to the Queen's right hand – not only Queen's Historian now, but also her new Castellan.

Thad sat tall in forest-green robes that fit his lean frame, not scribbling a thing as he watched the proceedings. Theroun let his gaze ease, as Metrene had been teaching him, to perceive *wyrria*. A curious phenomenon surrounded Thad. Rather than silver weaves like the Kreth-Hakir, or Theroun's strangely black ones that resisted turning silver like the Brethren to which he was now bound, vibrant green filaments eased out from Thad like eager anemones, snaring words as they left people's mouths. Those tendrils did the same with any document Thad shuffled from his stack of papers, and Theroun smiled more, watching that incredible *wyrria*. He'd always known Thad had a unique talent, but to finally be able to see it was a pleasure.

Thad shivered and turned, glancing to the column where Theroun stood. Theroun thickened his oilslick weaves. Confusion darkened Thad's alertness and his gaze slid by – causing Theroun a twinge in his old wound.

The meeting continued, the floor given now to the miscellaneous ambassador's table. Theroun watched the tall Jadounian warrior Duthukan stand and begin to speak. The man had risen to prominence during his time enslaved, and now gave a report of his countrymen who had been returned to their homes.

Valenghia and Alrou-Mendera had provided ample coin and goods to help restore razed villages in Jadoun and Perthe. The situation was still tense, with warlords trying to vie for dominance. But many of those who had been in the slave army now returned home as leaders, strong in mind and will from all they had endured.

It was a small victory, in a time of chaos and uncertainty.

Next to speak was a tall spearman wearing thin silk garb and a reed-woven breastplate, with a strikingly Alrashemni look. Lourden al'Lhesk, Captain of the *Riishalleth* of Ghellen in the Twelve Tribes south of Ghrec, gave an account of particular interest to Theroun. Battle had taken Lourden's city two months ago, attacked by a Menderian slave-army sent by Alranstone from Lhaurent. Involving Kreth-Hakir, the attack had been accompanied by an assault on the Twelve Tribes' coastline – the sea-battle that had been discussed at the Kreth-Hakir's Heraldation.

The fight for the Twelve Tribes had been vicious. But the Tribesmen were excellent warriors, joined by Berounhim *caravanserai* from the interior to wage guerrilla-style battles in the nighttime desert. Lhaurent's forces had been crushed, though it had been a drain on the Tribes. The spear-Captain Lourden sought compensation from Alrou-Mendera via trade agreements, now that the Alranstones were open. Elyasin nodded soberly and rose to tell the spear-captain that it would be done, inviting him and his cohort to stay the week, to continue their talks of peace.

The man nodded with a soldier's efficiency and sat, and the assembly moved on.

After all had been heard, a discourse raged. Most notably, the heads of military pinning Fentleith Alodwine over and over with questions about *wyrria* and how it would affect people – most of which he couldn't answer. When it was at last obvious that Fenton was becoming beleaguered, Elyasin rose and invited the Articles of the Coalition to be distributed. A few more clauses were introduced, voted upon, and added by Thaddeus to the main document, then given to Jenner scribes to copy in a fair calligraphy. The Articles were affirmed, the documents signed by royalty and witnesses, and it was done. As the signed copies were distributed back to their nations, each in a golden codex, Queen Elyasin stood.

"This is the beginning of a new era. Thank you all for being a part of the First Pact of the Coalition. I invite you to stay the week, or longer if you like. Enjoy the hospitality of Alrou-Mendera – as we have celebrations in honor of Darkwinter Night, the Pact, and the new year planned throughout the week. Rest, mingle, or explore our fair city. Refreshments will be provided here and in your rooms. The celebratory feast tonight in the Throne Hall will commence at sundown. For those of you who wish it, there shall be an Honoring of the Fallen in the Rose Courtyard an hour prior to sunset. Come and honor your slain, but then we shall make merry, for we have accomplished a great triumph today! Go with joy in your hearts. I will see you all at the festivities."

With that, Elyasin placed a palm over her heart and set one hand to the longknife at her hip, bowing to the assembly like a Kingsman. All rose and made a gesture back – a bow or sign of affirmation and respect from their own culture. As she straightened, Elsthemi whoops went up, and just like that the formality broke. Everyone rose and began to mingle, taking up chalices of wine.

Pride filled Theroun's heart. He couldn't help but think how proud Uhlas would have been to see this strong warrior-Queen, his daughter. To see how generous Elyasin was, how open-hearted and fierce, how unabashedly dedicated to truth and honor, right down to her marrow. It was fitting, that Elyasin had made this Unification a reality. Uhlas had been too careful and stoic. Alden had been too rash and righteous. But Elyasin was the perfect balance of both.

Even as Theroun's emotions elevated, the old war-wound in his right side twinged, sending a spike of pain through his chest. Theroun took a breath, stretching his scar. Lingering at the column, his fierce joy was cast into shadow – that everyone here could celebrate Elyasin's achievements except him. He was in little danger of being discovered. But his new allegiance also meant that he would never be able to join their revelry. Apart, he lost himself in wondering if this was what it felt like to be dead. To be a Black Ghost among the living. A true outsider, so lost to darkness that he could never again be part of the light.

So deep was Theroun in his musings that when a man stepped up beside him, Theroun's hand flashed to the longknife at his hip.

"Don't draw, General. If you value your secret, that is."

Fentleith Alodwine's low chuckle sent ripples of discomfort surging over Theroun's skin, like a march of fire ants. Theroun set his jaw and turned, lifting his hand carefully away from his knife. The once-Lieutenant moved into Theroun's line of sight, sipping from a chalice with a slight smile as his liquid-gold gaze scanned the assembly.

"Does it please you to sneak up on men, Scion of Khehem?" Theroun growled.

"Vastly." Fenton swirled his goblet. Standing at Theroun's shoulder, the flash of threat in his golden gaze was far from subtle. "You'll have to improve your Hakir skills far more, General, to conceal yourself from my eye. Which brings me to why I came over. What are your intentions here?"

"Can't you just pluck them from my mind?" Theroun growled. He raised an eyebrow and the *wyrric* lord laughed, resounding and bright. Heads turned their way, but he waved a hand as if dismissing something funny he'd just thought of, and people turned back to their conversations. But Theroun stood his ground, wary. He had seen Fentleith Alodwine in battle at the Aphellian Way – the man was a force of nature. Not to mention the raging Wolf and Dragon *wyrria* that kept his mind a flood of red fire to Theroun's perusal.

"Shall I?" Fenton gave him a sidelong glance, all friendliness dropped away. "Or shall I just blast it out of you? Mind-weaves are hard to keep when your flesh is on fire."

Theroun took a hard in-breath, though he knew the man was bluffing. Theroun couldn't read it, but he could feel it from years of experience. "Raise your magics against me, Alodwine, and upset this blissful treaty you and the Queen are trying so hard to orchestrate. Civil discourse will earn us more than a show of force. I am here to record the proceedings. Nothing more."

"Indeed." Fenton lifted a dangerous eyebrow. "If I had felt more from you, I would have killed you where you stand. Count yourself lucky that I'm a far more patient man than I was nine hundred years ago."

"I'm sure." Theroun couldn't keep the bite from his words. He didn't take well to threats. But he played a dangerous game here, all the more because of his relative newness to *wyrria*. "I'm not here to maim your Coalition. The faction I represent wishes the Coalition to move forward."

Fenton went very still at his side. "The Kreth-Hakir Brethren want to support the Unification?"

"Some of us do."

"The Kreth-Hakir rebellion." Fenton's voice was soft with wonder. "Then what I saw on the Aphellian Way was no trick. Khorel Jornath has turned against his Brethren."

"Indeed." Theroun set his jaw. "Khorel has a different opinion about how the Brethren need to be led. And he's not alone."

"But still far from being able to fight for dominance of the Order." Fenton's sidelong gaze held immense knowledge, and Theroun admired it. Fenton was shrewd, and now that Theroun knew part of the man's history, his respect was merited. Though Fenton's choices here would define how they moved forward from this moment – as enemies, or allies.

"I would like to speak with Queen Elyasin," Theroun spoke in his most clandestine bark. "Privately."

"Why?" Fenton's tone was curt, but not without interest.

"I need to tell her the truth of things."

Fenton eyeballed him, then sipped his wine and nodded pleasantly at a pair of Cennetian noblewomen in sheer silks wandering by. They gave him sexy smiles, full of lust and poison, but kept their distance, accepting a freshening of their wine from a young serving-lad.

"You want to clear your name to Elyasin?" Fenton asked once they'd passed.

"It's not about clearing my name," Theroun growled, "it's about the security of her nation."

Fenton took a deep breath. The sizzling, biting feeling that crawled over Theroun's skin eased. Fenton drained his goblet and set it down upon a tray as a serving-girl swept by. His gaze followed Queen Elyasin, now artfully extricating herself from the assembly with Thaddeus, his arms full of papers. They whisked out of the room and Theroun felt Fenton hesitate, before he gave a short huff.

"Break your glamour and be seen before I say so," Fenton spoke low, "or try any mind-manipulation, and become my enemy. Imminently. Come."

Without waiting, Fenton marched toward the open doors. Theroun was fast upon his heels, using the man's brisk wake to follow without touching anyone. In a moment, they were out the doors and into the vaulted hall. Elyasin and Thaddeus were turning into the Queen's resting-solar at the northern end, the doors shutting behind them and four Palace Guard moving into a flanking position.

Fenton strode down the hall, not looking around. They soon gained the doors and he waved the Guardsmen away. They snapped their heels, parting to their once-Lieutenant, who rapped upon the door. Elyasin's voice spoke from inside, and Fenton pushed both doors inward with a brisk, smooth strength. He moved in, waited a beat for the invisible Theroun to step inside, then shut the doors and lowered the massive beam into the brackets to bar the door.

The solar was thankfully empty, save for Elyasin and Thaddeus. A pair of hearths burned high, a far bank of windows admitting the long angle of the winter sun as it began to set over the Kingsmount. Elyasin stood by a series of bookshelves heaped with papers and scrolls, clearly the place where she and Thaddeus had been staging their Coalition conversations. Her golden eyebrows were raised and her arms crossed, a mildly peeved expression upon her features.

"Locking me into my study, Fentleith Alodwine?" She spoke with mild irritation. "May I ask why? You're no longer part of my Guard, you know."

"I have someone who needs to speak with you, Queen Elyasin," Fenton began. "His information may be of vast importance to the security of your nation. And of the Coalition."

Fenton's grave tone sobered Elyasin. She blinked, and her arms uncrossed. "Well, show him in. I will hear him straightaway."

Fenton glanced to Theroun. "You have five minutes."

"Five minutes is all I require." Theroun let his black weaves drop. The Queen inhaled, her hands flashing to her weapons. But Fenton held up a hand, forestalling her.

"General Theroun!" It was Thaddeus who spoke, his eyes enormous behind his spectacles. "How... what—?"

"Not now, Thad." Theroun chided the lad as gently as he knew how. He wanted to tell Thaddeus everything. He wanted someone to believe him, to know his loyalty. But this moment couldn't be wasted. He had only five minutes to state his intentions to his Queen, and Theroun wasn't about to squander that time.

With humility, he took a knee and bowed his head. "My

Queen. Only daughter of Uhlas and righteous protector of our nation, hear me. I come before you as a penitent, seeking absolution. I come before you as a traitor, pledged to a master I cannot escape. I come before you as a dead man, knowing my life is forfeit to the forces that move me, trying to stay alive as best I may. But most of all, I come before you as your devoted servant, to the bitter, galling end – if it comes to that."

He heard a slow, tense inhalation from his Queen. "Look at me, Theroun. What is it that you have come here to say? For surely you are beheld in the eyes of the Coalition as a traitor of the highest order. And yet – I have heard of your valor upon the Aphellian Way, despite your new allegiances. Lift your eyes to your Queen and explain yourself."

Theroun did as he was told. He did not rise, but held his Queen's furious gaze with a grim passion. "My Queen. I have a darkness within me. A darkness of *wyrria*. It has been recognized by the Brethren of the Kreth-Hakir as akin to theirs, and I have chosen to become a part of their Order because of it – a choice of life or death, as my rising *wyrria* was tearing me apart, and only the Brethren's arts could save me."

Elyasin heaved a hard breath, her green eyes fired with fury. Her fingers gripped the hilt of a longknife at her belt, brushing the wrapped leather. "Give me one good reason to not slit your throat right now."

"Because I am yours. Just as I was once your father's," Theroun spoke from his heart. They had no time for subtlety.

Elyasin hesitated, and uncertainty broke in her eyes. "Why have you come here?"

"Because I wish to be your liaison inside the Kreth-Hakir Brethren."

Elyasin inhaled a sharp breath. Her green eyes pierced Theroun like knives, but she was listening. "You wish to spy amongst them?"

"I may not be able to make report often, or hardly at all," Theroun growled. "I may not be able to escape them for many years. But I offer you, today, my eyes and ears inside their organization, as best I may. My mind – yours to eviscerate at will – when or if I am able to return."

Elyasin was silent for a long moment. At last, she breathed, "Why?"

"Because I've made mistakes, my Queen, from this darkness inside me," Theroun grated. "I allowed others to manipulate it, at the expense of my King and nation. Under the tutelage of the Kreth-Hakir, I have the opportunity to learn about it – tame it to my will and make it a weapon. To become the Black Viper that strikes the heart of the Brethren. For you. For Uhlas. And for us all."

Elyasin's gaze weighed him, as if weighing his soul against the steel of his words. "I believe you," she whispered at last.

"He employs no Hakir arts right now, Elyasin," Fenton's words were quiet at Theroun's side. "His words were spoken in truth, with no mind-manipulations."

"Theroun." Elyasin's eyes softened. Her golden brows knit, a sad grace upon her visage. "The Kreth-Hakir will do worse than kill you if they find out you spy for me. Fentleith has told me of their horrors. What they do to traitors," Elyasin shivered, standing with a hard regality. "It is worse than any punishment a Queen could ever devise. Why would you take such a grave risk?"

"Because I am dead if I don't." Theroun grated, feeling his heart break deep inside. "Because my love of King and country is the only thing I do love. And if I don't hold on to that—" Fear slithered into Theroun's gut, carving out a black nest and filling it with venom. "Then I will become the darkness in truth."

A deep sadness filled Elyasin's eyes. Slowly, she sank to one knee, reaching out to touch Theroun's cheek. "Have you seen the red eyes of the Demon, Theroun? Because I have. And he comes for all those who fall into darkness without any light to hold on to."

Tears filled Theroun's vision, burning like a viper's strike. "I have seen black arts, my Queen. I have felt them, these past nine months, stirring within me. The Demon comes for those who rise fast in Hakir *wyrria*, so the Brethren say. And I rise fast. Faster than anyone they have seen in a thousand years."

He heard Fenton's sudden inhalation and slow out-breath. Theroun felt the unspoken conversation Queen Elyasin had with Fenton, her eyes flicking to his. Her gaze shifted back to Theroun, and in their emerald depths was the brightest strength Theroun had ever seen. Slowly, she slipped her hand from Theroun's cheek, her sapphire and gold lion-sigil ring of House den'Ildrian proffered now beneath his lips.

"Swear yourself to me, General Theroun den'Vekir," she commanded. "And let your Black Viper's strike serve none other. Ever."

"So do I swear." Theroun grated, pressing his lips to her fingers and ring. "On pain of the Demon's annihilation."

"So shall it be." With stern grace, Elyasin rose. She stared down at Theroun from a height, like a goddess of battle. "Rise, General Theroun den'Vekir. Rise as mine to command, and mine to fell. Rise for your Queen, and do her bidding. Infiltrate the Kreth-Hakir Brethren. Keep all in secrecy. Report to me when you can. And hold fast against the Demon, for he is friend to none. Rise now, and do my will."

"My Queen." Theroun rose, nodding his head with a crisp clack of his bootheels, one hand upon the sword at his hip. They shared a long glance, full of things unspoken about Elyasin's father, her family – and how much Theroun would have given to remain by her side. Suddenly, Elyasin moved forward. Reaching down, she took up Theroun's fingers from his sword. Holding his hand, almost tenderly, her gaze pierced him.

"Theroun," she spoke softly. "All may fail in darkness, for we live now in strange and desperate times. But know that all of us hold within us a light, even though there is also dark. If you cannot be light in the days to come, then I shall hold that light for you. I will be your lighthouse to come home to. But know that within yourself, lies one of the strongest lights I have ever seen. A light that knows loyalty, and justice, and all things truthful and honest. My father saw that in you, Theroun, and I see it, too. Uhlas did not pardon you out of mis-applied mercy. He pardoned you because he saw that light, even in your darkest hour. Find it. Use it. And come back to us."

"My Queen." Theroun's throat choked. His shoulders trembled, a tight lance of pain devouring his old injury. But as Elyasin let his fingers fall, he knew he would die for her. He would do anything, for her. If his path was darkness, he would take it. He would take it and bend it to his will, and make it his to command.

For his light – and for his Queen.

Theroun gave a long exhalation and drew darkness down

around him like a veil. Elyasin's eyes betrayed no emotion, watching him disappear with calm readiness. Fenton raised the beam and pushed open the doors, stepping out into the hall first as if he was the only one exiting. Theroun turned from his Queen, stepping out behind Fenton. His last glance was upon Thaddeus as the doors closed, the lad's green eyes lingering as if Thad could still see him.

And then the doors boomed shut.

Theroun's heart clenched. Everything he loved was in that room. And nothing of that love would save him out here in the darkness, except what he carried with him. With careful breaths, Theroun used the will-weaving Khorel had taught him these past months. He took that last image of Thad standing by Elyasin and wove it away into the darkest corner of his mind. The blackest void inside himself, knowing that he could never share it even with Khorel. His memories of this day, he wove into a tight cocoon, impenetrable.

And hoped, that it would be strong enough to save his sanity against those who might use it against him.

Fenton had struck up a conversation with the Guardsmen at the doors. Theroun gave him a nod and Fenton gave a casual nod back, as if it was all part of the conversation flowing from his lips. Theroun turned away, feeling a prickle of lightning ease over his skin. And then moved off, toward a side-stair that would take him down to the Kingstone deep within the bowels of Roushenn.

Where Khorel Jornath and Metrene den'Yesh awaited him.

CHAPTER 52 – ELYASIN

Elyasin stood, staring at the closed door. Emotions swirled through her in the wake of Theroun's revelation. She could feel and yet she couldn't – understanding, so crystalline suddenly, what a man would do for honor.

The thought woke Elyasin to alertness, and she inhaled. Glancing around, she took in the palatial room of bluestone granite as the sunlight flashed out over the Kingsmount. It wasn't her original reading-room – much had been destroyed by Fenton and Lhaurent's colossal battle inside Roushenn, particularly the upper Tiers. But this room had been royally re-designed and outfitted from furniture discovered behind the palace walls. In shadowed halls that Elyasin had banished with Roushenn's re-design – just one of many secrets that had nearly ruined her nation.

But now, a secret faced her, one that meant everything to the survival of her people, her Coalition, and a loyal man's life. High clouds caught Elyasin's gaze, gleaming beyond the bank of windows. Heavy cobalt curtains with golden thread and tassels were pulled back by the vaulted windows, letting in the bright winter light. The world shone white and crisp beyond, turrets of blue-grey granite standing in stark contrast to the deep cerulean of the winter sky. Darkwinter – the shortest day of all the year. The day the light returned, but only because the darkness had gone before.

Fenton returned, closing the door softly behind himself. Moving forward, he did not take Elyasin's hand, but his persona radiated the calm readiness he was known for. Though he was something else now. Something she could see swirl briefly in his gold-brown eyes.

"Are you alright?" Fenton murmured. Thaddeus had moved into their circle also. He removed his spectacles, lipping them with a worried gaze.

"No." Elyasin heaved a deep breath, making a fist to stop

herself from rubbing her knuckles.

"What can I do?" Fenton asked, his gaze full of concern.

Elyasin paused, then spoke what had to be said. "Tell no one. Either of you. Theroun's revelation, his appointment – it cannot be known."

"And Therel?" Fenton's gaze was careful.

Elyasin pursed her lips and blew out through them softly. "I will tell Therel, when the time is right. For now, this silence is absolute. If Therel knows right now, he'll send men to track Theroun. Merra, or Ihbram, or someone else to rout out the Kreth-Hakir. I know my husband. He'll act. And this – we can't have action on this. Not yet."

"Unfortunately, I agree." Fenton's gold-brown eyes were steady.

Elyasin ran her hands over her new garments. A supple dove-grey leather, her high-collared jerkin was a gift from Therel to celebrate the Coalition. Her Elsthemi knee-boots held longknives, her weapons harness tooled with the Kingsmount and Stars, the Lion of den'Ildrian, and a wolf for House Alramir. Ancient sigildry flowed down the arms and spine, and every buckle. Reaching up, Elyasin touched her gilded keshar pendant beneath the white wolf pelt, stroking it. Her other hand settled to a sickled longknife of a dusky white metal inset with a ruby and runes. A matching longsword rode her back – items found when Lhaurent's corpse had burned away.

Turning, she gazed into a mirror near one bookcase. A coronet of the same white metal rested upon Elyasin's brow, discovered up in a fortress atop the Kingsmount when the Alranstones had opened. Though it held not a single jewel, it glowed like a morning on fire. Elyasin felt a shiver move through her, a *wyrric* breath upon her skin – an echo of the power she'd had while joined to Brother King Hahled Ferrian.

"I have to keep this secret, for now," she spoke at last. "And the two of you must as well."

Something sad moved in Fenton's eyes. But he bowed, saying, "As you wish," a sentiment echoed by Thaddeus.

Squaring her shoulders, Elyasin fought a great heaviness. The day seemed somehow dark as she faced Thad and saw the knowledge of her sacrifice in his eyes. "Where are we with the event scheduled for the Rose Courtyard, Castellan den'Lhor?"

"All is prepared, my Queen." Thad's green eyes held love and support as he spoke in a gentle voice. "The sarcophagi are in place. Morvein wrought wonders with them, these past two months. It's breathtaking."

"People should be making their way down," Fenton took up the conversation. "Aldris left orders for the Guardsmen to chaperone people a half-hour after the Coalition conference ended."

"And Therel?" Elyasin caught Fenton's gaze.

"He said he'd meet you there," Fenton spoke softly. "He's still in the Coalition-hall, extending a few notes to the Isle shipwrights on the rebuilding of Fhekran Palace."

Elyasin nodded, conflict surging through her. She slid her fingers over her sickled hilt, then straightened. "So it is."

Moving forward, she strode toward the doors of the chamber and pushed them open. Thaddeus and Fenton were on her heels as she moved down the hall to the grand staircase. Ambassadors flooded the hall, descending the stairs in small groups led by Palace Guardsmen. Elyasin nodded here and there, but her mind whirled as she moved down the graceful staircase, then through another ornate hall toward the Rose Courtyard.

Issuing through a set of palatial doors, Elyasin stepped out into a winter wonderland. The Rose Courtyard of Roushenn was gracious with silence, though every path was choked with people. The sun had set behind the Kingsmount, painting the winter sky in rose and gold, ochre and violet. A whispering wind rippled the pelt upon Elyasin's shoulders, her breath puffing cold in the gloaming. Torches and braziers had been lit around the grand gardens, bright in every arch and niche.

One of the few places that had been spared from the Battle of Roushenn, the Rose Courtyard was as Elyasin remembered it, lovely with drifts of snow that glittered beneath the torchlight. Charmed by the *wyrria* that now flowed in torrents beneath the palace and upwelled all over the city of Lintesh, the burbling fountains here had not frozen. Twining vines of roses bloomed out of season, in a riot of loveliness, though ice limned every petal. More than two thousand crystal sarcophagi were arranged along the snowy paths tonight, a glittering sea of loveliness punctuated by the somber movement of people walking the crushed gravel paths and remembering the fallen. The scent of roses filled Elyasin's nostrils as she moved to a low dais set below a bluestone arch wound with roses, then stepped up.

Before her, three honored warriors waited, entombed in smooth crystal vaults inscribed with ornate sigils that scattered the torchlight. Olea den'Alrahel was as beautiful as Elyasin remembered. Given a place of honor alongside the reclaimed bodies of Temlin den'Ildrian and Khouren Alodwine, Olea was luminous in the lowering night. Elyasin set her fingertips to Olea's bier, tracing the sigils that flared a gentle blue-white to her touch. Giannyk symbols, they were Morvein Vishke's – these two thousand sarcophagi her soberest gift of the past two months. Elyasin couldn't read the sigils, but Thad had said they spoke of peace, and the bliss of being released to the Void.

A hard lump filled Elyasin's throat as her gaze perused the face of her mentor – a woman who had been a friend, a protector, and a sister. Olea's corpse had looked wretched when Fenton had first led Elyasin down through the Roushenn's crumbled depths to the King's Tomb two months ago – yet another secret that Elyasin had never known about. But now, because of Morvein's gift, Olea's beauty had returned. Her blue-black curls shone glossy in the torchlight, her eyelashes dark and full, her cheeks rosy as if she might rise at any moment. Dressed in Kingsmen Greys, her hands rested upon the pommel of a sword inscribed with Alrashemni runes. A pin with the Lion of den'Ildrian pierced her collar, done in blue sapphires and gold filigree – Elyasin's last gift.

Straightening, Elyasin gazed out over the sea of milling people. Pennants of many nations fluttered in the breeze, crystal tombs throwing the hushed twilight and the flicker of torches across the roses limned in snow. Elyasin's gaze tracked the most notable faction as they knelt before biers with a salute to their Inkings. The surviving Kingsmen were few, but they had come dressed in their Greys tonight to honor their fallen.

Found, and brought home to rest at last.

Raising her arms, a hush settled around the courtyard, every eye turned her way. The ceremony was brief, and Elyasin spoke the words, hardly aware of them as they fell from her lips. Dignified platitudes of bravery and righteousness, they seemed hollow in the settling dusk – as if any words she could devise would never be enough to undo the injustice that had befallen the Kingsmen. Her eyes met others as she spoke, seeing the pain in their faces, seeing tears fall. Seeing a people, broken yet still standing tall, receive amendment for their slain. Elyasin's chest compressed, a choking sensation rattling her words. The night blurred and she blinked tears from her eyes as she finished the benediction, her last words easing away.

As one, the Alrashemni Kingsmen settled through the courtyard, down to one knee. Like a rippling wave, they bowed to her, palms to hearts between the ambassadors and royalty who looked on in reverent sadness. And then they rose, breaking the spell that drowned the courtyard in silence.

Though nothing could break Elyasin's dire understanding this night – of right and wrong, good and evil.

People began to move the paths again, as others siphoned from the courtyard and back inside the palace, to make ready for the revelry that would soon begin. Elyasin needed to go change for the celebrations, but found she was riveted where she stood, her gaze moving from Olea to the lion-maned man entombed beside her – Temlin den'Ildrian. Elyasin had never known her uncle. But gazing upon him now, entombed with a sword and shield blazing with the gold and cobalt lion's crest of den'Ildrian, she could feel his stalwart strength. She could feel his roar as she looked upon him, and remembered the stories she'd been told these past months of his bravery in holding her city and opposing Lhaurent.

Yet another death of a good heart known too late.

The paths were nearly cleared now, the sky shimmering into a deep cobalt dotted with diamond-bright stars. Someone stepped to Elyasin's side and she turned. She'd expected Fenton, but was surprised to see her Guard-Captain, Aldris den'Farahan. His green eyes were somber as he gazed out over the sea of crystal and roses, his golden mane catching the torchlight.

"You've done the Kingsmen proud, Elyasin," he rasped, a sad smile twisting his lips. "An honor the world will never forget."

"And neither should they," Elyasin spoke, facing him. "The Kingsmen died because of the secrets that crippled us all. This vigil is transparent for a reason – because all should see and know how darkness divides us."

Aldris' gaze moved to Olea's sarcophagus. Reaching out, he set a tender hand to the crystal, stroking it. "She would have loved to see this tonight."

"I would have loved to have her here." Reaching out, Elyasin set a hand over Aldris'. He startled at her touch, swinging red-rimmed eyes up to meet Elyasin's. "I can't thank you enough, Aldris. For bringing the Kingsmen back through Khehem's Alranstone. Words can never express how grateful I am, that you found them and brought them home."

"My Queen." Her glib-tongued Guard-Captain was of few words tonight. Aldris had been tempered by the ordeals he had undergone these past months. And though they'd only had a few moments to speak of his journey to Oasis Ghellen and the friendship he had formed with the Ghellani, she made a mental note to save time for him later.

Fenton moved up to the raised dais, breaking her thoughts. He and Aldris embraced in a subdued manner, clapping each other's shoulders. Fenton set a hand to Olea's sarcophagus, staring down at her with a complicated emotion in his gold-flame eyes as he stroked the crystal. "She was a light in the darkness. For all of us."

"Olea followed her heart," Elyasin spoke with strength. "A kind heart of honor and truth. I was wrong to doubt her. I hoped that someday I would have a chance to apologize for turning her away from my confidence. A regret I must now live with."

"She didn't hold it against you." Aldris glanced up, his green eyes tired. "Olea never spoke a bad word about you, in all the time we were in Ghellen. All she ever wanted was to protect you – to keep you and those she loved safe."

Elyasin's throat clenched; tears pricked her eyes. Reaching out, she set a hand to the crystal also, stroking its glossy surface. Her tears spilled, slipping down her cheeks like diamond raindrops in the frigid night. The sky was deep violet now, stars pricking the velvet darkness. Fenton stepped away from Olea's bier and knelt before the one that encased the Ghost of Roushenn – Fenton's grandson, Khouren Alodwine. A man Elyasin had never known, but who had saved every one of them with his honorable sacrifice.

Elyasin watched Fenton's gold eyes twist with power and pain

as he gazed through the glassy crystal at his grandson. She felt the
bonds of family and love as a slow simmer of golden fire broke out
around Fenton's person. As Elyasin watched, a tear trickled down
Fenton's cheeks. Setting his forehead to the smooth crystal, he gave a
soft sigh. And then stood, his hand slipping from the bier.

"Please excuse me," he rasped, stepping away without meeting
her gaze.

Standing next to Aldris, Elyasin watched him go. She didn't
understand the ancient being that was Fentleith Alodwine. Once the
Guardsman she had trusted for years, he was a different person now.
Elyasin's brows furrowed, watching him stride out into the night.

"May I have a moment? I'd like to say goodbye."

Elyasin blinked from her reverie, noting a beautiful woman
standing at the base of the dais. With an ornate sable braid and deep
violet eyes, the woman sported a newly-Inked Blackmark upon her
chest, clad in Elsthemi-style Alrashemni Greys. Eleshen had heard
tales of the fearless Eleshen den'Fenrir, but they'd not met yet.
Though now was not the time for introductions. With a genteel nod,
Elyasin summoned Aldris and they stepped down to a sprawling
bush of white roses that climbed a bluestone arch nearby.

Turning, Elyasin watched the fierce fighter from afar. Leaning
over Khouren Alodwine's sarcophagus, Eleshen set a hand to the
crystal, gazing upon the Ghost of Roushenn with her stunning violet
eyes. Her eyes did not gather tears and she did not weep. At last,
Eleshen den'Fenrir gave a haunting smile. A smile that moved
through Elyasin with a blissful sound like a trickling stream beneath
a midnight moon. With a kiss to her fingertips upon Khouren's bier,
Eleshen stepped away, off into the night.

"If you'll excuse me, my Queen," Aldris murmured, "I have a
few more people I'd like to say goodbye to before the revelry begins."

"Go." Elyasin turned to him with a soft smile. "Find your kin.
Lay them to rest."

"Thank you." His green eyes were grim in the darkening light,
but held fervency. "History will remember you, Elyasin, no matter
what else you do with your reign."

Her lips quirked. Reaching out, she clasped her Captain's
hand. "I don't care about memory and history, Aldris. I care about
the living. Go. Find your kin. No need to be Guard-Captain

tonight."

"I will never stop being your Guard-Captain," Aldris' lips quirked in his famed, cheeky humor at last. "And neither did Olea. I'll be back soon."

He stepped away, leaving Elyasin alone by the bluestone arch and winter-white roses. Their scent drowned her as night darkened. Leaning toward the arch, Elyasin surrendered to it, freeing her mind to the stars and the torch-flickers in the brisk wind. The moon was rising, a wan sickle out over the Eleskis. Elyasin watched it a long moment, as stars flickered to life in the longest night of the year. Her white wolf-pelt ruffled around her ears as the breeze toyed with it.

Turning, she stared at the roses climbing the arch. They would bloom all year, so Fenton had said, now that *wyrria* was back in the world. Many things had changed, and many things would, now that such power flowed through all the continents again. There would be years of adapting to *wyrric* dangers and oddities such as this. But the fey delight of having roses in wintertime charmed Elyasin. Leaning forward, she extended her chin to scent one ghostly bloom. When suddenly, a presence stepped in behind her. Wrapping her around the waist with one arm, the man reached in to pluck the rose from its thorns, moving its heady fragrance close to Elyasin's lips.

"It's not telmen," the man's darkly smoldering voice spoke beside her ear, "but it'll do."

"Therel!" Elyasin breathed, radiant at his surprise.

Moving close, Therel pressed his body against her back. He palmed her waist as he gave a smooth growl by her hair, pressing his lips in to kiss her neck. Elyasin forgot roses as she lifted her arms, threading them around his neck as he leaned in, reaching up a hand to span her throat. Elyasin sighed in bliss, arching for him. "You've been gone too long, Therel."

"It's only been five days since my last visit," Therel chuckled, roguish.

"Far too long." Elyasin's mouth blossomed in a full smile, as she turned in her King and husband's arms. Lifting her chin, she pressed her lips to his, and they kissed a long while in the drowning scent of the night. She could feel his heat as he pressed close, cupping her ass now so she could feel the hardness of how much he had missed her. It left Elyasin with high, fast breaths as he pulled back with a renegade chuckle, his wolf-blue eyes vivid in the torchlight.

The silver of his keshar-pendant shone in the gloaming, though it held no power now. The Brother Kings were gone, released from their Alranstones, and Elyasin and Therel's magic had gone with it. But staring up into her King and husband's grinning, regal face, Elyasin knew the truth. That they were better this way, just the two of them. Without dire, destructive *wyrria* racing through their veins — even though neither of them had lost the strange *wyrric* inkings of the Brother Kings. Gazing up into her beloved's eyes, Elyasin felt a power all their own blossom into the night, as drums of celebration began to pound inside the palace. Staring down, a winsome delight lifted Therel's face. His pale eyes were luminous as he beamed at her, reaching up to stroke her cheek.

"What is this amazing look a wife gives her husband tonight?" He chuckled.

"I love you," Elyasin spoke plainly, holding her husband's strong gaze.

"I love you, too." Therel bent his head, pressing the softest kiss upon her lips, lingering. A breath of wind eased around them, sealing their moment of bliss as they stood in the chill, inhaling the darkness and feeling love.

"Sounds like the celebration's beginning without us," Therel spoke at last, lifting Elyasin's fingers up to press them with a roguish kiss as his eyes glinted like a cocky raven. "Shall we make our way up and show them how to really start a party?"

"Absolutely." Elyasin broke into a wide smile.

"Then after you, my sweetgrape." With a flourishing bow and a swirl of his crimson cloak, Therel motioned her on. But Elyasin stepped in, hooking her arm through his with firm solidarity.

"We go as one."

Therel's eyes shone as he gazed down through the glittering night, then lowered his head to kiss her lips. "We go as one. Always."

CHAPTER 53 – ELOHL

The rebuilt Throne Hall of Roushenn Palace was a place of magic tonight. Elohl glanced around, watching the Darkwinter celebrations rage all around him. Holly and cendarie boughs twined every column, the trestle-tables laden so full of food, ale, and telmenberry wine that they dipped in the middle. White globes swirled into every vault, brightening crystal chandeliers newly installed from Roushenn's catacombs. The palace sparkled with life and revelry, packed with attendees from seven nations and more, all dressed in their finest. Elohl himself was clad in an exquisite midnight blue silk jerkin. Embroidered with golden thread in the pattern of his Goldenmarks, it was a gift from Elyasin, along with the new set of Kingsmen longknives in his black boots, and the sword he'd left in his rooms.

For this, the first night of their peace treaty and new Unification year.

But Elohl felt only emptiness as Elsthemi war-drums pounded through the hall, a rousing chorus of fifes and hand-clapping accompanying a raucous partner dance. Servants rushed about, making sure every goblet was filled, and Elohl's telmen wine was barely half-drained when a young woman refilled it with a wink and a smile. He gave her a nod. She sensed his mood and moved off, continuing to libate the festivities. Trestle-tables ringed the hall, but most everyone mingled through the space with their plates and drink, the Throne Hall newly adorned with chaises and high-backed chairs in extra dining clusters, plus indoor greenery that the gaily-adorned royals moved through like fish in a calm eddy.

Elohl had eaten little. He'd picked at his roast pheasant and plum chutney, his tastebuds dull. After a few bites he'd abandoned it, and now had no idea where his plate had ended up. Idling near a column with only his drink, the spicy scent of evergreen boughs was the only thing that came even close to soothing him. He sipped from a golden chalice, his eyes tracing the boughs that wound the tall bluestone columns like a living forest – faces of deer and nymphs staring out at him, newly carven by Fenton's *wyrric* arts and the diligent Jenner monks.

The shadows were the only place Elohl felt at ease. His sensate sphere had heightened since the opening of the world to *wyrria*. Every clap of hands and thunder of drums set his teeth on edge, his hearing almost painfully acute. The light-globes that swirled above were searing to his eyes, his wine too sweet upon his tongue. Elohl took another sip, trying to restrain himself from bolting back to the forest near the Elsce that he'd been haunting for the past two months.

"Nice place to hide. Couldn't have picked a better spot myself."

Fenton's calm baritone was the only thing soothing to Elohl's ears in all the cacophony. Elohl turned with relief to see the Scion of Khehem at his shoulder. Fenton was resplendent in a crimson jerkin with Wolf and Dragon tooling in gold. A pendant of dusky star-metal set with a ruby showed at his open collar, and the ruby ring of Leith Alodwine glittered upon his left index finger. He hailed Elohl with a lift of his gilded goblet, his eyes their regular gold-brown, though a tad reckless with drink. Fenton's confrontational but humorous glance spoke volumes. He wasn't going to berate Elohl for being absent from the world these past two months, but he also wasn't going to let Elohl slip away without facing it, either.

"I'm only here for the night." Elohl sipped his wine.

"You're not here at all."

Fenton's curt response wasn't what Elohl expected, and made him turn. "What do you mean?"

"You're not here." Fenton gestured, indicating the festivities. A Valenghian game of horseshoe-slide had begun in a cleared space, and Jadounian war-whoops went up as the southrons began to handily win every slide against the silver-haired folk.

"You're not among us, Elohl," Fenton continued, fixing Elohl in his keen gaze. "You're somewhere else. Don't think I can't feel it. Everyone here is celebrating the Rennkavi's Unity, except the Rennkavi himself."

"Not just me." Elohl's glance tracked to the one person he'd been watching all evening. Beautiful as a tundra night, Ghrenna's pale perfection outshone even the loveliest women in the hall. Her hair was braided in an ornate weave, curled up in a bun at the side of her slim neck, long tendrils escaping. She shone like a pearl in a gown of cerulean silk the color of her eyes, decorated with sapphires along the high collar – a collar that covered the burn marks over her chest and the sides of her neck. Her cheeks were vivid, her lips the same as she sipped from a pewter goblet, watching the revelry from the shadowed greenery also.

They were a pair, the Rennkavi and his Gerunthane.

Except that they weren't, not anymore.

Ghrenna glanced over, as if she felt Elohl watching. Her dark blue eyes devoured him, and all sound dropped from Elohl's ears. All motion dimmed as she became his world. But in that beautiful, sundering gaze, he saw only a lingering curiosity and sadness. Those blue eyes held a different woman than his beloved – someone he didn't know.

"She's not the same, is she?" Fenton's murmur stole into Elohl's ears, reopening them.

"She's Morvein Vishke now," Elohl spoke, cold. Ghrenna turned away, back to the throng. Lifting his goblet, Elohl took a deep swig, but didn't feel any better. Something dark had opened up inside him, ever since the White Tower and everything that had happened there. Deep inside his innermost self, he'd always held onto Ghrenna's love. But now that love had been severed, taken by the countless arguments and ways he'd tried in that first week to find Ghrenna within the woman who now occupied her body.

And found that his beloved was well and truly gone.

"She is Morvein." Fenton spoke again, his words knifing Elohl's heart and making yet another dark wound inside him. "I remember everything about her, Elohl. The way she moved, the way she spoke. The way she breathed and turned her head. Every way that Morvein was then, eight hundred years ago, Ghrenna is now. You'll have to face it, eventually."

"I *have* faced it." Elohl's growl was harsh as he swigged his wine again. Turning to Fenton, a flare of anger whipped him – an echo of the vicious, devouring beast of *wyrria* that had partially transformed him atop the White Tower. "I know she's not the same. What do you want from me?"

Fenton's mouth quirked, though the humor didn't touch the smolder of gold moving in his eyes. "Finally. Some other emotion than this self-suffering darkness you've been devoured by every damn time I see you."

"Fuck off." Elohl didn't want company. He swigged his wine, turning back to the hall.

"Don't be this way, Elohl."

"Leave me be."

"No." Stepping in front of him, Fenton placed himself squarely in Elohl's line of sight. "I don't leave my family alone when they're suffering. You and I both saw what happened to you atop the White Tower, when everything went bad against Lhaurent. I've convinced Thaddeus to keep his peace about it for now, but eventually, we'll need to discuss what happened. You've changed, Elohl, don't think I don't see it. We—"

But at that moment, a golden-maned Palace Guardsman in cobalt stepped up, a contingent of Twelve Tribes spearmen in desert-silk finery accompanying him. Aldris den'Farahan, now wearing the silver pins of Guard-Captain at his high collar, gave a bright laugh. Moving in, he embraced Fenton with a slap on the back.

"Fenton! Finally!" Aldris spoke, grinning. "Been dodging ambassadors all night to get to your side, asshole. And *wyrria*! Fuck off, man, when did you get all that?"

"Oh, I might have had it for a little while," Fenton chuckled, gripping Aldris' shoulder with a pleased smile, his intensity vanished as if it had never been.

"Longer than a little while, so I hear." Aldris gaze was keen suddenly, as if the lively persona was just a mask for a very shrewd mind glinting out from those emerald eyes. Aldris turned to Elohl next, his lively face dropping into seriousness. They had first met at the Queen's coronation, when Aldris had helped Elohl masquerade as a Palace Guardsman, but Elohl knew Aldris was one of the men who had been there for Olea's last moments. Elohl hadn't wanted to speak to Aldris, but now it was upon him. Reaching into the breast pocket of his cobalt jerkin, Aldris produced a small box of woven red reeds. He held it out.

"Elohl." Aldris eyes had gone dead, full of pain. "She would have wanted you to have this."

Elohl's throat closed. He didn't want to take the box. Reaching out, he claimed it gently, opening it. Within lay a single curl of glossy blue-black hair, lovely as a dragonfly's wing. Reaching in, he touched Olea's curl with reverent fingers.

"She was a warrior until the moment she died," Aldris spoke, somber. "Olea brought hope to an entire nation against Lhaurent's tyranny. Her death was not in vain."

"Thank you." Elohl's throat was tight. He couldn't see, his world blurring.

A tall spearman with brush-cut hair dressed in a white shawl with a red-woven border stepped forward next, setting hand to Elohl's shoulder. His sorrowful grey eyes met Elohl's, love radiating from his presence.

"She will be missed," the spear-captain spoke in a flowing accent. "*Olea-gishii* was the flower of our hope. She was the peace in our hearts."

Elohl could only nod, grief too keen inside him. Just then, trumpets gave a fanfare through the hall. Elohl tucked the reed-woven box away in his jerkin as the music died and the dancing halted. Heads craned, to see Queen Elyasin ascend the dais and take up a place before her throne. Clad in a vivid gown of gold and cobalt silk now rather than her leathers, she was escorted upon the arm of King Therel in his crimson and black formal attire.

They were the picture of bliss. Something woeful gripped Elohl, even as he was glad for them. Beaming at each other, the young King and Queen were the height of fierce handsomeness and effortless command. With a smooth gesture from Elyasin, the hall quieted. Releasing Therel's arm, she raised her voice, its strong rule echoing from every restored vault and pillar.

"Friends! Welcome to our Darkwinter Night celebrations, and the blessing of our Coalition's First New Year!"

Roars erupted through the hall from the Elsthemi, punctuated by battle-whoops from the Jadounians and polite clapping from the Valenghians and the rest. With a laugh, Therel gestured for quiet and the hall gradually came back to a boisterous, eager attention.

"I will be brief, but we have a few matters of ceremony before we commence with the rest of the revelry," Elyasin continued. Clad in dark green robes that fit his slender frame like a scabbard fits a sword, Castellan and Queen's Historian Thaddeus den'Lhor moved to Elyasin's side. Extending a ceremonial sword in a gilded scabbard, he paused, and Elyasin received it with a nod. Retreating a step behind her, Elyasin's new Castellan kept to her side.

"Our primary order of business," Elyasin spoke again, "is a reparation of grievous wrongs. High Rakhan Arlen den'Selthir of the Alrashemni Kingsmen and Shemout Alrashemni Order. If you would come forward, please."

At mention of the Kingsmen, Elohl's attention sharpened upon the dais. Watching closely, he sipped his wine, every sense alert. Tingling with attention so fully that it made his skin crawl in the packed hall, Elohl didn't know exactly what was happening, though it had the feel of a ceremony arranged ahead of time.

A lean lord with iron-blonde hair moved up the steps of the dais, until he stood a step below Elyasin. Elohl had found out about the Shemout from Fenton, but he'd never met this man. But he had an impeccable demeanor as Elyasin motioned him all the way up, and he came to stand before her. The feel of *wyrria* breathed over Elohl's skin as the man performed a crisp Kingsman salute with one hand upon his sword, the other over his elegant charcoal silk doublet trimmed with silver braid.

"High Rakhan of the Alrashemni Kingsmen, please kneel."

A breath of surprise flowed through Elohl's lips – a similar breath issuing out from the entire hall. Everyone was rapt, watching the proceedings. Elohl's skin prickled, his Goldenmarks simmering beneath his midnight blue jerkin. Light eased out from beneath his high collar, but Elohl ignored it, watching the dais.

Rakhan Arlen den'Selthir sank to one knee before Elyasin. Sliding the ceremonial sword from its scabbard, she dubbed it gently across Arlen's shoulders. "Through the presence of their chosen High Rakhan here today, and by the grace vested in me as Queen of Alrou-Mendera and Elsthemen, I hearby re-instate the Alrashemni Kingsmen as Friends of the Crown. I hearby rescind all annexation Alrou-Mendera has made upon sovereign Alrashemni lands and citadels. I release the Alrashemni Kingsmen from the accusation of falsely-instated High Treason by the Summons of the Kingsmen. And I release the Alrashemni Kingsmen of any obligation to serve the Crown, though they remain Friend to us for their support of this nation in dire times, proven throughout our mutual history. Please accept the Crown's formal apology, for the heinous atrocities wrecked against you these past ten years. And our sincere promise, to spare no expense in rebuilding your life in the years to come. We regret what has passed by our father's reign. And we seek to repair all wrongs, so we may move forward together."

A spreading hush filled the hall. In that moment of silence, Queen Elyasin sank gracefully to her knees in her cobalt gown, right before the High Rakhan of the Kingsmen. Placing the gilded sword into his hands, she bowed with her forehead all the way down to the floor and moved aside her golden hair – baring her long, lovely neck.

Gasps inhaled throughout the hall. The gesture was not lost upon anyone, and it made a rushing thrill burst through Elohl. Elyasin bared her neck to the High Rakhan of the Kingsmen. She bared her Queenship, offering it as reparation for the terrible wrongs done to the Alrashemni during Uhlas' reign.

Elohl saw Arlen hesitate. He saw the man's fingers grip the hilt of that blade, just for an instant. Though it was ceremonial, the edges shone in the hall's light, wickedly sharp. But with a smooth, slow out-breath, that Elohl felt shiver through him from across the crowded hall, Arlen set the blade aside upon the stone of the dais. Reaching out, he set a hand under Elyasin's chin. She looked up, meeting the raptor-keen gaze of the aged fighter, holding it with her own hard readiness.

"In the name of the Alrashemni Kingsmen," Arlen rasped, his hand lifting hers to his lips, the both of them still upon their knees, "I accept your apology. And I reinstate the Kingsmen as Friend to the Crown, in any hour of need. Especially for you. You make our nation strong, my Queen, and the Kingsmen would aid you in that. Let us be One once more, as we should have been these ten long years."

Arlen kissed Elyasin's fingers with a lordly gentleness, and a cheer went up through the hall. It shattered Elohl's ears, thundering every nerve. With a graceful fluidity, Arlen helped Elyasin rise, then moved in to give her an almost fatherly kiss upon either cheek. She blushed with a tremendous smile and stepped back, allowing Arlen to turn to the hall.

"Tonight," Arlen thundered, his voice ringing like well-forged steel, "we do more than re-instate the Kingsmen! We also add to our numbers, for the first time in ten years. Vhiniti Khenria Oblitenne of Valenghia, Dhepan Eleshen den'Fenrir of Quelsis! Please step to the dais and be recognized by the Alrashemni for deeds of valor in our time of need."

Elohl blinked, startling to hear Eleshen's name. His gaze roved the hall, searching for her curvaceous golden beauty. He'd not known she was here, and certainly hadn't known that she'd been involved in the events of the past few months. But as he watched two women step up the dais, confusion filled him. One was Khenria, the distinctly Alrashemni-looking, fierce young woman who had been Dherran's lover. Now the Vhiniti of Valenghia, heir to the Vhinesse, she was dressed in a crimson Red Valor uniform with royal gold detail.

But the other woman who approached the dais had cascading black hair sleek as otter's fur that fell in an ornate braid to her waist. Tall and willowy and wearing Kingsmen Greys but with Elsthemi styling, she had a warrior's way that reminded Elohl of Olea – fierce and bristling with weapons. As she turned to be recognized, Elohl saw a haunting face with level, dark brows, high cheekbones, and violet eyes so stunning they made Elohl's breath slip from his lips. "Aeon, who—?"

"I do believe I saw her in your bed once, Elohl." Fenton spoke with an amused quirk of lips, as they watched her receive a codex from Arlen, containing the Writ of her Eighth Seal. Stepping in, Arlen set his palm upon her chest, over her stark Elsthemi-style Inkings. He murmured words for her, and Elohl watched those stunning violet eyes shine with tears. But the woman was fierce, and did not shed her tears as Arlen stepped back, lifting his blade and piercing her, just a small welt of blood, in the center of her Inking. She bore it well, flinching not at all, her eyes proud.

Arlen moved to the Vhiniti next, repeating the ceremony. But Khenria received a piercing from Arlen and then a beaming smile. Elohl recalled some gossip, that Delennia's daughter and Dherran's paramour was also Arlen's daughter. Fatherly pride shone from the man's flint-blue eyes as he pressed her forehead with a kiss. Elohl saw her exhale, before she looked her father in the eyes with fierce readiness. Arlen concluded the ceremony, and the hall erupted in victorious roars, the Valenghian Vhinesse ascending the dais to stand with her daughter.

"Is that really Eleshen?" Elohl watched the beautiful warrior descend the dais now that the ceremony was concluded. She accepted a cup of wine from a serving-lad, her eyes strangely sad as she scanned the hall, though other Kingsmen in their Greys moved by, congratulating her. Seeing Elohl standing with Fenton, her gaze fixed. She smiled and began slipping though the crowd with a dancer's grace as Queen Elyasin bade everyone drink and make merry.

"That's Eleshen, alright. Hard as it may be to believe." Fenton tracked her approach. She was soon before them, stepping forward to set a hand to Fenton's shoulder and give him a kiss upon his cheek, her bell-chime voice low and ringing with cheeky laughter.

"Fentleith, you tease!" Eleshen quipped. "I've been looking everywhere for you!"

"Eleshen. Congratulations on your Dhepanship – and your Inking. It looks very well on you." Fenton clinked goblets with her. "You remember Elohl."

Elohl's heart leapt to his throat as those stunning violet eyes pinned him. The woman crossed one arm over her abdomen and beneath her elbow, swirling her goblet as she gave Elohl a very arch gaze with one eyebrow quirked.

"Well! Never thought I'd see the Rennkavi again. After you abandoned me in that *barn* of an inn. I heard you saved a Queen or something? Or was it the world? Oh dear, how could you possibly have kept track of a tagalong innkeeper during all that? Good thing I learned how to use my fry-pan after all."

"And a sword. And longknives. And *wyrria.*" Fenton chuckled into his wine, grinning.

"Eleshen!" Elohl couldn't believe it. She was entirely different, and yet, it was her. Her fierce, teasing pout that grinned around the edges. The fire in those defiant eyes. The way she crossed her arm just so, to make sure he knew where her breasts were, and that her chest had a stark Blackmark upon it now. She was Eleshen, even though Elohl could barely reconcile her manner in this new warrior's body.

"Hey, Kingswoman! Eleshen! Come here and get some congratulations!"

Elohl didn't have a moment to speak before Ihbram strode up, his russet braids clean and oiled and his beard trimmed, looking dashing in a crimson and gold jerkin similar to Fenton's and also tooled with the Wolf and Dragon. Wrapping Eleshen in a swaddling hug, he lifted her off the ground with a roaring laugh, and she shoved him off in a playful manner. It wasn't sexual, but sibling-esque, and it punched Elohl in the heart. Eleshen puffed up her chest at Ihbram, who playfully put out a hand to touch her Inkings, before she slapped his fingers away with a feisty laugh.

"You're such a bitch," Ihbram chuckled, massaging his hand.

"And *you're* a rogue!" Eleshen laughed. But her levity was arrested as she glanced at Elohl.

"Interrupt much, son of mine?" Fenton lifted a goblet from a server's tray, handing it to Ihbram. "Elohl and Eleshen were just getting reacquainted."

"Oh! Well. I think that pillar over there needs some judicious loitering." Ihbram had the grace to look chagrined. Eleshen's skin flushed, her gaze flicking away from Elohl's. But as Ihbram made to withdraw, nudging Fenton to join him, Eleshen reached out and snagged Fenton by the elbow.

"Stay."

Ihbram and Fenton exchanged a look. "We'll be just over there, getting a bite," Fenton nodded to a spot ten paces off, near a table laden with desserts and pies. Eleshen nodded, and Ihbram and his father moved off, though Ihbram and Fenton both gave a warning glance back to Elohl – a glance that spoke volumes.

Eleshen was fidgeting with her fingers when Elohl looked back. She was so different, but her mannerisms were the same. As he watched, she drew her long sable braid over her shoulder and began fiddling with the end of that instead. It made Elohl smile, and she looked up, meeting his gaze at last.

"I don't know quite what to say," she spoke plainly. "I'm so – so angry at you."

"You have every right to be." It hurt too much to say more, so Elohl lapsed into quiet.

Eleshen glanced over, and Elohl's gaze followed. To see

Ghrenna, lingering at her pillar, sipping and watching the crowd. She looked around, saw them watching, and looked away again.

"I thought—" Eleshen spoke again. "I thought you two would be together now."

"So did I." Elohl's words were stone as they dropped from his lips.

"Perhaps some things aren't meant to be."

Elohl heard too much in Eleshen's simple statement. He heard the deep knell of fate, like a resounding gong sounding a destiny he didn't want. He heard a chorus of dark laughter, like the celestial Void mocking him. He heard his own heartbreak in those words, and something else, that tore him apart more than his own woe.

He heard the darkness inside Eleshen, something she'd only hinted at before.

"I thought I could love you." Eleshen's arm cradled herself tight, her fingertips gripping her goblet, white. "I thought we could have a simple future, together. Fighting the good fight for truth and justice. I didn't even realize how naive I was until everything twisted. From right to wrong. From light to darkness. From known to... strange." She took a deep breath, and Elohl waited. "I'd like to apologize to you, Elohl."

"What do you mean?" Confusion flooded Elohl, feeling like he should have been the one apologizing. He stepped closer, feeling an urge to touch her, but she held up a quick hand.

"No. I need to get this out." Taking a long breath, she started again. "I need to apologize for following you that day on the road. If I hadn't, you would never have gone up to Gerrov-Tel. You'd never have been Goldenmarked. You'd never have been pulled around so cruelly by the weaves of fate. I see it in your eyes, how much you desire the steadiness of home and hearth. But I knew the moment you stepped up my porch-boards, that you were a man whose heart could never let him rest until he found *the one* that made him complete. I knew, but I pushed. I'm sorry. For both our sakes."

All words dropped from Elohl's lips. He stood staring at her, feeling too much. Feeling everything he had endured these past six months. Everything he had lost, all the ways life had uprooted him. And yet, staring down into Eleshen's lovely face, he couldn't blame her for that. Eleshen had been the instigator for him to take the path up to Hahled's Alranstone, but if she'd not been there, who was to say he'd not have been called on his own. He didn't know what expression was on his face, but something broke in Eleshen's eyes as he stood there, silent.

Her gaze shying away, Eleshen stepped in and gave him a peck on the cheek. "Don't hate me, Elohl. Please. I couldn't bear it."

Moving off to Fenton and Ihbram, she left Elohl standing alone by the pillar.

The party suddenly had no flavor left in it. Like a shadow, Elohl downed his drink and set it upon a server's tray, then turned and threaded through the greenery to the rear of the hall. Slipping out, he turned a corner and moved down a secondary stairwell, lit only by torches guttering in iron sconces. He wasn't even certain where his feet were taking him. Led by a tingle of his foot here, a brush of his leg there, he finally exited the palace through an ironbound side-door into a snowy midnight courtyard drowning with the scent of roses.

His *wyrria* chose the way, forming a ghostly picture of his surroundings of ferns and trees and gravel paths in the night. Some part of Elohl registered the familiarity of the garden, drowning in a midnight hush – the same side-door and garden he'd come through ten years ago when he'd first stolen into Roushenn on his dire errand. The specter of that time breathed around him in the night as he passed under archways and trellises, his feet crunching softly in the moonlit snow. Until he stopped, gazing down, and sank to his knees with his forehead resting upon Olea's sarcophagus.

Entombed in an elegant coffin made of smooth clear quartz, Olea's body was clad in Kingsmen Greys, her features restored to a timeless loveliness by the *wyrria* flowing through the crystal. But her beauty could not belie the pale cast of death in her features, nor the stiffness with which her fingers clasped the hilts of two Alrashemni longknives crossed atop her chest. Elohl's shoulders heaved. His heart cracked. Misery came flooding out in a terrible wave, and soon he was down upon his hands and knees in the snow, screaming.

The courtyard was emptied; no one came for him. No hands touched his hair to comfort him. No lips found his cheek to kiss away his grief. No hearts wound through his, to warm him upon this darkest winter midnight.

Until they did. A gentle hand touched Elohl's hair and he startled. Flashing to his feet with one hand upon his longknife, his heart pounded, his head wild like an animal. With steady eyes, Ghrenna stood her ground before him. Morvein Vishke – a wealth of heartache lining her lovely face.

"What do you want?" Elohl rasped, removing his hand from his blade with a will.

"She was your sister?" The white witch breathed, her gaze flicking to Olea's beautiful tomb.

"She was more than that." Elohl choked and turned away, staring at Olea's loveliness rather than face the woman behind him.

"Twinned souls." Morvein's low alto breathed through the crystal night as she moved to his side. Reaching out, she stroked the tomb. "My Brother Kings were twins, too – twinned souls. Where one went, the other was sure to follow. Where one had passion, the other did also. Though they were so different – my light and my darkness."

Elohl had nothing to say to that, and so said nothing.

"I miss them, you know," she spoke again. "They were my own true loves, just as you believe me to be yours. But all things sunder to time. I cursed my beloveds to writhe in misery for eons inside their Alranstones. All so that I could bring you – the Rennkavi – to this world."

Turning, she set a hand upon his arm, and Elohl couldn't help but face her. Gazing up at him with an ancient pain in her cerulean eyes, she gave a sad smile. "I don't remember our love, you and I. But something inside me knows it was there. It was bright, and it was good, and every sinew of my body feels it when I look at you. Though I don't love you, you feel like home to me, and that means more than you could ever know. My home is gone – destroyed, so long ago. And the ones I loved are now gone with it. We have nothing left, you and I. Nothing left, but the decisions we now make with the time we still have."

A small smile twitched her full lips, before it was gone. And seeing that smile, standing so close, Elohl suddenly felt his wretched heart cry out. Reaching out, he touched her snow-pale locks, cupping her face with his hand. Sliding a hand to her waist, he moved closer. Everything inside him felt her fire. Everything inside him knew her body, because it sang in tune with his. Everything inside him knew that she and he had been forever changed – the both of them dealt a hand of fate they could never escape. He felt all of her pain and glory, calling him just like her beauty had called him beneath the summer moon so long ago.

Pulling her close, Elohl lowered his lips, feeling their hearts resonate. Smelling her, clean and sweet like pines and wintermint beneath a tundra night. But she turned her head at the last moment. Breathing hard, she set her cheek to his instead. "Forgive me. My heart grieves for other men."

With a twist so deft he hardly felt it, she was out of his arms. And Elohl was once again alone – more thoroughly than he'd been in his entire life.

His heart concussed in his chest. A raw pain gaped inside him, devouring. But no one was there to see his tears now. No one was looking at a man who had lost everything, who had been used by the world and spat out again with more scars ripping through his heart than he wore at his wrists. No one was looking at a man who had aged eons in months, the hard grey of his eyes ravaged now like the climb-weathered skin of his hands. Who bore the Goldenmarks of the Rennkavi with his Blackmark, but who still could not find peace, or a home.

Because home was gone, and could never be returned.

With a gasp that was too hard to be a sob and too soft to be a roar, Elohl turned. Passing a hand over Olea's last rest, he stepped through the snowy courtyard and out a side-arch, into the deep midnight beyond.

* * *

"Thought I might find you down here."

Fenton's voice was smooth in the bitter darkness. Elohl leaned up against the wall of the bluestone cavern beside the massive ironwood doors of the Wolf and Dragon. He remembered this place as an alehouse, but it was different now. The space was open, no chairs and tables or racks of barrels, but full of crates as if it was used for storage. Roushenn's swirling globes gathered near Elohl with a hushed midnight glow, and he moved a hand through the air, brushing at them idly.

"So you found me." Elohl's words sounded flat even to his own ears. Fenton moved into the muted light and watched Elohl a moment, his expression unreadable.

"Come with me. I have something to show you."

"Where?" Elohl didn't rise, just continued moving his hand through those limpid lights.

"Just up the stone bridge, there."

Elohl glanced to where Fenton indicated – to the natural stone bridge that had once backed the wooden bar. The bar was gone, but the stairs carven in the stone up to the bridge's crest were still there. As a breath of midnight wind eased through the cavern from the crevasse high above that led to the rooftops of Roushenn, Elohl regarded the high, narrow arch cutting through the center of the enormous cavern, lit by a collection of swirling orbs. It was graceful in the darkness, like a bridge to some unbeheld realm that might save Elohl from this roaring, cavernous rage he felt inside.

With a hard sigh, Elohl pushed to his feet. Fenton turned, leading the way across the polished bluestone floor to the stairs. They ascended into the cavernous darkness in silence, a cool breeze lipping Elohl from someplace far inside the Kingsmount. Gaining the height, they stepped onto the far end of the bridge, and Fenton gestured to the center of the arch.

"Go ahead."

Knitting his brows, Elohl faced the vaulted arch. White globes swirled away from him as he moved forward upon the narrow stone spar, leaving the bridge in darkness. A hundred-fold stronger than it had ever been, Elohl's sensate sphere pulsed him onward as he moved to the middle of the bridge. Breathing in the cool, massive space, he felt a strange calm come over him. A calm that went deep to his bones, easing his tension and heartache. Easing every sadness and fury his mortal soul carried and breathing it away into that vast black nothingness.

Halting at the center of the bridge, the sensation of emptiness and peace came to completion, and Elohl heaved a sigh. Tension dropped from his shoulders. And as Elohl stood there, gazing into the black, something began to glow. It wasn't his Goldenmarks, but pricks of light in the darkness. As he watched, those pin-pricks strengthened, becoming tiny stars. A million burning lights surrounded Elohl in the dark, like diamonds scattered in the air, each twisting subtly with the same etheric flame that burned through his Goldenmarks.

Mesmerized, Elohl reached out a hand, causing one of the lights to flare at his touch. A brief mirage blossomed in the darkness, of a ravine of red rocks inset with a vaulted doorway, and then the vision shuffled. The lights rearranged, zooming past each other, opening out from pinpricks until the area Elohl had touched filled the cavern and a new constellation filled the darkness.

"What is it?" Elohl asked, mesmerized.

"As near as I can tell," Fenton moved up to stand at his side, "it's a map."

"Of the stars?"

"Not really." Fenton shook his head. "This map doesn't match any star-chart I've ever seen. I think it's a map of portals. Not just through our continent, but through many worlds. Portals like the Alranstones and the Valley of Doors, but far more ancient."

Reaching out, Fenton selected a different light. It flared blue-green and the image of an underwater temple blossomed, before the stars rearranged again. Zooming in more, they were sparser now, as if the map hadn't been charted that far.

"Who made it?" Elohl breathed, his woe tempered in a moment of fascination.

"Who else would mark this cavern with the Wolf and Dragon?"

"Leith Alodwine." Elohl glanced to Fenton, understanding. "He was charting portal-ways on our world?"

"Not just our world." Fenton's fingers selected another spot and an image flared of a jungle with foliage so fiercely red and orange that it smote Elohl's eyes. He saw three suns – one red, one yellow, and one black – before the map rearranged again. "As many worlds as he could find."

"How?" Elohl breathed.

"Even my grandfather's mysteries are mysteries," Fenton murmured, his voice holding wonder and awe. "Just when I thought I knew him from my mother's tales, I hear something different. Too many people assert that he was a good man, trying to do a good thing, even if his power led him astray. The Giannyk Bhorlen told me to investigate what lies inside me, Elohl. A passion so raw and ruinous I've not known what to do with it or how to handle it for centuries. But being at your side, feeling this amazing *wyrria* my grandfather wrought and channeled into your body... some part of me doubts that he did what he did for selfish aims. And now, his power flows through me a hundred times stronger, ever since the ritual opened up *wyrria* upon our world again... I feel it, rushing through me in a tidal wave. And I wonder, how it was possible for Leith Alodwine to hold all that back. And I also wonder, how in a God's age you're managing it, after what I saw on the White Tower."

"You're managing just fine." Elohl turned, eyeballing Fenton.

Fenton held his gaze, then raised his wrist. Turning back the sleeve of his shirt, he bared something Elohl had not noticed upon him before. A solid bracer made of dusky white star-metal the same as his pendant and Leith's ring rode Fenton's forearm. Studded with rubies, it was positively covered in strange sigils, and polished to a high gloss. Fenton rolled up his other sleeve and Elohl saw a matching bracer upon his other forearm.

"These were Leith's," Fenton murmured. "After we brought down Lhaurent, when Khouren died... I went mad for a day or so. I raged through the palace – burning, destroying. I was in a red rage, flooded with terrible power, and grief. I don't know how many people in Roushenn were killed that day, from me blasting through the halls."

"Sweet Aeon," Elohl breathed.

Fenton nodded, his face carefully blank. "But somehow I found myself down here. Here, on this bridge, in the darkness. And when I walked to the center, just as you did now, I came to stillness. I was calmed. Brought to a judicious center-point, a level-headed place where I could feel again, could think again. Roushenn was carven out by Leith because the natural upwelling of *wyrria* here lends itself to a clear mind, and clear emotions. To centeredness, from which good judgement can flow. And Leith chose this place as his study, to think and record all his experiments and trials, and his notes on the world he was building."

"His study? How do you know? And where did you find his bracers?" Elohl asked, gazing around. The lights were beautiful, but the cavern, other than the miscellany in the old bar, was empty.

"Come."

Fenton moved over the arch toward the far wall. His curiosity aroused, Elohl followed. They moved from the lights back to darkness, the portal-chart dimming out behind them. At the rear wall of the cavern, Fenton set his right hand to his left wrist, unfastening the pin that held his left bracer. Collecting the bracer in his right hand, he took a deep breath, and with a horrible shudder, set his bare left hand to the stone.

His eyes flared a twisting red-gold in the darkness. Elohl heard thunder ripple through the cavern, and then vapors of lightning began to curl around Fenton. It was lightning and it wasn't. Elohl stepped back a careful distance, watching. It seemed a mix of the white *wyrric* vapors Elohl's Goldenmarks produced, and also a swirling globe of flickers of lightning. As if Fenton created a galaxy around him in miniature, building its vapors in a lattice. The nodes around him began to brighten, vicious as suns, and with another out-breath, Fenton poured all those nodes through his body and out through his hand, into the wall.

Sigils brightened in a swirling vortex through the stone. It grew like a leviathan, spreading away from Fenton's hand like a writhing beast of white fire. A low growl ripped from Fenton's throat and he shuddered, his body shivering with power so thick it seethed over Elohl's skin like molten rock. He was drowning in the power, choking on it. And when he thought he could take no more, crushed under a weight like Alranstones, the wall beneath Fenton's hand suddenly rippled away – vaporizing before Elohl's eyes.

A vaulted hall lay beyond. Lit by golden candelabrum that rose up from the floor, set with curling white fey-globes, the small antechamber had seven arches leading from it into darkness. Elohl could feel the vastness of it, textures of rock and air alternating in his sensate sphere as the labyrinth burrowed deep into the mountain. Shelving lined the recessed alcoves under the buttressed dome – full of books, scrolls, codices, and cubbies of ancient vellum.

Above it all, facing them with snarls so vivid Elohl could almost hear them roar, was the ever-battling tableau of the Wolf and Dragon. Their gazes pierced Elohl, each of their eyes set with an enormous ruby. Moving forward and unpinning his right bracer,

Fenton set his left palm to the eye of the Dragon, and his right palm to the eye of the Wolf. A thunderclap flashed from his body and tore a scream from his throat, as a rush of etheric fire went rolling down each of the halls in its wake. Fenton collapsed to his knees and Elohl rushed in fast to catch him from falling to his face upon the polished stone floor.

Fenton breathed hard, his body a rictus of pain, his eyes burning with fire. Trembling like a live wire in Elohl's grasp, he clipped each bracer back into place and set the pins. Only once they were solidly on did he start to lose that dire shiver. At last, he was able to exhale a shaky breath and sit on his own, though he didn't yet stand.

"What in Aeon's name was that?" Elohl breathed, astounded.

"*That* was the *wyrria* of Khehem," Fenton growled. "And *this* is what it unlocks."

"What is this place?" Elohl asked as he helped Fenton up to his feet.

"I believe it's my grandfather's library," Fenton said with a wry chuckle. "But every damn book or scroll I pick up I can't make heads or tales of. I've not told anyone else about this place yet, though eventually Elyasin will need to know. I've only found one section I can read so far, down that tunnel." He gestured to the tunnel furthest left. "A section that seems to be planning journals and diagrams for Leith's palaces, written in Old Khehemni. But if we're going to find any knowledge about who Leith really was, and what he was up to, making your Goldenmarks to unite the world, with the strange and unsettling effect of turning you into a mythic beast – we'll find it here."

Gazing around the vaulted antechamber, Elohl felt a strange uplifting in his heart. It was still cavernous, but standing here, feeling the immensity of Leith Alodwine's design, he suddenly felt part of something greater – as if all his woe and wrath served a purpose.

"I heard it Fenton," Elohl spoke as he stared down the leftmost hall, now rippling with etheric flame in candle-sconces all along its shadowed vaults. "When I was about to kill Lhaurent on the White Tower. I heard the Red-Eyed Demon. It spoke to me, inside my mind. It wanted me to finish Lhaurent."

"I heard it, too," Fenton breathed beside Elohl. "It came to me when I burned Lhaurent's eyes out of his smug face in Roushenn's throne hall. And it stayed all the rest of that day, inside me... until I found my way here. I was called to Leith's bracers. I clapped them onto my wrists like the manacles they are, and haven't left them long off my body since. They dampen my urge to use my power – as I'm sure they once must have done for Leith."

Elohl stood, silent, absorbing that terrible revelation. At last, he turned to Fenton, the both of them sharing a long silence fraught with ancient pain and new fear.

"The Red-Eyed Demon," Elohl spoke at last. "Why does it want us? And why did Leith Alodwine build all this against its rise?"

"Find out with me, Elohl," Fenton spoke, reaching out to grip his shoulder. "I inherited my grandfather's terrible and tremendous *wyrria*, and you inherited his Goldenmarks, the pinnacle of his magical creations. There are factions of Leith's out there that I've let run riot, that need tending to, like the Kreth-Hakir Brethren. They know things I don't. Things my grandfather told them that I never learned. With the knowledge in this place, and ferreting out Leith's lackeys, perhaps we can answer these riddles. And maybe... maybe we can get some peace, when all this is over."

"Peace." The word felt foreign to Elohl. "And what about Ghrenna?"

Fenton reached out, gripping Elohl's shoulders with a kind firmness. "If there's anyone who could answer Ghrenna's dilemma, of how or why Morvein was able to take over her body after the Rennkavi's Ritual, it would be Leith Alodwine."

Reaching up, Elohl set his hands to Fenton's bared forearms above his bracers. At their skin contact, Elohl's Goldenmarks lit with a simmering glow, water-light patterns rippling through the antechamber. Fenton's eyes sparked with red-gold flames in response, and the two of them shared a breath in the ancient silence.

"We'll find answers, Elohl," Fenton murmured, setting his forehead to Elohl's. "I promise it. Don't give up. Don't give in to that darkness I feel inside you – the darkness that the Undoer wants to manipulate inside both of us. We're family, and we'll find what we require, to get the answers we need. Together."

"Together." Resting his forehead against Fenton's, a subtle strength sighed through Elohl. Curling with coils and muscled with fangs, it moved through their embrace with a languid grace. And as the Wolf and Dragon fought in their ever-dance upon the wall beside them, Elohl felt solace ease into his heart at last.

He wasn't alone. Whatever happened, wherever his journey led – he didn't have to be a lone wolf any longer.

EPILOGUE – JHERRICK

"Kehefnet! Khehfnet, lethnai!"

Jherrick groaned, waking from a black fugue, back into his wretched body. Wind whipped past his face and he had the sensation of movement, as if he flew through the air upon wings.

But that wasn't right. He was on his back, bundled in a quilt stuffed with bird down. Tawny feathers escaped the finely-woven red silk and tickled his nose as Jherrick turned his head to escape the small torture. Then wished he hadn't. A rolling sickness gripped his gut, and he clenched his teeth as his head pounded with a ten-day ache.

"Ah! Soubrithi ahkelnet!"

A man's voice spoke, and a strong hand cradled Jherrick's head, helping him lift up enough to drink from a leather flask. Warm water touched his lips, smooth with salts and fats. Jherrick drank and licked his lips, tasting butter of some kind, then drank more. The man cradling his head chuckled, and when Jherrick had taken his fill, the fellow let him rest.

Jherrick's head fell back into a pile of softness. He rested upon a thick mattress of feathers – he could feel them scratching through the silk upon his naked body. The wind sped by and Jherrick risked opening his eyes again, finding them less parched and gluey than before. Blue sky shone above, a beautiful dawn just ended to the east in pink and rose gold. Pinnacles of rock raced by, and Jherrick realized he was on a sledge of some kind, being whipped through the just-warming desert at a healthy pace. He heard the constant whisper of sand passing beneath the runners of the sledge, and a chorus of honking and hissing, like a flight of geese.

Trying to lift his head, Jherrick sought the origin of the noise. And was pressed back to the mattress by a kind, firm hand.

"You'll not want to move just yet." A man spoke to him in an amused baritone, his language a heavily-accented version of Old

Khehemni. Jherrick blinked up, and the man shaded Jherrick's eyes from the sun, so Jherrick could see his face.

And saw someone he never thought he'd see again.

"You!" Jherrick responded, speaking Old Khehemni back.

"You have some strength in you, *lethnim*." The Last King of Khehem, Leith Alodwine's golden eyes sparkled with wit as he pulled down a facewrap of grey silk to show a pleased smile upon his lips. "I thought we were going to lose you. You had traveled so very far out into the Void when my Berounhim found you. They thought you might never come back. And to tell you honestly, *ahlanati*... I wasn't sure you'd come back, either."

"The Blood Plinth." Jherrick croaked. Leith Alodwine offered him the flask again, and Jherrick drank deep of the refreshing water, feeling his mind clear a bit more.

"Blood Plinth?" Leith cocked his head, humor showing his golden-cinnabar eyes. "I do not know of such a thing, but it takes a strong will to come through a *Khehemnat Ithir*, a Way of the Ancients, without losing one's life or one's mind. I am pleased to see you still have both."

"Small pleasures." Jherrick struggled to sit up. Every bone in his body screamed at him. He grit his teeth, feeling like his body was made of glass, grating like the sand that whipped through the air. But he managed it, keeping the blanket wrapped around his nakedness. Leith let him manage his own body, rising to step to the front of the sledge and speak a few words to a man there who handled the reins.

Jherrick blinked, finally realizing what they rode in. It was a sledge, like the infamous dog-sledges of the far north in Elsthemen, but was constructed of some kind of tough, woven reeds. Lightweight, it hummed over the dunes upon wide runners of some thick yet flexible maroon material, and had a high crimson sail tooled with the Wolf and Dragon lofted from a clever series of pulleys to catch the morning wind and push the vehicle along. Six *berounhim* in dark grey desert silks sat crosslegged in the sledge, polishing weapons and talking amongst themselves. Some glanced at Jherrick with approving smiles. Jherrick caught a glimpse of the front of the sledge beyond the driver as they rounded a turn beside a tall pillar of red rock, and saw a line of two-by-six enormous, flightless birds running the sand with bony webbed feet and necks outstretched, pulling the sledge behind their traces.

The lean man standing at the driver's platform had their reins firmly in hand and leaned back against their pull like a Ghreccani charioteer. He shouted a few words against the wind to Leith, who nodded, clapped him on the shoulder, and stepped back to Jherrick's pallet.

"We make good time." Leith hunkered again by Jherrick, swaying lithely on the balls of his feet to the sledge's rocking. "We'll be home within the hour."

"Home?" Jherrick gazed around, seeing nothing but dunes and the occasional upthrust crag of rock. A swath of cliffs flanked them to the east, blue in the lightening morning – rising like a dragon's spine and continuing southward behind them.

"Khehem." Leith eyed him as the sledge bumped over a hard-packed area, then hissed through dunes. "You are from Khehem, are you not? Your *wyrria*, your accent, your manner – they are strange, but I feel the beat of the *Werus et Khehem* inside you. All those tales you told me in that strange realm – you had me worried, *lethnim*! But Khehem was safe upon my return, as you shall also see. Our city stands strong – the fairest jewel of the Tribes! Come. I have attire for you. We did our best to clean the sand off you, but you'll have a proper bath when we reach the palace. And whatever clothes you desire when we arrive. Whatever a King can do for you for saving his life, he shall. *Thouliet dannoua Khehem, yethan chelis.* Your heart remembers Khehem, and so my heart remembers you."

The man offered soft grey silks and a harness of weapons, his eyes honest. Jherrick accepted them, his brows knit in confusion, feeling as if he was still lost out in the Void. He shucked the quilt, not caring that the *berounhim* caravanserai gave nods of approval at his exposed body. Three of them were women, but they did not linger lecherously as he began to pull on the tight-fitted silk trousers. The shirt went on over his head and he pulled the laces, next donning the stiffer silk of the charcoal-grey jerkin over that, the jerkin's hood falling down his back behind its high collar. Leith extended a headwrap of a diaphanous grey silk to wind around Jherrick's neck, and he did. He pulled on knee-high leather boots soft as doeskin, and thrust two daggers into the boot-sheaths.

Buckling on the weapons harness and touching cold steel, he finally felt something like himself again.

The King of Khehem nodded, curious approval shining from his eyes.

Though there was also caution. Jherrick regarded the man back as the desert sped by, the rocky ridge ending and a hard, flat plain extending to the northern horizon. They bumped over stone, and Jherrick heard the tone of the runners change as they sped along a wide, flat white promenade of perfectly-fitted and polished flagstones. It went north to the mirage upon the horizon, as the day sizzled to a rising heat.

Jherrick didn't trust this man who had so blatantly started a war in the Noldarum's realm. Who claimed to be the long-lost King of a dead city. Jherrick didn't know if the man was delusional – it certainly was possible given the tremendous *wyrria* Jherrick had seen extend from him during the battle with Archaeon. But the man gave Jherrick equally careful eyes back. Though he had pledged his support for Jherrick saving his life – and he'd saved Jherrick's life twice now – he seemed equal parts curious and wary about Jherrick.

They held a tense silence as the sledge pulled by honking birds sped over the causeway. Suddenly, the driver gave a sharp whistle that sliced the morning air. Leith rose to his feet, raising his hood against the sun's glare and gazing to the north. A broad smile eased across his face, and he gave a throaty laugh of amiable pleasure. Clapping the driver upon the shoulder, he returned to Jherrick and offered a hand. "We've arrived."

"Arrived? You mean in Khehem? What's to see but blasted stone and ruin?" But Jherrick accepted the man's hand up, though every bone protested. He found his feet upon the reeds of the sledge, rocking like balancing in a boat at sea.

Leith clapped his shoulder and ushered him to the front of the sledge for a better view. The driver glanced at them as Jherrick stared out over the desert, seeing a city rising in the north like a leviathan from the deep. Two cities, one to the northwest and the other to the northeast. Like twin jewels, they commanded the land, their walls white and pristine in the high morning sun. As Jherrick watched the landmarks grow, he saw a causeway between them, formed of uninterrupted archways stretching all the way from one fair city to the other. The walls of both cities loomed toward the sky, and Jherrick saw greenery flooding over their reaches now, extending in patches of grasslands beyond the walls, where goats and other animals were being grazed.

Flocks of birds soared above, issuing throaty calls like mynahs. More of the flightless birds like the ones that pulled the sledge were kept in pens as the causeway neared a broad intersection with the pillared road. Jherrick saw fountains flanking the road now, where herders ushered their flocks to drink. Caravans of sledges similar to the one Jherrick rode but far more robust and filled with trade goods, stopped at the fountains to water their crew.

Crimson and gold pennants of the Wolf and Dragon fluttered from the sails of these, and the drivers hailed Leith's sledge with a shout and a wave. Leith stepped to the sledge's rim, grasping a sail-line and shouting a pleasantry back, before twisting his hand and throwing a curling, lively red-gold flame toward the sky. Trader's children shrieked with delight as they sped by, and herders waved.

Jherrick blinked, staring stunned at it all, as they turned up the pillared causeway and headed west, an enormous city rising before them. The causeway was crowded with a morning trade-rush, and Leith's sledge had to slow. They continued at a promenade-speed, herders moving their flocks as tall Alrashemni-looking people clad in colorful silks bowed backward with baskets of goods upon their heads.

Spearmen clad just like Lourden's warriors in red-crested silver helms vaulted to the rim of the sledge using their spears to pole them up. One with a silver breastplate imprinted with the Wolf and Dragon exchanged a few low words with Leith, who nodded, his face grim. At last, Leith signaled the man away. He vaulted down from the sledge, giving a sharp whistle to his cadre of spearmen and assembling into a vanguard following in the sledge's wake.

The doors to the walled city were thrown wide in the early morning. As the sledge whisked under that massive portcullis, hale and without a hint of char marring its luminous beauty, they pulled into the same wide plaza Jherrick remembered. But this plaza overflowed with greenery, burbling fountains, and people moving through a morning trade-market of colorful silk booths and stalls. As Jherrick watched it all, stunned, Leith clapped him upon the shoulder again.

"Khehem! Is she not the fairest jewel of the Tribes, my friend? Welcome home, Khehemnas. No matter how far your journey has been."

Jherrick stared around him in awe, seeing this very alive city, and contrasting it with the one he had seen that had been so very dead. But where that city had been a place of broken walls and shadow, of burned rock and ghosts, this was truly the oasis it claimed to be. A cool breeze whispered across Jherrick's skin, shaking the wide fronds of the towering palms, their shade shivering over his skin. Vines of jasoune-sweet white blossoms coated the inner walls and issued an intoxicating fragrance upon the morning air. Hummingbirds whizzed past, dipping their beaks into the long white flutes and taking nectar. Children ran by, shrieking in their colorful silk wraps, chasing the hummingbirds.

Jherrick gazed out upon Khehem, the oasis of the Wolf and Dragon, as their King, Leith Alodwine, vaulted from the sledge and greeted his people with a roaring laugh and embraces.

The King of Khehem was home. And Khehem surged around him with fire and life – hale and whole as if their war had never been.

THE END

The adventure continues in DRAGON OF THE DESERT, book one of *The Khehemni Chronicles*

Did you enjoy this book? Please leave a review at your favorite online retailer!

ABOUT JEAN LOWE CARLSON

Amazon bestselling and award-winning author Jean Lowe Carlson writes epic and adventurous fantasy fiction. Her raw and extensive worlds have been compared to such fantasy names as Robert Jordan, Brandon Sanderson, George R.R. Martin, Joe Abercrombie, and Patrick Rothfuss.

Jean holds a doctorate in Naturopathic Medicine (ND), and has a keen awareness of psychology and human behavior, using it to paint vivid characters set amidst nations in turmoil or societies with riveting secrets. Exciting, challenging, and passionate, her novels take the reader upon dire adventures while exploring deep human truths.

In 2016, she was the recipient of the Next Generation Indie Book Awards Finalist medal for her dark fantasy novel "Tears".

Find out more at: https://www.jeanlowecarlson.com/

APPENDIX 1 — PRONUNCIATION GUIDE

Word Beginnings:

Dh/Jh/Kh/Lh – Hard consonant, "h" is silent (Ex. Dherran [Dair-ren] like "dare", Jherrick [Jair-rick] like "jester", Khouren [Koor-en] like "kick", Lhaurent [Lao-rahnt] like "laugh")

Gh/G – Hard "g" sound (Ex. Ghrenna [Gren-na], Gherris [Gair-ris] like "good")

Ih – Long "ee" sound (Ex. Ihbram [Ee-brum] like "helium")

Th – Soft "th" combination (Ex. Theroun [Thair-oon] like "thespian")

Uh/U – Long "oo" sound (Ex. Uhlas [Oo-las] like "tulips")

O – Proper "oh" sound if begins a word (Ex. Olea [Oh-lay-a] like "ocean")

El – Open "eh" sound (Ex. Elohl [Eh-loll] like "elephant")

Il – Soft "ihl" sound (Ex. Ildrian [Ihl-dree-an] like "ill")

Middle of Words:

-i- If in the middle of a word, long "ee" sound (Ex. Elyasin [Ehl-ya-seen] like "do re mi")
Exception: Aldris [Al-dris, not Al-drees]

-ch- Soft "sh" sound (Ex. Suchinne [Soo-sheen])

-ou- Long "oo" sound (Ex. Roushenn [Roo-shen] like "frou-frou")

PHRASES IN HIGH ALRAKHAN:

Alrashemnesh ars veitriya rhovagnetari! Toura Corunenne!
Alrashemni are the true protectors! Long live the Queen!

PHRASES IN OLD KHEHEMNI:

Imendhe nethii hakkane!
Immortal ripping underworld!

Utrus! Khehe ahlwe——!
The Utrus! Battle it!

Hemna ahlmine!
Stay with me, dammit!

Thouliet dannoua Khehem, yethan chelis.
Remember you to Khehem, with your heart.

Kehefnet! Khehfnet, lethnai!
Hurry, hurry, let's go!

Ah! Soubrithi ahkelnet!
Ah! The dead sleeper awakens!

PHRASES IN LEFKANI:

Agate brithii discenzio!
Burning fires of hell! (Lefkani curse)

SAYINGS / TRANSLATIONS:

OLD KHEHEMNI
Ahlanati – Lord of dusk
Lethnim – Warrior
Shaper and Undoer – A common epithet from Leith's time
Seven fucks of Jeldhaia – An ancient curse from Leith's time

* * *

GIANNYK

Aliri – Light / enlightenment
Heldi – Memory / remember
Heldi aliri – Place of Enlightened Memory
Helta Wyrrin – High Magus
Karakhan nikh Obderheim – Riddle of the Obelisks
Kruk-heyya – Harvest / reaping
Utrus – Red-Eyed Demon
Warrik schlafin k'Utrus – Sleeping Warriors of the Undoer
Wyrrdani – Spirit / essence / wyrria

ELSTHEMI

Fenrir rakhne – Wolf's hells
Haldakir – Brute
Khrakane vishken – Kraken's talons
Kotar's Balls

CENNETIAN

Generalisso d'Iscurro – General of the Darkness aka King of Poisoners
Putistena – Whore
Gottio! – My God!

VALENGHIAN

My Living Vine – The way subjects address the Valenghian
Vhinesse

LEFKANI

Ghendii – "Fallen One", a term used by Lefkani Pirates

713

APPENDIX 2 – CHARACTERS

Elsthemen / Heldim Alir:
Therel Alramir – King of Alrou-Mendera and Elsthemen
Elyasin den'Ildrian Alramir – Queen of Alrou-Mendera and Elsthemen
Thaddeus den'Lhor – Queen's Chronicler
Luc den'Lhorissian – Queen's Physician
Ghrenna den'Tanuk – Alrashemni Kingswoman, Morvein Vishke reincarnated
Merra Alramir – High General of Elsthemen, older sister to Therel
Rhone and Rhennon Uhlki – Second-Captains to General Merra, twin brothers
Miri – A keshari rider, one of Merra's lieutenants
Mikka Khuriye – First Scout of the Bhorlen Rangers
Morvein Vishke (deceased) – High Dremorande to the Brother Kings
Hahled Ferrian – One of the Brother Kings of Elsthemen
Delman Ferrian – One of the Brother Kings of Elsthemen
Trevius Stranik (deceased) – King of the Giannyk, Heimhold Giannyk Clan
Vrennen Stranik – A Portalsmilth of the Heimhold Giannyk Clan
Bhorlen Valdaris – Master Portalsmith of the Dhuvvin Giannyk
Ulfgrad Stranik – Father of Trevius Stranik and the Four Giannyk Princes
Metholas Leifne (deceased) – Scribe to Morvein

Elsthemen / Ligenia / Kreth-Hakir:
Theroun den'Vekir – ex-General, Black Viper of the Aphellian Way
Khorel Jornath – A High Priest of the Kreth-Hakir
Metrene den'Yesh – The Kingstone, High Mistress of the Kreth-Hakir
Vitreal den'Bhorus – Captain of the Fleetrunners
Lhesher Khoum – Highsword to King Therel
Jhonen Rebaldi – First-Captain to General Merra, Dremor
Adelaine Visek – High Dremorande of Elsthemen
Magnus Yesh – High Master of the Kreth-Hakir
Brother Antonius Ossenheim – A Valenghian Brother of the Kreth-

Hakir
Brother Kiiar dhim'Erle – High Priest of the Watch of the Kreth-Hakir
Brother Caldrian hek'Khim – Priest of Wrath of the Kreth-Hakir
Brother Arlo del'Vonio – Priest of Letters of the Kreth-Hakir
Brother Coralim hek'Enni – Brother of the Kreth-Hakir
Brother Arno del'Legate – Brother of the Kreth-Hakir
Sage Pierce (deceased) – A Sage of the Kreth-Hakir
Lissendra del'Mira (deceased) – Theroun's wife
The Black Bastard – Theroun's black keshar-cat

Elsthemi Clans:
Blackthorn – Outriders, patrol Bhorlen Mountains near Valenghia
White Claws – Merra's personal guard, her most elite keshari warriors
Split Fangs – Merra's secondary guard

Valenghia:
Elohl den'Alrahel – First-Lieutenant of the High Brigade, twin to Olea
Fenton den'Kharel / Alodwine – First-Lieutenant of the Roushenn Palace Guard, Scion of Khehem
Dherran den'Lhust – Alrashemni Kingsman
Khenria den'Bhaelen – Friend to Dherran
Grump (aka Grunnach den'Lhis) – Friend to Dherran, the Greyhawk
Aelennia Oblitenne – The Vhinesse, Queen of Valenghia "The Living Vine"
Delennia Oblitenne – House of Oblitenne, once-lover to Arlen den'Selthir
Emeris ven'Khern – Personal Guard to Delennia
Chancellor ven'Rhenni – A Chancellor to the Vhinesse
Merkhenos del'Ilio – High General of Valenghia
Ghirano del'Letti – Red Valor Guard to Merkhenos
King Eleps des'Levanne – King of Praough
Greghane des'Finnes – Praoughian General at the Aphellian Way
Suxisse Osenneaux – Valenghian General at the Aphellian Way
Lieutenant des'Pannes – Valenghian Watch at the Aphellian Way

Suchinne den'Thaon (deceased) – A Kingswoman, first love to Dherran

Ennalea den'Alrahel / Alodwine (deceased) – Elohl and Olea's mother

Levennia del'Mira (deceased) – Fenton's first wife, Cennetian

Iccio del'Carrini of Legate (deceased) – Cennetian King

Roushenn Palace:
Lhaurent den'Alrahel / den'Karthus – Rennkavi

Khouren Alodwine – The Ghost of Roushenn

Ihbram den'Sennia / Alodwine – Veteran High Brigade

Arthe den'Tourmalin – King of the Tourmaline Isles

Uhlas den'Ildrian (deceased) – King of Alrou-Mendera

Alden den'Ildrian (deceased) – Dhenir of Alrou-Mendera

Evshein den'Lhamann (deceased) – King's Chancellor

Elemnia del'Letti (deceased) – Khouren's old Cennetian flame

Jhorenni al'Ban (deceased) – A lord of the Lhemvian Isles

Ruitia del'Mar (deceased) – Cennetian noble lover of Ihbram's

Helene del'Ilio (deceased) – Ihbram's first love

Minareth Alodwine (deceased) – Ihbram's sister

First Abbey of Lintesh / Gerrov-Tel:
Temlin den'Ildrian – King-Protectorate of Alrou-Mendera

Eleshen den'Fenrir – An innkeeper

Mollia den'Lhorissian – The Abbeystone

Brother Sebasos – Kingsman / Jenner brother

Brother Brandin – A young Jenner brother

Sister Nennia den'Thule – A Jenner / Kingswoman

Abbott Lhem den'Ulio (deceased) – Abbot of the Jenners

Abbess Lenuria den'Brac / Alodwine (deceased) – Abbess of the Jenners

Eiric den'Fenrir (deceased) – Dhepan of Quelsis, Eleshen's father

Moonshadow – Eleshen's keshar-cat

Sanctuary of the Noldarum:
Jherrick den'Tharn – Corporal in the Roushenn Palace Guard

Noldrones Flavian – Herald of the Noldarum, Albrenni

Noldra Ethirae – A Sister of the Noldarum, Albrenni

Archaeon Stranik – Giannyk / Albrenni warrior, the Key of Fire
Aldris den'Farahan (deceased) – Second-Lieutenant of the
Roushenn Palace Guard
Olea den'Alrahel (deceased) – Captain-General of the Palace
Guard, twin to Elohl

The Twelve Tribes:
Leith Alodwine (deceased) – Khehem's last King
Alitha Alodwine (deceased) – Leith's daughter / Fentleith's mother,
the Prophetess
Ordeith Alodwine (deceased) – Leith's grandfather, King of
Khehem, a tyrant
Lourden al'Lhesk – Spear-Captain of Oasis Ghellen

The Vault (Vennet):
Vicoute Arlen den'Selthir – Vicoute of Vennet, leader of the
Shemout Alrashemni
Purloch den'Crassis – Master of Purloch's House in the Bog
Khaspar den'Albehout – High General of the Menderian forces at
the Vault
Elyria Kenthar – A Dremor
Bherg – Yenlia's husband, a fighter of the Bog
Yenlia – Bherg's wife, a fighter of the Bog

APPENDIX 3 — PLACES AND THINGS

PLACES

ALROU-MENDERA

LINTESH (The King's City) – City at the base of the Kingsmount
Abbey Quarter – Location of the First Abbey
Tradesman Quarter – Near the Watercourse Gate
Watercourse Gate – Eastern gate of Lintesh

ROUSHENN PALACE – The royal palace at Lintesh
Rose Courtyard – Courtyard of roses in the Third Tier
Throne Hall – High Seat of Alrou-Mendera
King's Tomb – Secret tomb beneath Roushenn

FIRST ABBEY – Of the Jenners
Rare Tomes Room – Catacomb of ancient writings beneath the
Annex
Abbey Annex – Old cathedral of the First Abbey

GERROV-TEL (Mount Gerrov) – Fortress Ruins in the
Kingsmountains, site of Haled's Stone
Upper Gallery at Gerrov-Tel
Southwest tower
Armory catacombs

Alrashesh – First Court of the Alrashemni Kingsmen
Aphellian Way – Site of the Black Viper's slaughter, on the
Thalanout Plain
Bhorlen's Citadel – Ancient Giannyk city beneath the mountains
Bitterwoods – Forest near Vicoute Arlen's manor
Dhemman – Third Court of the Alrashemni Kingsmen
Elesk (The Kingsmount) – By Lintesh
Elhambrian Valley – Valley at the edge of Lintesh
Elsee – Lake in the Eleskis
Fhouria – Home of the Fhouria Thieves' Consortium
Gerson Hills – Location near Vennet

Gerthoun – City on the border of Elsthemen and Alrou-Mendera
Heathren Bog – Enormous bog north of the Aphellian way
(Purloch's Bog)
Hills of the Damned – Barrow-hills in the Thalanout Plain
Khenthar Rhegalatoria – Respite of the Rulers, Molli's valley at the
top of the Kingsmount
Lheshen Valley – In the mountains near Quelsis, has seen vicious
fighting, now well-protected
Long Valley – Valley on the Valenghian border just north of
Purloch's Bog
Pallisade Fhen – Location near Vennet
Port of Ligenia / Ligenia Bay – Coastal city, supply location for the
Aphellian Way
Purloch's House – Purloch's main city in the Heathren Bog
Quelsis – A city in the foothills of Alrou-Mendera
Southern Lethian Valley – Where the Menderian main war-camp is
(Camp Lethia)
Thalanout Plain – Where most of the fighting is against Valenghia
The Eleskis (The Kingsmountains) – Border of Valenghia and
Elsthemen
The Vault – Ancient Albrenni fortress southwest of Vennet
Thickhole Swamp – Swamp near Vicoute Arlen's manor
Vennet – A city on the eastern bogs, home of Vicoute Arlen
den'Selthir

ELSTHEMEN
Lhen Fhekran – Capitol city of Elsthemen
Fhekran Palace – Therel Alramir's palace at Lhen Fhekran
Valley of Doors – On Alrou-Mendera border, has ancient ruins, on
the Lethian Way
Northern Lethian Valley – Where the Elsthemi main war-camp is,
and the Valley of Doors
Lethian Way – An ancient canyon-road up through the river-gorge
in the Lethian Valley
Kherven Valley – The plains approaching Lhen Fhekran from the
west
Bhorlen Mountains – Elsthemi-Valenghian border, aka Bhorlen's
Ring / Bhorlen's Barrier

Mount Veldir – Elsthemi name for the Kingsmount
The Devil's Field – An immensely treacherous glacial crossing into Valenghia from Elsthemen
Lodresh Glacier – Glacier that holds the Devil's Field
Bitterrift Pass – The approach to the Devil's Field
Hokhar – City on the ice tundra
Mount Ghirlaj – Obsidian mountain to the south of the Devil's Field
Cannus Rift – Treacherous sheer gorge north of the Devil's Field
Fithri-Lhis – A lost city up on the ice tundra, home of Morvein
Dhelvendale – Ruined old capitol of Elsthemen
Blackthorn – Clan-fortress
Themi Sea – Eastern inland sea
White Ring – The site of the Rennkavi's Ritual
Heldim Alir – The Way Beneath the Mountain, Memory Vaults of the Giannyk

THE TWELVE TRIBES
Oasis Ghellen – An ancient city east of Khehem, capital of the Twelve Tribes
Oasis Khehem – A dead city west of Ghellen
Chiriit Crevasses/Oasis Chirus – North of Oasis Ghellen, protected by a vicious, secretive people
Oases Lukhaan, Niirm, Drashaan – Coastal oases of the Twelve Tribes
Oases Asyana, Vrenouhem – Northwestern mountain oases
Oasis Onaani – Far southeast mountain oasis
Oasis Aj Naab, Oasis Etrii – Eastern trade oases near the Ajnabiit lands
Oasis Revenhiim – Solitary central desert oasis
Oasis Bel'raa – Southern trade oasis to the Southern Desert (Ghistani lands)
The Blood Plinth – A cave sacred to Khehem

VALENGHIA
Velkennish – Capitol city of Valenghia
Palace of the Vine – The White Palace in Velkennish
Velkennish Valley – Valley where Velkennish is located
Weeping Sepulcher / The Weeping Woman – A weeping statue in

Velkennish
Cemetery of the Fallen – A veterans cemetery in Velkennish
The Falconry – Tower in the White Palace
Obelisk of the Vine – Aka the Stone of Milk and Honey, in the
Obelisk Quarter of Velkennish
Obelisk Quarter – Oldest quarter in Velkennish
Avenue of the Vine – The approach to the White Palace from the
south – Valenghian Royal Houses
Fluss Helmenthal – River in eastern Valenghia
Province of Leddi – Provence in eastern Valenghia
Wayfarer – A ruin in the Heathren Bog near the Aphellian Way

GHREC
Shelf of Lost Hope (Thuruman)
Sea of Ghrec
Ghreccan Desert

CENNETIA
Scovira Province – Northern Cennetia
Duomini – The City of Waterways in the Ciari River delta
Ciari River Delta – A primary river in Cennetia
Tellurium – A city in Cennetia

LHEMVIAN ISLES
Lhemvian Isles – Islands in the Archipelago of Crasos
Althumma – A city on the Lhemvian Isles

OTHER NATIONS
Aj Naab – Ajnabiit lands east of the Twelve Tribes, aka "The
Wasteland"
Cennetia, Praough – Nations annexed by Valenghia
Crasos – Island to the west of Cennetia
Jadoun, Perthe – Southwest countries to Alrou-Mendera
Southern Desert – Lands south of the Twelve Tribes (Ghistani
nomads)
Thuruman (Cape of Lost Hope) – Far eastern nation
Tourmaline Isles – Islands southwest of Alrou-Mendera
Unaligned Lands – To the northeast, nomadic lands

* * *

NOLDARUM'S REALM
Sanctuary of the Great Void – A citadel of learning and light
The Memorarium – Memory-chamber in the Sanctuary
Tomb of the World Shaper – Sacred resurrection tomb
The Void – The great cosmic space with souls live

THINGS
Aeon – God of the Air, like Zeus
Age of Chaos – The time of the Demon's Rise
Agne wyrdi (Creator *wyrria*) – The ability to create de-novo
Albrennus Fellasti of the First Darkening – aka the Albrenni
Alrashemni Kingsmen – Elite fighters and peacekeepers sworn to
the King of Alrou-Mendera
Annihilation – A Kreth-Hakir rite that breaks the mind into
complete destruction
Ashwood – A pale wood common to Valenghia
Asye wyrdi – Undoer *wyrria*, destroys anything
Aurus excelsianni – The the soul-excelsior finch, colorful and sings
Autumn Harvestfest – Autumnal celebrations in Alrou-Mendera
Barrow-vampires – Souls that haunt barrows
Beast's Awakening – A latent-awakened *wyrria* trying to
spontaneously change a person's flesh
Berlunid – Elsthemi battle-goddess
Berounhim – Caravanserai for the Twelve Tribes, their most elite
warriors
Bhorlen Rangers – Elsthemi rangers in the Highmountains
Byrunstone (Bluestone) – Common bluegrey stone in Alrou-
Mendera
Cendarie – Like a cedar tree
Champelion – A burgundy wine from Valenghia
Children of the Sands – Heart *wyrrics,* able to change future
outcomes
Citrene – Citrus
Commoner's Audience – The hearing of common petitions in
Valenghia
Consummation of the Goldenmarks – The final event in the

Rennkavi's Ritual

Council of the Coalition – Council of seven nations for a peace treaty

Darkwinter Night / Darkwinter Fest – Celebrations of winter solstice

Demon's First Rise – When the Red-Eyed Demon rose during the Albrenni / Giannyk Wars

Diamanne scorpions – southern desert scorpions, ridden by Kreth-Hakir

Dildrum the Egg-Man – Old nursery rhyme of Alrou-Mendera

Djinni – Elemental beings of the southern deserts

Dremor / Dremorande – An Elsthemi seer, with accurate visions

Elio lizard – A small green gecko with a yellow throat and a red stripe down its back

First Pact of the Coalition

First Rite of Proving – The first rite of passage in the Kreth-Hakir Order to become Initiate

Fleetrunners and High Brigade – Elite military brigades of Alrou-Mendera

Fyrrini – An ancient race, "born of salt and ash", keepers of the Key of Fire

Ghenje – A strategy game, like Go

Giannyk – A race of giant men from the north, *wyrric* portal- and sigil-makers – clans of Krethwathsten, Heimhold, Hakkim Beldir

Giannyk-Albrenni Wars – Ancient wars over 5000 years ago

Goldenmarked – Marked as the Rennkavi by Leith's *wyrric* sigils

Halsos – Like Hades, a god

Halsos' Hells / Halsos' Burnwater – Hell

Hellenthine quartzite – A smoky crystal

Heraldation – The Kreth-Hakir meeting for discussion of important events

Highsummer – Summer solstice

Honoress of the Albrenni – The Albrenni's High Priestess

Honoring of the Fallen – Ceremony to honor those who die in battle (Alrou-Mendera)

Illianti / Sons of Illium – Famous secret group of assassins in Cennetia

Ironpine – A stout hardwood

Jenner's Penitent – An order of monks in Lintesh at the First Abbey

Jinne wyrdi (Heart magic) – Aka jinnic *wyrria*, the magic of the pure heart

Kaf-Tesh – A relative of the coffee plant, native to Cennetia

Karthor – Elsthemi god of war

Keshar – A large battle-cat/saber-tooth cat, like a cougar but huge

Khehe wyrdi (Conflict magic) – Wolf and Dragon *wyrria*

Khehemnat Ithir – A Way of the Ancients, a portal in old Khehem

khemri-venom – Venom that gives Alrashemni fever-dreams for the Eighth Seal

Khets al'Roch – A massive black beast, lean with razor claws and fangs

Kiani-Hithrai – A battle to the death or domination, to ascend through the Kreth-Hakir

King Trevius' Sleep – Elsthemi fae-tale

Kingskinder – Children of the Alrashemni, not yet 21

Kotar – Elsthemi god of sexual stamina

Kreth-Hakir – Mind-bending monks from the Unaligned Lands, aka "Scorpions"

Kruk-tan – The Giannyk scythe symbol

Lefkani – Pirating culture from the west of Ghrec

Leithren / Khehemni Lothren – High council of the Khehemni, once aligned with Leith

Louve wyrdani – Dusk warrior, one who wields Dusk wyrria

Louve wyrdi – Dusk *wyrria* (Jherrick's magic)

Madrona – A red-wooded tree of the A-M lowlands

Mind of the Brethren – The Kreth-Hakir hive mind

Olea lithii – The Peace Olive, a dark and succulent fruit

Pact of the Coalition – Peace treaty of seven nations

Palladian – A costly white metal from Valenghia, more expensive than gold

Path of Initiate – becoming an Initiate among the Kreth-Hakir

Path of the Dead – Initiation rite for Dusk magic, aka "Way of the Dusk"

Pearlwood – A white wood found in Valenghia

Perthian rugs – Finest rugs in the continent

Pythian Resin – A flesh-eating resin, burns green/yellow

Rakhan –The leaders of the Alrashemni Kingsmen

Red Valor – Elite guards of Valenghia
Rennkavi's oath – Oath Fenton created to bind his bloodline to the Rennkavi
Rikiyasti, Fithri Ile – Ancient sites of the Tundra Kings
Ripfish – Like a pikefish
Rites of Kotar – Elsthemi rites for death
Rou – Currency of A-M
Roushenn Palace Guard – Cobalt-clad guards at Roushenn Palace
Scarde wyrdi (Scorpion *wyrria*) – A will-*wyrria* used by the Kreth-Hakir
Scorchgrass – Like mesquite
Shadow-will – The darkest manifestation of one's will
Sing-leaf – A tree with leaves that make a singing sound
Sirve wyrdi (Dawn *wyrria*) – Ability to access the natural world and the five senses
Sons of Illium – A secret bloodline of vigilante poisoners in Cennetia
Summons of the Kingsmen – Historical event ten years prior
Suna hebi – A vicious black viper form the southern deserts
Telmenberry – A blue-black berry from Elsthemen, like a blackberry
The Bitterlance – Term for Arlen and Delennia's coup
The Key of Fire – the Key of the World Shaper
The Noldarum – Knowers of the World Shaper's mysteries (a Mystery School)
Travelers – Like gypsies, put on plays and stories
Tundra-wights – Ghosts that haunt the tundras
Utrus – The Undoer, aka the Red-Eyed Demon
Wintermint – An herb like peppermint
Wolf and Dragon *wyrria (Werus et Khehem)* – Ancient battle-wyrria of Khehem, Conflict *wyrria*
World Shaper – Creationary deity
World Shaper's Key – Light of Creation
Wyrria – Magic - a term originating in the Twelve Tribes
Wyrric – A magic user
Yegovian cider – A strong pear cider, like brandy
Yither-wood – A white citrus wood from Valenghia

Alrou-Mendera Ranks of Lords (Least to Greatest):

Dhepan – Mayor of a town/city

Vicoute/Vicenne – A lower Viscount, manages a moderate area around cities/townships

Couthis/Couthenna – A higher Count, manages large areas including multiple cities

Duchev/Duchevy – A Duke/Duchess, manages major sections of the nation

Chancellor (King's Chancellor) – Advisers to the King

Dhenir/Dhenra – Prince/Princess of Alrou-Mendera

King/Queen – Monarch of Alrou-Mendera

Alrou-Mendera War Brigades:

High Brigade – Operate in the highest mountains in the Valenghian border

Longvalley Brigade – Operate in a well-protected valley on the Valenghian border

Fleetrunners – Messengers at the Valenghian border

Stone Valley Brigade – Special tactical unit, fierce fighters, called in where necessary

Printed in Great Britain
by Amazon